THE
MERCIES

THE
MERCIES

Kiran Millwood Hargrave

PICADOR

First published 2020 by Picador
an imprint of Pan Macmillan
The Smithson, 6 Briset Street, London EC1M 5NR
Associated companies throughout the world
www.panmacmillan.com

ISBN 978-1-5290-0510-3

1 3 5 7 9 8 6 4 2

A CIP catalogue record for this book is available from the British Library.

Interior artwork © Tom de Freston 2020

Map artwork by Global Blended Learning

Typeset by Palimpsest Book Production Ltd, Falkirk, Stirlingshire
Printed and bound by CPI Group (UK) Ltd, Croydon, CR0 4YY

Visit **www.picador.com** to read more about all our books
and to buy them. You will also find features, author interviews and
news of any author events, and you can sign up for e-newsletters
so that you're always first to hear about our new releases.

For my mother, Andrea,
and all the women who raise(d) me

VARDØ, FINNMARK. 1617

BARENTS SEA

NORWAY

Vardø

Hornøya
stac

headland

Hornøya
island

harbour

Vardøhus • • Vardø

N

*low
mountain*

• Kiberg

0   2 miles

0   2 km

BY ORDER OF THE KING

If any sorcerer, or faithful man, had the sacrifice of God
and His Holy Word and Christianity, and devoted himself to
the dævil, he should be cast down on fire and incineration.

FROM
Denmark–Norway Trolddom (Sorcery) Decree 1617,
ENACTED FINNMARK 1620

STORM

Last night Maren dreamt a whale beached itself on the rocks outside her house.

She climbed down the cliff to its heaving body and rested her eye against its eye, wrapped her arms across the great stinking swell. There was nothing she could do for it but this.

The men came scrambling down the black rock like dark, swift insects, glinting and hard-bodied with blades and scythes. They began to swing and cut before the whale was even dead. It bucking and all of them grim and holding like nets tight about a shoal, her arms growing long and strong around it – so wide and fierce she held it – until she didn't know if she was a comfort or a menace and didn't care, only watched its eye with her eye, not blinking.

Eventually it stilled, its breath melting out as they hacked and sawed. She smelt the blubber burning in the lamps before it stopped moving, long before the bright roll of its eye beneath her eye wore down to dullness.

She sank down into the rocks until she stood at the bottom of the sea. The night above was dark and moonless, stars scarring the surface. She drowned and came up from sleep gasping, smoke in her nostrils and at the dark back of her throat. The taste of burning fat caught under her tongue, and would not be washed away.

One

The storm comes in like a finger snap. That's how they'll speak in the months and years after, when it stops being only an ache behind their eyes and a crushing at the base of their throats. When it finally fits into stories. Even then, it doesn't tell how it actually was. There are ways words fall down: they give shape too easily, carelessly. And there was no grace, no ease to what Maren saw.

That afternoon, the best sail is spread like a blanket across her lap, Mamma and Diinna at its other corners. Their smaller, neater fingers are working smaller, neater stitches into the wind-wear tears, while she patches cloth over holes left by the mast fastenings.

Beside the fire there's a stack of white heather drying, cut and brought by her brother Erik from the low mountain on the mainland. Tomorrow, after, Mamma will give her three palmfuls for her pillow. She'll wrench it apart, stuff it earth and all into the casing, the honey scent almost sickening after months of only the stale smell of sleep and unwashed hair. She'll take it between her teeth and scream until her lungs wheeze with the sweet dirt tang of it.

Now, something makes her look up and out towards the

window. A bird, dark against dark, a sound? She stands to stretch, to watch the bay, flat grey and beyond it the open sea, tips of waves like smashed glass glittering. The boats are loosely pegged out against it by their two small lights, bow and aft, barely flickering.

She imagines she can tell Pappa and Erik's apart from the others, with its second-best sail rigged tight to the mast. The jerk and stop-start of their rowing, their backs to the horizon where the sun skulks, out of sight for a month now, and for another month to come. The men will see the steady light from Vardø's curtainless houses, lost in their own sea of dim-lit land. They're already out beyond the Hornøya stac, nearly at the place where the shoal was sighted earlier in the afternoon, worried into bright action by a whale.

'It will have passed on,' Pappa said. Mamma has a great terror of whales. 'Well eaten its fill by the time Erik manages to haul us there with those herringbone arms.'

Erik only bowed his head to accept Mamma's kiss, and his wife Diinna's press of thumb to his forehead that the Sámi say will draw a thread to reel men at sea home again. He rested a hand on her belly for a moment, bringing the swell of it more obviously through her knitted tunic. She pushed his hand away, but gently.

'You'll call it early. Let it be.'

After, Maren will wish she rose and kissed them both on each rough cheek. She will wish she had watched them go to the water in their stitched sealskins, her father's strung-out stride and Erik's shambling behind. Wish that she had felt anything at all about them going, other than gratitude for the time alone with Mamma and Diinna, for the easiness of other women.

Because, at twenty and with her first marriage proposal come three weeks before, she at last considered herself one of them. Dag Bjørnsson was making them a home from his father's second boathouse, and before winter was done it would be finished, and they wed.

Inside, he told her, panting hot, scratching breath beneath her ear, would be a fine hearth and separate food store so he wouldn't need to walk through the house with his axe like Pappa did. The wicked glint, even in Pappa's careful hands, brought bile to her tongue. Dag knew this, and cared to know.

He was blond as his mother, delicately featured in a way that Maren knew other men took to mean weakness, but she didn't mind. She didn't mind that he brushed his wide mouth against her throat, as he told her of the sheet she should weave for the bed he would build for them. And though she didn't feel anything at his hesitant caress at her back, too gentle and high to mean much at all through her dark blue winter dress, this house that would be hers – this hearth and bed – sent a pulse low in her belly. At night she'd press her hands to the places she'd felt the warmth, fingers cold bars across her hips and numb enough not to be hers.

Not even Erik and Diinna have their own house: they live in the narrow room Maren's father and brother tacked along the back edge of their outer wall. Their bed fills the width of it, is pressed flush against Maren's own through the divide. She put her arms over her head on their first nights together, breathing in the musty straw of her mattress, but never heard so much as a breath. It was a wonder when Diinna's belly started to show. The baby would be here just after winter left, and then there would be three in that slender bed.

After, she will think: perhaps she should have watched for Dag too.

But instead she fetched the damaged sailcloth and spread it over all their knees, and did not look up until the bird or the sound or the change in the air called her to the window to watch the lights shifting across the dark sea.

Her arms crackle: she brings one needle-coarsened finger to the other and pushes it under her woollen cuff, feels the hair stiff and the skin beneath it tightening. The boats are still rowing, still steady in the uncertain light, lamps glimmering.

And then the sea rises up and the sky swings down and greenish lightning slings itself across everything, flashing the black into an instantaneous, terrible brightness. Mamma is fetched to the window by the light and the noise, the sea and sky clashing like a mountain splitting so they feel it through their soles and spines, sending Maren's teeth into her tongue and hot salt down her gullet.

And then maybe both of them are screaming but there is no sound save the sea and the sky and all the boat lights swallowed and the boats flashing and the boats spinning, the boats flying, turning, gone. Maren goes spilling out into the wind, creased double by her suddenly sodden skirts, Diinna calling her in, wrenching the door behind to keep the fire from going out. The rain is a weight on her shoulders, the wind slamming her back, hands tight in on themselves, grasping nothing. She is screaming so loud her throat will be bruised for days. All about her, other mothers, sisters, daughters are throwing themselves at the weather: dark, rain-slick shapes, clumsy as seals.

The storm drops before she reaches the harbour, two hundred paces from home, its empty mouth gaping at the sea. The clouds roll themselves up and the waves fall, resting at each other's horizons, gentle as a flock settling.

The women of Vardø gather at the scooped-out edge of their island, and though some are still shouting, Maren's ears ring with silence. Before her, the harbour is wiped smooth as a mirror. Her jaw is caught on the hinges of itself, her tongue dripping blood warm down her chin. Her needle is threaded in the web between her thumb and forefinger, the wound a neat circle of pink.

As she watches, a final flash of lightning illuminates the hatefully still sea, and from its blackness rise oars and rudders and a full mast with gently stowed sails, like underwater forests uprooted. Of their men, there is no sign.

It is Christmas Eve.

Two

Overnight, the world turns white. Snow piles on snow, filling the windows and the mouths of doors. The kirke stands dark that Christmas, that first day after, a hole between the lit houses, swallowing light.

They are snowed in for three days, Diinna portioned off in her narrow room, Maren unable to rouse herself any more than she can Mamma. They eat nothing but old bread, settling like pebbles in their stomachs. Maren feels the food so solid inside her, and her body so unreal about it, she imagines herself pinned down to the earth only by Mamma's stale loaves. If she doesn't eat, she will become smoke and gather in the eaves of their house.

She keeps herself together by filling her belly until it aches, and by placing as much of herself as possible in the warmth from the fire. Everywhere it touches, she tells herself, she is real. She lifts her hair to show the grubby nape of her neck, spreads her fingers to let the warmth lick between them, lifts her skirts so her woollen stockings begin to singe and stink. *There, and there, and there.* Her breasts, back, and between them her heart, are caught in her winter vest, bundled tight together.

The second day, for the first time in years, the fire goes out. Pappa always laid it, and they only tended it, keeping it banked at night and breaking its crust each morning to let the hot heart of it breathe. Within hours there is a layer of frost on their blankets though Maren and her mother sleep together in the same bed. They don't speak, don't undress. Maren wraps herself in Pappa's old sealskin coat. It was not flensed properly and reeks a little of rotted fat.

Mamma wears Erik's from when he was a boy. She is dull-eyed as a smoked fish. Maren tries to make her eat, but her mother only curls into her side on the bed, sighs like a child. Maren is grateful for the blankness at the window that means the sea is hidden from sight.

Those three days are a pit she falls into. She watches Pappa's axe wink in the dark. Her tongue grows thick and mossy, the tender place where she bit it during the storm spongy and swollen, with something hard at its centre. She worries at it, and the blood makes her thirstier.

She dreams of Pappa and Erik, wakes dank and sweating, hands freezing. She dreams of Dag and when he opens his mouth it is full of nails meant for their bed. She wonders if they will die there, whether Diinna is already dead, her baby still paddling inside her, slowing. She wonders if God will come to them, and tell them to live.

They are both of them reeking when Kirsten Sørensdatter digs them out on the third night. Kirsten helps them restack and light the fire at last. When she clears the path to Diinna's door, Diinna looks almost furious, the dull gleam of her pouted lip catching in the torchlight, hands pressed hard either side of her swollen belly.

'Kirke,' says Kirsten to them all. 'It is the Sabbath.'

Even Diinna, who doesn't believe in their God, does not argue.

•

It isn't until they are all gathered in the kirke that Maren understands: nearly all their men are dead.

Toril Knudsdatter lights the candles, every one, until the room blazes so bright it stings Maren's eyes. She counts silently. There once were fifty-three men, and now they have but thirteen left: two babes in arms, three elders, and the rest boys too small for the boats. Even the minister is lost.

The women sit in their usual pews, hollows left between where husbands and sons sat, but Kirsten orders them forwards. All but Diinna obey, dumb as a herd. They take up three of the kirke's seven rows.

'There have been wrecks before,' says Kirsten. 'We have survived when men are lost.'

'But never so many,' says Gerda Folnsdatter. 'And never my husband among them. Never yours, Kirsten, or Sigfrid's. Never Toril's son. All of them—'

She grips at her throat, falls silent.

'We should pray, or sing,' suggests Sigfrid Jonsdatter, and the others look at her poisonously. They have been trapped apart for three days, and all they wish to talk of, all they can speak of, is the storm.

The women of Vardø are looking, all of them, for signs. The storm was one. The bodies, still to come, will be seen as another. But now Gerda speaks of the single tern she saw wheeling above the whale.

'In figures of eight,' she says, her ruddy hands arcing through the air. 'One, two, three, six times I counted.'

'Eight by six means not much at all,' says Kirsten dismissively. She is standing beside Pastor Gursson's pulpit with its engraved stand. Her large hand rests upon it, the broad thumb working over the carved shapes her only sign of nerves, or grief.

Her husband is among the drowned, and all her children were buried before they breathed. Maren likes her, has often gone about her tasks with her, but now she sees Kirsten as the others always have: as a woman apart. She is not standing behind the pulpit, but she may as well be: she watches them with a minister's consideration.

'The whale though,' says Edne Gunnsdatter, face swollen so tight by tears it looks bruised. 'It swam upside down. I saw its white belly shining under the waves.'

'It was feeding,' says Kirsten.

'It was luring the men,' says Edne. 'It set the shoal about Hornøya six times, to be sure we'd see.'

'I saw that,' nods Gerda, crossing herself. 'I saw that too.'

'You did not,' says Kirsten.

'I saw the blood Mattis coughed upon the table a week ago,' says Gerda. 'It has never scrubbed off.'

'I can sand that out for you,' says Kirsten smoothly.

'The whale was wrong,' says Toril. Her daughter is burrowed against her side so tight she might have been sewed to her hip by Toril's famously neat stitches. 'If what Edne says is true, it was sent.'

'Sent?' says Sigfrid, and Maren sees Kirsten turn a thankful eye upon her, thinking she has found an ally. 'Such a thing is possible?'

A sigh comes from the back of the kirke, and the whole room turns towards Diinna, but she tilts her head back, eyes closed, the brown skin of her throat gleaming gold in the candlelight.

'The Devil works darkly,' says Toril, and her daughter presses her face beneath her shoulder, cries out in fear. Maren wonders what terrors Toril has woven into her two surviving children these past three days. 'He has power set above all but God's. He could send such a thing. Or it could be called.'

'Enough.' Kirsten breaks the silence before it can deepen. 'This will help nothing.'

Maren wants to join her in her certainty, but all she can think of is the shape, the sound that brought her to the window. She had thought it was a bird but now it looms bigger and more unwieldy, five-finned and upside down. Unnatural. It is impossible to stop it leaking into the corner of her vision, even in the blessed light of the kirke.

Mamma stirs, as if from sleep, though the candles have been reflecting off her unblinking eyes since they sat down. When she speaks, Maren can hear the toll silence has taken on her voice.

'The night Erik was born,' says Mamma. 'There was a red point of light in the sky.'

'I remember,' says Kirsten, softly.

'And me,' says Toril. *And me*, thinks Maren, though she was only two.

'I followed it through the sky until it dropped in the sea,' says Mamma, lips barely moving. 'It lit the whole water with blood. He was marked – it was meant from that day.' She moans and covers her face. 'I should never have let him to sea.'

This brings a fresh wave of wailing from the women. Even Kirsten can do nothing to quell it. The candles stutter as there is a rush of cold air into the room, and Maren turns in time to see Diinna striding from the kirke. What words Maren could offer, as she puts her arm about Mamma, would be bitter comfort: *There was nothing for him but the sea.*

Vardø is an island, the harbour like a bite taken out of one side, the other shores too high or rocky for boats to be launched. Maren learnt nets before she learnt hurt, weather before she learnt love. In summer her mother's hands are speckled with the tiny stars of fish scales, flesh hung out to salt and dry like white drapes of baby's swaddling, or else wrapped in reindeer skins and buried to rot.

Pappa used to say that the sea was the shape of their lives. They have always lived by its grace, and long have they died on it. But the storm has made it an enemy, and there is brief talk of leaving.

'I have family in Alta,' says Gerda. 'There is land and work enough, there.'

'The storm did not reach so far?' asks Sigfrid.

'We will hear soon,' says Kirsten. 'I imagine they'll send word from Kiberg – the storm must surely have struck there.'

'My sister will get a message to me,' nods Edne. 'She has three horses, and it is only a day's ride.'

'And a rough crossing,' says Kirsten. 'The sea is still fierce. We must allow them time to reach us.'

Maren listens as others talk of Varanger, or more outlandishly, Tromsø, as if any of them could imagine life in a city, so far away. There is a small disagreement about who would take the reindeer for transport, for they belonged to Mads Petersson, who drowned alongside Toril's husband and sons. Toril seems to think this gives her some standing over them, but when Kirsten announces she will care for the herd no one argues. Maren can't imagine starting a fire, let alone keeping a herd of high-strung beasts through the winter. Toril likely thinks the same, for she drops her claim as quickly as she took it up.

Eventually the talk falters, finishes. Nothing is decided except that they will wait for word from Kiberg, and send for it if it does not arrive before the week is out.

'Until then, it is best to meet daily at kirke,' says Kirsten, and Toril nods fervently, in agreement for once. 'We must watch for each other. The snows seem on their way out, but there's no telling.'

'Watch for whales,' says Toril, and the light hits her face so Maren can see the bones work beneath her skin. She looks ominous, and Maren wants to laugh. She bites down on the tender spot on her tongue.

There is no more talk of leaving. Walking down the hill homewards, Mamma clinging so tightly it makes her arm ache, Maren wonders if the other women feel as she does: bound to the place now more than ever. Whale or no whale, sign or not, Maren was witness to the death of forty men. Now something in her is tied to this land, as tied as she is trapped.

Three

Nine days after the storm, the year newly turned over, the men are brought to them. Almost whole, almost all of them. Laid like offerings on the small black cove, or else risen by the tide to the rocks below Maren's house. They must climb to fetch them, using the ropes knotted strong for Erik to fetch eggs from the birds' nests woven into the cliffside.

Erik and Dag are amongst the first to come back, Pappa amongst the last. Pappa has one arm, and Dag is burnt, a black line drawn from left shoulder to right foot, which Mamma says means the lightning struck him.

'It would have been quick,' she says, not hiding her bitterness. 'It would have been easy.'

Maren presses nose to shoulder, breathes herself in.

Her brother looks as though he is sleeping, but his skin is filled with that horrible green light she knows from other bodies brought in by the tide. *Drowned*. Not so easy.

When it is Maren's turn to descend the cliff, she retrieves Toril's son, snagged like driftwood on the sharp-toothed rocks. He is Erik's age, and his body slips about in its bones like jointed meat in a sack. Maren smooths his dark hair away from his face, picks a whisper of seaweed from his collarbone. She and Edne must tie him by the waist and ribs and knees, to keep him together as he is drawn up to his mother. Maren is glad she can't see Toril's face when she is brought her boy. Though she is not fond of the woman, Toril's keens prick at Maren's chest like tiny needles.

The ground is too hard for burial, and so it is agreed that they will keep the dead in Dag's father's first boathouse, the cold keeping them frozen as earth. It will be months before they can break the surface to bury their men.

'We can use the sail as a shroud,' says Mamma, after Erik is taken to the boat shed. She eyes the mended sail where it lies in the centre of the floor, as if Erik is already beneath it. It is exactly where they had dropped it nearly two weeks before. Maren and Mamma have been dancing around it, neither wanting to touch it, but now Diinna snatches it up and shakes her head.

'A waste,' she says, and Maren is glad: she can't stand the thought of sending her father and brother into the ground with anything more of the sea upon them. Diinna folds the sail with deft movements, resting it upon her belly, and in her decisiveness Maren sees some of the girl who married her brother, laughing, a summer ago.

But Diinna disappears the day after Dag and Erik are brought back. Mamma is frantic that she has left to bring up the child with her Sámi family. She says some awful things, things that Maren knows she doesn't mean. She calls Diinna a Lapp, a whore, a savage, things Toril or Sigfrid might say.

'I always knew it,' Mamma weeps. 'I should never have let him marry a Lapp. They are not loyal, not made like us.'

Maren can only bite her tongue, and rub her back. It is true Diinna's childhood was spent travelling, living beneath changing stars even in winter. Her father is a noaidi, a shaman of good standing. Before the kirke was more fully established, their neighbour Baar Ragnvalsson and many other men went to him for charms against rough weather. That had stopped lately, with new laws brought in to ban such things, but still Maren sees the small bone figures that the Sámi say will protect against bad luck on most doorsteps. Pastor Gursson always turned a blind eye, though Toril and her ilk urged him to come down harder on such practices.

Maren knows it was only Diinna's love for Erik that made her agree to live in Vardø, but she doesn't think Diinna would leave like this, not when they have already lost so many. Not with Erik's baby inside her. She would not be so cruel as to take the last part of him away from them.

•

Within the week, they receive word from Kiberg. Edne's brother-in-law comes with news that besides numerous boats moored in the harbour, they lost only three men. When the women gather in the kirke to hear the message, it stokes their unease.

'Why did they not fish?' says Sigfrid. 'Did Kiberg not see the shoal?'

Edne shakes her head. 'The whale neither.'

'So it was sent for us,' whispers Toril, and her fear spreads across the pews in muttering waves.

The talk is too loose for a sacred place, full of omens and embellishments, but no one can resist the chance to gossip. Their words are like links they can hang fact upon, tightening with each telling. Many of them seem past caring what is true or not, only desperate for some reason, some order to the rearrangement of their lives, even if it is brought about by a lie. That the whale swam upside down is now beyond question, and though Maren tries to shore herself against the creeping terror their talk brings, she can't hold steady like Kirsten.

The woman has moved into Mads Petersson's house, the better to care for the reindeer. Maren regards her, standing firm by the pulpit. They have barely spoken since Kirsten dug them from the snow, except to exchange words of sorrow when their men were pulled rotting from the sea. Maren thinks to speak with her as the kirke meet comes to an end, but Kirsten is already out of the door, striding to her new homestead, bent against the wind.

•

Diinna is back the day they find Pappa. The first Maren hears of her return there is shouting at the boathouse and she runs, imagining all sorts of things: another storm though she can see for herself the sunless sky is calm, or a man found yet living.

There is a cluster of women about the door, Sigfrid and Toril at the fore, their faces twisted in anger. Before them stands Diinna with another Sámi: a short, square man who watches the women coolly. It is not Diinna's father, but he has a shaman drum at his hip. Between them they hold a furled length of silvery cloth. As Maren comes closer, dizzy with the effort of running, she sees it is birch bark.

'What's the matter?' she asks Diinna, and Toril answers.

'She wants to bury them in that.' The woman's voice is close to hysteria. Spit flecks her chin. 'Like *they* do.'

'Makes no sense to use cloth, not for so many,' says Diinna. 'This is—'

'And I will not have that, not near my boys.' Toril is panting worse than Maren, looking at the drum as though it were a weapon. Sigfrid Jonsdatter nods her approval as Toril plunges on. 'Nor my husband. He's a God-fearing man, and I'll not have you near him.'

'I don't remember you minding my help when you wanted another baby got upon you,' says Diinna.

22

Toril puts her hand across her belly, though her babies are long born. 'I did no such thing.'

'I know as well as any that you did, Toril,' says Maren, unable to keep silent at the lie. 'And you, Sigfrid. Many of you came to her, or her father.'

Toril narrows her eyes. 'I would never go to a Lapp sorcerer.'

There is a collective hiss. Maren steps forward, but Diinna puts her arm out.

'I should put a hole in your tongue, Toril. Perhaps it would let some of the poison out.' It is Toril's turn to shrink. 'And it's not sorcery, and it's not for them.'

Diinna turns to Maren. She is beautiful in the bluish light, the planes of her face strong, her eyes thickly lashed. 'It's for Erik.'

'And my father.' Maren's voice breaks. She cannot bear to separate them, and Pappa loved Diinna, was proud of the match made for his son.

'He has come back?' Maren nods, and Diinna clasps her shoulder. 'And for Herr Magnusson, of course. We will watch them. And any others that want it.'

'And will your mother be happy with this?' Toril rounds on Maren, and she is too weary to do anything but nod, her head heavy on her neck.

Eventually it is agreed that anyone who wants the Sámi rites for their men will be taken to the second boathouse, that was to have been Maren's home. Only two men are moved in next to Erik and Pappa: poor Mads Petersson, who has no family to speak for him, and Baar Ragnvalsson, who was often gone to the low mountain and wore Sámi clothing.

The second boathouse would have made a fine home. The start of the shed alone is as large as Diinna and Erik's room, and the main space rivals the one at Dag's father's house, the largest in the village. Their bed is laid out in planks ready for Dag's careful hands to knock together.

They take the wood for their fire, and lay her father and Erik on the bare ground. Maren has to leave Dag behind in the first boathouse: his mother, Fru Olufsdatter, has not spoken a word to her, will not meet her eye.

Maren snaps a lock of frozen hair from Erik's dark head, places it carefully into her pocket. As she leaves Diinna and the noaidi behind in the silent room, Maren loops around to the first boathouse. She sees one of the women has nailed a cross over the door, and it feels less like a blessing on those within than a warding-off of those without.

When she reaches home, Mamma is asleep, her arm flung across her eyes as though she is cowering from a nightmare.

'Mamma?' Maren wants to tell her about the noaidi, and the second boathouse. 'Diinna is back.'

There is no response. Mamma seems barely to breathe, and Maren resists the urge to place her cheek over her mouth to check for life. Instead, she retrieves the lock from her pocket, holds it before the fire. It frills into Erik's fine curls. She makes a slice in her pillow, places it inside with the heather.

•

Every day after kirke, Maren returns to the second boathouse, though she can't bring herself to sleep there like Diinna and the man with the drum. He does not speak Norwegian, and will not give an easy version of his name so Maren calls him Varr, vigilant, because it sounds a little like the beginning of what he says he is called before she loses the rest on her unskilled tongue.

Each time she visits her father and Erik she waits outside, listening to Varr and Diinna speak together in their language. They always fall silent the moment she puts her hand on the door, and Maren feels as though she's walked in on something indecent, or else intensely private. That she's broken something, clumsy just by being there.

Maren speaks Norwegian to Diinna and Diinna translates to Varr, her sentences always shorter, as though they have the better and more exacting words for what Maren is trying to say. What must it be like to have two languages in your head, in your mouth? Having to keep one tucked like a dark secret at the back of your throat? Diinna has always lived between Vardø and elsewhere, around now and again since Maren was a girl, trailing alongside her silent father who came to fix nets or weave charms.

'We lived here,' Diinna told Maren once, when Maren was still a little afraid of her: a girl in trousers and a coat edged with bear fur that she'd skinned and stitched herself.

'This is your land?'

'No.' The girl's tone was firm as her gaze. 'We only lived here.'

Sometimes Maren can hear the drum beaten, steady as a heartbeat, and she sleeps easier those nights though there is much muttering from the strictest kirke-goers about it. Diinna tells her the drum will clear the way for the spirits to break cleanly from the bodies, and not be afraid. But Varr never plays it when Maren is about. It is broad as a trough, skin stretched taut over a shallow bowl of pale wood. Small markings punctuate the surface: a reindeer with a sun and moon caught in its antlers, men and women linked like paper chains at the hands in the centre, and a twist of hideous almost-men, almost-beasts writhe across the bottom.

'Is that hell?' she asks Diinna. 'And that heaven, and us in the middle?'

Diinna doesn't translate to Varr. 'It is all here.'

Four

As winter loosens its grip on Vardø, and their food stores stand near empty, the sun heaves itself closer to the horizon. By the time Diinna and Erik's baby is born, they will have days flooded with light.

Maren feels an uneasy rhythm take hold of Vardø, her time finding shape. Kirke, boathouse, housework, sleep. Though the lines are beginning to be drawn more starkly between Kirsten and Toril, Diinna and the others, they pull together as men rowing a boat. It is a closeness born of necessity: they need each other more than ever, especially as food begins to scarcen.

They receive some grain from Alta, scant tørrfisk from Kiberg. Sometimes sailors stop in the harbour, row ashore with sealskins and whale oil. Kirsten has no shame in talking to them, and manages a good deal, but they are running low on items to trade, and it is clear that when the time arrives to sow their fields, no help will come.

Maren uses the between hours of her days to walk the headland that she and Erik would play upon as children, the scrubby patches of heather healing after a sun-starved winter. They will be knee high before long, and the air will be so sweet with their scent as to make her teeth ache.

At night, the grief is harder to manage. The first time she picks up a needle, the hair on her arms rises and she drops it as though scalded. All her dreams are dark and full of water. She sees Erik caught in stoppered bottles and the gaping, sea-washed hole of her father's arm: its white, white bone. The whale comes most of all, the dark hull of its body crashing through her mind and leaving nothing good, nothing living in its wake. Sometimes it swallows her whole, and sometimes it is beached and she lies with it, eye to eye, with her nostrils full of its stench.

Maren knows Mamma has nightmares too. But she doubts her mother wakes with salt on her tongue, the sea mottling her breath. Sometimes Maren wonders whether she brought this life upon them all with her wishing for time alone with Diinna and Mamma. For though Kiberg is close, and Alta not so far, no man has come to settle with them. Maren wanted time with women, and now all her days are so.

She starts to imagine that Vardø could go on for ever this way: a place without men, and still surviving. The cold is loosening its hold, and the bodies are in turn becoming soft. Once the thaw is root deep, they will bury their dead, and perhaps some of the rifts might be buried with them.

Maren aches for the feeling of soil beneath her fingernails, the weight of a spade in her hands, Erik and Pappa finally at rest, neat in their silver-birch shrouds. She checks the vegetable patch outside their home daily, scraping her nails across the ground.

•

Four months after the storm, the day her hand sinks into the dirt, she runs into kirke to declare they can dig at last. But the words catch in her throat: there is a man planted at the pulpit.

'This is Pastor Nils Kurtsson,' says Toril, voice reverent. 'He is sent from Varanger. Praise God, we are not forgotten after all.'

The minister turns pale eyes upon Maren. He is built slight as a boy.

Ousted from her usual spot, Kirsten slides in beside Mamma and Maren, leans close to whisper in Maren's ear.

'I hope his sermons are not so weak as his chin.'

But they are, and Maren thinks he must have done something awful to be posted at Vardø. Pastor Kurtsson is reedy, obviously unused to life by the sea. He offers no words of comfort for their particular trials, and seems a little afraid of the roomful of women who arrive each Sabbath's Day to fill his kirke. He scurries to his house next door after each final *Amen*.

The kirke newly sanctified, the women take to meeting on Wednesdays in Dag's father's house, Fru Olufsdatter reduced to a whisper in the rooms of her too-large home. The gossip is the same, but the women are more careful. As Toril had said, they are not forgotten, and Maren is sure she is not alone in her unease about what this might mean.

The week of his arrival, the minister writes for ten men from Kiberg, Edne's brother-in-law among them, and Maren feels an unexpected envy when they come to bury the dead. It takes them two days to dig the graves, and with the nights' darkness shortening they work late into them. They are loud, and laugh too much for their task. They sleep in the kirke, and lean on their spades to watch the women go by. Maren keeps her head down, but still she walks past the site to watch their progress hourly.

The graves are at the north-west side of the island, dark pit after dark pit, so many it makes Maren's head spin. The soil is heaped beside, and as Maren watches from a safe distance, she imagines the ache in her arms, the dirt tasting like a coin in her mouth, the sweat coming hard from her. It doesn't feel right, after all the women have seen, after gathering their men from the rocks and keeping vigil through the winter, to watch someone else dig the graves. She thinks Kirsten would agree with her, but doesn't want a fuss. She wants her pappa and brother in the ground, the winter over, and the men from Kiberg gone.

On the morning of the third day, their dead men are brought out from the first boathouse, already smelling a little, stomachs swollen in their cloth shrouds stitched by Toril. They are laid beside the open graves, stark white against the freshly turned earth.

'No coffins?' asks one man, plucking at the shroud.

'Forty dead,' says another. 'A lot of labour for a village of women.'

'A shroud is harder work than a coffin,' says Kirsten coolly, and Toril's cheeks pinken in surprise. 'And I'll thank you not to touch my husband.'

Kirsten sits on the edge of the grave, and before Maren understands what she is doing, she has dropped down so only her head and shoulders emerge, arms outstretched.

The men stare wordlessly at one another, and so Kirsten takes her husband herself, and disappears from view as she lowers him down. The next they see of her, she is pulling herself up, her stockinged leg flashing as she climbs out of the grave.

Toril tuts and turns away, and one of the men laughs, but Kirsten only takes a handful of earth from the mound and drops it onto her husband. Then she walks straight past Maren, close enough so Maren can see the tears on her cheeks. Maren should reach out to her, say something, but her tongue feels useless as a pebble.

'So she did love him,' murmurs Mamma, and Maren has

to bite back a retort. Any fool could tell Kirsten had loved her husband. She'd seen them often, walking together and laughing like friends. He took her to the fields and sometimes out on the sea. If she had gone with him the day of the storm, the women of Vardø would be even more lost than they are now.

Pastor Kurtsson moves forward to bless the grave. His jaw is tight, and Maren supposes he is embarrassed that Kirsten showed her boldness before these men. 'May the mercies of God be upon you,' he intones in his wavering voice, saying nothing much over the man he never knew.

'Kirsten should not have done that.' Diinna appears beside Maren, watching the minister. Her hand rests on her belly. The baby will come any day, and sorrow grips at Maren's throat: her brother pressed beneath the dirt before his child even breathes. She has a sudden urge to reach out and touch Diinna, to feel the warmth of her stomach and the baby inside, but not even the Diinna of before would have tolerated it. This new Diinna is hard as stone, and Maren doesn't dare ask.

No other woman has a hand in the burial of their kin. The men work methodically: two passing a body down to two in the grave. The families step forward to sprinkle dirt, Pastor Kurtsson blesses the grave, it is filled. No one wails, or falls to their knees. The women are tired, numb, done. Toril prays incessantly, the words rising and falling on the wind.

The cycle repeats until it is time for the second boathouse to be emptied, and Pastor Kurtsson raises a pale eyebrow at the silver-birch shrouds. Mamma plucks at Pappa's, looks from the minister to Maren.

'Perhaps we should ask Toril—'

'I have no cloth left,' says Toril.

'I have a sail—'

'No thread neither,' says Toril, and she turns her back on

them, walking home, pulling her son and daughter after. Sigfrid follows, and Gerda. Maren is sure that she, Diinna and Mamma will be left alone to bury their dead, but the other women stay to watch as Mads, then Pappa, then Erik, and at last Baar are lowered, covered over.

That night, when the men from Kiberg have left, Maren walks to the graves with Erik's lock of hair in her pocket, thinking to bury it with him. She has decided it is a macabre keepsake, that perhaps it is this poisoning her dreams, letting the sea seep in. The nights are no longer winter dark, and in the gloom the graves appear to her like a pod of whales on the horizon, humpbacked and menacing. She finds she cannot approach them.

She knows what they are: hallowed ground, blessed by a man of God, holding naught but the remains of their men. But here, with the wind whistling through the open channels of their island, and the lit houses at her back, walking towards them seems as ill-fated as stepping from a cliff. She imagines them crashing up, thrashing down, and the world seems to rock beneath her feet. In her confusion, she loosens her grip on the lock of Erik's hair. The wind plucks it from her slack fingers, and spins it away.

•

Later that night, the noise of the door wakes Maren. Mamma is curled on the blankets like a snail in its shell, breathing rank air into her face. She has insisted they still share the bed, though Maren sleeps the worse for it.

Maren sits up, body singing with nerves as the door closes. She can't see anyone, only sense them there. There is a grunting sound, a fast series of almost animal breaths. It sounds like a mouthful of dirt being choked on.

'Erik?'

She wonders if she has called him to her, conjured him with her dreaming and prayers, and it frightens her to the point where she is up and climbing over her mother, towards Pappa's axe. Then she hears Diinna's soft cry, a lurch of pain that sends the woman to her knees and Maren can make out her edges. A spirit wouldn't open a door, Maren chides herself, and an axe would be no help against it.

'I'll fetch Fru Olufsdatter.'

'Not her,' says Diinna on an outrush of breath. 'You.'

She guides Diinna to their hearthrug. Mamma is awake and cracks open the fire so its light spills over the floor, brings blankets and heats water, gets a strap of leather for Diinna to bite on, makes soothing sounds.

They don't need the strap – Diinna doesn't make much noise beyond panting. She sounds like a kicked dog: she whimpers and bites her lip. Maren stays by her head and Mamma removes her underthings. They are wet, and the whole room smells of Diinna's sweat. She is pouring with it, and Maren wipes a cloth across her forehead, tries not to stare at the dark mound between Diinna's legs, her mother's hands slick and working. She has never seen a child born before, only animals and often they did not live. She tries to banish the thoughts of slack tongues poking from between soft jaws.

'It is already nearly come,' says Mamma. 'Why did you not fetch us sooner?'

Diinna is almost dumb with agony, but whispers: 'I knocked at the wall.'

Maren dabs and murmurs at Diinna's ear, enjoying the closeness Diinna's pain is allowing them, like old times. Soon the light coming through the thin weave of the curtains at the window meets that of the fire, and they are all caught in a foggy white glow. Maren feels shrouded in sea mist as Diinna clings to Maren as if she were an anchor, holding her steady against the tides of pain. Maren presses a kiss to her forehead, tasting salt.

When it is finally time to push, Diinna flaps like a landed fish, bucking her body against the floor. 'Hold her,' says Mamma, and Maren tries though she has never been stronger than Diinna and cannot hope to be now. She sits behind so Diinna can lean against her, and whispers into her neck. Maren's own tears come to meet Diinna's as she gives another twist and, at last, a scream as an answering wail comes from between her legs.

'A boy.' Mamma's voice is bright with joy, and the sharp edge of pain. 'A boy. Just as I prayed for.'

Diinna falls back and Maren guides her to the floor. Maren holds her, kisses her cheeks, listening to the baby cry, the clatter of metal as her mother takes up a blade to cut the cord, then wipes blood from him with a rag. Diinna clings to her, crying harder, their bodies shaking, damp, exhausted, until Mamma nudges Maren off with her elbow and puts the baby to Diinna's chest.

He is tiny, crumpled, creamy with afterbirth. His lashes are dark against his white cheek. Maren is minded of a baby bird she found struck from its nest in the moss roof, so thinly skinned she could see the workings of its eye under the closed lid, the heartbeat quaking its entire frame. As soon as she touched it, thinking to put it back in the nest, it stopped moving.

His cries heave his tiny shoulders, his small mouth works. Diinna pulls down her nightgown, places her dark nipple into his mouth. There is scar tissue laced across one collarbone, a burn that Maren remembers came from a pan full of boiled water, though she can't recall who threw it. She wants to kiss there too, to smooth it.

Mamma finishes cleaning Diinna. She is crying, pulls herself up to lie on the other side of her, places a hand over Diinna's where it rests on his back. Maren hesitates only a moment longer before placing hers there too. He is shockingly warm, and smells of fresh bread, clean cloth. Her chest tightens, aches with want.

3rd of June 1618

To the Esteemed Mr Cornet,

I write on two counts.

Firstly, to thank you for your generous letter of the 12th January of this year. Your words of congratulations are most appreciated. My appointment as Lensmann over Finnmark is a great honour and, as you markedly say, a chance to serve our Lord God in that troubled place. The Devil's breath reeks there, and there is much work to be done. King Christian IV is working to solidify the Church's position, but sorcery laws were passed only a year previous, and though they are modelled on Daemonologie they are most lacking next to what our King James has achieved in Scotland and the Outer Isles. They are not even yet enacted in my Lensmannship. Of course, when I take up my post next year I will move to rectify this.

Which brings me to my second point. As you are aware, I am much admiring of your conduct in the 1616 Kirkwall trial of the witch Elspeth Reoch, which reached us even here. As I wrote at the time, while the public praise was all for that popinjay Coltart, I know how much you supported him and that it was your swift action that caught the incident in its earliest stages. It is precisely this pace that is required in Finnmark: men who can follow Daemonologie's teachings to 'spot, prove, and execute those who practise maleficium'.

I write, then, to offer you a place alongside me, to rout out its particular evils. Many of the issues arise from a segment of the local population, endemic here in Finnmark — a transient

35

community termed Lapps. They are somewhat akin to gypsies, but their magicks deal in wind and other weather. As mentioned, legislation against their sorcery is established, but weakly enforced.

You being an Orkney man, I do not need to tell you of the peculiarities of weather or season that come with a place like this. But I will warn you the situation is grave. Since the storm of 1617 (you remember it made even the Edinburgh papers: I myself was at sea and it was felt as far as Spitsbergen and Tromsø) womenfolk have been left to themselves. The barbarian Lapp population mixes freely with the whites. Their magicks are no small part of what we must move against. Their weather sorcery is even sought out by sailors. But I believe that with you, and a small number of other capable, God-fearing men, we can beat back the darkness even in the ever-dark of winter. Even here, at the edge of civilization, souls must be saved.

You would of course be remunerated for your efforts. I have it in mind to set you up in a sizeable dwelling in Vardø, close to the castle where I will have the seat of my power. Five years here, and I would write you a letter of recommendation fit for whatever endeavour you would wish to undertake.

Perhaps keep this offer close to you: I have no doubt Coltart would sniff it out, but he is not the sort of man I am in need of.

Think on it, Mr Cornet. I will await word of your response.

John Cunningham (Hans Køning)
Lensmann over Vardøhus County

Five

By the time her nephew is born, Maren's own body is becoming something she carries effortlessly, with pity and something like disgust. It is hungry, disobedient. When she stands, it is as if there are bubbles between all her bones, and they pop in her ears.

Grief cannot feed you, though it fills you. They have been ignoring that, but when Kirsten Sørensdatter asks for permission to speak at kirke, a clear six months after the storm, Maren sees it finally in the loose skin about the woman's jaw, and in the tributaries of Mamma's veins standing proud from her arms. Perhaps the others do too, because they straighten from the slump of their sermon-listening, watch her carefully.

'It will not change with more waiting,' Kirsten begins, as though picking up a conversation. Her brow is pulled down over her small blue eyes. 'Our neighbours have been kind but we all know kindness has its time. We must start carrying ourselves.' She straightens: something clicks. 'The ice is gone, we have the midnight sun, and there are four boats fit for sea. It is time to fish. We need twenty women, perhaps sixteen. I am one.' She looks about her.

Maren expects some of the others, Sigfrid or Toril or

perhaps even the minister, to say something, to raise an objection. But he is thinner too, and he had precious little weight to lose. It is sense, what Kirsten says, however briefly she chooses to say it. Maren's hand goes up with ten others. As she lifts it, she has the same lurching sensation that comes with leaning into the wind, and feeling it lessen just as you find your balance. Mamma eyes her, and says nothing.

'No others? This is crew enough for only two boats,' says Kirsten. Eyes drop and the women shift in the pews.

•

They thought it was decided. But though the minister raises no objection in the kirke, Toril arrives at the next Wednesday meet with news that Pastor Kurtsson found his voice, and has written a letter.

'How clever,' says Kirsten, not looking up from her work: she is making a pair of sealskin gloves, for helping grip the oars, Maren guesses.

'To the man who is soon to take over Vardøhus,' says Toril, and even Kirsten stills and looks up.

'The fortress? Here?' says Sigfrid, her eyes shining at the gossip. 'You're sure?'

'You know of another?' snaps Toril, but Maren can understand the question. The fortress has stood empty for her entire lifetime.

Beside Maren, Diinna and Mamma have stopped working too. The three women are salvaging an old net, Diinna resting it upon her lap beneath baby Erik in his cloth sling. She brings her head down so close she looks like a mother bird feeding her young.

It is impossible to forget the last time the three of them worked on mending together, and the needle feels spiteful. Maren places her hand on the fine thread, so as not to lose her place. Dag's mother, Fru Olufsdatter, has set out benches along the edges of her cook room and they sit around them as though they are ranged about the lip of a square boat. The firelight sets the floor unsteady.

'We will have a Lensmann there, Hans Køning. He is under direct orders from King Christian, and will be making great changes, Pastor Kurtsson says, with new strictures on kirke-going.' Toril looks directly at Diinna. 'And he is looking to settle the Lapps and bring them to God.'

Diinna shifts beside Maren, but holds Toril's gaze.

'He will not manage it with men like Nils Kurtsson,' says Kirsten. 'That man couldn't bring a beast to pasture.'

Diinna snorts, and goes back to her sewing.

'Pastor Kurtsson has told me his next sermon will be to stay you,' says Toril, narrowing her eyes at the top of Diinna's head. 'The Lensmann will not think fishing proper.'

'He isn't our Lensmann yet. And propriety doesn't feed us,' says Kirsten. 'Only fish can do that. I'll not be minding what a Scotsman thinks of it.'

'He's a Scotsman?' Sigfrid's eyebrows rise. 'Why not a Norwegian, or a Dane?'

'He was in the Danish fleet for many years,' says Kirsten, eyes on her needlework. 'Cleared the pirates at Spitsbergen. The King himself picked and placed him at Vardøhus.'

'How do you know this?' says Toril.

Kirsten doesn't look up. 'You aren't the only one with ears, Toril. I speak with the sailors who come to our harbour.'

'I see you do,' says Toril. 'It is most indecent.'

Kirsten ignores her. 'And whatever Pastor Kurtsson decides to mumble at us this Sabbath's Day, I shall not be able to hear him over the grumble of my stomach.'

Maren stifles a laugh. If it had been anyone but Kirsten who had put forward the idea of taking the boats, they should not have entertained it. But she has always been a certain woman, stubborn and strong, and on Sabbath's Day Pastor Kurtsson's mouthful of lukewarm warnings do nothing to stop them. He has had no reply from the Lensmann, and so Kirsten insists they go ahead.

·

Instead of the Wednesday meet, eight of them gather at the harbour's edge. They have lost a few of their volunteers following news of the letter to the Lensmann, and will only take one boat after all.

The women are dressed in their dead men's sealskins and caps, hands unwieldy in thick gloves, oars standing higher than their heads as they regard the jumble of mended nets, unintelligible as the tangle of hair Maren pulls daily from Mamma's fish-spine comb.

'Well then,' Kirsten claps her broad hands together. 'We need two between us. Maren? Help me.'

Though her hands are large, they are more skilled than Maren's, whose fingers chafe and catch on the thin weave of the nets. It is a good day, the sky light but clouded, free of the biting cold they have spent so many months living with pressed against their bones.

They spread two nets out on the harbour side, and the others have to weight them with slick black stones. Then, taking one at a time, Kirsten shows them how to work them into a fold that can be opened easily.

'How do you know this?' says Edne.

'My husband taught me.'

'Why?' says Edne, shock apparent in her thin voice.

'Just as well he did,' snaps Kirsten. 'Now the next.'

They are watched on all sides from windows and most keenly from the doorway of the kirke. Pastor Kurtsson's slight

40

frame is backed by the brightness of candles and the wooden cross glowering behind. They are being judged, unfavourably at that.

Finally they load the boat with the nets and themselves. Mamma has made Maren a meal, just as she used to for Erik and Pappa, of flatbrød sprinkled with flax, and a strip of dried cod from Pappa's last catch. She told Maren this detail proudly, as if it is a blessing and not as Maren feels it, an omen. A skin of light beer sloshes over her heart.

Before she steps into the boat Maren does what she has been avoiding for months now, and looks directly at the sea, slapping the side of Mads's boat with careless little touches. *Waves*, Maren corrects. The sea doesn't have fingers, or hands, or a mouth that can open and swallow. It doesn't watch her: doesn't think anything of her at all.

She takes up an oar, and with Edne at her other side, begins to row. None of those watching cheer, or wave them off, and once the women are on their way they turn their backs.

Kirsten matched them according to size. Edne and Maren are of a similar height and age, though Edne is a little thinner. Maren has to temper her stroke to meet her, and from the seesawing of their path she can tell that others have not yet grasped the need to make allowances and adjustments for the rhythm of your partner. The calculation of it is so distracting Maren doesn't much care that land is drawing further and further away, how soon they will be at the harbour mouth and how beyond that is the sea proper, full of whales and seals and storms, and men drowned and never returned.

Her arms ache within minutes. Though none of them live idly, this is a different sort of movement, this folding forward and straining back, all in your shoulders and arms and licking up your neck and down your back, the seat hard beneath your thighs. The birds begin to circle, feinting so low towards the boat that Edne squeals.

Maren's breath has a song to it, a wheeze she can feel tracing down into her lungs and bringing up stale air, tasting like dust. Her hair is dripping sweat and sea spray down the back of her coat, face numb already, lips cracking around her foul breath. It is no wonder that the men kept their beards long: with her bare face she feels as unsuited to the sea as a newborn.

They reach the harbour mouth and suddenly are at open ocean. The wind comes stronger as soon as they leave the inlet, and a couple of the women cry out as the boat rocks against the strengthened waves.

'First net,' says Kirsten, voice still steady. Edne and Maren unfold it as the others continue to row. They spread the net as though they are making a bed with fresh sheets and throw it. It settles like a blanket over the waves, and drops down, tethered to the surface by regular plugs of cork. They keep it trailing from the boat with rope and throw the other net over the opposite side.

'Drop anchor,' says Kirsten. Magda and Britta heave it overboard and let the heavy metal fall. The men would cast off entirely and go further out to set more, but they are loath to travel beyond the jut of Hornøya island. The ache in Maren's arms has pooled into heaviness, and she is working hard not to look at the stac crouching barely a hundred feet away.

With the boat secured and nets down, something close to joy spreads through them. Magda laughs at the swooping birds and this brings an echo to Maren's own mouth. They fall silent almost as fast, but something has lifted. They slouch back into the curves of the boat and share their meals between them. The clouds sweep aside and though she can't feel its warmth, the sun is starting to redden Maren's nose. She feels tired and happy, and does not think of the whale at all.

After an hour or so, a shadow crosses the sun, clouds turning swift and the sea swelling once again. An awful quiet passes through, but there is nothing to do but wait. Spitsbergen, where Kirsten says the Lensmann fought back pirates, sits beyond a horizon sparkling with ice. It could be that they can see to the end of the world, here.

'Nets,' says Kirsten. 'Come on.'

Maren knows it is good the moment they start pulling. The net is heavy and strains their sore arms, but as the first shift and flip of fish begin to break the green chop of the water they are shrieking joy through ragged throats. Pulling harder and faster, they soon spill a half-net into the bottom of the boat.

Aside from the skrei and other whitefish fit for tørrfisk, there are herring neat and silver as needles, and salmon that thrash until Kirsten picks them up, one by one, and smashes their heads over the sides of the boat. Edne shrinks back but Maren cheers with the others. The other net is nearly as full: a single redfish thrashes bewildered amongst cod. Maren lifts it almost tenderly, and takes firm grasp of its tail. The snap of its head against the boat sends a thrill through her aching belly.

'Well done,' says Kirsten, a hand on her shoulder, and for a moment Maren thinks she might blood her cheeks like a man after a hunt.

There is light enough for another cast-off, but they don't want to stretch their luck. They turn for home, and now they are facing the open water, broken only by Hornøya island and its stac of heaped rocks. Edne whispers a prayer beneath her breath, and Maren closes her eyes, breathing the air in deep, feeling the drag of her oar.

The row home feels fast, all of them finding each other's pace more easily, like a well-worn tune. There is no one waiting

43

as they draw in. Kirsten jumps ashore to tether them, and Maren watches the dark water and thinks that maybe the whale was shadowing them all along, and will now rise to break the boat across its back.

But soon she is being helped onto the harbour edge, the ground unsteady beneath her. Land has been made strange from even their half-day at sea: Maren wonders how sailors can stand to come ashore at all. The other women start to gather when they bring the catch to the troughs, Toril at their head. There is a subdued cheer as the nets are emptied, and Maren can barely believe how many fish there are.

'God provides,' says Toril, though the ache in Maren's arms tells her it was not God but they who brought this catch home.

Mamma comes to the harbour like an invalid, leaning on Diinna, and Maren can see baby Erik's hat over her shoulder. Diinna's lips are pursed. She doesn't like being left alone with Mamma: recently Mamma has become absent-minded. She gets in the way and does household tasks wrong, darns already mended stockings, leaves the lids off jars so they spoil. Diinna would rather be on the boat than at home with her child and Mamma, Maren is sure.

Maren helps sort the fish, and atop the regular meting-out of their portion, Kirsten gives Maren the redfish she killed. She thinks to tell Mamma what she did but Mamma shrinks away from it, and from Maren. She says, 'You have blood on your cheek,' then turns and follows Diinna, laden with their share of the catch, back to the house, leaving Maren to seek out the smudge herself.

When Maren reaches home she lets Diinna help prepare all but the redfish. She scrapes it clean of scales herself, draws a line from its mashed head to its narrow tail, and brings out the guts. She settles them beside the board, and doesn't let Diinna throw them away: they are blue and red and translucent.

She throws them instead on the fire, watches them sizzle and dissolve.

Maren uses Pappa's walrus-tusk tweezers to lift out the finest bones of the fish, and when she is done she cooks it straight away, though it would have been best smoked. She wants to eat it now, at its freshest, while she can still remember what it felt like to have it living between her palms.

Mamma watches her from bed with something like disapproval knotting her brow. She will not eat the fish, will not eat at all that night. She doesn't ask Maren what it was like on the boat, or tell her she is proud. She turns her back in bed, and feigns sleep.

Maren dreams, as always, of the whale. There is salt in her mouth, and her arms strain with effort. But the whale is swimming, not beached, and though it is black and has five fins she isn't afraid. She reaches out to it, and it is warm as blood.

Six

The next months are at once sharp and shapeless. There is no more talk of whether they should go to sea: they do, every week. More women join them, and soon they have three boats going regularly, even as the year switches on its heel and darkness begins to gather at the corners of the sky, like shadows at the rafters of a mighty house.

Pastor Kurtsson watches from the narrow stoop of the kirke, preaches sermons of growing intensity on the merits of obeying the Kirke and its servants. But even as his fervour builds, Maren feels a change, a turning amongst the women. Something darker is growing, and she finds it in herself, too. She is less and less interested in what he has to say, and more consumed by her work: fishing, chopping wood, readying the fields. In kirke, she finds she has drifted, like an untethered boat, and her mind is out at sea with oars in her hands and an ache in her arms.

She is not the only one losing interest in kirke ways. At the Wednesday meets, Fru Olufsdatter questions Diinna about the Sámi way of scenting fresh water, and enlists Kirsten's help in fashioning bone figures to mark her husband and son. When Maren visits Pappa's and Erik's graves, she finds poorly carved rune rocks laid like stepping stones amongst the settled dirt. More than once, she finds a fox skin on the headland, its meat left at the highest point of the hill. Remembrances, charms: she recalls such things from childhood.

She watches the women in kirke, wonders who snared it, bled it out. Who peeled the fur from its flesh and left it hollow, pinned down by rocks, an offering to the wind. She asks Diinna what a skinned fox means, and Diinna raises her eyebrows, shrugs. But whatever the hope wished over it, the women of Vardø are slipping back into the old ways, grasping for anything solid.

Toril must be unaware of it, or else she'd have told the minister. She and her 'kirke-women', as Kirsten calls them, spend more and more time in the kirke as the winter draws in and closes over them, atoning for the sins that took their husbands from them.

Still the divide is growing, sure as a crack in the wall tapped upon by ceaseless fingers, smoothed only slightly by fuller bellies. But they are still here, Maren reminds herself. Still living. They have a system – if you need hides you go to Kirsten, swap for dried fish or thread work, which is in turn exchanged with Toril for gut thread or fresh moss from the low mountain, where she refuses to go because it is full of Sámi and once rumoured to be a witches' meet place. All of them have their skills, their uses, interlaced and built up like a haphazard ladder, resting one atop another.

'It's a sort of triumph,' says Kirsten one Wednesday. 'What would our husbands say?'

'Nothing good,' says Sigfrid. She has fallen firmly in with Toril, but can't stand to miss the gossip of the meets. 'Pastor Kurtsson says—'

'Has Pastor Kurtsson planned the sermon for Christmas Eve?' says Kirsten.

'I imagine so,' says Sigfrid.

'I should like to say something,' says Kirsten. 'Speak on the storm. I think many of us would. It is time. I am ready.'

Maren looks around the room. She sees no likely candidates. She has no true words for it, even a year later. All of them have the same telling of the storm, now, passed through many tongues until its rough, difficult edges are worn smooth as sea glass.

'Maren?' Kirsten is looking at her, waiting for support. But Maren has none to give her, and nor does any arrive from Edne, or Fru Olufsdatter.

The others must feel, as Maren does, a comfort in it, all of them standing at the same point on the flat sweep of bay: as though they are collected and folded an eye behind an eye behind an eye, clustered around the same seeing scope. *The storm came in like that.* Finger snap. She can't remember who first put the action to it: it may have been Toril, or Kirsten. It may even have been her. They agree on this telling, this snap of fingers, as if by accident, though it's a sort of cowardice. She's sure they despise her for it, as she does them. They pull it across their eyes and tongues so they do not have to really remember. How the boats were there, and then gone.

Maren looks to the window. The relentless dark has a tinge of grey to it: a fog rolling in from the north. They come sudden, swallowing, a dampening cold that penetrates skirts, stockings, makes the familiar ground foreign and strange. Out there, beyond the final row of houses, is the harbour. She watches the sea even more carefully now. She is learning not to feel much for it, with their regular fishing expeditions. But with the anniversary soon upon them, she finds she has no desire to dwell on what it took from them, least of all speak about it in kirke.

48

She can feel Kirsten's disappointment, and seeks her out as Fru Olufsdatter dims the lamps and tells them it is time to go.

'I'm sorry,' she says, touching Kirsten's shoulder. 'I am sure the pastor would let you speak.'

'I don't need his permission,' says Kirsten, blue eyes narrowed. 'I'll think on it.'

•

Kirsten does not speak on Christmas Eve, though Maren wishes she had. Pastor Kurtsson's sermon is full of platitude, a vague repetition of his words over their husbands' and sons' graves. Maren finds no comfort in it, nothing of their lost men, nothing of the altered women left behind. How many times has she wished that Erik and Pappa lived? Pastor Kurtsson could never understand. No man could.

As she watches him bend to the shelf below his pulpit, and bring out a letter bearing a seal and tassel, Maren realizes she hates him a little: his weakness, his power over them. His constant talk of the mercies of God, when it is obvious to her that they do not extend so far north. Is His eye upon her, inside her head as she thinks these things? She holds her breath and gropes inside her mind, as though she could feel God there.

'This arrived yesterday,' says their minister, unfolding the letter. The seal is so heavy it bends the parchment almost in half, and Pastor Kurtsson must hold it out before him, so it blocks him from view. 'Our Lensmann is soon to take his seat at Vardøhus, from which he will govern all of Finnmark.'

Toril shifts in her seat, looks about the room as if to ensure they note it was she who first brought them the news.

'And, in addition, you,' continues Pastor Kurtsson, 'which is to say, we, are to have a commissioner live amongst us. He will be appointed by the Lensmann, to oversee the town more closely.'

'But Pastor Kurtsson,' says Kirsten, 'is that not what our minister, your good self, is for?'

'It is true that he might assist in spiritual matters,' says Pastor Kurtsson, frowning at the interruption. 'But I remain your minister.'

'Praise be,' says Kirsten, too brightly for the minister to do much but look dour.

When the letter is folded, and the kirke-women kneel to heap prayers upon prayers, Kirsten and Maren linger outside. It is so dark they must stand very close to one another, like animals pushing their bodies together for warmth. Kirsten's eyes are hooded.

'A commissioner,' she says. 'But no mention of his commission.'

'Perhaps he will be like a governor, as Alta has,' offers Maren.

'In so small a place?' says Kirsten. 'Alta has a great many more people. What need have we of an overseer, especially if Lensmann Cunningham will soon be at his fortress?'

They glance instinctively in the direction of Vardøhus, though the fog is pressed so tight against Maren's eyeballs it makes them sting. Kirsten looks back at her, considering. 'Would you like to come to my house? I have beer, and cheese.'

Maren would like, very much, to see what Kirsten has made of Mads Petersson's house. She has often wondered how Kirsten copes there, without farmhands, and she would like to see the reindeer. But Mamma will be at home and weeping over Pappa, and so she shakes her head.

'Thank you, but I must go.'

Kirsten nods. 'To be told of the commissioner on this day – is it significant?'

Maren blinks at her, surprised. 'I did not take you for superstitious.'

'I only wonder what it is the beginning of.'

'Perhaps it is an end,' says Maren, unsettled by her tone. 'A closing of a circle.'

'Circles have no end,' says Kirsten, and straightens suddenly. 'I'll see you tomorrow.'

They turn away from each other into the mouthing fog. The houses are quiet as Maren walks from the kirke, past Fru Olufsdatter's house, Toril's home, and to the outskirts where the light from their fire glows weakly through the slatted windows, dispersed into unearthly whiteness by the fog.

Maren wants to keep walking, past Baar Ragnvalsson's empty house, to the headland. It is an effort to place her hand on their door, to push her way into the cloying warmth. Mamma is stoking the fire, worrying at a patch of dry skin at the corner of her mouth, and Diinna is there with Erik pressed to her chest.

'I told her,' says Mamma, without looking up. 'About the commissioner.'

'What do you think?' says Maren.

'Not much.' Diinna is rubbing at Erik's gums with clove paste. Drool comes in great strings from his mouth, red in the firelight. Maren wants to shake her. She misses the way they used to talk. She thought Erik's birth would draw Diinna out of her husband's death, but she is more silent than ever.

'At least it will be someone new,' she offers. 'Another pair of hands.'

Mamma's tongue flicks at her cracked lip, and they fall into the silence that marks their evenings, and speak no more of the commissioner.

They imagine he will be like their minister, have as little impact as snow falling in the sea. They imagine that their lives will go on, and that the worst is behind them. They imagine all sorts of silly, inconsequential things, and every bit of it is wrong.

To the Esteemed Commissioner of Vardøhus, Mr Cornet,

New Year greetings to you! I thank you for your letter of the
19th October. I am greatly encouraged that it reached me with
such pace. One never knows how the ships will go.

It is with gladness I read of your acceptance, and urge you
not to tarry. I will inform King Christian of your agreement –
I have his ear and you can be sure your name will be poured
into it. The minister at Vardø has already been notified, and
will make ready for your arrival. Great things await you here,
and I hope we can grow the Lord's estimation of us Scotsmen
even further.

I enclose with this letter your passage to Bergen, where you
can proceed through Trøndheim, and on to Vardø. I trust you
will not find the journey too arduous.

Your idea of a Norwegian wife is a good one, though I
should not wait to come so far north. Bergen will have its spread
of good young women desirous of a husband of such standing.
Use your title and the sum enclosed to bring someone to keep
your bed warm. Perhaps someone who can sing? We will be in
need of entertainment.

My regards to Coltart, who I had not known reads your
letters. There will be none of that here.

Come safely and swiftly.

Hans Køning
Lensmann over Vardøhus County

Bergen, Hordaland,
south-western Norway
1619

Seven

Siv has lit the fires in the drawing room and hung the best curtains, so Ursa knows there has either been a death, or there is to be a marriage.

'Or maybe a lord come to our house,' says Agnete when Ursa has returned with a final warmed jug of water and the information. 'Or an actress?' Agnete has recently learnt of actresses, their father having organized passage for a theatre troupe travelling to Edinburgh on one of his remaining ships.

'Then it will be a dead lord, or a lord come to marry one of us,' Ursa says, pouring the jug into the tub. 'Same goes for the actress, only she will be here for Father.'

Agnete laughs, and then winces. Ursa can hear the draw of fluid rattling across her lungs.

'Hush, I should not have excited you.' She helps Agnete pull herself up on her pillows. Her leg drags, and Ursa smooths the sheets. 'Siv will not forgive me. Here.'

She places her hand on Agnete's thin front, leans her forwards over the enamel bowl. Beneath her palms her sister's lungs rattle as she spits. Ursa covers it over without looking as Siv tells her to do: she knows what colour it will be from the thick breathing that came against her ear all night.

When Agnete is done she helps her from her nightdress. It smells of sour sweat and sickness, so common to Agnete that Ursa barely notices it other than when the clean, bright smell of lavender-scented water is in the air. She helps Agnete into the tub, half-lifting her bad leg over the edge, specially scooped for this purpose.

Her sister is still child-thin, child-straight at the waist and hips though Ursa was nearly full-figured by thirteen. The doctors, who come monthly, measure her each time, but none see her naked as Ursa does, the sharp planes of her body hollowed, her bad leg shrivelled off as old fruit.

'Surely there's no one left to die,' says Agnete when Ursa has placed the bar across the tub for her to lean on as she soaps. 'So it must be marriage.'

Ursa had thought the same, and hopes Agnete can't hear the painful thumping of her heart.

'Do you not think so, Ursa? Father has found someone for you to marry!' Her voice is bright and hollow as a bell. Though there are seven years between them, Ursa often thinks Agnete feels what she feels, as they say twins do. Now Agnete is clutching her soaped hand to her bare chest, at exactly the point Ursa's is hurting.

'Perhaps.'

It means Agnete will be alone in this house, confined mostly upstairs, with only Siv left to care for her. Father rarely visits them except to say goodnight. Even if Ursa's betrothed is from Bergen, Agnete will have to learn to sleep alone in this room, spend her days with only herself for company. But Agnete doesn't say any of this, only nods for Ursa to pour a jug of water over her head.

When Agnete is out and dried, and in a clean nightdress, she stops Ursa from combing her hair and says, 'Come, let me plait yours. Siv makes it so severe.'

Her hands are gentle as she wraps and twists Ursa's hair into one long loop that gathers across the back of her head, scooping down to her nape and fastening behind each ear, and looks at her with such evident pride that Ursa feels self-conscious.

Siv raises an eyebrow at it when she comes to dress Ursa: she is as strict a Lutheran as they come, and wears only brown, and a square of starched white on her greying hair. She sniffs as she puts away the pale pink cotton Ursa was to wear, and crosses to the heavy armoire they used to share with Mother.

It is cherrywood, stripped from a ship come from New England, varnished with a dark brown that drags the colour out of it: much as Siv's clothes do her. But at its hinges and the battered carved nubs of its feet, the wood is deepest, softest red.

Siv draws out Mother's favourite gown: yellow and gathered at the sleeves. 'Your father wants you in this,' she says, reluctant. 'You're to meet a gentleman.'

'A gentleman!' Agnete is propped on her pillows and clasps her hands. 'And in Mother's gown, Ursa. I'm so jealous I could spit.'

'Neither jealousy nor spitting are virtues, Agnete.'

'What gentleman, Siv?' says Ursa.

'I don't know that. Only that he's a good Christian. Your father saw fit to tell me that. He's no Papist.'

Agnete rolls her eyes as Siv turns to unhook the buttons from their loops of silk. 'Did you find out anything important, Siv?'

'I can't think of much more important than that.'

'Oh, but is he tall, or rich, or have a beard?'

Siv purses her lips. 'This will be a little small, but I have no time to adjust it.' She motions for Ursa to crouch, and hauls the dress over her head.

Ursa waits in the rustling gloom of its skirts while Siv's hand searches, and makes no move to help. She breathes deeply, hoping for the lilac scent of Mother to come to her in the dark. But it smells only of dust.

•

The drawing-room door is open when she is summoned, the firelight glowing across the hallway carpet. They heard him arrive, rushed to the window to spy a wide-brimmed black hat standing beneath the windowsill, removed just in time for the door to be opened and the head disappear into shadows. Agnete squeezes Ursa's hands.

'Remember everything.'

The banister is very smooth, and throws up the scent of beeswax Siv has not buffed off fully. She hopes they will not have to touch. Of course they will not. But all the same she imagines him reaching for her hand and sliding right off, greasy with wax. He has no face and she realizes he soon will. And a body, a voice, and a smell.

It is her first time meeting a suitor, and she wishes Father had come to tell her something of him, or how he met him, or even if he is someone she knows. Herr Kasperson perhaps, Father's clerk, with his rosy cheeks and shy smile. He is twenty-five, only five years older than Ursa. She thinks she could like a man like him, though he has a strange habit of rubbing his lip with his thumb, which makes him look shifty. She could ask him to stop that if they were married. He seems the sort of man who would listen.

The patched step creaks. She looks up to where their bedroom door stands ajar, imagines Agnete listening for her, holding her breath. Ursa lit as many candles as she could before she came down, but still Agnete had been swallowed by shadow. It has been a long winter, stretching out over spring and freezing the windows closed. But then, this house is always dark at its edges, even in summer, even with all the drapes thrown back and the light so bright it makes Ursa sneeze. She may never spend another season in this house. Would she miss it, or only the people inside?

She turns from the staircase and rolls her shoulders back. Walking feels strange in her narrow silk slippers, with the weight of Mother's dress slipping close to her shoulders.

Deep voices flicker with the firelight. It isn't Herr Kasperson's voice that answers Father's, or anyone's voice she knows. It isn't, she notes as she readies herself to enter, even Norwegian. *English*, she thinks, dredges it up from the small, painful place where she keeps all her memories of her mother. Her mother couldn't read or write but, being the daughter of a merchant, she learnt English well enough and brought Ursa and Agnete up with it too. They used to speak it around the dinner table, practising their accents until they were smooth and only slightly inflected. Ursa clucks her tongue, once, twice, and steps across the threshold.

He is as tall as Father, and broader than any man she knows. He bows as Father places a firm hand at her back and sweeps her forward into the room, so even as she sits she has not seen his face.

The men have been sitting beside one another in the crimson-flocked chairs with the carved arms, and she is left to settle opposite them on the armless chair, careful to keep her back straight, hands folded in her lap.

'Ursula. After the saint, I presume.' His accent means she has to listen carefully to understand each word, though he doesn't speak fast. If anything, he speaks too slowly, and it distorts the words. He is turned in his chair, sideways towards the fire and her father. His voice sinks and burrs. She feels a blush rising at her throat.

Father jerks his head. She is meant to answer, then, though his tone gave no hint of a question.

'Yes, sir. And the stars.'

'Stars?'

Father coughs awkwardly. 'Ursula, this is Herr Cornet.'

'Commissioner Cornet,' corrects the man. 'Absalom.'

It takes a moment to comprehend this must be his given name, because he says it like a hallelujah or an *Amen*. She looks up more boldly.

He is tall, dark-eyed. She can't place him in age: not so young as Herr Kasperson, not nearly so old as Father. He is handsome, in his way. His austere, well-cut clothing can't hide how he carries a little weight around his middle, though not so much as she. Ursa watches his profile, the workmanlike heft of his jaw and brow made fine by his straight nose, his dark, slightly curling hair.

'Commissioner Cornet has come from Scotland,' says Father. 'He is to take up a prestigious post in Vardøhus.'

'Sent for by John Cunningham himself, who is upon the orders of your King,' says Cornet pridefully. She has not heard of John Cunningham, or of Vardøhus. 'And I'm in need of a wife.'

It is a moment before she realizes this is the marriage proposal.

'The wife of a commissioner,' says Father gladly. 'Ursula?' She can hear the question in his voice, knows she should look up and smile, reassure him that she is glad too. She searches herself, regards her lap. Her knuckles are white. 'We will arrange it at once.'

They talk back and forth, Father asking about the commission, Cornet enquiring whether it is true there are no trees so far north. Their passage will be on one of Father's ships, and Ursa listens to the rising rush in her ears. Siv laced her in to the joins, and she can't inhale fully. She thinks of Agnete, her wet breath. North. Ursa never guessed marriage would take her so far. She imagines ice, and darkness. Finally Father seems to remember her there, dismisses her. She stands so quickly her head spins, and trips from the room.

The wife of a commissioner. She knows she couldn't wish for better, but still her skin crawls with nerves. Since Mother's death, Father has made bad decision after bad decision: she sees it in the dismissal of all clerks except Herr Kasperson, the letting-go of all servants but Siv, the visits from the doctors reduced from weekly to monthly. She can read it in the drawing room shuttered up for all but the best visitors and Christmas, in the settling droop of Father's shoulders and the beer on his breath. This is a good marriage, will bring a little coin with it perhaps.

She passes the rack and leans towards Cornet's coat. It smells of wet leaves and her fingers twitch towards the pockets, but she can't bring herself to touch it.

Ursa makes for the stairs, taking them too fast and too loudly. Agnete looks startled as Ursa closes their door, starts immediately to grapple with the buttons.

'What's the matter? Was he ugly?'

The dress has to come off. She can't breathe in it. She is growing bigger inside it, or it is shrinking, and her head is gripped by the hairstyle and she has to be loose of all of it: her sister's careful braid, her dead mother's dress. How has he come here? How has he found her, in this quiet house on an unquiet street in Bergen?

'Can you help me?'

She sits beside Agnete on the bed, and her sister struggles to a sitting position, fumbles with the fastenings, but it is too tight about the waist. 'We need Siv.'

Ursa feels sick at the way it presses her. She goes to the

window, watching for him to leave. Her heart is loud as a clock.

'Ursa? What happened?'

The door opens, and her betrothed steps into the street, doesn't call for a carriage. She watches his black-hatted head fade in amongst all the other black-hatted heads.

'Ursa?'

Absalom Cornet. It sounds less like a prayer, and more like a knell.

Eight

Ursa expects to wake feeling different, but there is nothing to mark the next day as special. Siv rouses them early as usual, throwing back their curtains, though since they were swapped for cheaper cotton the light leaks right through. Ursa can remember the fine blue velvet ones she grew up with, hiding in their long folds while Mother sat at her dresser, brushing out the thick blonde hair that both daughters inherited. But they had to be sold five years ago, along with that dresser and the silver-backed combs, when Father made another poor investment. This room that was once her mother's dressing room is now their bedroom, the top floor shuttered up.

'It makes no sense with Agnete as she is,' Father told her when Ursa complained about moving from her large room. 'All those stairs. And it is too costly to run the fires, keep all that furniture in those empty rooms. I'm selling much of it, though we may yet rent it out.'

Ursa is glad the lodger is yet to materialize. She doesn't want a stranger sleeping in their house. And now, she won't have to worry about it ever again, for soon she will be sleeping beside a stranger in her own house. When she thinks of this, her hands shake. She hopes Absalom Cornet won't remain unfamiliar for long.

Siv sets a breakfast tray before Agnete. It's the same silver one she served the tea on yesterday and Ursa smiles at her, noticing the effort. Agnete has had another bad night, and the sheets are twisted about her legs. Ursa smooths them and helps her sister into a sitting position as Siv clears her spit bowl, brow creased with concern.

'Another dose of the vapours after breakfast, I think.'

'No, please, Siv,' says Agnete. Her voice is thick, her chest wheezes. 'I am fine, really.'

'Her nose is still sore from last time,' says Ursa. 'Can we not leave it today?'

'We have orders from the doctor,' says Siv. 'You know it helps.'

'It hurts,' says Agnete when Siv has gone to fetch the vapour bowl. She touches the tender red place beneath her nose where the skin is cracked and irritated.

'I know,' says Ursa, smoothing back her sister's hair. Despite her bath, it is already rank with sweat. 'We can cover your nose with one of Mother's silk kerchiefs.'

'The blue one?'

Ursa stands at once and goes to their mother's armoire. On the shelf above the rail there is a wooden box of kerchiefs and other effects that survived Father's purge, and she takes Agnete's favourite from it. She pins back her sister's hair as Agnete presses it to her face, running it through her fingers.

'Eat, Agnete.'

'We should be speaking English,' says Agnete. 'To help you practise.'

'He is Scottish.'

'But he speaks English, still?'

'Yes.'

64

'Well then.'

'Well then,' says Ursa, in English. 'Eat, Agnete.'

Agnete nibbles at the knekkebrød. 'It's so dry.'

'There is no blessing so complete as bread,' says Ursa, mock sternly, imitating their housekeeper's intonation. But it is increasingly hard to keep Agnete happy, with all her pleasures slowly being strictured. The doctors stopped her eating anything wet about a month ago, and she is still adjusting to it. Ursa suspects they are making up much of Agnete's treatment as they go along. She doesn't think her sister's poor lungs are caused by too much stew.

Siv brings back a cloth and a large bowl of steaming water, and the small bottle brought by the doctor. She starts to unstopper its lid but Ursa holds out her hand for it. 'I can manage, thank you, Siv.'

Siv eyes her. 'Seven drops, the doctor said. Seven drops or else there's no point.'

'I know.'

The housekeeper puts the bottle into her outstretched palm, presses a brisk kiss to Agnete's forehead, and leaves the room.

'You won't do seven, will you? One is fine,' says Agnete, peering anxiously at her. Ursa shakes four drops of oil into the bowl, swirls it so the yellowness spreads about on the water. The smell hits her nostrils and makes her eyes sting. She sets the bowl on the table beside Agnete, helps her sit up so she can lean over the steam, kerchief clutched tight to her nose.

She places one hand at her sister's forehead to support her, and brings the cloth over her head to trap the vapours.

'Breathe deep.'

She places her palm on Agnete's back, hearing as much as feeling her slow, painful inhale, the wet rush of her exhale. She counts aloud to one hundred breaths, and Agnete emerges red-faced from the steam, eyes streaming, the kerchief damp. She coughs, spits into the clean bowl Siv brought on her breakfast tray.

'How does it feel?' asks Agnete, as Ursa covers the bowl, and sets it aside.

'I was about to ask you.'

'It stings and it's horrible and I wish the doctors would listen when I tell them so. Now you.'

'How does what feel?'

Agnete rolls her watering eyes. 'Being engaged to be married.'

Despite her complaints, Ursa can hear that Agnete's breathing is easier. 'Much the same. Would you like to go downstairs today?'

'No. Tell me, what he is like?'

'I do not know much of him yet,' says Ursa. 'Only what I told you yesterday.'

'Tell me again?'

•

She has told her meagre story three times before the day is done. Father doesn't call on them that day, nor the next, and Siv tells them he is out to decide details at Absalom's place of residence, leaving Ursa to withstand Agnete's disappointment at the lack of courtship.

'Why does he not write?'

'It is only two days since we met.'

'Still.'

'What use would a letter be? I cannot read.'

'A song then. Something.'

Ursa shrugs.

'Perhaps it doesn't matter,' says Agnete. 'Perhaps it is enough that he saw your face and wished to marry you.'

Ursa supposes there is a romance to that. For someone not even to know you, and yet to love you.

'Do you think Father wrote to Mother?'

'She couldn't read, either.' Agnete's face falls, and Ursa takes pity on her. 'Maybe. You should ask him.'

She knows Agnete won't. She won't, either. Father crumples whenever Mother is mentioned, even after all these years. Lately Ursa has caught him looking at her with an awful sadness in his eyes – she knows she is looking more like her mother with each passing year. Perhaps that is why he stays so much away from her these days, though he used to speak to her on all manner of things. They were once so close, and now, his silence is catching.

Ursa wonders how different this moment would be if Mother had not died bringing their brother into the world. If both of them had lived, and there were a boy running about the house. If Father had not lost all his money, and all three of the siblings were hiding in the velvet curtains, watching their mother brush her hair until it crackled. But Agnete would still be ill, and she would still be marrying a stranger, going with him to a place she has never heard of.

Agnete reaches out suddenly for her.

'You will miss me?'

Ursa wants to tell her yes. She wants to tell her sister she is as air to her, that she couldn't have a better friend in the world. But she only takes Agnete's thin face in her palms and hopes she knows what it means.

•

The night before the wedding, they lift Agnete down the stairs in her chair to dine with them for the first time in months. It is an inelegant task, and all of them are sweating by the time Agnete is ensconced closest to the fire, wrapped in shawls. Siv

67

watches her, poised, as though she may keel over like an upturned boat at any moment.

But Agnete sits straight, and barely coughs, and Father pours Ursa a small glass of akevitt. It tastes bitter as medicine, but she swallows it down, the burn turning to a gentle warmth in her belly.

Emboldened by the akevitt and Agnete's presence, Ursa asks Father how it came to be that Absalom Cornet arrived at their door, and Agnete stops chewing to listen. Ursa knows her sister has imagined all sorts of fanciful things.

'I met him at the harbour,' says Father, not looking at Ursa. 'He approached me, admired my cross.'

Its chain glints from his waistcoat pocket. Ursa knows he often takes it out and keeps it held in his hand without even thinking about it: piousness as a tic.

'He told me of his posting to Vardø, his calling from God to serve there.'

'I thought the Lensmann had called him?' says Ursa, and winks at Agnete. But Father does not catch the tone, pours another akevitt.

'The Lensmann is beneath the King, and the King beneath God.'

'Your husband must be verily crushed,' says Agnete, winking back. Ursa clasps her sister's hand beneath the table. It is so soft she wants to bring it to her cheek, to kiss it and not let go.

'He was in need of a ship, and a bride—'

'In that order?' whispers Ursa, and Agnete snorts so suddenly she begins to cough again. Siv rushes forwards with her spit bowl, and Ursa tightens her grip on her hand until the worst is past. Father drains his akevitt, speaks more to himself than to his daughters.

'I gave him a good price for his passage.'

68

And for me, Ursa thinks.

Agnete must be carried up, and Ursa insists upon doing it, tucking up her skirts so she will not trip on the stairs. Her sister is hot and too light, like a newborn pup. Agnete wraps her thin arms around Ursa's neck.

'Not very romantic, is it?' she murmurs, her chest rattling.

'It'll do,' says Ursa. Agnete wrinkles her nose in disappointment.

For once, Agnete sleeps, but the akevitt fizzes through Ursa's body, leaves her legs restless. She stands to pace their room, presses her forehead against the cool glass of their window. She can see as far as the harbour, the ships like toys on the horizon. There are always men there, always busy and moving. *The world goes on*, she thinks, and beneath the weight in the pit of her stomach that is half Siv's cooking, half dread, she is glad she will soon be part of it.

•

Leaving their house in the morning is like walking through a dreamscape: everything familiar and made completely strange by the fact that she will not see it again, not for a long while. *Ever?* She banishes the thought. She is the daughter of a ship-owner: of course she will come back.

Father stops her in the hallway with a rare clasp of her hand.

'Your mother,' he begins, and she hears the catch in his throat.

She thinks he will not say more, is hopeful of it because her eyes are swollen enough by her tears with Agnete, despite Siv's cold compresses. But instead he draws her into the dimness of his study, lights a lamp and pushes the door to.

'You must have this.'

It is a small glass bottle, the one that always stood on

Mother's dresser before it was sold. Ursa takes and unstoppers it, presses the smell of stale lilacs into her wrists.

'Thank you, Father.'

She hopes it will make it easier for him, now there is one fewer to clothe and feed. Perhaps he can employ someone to help with Agnete. For although there has been no time to announce it in the society pages of the paper, and though her dowry comprises mostly of their passage to the North, some fragrance and her dead mother's dress, it is a good marriage. Her husband is a commissioner with a letter from a Lensmann in his pocket.

Father kisses her on the forehead. His hand trembles and he smells of old beer: yeast and sharpness. Later, her husband kisses her on exactly the same spot to seal the marriage, and he smells of nothing at all. Clean as snow.

Nine

It is still early when Cornet holds the door of the tavern he has booked a bed in open for her, and goes to the bar while Ursa retires to their room.

She prepares as best she can, presses the lilac water to her wrists, and at the place where her pulse moves the thin skin beneath her earlobe. She imagines that he will kiss her there, and it makes her hands quake. The linen of her nightdress scratches at her shoulders and breasts. It has a high neck and doesn't seem to be designed to lie down in, but as it is Siv's wedding gift, perhaps that is the idea after all.

Siv starched it herself, and Ursa knows that was a luxury of time she did not have. Ursa smelt the boiling bran, saw Siv soaking it the three days between betrothal and wedding. The nightdress still smells of sour water, though Siv had worked it across the slickstone to take out the worst of it; it still crunched the first time Ursa laced the ribbons at the front.

Agnete gave her the blue silk kerchief, her favourite of Mother's. It clinked when Ursa took it. Inside were five skilling, Agnete's share of what they were given following the sale of Mother's things.

'I cannot take this.'

'You must not go so far without the means to come back.'

'I can ask Absalom for the money.'

'You should have your own,' Agnete said, though she had no idea of the cost of such a voyage, any more than Ursa did. 'Just in case.'

Ursula's eyes are small and mean in the dark, greasy window: her lip trembles like a sulking child's. She draws the thin curtains.

Her husband, for all his pride in his title, is obviously not the lavish sort. Their lodging is within smelling distance of the trade port, with its perpetual reek of tobacco and decay. It seeps in through the rotten frame of the window on the bleak chill and she presses her wrist to her nose.

The lilac brings back easier days, before Mother died, when the house was lit like a Christmas tree throughout the cold winters and long, luminous summers, and all of them dressed and fed by four servants and a cook. Mother and Father had dinner parties with other merchants and their sparkling wives, and Ursa would be permitted to sit up with them in the drawing room before they descended into the dark glitter and chatter of the dining room.

She never had much thought for her wedding breakfast, but supposed it would be something like one of those parties. She'd certainly imagined guests beyond Siv, Father, and Agnete made breathless by the cold air. Though she had no friends to speak of, Father having withdrawn them so much from society, still she'd imagined women like Mother used to dine with, their long bare throats backed by bright collars, golden hair twisted about their heads. Men in fine suits with ruffs jutting at their necks like well-wattled birds, bearing gifts of sugared plums and silk. Pomade and lavender in the air, a table laid with roasted goose and creamed spinach, a whole salmon poached with lemon and chives, carrots heaped with butter. Candles burnishing the scene golden and precious.

Not the back room of Gelfstadt Tavern, convenient to the kirke and the harbour, a bottle of brandy between the men, Father misty-eyed and remembering. He looked old in the glow from the draughty fire that kept spluttering soot and chill wind through its fireguard. The candles were stubs melted together from many ends: yellow and gutting.

When the time for goodbyes came, Cornet turned his back as though her tears were something indecent. Agnete stood without aid, to show she could, leant only a little on her on the walk to the carriage. Father had drunk too much and they had already said their goodbyes in his study. There was nothing Ursa could say to Agnete but they clung to each other until Siv pushed them gently apart.

'Take care, Mistress Cornet.'

And then they were away.

She imagines her husband downstairs, the band she placed onto the base of his finger clinking against his glass, perhaps toasting her. And because they will use his customs for naming, she is Mistress Absalom Cornet. Herself, lost inside his name.

She hopes to please him, and knows some of this begins tonight, in this square room with its overlarge bed, here in this tavern on the Bergen docks, their ship to Finnmark waiting outside on water so chill she hears men at the hull breaking ice from it. An accusatory Siv told Ursa a little of what to do, cheeks flushing – *nightdress, bed, don't watch him for it is too wanton, prayers when it is done.*

She removes the chamber pot from sight, slides the warming pan from one side of the bed to the other. There are pale stains on the mattress, and the straw has broken through in places. She can't face the greying pillow and so wraps her old nightdress about it.

She lies ever so carefully, makes sure her hair is about her shoulders the way Agnete told her makes it look like she lies in a field of shining yellow wheat. Lamplight comes irregularly from the dock, and through the wooden walls she hears coarse voices speaking English and Norwegian and French and other languages she can't recognize.

Beneath it all sits a creaking sound, like their stair at home, or Father's knees when he sits. For a long while she can't place it, and wonders if it is inside her own mind. But then she realizes: it is the ice, relocking about the ships.

Soon she will be on that sea, and moving further and further from Agnete and Father and Siv, from their house on Konge Street, and from Bergen with its broad, clean roads and busy port. Leaving the finest city of the world, and all she has ever known, for what? She has no picture of Vardø, the place she is to live. No idea of the house they will share, the people she will meet.

The creaking grows until it is all she can hear. She presses her lilac-scented wrist to her face, and sucks in air like water.

•

The rasp of a door and gutter of a candle wake her, and she rolls over, reaches for Agnete. Her nightdress is creased beneath her cheek, hands frozen on the sheet. And in the small circle of the candlelight, Absalom – her *husband* – is undressing, the dark nap of his head bowed as he sways and struggles with his belt.

She doesn't stir. She barely breathes. In her sleep she has ruined her careful arrangement of hair: it is about her neck like a noose. Her nightgown has rucked up to her waist but she dares not move to pull it down.

Absalom Cornet has removed his trousers, and now that her eyes have adjusted she can see his underthings have come

74

off as well. He is even paler beneath his clothes, like a sea creature winkled from its shell. She closes her eyes as he comes towards the bed, and the straw wheezes staleness as the weight of his body falls upon it.

A rush of cold air sweeps beneath the blankets as he moves under them, and she feels her cheeks flush when she realizes what he must be able to see: her underthings, childish with their ribbons drawn through. The room is filled with a sharp smell of alcohol and smoke. She had not taken him for a drinker. Her heartbeat is painful in her ears.

Nothing happens for a long while, and she wonders if he is asleep. She opens an eyelid and sees his eyes are still wide and staring at the ceiling. He is taking deep breaths, his hand clutching at the blanket, white-knuckled, and it comes to her that he is nervous. That is why he has drunk so much and come so late. She is likely his first. She is readying herself to reach out to him, to tell him she is shy of it too, when he turns his head and looks at her.

She knows the set of his eyes, has seen it in the men who arrived at the dinner parties steady and clear-eyed, but left staggering. Something sharp enters his gaze as he props himself sideways. She remembers Siv's instruction not to look him in the eye, and with an urgency that is almost painful her hands contract about her nightdress, pulling it down.

He rolls himself suddenly on top of her; so clumsy and heavy her breasts are crushed. The possibility of breath narrows to such a point that it is only when she feels the hardness of him already on her thigh that she thinks to take one, a gasp that heightens to a cry. He is fumbling with the ribbons, then lower, at the seams. He pulls: it gives. He moves along her, and her body doesn't give so easily.

Another cry comes, a sound she has never heard herself make before. It frightens her more even than he does. He has cut her, she thinks wildly, he has stabbed her. There is a centre to her she never knew existed: a bright, throbbing place so sore she could sob.

His face is in the pillow, and he is breathing bitter breath against her ear and hair. His arms are braced either side of her shoulders, and his chest knocks against hers with an awful force. She drags her awareness away from the hot point of hurt as he burrows further into her, sending it to the ache of her legs, caught and cramping beneath his. When she tries to move them he raises himself slightly and lays one arm flat across her collarbones, and she knows he means for her to lie still.

The bed makes a wild squeaking sound, like an animal in a trap, and finally tears come hot from the humiliation of it, the tearing of it. His whole body bucks. A moan hits her ear.

The coming-out is nearly as painful as the going-in.

He stands unsteadily and pisses in the bedpan: she can hear he misses. There is something warm between her legs: blood and something else that doesn't belong to her.

When he has dragged on his nightshirt, blown out the candle and slumped into bed with no part of them touching, she rolls the other way and brings her legs up to her belly, trying to soothe the stinging.

She couldn't have guessed at it: this hollow knowledge that wives must carry with them, that their husbands tear themselves a place in their bodies. Is this really how babies are got? She bites on her hand to keep from crying. How is she to tell Agnete of any of this – how is she to warn her that even with a man appointed commissioner, with a beard that smells of clean snow and who prays hard as a minister, there can be no safety? Beside her, with the first light of morning coming through the thin curtains, Absalom Cornet opens his mouth wide, and begins to snore.

Ten

There is a hierarchy to a ship stricter than in the finest house. It is close to covenant, and Ursa decides, for all her limited knowledge of the world, that there must be no country run harder or neater than a ship.

In place of beasts are the monkeys, the boys of twelve or thirteen who climb the rigging and swab the decks: even the ship's cat is treated better. They accept beatings and yellings dumbly as horses, are as pitiable. Then there are the sailors, older, rougher. They are skilled and coarse, going about their tasks with a rhythm inscrutable to Ursa's eye. The captain, it seems, is higher than a king, though lower than God. The sea is that to them, giving grace or committing violence, always spoken of in hushed, reverent tones. Ursa isn't sure where her husband and she fit – she supposes they do not.

Why any man would choose a life at sea is beyond her. From the moment she steps aboard the *Petrsbolli*, she wishes to turn around and step straight back off it. Everything, from its dark wood to its slimed guard rail, seems glowering and forbidding.

It is a rudimentary ship, even to her untrained eye. It isn't that Father has not made an effort: there are clean linen sheets on the bunk, made double size for their marriage bed, and he has sent a tiny clothes chest of cherrywood, same as Mother's armoire, fitted with a brass lock for which she has the only key. In it she keeps Mother's lilac water and blue kerchief, Agnete's money. But these fine details make the whole thing worse. It is dark, the floor is slippery with unknowable grease, and it is tiny – her husband could brush the walls with his outstretched fingers, and when they lie down his feet will dangle over the end of the bunk.

This, she knows, is the best they could do. They can't afford passage on a better ship. She wonders if Absalom regrets her father's offer. It isn't even a merchant ship made for fine goods: their cargo is local wood, milled in the forests of Christiania and brought by fjord to be taken north, where there are no trees. This thought is as strange to her as the sea: all about Bergen is forest.

Not for the first time, she is glad she was not Father's son, and had no need to be trained in the shipping business. The ground never steady beneath your feet, so that at one moment you may be taking tea below decks with your husband and the captain in his cabin and, despite the swaying of the minute horn lantern and the cups braced by small lips to keep them from sliding about the table, almost imagining yourself in some sort of decent society, and at the next the whole world is tipped sideways.

And then there is the sound. Not only from the sea, which her night in Gelfstadt Tavern gave some notion of, but from other people. The sound of so many men: their heavy tread on the boards above and below; men's laughter, always too loud and too long; the grunt of men's effort as they haul ropes or clean decks or move cargo. The cargo must be turned and checked for rot every other day, the ship's cat loosed to flush out rats.

This isn't a ship made, nor fit, for passengers. Their cabin has been nooked out of the men's sleeping room, marked off by thin walls of cheap wood that sway and strain in the joins. They share a doorway, left to the cabin, right to the large space of the men's room. She waits to rise until most of them are up at work, but on a ship no one sleeps all at once so she still catches glimpses of hammocks strung like great cocoons fore-and-aft, two or three sleeping as close as bats clustered in the dark. But worst are the noises of night-times, the snoring and other bodily effects, occasionally sounds that make her cheeks burn and her body tense.

The men, for all their coarseness, still call her 'Mistress Cornet' when they pass each other below decks, but in bed she knows her true place. At first she thinks she must be doing something wrong. Though her husband gives her time to take off her underthings after that first night together, and though she learns to keep her legs open so as not to feel so trapped, and pins her hair back so it doesn't catch beneath his hands, there is always pain. There isn't always blood after, but there is a constant soreness.

Every morning, every night, and after each meal, he drops to his knees and prays so fervently she doubts she could pull him from it were there fire licking his soles. He prays with a care and focus he does not show her, his lips working, his forehead pressed against his clasped hands. Inwardly she rails against Agnete's beloved stories, at Mother's tender glances at Father, at the bawdy laughter of the kitchen maids back when they had them, when the delivery boy came calling.

Did they all know what love was, and lie?

•

To survive, she is cultivating distance. Even before Agnete was born, Ursa craved company, always shadowed Father and

79

played in the same room as Mother, always talked too much though she knew it risked being banished to the playroom with its dolls and blocks. Now, she is making a silence of herself.

She barely speaks, barely opens her mouth wide enough to eat the small squares of tough meat and wrinkled carrots, the mush of oats or fish, made edible with fresh herbs that quickly wither and turn brown. She is working on turning invisible, sits very still at the formal meal, which they take daily with the captain, her mouth a dark line like a closed hinge. Even when she joins Absalom on the floor to pray, the wood hard beneath her knees, she is sure not to raise her voice above a whisper on the *Amen*.

Sometimes Captain Leifsson and Absalom have whole conversations without so much as gesturing at her. The captain's English is heavily accented, and Ursa must listen as carefully as she does to Absalom. Her husband is often boastful of his appointment as commissioner: she learns a little more of him this way. How, at thirty-four, he is the youngest commissioner Lensmann Cunningham has selected, that he comes from the same area of Scotland, though is lower-born. That his name has been mentioned to the King himself.

'And why is he bringing you?' asks Captain Leifsson. 'It is a long way from Scotland.'

'We are to root the Church more fully into the land there,' says Absalom, with the same passion with which he prays. 'And destroy its enemies.'

'I am sure you will not find many of those,' says Captain Leifsson, sipping from his cup. Ursa can see a small smile at the corners of his lips. 'There is barely anyone there.'

She keeps all this information held hard in her mind. She wants to take as much from her husband as she can, without having to give too much of herself in return – she feels the scales must eventually tip in her favour, that soon she will have some power in their relations. That he desires her is obvious, but tenderness seems distant as their destination. Perhaps by the time they reach the edge of the world, they might draw closer together, but then again, she is not sure, any more, that this is what she wants.

What she wishes for, prays for, is some sort of control. She finds it only alone, in the cabin that has been her world at sea so far. Her husband goes elsewhere in the days. He is exactly as his profile suggested to her in Father's sitting room. Brutishness made palatable by touches of fineness and manners.

Their journey is punctuated by stops along the coast. They are to be at sea over a month – 'Perhaps two,' shrugs Captain Leifsson, unconcerned as Ursa feels herself blanche – though the journey would be far quicker aboard a ship that did not have business at seemingly every port. Ursa supposes Father must exploit any opportunity for trade.

Each day, though she spends them mainly alone, she dresses carefully as Siv taught her, hooking the buttons with a claw designed for this purpose. Siv must have one, to dress herself – or does her dress do up at the front? Ursa wrinkles her nose, tries to remember. She wants no detail of home to slip away. The monotony is broken by occasional nausea, which she eases by lying back with one foot placed on the floor.

It is ten days since they left Bergen, and she is arranged just so when there is a knock at the thin door. Captain Leifsson stands crouched beneath the low beam, smiling.

'We are about to enter Christiansfjord, Mistress Cornet, to begin our approach to Trøndheim. It is fair weather, and the cliffs standing clear. Perhaps you should like to come and see?'

He has a voice like a minister, or a judge. A voice that makes a suggestion into an order, impossible to disobey. He is a head shorter than her husband, and with a thinner beard, blond where Absalom is dark. He is kinder-eyed, too. She wishes Absalom would look like that at her, wonders if this is her lot now, judging all men against the length and breadth of her husband.

He waits while she slides on her cloak and follows behind him. The passageway is busy as ever, men coming running along the length and pausing to allow them past, before disappearing into the shadows again.

'I hope you are finding the journey comfortable?' says Captain Leifsson.

'Most comfortable, thank you, captain. I hope we are not too much of an imposition.'

'It is your father's charter.' She notices he doesn't say that it is Father's ship. 'It is good,' he continues, perhaps to soften his sentence, 'to have reason to light the lamps in my cabin, and I know the cook enjoys the challenge of creating such culinary delights as are appropriate for a lady from Bergen.' He turns briefly back to her, a twitch of a smile in his beard. 'And besides, I have not gone so far as Vardø since my whaling days. Here we are. Might you wish to ascend first?'

The ladder is steep, barely slanted. She would like to go ahead, to have someone behind in case she loses her grip, but her dress means it would be improper. She gestures for him to go. The rungs are slick and chill, seeping instantly through her gloves and thin soles. Could Father not have sent her with boots?

Captain Leifsson waits at the top and helps her up, taking her weight where she stumbles slightly on the iced-over top step. Though his touch is gentle it feels bruising even through clothes: she can't suffer a man to touch her, however well meant. He leads her to the raised back of the ship.

The day is impossibly bright: the sort of crystalline clarity that comes when winter still sits in the air. They have already entered at the narrow mouth of the fjord, and the cliffs rise sheerly either side, a clean hundred feet, the black rock raked with lines of lighter grey. The sea is green and glitters with chips of ice, and as soon as the wind bites at her face and brings up its blood, chilling her lungs, she feels better than she has since she left home.

'They are magnificent, are they not?'

'They are,' she breathes, and is embarrassed by the keenness in her voice. 'Though you must have seen mightier, captain?'

'I take each sight for itself alone, Mistress Cornet. Come.'

He offers her his arm. She looks about for her husband, but can't sight him. The deck is full of men, leaning out each side of the ship, calling back in a chain of voices to the second mate, Hinsson, who stands steering at the whipstaff towards the rear. The sail stands over them, snapping in the wind like a canvas cloud: monkeys scurry up and down the rigging, and stronger sailors sit astride the beams, adjusting the vents of the canvas to control their speed.

It feels good to be amongst such action. Ursa takes the captain's arm out of necessity more than anything, and they begin to walk. Her legs are stiff and soft all at once, begrudging and grateful of her weight.

'You should come up here more often,' he suggests. 'It would be perfectly appropriate for you to walk the stern, even alone. No one would trouble you.'

'I'll think on it,' says Ursa. It sounds harsher than she meant, and she adds a hurried, 'Thank you, captain.'

'Have you been a-sea before, Mistress Cornet?'

'Never.'

'I am amazed,' he says. 'Your father was so often at sea. To travel seemed his great passion. I would have guessed at him sharing it with his kin, girls or no.'

'Father has not sailed for years,' she says, surprised. 'He gave it up when I was born, and once my mother . . .' She hesitates. The clean air brings confidences up easily, and with the wind snatching her words from her as soon as they are out she doesn't feel as though she need conceal it. 'Mother grew frail, he did not wish to leave her.'

'Ah, yes. I heard Merida had passed. I started to write, many times, but . . .' He gestures about him, and she thinks she understands what he is trying to say. A ship feels a different place entirely. 'Six years?'

'Nine. Forgive me, I did not know you were so well acquainted with my parents.'

He stops. 'Do you not recognize me, Ursula?'

Her name, unshrouded by her husband's for the first time in ten days, is a shock. But she finds nothing familiar in his face. She shakes her head.

'I am sorry, captain. Should I?'

'I dined at your house on several occasions, when Merida was still living. You were often at play about us, getting beneath our feet. I sometimes passed you food beneath the table, like a dog . . .' He stops again and turns to her, eyes wide. 'I did not mean offence, only you were a mischievous child.' But she is smiling at his alarm, gives his arm the lightest of squeezes.

'I take no offence, captain.'

'You are up, wife.' Absalom Cornet is before them, sudden as a squall, leaning on the guard rail, with his face to them. How decent he looks. But something in her throbs with panic. She gives no sign of it, but the corner of her eye starts to flutter in time with her heart.

'The captain willed it, husband. He wished to show me Christiansfjord.'

Absalom eyes the cliffs as though they just occurred to him to be worth looking at. 'Named for your King, I suppose.'

'There is some debate over that.' Captain Leifsson's voice is firm but light.

'That they are named for him?'

'That he is our King. Some still rebuke the treaty.'

'It is law,' says her husband without humour to match that in the captain's voice. 'There is surely nothing to rebuke?'

'Of course.' The captain gives a neat bow. She realizes she is clinging to him and eases her grip. A muscle is working in Absalom's jaw. 'We are walking the deck, if you would care to join us.'

Absalom gives a tight shake of his head and turns back to his staring. She notes that his hands are clasped on the rail and wonders if he has been praying.

Silence falls between them. Their exchange with her husband has reminded her to feel afraid. The back of her neck creeps as she catches the smell of ice on the air: of clean nothing. The knot that had eased in her belly is done up tight again and squeezing, even as they walk away from Absalom. The fjord slides a mighty shadow over them, and in its jagged cool she tries to relax.

'You do not remember, then?' Captain Leifsson's voice is soft, as though he recognizes her panic.

Those dinner parties were over with by the time she was eleven. Even without the fug of distance, the faces of adults were all the same, all glamour and whiskers and age. She never watched them with any specificity, only revelled in her access to this world of laughter and smoke. She barely remembers hiding beneath the table. It must have only been on one or two occasions, when Father was too involved in conversation to notice, Mother turning a blind eye.

'I am sorry.'

'No need, no need.' But she is sure she has disappointed him somehow. Wanting to pull him from it, she casts about for another question.

'Have you been to Vardøhus before, captain?'

He gives a tight nod.

'Is it a castle as everybody says?'

'Of a sort. It is certainly a sizeable structure to have been built so far from anything.'

Her dismay must show clearly for he pushes on. 'But I have heard it is to become grander beneath Lensmann Køning. He has the King's ear, and I hear he has great plans for Finnmark. What has your husband told you of it?'

'Very little.'

'Your father, perhaps? I know he ran whaling boats at Spitsbergen. Did he go east to Vardø?'

She bites the tender inside of her cheek. 'Not that he spoke to me of, captain.'

They are approaching the whipstaff, where Second Mate Hinsson lifts a meaty hand in greeting. Before him, one of the monkeys, a thin boy of about Agnete's age, is sorting frayed ends of rigging.

'Would you tell me of Finnmark?'

'I only know it from the sea.'

'I know of it not at all. I have not been north of Bergen a day in my life.'

They have reached the stern, where St Peter for whom the ship is named is carved in miniature with brute efficiency and attached to the rearmost mast. Piles of rope are stored in tight whorls big as barrels. The captain lets go of her arm and leans against one, looking back over the stern. Behind, the boat is throwing out long draglines of froth. The captain withdraws a stained pipe from his jacket.

'Do you mind?'

She shakes her head no. He brings out a small pouch of tobacco and tamps it down, strikes his lighting flint, shields it from the wind. The sudden flare of the tobacco catching makes her realize it is growing dark again, the bluish light fading to

86

a darker spread of deep blue. Soon the first stars will be out. She has not seen them in days.

He takes a long drag, exhales white smoke. 'What do you wish to know?'

Ursa considers. 'What's the furthest you've been?'

'From where?'

Ursa flushes. 'From Bergen.' She had forgot it was not the centre of the world for everyone.

'Spitsbergen, as I said.'

'Is that very far?'

He chuckles, a throaty sound made mellower by his mouthful of smoke. 'The furthest most go north.'

'And Vardø is not so far as that.'

'No, not so far.'

That comforts her, a little. 'What is there?'

'Whales. Ice. Some Sámi cross the ice in winter to summer there, return when the sea refreezes.'

'Sámi? You mean the Lapps?'

'No, I mean Sámi,' Captain Leifsson replies, firmly.

'You've met them?' The thin skin at the edges of her eyes stings.

'Some of them.'

'What are they like? Are they fearfully wild?'

'No more than the next man.' Something between them shifts. He seems annoyed with her, and Ursa grapples for something to say to pull herself back into his confidence.

'Is there anything beyond Spitsbergen?'

He sniffs, rubs at his nose. The moment of uneasiness passes. His pipe has already gone out and he empties out the burnt endings, refills. For an instant she wonders what it would be like to be married to a man such as this, who speaks to her so easily and takes her arm so gently. He strikes the flint, and the tobacco flares in the dark hollow of his palms.

87

'Educated types say there is a black rock there. A mountain, high as the sky, made out of magnetic rock, and that is why our compass needles drag north. Some think the sea pulls towards it the nearer you get, too. That if you cross the gulf, you will be carried along on its current, all the way to the black rock.'

'And you'll be dashed upon it?'

'Sucked down.' He takes a long draw. 'They think the sea stops before it, drops like a waterfall, right through to the bottom of the earth. But I do not believe it,' he says, straightening and rolling back his shoulders. 'The Sámi do not speak of it, and they go further than any Norseman has.'

'What do you think is there?'

'Perhaps there is a black rock. It makes sense that the compasses point that way for a reason. But I do not believe the sea turns river and drops away. I believe it flows all the way around.' The bowl smoulders redly. 'And that is quite terrifying enough.'

He tamps out the pipe, pulls another pouch from another pocket, loosens the drawstring, and holds it towards her. 'Aniseed?'

'What is it?'

'A herbal seed, from Asia. It's sweet.' Ursa holds out her palm and he tips a small greenish seed onto it. When she bites into it, it's bitter and she grimaces. Captain Leifsson laughs.

'You are meant to suck upon it. See?'

He places one in his mouth. His cheeks hollow in. Ursa turns away to spit the seed into her palm, throws it over the back of the ship. The captain gives her another, and she sucks, very aware of his eyes upon her mouth.

'Wife.' The word is curt, a summons. 'Captain, we should ready ourselves to dine.' Her husband stands with his hand outstretched. 'Come.'

She had not been conscious of how close she and the captain had been standing. She steps away.

'Thank you for the company, captain.'

'A pleasure, Mistress Cornet.'

When Absalom takes her hand, his grip is too firm. As soon as they are out of hearing distance, he bends his head towards her.

'Do not speak Norwegian with him in my presence. A man should understand what his wife is saying.' He drops her hand. She follows him at as much of a distance as she dares, and they ready themselves in silence for dinner.

His mood seems to pass quickly, and he calls her beautiful when they are both changed, her hair freshly combed and pinned. He places his hand at the small of her back when they go to the captain's cabin, sits close to her at the table.

'I have been thinking, captain. I should like to make further efforts to learn Norwegian. I hear you butcher my language enough. It is only fair I have a turn at yours.'

'Certainly,' says Captain Leifsson jovially. 'I'll speak with Dr Rivkin, he has some experience teaching, I believe.'

Ursa feels a noose slip about her neck. Soon she will have nowhere to hide, not even her mother tongue. She excuses herself early, leaves them talking in the lamplight. She feels, once again, quite alone.

Eleven

They arrive at Trøndheim in the dark. Her husband still hasn't come to bed from the captain's cabin, and despite herself she wishes that he, someone, were there beside her as she listens to the boisterous noise of the port.

She tries to sleep, but before the light arrives she gives up. The men's room is empty, the sacks of the hammocks hanging loose in the scant light. The lanterns aren't lit in the passageway, but the captain had taken her along a straight route to the ladder. The terror of the dark almost sends her back, but she can hear Agnete's voice in her head, urging her on.

Feeling along the rough wooden walls, she begins to make her way to what should be the hatch to get above deck. The sounds guide her and soon she is at the ladder. The trapdoor is closed and she is in near blackness, but starts the climb anyway. About halfway up there is a sudden light, and a crash rings down as the hatch is opened.

A bare foot slaps on the top rung.

'Wait,' she calls out. 'I'm coming up.'

A thin face looks down, and she sees it is the boy she noticed yesterday sorting rope ends.

'Sorry, Fru!' He hurriedly vacates the top of the ladder, and when she reaches it his hand extends and, thanking heaven for her gloves, she takes it.

'Thank you.' She smooths her skirts. 'Have you seen my husband? Commissioner Cornet?'

'He's gone ashore, Fru Cornet.'

'Mistress Cornet.' She corrects, and looks about her. Trøndheim is ablaze with lamps and a winch is being rolled to them on the low stone harbour, the ship ready for unloading. The harbour curves fully about them. From here, it looks similar to Bergen, and she is heartened. 'Is Captain Leifsson about?'

The boy shakes his head. 'No, mistress. Ashore.'

'Do you know where?' She had imagined one of them would be here.

'No.'

'Then I shall go ashore also. Would you find someone to escort me?'

He gives a short nod and darts off. The sky is lightening, and she can see that the houses lining the harbour are as brightly painted as in Bergen.

The boy is back. 'Second Mate Hinsson says I am to assist you, mistress.'

'Is there no one else?'

'No one else to be spared.' He has a slight lisp, and she wonders if he is in fact younger than Agnete, still losing milk teeth.

'Do you know Trøndheim?'

'No, Mistress Cornet.'

'Well,' she says, resisting the urge to throw up her hands. 'Shall we?'

He leads the way along the narrow gangplank, darting ahead with his bare feet. She should have at least asked him to put on shoes – the ground must be freezing.

She scrambles after him, the ship made unsteady by the unloading. The men crossing the gangplank stop to allow her across, but as soon as she steps onto the damp wood, a slam of wind pushes her sideways. She grips the rope so tight her palms ache, and regains her balance, but the pins are pulled from her hair, sending it in a whipping sheet across her face.

Teeth chattering, she edges her way forwards until she reaches the harbour edge. The ground is so still it makes her stumble, and for the second time that morning a small, dirty hand steadies her. 'Careful, mistress.'

'Are you all right?' A man stands a respectful distance off, hand half out as if he is about to offer to help.

'Quite all right.' She manages a weak smile. 'Is there anywhere we may have something to eat?'

He points to a narrow wooden structure painted an uneven yellow. A murky sign depicting a bell sways slightly in the wind. She nods her thanks and, trailing the boy behind, takes several uncertain steps to its front door. The open sewer before it is frozen and she averts her eyes as she crosses the plank and pushes her way into the inn.

It is near full though the hour is early, but the boy finds them a small table in a corner furthest from the fire. There are some finely dressed women dotted throughout the crowd, accompanied by their husbands, and she knows it is irregular for her to be there without Absalom. But she is frayed from her sleepless night, and sends the boy to the bar with a skilling of Agnete's gift to buy light beer and a plate of whatever they have.

He returns with her change and some raspeball, which are hot and surprisingly good, filled with highly salted meat, the potato well cooked and warming. He hovers uncertainly as she begins to eat, and she has to pull him bodily onto the stool beside her and place a dumpling in his grimy hand before he will eat anything. She smiles at the boy and he looks so surprised she wonders what her face has been doing before now. In an effort to reassure him she asks his name, and he tells her it is Casper.

'How did you come to work aboard the ship?'

He shrugs, looking at the raspeball, and she pushes the plate towards him. Silence is fine with her.

As they leave, one of the sailors opens the door with a mock bow and though she doesn't dignify it with an acknowledgement she leaves with a smile on her face.

'The way they were staring,' she says to Casper, 'you'd think they'd never seen a lady before.'

'There were ladies in there,' says Casper. 'But they were not the same sort.'

'Same sort?'

'The sort such as what you are, mistress.'

She recalls their rouged cheeks, the bright colours of their dresses. Finally understanding, she flushes and wonders if the sailors took her for a whore, too, and whether those women at least receive something for their shame.

They make their way through the slowly waking town. The streets are narrow and the houses seem to lean in either side, as if conspiring. It isn't so fine as Bergen, of course, despite it being their capital.

They find a market in a large trading square, and Ursa buys boots and a vizard, and though he protests, a pair of gloves for Casper.

'I saw you sorting those odds of rope. These will keep your fingers nimble.'

She tries to offer him boots too, but he refuses to try any on, which the cobbler seems glad of. 'It is better to be barefoot, mistress, while I'm still growing. I'll out of them in a month. That's what Second Mate Hinsson says.'

When they return to the ship her husband is waiting at the top of the gangplank. He clips Casper lightly about the head and the boy disappears into the bustle of the ship, which has been emptied of much of its wood and sits higher in the water. Absalom glowers at her packages.

'It is the first day we have had a kirke at our disposal. The very kirke where your Kings are crowned, I believe. And you take the chance to purchase *things*.' He jerks his head at her full arms. 'Where did you get the means for those?'

'My sister gave me a little coin.'

'A husband should know of his wife's money,' he says, turning his dark eyes on her. 'Your father should have told you that.' He holds out his hand and after a moment's pause she reaches out to take it, but he flinches away. 'The money, wife.'

Later, when he is snoring beside her, she will dig her fingernails into the soft place beneath her ear, and curse herself for handing it over. Because though the lie would have come easy – 'I am sorry, husband, I have spent it' – she doesn't speak it. Something in him compels her, even as it repels. She reaches into her belt and passes over Agnete's coins.

He turns and leads her down the ladder, to their corridor. She wonders if, as he has been at kirke and so it is a sort of Sabbath, he will not lie with her that night. But he does, and it is as if he is trying to bed down something into her, plant her penance deep.

•

Ursa often wonders what she would say to Agnete, were she here. She doesn't have the words for the confusion of it: the way her body has become something unhomed, how she has already learnt the way to wield silence like a weapon.

She withdraws again from Captain Leifsson, though he has

94

been nothing but kind, even giving her a pouch of aniseed. She can trust nobody with her thoughts: fearful and limited though they are. Inside her, they are safe, a locked box stronger than her father's cherrywood gift. She needs them, every word, to herself.

But she does have somewhere, at last, to go. The day after they leave Trøndheim, she clothes herself as warmly as she can. She slips an aniseed onto her tongue, pulls on her boots and, tucking her vizard under one arm, opens the cabin door.

The trapdoor is closed, so she knocks until it is lifted, and doesn't take the hand that offers to help. She looks for Casper but he isn't above decks, or at least she can't discern him from the other monkeys scrambling in blankets up the rigging, unfurling the *Petrsbolli*'s sails to take them north.

Moving along the ship without Captain Leifsson's arm to steady her is disconcerting, but she doesn't trip as she had on the gangplank. She returns to the rear of the ship, just behind the mast where St Peter holds out his placating hand. Reaching the thick coil of rope twisted into a seat of sorts, and checking no one is nearby or watching, she heaves herself up.

She rests her feet primly on another coil of rope, and sits bundled in her coat and with her vizard over her face, the hard bite of her teeth against its holding bead comforting as a sweet. Through its narrow eye slits, everything feels more manageable. She wonders if this is how a horse feels, blinkered from the sights either side, only able to look ahead. She can see Second Mate Hinsson at the whipstaff, but he pays her no mind. As they move further north, she turns her thoughts before them, to the edge of the world.

Twelve

Baby Erik is approaching his eleventh month when Pastor Kurtsson receives a second letter from the Lensmann, telling them the commissioner has started his journey from Scotland, and they are to make the second boathouse ready. It is to be converted into a home for the commissioner.

Pastor Kurtsson, to everyone's surprise, seeks out Kirsten at Wednesday meet, and asks her to help.

'He tells me I am a calming presence,' says Kirsten to Maren and Mamma as they leave Fru Olufsdatter's. 'I wonder what has possessed him?'

'He likely wants allies before this commissioner arrives,' says Maren.

'Toril will not be pleased,' says Kirsten, smiling.

'Toril cannot ready a house. Our minister neither,' says Maren. 'You can, Kirsten. Toril knows her beloved Pastor Kurtsson has not offered the same steadiness as you.'

Kirsten shrugs off the compliment. 'He is sending men from Kiberg to help, but the commissioner is fetching a wife from Bergen, so she will be in need of some comforts. There is a limited purse, and Lensmann Køning has sent wood. I am to slaughter enough meat to last them the summer, and I thought you could stitch the pelts into something?'

Maren looks up at her, surprised.

'Toril is the best one for such a task,' says Mamma.

'Perhaps,' says Kirsten. 'But Toril is like to weave bitterness into it along with pretty patterns, and I would rather give the coin to you.'

It is decided then, that Maren will fetch the hides the following week, and the meat is to be salted and smoked in the shed Dag built.

'Very well,' says Kirsten. 'Between us, we'll make that boathouse fit for a commissioner.'

It is a kick to hear it, though of course the boathouse was never Maren's. It was a kindness that Dag's mother even allowed them to lay their dead there. Maren has no claim to it, and yet she still takes routes past it wherever she can, touches the carved runes of the door frame, and Herr Bjørn's carvings beneath. She still walks its circumference in the blue nights when she can't sleep because Erik is crying, or Mamma is crying, or Diinna's silence is too accusing. Now it is truly lost to her.

'What about fishing?' asks Maren.

Something troubled crosses Kirsten's weathered face. 'No more of that, I think. Not while things settle.'

Maren nods, suppressing a sigh of disappointment. 'I'll come for the furs next week.'

Kirsten waves them farewell, turns for home.

'We have forgotten our place in the world,' remarks Mamma as they walk the other way. 'That Kirsten Sørensdatter ought to be careful. She thinks herself our Lensmann, I can see that arrogance in her.'

'She has been, of sorts,' says Maren, as they pass the second boat shed. 'Kirsten kept us alive. She is a better Lensmann than the one soon to sit at Vardøhus.'

'Lensmann of what? A place of women. We are no better than a pack of cards to that man. He has allowed us to build ourselves higher than we thought we could, and he may choose to knock it all down.'

It is the most Mamma has spoken in weeks. Her grief seems unending, and at times Maren wants to shake her, just to shock her from her weeping. During the long winter nights now thankfully past, when Mamma had latched onto her side like a babe with its mother, Maren longed to dash her mother's hands from her, to sling her from the bed. The frustration is edged with hurt, she knows: hurt that Mamma seems not to acknowledge that Maren has lost just as much, and a near-husband besides, and with that a home of her own.

Maren is grateful that her mother has found her voice again, but she thinks her worry misplaced. Their seagoing will not be found out, and if it is no one can begrudge them trying to feed themselves. The commissioner's anticipated arrival marks a change: an investment of sorts being made in the village. They are not forgotten after all; whether for good or ill they will soon see.

Diinna is outside the house, running a slickstone over the boards of the steps. Maren can hear baby Erik wailing from within, and feels a sharp stab of alarm.

'He's crying,' says Mamma, rushing forward.

'He had a splinter,' says Diinna. 'I removed it.'

'But he's still hurting,' says Mamma. 'You should calm him.'

'I am smoothing the steps, so it will not happen again.' Diinna doesn't look up, even once. She is bent close over the slickstone, intent on her work.

Mamma mutters something Maren can't catch and treads deliberately over Diinna, foot very close to her hand. There is a tension between them as balanced as an oar in its thole:

they are close to losing balance. It is left to Maren to act as bridge between them, and she is close to abandoning her patience with them both.

She feels worse for baby Erik, who does not seem to soothe any of the unspoken hurt. Where Toril walks about with her bundled child on her hip easy as a basket made for her, on Diinna's narrow body Erik looks like a burden, or a growth. Diinna doesn't call him Erik, which Mamma insisted on, but Eret, which is the Sámi way of saying it.

There is something unnatural in how she is with him. Maren thinks Diinna watches him with her hooded eyes as a wolf watches another wolf: he is kin, but she is wary. It is as if he takes something from her she doesn't want to give, from her breast, from her arms, with his hands tugging at her hair. She never shouts at him, but watches. There's no cruelty there, but there is also little warmth, other than in the quiet times at night, when through the wall Maren can hear Diinna singing to him, always the same song.

'What is that lullaby?' Maren asked once.

'His *joik*.' Diinna narrowed her eyes. 'It is not a lullaby. It's his song, the one I made for him.'

'Do you have one, too?'

'We all do.'

'Do I?'

'No.' She offers nothing further, and Maren must soothe herself, make tender excuses in her head: *I am not Sámi, that's all*. But Diinna's constant refusal of their familial connection wounds her: Maren thought their bond stronger, able to survive without her brother. She was wrong about so many things that she feels she must each day assess her life anew. Sometimes, Diinna straps her son onto her back in a reindeer-pelt sling and walks – Maren watches her take the road to the headland, or sometimes even a boat to the low mountain, and she comes

99

back smelling of heather and clean, cold air of the kind you get only there.

Maren loves the boy with a fierceness approaching violence, though she worries there is something truly the matter with him, that they harmed him in his coming. He doesn't smile, or wail, or throw things in anger or frustration. When Diinna leaves him with Mamma and Maren, he mostly sits in the soft corner of the house Mamma made out of blankets and hides, and watches mutely.

Erik would have loved his son. Maren sometimes lets the full pain of what could have been come to her, when she watches the baby blow bubbles of spit from between his pink lips, or raise his small arms to her to be held.

'Was it a bad splinter?' she asks Diinna, watching her work at the step. Erik has already stopped crying: was obviously calling for attention rather than out of pain.

Diinna shakes her head. 'A scratch.'

'We have been at Fru Olufsdatter's,' says Maren.

'I know. It is Wednesday.'

'Kirsten says there is to be a commissioner, come to live in Vardø. The Lensmann soon to be in Vardøhus has sent for him.'

Diinna continues to work the stone: the noise is loud in her silence. The step sags beneath the force.

'He is to live in the second boathouse. He has a new wife.'

Finally Diinna sits back. She is squatting, long skirts making it just about decent, but still Maren wishes she wouldn't do things that give Magda and Toril reason to whisper about her. Diinna replies with the frankness she has had since childhood.

'Your and Dag's house?'

Maren feel a warm tingle of gratitude, thinking Diinna understands, perhaps, how hard it is. Diinna nods back, briskly, and rises to her feet.

'Makes sense. It is a good space. It will be a good home.'

Diinna's hair is loose and falling across her face. She bends to give the step a last swipe and Maren can only gape after her as she takes up the slickstone and turns to move inside. She doesn't follow Mamma, but enters her own door, leaving Mamma to deal with the baby.

Maren doesn't want to go in at all. She had thought, for a moment, that Diinna would ask her how she feels. That perhaps they would talk as they had when she and Erik were first married – like sisters.

She stands on the polished stair a long while and lets the hurt stab at her chest. She doesn't go in until she is numb with it and the cold, and can feel nothing at all.

•

As promised, Maren goes to Mads Petersson's farm eight days later. She still thinks of it this way, though it is nearly a year and half since Kirsten moved in. She knows it is time to fetch the skins because the night before the wind was coming in hard from the east, and Maren heard the sharp panic of the reindeer as Kirsten picked which were for the slaughter. Maren hummed tunelessly to drown it out but Diinna went outside with Erik and stood on the step while the cries dropped like stones against the windows.

Maren takes the fastest route, through the centre of the town. The warmer weather has brought the women outside, and they sit about on stools, draped in shawls, stopping their chatter when she passes. Toril sniffs as she goes by, pointedly stabs her needle into the pillowcase she is darning. So the news that Kirsten came to Maren about the skins has reached her. Maren takes delight in smiling broadly at the woman.

The Petersson farm is hunched at the opposite end of the village to Maren's house, its boundary sprawling across a mix of sown fields and scrubland to the sea. Maren spots the reindeer grazing the slope before she sees the house, their white and grey pelts showing more clearly now the ground is turning green, and heather is beginning to arrive. Their smell comes too, musty and full, following the same passages of wind the cries of their slain companions had the night before.

The house is set apart from the village, its front door and windows turned to the sea. Maren doesn't know how Kirsten stands it: when she moves to knock on the door, her back is directly turned to Hornøya with its hundreds of shrieking birds and its stac. Mads Petersson likely had the best view of all of them of the whale.

When Kirsten answers, she is flushed and smelling of blood. Crescent moons of crimson sit beneath her fingernails as she gestures Maren inside.

'Nearly done. I've slaughtered six, so there are enough for the bed and the floor.'

The room is bright and cluttered, almost as large as the second boathouse. There is game hanging from the ceiling: rabbits stripped of fur and pale as naked babies. A side door is open, and beyond it Maren can see the herd moving across the field, and in the near-distance the purple and yellow mess of the skinned reindeer waiting to be hung. Maren remembers the foxes on the headland, but can see no sign of dolls like Fru Olufsdatter has.

What she does see is Kirsten, in trousers. She stops just inside the door, staring down at them.

'What?' Kirsten looks down at herself. 'Oh, come now, Maren. You're not going to faint, are you?'

'Of course not,' says Maren. She has seen Sámi women in trousers, after all. Diinna wore them all her childhood. But there is something about Kirsten, standing as she is with her legs wide apart like a man, which unnerves her.

'They're Petersson's,' says Kirsten, pulling Maren in so she can close the door. 'I don't think he'd mind.'

'You should be careful, Kirsten,' says Maren. 'What if it had not been me at the door? What if it had been Toril, or Pastor Kurtsson?'

'They most certainly would have fainted,' says Kirsten breezily. 'It's no matter, Maren. Do you want beer? I have cheese, too. Made this past month.'

Maren nods to both, and carries her meal out to watch Kirsten finish flensing the skins. Fat is still looped in yellowish strings against the smooth underside of the hide, and Kirsten scrapes a seal knife across it.

'No time for tanning.' Kirsten is not even looking at her work. She is looking out towards the sea, her profile strong and hawk-like. She is Mamma's age, but her skin has the weathered aspect of a man's. It makes her look older and timeless, all at once. This farm life seems to suit her, and when Maren tastes the beer it's good: free of the bitter aftertaste Pappa's brews always had.

Maren knows from gossip that Kirsten has lost four children, delivering them herself before they were formed properly. But Maren can't imagine her a mother anyway. She isn't exactly a friend, either: Maren feels for her as she once felt for their previous minister, Pastor Gursson, who went down in the boat with her father and brother. He had the same calm energy, the same solid centring to him. He had sharp blue eyes like Kirsten too, that Maren couldn't look long into without blushing. If Kirsten were a man Maren thinks she would be more than an unofficial leader of their village, rather a minister or a man of the law, perhaps even a commissioner.

'I've had more from Pastor Kurtsson,' says Kirsten. Maren raises her eyebrows. 'I know. He held me back, after kirke. Toril hovered like a hawk. I think you were right, about him wanting allies. I think he anticipates some sort of tussle with this commissioner.'

'Will you back him?'

Kirsten snorts. 'I'll back myself. And you. But I've a sense the commissioner will be a hardier man than Kurtsson. He is a Scotsman, like Lensmann Køning. And his wife is a ship-owner's daughter from Bergen.'

Maren's eyebrows work their way higher, and Kirsten laughs, a throaty sound, mimicking Maren's expression as she strips another length of fat from the fur with a ripping sound. 'I know. Shipowners' daughters aren't common in Finnmark, are they? They tend to stop at Tromsø, or Alta at the very least.'

'I wonder what the Lensmann promised to warrant a lady to leave her city life.'

'Perhaps her husband is very handsome.' Kirsten eyes her slyly, and Maren sees her chin is speckled with blood. 'Do you think it a shame, that he is bringing a wife?'

Maren frowns. 'How so?'

'Perhaps he would have picked one here.'

Maren feels a blush creep to her cheeks, brushes at them as though she could wipe it off easy as blood. 'I doubt I'd get far even if he had.'

'Dag Bjørnsson liked you well enough,' says Kirsten, and her voice is gentler.

'Yes.' Maren swallows. 'I suppose most men would prefer a city lady.'

'You're a good woman, Maren. Good enough for anyone.'

Maren can't meet her eye, feels her blush deepen. 'Is he a sailor, like the Lensmann?'

'A godly man.'

'A minister?' Maren sucks in her cheeks. 'No wonder Pastor Kurtsson is worried.'

Kirsten stabs the blade into the ground at her feet, and dips her hands into a bucket of water beside her, already rusty with blood. 'He is not of the cloth but he does God's work.'

'A pious man who can marry? Toril will be pleased. The wife should watch herself.'

Kirsten snorts, and stands to stretch, reaching towards the sky. 'They arrive within the week. The Lensmann, though, he's already being felt in Varanger and Alta. In Kirkenes too. There have been arrests.'

'Arrests?'

'Witchcraft,' says Kirsten. Her voice is grim. 'Sámi.'

Maren's heart thumps as she thinks of Diinna. 'What for?'

'Wind-weaving, drums.'

Maren swallows. 'Wind-weaving is for sailors.'

'And drums?' Kirsten collects the pelts, heaping them so the fur is touching fur, and skin touching skin. 'Don't worry. I'll keep a weather eye out.'

'Toril has a loose tongue,' says Maren. 'Perhaps I should ask her—'

'Ask nothing of her,' says Kirsten, holding out the pelts. 'There's no reasoning with such a woman. It will pass. The Lensmann only wants to flaunt his power. But we would all do well to mind ourselves.'

'It is you who must learn to mind herself most of all,' says Maren, glancing down at Kirsten's trousers.

Kirsten doesn't reply, and Maren reaches out to take the pelts. Instead, her fingers wipe the smear of blood from Kirsten's chin. The action surprises them both equally, and Maren can't meet her friend's eye as Kirsten hands her the pelts. They are heavy and smell strongly of raw meat and the sweet air of approaching summer.

'Shame there's no time for tanning.' Something drips and lands at her feet. 'Scraping's the best I can do.'

'That is good enough.' Kirsten leads her around the side of the house. The sea glimmers about the stacked rocks. Maren wants to ask if it scares her, if the whale comes to her at night. But looking at Kirsten, hands in her trouser pockets, she thinks Kirsten sleeps soundly as baby Erik.

'You should get out of sight,' she says, and Kirsten laughs, tucks a wind-caught lock of Maren's hair behind her ear.

'And you should not worry so much.'

Maren can feel Kirsten's eyes upon her as she walks home, laden by the skins. Bright spots of red sprinkle the ground, and trace her path like stepping stones.

Thirteen

Now that Ursa has her place above decks, she is better able to bear what happens below. She never before would have guessed she was someone happiest outdoors: felt sure she was bred for parlours. But though the ship's stern is just a larger cage than her cabin, the air it moves through is free and clear, and it is easy to imagine any number of things being possible.

The sun starts to stick better to the heights of the sky, and on the skin about her eyes uncovered by the vizard, she sometimes feels its warmth, like Agnete's laboured breath at night. She wonders if Absalom can taste the sea salt on her skin, if he notices the ring of reddened flesh about her wrists where her coat and gloves do not quite meet.

The *Petrsbolli* stays close to the shore, keeping it within sight on the clear days. At the horizon, the smooth plains about Trøndheim give way to a snarl of mountains, rising sheer as waves at the sea's edge. When they slip into the orbit of the Arctic Circle there is little change in the view. Trees crouch at the throats of the fjords, still thick enough for Ursa to make shapes and troll faces in them; snow settles the crowns of the mountains. She watches islands slide by, defiant juts of land.

As they make their turn east, she sees her first iceberg, a

massive siding of white so bright it is blue and green, big as their house in Bergen, moving impenetrable as rock through the water. Captain Leifsson orders the ship in a wide circle about it and tells her that what is beneath the water is the most dangerous. She imagines it stalking her all the way to Vardø.

After stops at several minor ports, they reach Tromsø. She doesn't go ashore, but watches from her place on deck as they approach the port in a bluster of wind and sea spray. The town stands small on a rocky island that seems to slam against the water as much as the waves slam it, grey upon grey. They stay long enough for her husband to pray in the crouched kirke, and for fresh supplies to be brought aboard for their final push to Vardø.

At the last moment she sees Casper crossing the gangplank before it is drawn up. He stands a little hunched, clutching a bundle and still shoeless. Ursa removes her vizard, leans across the side of the ship and calls out to him, but he has already turned and gone. She feels something close to panic, a hot shard in her ribs. She approaches the second mate, pokes him in the shoulder like a hoyden.

'Herr Hinsson, Casper is left behind.'

The second mate turns and looks at her blankly. 'Mistress Cornet?'

'Casper. The boy, the boy who was always sorting ropes.'

'Sorry, Mistress Cornet, I'm not sure which boy you mean.'

She points at his usual place. 'There, he'd sit there.'

'We let the boys come and go according to where there is work for them. After this we are on to Spitsbergen and some aren't made for whaling grounds.'

'I did not know this was a whaling vessel.'

He shifts his feet. 'We do whatever is profitable. Bergen is flooded with cod, and your father wants something more in demand.'

There is something in his tone she doesn't like, but leaves it unremarked. 'He did not want to go whaling?'

'Or he was unsuited. Not strong or some such.' He looks back at the deck, and she realizes the crew are poised, ready for him to take his place at the whipstaff.

'But I did not . . .' She lets the sentence slide back down her throat. Second Mate Hinsson is unlikely to care. She isn't certain why she does, so much. But the sight of Casper's bewildered face, his bare grubby feet cringing against the harbour – he looked so insubstantial. And now the second mate turns away from her, their conversation finished, and she glances back to the port. It is as though the boy was never there at all.

She is sorrier than she can explain that he didn't say good-bye, though they had not talked since their day in Trøndheim. She had thought, with a comforting vagueness, that he might stay in Vardø and be a sort of houseboy, and was going to ask Absalom or at least try to make him suggest the idea. It was a thought left unfinished.

They are drawing away from the harbour now. She can feel the ship swaying, the men back at their practised posts, heads already turning to sea. Soon they will be at Vardø, and it will be she who is left behind.

•

A few days before they are due into the harbour at Vardø, Ursa feels an ache in her stomach.

It spreads along her back and into her head, pushing its blunt fingers into her temples and down the backs of her thighs. A griping sensation grips her body, and sweat comes cool across her top lip, beneath her arms. She looks about for the captain, wishes Casper were still aboard. She thinks of calling out to Second Mate Hinsson, but something within her stays her voice: a dark, animal sense, that tells her not to share that she is hurt.

She lowers herself from the ropes, and a spasm crosses her back, so sudden she bites her lip. Is she poisoned? She straightens, breath coming fast through her mouth, just catching it when the pain builds suddenly again, and crashes against her lower body like a white-hot wave.

This time she knows better than to move before it recedes. As soon as she can, she begins a slow edge along the deck. The bead of her vizard is clenched between her teeth and so no one sees that she is sweating, that her eyes are smarting, filling with tears.

The ladder down might as well be a mountain. She counts beneath her breath from ten to one and again and again until she feels floorboards beneath her, closes her eyes and stumbles along the passage, focusing on controlling the pain when it comes, breathing through it.

It is less of a confusion now: she can trace its origin; map its sear across her body. It's a little like her monthly pains, but tenfold. Beginning at the space her husband has made inside her, it sends shockwaves rippling first down her legs and lower back, and eventually up to her head. It feels as though her insides are trying to come out, and she wonders if her husband has torn something vital, or even if the ship's cook's culinary experiments have killed her at last.

She fumbles the lock of their cabin, fingers slick with sweat and numb with cold, bolts shut the door and crawls to the chamber pot. It has not been emptied that day, and a yellow pool lies at its base. The pain fades and ripples, like water settling.

Finally she blinks and is clear-eyed again. She is crunched between the bed and the wall, knees imprinted against the wood frame, spine flush against the thin divide. She wonders if she made any noise: she can't remember. Her skirts drop about the chamber pot, and she doesn't look as she wipes herself carefully.

She throws the rag over the chamber pot and it drops a little, soaks red. She holds her breath and lifts it, looks. Beneath the rag is a soft blot. She saw enough of her mother's difficulties to know what it is.

She should cover it over again, unbolt the door. The cabin will be near empty: she could go to the porthole and empty the pot through it. The contents would barely mark the water with their entrance.

But she can't carry it, can't touch even the pot, which she places in the dark corner of the room, beside her chest, then lies down on the bunk fully clothed, sleep coming choppy as waves.

•

When she wakes she can hear snoring through the thin wall, and her husband is already sleeping beside her. She sits up with panic, and, careful not to wake him, moves to the chest. The chamber pot is empty. Her heart races painfully. Absalom must have removed it, and let her sleep on.

A rawness opens over her breastbone, and she presses her hand to it. She slides back into bed, lets herself move a little nearer to his slumbering warmth. He rolls over and slides his arm beneath her, gathering her in close as a stowed sail.

ARRIVAL

Fourteen

They arrive just ahead of the rain. Mamma fetches Maren out to watch, and together with baby Erik and Diinna they go closer to the harbour edge, standing beside Magda's house to see the ship approaching. Behind it a great bank of cloud is building, already swallowing the horizon with grey slathers of sleet.

Magda's son stamps his small feet and claps his hands and cries, 'It's giving to them whalers, it's giving to them good!' without thinking about the fact that it will be giving to them just as well within the hour.

'They'll never get in,' says Mamma, and it's true that even at this distance the ship is incongruously large, the neck of the harbour shrinking smaller as it nears.

Maren makes no effort to answer, only watches the huge sweep of cloud. The last time they had all stood watching the sea like this it had folded itself entire over forty men. She clenches her teeth.

The wind picks up, and the ship drops anchor outside the narrow mouth of the harbour. Pastor Kurtsson strides out from the kirke, a dark cap clutched to his head. He looks like a doll, like one of Fru Olufsdatter's poppets, and Maren imagines the wind filling his clothes and flying him into the sea. He has moved into the weather too early, and now stands awkwardly at the harbour side. There is no movement from the ship for a long while. Mamma begins to tremble.

'You should go inside,' says Maren, but doesn't move to usher her home.

It is shameful, but she can hardly bear to touch her mother now. There is something indecent about how obviously she wears her grief, and Maren is worried that whenever they touch it will leach into her skin. She wants to be away from the house, or wants it to herself. If it weren't for baby Erik she might have already done just that, and gone to lodge with Kirsten. It has been a low taunt to see the second boathouse made fine enough for the living of a commissioner and his wife.

At last, there is movement on the deck. Maren can see dark figures against the grey sky and then, incongruous as the sun in winter, a burst of bright yellow appears from somewhere below deck. It isn't a colour Maren has seen before, and she keeps her eyes upon it, almost hungry.

Five of the figures, including the one in yellow, are lowered slowly in a rowing boat. There is a spray of white against the sea as the boat is dropped onto the waves. The yellow figure makes a jerking movement, as though about to fall.

'Nearly,' says Diinna. Erik is dozing over her shoulder, and she has one hand on his back, patting irregularly.

At the harbour side, Pastor Kurtsson is stamping his feet and blowing on his hands. He is always telling them how God's love is the only warmth needed to weather the cold, and it gives Maren a little twist of satisfaction to see him shivering. Kirsten joins him on the dock, and hands him a coat. Maren can see the reluctance in his stance as he takes it and puts it on.

In the boat, two have taken up oars and are rowing towards

shore. The yellow figure sits in the stern, wind blowing their hair about their face, and now the boat is closer it is obviously the new wife from Bergen. Her outfit is an absurdity, especially in bad-tempered weather.

Beside her, steadying her, must be her husband: their commissioner. He is stocky and upright, turned slightly towards her. Between the oarsmen sits another man, his broad back to land. As the boat draws alongside the dock and Pastor Kurtsson raises a hand in greeting, he turns but doesn't return the gesture.

The oars go up like flagpoles, and it is Kirsten who catches the rope and knots it about the mooring.

Mamma sucks in her cheeks. 'She should be careful.'

For once, Maren agrees. They all know things must change now, even Kirsten, with a direct eye from Vardøhus amongst them. The usual hierarchies must be observed; the ones usual to the world rather than to Vardø. A lift of panic quickens Maren's heart as she thinks Kirsten may offer her hand to help the passengers ashore, but Kirsten steps back and allows Pastor Kurtsson forward, grown large inside his borrowed coat.

The broad-backed man steps heavily from the boat, leaving it rocking in his wake. The woman clutches at its wooden sides. Maren is too far away to make out his face clearly, but his features are even, lower half obscured by a black beard. The woman's companion steps nimbly from the boat and shakes Pastor Kurtsson's hand before turning to help her. She shakes her head, says something.

'She wants to go already,' says Diinna drily. 'It's a long way back to Bergen.'

Pastor Kurtsson beckons Kirsten forwards and she bends her head down to listen, then looks up suddenly towards the houses. Her eyes find Maren's and though Toril is closer, she starts to walk towards them.

'What did you do?' says Mamma, but Maren takes two steps towards Kirsten.

'Coat,' Kirsten says, voice thrown by the wind. It makes no sense for Maren to go, their home being furthest from the harbour, but Kirsten is looking directly at her, so Maren pushes her way through the gathered women and runs to their house, the wind at her back. She takes up her winter coat from its hook, lined with the fur of rabbits snared on the mainland, brings it out, slamming the door behind her. She runs against the wind and skids back into place, making Mamma jolt.

Kirsten stands a little way off, Mamma eyeing her with open dislike. Maren folds the coat over her arm and steps clear of the women, narrow skirts whipping about her ankles.

'What is it?' she asks when she reaches Kirsten, who turns and starts again to the harbour.

'The wife is worried her skirts will fly up.' There is a smile in her voice. 'And I can't say I blame her.'

The woman in the boat looks abruptly towards them, and though there is no way that she could have, Maren feels that she heard them. Maren sees a plump face, with large, light brown eyes and very blonde hair that is whipped to froth about her face. She looks at once insubstantial, as though she might fade at the edges and become sea spray, and overly large, garish in her yellow dress.

'A coat, Fru Cornet,' says Pastor Kurtsson, pulling it from Maren's grip and offering it spread across both arms. 'Not so fine as you are used to—'

'But it's clean enough,' says Kirsten, and Maren's cheeks burn as the broad-backed man turns his gaze on them. He is forbidding up close, as dark as the woman is pale, holding space easily, the same way Kirsten does. She feels herself shrink a little, rounding her shoulders against his scrutiny.

'My wife,' he says, in heavily accented Norwegian, 'isn't used to the cold. And shall be addressed as Mistress Cornet.'

This is her husband? Why did he not sit beside her, offer his hand to help her? The woman's lips are trembling, and part slightly as though to say something to her husband, but she instead looks past Pastor Kurtsson, straight to Maren.

'Thank you.' Her voice is steady and there is a sudden set to the soft line of her jaw, a muscle working in her cheek.

She reaches out for the coat, and the man Maren took for her husband, but whom she now sees is old enough to be her father, motions Kirsten and Maren forward. 'Here, please.'

They stand before the rocking boat, and the man gestures at the oarsmen, who obey so immediately Maren realizes he must be high in their chain of command. The captain, perhaps. They look down, shoulders still heaving from the effort of the row. They will be against the wind on their return.

'Give her the coat,' says the captain to the minister, and Maren takes the coat back from the frame of Pastor Kurtsson's arms. There are two pink blooms high in the woman's cheeks as she takes the captain's arm to steady herself in the rocking boat, and, keeping her other hand tightly clasped about her bunched skirts, stands quickly. Kirsten moves to block the woman from view as her skirts swirl about her in the wind. Her grip is white on the man's arm, and the set of her lips pressed thin.

She is embarrassed, and Maren is embarrassed for her. She has never seen so much cloth, has a job scooping the woman's shaking frame into her coat's sleeves, stiff with their fur lining.

The woman is shorter but plumper than Maren, and the coat sits rigid about her, arms held at an angle and straining across the back. In that moment, though her body is a woman's, the dress cut to emphasize her shape, the dazed look in her pale eyes makes her look like a girl. But once Maren has helped her with the buttons, the dress is kept down about her knees, and she can at last step from the boat.

'Thank you,' she says again, her hot breath hitting Maren's cheek. There is something sweet on it, so unexpected it makes Maren's mouth tingle.

Maren nods, keeping her own lips firmly shut about her teeth. Even aboard a ship this woman has kept herself better than any of the Vardø women, and it is Maren's time to blush at how she must look. Only a moment ago she had felt sorry for this woman, and now she feels a sorry sight herself in her shabby skirts and Pappa's coat, made no more fragrant by months of her seagoing.

The woman's husband has watched the whole scene dispassionately. When his wife is at last steady on the dock, he turns to Pastor Kurtsson. His eyes don't fall on him though: they search the houses clustered about the harbour.

'You the minister?' Maren isn't entirely convinced that his curtness is only due to a lack of confidence in their language.

'Yes, I am, Commissioner Cornet. Welcome to our—'

'Thank you, captain, for our safe passage.'

He offers his hand to the shorter man, who still has the wife attached to his arm.

'Not at all, Mr Cornet. It has been my pleasure.'

He nods briefly and turns again to the minister. 'That the kirke?'

'It is. Allow me—'

But the man doesn't let him finish before he turns sharply on his boot and makes for the kirke, long dark coat flapping behind him like a flock of crows. Pastor Kurtsson dithers a moment, and Maren could swear he actually dances from one foot to another, like a child. Though he isn't theirs, not really, she again feels that stab of embarrassment for him.

'You can go ahead,' says Kirsten to the minister. 'We will take Mistress Cornet to her home.'

Pastor Kurtsson straightens, trying to regain some control over the situation. 'Yes. I will show the commissioner the kirke, and you can oversee the luggage.'

He follows the commissioner without, Maren suspects, fully appreciating what he has just said. Kirsten gives a slight shake of her head and looks to the captain.

'Is that everything, captain?'

The bow of the boat is laden with three cases, a smaller package, and a neat reddish-wooden chest. It is finely carved, and has a brass lock. When the oarsmen begin to unload, the woman flutters about it, one hand clasped at the coat, eyes trained on the chest, brow furrowed.

The captain himself lifts the chest with care, and the men carry the three cases between them. Kirsten takes up the small package, leaving Maren uncertain whether to follow. No one gives her a sign, and she repeats Pastor Kurtsson's dither a moment too long. The five of them vanish between Toril and Magda's houses, the women and their children turning to watch, the snatch and flutter of the woman's yellow skirts disappearing out of sight as they turn towards the second boathouse.

The commissioner's wife doesn't look back, and Maren isn't sure why she wants her to. She feels a detached sort of panic, and hopes Kirsten will be kind.

She leaves the dock, feet crunching over the cold-hardened ground. Mamma has gone, but Diinna still stands behind Magda's house, with Erik slumped over her shoulder, her hand tapping its senseless rhythm into his back. They walk home together, and Diinna doesn't speak until they reach their house.

'This will bring nothing good,' she says, gaze fixed over Maren's head, in the direction of the boat straining against its moorings in the harbour. She tilts her head, as though listening, then turns and vanishes around the side of the house. Maren hears the slam of her door as she goes into her and Erik's room.

A moment after, the clouds that had followed the ship open above her head, and rain begins to fall.

Fifteen

Though Maren has the excuse to visit the boathouse, the reindeer hides being stitched and ready by the door, she instead spends the three days until Sabbath pacing their house like a tethered beast. The rain is fierce, churning the softening ground to mud, and she doesn't want her first visit there to be as a bedraggled mess.

Everything is made blurred and grey by the weather, and the commissioner's wife has set an uneasiness rocking inside her, though she can't name why. She feels she must know her. The yellow dress ghosts through Maren's daydreams: she has become obsessed with recalling it. How soft and giving the woven fabric was against her wrist as she pulled tight the coat, how bright it was, how much was gathered into its loose pleats, enough to wrap three people. The woman's sweet breath, her fingernails pale and delicate.

Maren's own clothes are stiff and itchy about her, the reek of herself so apparent she wonders how anyone can stand to be near her. She washes in the grey water from chores, tries to work her hair into a neater tie. The place where the needle pierced her hand the night of the storm has faded completely, but she worries at the thin webbing between forefinger and thumb until it is raw again, skin shrinking over her hands. Her fingernails are brittle and greyish, her mouth furred though she brushes with a birch twig until her gums sing and she spits the copper of blood into the mud. She wonders if she will ever be clean, has ever been. She takes to cleaning baby Erik more often too, but even his breath is foul with Diinna's milk, his hands mucky with crawling. Perhaps they are born to it.

The rainclouds affect an odd light on their house; the glow of snow gone and inside drab and dark. Maren used to welcome this restless time, the whole village stretching out from winter and everything being readied beneath the never-set sun before they begin their slow dance back together, cold forcing them once more into each other's pockets. Now, it is a reminder of how different their lives have become, and how, with the arrival of the commissioner, they are set to change again. *Just as we've found our feet*, Maren thinks.

When Pappa and Erik lived, they would take the boat for days at a time, and Maren and Mamma would strip the house of all its furs and cloth, beat them out and scatter fresh rushes on the floor. Last summer it had been Maren who had gone to sea, and the house had stayed closed and cloistered, furs collecting dust until Maren grew certain she inhaled lungfuls of herself. Soon there will be excursions across the sea to the low mountain, and the traders will come from Kiberg and Varanger. But the rain has trapped her, and though Mamma is gladdened by how it will ready the soil, encourage moss and lichen, Maren is bored. She unpicks the hem of the reindeer pelts, stitches them back together with more careful hands, burns the last of the dried heather and places the hides over the smoke to try to get the musk out.

•

Sabbath dawns dry, and almost painfully bright. Maren goes ahead of Mamma, passing close by the second boathouse, slowing slightly to try and divine if the commissioner and his wife are inside. The house is still, the flat sunlight hitting the high windows and making them inscrutable. She picks up her pace against the mud.

A group of women are already clustered about the door of the kirke: Maren can see that at their centre is Kirsten, standing a head taller than the rest. They are gossiping, she can tell, because as she draws nearer the women turn to check who is approaching before leaning back towards each other. It isn't a warm day, and they have to shuffle about lest the mud suck at their feet, but none of them want to miss the arrival of Commissioner Cornet and his wife.

'And what did you make of her?' says Toril the moment Maren arrives at the group. 'What did she say to you?'

'Only "thank you",' says Maren. 'Not enough for me to know the make of her.' She looks to Kirsten. 'What happened after you took them to the house?'

Kirsten shrugs. 'I stayed long enough to show the stores and light the fire. She didn't say a word. The captain was nice enough.'

'And her husband?'

'Not back from the kirke before I left.'

'Pastor Kurtsson says he prayed for hours before he visited Vardøhus,' says Toril, sickly with admiration. 'He will be a goodly thing for us.'

Maren feels pity for his wife, left alone in her new house while her husband prayed.

'Did you take the hides?' says Kirsten. Maren shakes her head. 'I told her to expect you.'

Maren grips at the sore skin between her forefinger and thumb, is about to say something about the rain or the mud or the re-hemming, but is saved from it by the sudden hush falling as a broad figure comes striding into sight, trailing a shorter one wrapped in Maren's coat, flicks of dark blue kicking about her ankles.

The women draw apart from each other: Maren drops her head without quite knowing why. The commissioner's muddy boots move in and out of her sight, the slippered feet of his wife a few paces behind.

Maren looks up in time to see a pale halo of hair disappear into the candlelit dark of the kirke. She seems so small against the bulk of her husband, and Maren imagines her walking into the belly of a whale. Kirsten follows in after, the women peeling off in a mute stream.

Maren waits another few minutes for Mamma to arrive. She comes huffing, hair unbrushed.

'Have I missed them?'

'Everyone is inside already. Is Diinna not coming?'

'She says she doesn't feel well.' Mamma's disapproval drips.

Pastor Kurtsson has abandoned his place by the door, is bending to speak to the commissioner, who sits in the front pew. Maren manoeuvres Mamma until they are sitting across and behind, so she can keep them both in sight. The pews around the new arrivals are crowded, though usually they spread out. The candles splutter as Toril performs her usual duty of shutting the door, and Pastor Kurtsson takes his place at the pulpit.

Maren barely hears the sermon. Her eyes are trained on the commissioner and his wife. All about her, heads are similarly turned, and when they pray Maren wonders if the other women are also trying to pick out the thread of the wife's voice in the knot of theirs.

Absolute quiet comes when they have said the final *Amen*. Maren's eyes are fixed on the back of the commissioner's head, which remains bowed for a full minute past the prayer.

'Surely he will say something?' Mamma's voice is quiet as the spit of the candle.

Pastor Kurtsson has vacated the pulpit, stands uncertainly before the commissioner. His wife stares straight ahead. Her collar is high about her pale neck, the roundness of her cheek made copper in the candlelight. The sort of skin that will change to suit whatever light hits it. Maren looks down again at her chapped hands, raw and ruddy, Mamma's just as coarse beside her.

At last, the commissioner straightens his neck, stands. The kirke is so quiet she hears the movement of cloth against cloth, the swallow of his throat before he turns to them to speak. His feet plant in a wide stance, hands clasped behind his back, and she wonders if he was a sailor or a soldier. Again Maren feels that strange pull of energy from him she had felt in the harbour, something coiled and magnetic, almost dangerous in the size and heft of him.

He wears a suit of black cloth, not so fine as his wife's clothing but well fitted: though it is sombre he wears it like an aristocrat. He has trimmed back his beard, revealing even, heavily bowed lips and a strong jaw.

Maren supposes he is handsome, but there is something wild there too. Something kept back that when left unchecked could turn his face cruel. Mamma draws closer to her and Maren doesn't slide away.

'I have only a little Norwegian. Pastor Kurtsson will translate as necessary. My name is Absalom Cornet, and I am from the northern isles of Orkney, Scotland. This –' he draws out a letter from his pocket, creased with rereading – 'is my commission from Lensmann Cunningham, stating that I have been appointed Commissioner over Vardø, and so you all.'

He changes to English. She knows only brief words of it, what she has picked up from rare whalers blown off course

127

from the main trading routes, or those who settle in the larger towns nearby.

She listens carefully, picking up unconnected words like driftwood on the current of his voice. Pastor Kurtsson is stumbling in his translation, and Maren suspects his English isn't as good as he led the commissioner to believe. His brow is furrowed with concentration, giving no particular emphasis to the words so it is left to them to decide what is most important.

He tells them it is his duty to be the eyes and ears of not only the Lensmann John Cunningham, which Maren realizes must be Hans Køning's English name, but also those of God.

'Does this mean the Lensmann will not come at all?' whispers Maren to Kirsten, but Kirsten ignores her, eyes narrowed at the commissioner. He tells them a little of his life before, in Orkney and then Caithness, places Maren has never heard of, and of his involvement with the trial of a woman. He says that it is this that brought him to Finnmark, to Vardø. He says that he knows they lost many men to a storm; there is a ripple around the room, a collective reel at the mention of their men in this stranger's mouth. He says that he will make a register of all their names, a census, for the Lensmann so he knows how many and who they are.

'This should have been done before,' translates Pastor Kurtsson duly, without noticing the barb in it.

The commissioner asks his wife to stand and she does, turning her moonish face to the congregation and dipping a curtsey that makes Mamma snort. He introduces her as Mistress Cornet and Maren whispers it under her breath, wonders what her given name is.

The woman's gaze barely lifts. The skin beneath her chin creases when she nods her acknowledgement, her pale hands stark against her dress. Her hair is neatly pinned though slightly lopsided, and Maren guesses she is used to using a looking glass, if she is used to arranging her own hair at all. She wills the woman to look up, to see her and know her as the one who placed the coat about her shoulders, but Mistress Cornet sits as soon as her husband motions her to do so, several moments before Pastor Kurtsson's translation catches up.

'Think of me as a Lensmann of sorts, a judge. You can trust me as you do your minister. Too long you have been left here without guidance. I am here to offer it, and I must ask you be vigilant.'

Commissioner Cornet returns to his clumsy Norwegian.

'I will take the names, now. And any questions and issues that have arisen – I hope to be a mediator.'

In many ways what he describes should be the duty of a minister. Perhaps Lensmann Køning realizes he sent a weak man, and is now trying to remedy it by sending a strong one. Hands have been raised, and the commissioner gestures to the back of the kirke. Toril's voice comes loud behind them.

'What of those who do not come to kirke? Should we give you their names?'

His face is so still Maren wonders if he has not understood. Pastor Kurtsson obviously assumes the same and moves to speak in his ear, but Commissioner Cornet turns to fix him with such a stare that the minister draws back.

'There are those who do not come to kirke?'

Maren notices a patch of damp plaster beside the cross, dark on the wall.

'Not many,' says Pastor Kurtsson. 'Lapps, some old—'

'There will be no more of that,' he says, looking to the back, to Toril. 'Give me their names.'

Sixteen

Ursa's husband is furious. Their house is stale with it, a thick fug of tension that roils from him like a storm cloud. The news that he has heathens among his people is only the latest of it – it began the day they arrived, and he was turned away from Vardøhus.

They had dropped anchor and Ursa had been almost afraid to look to land. The fortress was built of grey stone, visible from the sea, as high-walled and forbidding as a prison, which Captain Leifsson told them it oftentimes served as. Further along the coast were nooked a collection of houses at irregular intervals. Without trees the land seemed flat and featureless as a blank page.

As they had rowed ashore in that terrible wind, Ursa had wanted to cry. Captain Leifsson was sitting beside her and she trained her eyes on his knees as the wind slapped their cheeks.

Absalom was coiled as a spring, though lately he had been almost kind, albeit not in ways that others would notice. He had started calling her Ursula instead of 'wife', asking how she was feeling in Norwegian, small gestures at effort, perhaps even affection. Since the night she was unwell he hadn't touched her, and as they approached Vardø, he requested that she change into her yellow dress, placed his hand beside hers on the guard rail and moved it so close she could feel the dark heat and bristles of his hands through her thin gloves.

The women who helped her at the dock were snow-burnt and smelly. The larger woman, who introduced herself as Kirsten, had been brash and brusque. The other, similar in age to Ursa, bundled her into a reeking coat. This young woman looked haunted, her grey-blue eyes the same shade as the sea, her cheeks hollowed. But Ursa had come to feel grateful for the loan of the coat when they were shown to their house.

House. Now, the word burns in Ursa's stomach as she watches her husband pace the short length of the room where they must sleep, eat and otherwise exist – she isn't sure a life spent here is worthy of the label of living. She had thought their circumstances in Bergen were grave since Mother's death, with only one servant and rooms kept closed, but this is another thing entirely.

It has only four high, small windows that she can barely see through. The bed is large and takes up a full side of the room – above it are beams and long loops of rope from which hang rough curtains to portion it from view. The fire takes up another side, two pans and a large pot arranged on the drift-wood shelf. There are no rugs on the floor, only unnailed boards suspended over dirt. The ground beneath sends up a fierce cold though Kirsten, who showed Captain Leifsson and Ursa to the house, said that they have arrived into summer.

There is a second door at the back corner of the room. When Kirsten opened it, Ursa could have been sick. Great headless carcasses hang there, split from neck to belly and restitched.

'Enough there to last to winter,' Kirsten had said, before setting a light to the heaped moss in the grate. Captain Leifsson set Ursa's chest down in one corner. He couldn't meet Ursa's eye.

'Mistress Cornet, it has been a pleasure.'

He gave her a formal little bow and she wanted to throw her arms about him, cling to him. He held out a black pouch and she loosened its string tie.

'More aniseed,' he said. 'I know you like it.'

She didn't trust herself to speak, even without Absalom there, and gave him a nod of thanks. She wondered briefly if he would tell her to come with him, if he could take her back to Bergen. But he walked out with Kirsten, leaving her to this room with its small windows through which she watched his retreating back. He didn't turn. Within the hour the ship weighed anchor and was gone into the rain-smothered horizon. She sat heavily on the hard bench beside the table, folded her hands in her lap, and waited for Absalom to come.

Without a sunset Ursa feels untethered. She cannot think how long she sat there that first day before Absalom arrived to find her still on the bench, the room barely warmed by the low glow given out by a nearly spent fire. He didn't scold her, only heaped it again and said, 'Are you hungry?'

She shuddered no, thinking of the slaughtered beasts next door. He nodded tautly, looked about the room. 'Not like you're used to.' There was something close to an apology in his voice.

She was fearful he would be angry at her disappointment, but instead he sat across from her at the broad table, and took out a letter.

'I had thought myself made,' he said, and not entirely to himself. She waited. 'I went to Vardøhus. The Lensmann isn't yet at seat there. There was hardly anyone there at all. I spoke with an old man serving as a guard. They do not know if he will even come, may keep his base elsewhere.' His fist clenched upon the table. 'He mentioned none of this in his letters.'

Absalom looked up so suddenly Ursa flinched, but his face

was closed off and sorrowful, and she could almost bring herself to reach across the table to him.

'I grew up in a house like this,' he said. 'On an island not much bigger than Vardø. I got out as soon as I could, went to the city. There I made something of myself.' His fist hits the table. 'But here I am back again.'

Ursa didn't know where the words came from, but she said, 'You may make something more, here.'

Absalom's expression changed, as if a light were lit beneath his skin. He looked at her, seeming to see her for the first time. And then he stretched his long arm across the table, and took her hand.

They sat together, rain falling heavy on the roof. It must have been past midnight when he called her to bed, though the grey light outside was of a perpetual dusk. He was gentler than ever before, but still she couldn't ignore the rigid frame of the bed beneath her, the rain coming hard against the walls, and so sent her mind far away.

Seventeen

Absalom leaves the house twice a day in the three days until Sabbath, for hours at a stretch. Each time he comes back sopping.

'No one there,' he says. 'Not at kirke, not in Vardøhus.' Ursa knows he wants comfort, but it is something she can't give him. The look on his face when she had soothed him on their first night had made her afraid: he is hungry for her approval and she has no idea why. She wants to go back to being invisible.

She senses his mood deepen, but when the rain clears on Sabbath it feels like a sign that all may yet come good. She puts on her darkest dress, and follows her husband into the mud.

As they walk, he tells her their nearest neighbour is Fru Olufsdatter, a woman who, like so many of them, lost her husband and son in the storm. Her house is easily the finest: a two-storey stabbur with thick turf overlaying silvery birch. Carved wooden pillars fence the porch, and through its light-framed windows Ursa sees colour: yellow and red adorning the walls. She wonders whether she can ask Absalom if they might decorate their house. She doesn't think she can stand another moment of its bareness. Otherwise the houses are square, windowless, and single-floored, none so large as theirs.

The kirke is of a good size, standing high as their house in Bergen and in a style more ornate than the new Lutheran churches in her city. It looks older too, all dark wood angling at the sky like an ancient ship brought to settle on land. A dozen women wait outside, and from the way they fall silent and spin away from each other on their approach, Ursa can tell she and her husband are the subject of their talk.

She shrinks inside the borrowed coat, feels all their eyes scratching over her. Kirsten is there, and so is the young woman who helped her with the coat. Ursa wonders about smiling at them, thinks better of it. She feels ridiculous in her mud-clad slippers, should have worn her boots from Tromsø. She hardens the set of her shoulders as they walk past, and then wishes she had smiled. She will need friends here, or she really will go mad.

They are greeted by the obsequious minister, who seats them in the front pew. There are lighter patches on the walls behind the wooden cross, as though something else had hung there, and a massive dark stain beside it that Ursa sees all sorts of patterns in. All through the service she feels a sort of warmth upon her, a scrutiny that has an almost physical weight.

Her husband's eyes are fixed upon the minister with an intensity he usually reserves for the middle distance. His hand is motionless on his knee: he barely seems to breathe.

She tries to look more alert when he rises to address the congregation. Pastor Kurtsson's translation is rudimentary, and the dissonance between them grates on Ursa's nerves so that she nearly misses her cue to stand and show herself to the people of Vardø. Their collective gaze falls against her like stones. She should straighten her back, meet their eyes. She dips a little, out of politeness, hears a faint snort from the back of the kirke. Before Ursa takes her seat again she looks briefly: the thin woman who gave her the coat sits beside an older, thinner version of herself, their twin sets of blue-grey eyes on her. Was it her who laughed? Ursa feels a betrayal though she owes her nothing. Heat rushes into her cheeks and the back of her neck as she waits for her husband to finish.

It takes a full hour to collect all the names for the census, though they are so few. Some women are keen on speaking with him: he turns his steady gaze on each of them, even lets loose an easy flash of teeth. He trimmed his beard ready for the service, and is wearing the suit he wore to meet and marry her. The ship's diet has shrunk his middle, the morning's prayer given him a softness about his brutish jaw which fades and re-hardens only when there is mention of those absent from kirke, candlelight finding red-gold darts in his beard.

Briefly Ursa can see him how she thinks they must. A town of women, with only a weak-chinned minister and two old men amongst the congregation, the others boys: a man like him is welcome here. And as she trails him back to their house, she knows that she isn't. They watch her go like an unkindness of ravens: as soon as the kirke is out of sight she hears them cawing.

In the stark daylight he looks older, the furrows in his forehead deepen. 'Six not come,' he says. 'How has the pastor allowed it?'

Ursa's lips twitch: she still doesn't know if his questions are for her. She assumes this one wasn't, for he doesn't break his stride. He knows the route already from his twice-daily prayers and pilgrimages to the fortress, past three blocky houses close together, between two larger ones, boundaries marked with rocks.

Ursa tries to learn it, commit it to memory. The village has the curious sense of being crammed together and spread widely out: it bunches and then releases, land standing uneasy between buildings of wood and stone, turf and mud. Absalom has told her next to nothing of the town, only that it was the worst hit by the storm, and that it is a place of women now. She had imagined sisterhood, but is now uncertain if there is anything for her here at all. A single tern wheels ahead, climbing into the sky.

Outside their house he stops so suddenly that she must swerve, catches her hip against his.

'Husband?'

His eyes are narrowed. 'There. See?'

Ursa does, but isn't sure what she is seeing. Over the lintel, roughly carved into the wood, are a scramble of shapes. A circle, with lines waving from it. A sun? And beside it a fish, as basic as a child's. They are in turn obscured by more carvings. At first she thinks someone has tried to erase them, but the crossings-out are too regular, deliberate.

'Runes,' breathes Absalom, and there is something in his voice so foreign she doesn't at once recognize it for what it is. His hands clasp his jacket convulsively. Her own fear rises to meet his.

'Husband?'

'They are runes,' he says, and his voice is shaking. He turns and scans the houses about them. Ursa watches as he strides to the nearest and knocks on the door. No one answers: they are probably still gossiping at the kirke. He comes back.

'It is as the Lensmann said. Worse, perhaps.' His gaze has taken on a feverish edge. The mud has started to swallow Ursa's slippers but she doesn't want to go inside.

There is a squelch of footsteps behind and two figures approach, one supporting the other. Ursa sees it is the young woman whose coat she wears, and the older woman who shares her thin cheekbones and eyes: her mother.

'You,' says Absalom. The women's heads were down, and now they jerk to a stop.

'That,' he says, and his fear has resolved into something Ursa understands better: anger. 'Why are they there?' He points at the marks over the door. 'Runes, yes?'

The young woman follows his finger. She nods.

'Who put them there?'

'Diinna,' says the mother. Ursa looks to the young woman.

'You are Diinna?' says Ursa, and the young woman shakes her head, doesn't meet Ursa's eye.

'This is my daughter, Maren,' says the mother. 'I am Freja, and my son's widow Diinna made those marks.' It is not lost on Ursa that she introduces her daughter-in-law so, at such a distance. 'We gave our names and hers to you just now.'

'Was this Diinna not at the church?' says her husband. 'Why?'

'She is sick,' says the daughter, Maren. 'She has a small boy – she must get better for him.' Freja looks at her sharply.

'Why are they there?' His finger jabs at the air, his voice disgusted.

'This was the resting place for my father and brother,' says Maren. 'For her husband.' She looks from Ursa's face and back to Absalom, sees they do not understand. 'After the storm, this is where we brought them.'

Dead, realizes Ursa, and something inside her twists. Drowned people have lain in their house, on that floor. She thinks of the hanging carcasses in the store, and bile stings her throat. *For God's sake, do not be sick.*

'Why were we not told?'

'It was a resting place, only.' Maren must scent danger, because her whole stance changes. She makes her slight frame smaller, rounding her shoulders. 'Commissioner, we mean no offence. This was once a boathouse, the only place in the village we thought large enough to befit you.'

It is artfully done, thinks Ursa. Absalom's stance softens in the face of the woman's obeisance, and she wishes she could bring herself to be like that for him. She feels always either too bold, or too meek.

'We should have been informed.' He turns and looks up at the carved figures. 'These aren't Christian symbols.'

'Diinna is Sámi,' says Freja. Maren's jaw clenches, bone pressing white against her pale skin, and Ursa knows she would not have wished this to be revealed.

'A Lapp?' He shakes his head suddenly, a bull throwing off a fly. 'They had Lapp rites?'

'No,' says Maren, earning another pointed glance from her mother. 'They only watched the bodies. They did no harm.'

'Anything that isn't the dominion of the Lord is harmful, however it comes. They used no drum?'

'No.'

He narrows his eyes at her. 'I'll be telling the Lensmann of this.'

He goes inside. Maren's blue-grey eyes have a bright intensity to them, a skein of panic. Ursa fights an urge to reach out to her.

'Ursula!' Absalom's shout breaks their stillness. She thinks to say goodbye but the two women have vanished around the side of the house.

The mud has taken in her slippers, and she imagines sinking down to her knees, her waist and her throat, until she is stuck into the belly of the earth, lying there cool and smothered and safe.

'Wife?' Absalom is in the doorway, the fire coaxed to bright flickers behind him and throwing his broad shape into shadow. In his hand he holds a flat instrument, a chisel of some sort, and beneath his other arm is the bench from their table. 'Make dinner.'

139

She looks at him dumbly, and down at her stuck feet. He sighs and places the bench and chisel down, puts his hands beneath her armpits and heaves her free, depositing her in the doorway. Her head spins: how often had she and Agnete imagined a man lifting them into the doorway of the home they share? How different it is, how foolish she feels. Her slippers are ruined, and he closes the door on her.

She makes her dazed way to the cold store. They are almost out of fish and bread, what had been left for them by the women. Soon she will have to make dough. Siv let her household teachings lapse since Agnete's maid was dismissed and Ursa took over her care. She knows how to heat mint oil in water and rest Agnete's head in her hand so she can breathe over it, but can't brew light beer. She can lift and wash Agnete's sore leg, but can't keep a house.

And even if she could remember how to make bread, Absalom will not be happy with only that. Surely he will not expect her to butcher the meat in the store? Her body shakes and she turns her back to its door. She had expected a maid at least. Her father must have too, or else he wouldn't have sent her so ill-equipped for her duties. She hacks at the hard loaf, but her fingers are chilled.

She wishes she could write, and could send a letter to Father. She would tell him Vardø is not fine at all, but an island full of bereaved, watchful women, some of whom are not church-going. That it is cold though it is summer, and the sun doesn't set. That they do not have a house fit for a commissioner, or in fact anything that he would recognize as a house, but a room with runes carved over its door, because it used to hold the dead.

She presses a cold hand to her mouth, breathes the cupped air in and out to warm it. What could he do? She can't leave her husband: the disgrace would follow her like a mangy dog to Bergen. She could not marry again, would be a spinster, a burden. Agnete is unlikely to find a husband of any sort, and Ursa sends up a small prayer of thanks for that.

Scraping sounds filter through from outside as Absalom takes a chisel to the runes. It sets her teeth on edge: her vision flickers. She holds the knife more tightly, until the faintness passes. When Absalom comes inside, the table is laid with its mismatch of crockery. They eat the last of the bread.

•

Each day he strides out to pray, and to learn Norwegian with Pastor Kurtsson, and to stand at Vardøhus's gates for news. Ursa knows he is waiting for a letter from the Lensmann, for an invitation. She wills it to come too, and not only to lighten his stormy mood. She needs to be out of the house, to eat something that isn't tørrfisk, the dried cod that fills their store. Something fresh: a carrot, a herb. She dreams of fruit, of sweetness. She rations each piece of aniseed, places it inside her cheek until it is soft and barely crunches between her teeth. She dreams of a meal shared with anyone but her husband.

But when he leaves to visit, or to check on the unarrived Lensmann, there is worse. Then, she is alone. Even his company is better than her own.

Eighteen

The commissioner and his wife have been here a week, but the stitched pelts are still folded ready by the door of Maren's house. Their exchange with Commissioner Cornet made her uneasy, though Maren knows it could have been worse: she might have been too slow to stop Mamma mentioning the drum.

When she chided her at home, her mother had closed up like a shell, and Maren grew less sure her loose talk of Diinna was in error. She will have to watch them, the women she calls her family – they have grown apart so starkly it feels dangerous. Almost as dangerous as the commissioner's face when the Sámi rites were mentioned.

She knows, of course, that such things are looked down on. Pastor Kurtsson had frowned at the silver-birch shrouds, but he had allowed it. Commissioner Cornet seems not to understand that things work differently here. This was Sámi land, though they would not call it that. Sailors still sometimes call on Sámi for good wind, for good fortune, and Toril, despite all her protests, went to Diinna when she needed help bearing a child. But the commissioner's disgust has sharpened her to things she had not noticed before: how the Sámi who used to set up their laavus on the headland in summer have not come in years, how Diinna is the last Sámi left living in Vardø.

When she tells Diinna of the exchange, she only shrugs as Erik grabs at her thick braid, chewing the end between sore gums.

'I am used to such ignorance,' Diinna says, eyes fixed on Mamma's back.

Maren feels alone in her disquiet, as if she is the only one seeing a storm approach.

It isn't until her mother grows tired of tripping on the skins and snaps that she will take them herself, that Maren finally scoops them up and makes for the second boathouse.

The day is crisp and she is comfortable in her woollen dress. The mud has hardened into its churned ridges, digging into her soles. Toril is beating a blanket on her front step and the women studiously ignore each other, Toril sending a cloud of foul-tasting dust into Maren's mouth. She slaps the worst of it from the reindeer skins.

The second boathouse is closed up and quiet, but smoke is rising from the stack and the place where the runes had been is painted in fresh, gleaming white. She isn't sure where they got the paint from: no one apart from Dag's mother insists on a job that only creates more work rather than lessening it. She listens a moment before she knocks, but can hear nothing.

A minute later, the commissioner's wife, Ursula, opens the door, her hair loose about her round face.

'Good morning, Mistress Cornet.'

'Maren, yes?'

Her name in the woman's mouth sends a tingling across her breastbone. She nods. 'Maren Magnusdatter.'

'My husband is not here. He's at the kirke with Pastor Kurtsson.' She doesn't meet Maren's eye. Her eyelashes are so blonde they are almost white against her cheek. She is wearing the dark blue dress she wore at kirke, and there is mud still about its hem. Maren wonders why she has not yet washed it.

'I brought these.' She holds up the skins. The woman recoils a little. 'The Lensmann ordered them from Kirsten for your arrival. They're for the floor.'

'Oh.'

'I stitched them.'

'Thank you,' says Ursula, but she doesn't reach out for them. She is eyeing them as though they still have living flesh inside them, are something to be wary of.

'I can lay them if you like?'

She opens the door wider to allow Maren inside, and her face is so grateful it makes Maren wince.

The men from Kiberg have made a good job of it. There is a broad bed across one side of the room, with a curtain for privacy. There is a solid table and, under it, a bench and an array of pots and pans hung across the mantel that look untouched. Beside the grate where Dag used to kiss her is a wooden shelf set into the wall for the washbowl. A stack of plates sits beside it. The door to the store where he first took her hand has a cobweb growing across it. She digs her fingernails into her palm. Though it looks well, there is something decidedly unhomely about it. Aside from the crucifix over the fire, there is no ornament. The fire has been fed poorly and is smoking, giving meagre light and heat.

She can feel the cold of the floor leaching through her boots. No wonder Ursula is shivering, though she tries not to show it. A rough woollen blanket is thrown over the back of one of the chairs and she wonders if Ursula had been wearing it when she knocked, had taken it off for appearances' sake. When Maren looks about her she sees that the washbowl is full of grey water. More cobwebs lurk in the corners of the room, above the bed, and the rushes beneath her feet are muddy and wilted.

The house smells of closed-up must, but there is no trace lingering of the rot that Maren smelt the last time she stood in this room. Of course there wouldn't be, it is eighteen months since her father and brother lay there – her eyes flick to the spot before the fireplace and it seems to her the ground is darker there. Ursula follows her gaze.

'Is that where?'

Maren nods before she can think better of it, and Ursula sways. She is paler than before, Maren thinks, and shadows are pressed beneath her eyes, though her cheeks are still plump. 'Are you all right?'

'I'm sorry,' says Ursula. She places her hand upon her stomach. 'We were not informed. It is something of a shock to know there were dead kept here.'

'There's nothing bad in it,' says Maren. 'The dead are often rested inside in winter. Usually we would have kept them at home but . . .' But there were two of them. They would have taken up the whole room. 'This was a boat shed, once. We did not know it was to be your home.' She wouldn't have allowed cobwebs to settle across the doorways and ceilings. There would be woven curtains at the windows, the pots hung over the fire and full of reindeer stew.

She needs to be out of this house.

'Where do you want these?'

Ursula looks about her, as though she has misplaced something. 'I . . .' She gestures to the floor before the fire.

'There are two. Perhaps,' says Maren, 'one there, and one before the bed? It is not nice to place your feet straight from the warmth of bed onto the cold floor.'

Ursula flushes as she nods, and Maren wonders if she is shy of her mention of the bed. Perhaps in Bergen they are more private about such things: she knows that Dag's father insisted on two levels to his own house, so their bedrooms could be separate as in their house in Tromsø.

Maren takes up one patchwork of skins and lays it before the fire. It is fine fur, and she has worked the white breast of each animal into the corners so it looks almost like a design. She smooths it, looks to Ursula for approval; but the woman's eyes are far away, and she is still holding herself about her waist.

The second stitched pelt she lays beside the bed. It is made, but the blankets are rumpled. Before she stands, her back to the room, Maren places her hand over the place: it is still warm.

Ursula is raking the fire, poking through the smoking ash. It is perhaps not her place, but Maren can't watch without commenting.

'You need fresh.' She gestures at the store door. 'There'll be plenty in there, Kirsten saw to that.'

'Yes, I . . .' Ursula stands: her eyelids flutter. Maren hurries forward and hooks her hand beneath her elbow, feeling the gentle give of her arm. Ursula places her own hand on Maren's shoulder to steady herself, and Maren is taken back to their first encounter on the dock, the woman's hand soft and cold upon her.

'Are you all right?'

Ursula's eyes are closed. Her lids are palest pink, like the insides of seashells, or a newborn's fingernails. Her breath is coming a little too fast and uneven: there is still that sweetness upon it, and it sets Maren's teeth on edge.

'Yes. I'm sorry.' She takes her own weight, and Maren lets go of her elbow, places her hand at her back. 'I am a little faint.'

'Would you like some water? Some bread?' Maren manoeuvres her gently to the nearest chair, places the blanket about

146

her shoulders. She turns before Ursula answers, is already at the pitcher – it is empty.

'You're out of water.'

'Bread too.' Ursula's voice is flat and quiet. 'I don't know how.'

'How?' Maren looks closer at the washing bowl: the water has a skim across it. The house isn't simply poorly kept – it is squalid.

'How to—' Ursula breaks off with a sharp inhale of breath.

The tingling point in Maren's chest squeezes as she takes up the pitcher. 'I can fetch water. You stay there.'

'I'm sorry, I should—'

Maren hears a rustle of skirts. Ursula has braced herself on the table. The soft skin at her wrist is creased, her face crumpled. Maren looks away again, addresses her feet. 'You should sit. Rest. I'll not be long.'

The chair creaks and Maren goes out into the bright day, relieved to be outside the house, and urgent to be back. She takes a deep breath of fresh air and hurries home. Toril has gone inside and the rug she had looped over her gate to air has fallen onto the ground: Maren stomps over it.

Mamma, who is watching Erik play beside the fire, looks up sharply when Maren returns. 'You were gone a while.'

'I went in to lay them.'

'She's too fine to lay her own rug? How is the house?'

'She's not well. She's feeling faint.' Maren crosses to their drinking bucket, fills the pitcher. 'The house is . . .'

She doesn't know how to speak it, the sadness she felt, coming from Ursula and the dusty floor and the warm bed, the whole place seeming more abandoned than it ever had when she and Dag were there, or even when Diinna and Varr watched over their men. Erik grips at her skirt as she passes him to take a loaf of black bread from the basket.

'What's that for?'

'They have no bread.'

Mamma snorts. 'The commissioner, out of bread? His fat wife likely ate it all.' She narrows her eyes, the hollows of her cheeks showing. 'We don't have it to give.'

'We have enough for the week,' says Maren, wrapping the bread in cloth and placing it over the mouth of the jug. 'They will give us the loaf in return, when it's made.'

'Lazy dritt,' says Mamma, so viciously Maren stares at her. 'What else does she have to do all day? Not like her husband, out all hours visiting.'

'He visits?'

'Toril and Magda said he prayed with them. And I imagine he has his eye on Diinna too.' Mamma licks at the corner of her mouth, the skin there dry and weeping. 'He'll maybe come soon.'

'Maybe.' Maren disguises a shudder as she drapes her shawl over her shoulders. 'I won't be long.'

She gives Toril's house a wide berth. She wonders if he is in there now, praying with the family instead of keeping his wife company. She walks across the fallen blanket again, grinding in her heel.

The door to the boathouse is ajar, and the crisp chill is seeping inside, making the struggling fire stutter. Ursula is sitting where Maren left her, knuckles white and clasped about the blanket. Maren swallows down her impatience – why could she not have closed the door?

'Here,' she says, putting the pitcher down heavily on the table. Ursula starts as Maren closes the door. 'Water, and bread. Where are the knives?'

'There.'

Maren sweeps the stale crumbs from the chopping board. The knife is dull and she can see no sign of the sharpening

148

stone. She saws two pieces roughly from the loaf, brings them on the cleanest plate she can find and sets them down along with a horn cup that has a stain about the rim.

She is wondering whether she will need to place the woman's hand upon the food, perhaps even feed her, when Ursula blinks and looks up at her for the first time, her hand taking Maren's.

'Thank you,' she says. 'I'm sorry, I—' She breaks off, swallows. 'What must you think of me.'

'Not for me to think anything of you,' says Maren, feeling her cheeks redden. Ursula's hand is warm from the blanket, and so soft she can't find a bone in it. Maren feels her own all angles, hard and dry and cold as the dirt outside. She pulls from the grasp. 'It's no trouble.'

'I can pay you.' Ursula makes to rise. 'My husband . . . I can ask him . . .'

'All I ask is for a loaf in return.'

'Yes, of course. Please, join me.'

Maren could laugh at that, being invited to share in her own bread and water, but instead she sits in the chair beside Ursula, takes a slice.

She watches how small Ursula's bites are, dainty as a bird's. Her teeth are very white, her lips pinker now she is warming beneath the blanket.

Maren hesitates as Ursula takes another bite of bread, a sip of water. 'If you don't mind me asking, Mistress Cornet.'

'Ursula, please. Or Ursa.'

'Ursa?'

'You can call me Ursula if you'd prefer, of course. But those I'm close with call me Ursa, and now we have broken bread together . . .' She smiles weakly and Maren smiles back, her face feeling tight.

'Ursa.' She tries it. 'If you don't mind me speaking plainly. There's plenty of flour, and Kirsten left five carcasses in the store.' Ursa stiffens. Maren hurries on. 'I only wondered if everything was well.'

Ursa chews a long while, until the bread must be mush in her mouth. Her swallow is loud in the silence. She meets Maren's gaze again. Her eyes are very light brown, almost gold. 'You must think me very foolish—'

'Not at all—'

'But I cannot make bread.'

Maren's lips form a silent *Oh* as Ursa speaks on. 'I cannot butcher meat, have never seen a dead animal whole, cannot bring myself to even enter that room. I can barely keep the fire going, and my husband must start it when it dies. I cannot keep a house.' She gives a wild little laugh, and Maren's pulse quickens. 'I am not much of a wife.'

'I am sure that isn't – well, that is not so . . .' Maren wants to reassure her, but how? Butchering she can understand, perhaps: her mother was squeamish about such things, and leaves even the fish to Maren mostly. But bread, a broom? They aren't such hard things to know.

'It is bad,' Ursa interrupts, and her face flickers with anger that Maren knows is for herself. 'But I do not know what to do about it.' She reaches out again for Maren's hand, clasps it in her own. 'I need help, that much is evident, I'm sure. And we have some coin. I wonder if you . . . might you help me?'

'Help you?'

'Teach me. You would not be a maid so much as a friend, a teacher. Unless it is a silly idea. You can tell me.'

Maren wonders if she should feel offended. It sounds exactly like being a maid. 'I am not the best housekeeper myself.'

'The standard is not so high.' Ursa gives another weak smile. Maren looks about her, at the dying fire, the windows grimy with smoke, the cobwebs. 'Of course, if you do not want to, it is all right. I do not even know if Absalom . . .'

She trails off, her face sombre again, loosening her grip on Maren's hand. Maren tightens hers in response.

'Yes,' she says. The word is out before she can really think about it.

'You are certain?' Ursa smiles. 'Thank you. I'll speak with my husband.'

Maren rises suddenly. 'I'll tell my mother.'

'Yes.'

'See you on the Sabbath. You can tell me what the commissioner says.'

'I will.' Ursa follows her to the door. Her brown eyes are bright with relief. There is a crumb caught on her lower lip, and Maren must clutch her skirts to keep from brushing it off.

'Thank you, Maren.'

The door closes, and Maren feels it is she who is plunged into an airless room.

Nineteen

'I know we aren't so fine as her from Bergen but we are no servants.' Mamma is pacing the small floor of their house, licking at the cracked edge of her mouth, glaring at Maren. 'Whatever possessed you to say yes to that fat dritt?'

But Maren can't explain it. She knows they have enough trouble with baby Erik and Diinna to keep them busy, enough work to do in the remaining month of the midnight sun to ensure they survive the winter. There are crops to be planted, last year's harvested. They will have to go to Kiberg for fish, sell furs to trade, make trips to the low mountain for fresh heather and moss for the roof where last winter ice found its way in and swelled, letting in damp when it melted.

This means Diinna will have to pick up the slack Maren creates, as will Mamma. And Mamma is getting older, getting frailer, and inside her is growing an anger towards Diinna that frightens Maren when she sees it, even more than her mother frightens her now.

As Mamma tells her over and over how foolish she is, that she supposes there is no way out of it without offending Mistress Cornet and so the commissioner, Maren can't disagree. She can't explain what happened, why she felt she had no choice in the matter. The only thing she could offer – though she will not offer it – was that when Ursa loosened her hand, she felt as though something important was slipping away from her and that she must grab it. She had to say yes. She had no choice.

Though something is decided, she is unsure how the arrangement will work. It feels strange to take money, but Mamma will not accept her helping for nothing. She doesn't know how to broach the subject, or whether she should go unbidden to the house. It is only another day till the Sabbath – she supposes she will hear more then.

She tries to go about her tasks with her usual care and attention, but the thought of being out of the house has sent something singing through her blood, something restless and hot and almost painful. Though she isn't to go to the sea to fish as they had before the commissioner arrived, it is still a change of scenery, and a place where she had kissed her betrothed and watched over her brother and father. In another version of her life, the boathouse is hers, and now she has a chance to claim a small ownership to it.

And Ursa – she too sets something moving through Maren's body. It feels almost like the ache when she watches Erik sleep, but it is ridiculous to harbour such tenderness towards a grown woman, even one seemingly clueless as a child. Maren is startled by her. What kind of life must she have had in Bergen, to arrive so unprepared? Though it is as unthinkable as Mamma says, Maren feels no scorn, only a crushing pity.

The day that passes between the making of their agreement and their meeting in kirke is filled with thoughts of Ursa alone in her large house, sitting still as stone by the table beneath the blanket, or lying in bed once her husband has left. Maren imagines her bare toes falling on the pelt she stitched, the gentle attention of her eyes as she slices the bread Maren brought her. The birdlike close of her lips about it.

Though Maren is in a hurry to get there, she still knocks at Diinna's door and urges her to come to kirke on the Sabbath.

'He doesn't approve,' says Maren, 'of people not attending.'

'What do I care for his approval?'

Maren can't make her dull-eyed sister-in-law understand, that he isn't like the minister, how this man's favour has a heft to it, that to fall out of it would have an even greater weight.

She hasn't told Diinna what Mamma said to him about the runes and the rites, though she supposes she may have over-heard them discussing it, through the wall. But Diinna gives no sign that she has heard, gives no sign of caring what anyone says, even Maren. The dislike between her and Mamma pulses, is growing teeth. Maren reaches out for her hand. It is sticky with something.

'Please, Diinna. You should come. He may have more ques-tions for the census.'

She shrugs. 'He knows where I am.' Her dark eyes slide to the wall. Perhaps she did hear after all, knows Toril gave her name and that Mamma confirmed she lived here.

'At least let us bring Erik,' says Maren, impatient to get away.

Diinna holds him out, a wordless *Take him*. So Maren takes the boy, places him gently on the floor. He sits heavily, like a child much younger than his near fourteen months. *He should be walking more, and babbling*, Maren thinks, *or at least trying to*. His small face regards hers seriously. He has Diinna's eyes, his father's narrow face and lips. The lower one trembles, but he doesn't cry.

'Hello, Erik. You're coming to kirke with me. Would you like that?' His gaze moves to her face, then slides away.

Diinna shuts the door and Maren hoists Erik back to her

hip, carries him to their house, kisses him upon the forehead. The smell of clean cotton is long gone: he smells of wet wool, and his hair is greasier than it should be. She calls for Mamma to hurry up, and bring a blanket for Erik. He has been handed to her in a shift. Mamma comes out grumbling.

'She should take her own child to kirke. And what's she thinking of, sending him out in so little?' She doesn't bother to keep her voice down. 'The Devil's in that woman.'

'Hush, Mamma,' snaps Maren, glancing around. 'Don't say such things.'

Mamma tuts as she wraps Erik in the blanket, swaddling him like a newborn. He struggles briefly to free his arms as Mamma takes him. She babies him, and Diinna treats him as though she can't wait for him to be grown up and out of the house.

What will become of him? Erik's child, who is as serious as his namesake. She and her brother lived lives apart from a young age, Maren inside the house, Erik learning the land and, later, the sea. They played at the headland sometimes, in those rare, in-between years when they were old enough to be un-supervised and young enough to be more use out of the way than trusted with housework. Whole worlds sprang up from Vardø's flat ground – troll lands and faerie kingdoms.

In company outside of her own, he was quiet and she always talked for her little brother. Now she remembers it, Erik did not speak until late, two or three. But that was because Maren did it for him. Who will speak for his son? As an adult, Erik was a man of few words. Even Diinna, always bright and laughing in those days, could not make him speak beyond what was necessary. And now his wife is silent as he was, and sullen besides.

•

The novelty of the commissioner and his wife has not worn off enough for the women to go straight inside. They are ranged about the door of the kirke again, Kirsten a head taller than everyone else. Pastor Kurtsson is there too. As Maren draws closer, she can see there is a faint break between the groups – most have set themselves close to the minister, but a handful, mostly the seagoers, are speaking with Kirsten.

Mamma makes for the minister's group, Maren moves towards the other. She hears the women make half-hearted coos over Erik, though he is too large for them, and she knows most do not like Diinna any more than Mamma seems to.

'No Diinna?' says Kirsten, watching Mamma's back. Maren shakes her head. 'You should have made her come.'

'I can't make her. I tried.'

'You should have tried harder,' says Kirsten. 'Edne managed to bring her father though he is nearly blind. The census . . .' She lowers her voice. 'It would be good to have her say her own name. Especially with the killings at Alta and Kirkenes.'

'Killings now?' Maren feels a chill steal across her neck.

'Three Sámi, all weather-weavers.'

'But Diinna doesn't—'

'It doesn't matter much what Diinna does, only what she is. This Lensmann, he is determined to put a stop to the old ways.'

'He is not even at Vardøhus.'

'Nor at Alta,' says Kirsten. 'But he has his commissioners, and Cornet should see Diinna in kirke.'

Maren understands. To not come to kirke is one danger; to be Sámi and not come is another. 'I've no time to fetch her now.'

'Perhaps he won't notice,' says Kirsten, but Maren knows as well as she that he is the sort who notices. It is why, when she sees him striding towards the kirke, Ursa in a lighter blue dress behind him, she shrinks herself small as she can.

'Good morning,' he says. The women chorus back like girls. Kirsten grimaces.

'Good morning,' says a quieter voice, a voice Maren feels is just for her. Ursa has stopped beside her and Kirsten, is smiling nervously. Her hair is neater than last Sabbath's Day – she must be getting used to the lack of a mirror.

'Good morning,' says Kirsten.

'I was hoping we could begin our arrangement tomorrow?' says Ursa.

'Of course.'

Ursa smiles more broadly, showing even teeth. 'I have not forgotten the loan of your coat. Perhaps I could buy more skins from you, Fru Sørensdatter?'

'Certainly,' says Kirsten. 'I can bring them tomorrow, if that is agreeable.'

'Most agreeable. And maybe Maren could give you a list of what more we need – I understand you have a good store of grains and the like. You sound most enterprising.'

'Thank you very much, Mistress Cornet.'

'Ursula, please.'

Maren becomes aware of others watching them, Toril's attention torn between the commissioner and their conversation with his wife.

'Until tomorrow,' says Ursa, following her husband inside the dark mouth of the kirke.

'You have an arrangement?' says Kirsten, the curiosity apparent in her voice.

'She needs help with the house,' says Maren. There is a spiralling in her stomach. It feels like a strange sort of triumph. 'I offered.' Kirsten's eyebrows are raised. 'She's paying. Good coin. Bergen coin.'

Kirsten nods slowly. 'Get that list to me after kirke. And Maren?' She looks intently at her, her eyes direct as her words. 'Be careful.' She squeezes Maren's upper arm, and goes inside before Maren can ask of what.

Twenty

Absalom leaves early the next day for Alta, before Ursa can ask him for his approval of her plan to bring Maren into their home. He has a new tactic, he tells her.

'I am done with waiting at the fortress gates day after day. Until the Lensmann arrives in Vardøhus, I will make myself useful. There has been some action at Alta that I am keen to gain the measure of.'

Ursa guesses he is also resolved to meet the other commissioners to get some idea of their relationship with Lensmann Cunningham. She knows it enrages him that others may be in communication with the Lensmann while he is left in Vardø, and Ursa hopes their situation is common among the commissioners, prays he will not return with even more anger in his heart.

He tells her he must take a small rowing boat a few hours up the coast to Hamningberg, manned by a fisherman from there, where a larger whaling ship will carry him on to Alta, which lies two days to the west. They must have passed the town on the way from Bergen, but Ursa doesn't remember stopping there.

The journey and visit will keep him away at least a week,

and she feels the same mix of relief and anxiety she felt the night he didn't come to her on the ship. The house is already becoming familiar, seeing as she doesn't leave it all day, but at night, even with him snoring beside her, she thinks of the bodies in the store, the runes painted over the door, and the space before the fire beneath Maren's hide covering, where drowned men lay.

Though she has not told him of Maren, he was impressed by the coverings and so agreed when she asked for some money for additional pelts and supplies promised to her by Kirsten, and guessed at a little extra so she could pay Maren. She can't think he would have denied her: the embarrassment of their home was suddenly apparent after Maren's visit. It had been all right when she had been left to sit in the creeping squalor alone. But when Maren had come, holding the skins that now adorn the floor, she had noticed the disarray for the first time.

She had done her best in the small time between Absalom's departure and Maren's arrival, sweeping with the bristle broom and sending plumes of dirt and dust into the air. She had fetched water from the well, and tried to scour the mud from her blue dress with a brush and board. She imagined Agnete's raised eyebrow, and most of all Siv's thin, tired face, her hands blistered and cracked, her nails kept so short the sisters would laugh about them being mannish.

Ursa's face flushes with the memory, the casual cruelty and complete stupidity of it. Her arms ache from the minutes over the scrubbing board, and she feels her hands greasy with tallow soap, stained with ash. She should ask Absalom to write to Siv, so Ursa can thank her for keeping them clean and fed and, in her own stern fashion, loved. Ursa longs to feel this way again, and for the bathtub before the crackling fire, the warmth that easily reached her bones. The press of her sister's bony spine against her back as they sat facing away from each other in the tub, the buzz of Agnete's laboured breath like bees cupped against her ribs—

Maren is on her doorstep before Ursa has washed the tears from her face. In her hands is a bundle of cloth, and she sets it on the floor beside the table with great effort, bending carefully. Ursa offers her tea.

'With what?' says Maren, looking at the meagre shelves.

'My husband brought bilberry leaves from Bergen. I'm sure he can spare us some.'

Maren nods, and moves to the fireplace.

'Let me,' says Ursa. 'I know how to make tea.'

It is the simplest of tasks, but she has not been watched doing it before, and she can feel Maren's eyes upon her just as she had in kirke. It makes her stand a little straighter, take the cups from their shelf with greater care, flourish a little with the leaves as she drops them to boil. She enjoys the woman's attention upon her: it doesn't feel like malice, as though she is watching for her to make a mistake, but rather more like care, the way Siv would supervise Ursa with her needlework.

Maren takes the cup between cold fingers – Ursa notices the nail beds are raw pink and stretched as though freshly scrubbed. The pads that brush against her own hands are rough as her husband's. She feels shy of her own palms, soft and unskilled as a baby's, hides them in the folds of her skirts. They must be of similar age, but they are made so differently. Ursa feels too big in Maren's presence, cumbersome and absurd in her petticoats. Maren's eyes are large and softly coloured, but her gaze is sharp and clever.

The last time they had been together in the house like this, Maren had taken charge immediately, and Ursa waits for her to do the same again now. But Maren seems uncertain of herself, her eyes lowered to the steam of her cup. It sets off uneasiness in Ursa, a discomfort. She becomes aware of her breath, too loud in the quiet, tries to breathe more shallowly, which makes her chest tighten.

They sit wordlessly together at the table, and Ursa realizes that though she is vague on the perimeters of their relationship – Maren isn't a servant, like Siv, and so she isn't this woman's mistress – she must be the one to speak, to begin.

'Thank you again for coming.'

Maren's eyes are still fixed on her cup.

'I am glad your mother could spare you. With luck I will be quick to learn and she can have you back. Summers must be busy here, being so short.'

Maren is bent so low over the steam of her cup, perhaps warming her nose, that Ursa can see the small hairs pulling at the back of her neck where her bun is tight, the collar of her dress creased and worn, the nubs of her spine beneath. The bundle sits at her feet, lumpen.

'What have you brought?'

Maren bends, brings it up to her knees, the cloth and her arms straining, the hollows about the base of her throat deepening. Ursa reaches out to help, catching her hands beneath it to help raise it to the table.

'Why, it's heavy as a rock,' says Ursa, standing now beside her chair, and Maren's narrow fingers work at the knot, tightened by the strain put upon it. Her ragged nail catches and she sucks in a breath. 'Shall I cut it?' She fetches a knife, but at last Maren is roused to speech.

'No, if you'll please, Mistress Cornet.' There is an urgency beneath the formality, and both surprise Ursa. Maren's cheeks are red, and she moves so the bundle on the table is hidden behind her, as though protecting a small child from Ursa's blade. 'It's my mother's.'

Now it is Ursa's turn to flush, and she takes her time

returning the knife to its place. It isn't Maren who put the distance back between them at all, but her, treating the cloth like something that could be easily got, easily disposed of, easily replaced. *That is your old life*, she tells herself.

By the time she turns round again the cloth has been carefully eased out from under its cargo, and folded neatly beside. Ursa had not been wrong in her first estimation: beside a smooth column of stone that she recognizes as a rolling pin, sits a rock, grey and shaped like a mound with a flattish top, about the size of her mother's belly when she was pregnant with the brother that wasn't to live.

'Is it a slickstone?' she asks, and Maren snorts, an abrupt sound, bringing her hand up to her mouth.

'I am sorry, it's only . . .' Another snort escapes her, followed by a thin peal of laughter. She looks immediately contrite, which makes Ursa laugh, too. 'I am sorry, I am sorry.'

'Do not be sorry,' says Ursa, feeling the distance closing between them again. 'Only, please, explain to me what this is. And perhaps,' she smiles, 'why it is not a slickstone?'

'A slickstone is for smoothing, or for starching. It fits like a hand in a hand, just so—' Maren holds out her palm, and in a gesture that is more reaction than intent, Ursa reaches her hand out too, and places it atop Maren's palm. She barely feels the cool dryness of it, the rough callouses, before Maren jerks away, clutching it to her as though burnt.

'I—'

The door is knocked upon: three sharp raps displaying a confidence that sets Ursa in mind of her husband. Her chest thrums, but Maren recognizes the sound.

'Kirsten Sørensdatter,' she says.

She knocks like a man, thinks Ursa, as she opens the door. Kirsten stands there, her arms piled with bundles, a covered bucket hooked over her elbow, and two skins tied like a cape about her neck. She doesn't wait for an invitation to enter, only strides inside and drops the whole lot upon the table.

'Good morning, Ursula, Maren.' She stands smiling at them both, as though aware she has walked in at a strange moment and understands it better than Ursa herself. Ursa is again prompted to draw a line between Kirsten and her husband: she is so certain of herself, so solid in the middle of the room that Ursa fancies she can feel the air pushing itself backwards to make more space for her. And though Maren's exclamation comes immediately, it still takes Ursa another moment to register that the woman is wearing trousers.

'Kirsten, are you mad? I told you this must stop.'

Maren is standing before her friend, and though Ursa can't see her face from her place beside the open door, she can hear the fear upon it.

Kirsten looks down at herself. 'What would be madness is slaughtering in skirts.'

Ursa notices the dark stains over her thighs, speckling the bottoms of the trousers, which are a little short, the waistband tied with rope. She checks outside the door: there is no one looking from the neighbouring windows, no one on their steps. She closes it and moves back to the table quietly. Maren is mouthing wordlessly, standing very close to Kirsten, as though to shield her from Ursa's view. There is something between them, she thinks, a deeper friendship than two who gossip outside kirke once a week.

'No one was looking,' Ursa says, hoping to break the thread between them.

'Still, someone will have seen.' Maren clutches her hands together as though in prayer. 'Someone always does. What if word gets back to Pastor Kurtsson, or to Commissioner—'

She gasps and wheels about to Ursa, who recoils. Maren's energy feels dangerous and desperate, like a fox in a trap.

'Mistress Cornet, Ursa, you will not . . .' She gathers herself. 'Please, would you please not . . .' She turns back to Kirsten. 'You have come to the commissioner's house, Kirsten. The commissioner's house, in trousers!'

'They are my finest trousers,' says Kirsten, her voice mock-affronted.

'And yet you slaughter in them?' says Ursa, playing along. Maren's face is still wretched, and Ursa tries to soothe her. 'I will not tell my husband, Maren. Fru Sørensdatter, you have my word. Or should it be Herr Sørensdatter?'

Maren doesn't laugh, but Kirsten lets out a boom and doffs an imaginary cap. 'Milady.'

'Do you not see how dangerous this is?' Maren twists her hands into her skirts. 'It was one thing in your own house—'

'What is dangerous is your glower. If the wind blows the other way you shall be stuck like that, and even the trolls will run away.'

'Trolls are for children,' says Maren. 'This is serious.'

'And yet you leave crumbs out every midwinter.'

'We do not follow such customs.' Maren's voice has a note of hysteria, and Ursa finally realizes that she is again the cause of Maren's distress. It is her husband Maren fears, his displeasure at the runes and, no doubt, at trolls. Ursa despises him at that moment: how she wishes these women knew that she is as scared as them. This time she comes close to Maren and places a hand upon her shoulder.

'Please, Maren, you do not have to worry. I will not tell my husband of any of this. He is in Alta this week, and no doubt Pastor Kurtsson is taking full advantage of his absence to rest from his Norwegian lessons. And besides –' she gives her a hesitant smile – 'I, too, leave food out for the trolls in midwinter. In fact, my sister and I would insist on whole herring, prepared with a potato, and a sweet cake.'

'I should like to be a troll in Bergen, to eat so fine as that,' says Kirsten, and though Ursa decides to take it in good humour she hears the barb in it, chides herself again for her display of extravagance.

Maren searches her face and, at last, seems to take her at her word. She nods carefully, her pointed chin uncreasing. 'Thank you.'

'All the same, Kirsten,' says Ursa, determined to take charge, to show confidence so Maren can take assurance from her. 'You had better borrow something to return home in.' She lifts the lid of her cherrywood chest, draws out her grey wool skirt. 'This is a little long anyway.' She holds it out to Kirsten, and for the first time sees uncertainty cross her broad face.

'I can't wear that,' she says. 'It is too dear.'

'Nonsense,' says Ursa. 'I insist.'

'I will muddy it with my boots.'

'I am learning how to take mud out of cloth. It is no trouble.'

Kirsten takes it with reluctance, and removes her boots before stepping into it. It comes up a little short, but the trouserlegs come up shorter.

'All this worry over some trousers,' says Kirsten, relacing her shoes. 'I am like to cause as much of a fuss in so fine a skirt as this. Best be careful, Mistress Cornet, or you'll have the kirke-women at the door, begging alms of lace.' She straightens. 'I brought everything you asked for.' This to Maren. 'Flour and such. And even found some fennel seeds among Mads's things. I have no use for them.'

Ursa fetches what she owes Kirsten for the supplies, and the woman places the coins into her trouser pocket beneath the skirt. 'Thank you. I hope your lesson goes well, though why you have picked such a teacher I will never guess.' She smiles warmly at Maren, whose face still holds the last vestiges of worry. 'I will see you on Wednesday.'

Twenty-One

Maren could weep. Damn Kirsten, with her arrogance and her stupidity and her need to be seen. She doesn't believe for a moment her attire was only for the slaughter. It was as much for show. She wanted the measure of the commissioner's wife and now she has it. Maren hopes she is ashamed.

The door closes heavily, and Maren jumps.

'Please,' says Ursa. 'You must not worry.'

Maren tries to smooth her face, which aches with the effort of it. She isn't used to being noticed in this way. But Ursa is looking at her as though she could see straight through her skin to her thudding heart. Maren brings her arms across her chest, holds herself.

'I am not worried.' She clears her throat, gives herself a sharp pinch beneath her shoulder blade, and then moves back to the table where the rock sits. 'Will you help me move this to the fire?'

'We are to burn it?'

'Rocks do not burn,' says Maren carefully, checking Ursa's face for jest, and finding it. She smiles back. 'It is a baking stone.' She unties the nearest bundle, checks inside and brings out a closely woven packet of something. She opens it carefully, rubs it between her fingers, feeling for the grain. 'It is good Kirsten brought fennel, all she has given is potato flour.' She dusts off her hands. 'We are going to make flatbrød.'

Ursa nods. 'I think I have had that, at Christmas time with herring and onions.'

Maren winces. Flatbrød is what they eat more than anything, and certainly never with onions. She hopes Ursa likes it – there will not be fresh bread waiting in her pantry often.

She doesn't elaborate, doesn't tell Ursa that the reason she has chosen this for their first meeting is because even a child could make it, as it is near impossible to burn or make bitter. She has been making it with Mamma for as long as she can remember, since before her brother was taken by Pappa to hunt or to fish. They spend a whole day on it every few months, Mamma rolling and Maren baking.

'This kind of stone, it holds warmth very well. We use it for our beds, on very cold nights.'

She used to go with Mamma, sometimes even Pappa, to the low mountain looking for these rocks. Firestone, Pappa called it, because it was warm from even a touch of sun. She strokes her hand across it. This was their second baking stone, more recently fetched, ten years ago perhaps. The one left at their house is better, scooped like a bowl from years of use. She thought to make this one a gift for Ursa, is shy to propose it. Mamma is unlikely to notice it gone. She notices nothing much at all any more, as though a film has grown across her eyes and thickens every month.

'Like a bedpan?'

Maren doesn't know, nods anyway. 'It keeps the heat even, keeps the air out of the dough. The bread will keep for months, years.'

They heave it up between them, Ursa exclaiming at Maren's ability to carry it alone to the house, and settle it atop the grate. 'It will take a while to heat, but we can begin anyway.'

She lays out what Kirsten has brought: there is plenty of flour, a bucket of kjernemelk with a thin skin on top that makes Maren's mouth water just to look at it. Kirsten, Maren realizes as she unpacks smaller packets of seeds and even a small hard crystal of salt, is even more comfortably off than Maren guessed.

She fetches Ursa's pestle and mortar, made of cool grey stone, and sets Ursa to grinding the fennel seeds while she begins measuring and sifting the flour. The seeds will be too overpowering whole, will throw the balance of the bread out and make the places where there is none taste lacking. That is how she feels, standing beside Ursa: chalky and thin as plain flatbrød.

Ursa scatters the ground fennel into the mix and Maren must start to sift all over again: Ursa has not put great effort into it and the seeds aren't of the fine powder she would have preferred. But the woman is looking anxiously into her face and so Maren nods and says thank you. When the flour mix is a little less gritty, she has a small mound of fennel husks beside her on the table. Ursa reaches to sweep them away and Maren puts her own hand out. She is prepared, this time, for the contact, doesn't feel the surge that came a little like panic when Ursa had placed her hand in her palm.

'Keep them. We can use it all.'

Ursa does something very strange. She covers her face, makes a sound of irritation, much like a chided child.

'I am sorry,' she says. 'I feel so foolish. You must think me awful, to be so wasteful.'

'I think no such thing,' says Maren. 'I only think you lived differently in Bergen. I hope you will come to like your life here.' She feels heat flush her neck. 'Not that I think you are struggling.'

Ursa lets out a hollow little laugh, a wretched sound that pulls at Maren. 'Oh, but I am.'

It is a moment of confidence that fills Maren with tenderness. 'All will be well, Ursa.'

Ursa looks at her with such simple gratitude that Maren blushes. 'You are so kind. I am so glad of you.'

She reaches out to Maren, and though Maren doesn't hold people easily – the last time was perhaps with Diinna when she lay collapsed on their floor as Mamma held the newly born Erik – something compels Maren to let her.

There is no reluctance or self-consciousness in the way Ursa folds into her arms, fitting beneath her chin, her hair smelling of sleep and perfumed water. Ursa mentioned a sister, and has perhaps missed holding her, for she clings to Maren with an unsettling need.

For her part, Maren grows bolder, and tightens her grip about Ursa, feeling the softness of her shape beneath her fine dress, the gentle swell of her shoulder blades, like low waves across her back. She doesn't want to breathe, to create the space between them for her chest to grow into. But then Ursa is loosening her grip and pulling away.

'Thank you,' says Ursa, and turns back to the fennel husks. She seems soothed by the embrace where Maren has been disquieted. 'Should I grind them finer?'

There is a double pulse in Maren's body. She motions yes and begins adding the kjernemelk, skimming the butter from the top to reach the liquid below. The action requires focus, and calms her. She wraps the butter in the clean cloth Kirsten has given for this purpose, and the creamy smell coats her nostrils. They went without butter last year, and she has missed the richness of it, the salt dried from a pailful of sea and churned until it is golden and smooth and perfect.

When she has added enough buttermilk she mixes it in

carefully, tilting the bowl so Ursa can see as she stirs it about until the mixture is firm and consistent, sitting mounded like a small mimic of the baking stone heating in the fire.

She scatters flour over the tabletop and Ursa passes her the heavy rolling pin. It is made from a different rock than the baking stone, cooler, to keep the dough from sticking. She portions palmfuls of dough, sets one before Ursa.

'You want it thin as a biscuit.'

Ursa nods, but the moment she starts rolling Maren knows she has not made biscuits before. The shape that forms is nothing like a circle. But when she looks to Maren for approval, a flour stain on her forehead near her hairline, Maren smiles encouragingly, watches as she carries it carefully to the baking stone and drops it on top. It is off-centre, one side edging over towards the licking flames, and Maren already knows it will burn there and cook unevenly elsewhere.

'How long?' Ursa is staring at the baking stone.

'We wait until all the water is gone, until it is crisp and good for cracking. Will you watch it?'

With Ursa given her task, Maren takes up the rolling pin. It holds none of the warmth from Ursa's hands. She rolls out the remaining dough into neat discs. She isn't so skilled as Mamma, but they are even and speckled like the rare eggs they find tucked in the gaps between rocks in the cliff below their house. They have not checked since the storm. Perhaps she should suggest it to Mamma – after well over a year undisturbed the birds will likely have forgotten the danger of people.

After a few tries of Ursa rescuing the flatbrød too early or too late, she learns the point at which she must clamp the breads between the tongs and rest them to cool. They find an easy rhythm between them, do not speak except through glances and nods, and when the dough is rolled and stacked, Maren takes up the pot without asking and begins to brew some more tea. The fireplace is double width, as Dag intended, and so they can stand shoulder to shoulder before it. By the time the tea is brewed the first breads are dry and cool.

Ursa prods them. 'They are good?'

'One way to discover it.'

They sit together at the floury table. Ursa takes her own attempt and cracks it, sending crumbs and flakes of seeds scattering into her lap. She brushes them carelessly to the floor as she chews.

'They get better the longer you leave them,' says Maren.

'They are good already.' Ursa's smile is broad and Maren returns it gladly. 'There is no blessing so complete as bread.'

'What?'

'Something Siv used to say.'

'She is your sister?'

'Servant.' Ursa seems to catch herself. 'But also my friend. Agnete is my sister.' She blinks, her pale lashes brushing her cheek. 'She's ill.'

'I'm sorry.'

'She was near drowned when she was first born. The doctors say it's because she came in my mother's bath, and there's still water on her lungs. I used to care for her.'

Maren can't think what to say. She takes some more flatbrød, catching the crumbs neatly in her palm and placing them atop the flour.

'They did not think she would see her first birthday, but she's thirteen years old now. She will be grown when next we meet.'

The silence widens. Ursa doesn't finish her piece, only passes it between her fingers, hand to hand. In her face is pain so apparent it feels indecent to witness.

'My brother was younger, too,' Maren says finally. 'By a year. But still he was married before me.'

'At least I have beaten Agnete there.' Slowly, Ursa meets her eye. 'You must miss him.'

To that there is nothing Maren can say. She feels a dark draw of energy from the spot before the fire, where Erik lay in his greenish skin and seemed to shrink before her eyes. She couldn't bring herself to touch him in the weeks he'd lain there, had not thrown herself over him and keened as Mamma had. Though the Kirke talked of souls, Varr and Diinna of spirits, from the moment she saw him dead she had felt there was nothing left of him in this world, or any other. There was only a body, empty as the shapes in the store. Erik was not this shrunken form, was not caught like a bird fluttering at the windows, was not in the sea or the whale or the sky. He was gone, and Maren could find no comfort for it.

'I'm sorry,' says Ursa. 'I have spoken out of turn. Agnete and I, we did not converse much with others beyond Father and Siv.'

'We don't speak much at all in our house,' says Maren, briskly. 'We should store these. You have bread barrels?'

'Not that I have noticed. Though perhaps . . .'

Ursa looks towards the store. The cobwebs have gone, but Maren suspects they have been cleaned away rather than broken by entry.

'I'll fetch them,' says Maren, rising to her feet, but Ursa stands with her.

'Let me.' There is that determined set to her chin that Maren noticed when she stepped from the boat in her yellow dress. 'I can do it.'

She crosses the room, places her hand upon the latch. Maren watches the small lift of her shoulders as she takes a breath and opens the door, leaving floury smudges on the frame. The store has a small, narrow slit of a window set into the far wall, and the light filters through the hanging shapes of the carcasses to illuminate the wispy hairs that spring up about Ursa's ears, escaping her neat knot.

She hesitates a moment before moving further into the store, and out of Maren's sight. She sees the sway of the slaughtered reindeer, their bodies dark red and sinewy. They will be gamey now, rich and salty. She should offer to teach her how to butcher, but perhaps that is too much too soon. There's a scraping sound and Ursa comes back out, rolling a barrel before her, flinching as the swing of a carcass brings it brushing against her. She pulls the door closed behind her, lips a thin line, and rolls the barrel to the table, righting it and resting her palms on it.

They wrap the flatbrød and stack them inside the bread barrels. When it is done, they wipe down the table, sweep the floor. Maren washes the cups in the grey water of the bowl, her hands wrinkling as she rubs a fingertip across the lip of Ursa's cup.

They edge the stone out of the fire using the pokers. 'Leave it until tomorrow,' says Maren. 'It will be cool by then.'

'Shall I bring it to you?'

'You can keep it. And the roller. We have another.'

Ursa reaches out with her easy familiarity, and takes her hand. 'Thank you.'

'I don't have to go just yet,' says Maren, though it isn't true. She had promised Mamma she would be home for their own baking. But returning to their small house, full of silence and sadness so thick it reeks, feels an impossibility just now, in this warm room, with Ursa's soft hand in hers. 'We could make a start on those hides.'

'How thoughtless of me,' says Ursa. 'You must be missing your coat.'

'Yes.' It is an easy lie; she has her father's at home. 'It would be good to have it back.'

174

'But won't your mother be needing you? I could do without the coat. I have nowhere to go but kirke. Besides, it is a few days till Sabbath and warmer all the time.'

Maren feels her chance slipping. 'I wouldn't want to leave you without it. It will not take long for me to teach you. Though of course it would be quicker with two. We could have it made before turn of day.'

Why does she not just say she wishes to stay? This isn't how they speak here, if they speak at all, this to-and-fro like currents whirled away and together again by a quick wind.

'It is no trouble for me if you stay. In fact I would prefer it, with Absalom gone to Alta.' Her eyes shine as she turns them upon Maren. 'We could sit beside the fire together, talk a little as we sew. If you would like it. You don't have to . . .'

Again Maren feels that reach from inside her, a third, ghostly arm stretching out to seize hold of Ursa, as though she were drowning and found a raft among wreckage.

'Yes,' she manages. 'Yes, I can stay.'

Twenty-Two

They spread the hides out upon the floor, and Maren fetches a knife to score them at the right points. She must reach about Ursa with string to measure her, and even this makes her flush. She slices the hides into various shapes, and as Ursa watches her, Maren can feel she wants to say something.

'Is the Wednesday meet a regular occurrence?'

Maren stops slicing, rests on her heels.

'The Wednesday meet Kirsten spoke of,' says Ursa. Maren can barely recall any of Kirsten's visit. It feels a great distance away. 'Is it just the two of you?'

'No. Many of us meet, in Fru Olufsdatter's house.'

'She is our neighbour, yes? I perhaps could come. I should like to meet some people outside of kirke.'

Maren flinches.

'I won't mention any of this to them if you do not wish it. I could pretend not to know you at all.'

Maren knows she says it in jest, but still she is too slow to hide the hurt in her face. 'You may do as you like.'

Ursa rises and goes to her cherrywood chest.

'Aniseed?' Ursa tips two smallish seeds onto her palm, holds it out to her. 'You place them on your tongue. They taste strange, but good.' She takes one and puts it in her mouth, sticks her tongue out to show it. 'If you do not like it,' says Ursa, covering her mouth, words slightly stilted by the aniseed, 'you can leave it.'

Maren takes it from Ursa's hand, closes her lips around it.

'It is good, yes?'

'I have never tasted anything like it. From Bergen?'

'Asia. Captain Leifsson, who ran the ship that brought me. He gave me some.'

They set to work again, Maren bringing the sleeve pieces together to the table for them to stitch, one each. She makes holes with a pointed bore, shows Ursa the cross-stitch she must use to make them strong.

'I hope you do not mind me asking about the Wednesday meet,' says Ursa. 'I should understand if I were not welcome. It is only that I have so enjoyed this day together, and I should like to meet some others, if they are all as kind as you.'

How can Maren explain the knot in her chest at the thought of Ursa becoming friends with others? It is childish to feel jealousy over such a new friendship. And there is the complication of having the commissioner's wife in such an informal atmosphere. She trusts that Ursa will not tell anyone about Kirsten's trousers, but what else will she hear?

'I understand I am a stranger here,' prompts Ursa, 'but I should dearly like not to be.'

'Come, of course.'

'Will you fetch me? I should not like to arrive unannounced the first time.'

Maren can do nothing but nod.

'Good,' smiles Ursa. 'It's settled.' She turns her attention back to her work. 'Now, where have I gone wrong here?'

The answer is immediately, and Maren helps Ursa unpick her work, shows her more slowly so she can follow along. The fire burns down twice before they are done. The world is still and grey at the small windows, the night so quiet it is as if everything living is holding its breath.

Ursa's thumb is reddened and bleeding from pushing the needle through the coarse hide without a thimble. Maren will bring her a piece of leather next time, she thinks.

'You should try it on.' She holds the coat out for her, and Ursa slides it over her arms.

'How do I look?' Ursa asks, spinning. 'Like a Vardø woman?'

She looks nothing like them, any of them. Maren's chest aches and she dips her head to mask her confusion, begins to ravel the remaining gut thread.

Ursa takes the coat off, hangs it from the hook beside the door, takes the one beside it and holds it out to Maren.

'Thank you for the loan of it.' She crosses again to the chest. This time there are two seeds in her palm, and coins.

'Here.'

The coins sit in Maren's hand, cold and glinting. 'This is too much.'

'Not with the stone and the rolling pin and so forth,' says Ursa. She closes Maren's fingers about them. 'We have done far more than I ever thought to achieve. Why, I am nearly a housekeeper already.'

'And the aniseed—'

'One for now, one for later. Until Wednesday?'

Maren wants Ursa to stay her yet again, to barricade the way, to keep her at least until the day returns. But she only opens the door, and lets her disappear into the misty, sunlit night.

Her time with Ursa makes her feel noticed in a way she has not since Dag came to her trembling, and asked to marry her. Even her friendship with Kirsten, though dear, is built on different terms.

The money is more than she has ever seen before, their village running more on trade than coin. It jangles in her skirts like a taunt. It makes their time together nothing more than a service, she nothing more to Ursa than Kirsten is. Still, she knows it is too much, will pay many times over for their usual orders from the traders from Varanger when they come in midsummer. And besides, Mamma will not allow her to return empty-handed, would forbid her from going back.

Would Maren listen? She doubts her mother's disapproval could keep her from that house, from Ursa. She is the first friend Maren has made in years, and untouched by the hardnesses of a lifetime in Vardø. Even before the storm, none of them were so soft as her.

When home is in sight, light leaking from its windows and making it seem a ship poised on a fogged sea, she takes three of the smaller, heavier coins from her pocket, and moves them to the other, stifling them with a scrap of cloth. She doesn't know what they are worth, can't make sense of their surfaces, but something in their heft and colour makes her sure they are the most valuable.

These she will keep for herself, for some purpose as yet unclear to her. Perhaps she will go to Trøndheim and buy woven cloth, make herself a dress in the style of Ursa's dark blue one, with a collar that scoops daringly close to her shoulders, and has a trim of lace about the cuffs. She wouldn't fill it so pleasingly, but it would be good to have something new, something that isn't frayed about its edges and seams. She squeezes the coins until they grow warm at her touch, looks up to the sky. The sun is low and diffuse, its light shifting always to the corners of her sight. Perhaps she could even build a house of her own some day.

Her mother is awake and standing before the fire, the baking stone crouched in the flames like a toad, a stack of flatbrød beside her, more dough on the table. She doesn't look around as Maren closes the door. The room is close about her after a day at the commissioner's house, and though it is well swept, there is a smell that she has never noticed before: smoke and unwashed hair. She clears her throat, tastes aniseed.

'Mamma?'

Her mother reaches with her hands to the baked bread, taps it, and flips it out onto her palms. It is steaming but she takes her time carrying it to the rack, lowers it gentle as a prayer. *There is no blessing so complete as bread*, thinks Maren, as her mother takes up another circle of dough, lays it atop the stone.

'I'm sorry I'm late,' says Maren, taking off her coat. She is caught suddenly about the chest, remembering Ursa. How she had made the new coat look like something rare and lovely, the way a bird wears its feathers.

She doesn't know that Maren stitched two small runes into her sleeve, the ones Diinna once taught her meant protection from harm, and care. It pleases her to think of it now, like messages scrawled in invisible ink, worn against Ursa's pale wrist, the smooth passages of her veins green as meltwater.

Mamma still doesn't speak, but there is a tense set to her shoulders, inched up towards her ears, and when Maren moves to the fire there is a grim twitch in Mamma's jaw as she flips the bread. Her hands are so used to the motion she doesn't look down but straight ahead, the heat bringing sweat beading about her face. Her skin glows with it, the constant scab at the edge of her mouth flaking. She looks like a stranger.

'Mamma?'

Maren holds out the coins, and at last Mamma looks at her, then at her hand. Wordlessly she nods towards the pot where they keep their meagre purse, the string of beads that came from Diinna's father on her marriage to Erik, and the grey pearl their father found in the mouth of a shell that she thought to give Dag as a marriage gift. Maren adds her coins, and comes to hand Mamma the next flatbrød.

They work shoulder to shoulder, and the silence is both harder and easier than it was with Ursa. They have done this together so many times, they are like parts of the same body.

'What is she like?' says Mamma, eventually.

Maren thinks of Ursa's soft hands, her smooth cheek, the crease of her chin when she thinks or is embarrassed. She thinks of the aniseed on her breath, how she shares it now, like a secret. 'She is not as you would expect.'

Mamma snorts her disbelief.

'You will know her soon enough,' says Maren, passing the last of the uncooked breads as Mamma moves another to the rack. 'She is coming to the Wednesday meet.'

The mention of it brings the same confusion she'd felt when Ursa had raised it. Their friendship is still new and unformed, not yet hardened into something solid enough for her to feel confident in it. What if Ursa finally realizes that she has chosen someone wholly middling to assist her, when she could easily have her pick of teachers? Toril is the most skilled at needlework, Gerda the fastest at churning, Kirsten the best at butchering. Her mother is better at cooking, baking – Maren doesn't even have as good a temperament as most.

'Is she now?' Mamma's eyebrow rises. 'That will be interesting. What will your Kirsten have to say on that?'

'Why would she have anything to say?'

'She likes to be the centre of it all, doesn't she? With the commissioner's wife there, she will not be able to take charge so easily.'

'She will not mind. She is the one who mentioned it in front of her.'

'We will see,' says Mamma. She begins to stack the breads into their barrels, and Maren moves to help. Through the thin wall, Erik is at last quieted, and Maren hears a low song coming, Diinna speaking in her language. Erik's *joik*.

They go to bed just as the morning slips its noise beneath the door, and Maren must wait until Mamma is asleep before she takes the remaining coins and aniseed from her pocket and places them in the rip in her pillow. She shifts the aniseed so it will sit small and hard against her cheek, and she fancies she can smell it through the greying cloth. She should make the most of one of the long summer days, row to the low mountain. She has not replaced the heather since the storm, and it is as crisp as burnt bread. Perhaps now that Ursa has her coat, she will want to come with her.

Diinna's singing still comes through the wall. Erik must be waking, and Maren places her palm against it, letting her eyelids close against the brightening day. She sinks, and the whale that came for her father and brother surfaces, calling her to the sea.

Twenty-Three

Mamma works Maren hard in the day before the Wednesday meet. She is sent to Toril's to fetch mended winter vests, and the woman is stiffer with her than ever. Toril was always a difficult woman to like, cool even to those she had known all her life, but since the storm she has taken to wearing her faith like armour, wielding her piousness like a blade. Maren counts five crucifixes on the shelf over the fireplace, ranged like newly forged weapons. More line the walls, delicate fashionings of woven sea grass and twine.

'That for Commissioner Cornet?' Maren nods at them.

'For God. He comes most days,' says Toril.

'God?'

'The commissioner.' Maren sucks her cheeks to keep from laughing at Toril's furious face. 'Though not today. Today he is in—'

'Alta.'

Toril's knuckles turn white on the vests in her arms. 'He told you?'

'You aren't the only one who knows things, Toril,' says Maren, irresistibly reminded of how Kirsten took the wind from Toril's sails with her information about the Lensmann.

She holds out her hands for the pile of restitched cloth, but the woman doesn't pass it to her.

'He has not visited you.'

Maren shrugs.

'I know he has not. He would never, not with that Lapp and her bastard under the roof.'

Anger comes quick and hot to Maren's chest. 'Erik is no bastard. They were married, you yourself danced at their wedding feast.'

'I did not dance,' says Toril. 'I would not dance at such a devilish union.'

Maren's palm itches. She longs to slap Toril across the face, to tear at her hair. But she only snatches the vests from her. 'You had best mind your tongue, Toril Knudsdatter.'

Toril loses her balance and stumbles, her shoulder catching at the shelf beside her and sending several of her crucifixes to the floor. Maren turns and leaves her scrabbling about on the ground for them, heart thumping.

Vardø is busy in a way it only is in summertime, women sitting outside their houses with butter churns, scaling fish brought from Kiberg. The smells, the low talk, familiar as it is, can't soothe her. She goes straight to Diinna's door, knocks with her elbow.

Diinna takes her time answering. She is sallow-skinned, mouth a tight line, her hair loose and lank. Maren is minded of her expression the day Kirsten dug her from the snow that first winter. Behind her, the room is dark and airless, and smells of sour milk. Maren can see the small figure of Erik still tucked into the blankets, the slow rise-fall of his breath just visible.

Diinna reaches wordlessly for her vests, but Maren shakes her head, gestures for her to come outside. The door closes softly behind them, though Maren wishes she could tell her to leave it open, to let some fresh air into the room where her son sleeps.

'I have just come from Toril's house.'

'So I can see.' Moved fully into the daylight, Diinna looks more wretched than ever. Her eyes are pouchy and deadened, and if Maren didn't know that there was no way for her to have gotten hold of any, she would have thought her drunk on spirits.

'She has been speaking of you. Speaking unkindly.'

'What does it matter?'

'She said you and Erik were not married, not truly.'

Pain crosses Diinna's face. She puts an end of her hair into her mouth, sucks upon it. 'She was there, she saw us marry.'

'She called it –' Maren lowers her voice so Mamma will not hear – 'a devilish union.'

Diinna shrugs. 'She has always been like that. Even when we were children. She threw a hot potful of water at me once.' Her hand goes to her shoulder where the scar tissue sits like lace across her shoulder, and Maren remembers at last that it was indeed Toril who inflicted it. 'Why are you coming to me with old tales?'

'But this is no idle chatter,' says Maren. 'She has the ear of the commissioner now. He sits with her most days to pray.'

Diinna snorts. 'Is that what they are doing all hours?'

Maren lets the vests drop to the ground, takes her by the shoulders. Her bones come hard beneath her fingers. 'Diinna, please. Come to kirke on the Sabbath. He should see your face, see you there.'

Diinna shrugs her off. 'I send Erik, for you and for your mother. That should be enough.'

'It is not for me.' Maren wants to shake her. 'It is for you, and if not for you, for Erik. It is in the commissioner's census that you do not go to kirke.'

'Census?'

'In his book. It is written, and once written, things aren't easily forgotten. And you are . . .'

'A Lapp?' Diinna's eyes are narrowed.

'I would never use that word. But I told you what Kirsten said of the Sámi men put to death in Alta, and another in Kirkenes.'

'They were wind-weavers only.' Diinna's carefully smooth face creases in sadness for a moment. 'Innocents.'

'That is exactly why you must be careful.' Maren grits her teeth. 'And at his first meet,' she continues, remembering suddenly, 'Commissioner Cornet spoke of his involvement in the trial of a woman. It may not be all he is here for, but it is some of it. You must come to kirke.'

'Seems to me the best idea would be to stay far from his sight.'

'But he knows of you. Toril spoke your name in the kirke, and it sounds as if she speaks it still to him.'

'I should have put a hole in her tongue when I threatened it,' says Diinna. 'It would do us all good.'

Maren had forgotten that warning made in those terrible, early days after the storm, and it sends a fresh broil of nausea through her.

'You should not say such things.'

'Why, do you think me a witch, too?' Diinna's gaze is unblinking.

Maren digs her nails into her palms, desperation verging on annoyance. 'You will not come?'

Diinna looks into the middle distance.

'It would be good if you would come more often to see the others at least,' she says. 'You used to like some of us.'

You used to love me, she thinks, collecting up the vests. Diinna doesn't move to help. She still has a slick snake of hair trailing from her lips, and the sound of her sucking it fills Maren's own mouth with bitterness.

'Perhaps come on Wednesday? You used to come. Toril doesn't attend, nor most of the kirke folk.'

'Your mamma does, though. And I thought you were all kirke folk now.' Diinna's voice is dry.

'You know I am not one of them,' says Maren, straightening and holding out the vests. 'Kirsten and Edne and many of us, we aren't like them.'

'Yes,' says Diinna, taking the soft garments. 'But I am not one of you, either.'

Inside, Erik begins to moan.

'You'll come to the meet?' says Maren, desperate as Diinna opens the door and turns to close it behind her. She gets no answer.

She paces back and forth before her door. She feels it, a trap being set about them, has felt it since Toril gave Diinna's name in kirke. The news from Alta makes it worse. That the sailors have been going to the Sámi for weather charms since they settled here held no currency in the court. Kirsten said they were sent to their deaths within a day.

She knows it is against Diinna's beliefs, against the Sámi ways, to go to kirke but she cannot help that it matters less what they believe now than what they pretend to believe. She sometimes wonders if she is pretending a little, too. The eye of God feels turned from her, has done since the storm, and since the commissioner's arrival she fears Cornet far more than any God.

Inside, Mamma is wrapping salted fish in clean cloths. They are spread across the table, a dissemblance in various shades of white, blanched by salt. The bones sit in a wispy pile, ready to be sorted into those that can be used as needles or combs, and those that will be boiled for soup.

'What was that about?'

Maren places the vests on the shelf, comes to join Mamma at the table. 'Diinna will not come to kirke.'

'Nothing new there.' Mamma turns a sharp eye upon her. 'Why did you try?' Maren takes up a fish and some tweezers. She doesn't want to go over it again.

'Ah. Toril?' Maren nods, and Mamma sucks her teeth. 'I told Erik when he married her there would be talk. And now he is not here to protect her from it.'

And you do nothing to help her, thinks Maren, pulling bones from a butterflied cod. 'I invited her to the Wednesday meet.'

Mamma's eyebrows raise. 'Her, and the commissioner's wife? You think that a wise combination?'

'Urs— Mistress Cornet is not like the commissioner. It will be fine.'

'We will see.' There is something glinting close to excitement in Mamma's voice, and not for the first time Maren considers that her mother's dislike for Diinna has grown more akin to hatred. Whereas before Mamma worried about Diinna disappearing to the low mountain, now Maren suspects Mamma would prefer it, so long as Erik was left here.

'Besides –' Mamma's tongue flicks at the corner of her mouth – 'whatever will come, you can be sure Diinna brings it upon herself.'

Twenty-Four

Though Ursa had been worried about sleeping alone, her body is so unused to any sort of exertion that it drags her down into a deep sleep as soon as she closes the door on Maren. She wakes in confusion early the next day, her head throbbing, in her swept and tidy house, the new coat hung like a presence behind the door.

She wonders about putting it on, going for a walk perhaps, maybe to find Maren. While it would have been unthinkable for her to go out unaccompanied in Bergen, in this place of women it seems to hold no cause for gossip. But she doesn't know the way to anywhere but the kirke, and she has no desire to go there.

From Wednesday, she tells herself, she will know more people, and perhaps can go visiting. With her coat and boots, she feels steadier. She makes herself tea, eats a square of flatbrød spread with some of the butter Maren skimmed from the kjernemelk. Even a day with Maren has given her fresh eyes, and where before she saw no work to be done now she knows she must replenish the fuel for the fire, and perhaps use some of the leftover flour to make small fresh loaves that she and Absalom can eat together upon his return.

It comes far sooner than she's prepared for. On Wednesday morning, she is up early and dressed, boiling water for tea, when the door opens roughly behind her. She turns, thinking it might be Maren, come early to collect her for the meet, but the doorway is filled by Absalom Cornet, taking off his black hat.

'Husband.' She catches her smile before it drops. 'Back so soon?'

'The wind was against us, so I took measure of the situation in Alta from Hamningberg.' After all that, he had only reached the next village up the coast.

Ursa studies his face, but there is no sign of temper. He is looking her up and down. 'Have you been to the kirke, wife?'

'Forgive me, no, husband. I only wanted to look presentable.'

His thick eyebrows rise. 'For whom?'

'Later I am to meet with some of the other women.'

She had feared his reaction, but he nods. 'That is good. Did Toril Knudsdatter come to invite you?'

'No, husband.'

'Sigfrid? They spoke of doing so.'

She shakes her head. 'I do not know these women.'

'They help at the kirke, and I have been overseeing their spiritual teaching with Pastor Kurtsson.'

Ursa pours the boiled water, sending the leaves spinning.

He frowns as she passes him a cup of fresh-brewed tea. 'Who, then?'

'Our neighbour, Fru Olufsdatter.' She doesn't want to give Maren's name, and certainly not Kirsten's.

'I see.' He takes a sip.

'How was Hamningberg?' Now that he has not raised an objection outright to her attending the meet, she wants to move him from the subject.

'Fine, fine. The commissioner from Kiberg was also stuck there. Larsen. He's a good enough man, though a little full of bluster. Had all the news sent from Commissioner Moe in Alta. The trial was a clear-cut one.'

'You were to attend a trial? What for?'

'It was already over – I only wished to take measure of the situation. Though they have two more Lapps in their gaol, so I intend to return when the wind blows more favourably.'

'What did the Lapps do?'

'It is not so much what they do as what they are born to. Sorcerers.'

'They are witches?' Ursa's arms come across herself.

'Often as not,' says Absalom. He is flattered by her interest, she can tell.

'How is it proven?'

'There are tests.' He leans forwards, and though there is an undeniable frisson of excitement in his voice, there is fear there, too. 'Our King James in Scotland has written a book on how to spot and test a witch, but the Lapps are easy enough to catch. They have drums of stretched skin, and they beat them to summon demons.' He crosses himself, and Ursa feels a chill slide beneath her skin.

'Demons? They can do that?'

'Surely as a minister can call on God,' says Absalom gravely. 'Old times, before King Christian ordered it, they were not even bound by law to destroy such instruments. Moe's letter says they have one they seized – they dare not burn it in case it releases something.'

Ursa shivers. 'You truly think it possible?'

'I have seen such things are possible.' Absalom's voice is a whisper. He is remembering something that makes him afraid, and it unsettles her. 'In Scotland, we had a great many trials. I did not need to make such a journey to see another, but I thought I could learn something from Commissioner Moe's ways of operating. I certainly can have no knowledge from Larsen.' He leans back in his chair. 'He had not even thought to conduct a census before I suggested it.'

'He has seen the Lensmann?'

'He has, in Alta.' Absalom's face closes back to its usual inscrutability. 'A lot of the other commissioners, they are old friends, old seagoers.'

'Then it is a great honour, is it not, husband?' He looks up at her. 'That you have been brought all the way from Scotland, on your reputation alone.'

His shoulders straighten a little, and he looks at her with the ghost of a smile at the corners of his lips. 'That it is, Ursula.'

He drains the cup, stands with a renewed vigour.

'I am to kirke. I hope your meet is pleasant – but, wife?' She looks into his face. 'Keep your ears open. If you hear anything of use . . .' He trails into silence, and then he is gone again, closing the door behind him.

Ursa can breathe again. She did well with him there, showing an interest in Alta and the trial, though it turned her stomach. Devilry felt a more distant thing in Bergen, but here? Perhaps such things are possible. She cleans his cup immediately, and makes another pot of tea. She doesn't want to drink from the same dregs.

•

When Maren arrives just past high sun, she is trailing two others. Ursa recognizes Maren's mother, and makes a neat curtsey that the woman doesn't return. Instead she looks past Ursa, into the house, and there is such hostility in her gaze that Ursa doesn't invite them in, only slips on her coat and closes the latch.

All three have bundles strapped to their fronts, and Ursa recognizes the cloth she thought to cut, bound to Maren's mother. She hopes Maren did not tell her of her ignorance. The sky behind them is grey and blue, like a day-old bruise, their misshapen figures pegged out against it.

'This is Diinna,' says Maren, strain apparent on her face.

The other woman meets Ursa's eyes steadily. She is carrying a bundle big as her torso, and has a broad face and high cheek-bones. Ursa has not seen her in kirke, realizes this must be the Sámi woman who Maren tried to protect from her husband's questions. The one who drew the runes over the door.

Though she is thin as Maren and her mother, she suits it better, carries herself with more ease. Her hair looks stringy and long unwashed, matted into knots at its ends. She jigs the bundle on her front, and it is another moment before Ursa realizes it is a young child, but not so young as it should be carried like a baby.

'This is Erik,' says Maren. 'My brother's son.'

'And mine,' says Diinna, the edge of a challenge on her tongue. There is something disconcerting about the three of them, and Ursa walks beside Maren the short distance to her neighbour's house.

The door is ajar and chatter comes from within, along with the now familiar smells of fresh bread. There is no time for Ursa to gather herself before Maren pushes the door fully open, and plunges into the yellow room.

There are benches set along the sides, women ranged on them in clumps, chattering with needlework on their laps. There is a shelf set into the wall with what looks like an assortment of pale stones upon it. The table is pushed before the fireplace, and laden with bread and fish, and jugs of water and light beer. She wonders then if she should have brought something, whether she should fetch the small loaves she made yesterday.

At first the talk goes on, but heads turn as Ursa enters, faces she knows from kirke but for which she has no names. Finally there is silence apart from the children playing on the floor at their feet. It feels like the first time in kirke, and Ursa shrinks, studies her skirts.

It is Kirsten who breaks the quiet. 'Did I not tell you she'd come?' she says to a mousy-haired woman beside the fire. 'I'll bet you're glad of your good platters now.'

The woman rises to her feet, crosses to Ursa, hand out in a gesture of welcome. Fru Olufsdatter, the owner of the house. 'I am very glad you have come, Mistress Cornet.'

'Ursula, please. Your home is lovely.'

'My husband's father built it,' she says. She moves to her right slightly, and Ursa wonders if she is trying to obscure the shelf beside the fire. At Ursa's side, Maren shifts from one foot to another, but the woman's focus is fixed on her, almost reverent. 'Thank you for coming.'

'It is Maren who invited me,' says Ursa, still keen to prove the validity of her presence. The woman studiously ignores Maren, and Ursa realizes that something is between them, some distance.

'I am glad,' she repeats, motions towards the table. 'Would you care for something to eat, to drink?'

'I am a little thirsty,' says Ursa, and the woman bends to the table to pour from one of the jugs. She takes the opportunity to look more closely at the shelf – the objects aren't all stones; she can see two figures carved roughly from bone placed in the centre.

Fru Olufsdatter straightens and brings her a cup. It isn't water or tea, which is all she has drunk for weeks since the akevitt on the ship, but some sort of clouded liquid. Ursa sniffs at it, not wishing to be rude.

'It's sorrel water,' Maren tells her. 'It's a little sharp, but I think you'll like it.'

With Maren so close, Ursa can smell aniseed on her breath. It comforts her and she takes a sip, tries not to wrinkle her nose. It is very bitter, but with an ending of sweetness, like the cooking apples Siv buys for Christmas time. Agnete loved them before her doctors imposed her diet of dry food, used to chomp through them like a horse, pulling her lips from her teeth. Ursa's insides clench with missing.

Fru Olufsdatter peers at her anxiously, and so she smiles and nods for more, though it will take some getting used to. Room is made for them on a bench to the right of the fire, and though there is space enough for Diinna's slight form, she stays standing beside the door even once she has deposited Erik with the other children. Her presence has as much effect on the others as Ursa's. Though Ursa feels badly for Diinna she is glad that the attention on her is closer to wariness than open dislike.

The chatter starts up again, but it is quieter, each speaking to her neighbour and not across the room as before. She looks at Diinna from over her cup. Herr Kasperson, her father's clerk, had spent some time in Spitsbergen as a bookkeeper at a whaling station. He told them Lapps were short and wild-looking, with teeth tiny and needle sharp, that they dressed in knotted wolf tails about their necks, and pointed hats on their heads. But there is not much to mark Diinna out as different, beyond her darker skin, higher cheekbones, and the other women's attitude to her. Ursa thinks of the trial in Alta, wonders if Diinna knows about it.

Erik too sits a little apart from the other children, legs straight out in front of him. He is more markedly distinct: there is something slack about his jaw, a looseness. Ursa wonders if there is something wrong with him. Agnete, too, had been a slow child. But despite her illness, her mind had grown sharp. Perhaps it is the same with Erik.

Maren takes out a large piece of cloth from her bundle, unwraps a fine needle and piece of thread. Kirsten has a pair of boots – large as a man's – on a low stool before her, and is cutting pieces of fur to line them. Ursa realizes she should have brought something to do, too.

'Would you like some help?' she asks Maren, who looks at her, surprised. Ursa supposes she is remembering her handiwork at the sleeves. But she must also recognize Ursa's need for something to focus upon, and passes her a smaller piece of cloth, a pillowcase perhaps, and a thicker needle that will not so easily sink into her fingers.

She is well aware of eyes upon her as she threads the needle, finds the worn patch and takes up a fresh piece of cloth to cover it. But just as she is about to make the first stitch the door is opened again.

A pinch-faced woman comes in with two children, another woman following behind accompanied by a young girl with matching blue eyes and thin lips. This silence is more abrupt than the one that greeted Ursa's arrival. Kirsten moves aside the stool with the boots, stands with her arms folded.

'What are you doing here?'

'Last I checked this was not your house to ask such a question, Kirsten Sørensdatter.' The woman is carrying two baskets, and she lifts back the cloth atop one, holds it out to Fru Olufsdatter. 'I do not come empty-handed.'

Fru Olufsdatter doesn't take it. She looks caught by some invisible current, pale and suddenly afraid. Her eyes flick to the spot on the shelf beside the fire, where the small bone figures and stones are arranged. The woman purses her lips, and places the basket on the table. Ursa notices she wears a cross about her neck, realizes she is one of the kirke-women her husband keeps council with.

'Sigfrid and I only came to keep company. And to speak with Mistress Cornet.'

It is a few heartbeats before Ursa realizes that she is Mistress Cornet. The name still doesn't feel as though it belongs to her: it is a thing apart, like the needle in her hand, and as sharp.

'Me?'

'What are you wanting with her, Toril?'

Maren has stiffened beside her, and out of the corner of her eye Ursa can see open dislike on her face.

'That is no matter to you,' says Toril.

Ursa touches her leg against Maren's to stay her. 'How may I help you, Fru . . . ?'

'Knudsdatter.' Toril frowns. 'I thought your husband mentioned me.'

'And me,' says Sigfrid. 'He wished us to come and keep company with you.'

'She has company enough,' says Kirsten, gesturing around. The other women are looking shiftily about themselves, and Ursa isn't sure whose disapproval they are shrinking from, Kirsten's or Toril's. There is obviously some struggle for power between them, though they seem very unmatched to her. She would wish to stand beside Kirsten any day.

'He hopes for a better sort of companion for his wife,' says Toril, and Ursa's cheeks flush with Absalom's interference. She should not have spoken of her plans with him. Toril stands before Ursa, and eventually Maren's mother moves along the already cramped bench. Toril sets her other basket down on the floor and slides in beside her.

Fru Olufsdatter still looks imperilled. She has again positioned herself before her shelf, and Ursa notices her move a jug to cover the bone figures.

Sigfrid too finds a spot on the bench, knocking over Toril's basket, sending scraps of lace and spooled thread tumbling.

'I'm sorry,' says Sigfrid, crouching to right it. There is much tutting from Toril as some of the women rise to help gather everything together. Ursa notices Kirsten doesn't, nor Maren, and so she stays in her place.

Diinna retrieves a needlecase, holds it out to Toril. Toril looks at her sharply, and makes no move to take it. 'Do you threaten me?'

'Threaten?' Diinna snorts and drops the case into the basket.

'I've not forgotten how you thought to thread a needle through my tongue,' spits Toril, and the room ripples with muttering.

'Toril,' says Kirsten, warning sharp in her voice. 'She was only helping.'

'I need no help from the likes of her,' says Toril. Maren is tense beside Ursa. Diinna looks as though she may say something, but she only sucks her teeth, and scoops up Erik. She leaves the house without a gesture of goodbye, letting the door bang behind her. Maren starts, looks as though she may go after her, and Ursa is certain it's only her presence that makes her stay.

Toril meanwhile makes no attempt to start a conversation with Ursa. She just sits, a little too close, and brings out some cloth to darn. It is immediately apparent that she is very skilled at it, her narrow fingers working deftly and closing the tears at the edges, frilling it with a stitch she has not seen before.

'So, Ursula.' Kirsten's voice is like a bell, ringing into the hushed room and bringing it to silence. 'What has Maren taught you so far? I can see you have a fine coat from the hides I brought.'

Beside her Maren shrinks a little. Perhaps it is as Ursa feared, that she is embarrassed by their arrangement. But it is too late now.

'She is a fine teacher. I have enough flatbrød for a decade, I feel, and the coat will serve me well.'

'A coat,' says Toril. 'You?'

She speaks past Ursa, who wishes she were thin as Maren and could press flat to the wall. Maren doesn't answer, keeps her eyes fixed to her work, but Ursa sees the slight shake of her fingers.

'Yes,' she says. 'Maren helped me make something warm. I did not bring anything suitable from Bergen.'

'Mistress Cornet, I would be happy to help you with any clothes-making. It is something of a speciality of mine. It is well known throughout the village.'

No one speaks in her favour, though Sigfrid nods like a lackey.

'I am happy enough with what I have, thank you, Fru Knudsdatter.'

'Toril, please.' She moves, if it is possible, even closer, her knee angled towards Ursa's thigh. 'Your husband thought it would be pleasant for us to meet together regularly. He thought you would need some more educated conversation, being from Bergen. My own mother was from Tromsø—'

'Fru Olufsdatter is from Tromsø,' interrupts Kirsten. 'If Mistress Cornet wants educated conversation she should not come to you, Toril. Unless she wants her Bible learnt by heart.'

'You say that as though it is a bad thing, Kirsten Sørensdatter,' says Toril, snappishly. 'You forget who our commissioner is. As much a man of God as Pastor Kurtsson. He wishes his wife to have better companionship than this and, most like, a better coat than Maren Magnusdatter can manage.'

Ursa thinks she should speak in Maren's defence but her voice feels as caught as her skirts beneath Toril's thigh. The woman seems to gather herself, her voice turning sickening sweet again. 'Perhaps you would like some company in the days. I know he is often at kirke or on important business in the district—'

'I have company, thank you, Fru Knudsdatter.'

She feels Toril's gaze pierce through her and into Maren, who has still not spoken a word in her own defence.

'Very well,' says Toril, and there is a break in her voice.

'Is that it now, Toril?' says Kirsten. 'Can we all be free of your kind company?'

Toril throws her needlework into her basket, then pauses, running her fingers over the scraps.

'Who took my lace?' She scans the room.

'Lace?' Kirsten sounds bored.

'Was it you?' Toril squares up to Kirsten, the mismatch in their heights like a child to their parent. 'I had lacework in here.'

'What use have I for lace?'

Ursa holds her breath, but Toril seems to think it not worth the fight. 'Elsebe, Nils, we are going.'

She stands suddenly and gathers up her children, who follow her mute and neat as her stitches. She turns in the doorway, Sigfrid hastening to pack her things and usher her daughter out.

'Don't think I have not seen what sits aside your fire, Fru Olufsdatter, and who fled your house when we arrived. The time for such things is past. Commissioner Cornet has not the patience for it. There are men burnt at Alta—'

'My husband,' says Ursa, temper flaring, 'doesn't mind how people keep their houses.'

The room seems to hold its breath. Ursa is aware of absolute silence as Toril turns her imperious face upon her. She is minded of Siv when she is back from kirke and the prayers still sit fresh in her: unbowed, strengthened by them.

'As you say, Mistress Cornet. I will tell him you have chosen your company.'

'I can tell him myself.' Ursa's heart is thumping. Burnings? Absalom had neglected to tell her this detail.

Toril stands aside to let her children out before her, speaks again to Fru Olufsdatter. 'You would do well to use my gift for you.' She jerks her head at the table. 'I'll have the basket back. God bless you.'

Twenty-Five

Once the door has slammed shut behind Sigfrid and her daughter, Maren feels she can breathe again. Kirsten slaps her hands together and lets out a hoot.

'Mistress Cornet, you have a heat to you that I confess I hadn't foreseen.'

'I only spoke my mind,' says Ursa steadily, though her body trembles. Maren wants to take her in her arms and rock her like a child. 'It is no business of hers how I choose to spend my time.'

'The poppets,' says Fru Olufsdatter. Her voice reminds Maren of a worn-out rag, her face as grey. 'I had forgot them, Mistress Cornet. They aren't – I had them given me after my boy and husband died. Many of us had them . . .'

She looks about for support: heads bow to their work.

'They do not mean a thing. I should throw them in the fire.' But she doesn't move, only looks at Ursa with desperate eyes.

'I do not mind what you choose to keep in your house, any more than I would wish you to tell me how to attire my own.'

'Sounds as if that is what Maren has been up to,' says Edne. Maren casts her a sharp glance.

'I am only helping a little.'

'Who was that woman?' says Ursa, and Maren is pleased to hear dislike clear in her voice.

'She helps Pastor Kurtsson at kirke,' says Kirsten. 'And seems to me she is now your husband's anointed emissary.'

No one else would have dared such a remark, but Kirsten is rewarded with a sudden peal of laughter from Ursa that sends an echoing ripple around the benches, and a jab of envy through Maren.

'Do not worry on your poppets, Fru Olufsdatter,' says Kirsten. 'Ursula doesn't mind them, and she knows her husband's thoughts better than Toril Knudsdatter.'

Ursa doesn't laugh this time. A crease appears between her eyes.

'What gifts has she given you?' asks Edne.

Fru Olufsdatter doesn't move to look in the basket, so Kirsten bends over it, snorts and brings out a cross of cloth and twine, like those Maren had caused Toril to knock from her shelf. 'There must be near two dozen in here. Enough for all of us.'

She throws one to Maren, who catches it without thinking. She places it into her bundle, wanting to drop it as quickly as possible. It feels a threat, rather than a gift.

Their meets usually go on until evening, but Maren has no stomach for food or conversation. It is a relief when, after a period of uneasy silence, Ursa begins to shift uncomfortably, leans in to her, says, 'Shall we go?'

Mamma is talking to Edne and so they go together, rising to another silence, and leaving in an outbreak of whispers. Fru Olufsdatter sits crumpled in her place, watches Ursa leave like a thing hunted.

As they reach Ursa's door she hesitates, her jaw tense. Maren listens, hears a low rumble that must be the commissioner, and a woman's voice answering. Maren recognizes its syrupy undercurrent: Toril, speaking to authority. Ursa begins to back away, but her foot creaks upon the step and the voices stall. Heavy tread on the floorboards, and then Commissioner Cornet is at the door, brows pulled down over his eyes.

'Wife,' he says, ignoring Maren completely. 'Inside.'

Ursa's face pales, but she straightens her shoulders, turns to thank Maren before stepping through the doorway. Maren can't see past his bulk, but Toril's greeting to Ursa reaches her clearly. The commissioner slams the door on Maren, and for a moment she waits. But what will she do? She will not push open the door, nor listen at the latch. Over the door the runes are not fully smoothed out. Their shadow is still visible, showing beneath the whitewash like scars.

She could go back to the meet, but the poison Toril had spread about the room remained. Mamma never used to like Toril, but recently Maren thinks that has changed. She noticed the look of satisfaction on Mamma's face as Toril delivered her speeches, and at Diinna's departure. Toril was always against the Sámis visiting the village, and Kirsten was always headstrong. But the women and their divides have strengthened, are growing swallowingly large, deep and dangerous as a pit.

Even Kirsten is irritating her with her brashness. Maren is still not over her appearance at Ursa's house in trousers – at least Toril had no mention of that, and so must not have seen it. She wouldn't have missed the opportunity to spread such a piece of gossip.

Maren barely notices her feet carrying her home. She is pushed far inside her body, hearing only the jumble of her thoughts tangling like a fishing net. Diinna's departure was delayed just long enough for her to give Maren a look of such venom that if Maren believed some of the kirke-women's stories of the Sámis, she would have thought herself cursed. Diinna can't think that Maren knew Toril would come?

She speaks this through Diinna's closed door, though she will not answer. There is no noise from Erik either. Diinna's silence is a wall that grows into a wave, pushing Maren from her door and onwards, out past Baar Ragnvalsson's house, the roof rotted and collapsed in, the stones scattered about as though thrown by a troll. It was a fine house, once, but when he started spending summers with the Sámi on the low mountain it became less a place where he lived, and more a place where he existed. She would see him outside in his embroidered tunic and hat, sitting in even the coldest weather, with his head tipped to the side, eyes closed, as though listening for something.

The memory hits her like a blow, and she presses her fist to her heart. She never mourned for him, though his body lay beside Erik and Pappa's all those months. She can't even recall his injuries, if he had any. Perhaps that is better. She says a small prayer to the wind, which has begun to gust full behind her, like an insistent hand at her back, throwing her skirts before her. Her hair is across her face so she must focus on her feet and can't see the tumble of Herr Ragnvalsson's house any more, or his remembered form outside it.

She walks past the boundary wall and on to the green, boggy land beyond. How quickly what little grasp they have on the land vanishes, as though beyond the boundary there were never people there at all and she has wandered full into the land of trolls. As children, she and Erik used to go hunting for them, under pretence of foraging for the sweet clover that sometimes grows here, and that their mother would boil until the leaves softened and leaked milky liquid, good for settling stomachs sore through hunger. They would comb through the moss and short grasses, searching for marks and stone circles, for small doors set into hillocks and rocks. They'd speak half-sentences, telling each other that they'd trodden on a knoll and were cursed to death, losing each other in the mists that sometimes stumbled over the headland from the sea.

She remembers finding herself suddenly alone in one once, all about her an endless grey, chill soaking through to her bones. She should have stayed still, crouched to keep warm, but she carried on walking until she thought she had crossed over. The terror of it had struck her dumb, and when the mist lifted, sudden as a skein of birds taking flight, she found herself a mere step from a drop of sixty feet, the sea churning white at the base of the rocks. Erik came running over the spongy ground calling for her: he had done as she should have, stayed still and waited. His cheeks were snot-streaked and blotchy with tears and she had shoved him and called him a coward, though he wore her face, had her frighted heart beating in his narrow chest. It was one of many small unkindnesses she wishes she could take back, thoughtless moments or worse, instances engineered to hurt.

Her feet have brought her here, to that spot. Now the sky is clear and crisp, the light that bluish grey that means they will find frost on the inside of their doors though winter is months away. She goes as close to the edge as she dares. Sometimes, in that terrible year when the pain was so immediate it was like living with a knife through her chest, she came here and stood with her toes so far over that one good gust of wind could cause her to fall. It would be quick enough, faster than a blade or some nightshade steeped like tea and drunk. This place is out of sight of the village, and the current that keeps the channel clear of ice would drag a body clear into open sea. It was something remarked upon by them all, that it was lucky the storm had not occurred this side of Vardø, or they never would have had their men brought back.

When she stood there it was both challenge and offering. She was waiting, like Baar Ragnvalsson, to be given permission to go home and continue living, though she often wondered if she wanted that at all. Since the storm, there has felt so little to exist for. But something has changed that; she feels it now, certain as seasons. Someone has changed that.

There are small yellow flowers growing on wiry stalks at her feet. She uproots one for her father, one for Erik, and a third. This one she cups close to her lips, as she lets the wind carry the others before her, over the edge.

•

The whole week Maren fears a knock at her door, telling her she isn't needed, that Toril has managed to take her place in the commissioner's household. She must bear this alongside increased hostility between her mother and Diinna, who on Friday have a disagreement over Erik's lack of movement, which grows to a fight of such ferocity that Maren scoops up Erik and walks him ten times around Herr Ragnvalsson's house before they are done.

But the knock doesn't come, and at Sabbath, though Ursa is locked tight to her husband's side, and though she is greeted by name by Toril and Sigfrid, it is Maren whose face she seeks out, Maren who she makes for after the sermon while her husband is engaged in conversation with some of the women.

'You will come tomorrow?'

Maren can barely speak.

'He is usually away by mid-morning.' Ursa brushes her fingers against Maren's, a gesture meant as comfort. There is a circle of bruises on her wrist, and when she notices Maren looking she snatches her hand away. She pulls down her sleeve and is beside her husband again so fast Maren feels she may have imagined it.

The next day she arrives at Ursa's door with her frame

loom tucked beneath her arm, feels her body unknot as she steps inside and it is just her and Ursa. They spend the day weaving cloth for curtains, slow and full of mistakes and easy silences, easier touches that make Maren feel loose and formless as Ursa's weave.

'What did Toril want?' she says. Ursa is frowning at the loom as though it has betrayed her, her tongue a pink blot between her lips.

'She lost some lace at the Wednesday meet. She said she wanted to borrow some of the lace Kirsten gave me, but I think she thought Kirsten had stolen it.'

Maren sets down her shuttle. 'Did she say so in front of Absalom?'

Ursa nods, focusing on the loom. 'Don't worry, I set her right. I am sorry that Absalom was rude to you.'

'I did not mind.' She had expected no less. 'Did she tell him of the poppets?'

'Perhaps,' says Ursa. 'He was certainly displeased to hear of Diinna's attendance. I told him the meets are nothing, that they are harmless.' She puts the loom onto the table with a sigh, at her trouble with it or Toril's interference Maren does not know. 'And that Toril should not be taken from her study with him, and her Christian duties are much fulfilled by her work for the others. That it wouldn't be fair to have her all to myself. You, on the other hand,' she says, with a sly smile, 'are completely dispensable. Cheap, too. And perhaps we can save your soul from living with a Lapp.'

The word is ugly in Ursa's mouth, but the rest of what she says so pleasing that Maren doesn't speak against it.

'Moreover, he agreed that you must come twice a week from now. The more you are out of that house and influence the better, don't you agree?'

Maren's face aches from smiling, the dry skin of her lips

stretching, but as Ursa reaches for her loom, she again sees the bruises, dark as dirt about her wrist.

'What happened?'

Ursa looks down at her wrist as though it does not belong to her. 'Nothing.' Maren stares at her. 'Absalom, sometimes he does not know his own strength.'

'It was not because of Toril, because of me?'

'No,' says Ursa, cheeks flushing. 'It was not done in anger.'

'He should not touch you like that,' says Maren, understanding. Her rage is quick and frightening, hot as a brand inside her.

'Isn't it a wife's duty to be touched by her husband?'

Maren's cheeks redden at her frankness. 'I would not know of it.'

'You were never married, before the storm?'

Maren doesn't want to call Dag to her, not now. She shakes her head. 'No.'

•

From that day on she is at Ursa's house Monday and Thursday, watching for more bruises, finding none. She wonders about the pale expanse of Ursa's body, if she is marked in places Maren can't see.

Wednesdays Ursa comes to the meets, her presence quickly losing intrigue. Maren notices the poppets and runestones are gone from Fru Olufsdatter's shelf, one of Toril's crosses planted in their place, but the benches are less full. Toril and Sigfrid do not return, Edne no longer comes, and after a couple more weeks, nor does Maren's mother.

'Toril is having a meet at her house,' says Mamma. 'The commissioner will be there, to lead us in prayer. You should come, Maren. No doubt his wife will.'

But Maren knows Ursa will not, and so goes with her to

Dag's mother's house, where Kirsten holds court and makes ever-cruder jokes about the kirke-women, and Maren tries not to imagine what is said of them in return. Ursa seems unfussed by the rift, perhaps doesn't notice it, or maybe feels herself above it all. She doesn't speak against Toril except to Maren, and she suspects that she alone is the recipient of Ursa's true thoughts.

Twice a week is too much for a household of one room and a family of two. Maren herself generates as much mess as she helps sort out. They get their work done slowly, Ursa more and more capable so that she is like not to need Maren there at all, but there is no suggestion of her stopping coming. They butcher two of the reindeer, make stews with cloud-berries that Ursa leaves too long on the fire so they must spend hours scouring the pots with sand. Maren teaches her to bank the fire so in the mornings she can break the crust and it will be fierce enough for boiling water almost straight away.

Beyond the faded bruises, Absalom's presence is merely an impression upon the house: she doesn't see him but at kirke. Ursa speaks a little of him, tells her of his growing frustration at the lack of communication from Vardøhus, and Maren doesn't ask more because she doesn't want to hear it. She changes the sheets and helps with the washing, knows Ursa's bloods come monthly upon her, allows herself to hope that they do not lie together much at all, though there is only one bed and no chair suitable for a man to sleep.

When they are alone she can imagine that it isn't the commissioner and his wife who live there, nor even another version of life in which she and Dag made their home here, but rather she and Ursa. And though she knows it is a wrong thought, a dangerous thought, she allows herself to slip into this dream more and more as their weeks together stretch to a month, and they begin to span their time into the late, light evenings when Absalom is away travelling to Alta or elsewhere. Maren does not care where he is, only longs for him never to return.

In these times they walk through the village together, when most are inside or sleeping, the distance between them stinging like a hook in Maren's side. They speak of their childhoods. Ursa tells her that once their family was rich and now they are not, and when she mentions Agnete, Maren can feel the sorrow coming from her like cold. Maren tells Ursa about troll-hunting with Erik, and it makes Ursa laugh.

She takes Ursa to the headland, watches how the colour of the thin skin at her throat changes in the endless low light, how the wind throws her dress more tightly against her body, as it did the day they met and Maren thought her as much a fool as Mamma still does.

Ursa is telling her about the black rock at the end of the world, that pulls currents towards it.

'Captain Leifsson, the captain of the *Petrsbolli* – you know, the ship we came in – he thinks there are no waterfalls, perhaps no rock at all.' She turns to Maren and her eyes shine. 'But I think there is. I should like to see that rock, some day.'

Maren wants to reach out to Ursa and hold her, but not in the easy way they embrace now when she arrives or leaves. She wants to press her whole form against her, like Dag in the boat shed.

Sometimes this thought comes to her at night, and she feels a low throb in her belly, and must keep her hand from moving to herself. Even with her mother snoring beside her, it isn't easy, and her dreams are full of slick mouths that moan her name, sometimes in Dag's voice, more often in Ursa's, her face smooth against her, her almost-boneless hands supple against the blunt thinness of Maren's ribs.

She thinks she keeps it well from the world, speaking as

little as she can to Mamma of Ursa, and even less to Diinna, who would see something on her face or in her voice, she is sure of it.

Most of all she guards it from Ursa, knowing the absurdity of what she feels. But she doesn't pray for it to pass, doesn't pray at all but for Erik and Pappa in kirke. The secret doesn't gnaw at her. Rather she feels strengthened by it, forged into something glittering and rare. She doesn't tell herself she loves Ursa, but knows it is something closer to love than she has ever known. With it inside her, she feels bold as Kirsten in trousers, and though she relishes the feeling, she knows it is just as reckless, as dangerous.

Twenty-Six

The letter from the Lensmann comes almost four months to the day after their arrival in Vardø. Ursa's time is pegged out by her days with Maren, and the others which she must survive without her. Maren is now where she flies to in her head, when her husband moves upon her. Walking with Maren, into the wind on the headland, the ground so uncertain beneath her she never fails to stumble and reach for her friend, gasping with laughter, Maren's strong hands holding her steady as his grip leaves more bruises on her wrists.

The nights they lie together he doesn't have the same anger in him, though it is still nothing pleasurable. He doesn't even make much sound, and she wonders if it is become a duty for him, whether it would be best for them both if she were to bear a child, and then maybe they could be done with it.

She tries to imagine her life with a baby in it, but that again is another country, much how she felt about Vardø before they arrived. She supposes she would adapt as she has to this place, and with Maren to help her in this as well perhaps it wouldn't be so difficult, but the thought of her soft belly hardening and filling makes her queasy to the point of dizziness.

As for the coming of it, the little she knows of that was

learnt from Mother's birthing of her many dead siblings, and Agnete. Even a living baby brings so much blood. She wonders sometimes to speak with Maren about it. Her reaction to the bruises had made her think not, though she doesn't think Maren would be prudish. She would have some knowledge, what with Diinna and Erik, but there is always something more important to speak of, or a silence to be had, so comfortable Ursa feels she could stretch out in it for ever.

Maren has never spoken of a betrothed, or a want for one. Spinsters were a rarity in Bergen, but then, so were widows before middle age. Men, sailors mostly, come to Vardø's harbour to sell fish, to shelter their boats in squalls, to trade for furs and needlework. But they stay at the boundary, not even leaving their boats sometimes, and Kirsten strides down to meet them. Ursa thinks there must be some talk of this island, with all its drowned men, that keeps the living ones from it.

Absalom is like to hear of such talk. He travels successfully to Alta, and on his return sometimes speaks of more trials, more Sámi arrested, and now Ursa knows that this means burnings she doesn't ask for details. She could almost forget there is a world outside Vardø, especially on days when the sea sends a mist creeping over everything, and she and Maren must knot arms and stay close, walking slow along the headland. It is a strange landscape even on a clear day. No forests, no shrub above hip height, and even in the time of the midnight sun it was cold enough for her to need her coat most nights.

Now the weather is turning properly, and winter will arrive soon. Ursa has no guess at its brutality, though as the days shorten, the cold digs so sharply into her joints they seem to creak. In Bergen they would close off half the house, heat the remaining rooms to such a peak she and Agnete would have worn nothing but their shifts had Siv allowed it. Here she will wear her coat all the time, even in bed with her husband, the reindeer hides pulled over their bodies.

She receives no word from her father or sister. She supposes she could send some pressed heather from the headland, or some of her poor weaving, ask Absalom to write her a note, but she does not. Now they are at a distance of months she almost wishes she could forget their faces, the way her sister's rattling body felt curled at her side, knees digging fit to bruise, how their bed was clean every night, and at dinner there was cheese and meat that she didn't have to cut from carcasses herself. She misses her life in Bergen as impossibly as the landscape misses trees.

Absalom writes many letters, to the other commissioners and the Lensmann, she assumes, but receives few, and so when he strides into their house waving a square of paper, an invitation is the furthest of her guesses.

'Lensmann Cunningham has arrived!' His face is slick, his eyes radiating triumph. 'He is at Vardøhus, and we are invited to the fortress, to dine.'

They will be there a night at least, Absalom tells her, will be expected to stay though it is a mere mile away. Ursa has no overnight bag, only her chest and her large case, and so gives her fine dress, petticoat and underthings to Absalom to pack in his case. It makes her queasy to think of their garments pressed together. She escapes the house when he goes to kirke to tell Pastor Kurtsson the news, and hurries to Maren's home.

Maren looks harried when she opens the door, but her expression softens when she sees who has knocked. 'Thank goodness. I was about to wring my mother's neck. Walk?'

Ursa wishes she could say yes, but she shakes her head. 'I only came to tell you, we are invited to the Lensmann's. To stay the night.'

Maren raises her eyebrows. 'In the fortress? But it is so close.'

'I know,' says Ursa, 'but Absalom is greatly excited.'

Something crosses Maren's face, a shadow, as it always does when Ursa mentions Absalom.

'All right,' she says. 'Will you send word when you return?'

Ursa nods. 'I will, of course.'

Maren glances back at her house, and Ursa clasps her hand the better to impress upon her what she says next. 'You should go for a walk, though. It would do you the power of good.' She raises her eyebrows at the raised voices issuing from inside. 'Better than being held for murder.'

A brief smile flickers on Maren's cheeks. Her sea-tinted eyes are inscrutable. 'Be well,' she says.

'Be well.'

•

The next morning, Absalom has her up early and in her boots to walk, but they are only steps from their house when there is a noise Ursa has not heard since Bergen: the clack of horse-shoes, the rattle of a carriage. Absalom is gleeful as it draws up.

'We are made now, Ursula.'

She changes back into her slippers before they step out to the carriage. The horses look half starved and sway in their harnesses: they must have been brought by sea on one of the ships passing by, and it has not suited them. But the carriage is made of light wood and covered over so it is better than a cart. All about them, their neighbours are coming out to watch as Absalom helps her inside. She leans forward to look out, to try to sight Maren. She would like her to see, so they can laugh about the absurdity later, their mile-long carriage ride. But Maren is not there. She instead sees Toril standing mean-eyed, and Fru Olufsdatter already shrinking back inside her fine house.

The fortress is visible as soon as they are out of the village proper, a bank of earth and tufty green shielding grey stone walls, the whole thing rising from an otherwise flat and feature-less plate of land. It is entirely underwhelming, though she knows from Captain Leifsson this place was the subject of a brief struggle between Novgorod and Norway–Denmark, this land fought over, and that is why the Lensmann was installed.

'Were it not for the fishing and whaling, I doubt they would have bothered,' he'd said. 'But whoever runs Vardøhus controls passage through the Barents Sea, and come summer there'll be thousands of skilling made.' It doesn't look like a rich place to Ursa, but the Lensmann is only just arrived.

The ride is over as soon as it is begun. The Lensmann isn't there to greet them, and though her husband doesn't say anything, she feels the cold throb of his disappointment fall over her like a rain cloud. The bank, she notices, is raised by grey stones of the same kind as the walls. Maren has never brought her here on their walks, and Ursa realizes that she has held a horror of it since sighting it from the ship. She shudders as they pass through a slice in the fortification, manned by two guards. She has seen more men in the past few minutes than she has for months. They are led across an empty moat on a road of flagstones, slick though it has not rained the past two days. Ursa must take Absalom's arm to keep from slipping.

At the base of the wall, a door sits mounted on metal hinges. A barred grate is set into it and they are eyed before it is opened. Once they are across the threshold, the door bangs heavily shut behind, and Ursa jumps.

'Feels like a prison,' she says.

'It is,' replies Absalom.

It isn't the castle she had imagined. Inside are several buildings, arranged along the edges of the wall. Absalom points out one, speaks to their guide to confirm. 'That is the gaol, yes?'

The guard gives a brief nod. 'The witches' hole.'

'Any witches?'

Ursa's attention piques as she regards the structure. She has never seen a prison before. It is long and narrow. Bars line small, high windows.

The guard gives a slower nod, shifting his shoulders. He answers in the rough English many sailors learn. 'Two. Sorcerers. Lapps from Varanger.'

'May I see?' Absalom's voice has something tight in it. An excitement.

The guard indicates the largest of the buildings. 'Lensmann Køning wishes to meet you, and then it will be time to dine. The Lensmann likes things run to time.' The man's stance sharpens. 'He was a captain of our fleet. Ran the pirates out of Spitsbergen.'

'We have corresponded,' says Absalom, defensive. 'I know.'

The guard gives a deferential nod, and Ursa is reminded of Maren, making herself small in her husband's presence.

Turning their backs to the gaol, they cross the slippery flagstones to the main house. It stands taller than the other buildings, built in a style unfamiliar to her, broad at its front with the door set in the centre, made of stone like the wall, but with wooden touches about the windows and even carved gables beneath the roof. The guard doesn't knock, but opens the door and leads them into a wide corridor. It doesn't look as though it has only recently been inhabited. There is a woven rug beneath Ursa's feet, its pattern a garish pink and yellow, its softness disarming.

The guard takes them left, into a room where a fire is

crackling and china cups have been set out on a low dark-wood table. There is smoke-stained wallcloth, and the windows have heavy curtains and sashes of red that clash with the rug. There is even a vase on the table beside the teapot, with five lilacs standing from it.

'Please, wait here.' The guard closes the door softly behind him. The settle is upholstered in the same colours as the rug, but its pattern is faded and threadbare, stuffing frothing from the arms as she arranges herself upon it. It is hard beneath her, like a church pew.

She looks closer at the lilacs: they are paper. She can see now that the vase has no water, and that dust has settled in the petals' creases. But still, it cheers her to see them, and the gesture at homeliness.

Absalom doesn't sit, nor move to pour tea. Ursa watches, throat dry and tongue thick from sea salt in her mouth, as her husband paces the broad width of the room, his long black coat setting the fire to quiver every time he passes.

He is nervous, she thinks, and wonders whether to say something to calm him before realizing it is exactly this power she lacks. Her mother could settle Father with a touch of her fingertip to his wrist, with a soft exhale of breath. He'd bend towards her like a reed bowed by the wind, the lines of his face loosening. Absalom notices her staring at him. He frowns and turns his face away.

The door opens and she rises hurriedly, but it is only the guard.

'Apologies, Commissioner Cornet. The Lensmann has urgent business and will be delayed. Perhaps –' he notices the untouched tea – 'you would like some biscuits while you wait?'

'No,' says Absalom, a muscle in his cheek working beneath his trimmed beard.

'Mistress Cornet?' The guard turns his gaze on her.

Ursa's mouth floods with want, for butter and sugar and perhaps some currants—

'No, we are fine.' Her husband casts her a stern look. The door closes.

Ursa wonders if they will ever have an easy silence, akin to those she shares with Maren. Absalom sits and pours her a cup of light brown tea that smells of damp wood and something medicinal. She drinks it in small sips – it is already cold, but it is something to do – while he fixes the door with such an intense stare she wonders if he is trying to summon the Lensmann. She thinks of the witches in the gaol, the . . . what had the guard said? Sorcerers. Absalom shifts in his chair, takes a swig of tea, grimaces, sets it down.

'Do you like that stuff?'

He says it in Norwegian, and his accent is improving. His address is always a shock to her body, a cause for her heart to race and her palms to sweat. She sets down the cup so it will not rattle against the saucer. *Calm*, she tells herself.

'It is all right.'

'Why do you do that?' He is leaning back in his chair, looking directly at her. She wills his attention to return to the door. 'If you do not like something, you should leave it.'

There is disapproval in his voice. She can't be right, can't please him. She takes the cup back up, finishes it. 'I like it now.'

He crosses his arms, goes back to eyeing the door. They are left perhaps another half an hour – there is no clock in the room – and this time when the door opens it isn't the guard but a woman trailing a serving boy.

'Commissioner Cornet, I am Christin Cunningham.' She inclines her head as they both stand. 'You must excuse my husband. Some trouble with tax, I suspect. It usually is.' Her voice has only the touch of an accent to it, Danish, Ursa thinks, like her father's once-associate Herr Brekla. Her eyes are large and framed by thick, straight lashes. She flicks them towards Ursa.

'You must be his lovely wife fetched from Bergen.' She holds out both her hands and Ursa takes them, feeling embarrassed and buoyed by her familiarity. 'Forgive me, I do not know your name.'

'Ursula, Fru Cunningham. Ursula Cornet.'

'A beauty,' smiles Christin. She has a motherly warmth to her, Ursa decides, though she can't be much more than thirty. She is wearing a white cap of the sort Siv wears, but it is trimmed with white lace and stylishly starched, pushed back off her forehead so the neat parting of her dark hair is revealed.

'You have done well, commissioner.' She turns to the boy. 'Oluf will take you to John's study. And we –' she tucks Ursa's hand beneath her arm – 'we can go to the kitchen. It is cosier there.'

She guides them back to the corridor, and the serving boy takes Absalom ahead and to the right, while the Ursa and Christin go down a small set of stairs into a squarish space only slightly smaller than the drawing room. Two women look up from peeling carrots. A large stew is bubbling over the fire, and everything smells rich and nourishing.

Christin switches to Norwegian, and her accent is more pronounced. Ursa is relieved not to have to attempt her clumsy Danish, learnt from brief exchanges with her father's clerk.

'It is very good to have you here. Many of the other commissioners are churchmen and not much interested in wives, or else they are old or live far away.'

Christin leads her to a couch beside the fire, and one of the women stops peeling to bring them more tea and – Ursa's stomach clenches – round, dark biscuits, which she sets on a low table before them.

'I hope you do not mind this,' says Christin, pulling off her cap. Her hair is drawn into a neat coil. 'I much prefer it to upstairs. We sent ahead to have it redecorated a little but it still feels drear, don't you think?'

Ursa catches herself. 'It's very fine, Fru Cunningham.'

Christin waves her hand in a parody of graciousness. 'Christin, please.' She takes up the plate of biscuits, holds them out. 'Pepperkaker? More suitable for Christmas time I know, but it's still cold enough to be Christmas here, don't you think? They are my favourite, and John gets a good supply of ginger from his connections in Bergen –' something twists in Ursa's chest at mention of her city – 'though we are running a little short. Did you bring spices with you from home? No? Pity.' She takes a biscuit as well, eyes it critically. 'They are a little burnt. Fanne, you must take more care.'

But Ursa can smell the ginger, is so grateful for its sweetness she doesn't mind the bitter foretaste.

'Now, you must tell me all about yourself, and your husband too. Handsome man, as these Scots often seem to be, if a little . . .' She wrinkles her nose, lets out a little, high laugh that sets Ursa's teeth on edge. 'And you are so lovely. Wherever did he find you?'

'Bergen.'

'Yes, Bergen I know, but where? How?'

Ursa recounts their meeting.

'Did he tell you what it was like here?'

She shakes her head. 'He knew little of it himself, I think.'

Christin sighs, a theatrical sound such as Agnete might make while throwing herself back, hand to forehead.

'I did warn John, I told him to tell everyone. But he's a seaman, he's used to it. You've heard about Spitsbergen? Not that it will make a difference if you have or not – he'll tell you all about it himself at dinner.'

Her dark eyes glitter, but there is no malice there. It is

strange to have found a woman like this in such an austere place. She is fey and sharp all at once. She is just the sort of person who would have attended their dinner parties in Bergen, been friends with Mother.

'He's the King's favourite, if you can believe it. And this is where the King's favourites end up – can you imagine where the enemies go.'

Ursa notices the servants eyeing each other, and suspects they do not approve of their mistress.

'How long have you been here?' she asks, feeling a little bolder in this room of women, with the taste of sugar still on her tongue. 'We did not see you arrive.'

'We came in at night, two weeks ago,' says Christin. 'You are surprised?'

Ursa hopes her husband does not know it was so long between their arrival and his invitation. 'Only that the house seems so settled.'

'Castle,' says Christin, a little too sharply. 'That's what the King called it. Vardøhus Festning.' Her eyes go a little far away. She is not quite right, thinks Ursa. Her brightness is too keen, a little slanting and strange. 'We were wed in Copenhagen. A captain! I'd thought . . .'

Ursa knows, because she had also thought. She has a compulsion to reach out to Christin with both hands, as Christin had to her in the drawing room. Male voices fill the corridor upstairs, and Christin seems to snap from herself. 'Dinner soon, yes?' She stands and smooths her dark skirts. 'I must ask John something.'

They go up into the corridor and see the front door close. Absalom is there with another man, perhaps ten years his elder, with a weather-beaten, bearded face like Captain Leifsson's, which broadens into a smile.

'You must be Ursula.' His Norwegian is flawless. Absalom

isn't looking at the women, but at him, with rapt attention. Ursa guesses he does not know of the delay in the Lensmann's contacting him. 'It is very good to meet you.' Cunningham switches to English. 'Tell me, can you sing?'

'Sing?'

Absalom gives a simpering laugh. It is so unlike him it causes her to stare, but his eyes are fixed on the Lensmann, who claps him on the back, chuckling.

'Never mind, never mind. You must be ready for dinner. I like to dine at seven o'clock sharp, just like we did on the *Katten*. My second ship, you know. The one I took to Spitsbergen. Good to keep a routine, yes? Fanne will show you to your room.'

A stone-faced Fanne leads them upstairs. Their room is above the drawing room at the front of the house, and just as faded and fine, though it smells unpleasant, of closed, forgotten cellars and something else more insistent, greasy and cloying, like fat left to congeal at the base of a pot.

It feels half a world away from their home just a mile down the road, though. There is even a tarnished mirror on the dresser. It has been a long time since Ursa has seen her face but in dark windows, and she notes how it has lost some of its plumpness, how the weeks on the ship's deck and days walking with Maren have given her cheeks and nose a smattering of freckles that Siv would have called common. There is a different set to her face too – a worry line has come in between her eyes and she smooths it with her forefinger but the wrinkle stays there, faint as a whisper.

Ursa's dress has been placed on a chair to air, and the overnight bag is empty and sits atop the chest of drawers. Their things have been folded into the drawers and it discomforts Ursa to think of someone touching them, seeing the stains she has not managed to soak away. She used to be so at ease with their bevy of servants, found it a nuisance when they were left only with Siv, but now she is unsure about it again. Someone seeing your soiled clothes, your mucky belongings, the mess of your house and body.

Absalom is happy, perhaps even a little drunk. He sits upon the end of the bed and holds two pieces of paper in his hands, tied with green ribbon and sealing wax.

'Was your meet with the Lensmann good, husband?'

'He has shown me my purpose, wife. He is a greater man than I had hoped for.'

'I am pleased for you.'

Then Absalom does something that astonishes her. He stands, takes her chin in his hand, and presses his lips to hers, softly, chastely. 'God did this, Ursula. I am assured of that now.'

She waits until he has turned his back to wipe her hand across her mouth. Still she can feel the tickle of his beard upon her, the gentle press of his thumb under her lip.

It was so tender she wants to weep.

Twenty-Seven

There is a screen in the corner of the bedroom, painted with black birds and slicked in a thick layer of varnish, and Ursa takes her dress behind it when Absalom begins to unbutton his shirt. The mirror and light of the room have made her more conscious of her appearance than she has felt in months, and she can see her shape dimly in the varnish. Though Absalom is nearby, she takes off her underthings and stands regarding the round edges of herself, her nipples like dark holes at the centres of her breasts, the pale fuzz between her legs, the curve of her belly only slightly diminished by her changed life.

It's like seeing a ghost, and she changes quickly, comes out to stand before the mirror again, tries to slick and twist her hair the same way Christin had. The pins bite at her head.

They go down, and find Christin emerging from the kitchen, wearing a deep yellow dress, the velvet so fine it shines nearly golden in the lamplight. She nods approvingly at Ursa's hair, pats her own to show she has noticed.

'Excuse the smell,' she says as she leads them towards the drawing room. 'My husband accepted tax from the Ruskis in whales. Blubber, oil.' She grimaces. 'It does reek.'

So that is the smoky, greasy smell, so hard to ignore. The

burnt gingerbread roils in Ursa's stomach. They have tallow burners in Bergen, the smell disguised with clove.

'A wise trade,' says Lensmann Cunningham, emerging from what Ursa presumes is his study. He is wearing a small ruff over his black tunic: it is a little tight and she watches as his Adam's apple squeezes up before disappearing back down. 'Prices are rising weekly now the channels are closed.'

'You closed them,' says his wife.

'Exactly.' He pulls the door to, gestures for them to follow him. 'Here we are.'

The dining room is wood-panelled, so fresh Ursa can still smell the forest on it, with a table built large enough for thrice their number. Candlesticks line it, and Ursa is grateful to note there are no blubber lamps here, only the candles with their soft light. She feels their glow settle over her like a lick of kindness, smoothing her dry hands, casting her husband in gentleness. There are two rows of cutlery, and polished china plates, a square loaf of black bread on the table with a knife lying beside it.

They sit with the Lensmann at the head of the table, his back to a large window. The curtains have not been drawn, and the darkness seeps into the room, edging at the candlelight. The women sit together, facing Absalom.

Fanne enters with a tray of small glasses half filled with clear liquid, etched about their rims. It is sharp, herbal-smelling. She leaves the bottle on the table beside the Lensmann, an elegant, long-necked thing of blue glass.

'Akevitt,' says Lensmann Cunningham. 'Normally an after-dinner sup, I know, but it's a habit I got into aboard the *Katten*. A glass before food wakes the tongue. *Skol!*'

He raises his glass, drains it in one. Absalom does the same and begins to cough. Lensmann Cunningham slaps him between the shoulders as Ursa looks to Christin for guidance, but her glass is empty, too. Ursa sips at the akevitt, winces. It burns down.

Beside Absalom there are two seats empty. 'We are to have company?' he says, and Ursa wonders if Lensmann Cunningham can hear his disappointment too.

'Commissioner Moe from Alta,' says the Lensmann, taking up the knife and beginning to slice the bread. 'I believe you have met? And Herr Abhorsen, a wealthy trader up from Bergen.' He nods at Ursa. 'I thought it would be nice for you to hear the gossip.'

Ursa nods back politely. She never heard gossip when she lived there and was old enough to care. She and Agnete speculated, but their father couldn't employ a chaperone after Mother died, and so they were mostly left inside with their imaginations and chatter.

'But they must be delayed coming from Alta. We can begin without them.' He pours more akevitt, this time filling only his and Absalom's glasses.

'Tell me, Ursula,' says Christin, resting her hand lightly upon Ursa's. 'What of your family? What does your father do?'

'He's a shipowner, wood mostly. From Christiania.'

'Oak, then?' interrupts Cunningham. '*Katten* was a pine ship. Lighter, faster.'

Christin speaks as though her husband has not. 'Have you brothers, sisters?'

A bitter taste fills Ursa's mouth, and she takes another sip of akevitt to wash it away, welcoming the burning channel it carves down her throat, the heat it brings to her stomach. 'A sister.' There is a silence, so she heaves up her name too. 'Agnete.'

'She is crippled,' says Absalom. Ursa flinches. 'Something wrong with her leg, her lungs.'

'She is well in her mind,' says Ursa. 'She is thirteen, nearly fourteen.'

'So much younger,' muses Christin. Fanne enters with a plate of something silvery and gelatinous and sets it at the centre of the table, leaning across between Cunningham and Absalom. The Lensmann's eyes follow her out of the room. 'Why did your mother wait so long?'

Ursa checks her husband's face. But he is looking off over her shoulder, his attention sleeping until it is called to wake by his master.

'She had several losses, I know.'

'Any boys?' Cunningham asks, reaching forward to spear a chunk of silver herring from the plate before them.

'I do not know,' says Ursa. It is strange to be discussing her mother's failed birthings at dinner with near-strangers, but she doesn't feel she can refuse the information.

'What does she think of you living up here?' He is now mashing the fish flat on a slice of bread with the back of his fork. It pulps and glints. Ursa feels nauseous.

'She's dead,' interjects Absalom, but it isn't done to save her, only to get a foot in the conversation.

'I am sorry,' says Christin, moving her hand from Ursa's and taking up the plate. 'Herring?'

Ursa takes some, the jelly sliding through the tines of her fork and soaking the rye bread. They chew and Fanne brings a small platter of sliced onions.

'These are to come out with the fish next time,' says Christin. Fanne bobs, brings around a flagon of honey-coloured liquid and pours each of them a large glass though the akevitt is still on the table, Absalom's second glass full and untouched.

'Your husband has told me some of his suspicions of Vardø,' says Cunningham. The contents of his mouth churn in the candlelight. 'What is your opinion?'

'My opinion?' repeats Ursa.

'Of the women.' He swallows; his Adam's apple wrestles its way past his ruff again. 'Women often see things we miss, don't they, sweetling?'

'And things you hope we would miss,' says Christin, voice arch as Fanne leaves the room again, the Lensmann's eyes trailing her.

'They seem . . .' Ursa searches for the right word.

'Do not worry about tact, Mistress Cornet. I have encountered enough of these Finnmark women to know they are a hard sort, and those from Vardø have a special reputation even here. After the storm – you'll have told her all about that, I'm sure.' This he addresses to Absalom. But her husband has told her nothing. What she has heard she gleaned from Captain Leifsson, or else from Maren's mention of her father and brother.

'It killed a handful in Kiberg, made widows. They remarried. It struck worst here. But the women of Vardø . . .' He chews, shakes his head. 'About six months after the storm, I received a letter from their minister. Pastor Kurtsson – what do you think of him?'

Absalom shrugs his broad shoulders. 'He is a good-hearted man, but not a strong one.'

Cunningham nods until the movement takes on its own momentum, tears another piece of bread. 'He sent me word the women were planning to fish for themselves. Can you imagine?'

'I can, actually,' says Christin. 'Women are different here. They till the land, tend the livestock.'

'Peasants do that all over,' says Cunningham. 'But none go to sea.'

The runnels of their exchange sound smooth, as though they have gone over this ground many times.

'What else were they to do?' says Christin. 'Starve?'

'I provided for them.'

'How?'

'I sent money to Kiberg for them to send fish and grain.'

'You were not here,' says Christin. 'How can you be sure it reached them?'

'I did not need to be here to do my duty.' Cunningham's voice rises. 'They would not defy my authority. A woman has no place on a boat. And besides –' he takes another bite of bread, eyes Ursa – 'that storm was no ordinary one.'

Her heart pounds in her chest, and in the corner of her vision she sees Absalom lean forward, elbows on the table.

'You are certain of it?' he asks, his breathing a little ragged.

Cunningham does not look away from Ursa when he answers. 'Quite certain. I have been a-sea more often than on land for most of my life. I know what the weather can do, and what it cannot. Forty men, dead in a moment?' He shakes his head in disbelief. 'And after what your husband told me of the runes . . .' He crosses himself, his hand clutching bread. Absalom follows suit, and finally Cunningham turns his attention back to her husband. Ursa can breathe again. 'You can surely see why I posted you here? We have some handle on it in Alta, in Kirkenes, but here . . .'

Ursa waits, but the end of the sentence doesn't come. The door opens and Fanne enters. She is carrying a broad polished tray with five bowls of the stew they had smelt in the kitchen earlier. 'Commissioner Moe is here, Lensmann. He's just washing for dinner.'

She sets them down, and one at the place beside Absalom. They wait, the smell of the stew making Ursa's stomach murmur inside her dress, until Commissioner Moe arrives.

'I beg your pardon, Lensmann Køning,' he says in Norwegian. 'The crossing was rough as anything. Waited for it to calm and it only got worse. Daniel begged off the journey and has gone to Hamningberg. You know these Bergen folk.' He winks at Absalom, who looks back blankly. He has whiskers like her father's, and their disarray attests to the rough crossing. Ursa places him about the Lensmann's age, and he is her height.

'It is good to see you again, Commissioner Cornet,' he says, changing to English as he bows to Absalom, who nods shallowly back. 'And this must be your charming wife.'

Ursa can't imagine he got that description from Absalom. 'Commissioner.'

'Moe, please. Now then —' he slaps his hands together — 'what are we having?'

Twenty-Eight

The three men speak so loud and continuously, over and around each other, it is like listening to ten. Christin barely touches her food, takes the occasional sip of mead, and watches them, eventually leaning in to Ursa and saying, 'He doesn't speak Norwegian?'

'He has a little. He is working on it with the minister.'

'Could you not help him?'

'I am not sure he would like that.'

Christin nods, and Ursa knows she understands her meaning. 'Tell me then, truthfully. How is it in the village? My husband has told me enough to ensure I am unlikely to visit.'

'It isn't so bad.'

'You aren't afraid?'

'Of what?'

'Cornet wrote to us of the runes, of the poppets. Well, he wrote to my husband, but John reads me many letters. He loves an audience.'

Ursa takes another mouthful of ptarmigan. 'I am not afraid. Do you not feel afraid, with the gaol so near?'

'Ah, yes.' The woman sips her mead, but her voice remains

dry as ever. Perhaps this is the key to surviving here – emptying your glass. 'The Lapps. My husband has a particular fascination with them.'

'My life's work,' booms the Lensmann. Ursa jumps – she had not been aware they were being listened to. 'The reason I am here. My predecessor but one was not so lucky.'

'Kofoed?' says Moe. 'Knew him as a boy. Nasty business.'

'What happened?' says Ursa.

'Lapps got him,' says the Lensmann darkly. 'Cursed him. They say he shrivelled like an uprooted plant. Overnight.'

Commissioner Moe makes the gesture of the cross over himself. 'Watched the burning of Olson myself. He was the ringleader. When they lit him the smoke burnt black as hellfire.'

Ursa puts her fork down but the others carry on chewing, eyes intent on Commissioner Moe.

'Were there other signs, before Kofoed?' asks Absalom.

'Oh, yes,' says Moe darkly. 'Livestock deaths, put down to wolves until Olson confessed. Girls pregnant without husbands. And those who watched him burn, we were all of us sick for days after. It felt as though I had blots upon my lungs.'

There is a heavy silence. Ursa feels sick, the akevitt turning her stomach. She drinks more.

'You have two sorcerers now,' says Absalom to Cunningham. 'What are they imprisoned for?'

'Wind-weaving,' says Cunningham, and Ursa can't stop the small laugh that escapes her lips. The others look at her with implacable faces. She can't tell them she had been thinking of her weave, large enough for fingers to move through, how Maren had waggled them at her and said they won't be setting any ships to sail with them.

'I am sorry,' she says. 'I have never heard of such a thing before today.'

'It is nothing to be laughed at,' says Lensmann Cunningham,

and Ursa feels like a child chastised. 'Weather has always been their weapon of choice. You should know it, living in Vardø.'

'Perhaps it is only that we do not have witches in Bergen.'

'That may be so,' says Cunningham seriously, his eyes unfocused, his grip on the arm of his chair unnaturally tight. 'Though there was a witch's hill near Bergen, was there not, Moe?'

'There is. Lyderhorn, I believe.'

'I read of it,' nods Absalom. 'Mons Storebarn and Mons Anderson met there, plotted against the Kirke.'

'Said he was good, didn't I, Moe! We know our stuff, we Scotsmen.' He reaches across to clink glasses with Absalom. 'But still, they usually lurk at the edges of the world. That's what I told you, isn't it, Absalom?' Cunningham is leaning forward in his chair. 'In our letters. The candle's light is weakest in the corners. We are here to shine the light more fully, to seek out darkness and burn it up. Swallow it with the fire of God's love.'

His eyes are shining. Though he speaks to Absalom, his gaze is fixed upon her. He looks possessed, and Ursa has a sudden terror he will throw himself across the table at her, grip her about the throat and squeeze and squeeze. But he only slumps back in his chair, motions for his wife to pour another glass.

None of the others seem to notice they are caught in this room with a bear.

'That is why the King placed me here, over one of your own.' He nods at Moe. 'In Scotland we are gaining ground, but of course that is without the complication of Lapps to contend with. I knew we had to meet sooner rather than later, especially after your last correspondence, Absalom. The news of the Lapp, the poppets.'

Ursa's skin crawls. She had hoped Christin's reference to

the poppets earlier had been conjecture, but Toril has talked, as Maren feared. And the Lapp – she must tell her Diinna has been mentioned.

'Until now our concern has been with the Lapp sorcerers, the men – they call themselves noaidi, you know the sort. Shamans, like Olson, the two in the gaol. But the women have become trouble too, and not only the Lapps. Your husband –' his eyes are again upon her and she hears her heart loud in her ears – 'is a man of particular talents, as you no doubt know.' He raises his eyebrows at her blank face. 'Surely you know that is why he was sent for? One of the very finest, even amongst us Scotsmen.'

'I am sorry,' she says, looking to Christin for support, but she is looking at the middle distance, her lips slightly parted.

Cunningham turns to her husband with a theatrical look of alarm that makes Commissioner Moe guffaw, the sounds choked by his mouthful of bread. 'Absalom, do not tell me your wife doesn't know of your achievements?'

Absalom shrugs modestly, and Ursa could hit him. 'I have not spoken of it.'

'Well, then, I must speak of it. Tell me, Ursula, have you heard of a woman named Elspeth Reoch?'

'Forgive me, I have not.'

'Forgive me, for I am about to tell you.' His voice is full of relish, and Ursa determines to meet his eyes, to not look afraid. 'She was but twelve years old, was she not, Absalom, when she made promises with the Devil? Twelve years old when she washed her eyes in his tears to make herself see what it is ungodly to see. She compacted with him. You know what compacted means, Mistress Cornet? What a woman must do to gain such powers of witchcraft?'

'I am sure she can guess at it,' interrupts Christin. 'Do not be so vulgar, John.'

'But it is vulgar.' Cunningham slaps the flat of his hand upon the table. 'It is depraved, disgusting. She bore him a child, did she not, Absalom?'

'Two,' says Absalom gravely. 'Though her secret was not found out until the trial. She claimed to have lost her voice, lived as a mute for years after her pact. Her brother tried to beat the voice from her – he was a godly man, brought her to Coltart's attention.'

'Coltart,' spits Cunningham, dislike apparent in his voice. 'A fraud if ever there was one. It was you who was the power behind his conviction, and do not deny it. Modesty is a fair trait in most cases, but this is not one of them.'

'How did you make her speak?' says Moe.

'Ducking. Irons.'

'You bound her?'

'Branded her. With crosses at her throat and arms.' Absalom is not looking at Ursa. She hopes it is because he is ashamed, but she hears none of that in his voice.

'Go on.'

'She cried out in a demonic language, and then sang like the Devil's bird she is.' Ursa's dress feels very tight as she watches him enjoy the Lensmann's attention. 'Confessed the whole tale, to seduction of four men and to theft, to a half-dozen meets with the Devil.'

'But what marked this so apart was her execution – a masterful stroke,' says Cunningham.

'You did not burn her?' asks Moe, as though enquiring as to the weather that day.

'We did,' says Absalom.

'They did,' echoes Cunningham. 'But first, to make right her crime of deceit in her claim of muteness, they strangled her. Did you not, Absalom?'

'Yes.' Now he looks at Ursa quickly, as though he wishes

237

she were not here, and she realizes they have not yet heard the worst of it. She presses her palms very hard against the table, bracing herself.

'Go on,' smiles Cunningham. 'Tell them how.'

'With a rope, sir,' says Absalom, and finally she hears the looked-for shame in his voice.

'And your involvement?'

Absalom's voice is barely audible. 'Had hold of one end of the rope myself, Lensmann.'

'See,' says Cunningham, leaning forward to slap Absalom on the shoulder. 'A man of quality. Not many men could mete out their punishment themselves. I'll bet it was not Coltart who had hold of the other end of that rope.'

'It was not, Lensmann.' He does not look at Ursa again, and she is glad. She could not hide what she is feeling at that moment, not for all the world.

'That was when I knew I must have you here,' continues Cunningham. 'In the heat of it. Anyone can set a fire – it makes killing no harder than boiling a cup for tea.'

'The kettles shriek louder,' says Moe.

'Please,' says Christin.

'Sorry, sweetling,' says Cunningham, a smirk at his bearded mouth. 'Moe, you must not forget our company.'

Ursa can't speak. She hates him, she knows now. Hates all of them. She knew of the trial from Absalom's mention of it in the first kirke meeting, but had not guessed that the woman had been put to death, that her husband with his own hands murdered her. *Branded. Strangled. Burnt.* The words repeat like a child's rhyme. She shudders, and it doesn't escape Fru Cunningham's notice.

'It is brute to hear such details, but you must feel no pity for a witch, Ursula,' says Christin, sympathetically. 'It is through the soft places that they take hold, through the hurt

238

heart, the tender mind. Even in Tromsø, in Bergen, we women must be taught this.'

'And you need fear them less than most,' says Cunningham. 'With such a man for your husband.'

Ursa watches Absalom across the table. She had not guessed at the pride he takes in the telling of this story. She can feel his pleasure in the admiration from the others coming off him, tangible as the smell of drink off Lensmann Cunningham.

Talk turns to the fishing channels, to the whaling at Spitsbergen and, finally, endlessly it seems to Ursa, to Lensmann Cunningham's time on the *Katten*. The dinner closes with a rømmegrøt of such proportions the candlesticks must be moved further apart so the great dish of cream can be placed between them.

Ursa takes enough to seem polite, but the cream feels wrong in her mouth, too rich after months of ship and then Vardø food. All this time she had been craving tastes like she used to have at home, cream and cinnamon and sugar, but it slides down thickly, sits heavy and malign in her stomach.

She notices that Absalom barely touches it either. His hands, large as hams, are resting on the table, the small hairs at his knuckles catching the candlelight like cobwebs. She feels tightness in her throat.

Commissioner Moe excuses himself soon after, red about the nose, citing his long journey. 'I am invigorated,' he says, grasping Absalom's hand. 'Let us get to work.'

Christin is grown very quiet beside Ursa, and she suspects it is the effect of the same drink that makes the Lensmann so expansive. Ursa too has drunk more than was perhaps polite. Her mouth feels tingling and raw with the liquor. As the plates are cleared and Absalom and Lensmann Cunningham rise to retire to the Lensmann's study, she brushes her fingers across her lips. They feel very soft, and not her own.

'Ursula?'

Christin is standing behind her pushed-in chair, watching her. 'I hope you do not mind?'

'Mind?'

'I am quite tired. Would you like me to see you to your room?'

'Oh . . .' Ursa hurries to stand, her skirts catching beneath the chair legs as she moves it backwards, Lensmann Cunningham moving too slowly to help. 'Thank you. Thank you for the dinner. It was very fine.'

'We found Fanne in Alta,' says Lensmann Cunningham. He is standing a little close to her, and she can smell sourness and cream on his breath. 'She is a good cook.'

'I wouldn't go so far,' says Christin crisply. 'But I am glad you enjoyed it.'

'Do you have help?' asks Cunningham, squinting at Absalom. 'Any Vardø women know how to keep a home?'

There is a leer in his voice that makes Ursa's skin crawl.

'My wife has some aid,' Absalom answers. 'Though not of my choosing. She is kin with a Lapp.'

'They are not kin,' says Ursa, fear making her bold. 'They are not blood. She comes to kirke, husband. She is a good woman.'

Absalom looks as though he will say more but Cunningham waves his hand diffidently.

'It is best to leave such matters to the women,' he says. 'You have enough to worry yourself about, especially with our conversations to act upon.'

'Shall we?' Christin is all but tapping her foot. She is obviously anxious to be abed, and Ursa doesn't mind. She longs for the oblivion of sleep, for it to be morning and to return to their house, to Maren. In her blurred mind she tells herself that there are things she must warn her of, like the mention of Diinna and the poppets. She digs her fingernails into her wrist, to make herself remember.

They go out into the corridor and say their goodnights to the men, who are already back into conversation, breaking off only briefly, Lensmann Cunningham to bump his mouth against his wife's high cheekbone, Absalom to give her another disconcertingly soft brush of lips, this time against her cheek.

'You must be proud, to be wed to a man such as that,' says Christin as she leads her up the stairs. Ursa wants to laugh, to ask which part she should be proud of – his slavish attention to the Lensmann, his intimate part in a woman's death, or his satisfaction in it?

'Your husband really had no say in the appointment of your servant?' Christin continues.

'She is not so much a servant, more a companion.'

'It is best to keep such people apart from yourself. And from your husband,' says Christin as they reach Ursa's bedroom door. Christin opens it, stands aside. As Ursa moves to walk past her Christin brings her hand up, brushes Ursa's neck where her knot has slipped its pins. The spot feels tender. 'Though you are so lovely, I am sure you do not need to worry.'

Ursa feels a blush rise up her constricted throat. 'Worry?'

'Drink, cards.' She blinks slowly at Ursa. 'Serving girls. Even great men have weaknesses. And it is we who must bear them.'

Ursa suddenly wants to confide in her, of her life with Absalom, all its small terrors and confusions, but Christin has already dropped her hand and is moving off to the other end of the corridor. She is not unsteady, only too careful.

'Goodnight, Ursula. I will put you in my prayers.'

Ursa closes the door. Light is coming around the edges of the drawn curtains, and the bedspread has been folded back, the linen smooth beneath. Can it be true, that Fanne and the Lensmann lie together? Perhaps in this bed, when there are no visitors.

She lets her hair down, collecting the pins in her hand as she crosses to the window, hooks aside one heavy drape with a finger. The other buildings in the complex are still lit, with the exception of the gaol. She listens: is that the sound of men moaning, or only the wind, the sea? The dark windows seem to stare back, and she lets the curtain drop, hurries to complete her ablutions, anxious to be asleep when Absalom comes to bed.

Before she slips between the clean sheets, she kneels beside the bed, the way she and Agnete used to, says a prayer for the sad-eyed Christin, for Maren out in the dark somewhere, and for herself. And though it may be an unnameable blasphemy, for Elspeth Reoch, who died at Absalom's hand. Witch or no, she wouldn't wish it on anyone.

Twenty-Nine

Ursa thought the worst of the evening was behind her, but she doesn't manage to sleep before Absalom comes to bed. The noises of the house are too strange, the sea much closer and the sound of it against the shore unsettling. She thinks she hears his hand on the door many times before he actually pushes it open.

'You awake, Ursula?'

There is no point pretending. She pushes herself up, pulling the sheets to her chin. He removes his boots, goes to the chair by the fire. He has a small glass in his hand, more folded paper in the other.

'I hope you enjoyed your dinner?'

'It was very rich, I have become unused to it.'

He sets his glass down on the fireplace, ducks his head so she can see his face only in profile as he gazes at the flames. When he speaks, it is into the flames too, and she doesn't catch his words.

'Sorry?' she says.

He speaks a little louder. 'I had not meant you to find out like that.'

She thought she would feel afraid upon his return, but now

she is full of the same righteous anger she felt in the dining room. It makes her bold.

'That you murdered a woman?'

The silence stretches, yawns like a pit. Ursa can hear her heart louder than the sea in her ears. She wishes she were wearing more than her cotton nightdress.

Finally, slowly, he straightens, turns back towards her, the flames glowing about his legs. His lips are pressed together thinly, and when she drags her gaze to his eyes, she sees they are glassy, a little unfocused. Is he drunk as the Lensmann?

'Murdered a woman?' he repeats, unable to make sense of the words. 'No. No –' he shakes his head as though dislodging a fly – 'I tried a witch, wife. She was sentenced to death by the court of my country. She was guilty, in the eyes of the law, and of God. "Thou shalt not suffer a witch to live." God commands it.'

'But you, husband. You had to be the one to kill her?'

He looks pained as he lifts his small glass from the fireplace, and, still clutching the papers, sits heavily in the chair beside the fire. 'It was a grave matter. I took no joy in it, though she deserved to die, and I prayed for it after. God forgave me. I am not an arrogant man, Ursula.' She stops herself from snorting. 'But I am proud of my service to God. I hope for my wife to be so, too.'

She knows the wisest thing is to say she is proud, as Christin thinks she should be. It would dispel the tension between them, and perhaps he is drunk enough that he would not remember the detail of their conversation in the morning. But she says nothing, only watches him.

He tilts his head against the hard back of the chair, so she can see only a little of his eyes, which seem almost black. 'I do like that you are from fine stock, Ursula. I could hardly believe my luck when your father told me of you. A shipowner's daughter.' He sucks in his breath. 'You are better than I could have hoped for.'

She wishes he would stop speaking, stop looking at her. 'You are a commissioner. You could have chosen finer.' She wishes he had. In that moment, though it would mean she would never have met Maren, she longs to be back at home with Agnete, tucked up in their shared bed, unwed and unaware of Absalom Cornet.

'I did not start so high,' says Absalom. 'Not like the Lensmann, lifted already at birth. I was the son of a sheep farmer, did you know that?'

'I did not. You have never told me.' *Careful*, she tells herself. *Not so sharp.*

'You have never asked.' He pauses, as though waiting for her to do so now, but she doesn't trust herself to speak.

He takes a swallow from his glass. 'I was born on a tiny spit of an island. Only a bit larger than this, as I once said. Nothing but sheep. It stank. And then they built a kirk on the next island over, and that was clean and smelt of candles. It was the finest place I'd ever known.' His eyes close, as if he is picturing it. 'The minister there, he could see something special in me. It was he who recommended me to Coltart, when the witch was caught.'

Bile rises in her throat.

'Isn't that a miraculous thing? The son of a sheep farmer, become a witch-hunter, and then a commissioner?' His dark eyes gleam at her.

'It is, husband.'

He shifts in his chair. 'Why do you not call me Absalom?'

'I will if you prefer it, Absalom.' She can feel a great sort of danger approaching, is searching for how to avoid it.

'Do you know what my name means?'

She shakes her head.

'Father of peace.'

Ursa almost laughs, catches herself in time.

'That is all I want. To rid the world of witches, so we can all live in God's peace. And if the only way to it is through war, so be it.'

He closes his eyes again, and does not say anything for a long time. She thinks he is asleep, and the knot in her stomach loosens slightly. But a moment later he speaks. 'I was destined for this, Ursula. The Lensmann has great faith in me. He sees me as special, just as the minister in Orkney did.'

He stands, so suddenly Ursa can't stop herself from jumping. He drains and sets down the glass, comes to the bed and sits beside her. His breath is hot on her cheek. 'Do you think me special, Ursula?'

She turns to face him. Her hands tremble on the sheet. 'Yes, Absalom.'

He closes one of his hands over hers. It is warm and strong and dry. He holds up the folded pieces of paper. 'The Lensmann gave me these. They have been arriving the past two months at Vardøhus. Letters, from Bergen.'

Her heart leaps. 'From my father?' She wants to reach for them, but her hands are held steady by his. He nods, drops them on the bedspread.

'They are opened,' she says, recognizing her father's writing, but nothing of what he says.

'A husband should know what his wife's affairs are.'

'They are my letters,' Ursa says, trying to stay calm.

'Can you read them?' His tone tells her he knows she can't.

'Can you read Norwegian?' she snaps, the words out too fast to catch them. His hand is upon her shoulder and squeezing before she can pull away.

'Careful, wife. They are in English.'

'I did not mean — of course my father knows you would

have to read them to me.' The pressure on her shoulder is painful. 'But could you not have waited until we were together?'

'It was my duty to read them. What if there had been bad news I had to prepare you for?'

Ursa's heart thumps. The fine dinner churns in her belly. 'There is bad news?'

He says nothing, only lightens his grip on her shoulder.

'Please.' She feels as though she is about to cry. 'Absalom, is it Agnete?'

He reaches for the letters again, plucks them from her hands. He sorts through them, and she grows certain he is searching for the one that brings news of her sister. Of her death.

The tears are already spilling down her face when he shakes his head slowly.

'Nothing like that. All is as it was.' He rifles through the sheaf. 'Your sister has a new doctor. They have bought a new rug for her room. Small, petty things like that. They want to know of your life here.'

She wipes her tears away, trembling. 'Can you read them to me?'

'It is late.'

'Just one, then. The latest one.' Ursa feels desperate as a starving animal. 'Please, husband – Absalom,' she corrects, 'please would you read one to me?'

He looks at her a long moment, then reaches out and touches the last of her tears. He rubs it between his fingers, considering, then takes up one of the letters. She wants to weep again, with relief, but controls herself.

'This was sent on the twenty-third of May.'

'But that is months ago,' says Ursa before she can catch herself.

'We are months away. Letters are slow to arrive.' He is placid at her interruption, but she reminds herself to not speak further. 'It says, "Dearest Ursa" –' he pauses. 'Is this what they call you?'

She nods.

'It is inelegant. "Dearest Ursa, you are not long gone but already we feel your absence sharply. The days are a little drabber, the house a little less full of light."'

Ursa closes her eyes, tries to imagine her father's voice.

'"Though it is a comfort to know you have taken your brightness north. I think they may need it even more than we. Agnete is no worse. Siv is thinking of employing a kitchen girl, so she may be more of a maid to her. Though Agnete insists that no one can rival you for a nurse. She wishes you to know that she loves you, though she is missing the blue kerchief, and would rather like it back."'

Ursa smiles as Absalom stifles a yawn.

'It goes on so.'

'Please, a little more.' She places her hand on his, hating herself for needing him so. 'Please, Absalom.'

He fixes her then with a more focused look, and she recognizes his desire, rubs her thumb slow across his. He resumes, and she removes her hand as fast as she dares.

'"I hope Captain Leifsson cared for you well. He will be returning to Finnmark in early next year, and we will send gifts. Do let us know if there is anything particular you require. Should Absalom's business bring him south, be sure to accompany him. Ursa, it is only now that I realize how much I relied upon you. You can be sure that I am loving Agnete for us both, and am resolved to be the father she needs in the absence of her much-loved sister."'

Ursa can't stop the tears this time. The words are so lovely she knows Absalom has not made them up: her father really has written just what her husband has read out. She feels nauseous with relief.

248

'Told you, nothing much to report.' Absalom throws the letter to the bed, reaches for her. But she is too slow to act: she flinches, still raw from her father's words, the obvious love and care in them. His gaze sharpens further, and he gathers up the letters. They scrunch between his fingers.

'Careful,' she pleads, but in one fluid movement, he stands, crosses the room. She knows his mind in an instant, rises from the bed, runs to stop him – but it is too late. He throws the letters into the fire.

She presses her hand to the sore throb beneath her breast as he turns to her. He takes her head between his hands, so large they encase her cheeks, and raises it so her neck is bent, arching up to him. She imagines him squeezing, her skull caving, but then he brings his mouth down on hers and kisses her, so softly it makes her skin crawl.

'I will write to them for you,' he says, breath hot against her cheek as he brings his lips again to her. She can feel his hardness pressing against her belly, and knows there is a silent condition to his offer.

Behind him, the letters from her father shrivel into ash, and are carried up like smoke signals to the night.

HUNT

Thirty

Though Ursa is only gone Wednesday and Thursday, it is twice what Maren had prepared for, and she feels each moment keenly as a blade. The meet is full of speculation on their Lensmann, on the gossip Ursa will come back with, and at every mention of her, Maren's nape tingles.

She doesn't know how she existed before her, now that mere days feel interminable. She matches Mamma for skittishness, Diinna for irritation, Erik for silence. She goes about her tasks with a caught anger that makes her fast, escapes to the headland, the only place she can see over the walls of the fortress, and watches the lights from the windows. She can see the whole of Vardø spread out in its gentle roll of valley, the two halves of the island matching each other almost exactly, like a book opened. Both nights she paces the cliff edge until the grass is flattened and churned.

She hears they are back on Friday morning, when Kirsten comes with salt and blood for blodplättar, and a message from Ursa. Mamma will not speak with Kirsten, barely speaks to Maren any more.

'Be sure she tells you all,' says Kirsten from the threshold. 'I am interested to have a measure of our Lensmann.'

'If you came to Toril's meets,' says Mamma to Maren, pummelling the butter churn though Maren can hear the thud that means it has been overworked, 'you would have heard all already. Commissioner Cornet speaks often of the Lensmann's work, his plans for us all.'

'I am interested in Ursula's measure of him, though,' says Kirsten. 'I will see you Sabbath Day, Maren.'

'What plans?' says Maren when she has closed the door and set the pail of blood upon the table, though she doesn't much care to hear. The sound of the over-churned butter clagging in the milk is pounding in her head and it is all she can do to keep from knocking the paddle from Mamma's hand.

'Good things. Godly things.' Her eyes flick to the place where her cloth cross from Toril is hung from a nick in the wadding of the wall. She had left one outside Diinna's door too, and Maren had found it unravelled and left in a pail of water two days later. Diinna must have been using it as a washcloth.

When did Diinna's dislike of Mamma grow to be such a monster? she wonders. Not that Maren's dislike is much less. She tries to quiet it, but sees only the vile cracking beside her mother's mouth where she constantly licks, the narrow hard face too like her own, the sweat coming heavy through her work dress. Is this the woman who used to soothe her pains, who laughed and span her when she came home with news of her proposal from Dag, who made her brother and delivered his son with gentle hands, that now sit crabbed about the paddle? Even her breath scratches at Maren's ear, loud with effort.

Maren doesn't ask anything further, but begins on the blodplättar, her stinging heart soothed a little by the knowledge that Ursa has been returned to her, is nearby at this very moment. When she has mixed the flour fully with the

254

blood, she goes out with a rope to the cliff and ties it about the post Erik knocked into the ground for this purpose five years before.

She lets a basket down, and her eyes linger a moment too long on the rocks below. The whale has come to her less and less, but now she sees it sprawled on the toothed jags, its sides heaving. The smell of salt and rot comes into her nostrils, and she wipes it away, blinks until the vision is gone.

She bends and ties another rope over this one, tugging the knot to make it strong. The other end she knots about her waist, tucks her skirts up into the rope and takes the easy route down to the nearest guillemot nest, her mind too full to attempt the trickier path. The birds lift, shrieking, and her head rings with their cries. She works methodically, taking five eggs from three nests, extending mercy to the smallest ones, the ones with fine freckles or that are pale as cream. Below it is low tide, and she remembers pulling Toril's son from the waves, his body slack and moving about on its bones.

She climbs up quickly, brings up the basket, and goes back to the house. She cracks the eggs one after another into the blood and flour, the shells breaking easily and speckling the mixture so she must scoop with her fingernails, draglines of blood drying quickly beneath them.

They have a blodplättar between them for lunch, the house filling with the smell of iron and salt. Her mother is mercifully silent as they eat: Maren knows she will be thinking of Erik, how these were his favourite. When Maren wraps one, still steaming, in a piece of cloth to take to Diinna on her way to the headland, Mamma doesn't raise an objection.

•

'Thought I could smell blodplättar,' says Diinna. She is sitting on her step, Erik playing in the earth below. She takes the cloth

255

carefully. 'Saw you going to the cliff. Did you check the knots?' She unwraps it, breathes it in.

'No need to thank me,' says Maren, her annoyance a bubble bursting. She turns to go, but Diinna reaches out with her strong hand, grasps her softly about the wrist.

'Thank you, Maren.' It is a shock sudden as a slap to see Diinna's dark eyes shining. 'If you need me to help you next time, ask. I am a better climber.'

Maren nods, swallows. She rubs the top of Diinna's hand. 'I will.'

As she steps from the shadow of their house, she hears Diinna coo softly to her son.

'Come, *ráhkis*. Come and taste. Your father loved these.'

As Maren walks she thinks only of Ursa: whether she will be at their agreed meeting-place, what she will do if she isn't. The alternate pleasure and panic have her almost breathless, so when she sights Ursa's figure in a light grey dress at the headland her head spins and she must slow her tread to keep from stumbling.

For a thin moment the double trick of the low sun off the sea is dazzling, and she thinks perhaps it isn't her at all. The face is mask-like at this distance, the pale blonde hair whipped to frenzy about the head, the dark eyes two holes set deep and swallowing beneath knitted brows. But in another moment Ursa is smiling, herself again, and raising one hand to wave, the other at her swirling skirts, and it is all Maren can do to keep from running to her and sweeping her up in her arms.

She stops short of embracing her, for though Ursa's mouth is wide her eyes are strained, hollows like bruises beneath them. Maren resists the urge to reach up, place her thumbs at them to soothe them.

'Kirsten found you then? I thought it best not to come directly, but did not wish to wait till evening.'

'You are unwell?'

'It is so obvious?' says Ursa. 'I kept to bed all day yesterday. It is why we were another day delayed. I hope you did not wait for long.'

Maren says nothing of the night before, her anxious pacing of the cliff. The ground at their feet is scuffed and worn by her tread, and she shifts to cover the worst of it.

'What ails you?'

'A poor stomach, only. You have given me a peasant's appetite.' She smiles more weakly. 'The cooking at Vardøhus did for me. And, perhaps, the drink.'

Maren imagines her made slack-limbed by it, like Pappa at midwinter.

'You are shocked?' says Ursa. 'You would have drunk in such company.'

'Your visit was not good?'

'My husband would say it was. The Lensmann is a great admirer of his deeds.'

'That is good for you. It means you are like to stay?'

Ursa looks at her, forehead creased.

'The Lensmann was a beast. All of them were, even his wife.' She takes in a sharp breath, holds her hand to her side. Maren moves closer.

'Perhaps we should go somewhere to sit? You are very pale.'

'My husband is at home. He is writing, some edict or another. We will hear all at kirke. But I wanted to tell you – Diinna is mentioned.'

'Mentioned?'

'My husband told the Lensmann of the runes, and he was not greatly pleased. The poppets too. I have a thought to tell Fru Olufsdatter, but I wanted to tell you about Diinna first.'

'You think it a bad thing?' says Maren, though she knows

it is. She is trying to grasp the edges of the situation, feel out what sort of trouble Ursa's confidence holds.

'My husband will not tell me more, but there was talk of witchcraft. There were two men in the gaol. Lapp men.'

'It is not witchcraft, what Diinna does. The runes were only what prayers are to us.'

'You should learn a better argument,' says Ursa. 'It wouldn't please him to hear you say such a thing. I have certainly spoken well of her to my husband, but the Lensmann has his mind and I discovered he has some past in dealings with witches.'

'Diinna is no witch,' snaps Maren, her panic making her voice harsher than she meant it to be.

Ursa's voice is deliberately calm. 'Perhaps she should come to kirke?'

'I will have no luck with that.' Maren's throat feels tight. 'Especially after Toril turned up at the Wednesday meet. She doesn't trust my opinion on such things.'

All her joy at seeing Ursa again has been snatched to pieces by this news, and she begins to pace a small path before her, a route in miniature of what she trod waiting for Ursa.

'Perhaps I could speak with her?' Ursa's hand rests upon her forearm, stilling her. 'I really think it important.'

Maren can't imagine it having more of an effect, but her touch sets more nerves jangling. 'What else did they say of her?'

'Nothing. But the talk . . . it was none of it good.' Ursa brings her hands up suddenly to her face, speaks in a strangled voice. 'Forgive me. I did not know the man I married. If I had, I would have warned you, wouldn't have brought you close to me, to us.'

Maren holds herself. 'I was mentioned?'

'Goodness, no,' says Ursa. 'I would never have let your name be spoken in such a way. I wouldn't have allowed it.'

She takes both Maren's hands in her own, holds them tightly. 'You are very dear to me, you know that, do you not? I could never let harm come to you.'

This is the time, thinks Maren with Ursa's fierce, lovely face before her, their gazes locked, that she should kiss her. The thought is terrifying: but Maren is certain that if she were a man, she would close the distance and press her mouth to Ursa's, stop up her words with kisses. But she only nods. 'I do.'

'Shall we go then?' Ursa says, the moment broken. 'To speak with Diinna?'

'It will not do any good,' says Maren. She doesn't want their time together to be over so soon, to go back to the village and to other people. But she allows Ursa to lead her back anyway, her head dipped against the wind so the creamy nape of her neck shows.

'What more of Vardøhus, of the wife?' Ursa asks.

'Nothing. It is a drear place however mightily built. And she . . .' She hesitates, reaching for the right word in a way that makes Maren think she has not thought long on her after. It makes her very glad. 'Is lonely there, I think. I did not care for her.'

It was not a danger she had considered, that Ursa might like Fru Cunningham enough to take her into her confidence. Maren feels a swooping sort of relief, as though a pit has been narrowly avoided.

'Are runes really only like prayers?' Ursa asks. 'Aren't they meant to call things, summon things? They spoke of wind-weaving.'

'Diinna doesn't do that. The runes were harmless.' To guide Maren's brother and father's soul to safety. She had believed it, because in those months she was grasping for something, anything, to order the chaos that the storm set amongst them. From Varr's drum to the runes, she had found comfort in it.

Though she could swear against it in a court if she must, it would be a lie.

Does Commissioner Cornet also know of the runestones left on the headland, of the skinned foxes and the talk of five-finned whales? With Toril close in his ear, she can't doubt it. None of that was Diinna, Maren is almost certain, but blame could easily be laid at her door. It can be claimed as simple superstition, of course, but now she sees it was ignorantly done, just as the fishing had been. And Commissioner Cornet's arrival, though it has brought Ursa to her, has pulled back that protective veil in a way that Pastor Kurtsson's presence never did.

Diinna is still on her step, Erik on her lap. His head is drawn into her chest, and Maren realizes suddenly that Erik's mouth is around his mother's nipple. Ursa comes to a sudden halt, her purpose fading as a blush reddens her cheek.

Diinna looks up at them both, and Maren, suddenly, sees her as a stranger would, as Ursa must. Her legs apart the better to bear the weight of her too-grown son, her heavy breast slipped between the folds of her jerkin. Veins stand out, rivers against the thin skin. Her hair is greased and flat to her head, her eyes dark with challenge. With Erik clasped to her, she looks like some sort of deity, powerful and strange. Maren can't stop her eyes going to her breast. She turns away, her mouth dry.

'We should not be here.'

'She should not be doing such a thing outside,' says Ursa, voice faint. 'What if Absalom were to see?'

Maren looks about them. They are shielded from all houses but the ruin of Baar Ragnvalsson's, the wheeling birds their only witnesses.

Diinna has moved Erik from her breast and set him on his feet. She rebuttons her jerkin. She doesn't look even a little ashamed.

'I had thought you would be away for longer,' she says as Erik reaches up to her front. She pushes his hands away, stands. 'You are usually a long time at the headland.'

There is a sharpness to her voice that makes Maren uneasy. 'Mistress Cornet wished to speak with you,' says Maren. She feels furious, and isn't sure why. 'You have a perfectly good door – why do you not use it?'

'What is it you wish to say?' Diinna turns her heavy-lidded eyes upon Ursa. 'Mistress Cornet?'

Ursa gets straight to it. 'I have just come from Vardøhus. My husband was invited to dine with Lensmann Cunningham. There was talk of you, at dinner.'

Diinna does not expect this, Maren can tell, though she hides her surprise well. There is only a slight movement at her jaw and Ursa, missing it, tries harder to impress upon her the situation.

'There were two Lapps in the gaol there.' Her jaw tightens further. 'They were wind-weavers.'

'I do not do that,' says Diinna.

'But the runes were mentioned, Diinna,' says Maren. 'The poppets too.'

'Fru Olufsdatter made those herself,' she says. 'I only told her which herbs to burn for remembrance.'

'And she is like to be in trouble too,' says Maren. 'But it is you we must concern ourselves with.'

'You need not concern yourself with me at all. The time for that is long past.'

'It is Ursa who wanted to tell you,' says Maren, turning away so Diinna doesn't see the hurt in her face. 'She thinks it important.'

'You should come to kirke,' says Ursa. 'I do not think the situation beyond remedy.'

'You don't?' says Diinna, disbelief in her voice, and Ursa

shifts, uncomfortable beneath her gaze. 'With two Lapps, as you say, in the gaol, no doubt waiting to burn?'

Maren waits for Ursa to refute it, feels a mounting pressure in her throat when she doesn't.

'I do not believe my husband to be above mercy.' There is nothing convincing in Ursa's voice.

'I have heard what happens when my people throw themselves upon the mercy of men like your husband, Mistress Cornet.' She bends and picks up Erik, holds him at her hip. 'I wouldn't be so certain.'

Diinna strides across her threshold and closes the door. Maren hesitates a few moments before she follows her. She doesn't knock but pushes full inside, catching Erik on the leg with the door so he lets out a soft wail. Maren shuts Ursa out, and turns to the room. It has been years since she has been in here, perhaps even since it was newly built and Diinna and Erik just married, and she filled the room with small white and yellow flowers, helped bring them their gifts of skrei and strung them from the rafters like miniature sails.

There are no flowers here now. What had felt cramped for a newly married couple feels somehow tinier with a mother and her son. The fire is banked and a thick blanket is hung at the window, so the whole room is in shadow and Diinna blinks at her through the gloom like some nocturnal bird. Erik goes to a corner that is scattered with small cloth shapes, some sticks, like a nest. It smells of off milk, and blodplättar, seeping in from their house. Her brother's boots are beside the fire, in echo of where Pappa's are next door. One is unlaced, its tongue gaping, the inside dark as a mouth.

Maren had come to accuse Diinna of rudeness, to tell her she spoke falsely when she said she was no longer Maren's concern, but in this room that feels impossible. They have failed her, failed Erik, failed Erik's memory.

'Diinna . . .'

Then she sees a knotted figure over the fire, wrapped in Toril's missing lace. The sight makes Maren stumble. There is a silver needle, stuck into its side.

'What is that?'

Diinna follows her gaze, then takes up the poppet. 'Nothing. A doll for Erik.'

'That is Toril's lace.'

Diinna pulls the needle from it, unwraps the scrap of lace. 'You want to give it back to her?'

Maren shakes her head, and Diinna drops it onto the fire. Maren makes a convulsive movement, as if to rescue the fabric, but it has caught, is already twisting and curling up.

She looks about the room, spies runestones beside the bed, a handful of rabbit spine bones next to the empty boots. The hairs on her arms lift.

'Diinna, what is all this?'

'All what?' Diinna lays the poppet at the centre of a large square of cloth spread flat on the bed. On top of this she puts a fox-tail scarf, thick mittens, her knife, a tunic.

'What are you doing?'

'You must not tell anyone,' she says, not stopping. 'Not even her.'

'You can't go.' Maren feels a flutter of panic. 'Diinna, you are no witch.'

But there is uncertainty in her voice, and Diinna looks up at her sharply. 'You don't sound so sure.'

Maren's hands tremble, and she realizes she is a little afraid. 'The poppet—'

'A doll,' says Diinna. 'For Erik. I took the lace out of spite, and to make the fabric less coarse.'

Maren's eyes trail to the bones, the runestones, and Diinna lets out a sad, low laugh. 'I remember once when runes gave you comfort, when sailors came to my father to cast bones and tell them of their time left to come. They are a language, Maren. Just because you do not speak it doesn't make it devilry.'

Maren nods, ashamed. She wants to apologize, but knows it will sound weak. Instead she repeats herself. 'You're no witch.'

'It doesn't matter what I am, only what they believe I am.'

'Ursa thinks it will be all right, thinks he will—'

'What does she know of any of it?' Diinna's voice frays. 'What do you know? I have stayed for you, so Erik may know his family. But it is not safe here.'

'You aren't taking him?'

'He is my son,' she says. 'You can't think me able to leave him behind.'

'How will he survive, on the low mountain?'

'We will have to go further than that,' says Diinna. 'But wherever we land he will survive better than he has here.' She looks about the squalid room. 'This is no place for a child. He needs air, he needs trees, he needs people who will not look at him as though he is something broken, or half made.' She shoots a poisonous look at the wall through which Maren can hear her mother still at work with the butter churn. 'I should have taken him when his father died.'

Maren catches Diinna's hand, tries to delay her. 'Please, stay.'

'It isn't safe.'

'I can keep you safe.'

She shakes her head, brings her hand up to Maren's cheek. 'We are nothing to them. We are as men to the sea, caught on their currents.' She rests her forehead against Maren's. Her skin is dry as sand.

'You could come too,' she says. Maren jerks away. 'Varr summers beyond the low mountain, in the forests south. They

264

will not follow there, and if they do, we know how to hide if we must.'

'I can't leave Mamma.' She can't leave Ursa. 'And there is no danger for me here.'

Diinna looks as though she wants to say more, but she only knots the first bundle, takes another blanket from a shelf, and spreads it out to start another.

There is so much Maren wants to say, manages only, 'When will you go?'

'Tonight. I will take Baar's boat—'

'It's a ruin,' says Maren. 'Take Kirsten's. I know she will not mind.'

Diinna nods. 'She can say I stole it. I'll leave it safe on the shore.'

Maren scoops up Erik, holds him to her, breathes in his milky smell. 'I have something for you. Some coins—'

'Keep them,' says Diinna. 'I'll have no use for them in the forests.'

'What if you are caught—'

'Tell no one,' says Diinna. She comes before her again, wraps her arms around them both, and Maren clenches her jaw so hard she hears something pop.

'Be careful,' whispers Diinna, her breath tickling her ear. 'Even of her.'

She draws back, places her thumb on Maren's forehead. 'Should you need to find me.'

Maren clenches her eyes shut, remembering Diinna pressing the same thread to her brother's forehead before he left that Christmas Eve. 'Diinna . . .' Maren catches her hand before she draws it away. 'Will you sing it to me? His *joik*?'

She is sure Diinna will deny her, but instead she brings her mouth close to Maren's ear and sings. The tune is lilting and soft, and Maren recognizes some of it from through the wall, but it is altogether stranger and more beautiful against her cheek. When it ends it feels as though something has been snatched from her. Erik is calm and smiling after the song, and Maren presses a last kiss to his cool cheek, breathes him in, before passing him back to his mother.

She tumbles from the house bewildered, a sob caught in her throat. Ursa's hair is bright after the gloom.

'Will she come to kirke?'

'She will,' says Maren, because it is easier, and Ursa's face lightens at the lie.

•

That night, Maren hears no sound though she sleeps in her old bed, presses her ear to the wall. She thinks Diinna must have changed her mind, goes at first light to her door.

It is unlatched and opens at her touch. There is nothing within but Erik's boots, empty beside the dead fire. Maren goes to the neat bed. She wants to throw the curtains wide, to let air and light touch the places so long held in dark. But she doesn't.

She only closes the door behind her, sits heavily on the bed. This is where her brother lay, where her nephew was got. She spreads wide her palms, presses them to the frame, trying to call something of them to her. Maren feels suddenly alone, as she had in the mist when she lost Erik on the headland. But this time, the mist will not lift. There is no one coming for her. Not her sweet, quiet brother with his heavy brows and slow laugh. Not Pappa, not even Mamma.

Her cry catches, sharp as a hook. She touches her fingers to the spot Diinna placed a thread to reel them together again, and something in her knows that just as it did for her brother, the cord has already been broken.

Thirty-One

Absalom spends the following day at home, sitting at the table. Ursa is unused to his company, can't settle to any one task. Their trip to Vardøhus had been illuminating and horrifying in equal measure, and now she feels she can never come close to liking, let alone loving, him.

He is absolutely focused, the two letters the Lensmann has given him lying with their seals broken before him, while he brings out the census he made in kirke the first day and runs his fingers down what she knows to be the lines of names, then writes on a third piece of parchment in small, cramped writing.

'What are you working at, Absalom?'

'A list.'

He is excited: she can feel it sloughing off him, just as it had in the Lensmann's dining room, and it makes her afraid. She wishes she could escape to Maren, but doesn't want to draw his attention to their closeness, not with Diinna in her perilous state. She feels as though they are all of them balanced upon a precipice, and her husband is chipping at the stone beneath their feet.

'A list?'

'For the Lensmann. You will see.'

That night he wants her fully naked despite the sucking cold of the dark room, and when he moves into her, he places his hands beneath her shoulder blades, moves his thumb up and down their length. It feels to her as though he is fingering a wound, making her skin raw. She thinks he is trying to be gentle, but she can't make herself open enough for him, and he must push in a way that makes her lock up further.

When he is finished, he watches as she pulls the nightdress back over herself. He doesn't roll over to sleep, but takes her hand and looks up to the ceiling. She lets it settle in his vast grasp, turns her head away, feeling his stickiness coming from between her legs.

'Will you have a child soon?' His breath is still heavy. 'The ship. The chamber pot. That was one lost, was it not? Are you like your mother?'

'I hope not, husband,' says Ursa.

'I hope not, Ursula,' he repeats. 'I shall want sons, five sons. I had four brothers that lived. We were all of us the terror of our town. It was a good way to grow.'

'We couldn't keep five boys here,' she says, faintly.

'That will soon be sorted.'

She doesn't like the way he says it, as though he has a secret.

'Have there been more?' he asks.

'More?'

'Losses.'

Her cheeks grow warm. She doesn't want to speak of such things, not with him. 'No.'

'I hope you are praying for our sons.'

'Yes,' she says, though she knows she will not pray for five. She wouldn't mind one, hopes he will be no terror. If she were to bear Absalom a child, she would wish for a daughter, with Agnete's smile and nothing of him. Though the world is not

268

tender for girls, she would want someone to understand her the way Agnete did, to love her as she loved Mother.

'Pray with me now.' He rolls onto his side so they are facing each other, catches her hands in his and closes his eyes, mouthing silently. She studies the brute force of his face, made restful in prayer, repeats his *Amen*. He smiles at her. 'We will have a legacy fit to match my work here. I will write that letter for you soon,' he says. 'Is there anything you would like me to say especially?'

'I will leave it to you.'

'Good,' he says, plants a final kiss on her forehead.

They drop hands, roll to their sides of the bed, and she presses her hand to her lower belly, willing his seed out of her.

•

Ursa wakes to an empty house, a dirty cup on the table, shudders when she thinks of him watching her as she slept.

She climbs from the bed and pours water still hot from the fire into her washbowl, scrubs at herself with a rag, reaching up inside until she is as sure as she can be that she is free of him. She begins to dress, fast in the cold room, thinking to walk to Maren's, to check that Diinna has taken her words to heart, but there is a cry from outside, sounding very close by, which spurs her into action.

The cry comes again, and outside it is louder but she is less certain of its source. Someone comes running past her – Ursa can't remember her name: Edne, Ebbe? – holding her skirts clear of her legs. She is running towards Maren's house, and for a terrible moment Ursa begins to follow her. But a loud sob, imploring, comes from behind.

Fru Olufsdatter's door is wide open on its hinges and slapping at the wall. From this angle Ursa can see nothing within, but as she watches, a man she doesn't recognize, slight and tall, comes to the doorway and closes it. A semicircle of women stand about outside. She is too far off to note their expressions, but several have their hands at their mouths.

She sees other faces at other thresholds, other shapes moving between houses like animals between trees towards the sound. She wants to go back inside, makes for the door. Fear grips her at the backs of the knees, loosens her legs, and for a moment she must cling on to the latch.

The women's attention breaks from the house as she approaches. Several scatter, faces downturned, but Toril walks towards her, grips her upper arms painfully, delight plain on her thin face.

'He has acted, at last! Mistress Cornet, it is a blessed day indeed.'

Ursa shrugs her off. 'Acted? What is happening?'

'Surely he told you?' The woman doesn't even bother to hide her smile. 'Mistress Cornet, he is in there now, with Fru Olufsdatter. He is arresting her.'

Her heartbeat becomes painful. 'Arresting her? What is her crime?'

'We do not know exactly,' Sigfrid says, coming to stand beside Toril. She is paler, less triumphant, but her voice is breathless with exhilaration. 'But no doubt her crimes are numerous. Their workings are apparent once you spot them.'

Toril squeezes Sigfrid's shoulder. 'We will be safer now, my friend.'

Ursa looks to the other women. She knows none of them well – one, Gerda, comes to Wednesday meets but doesn't speak much. The others must be the kirke-women, as Kirsten named them.

The door is thrown open, and Fru Olufsdatter comes out, bound at her wrists with the thin stranger beside her, a stripe of blood upon her white apron though she looks unhurt. Absalom walks close behind, his sheaf of papers tucked to his chest. His face is grave, mouth twitching with excitement. He spots Ursa – she sees his sharp intake of breath – but doesn't speak to her, only brushes past.

'Husband,' she says. 'Absalom. Where are you taking her?'

'To Vardøhus.' He speaks not only to her but lets the words ring out. 'To the witches' hole.'

'She is no witch,' says Ursa, desperate, remembering the squalid building where the Lapps were kept. 'I have been often to her house, prayed there often—'

'I knew her for it,' says Toril, a sheen on her upper lip. She is rank with agitation; Ursa can smell it in her sweat. 'Witchcraft. Her fine house – how would she keep it so well alone, other than with help from familiars? And the poppets—'

'And the marks upon my arm,' says Sigfrid. 'Twelve small black holes, like a beast's bite marks.'

Ursa blinks at her. She sounds mad. But Absalom nods gravely at them, places a hand upon each of them as though in benediction.

'You will be called for testimony,' he says. He follows as Fru Olufsdatter is pulled away. She is weeping, bound hands scrabbling at her face. Ursa can't bring herself to go to her. Instead she rounds on Toril and Sigfrid.

'What are these marks? Show me.'

'It isn't decent,' says the woman, flushing.

'God damns a liar, Fru Jonsdatter.'

'She is no liar,' says Toril.

'Was it you who told my husband of the poppets? They were gestures of remembrance, nothing more.'

'They were poppets,' says Toril. 'We all saw them for what they were.' The other women nod. 'She got them from that Lapp. She is next, no doubt.'

Ursa runs, skirts pulled over her knees. Maren's door is open too and for a terrible moment she thinks she is too late, her husband's men already inside, but as she calls for her Maren emerges, Edne's frightened face pale within. Beside her sits Maren's mother. The relief stabs at her side like a stitch and she grasps at her ribs.

'She told you?'

'Yes.'

'You must warn Diinna. I thought she had time to make amends, I thought—'

'She's gone.' Maren says this low, so only Ursa can hear.

'Gone?'

Maren holds her finger to her lips. 'In the night. They will not catch her now.'

Ursa sways, her breath still difficult, and Maren steadies her with a hand beneath her elbow. Her words and touch are so welcome Ursa wants to catch up her hand and kiss it.

'Come inside.'

Despite their months of friendship, Ursa has never entered Maren's house. It is laid out similarly to theirs – a single room with the fire at one end, a bed at the other, and a narrower bed snug in a corner – but it is barely a quarter of the size. With the four of them inside there is hardly space to crowd around the table as they sit, knees knocking together.

'What happened?' says Maren's mother. 'We can get no sense from Edne beyond that your husband is coming.'

'They have arrested Fru Olufsdatter,' says Ursa, the words feeling unreal in her mouth. 'For witchcraft.'

Maren's mother inhales, her breath a hiss through gapped teeth. 'Does Toril know of this?'

'It was Toril who accused her.'

The woman's tongue darts out the side of her mouth, licks the sore spot. Ursa looks away.

272

'You knew this was coming,' says Maren, her hands clenching compulsively on the tabletop. 'Didn't you?'

Her mother's silence is confirmation enough, and Maren flies to her feet, knocking her chair to the floor. Ursa rises too, ready to get between them, but Maren only begins to pace the short length of the room, finger pointed in accusation at her mother. 'And you would let them take Diinna too? Leave your grandson without a mother?'

'Better no mother at all than a witch.'

The knock comes into Maren's stunned silence, and Ursa is the only one who moves when it comes again, harder this time. Absalom is there, his eyebrows rising.

'You are here, wife?' He strides inside. The remaining air is squeezed from the room. 'Where is the Lapp?'

'Next door,' says Maren's mother, standing slowly. 'I will show you, commissioner. My grandson may be upset. I will keep him safely.'

Edne follows them out, scurries back to the other houses. Maren is frozen by the door, and Ursa can hear her husband's heavy tread, his heavier knock, and the lifting of the latch.

There is a moment's silence, and then a wail, high and anguished from Maren's mother, words fading in and out of understanding.

Absalom's tread comes faster this time and he is back in the room, face furious. 'Where is she? Where has she gone?'

'She is gone?' says Maren faintly, and if she had not whispered the news to Ursa a few minutes previously, Ursa would have believed her shock. 'And Erik? My brother's child, is he there?'

The tears that come to Maren's eyes are as real as any, and Ursa can't stop herself reaching for her across the table. 'Absalom, please. This is a terrible shock for them.'

He snarls with rage. 'She can't be far. We will find her.'

He storms from the house, leaving the door wide open, and Ursa can breathe again. Maren's tears do not stop for a long while, and through the wall comes a high keening, like an animal in pain. Maren presses her hands over her ears, jaw clenched.

'Maren,' whispers Ursa. 'Let's go. Come, let's go.'

Maren lets Ursa help her to her feet, and she is barely any weight at all. Though Maren is the taller, she slumps against Ursa, drags her feet as they pass the open door where Maren's mother sits on the floor and weeps.

Ursa considers their options. They could go past the ruined house and into the wild land. But already Ursa can see small shapes upon it, more men dressed in black, looking for Diinna and her son. The sight sends a terror through her, the swarming men dark as insects on a carcass.

Though all she needs is a quiet place, a lonely place, she turns them for home, keeping her head down, Maren's hand shielding her face. As they reach it, there is the sound of raised voices, and they round the house in time to see the same group of women who watched Fru Olufsdatter be led away gasping and parting as the solid, unmistakeable figure of Kirsten shoves another black-clad stranger full to the ground.

'Kirsten!' cries Maren. She straightens, hurries forward. 'What are you doing?'

'This dritt thinks he can lay hands on me.'

'He is the commissioner's man, the Lensmann's guard!'

'He is not my husband,' says Kirsten, looming over the man, who is skidding backwards on his heels. 'And should not touch me.'

The guard gets to his feet. He is a head shorter than Kirsten, as shrunk by her rage as she is grown by it. But more strangers are coming from the direction of Vardøhus, more men than Ursa has seen since the ship. They must have been sent from elsewhere, Alta or Varanger.

And there, emerging awful as a nightmare from between two houses, her husband, approaching Kirsten with triumph glinting in his eyes. How had she ever thought him handsome? His face is brute and cunning as a wolf's.

He closes the distance, more men at his back. How long has this been planned? she thinks. How long has the noose been closing without her, who was closest to it all, guessing at it?

'A step ahead of me again, wife?' he murmurs as he passes her.

'You are not to resist,' says the thrown man, emboldened by Absalom's presence, brushing himself down. 'You are accused.'

'Who accuses me?'

'I do, Kirsten Sørensdatter,' says Toril.

'And I,' says Sigfrid.

'And me,' says a tight voice behind them. Ursa turns to see Maren's mother, face wild with tears, lift a trembling hand and outstretch her finger. 'Witch.'

Thirty-Two

Maren watches as the word ripples around the assembled women like a current. One by one they raise their fingers, hatred so bald and terrible on their faces it makes Maren's breath catch in her throat. All the kirke-women, Toril and Sigfrid and Lisbet and Magda, and even Edne, who came to warn her of Fru Olufsdatter's arrest, who sat beside her in the boat and rowed until their arms ached and grew strong.

Maren tries to catch her eye, but Edne looks about the group, to Kirsten and to Absalom. His gaze falls upon her in return, and Edne, too, raises her hand, so fast it is as if it has been pulled on a string. Kirsten stands alone in the centre of their arrowing hands, and the fight seems to flood from her sudden as blood.

'Of what am I accused?'

'You will hear your charges in court,' says Absalom. 'But they are most grave.'

Maren can't let her stand alone, starts forward, but Ursa catches her about the wrist, digs her fingernail in. 'No, please.'

No one else could have stayed her in that moment. But she is helpless at Ursa's touch, undone by the need in her voice.

She watches, betrayal thumping its drum in her chest as Kirsten is bound at the wrists and led in the direction of Vardøhus.

With the focus of their accusation removed, the women drop their hands, blink about them as though emerging from a daze. Edne is breathing hard, places her hands on her knees and retches. Toril rubs her back, satisfied.

'You did well, girl.'

Edne pulls away, straightening with the same jerky motion that made her raise her hand. 'I am no girl. I am a woman same as you.'

Edne looks around, and Maren know she is looking for her. Their eyes meet, and Maren sees the wretchedness in Edne's face. It sends cold fury thrumming through her, and her hands itch, but she dare not approach with the men still circling the village.

'Come away,' says Ursa, perhaps sensing her impulse and pulling softly on her.

Maren follows her to the second boathouse. The door closed, Ursa pulls Maren in to her, tucks her chin over her shoulder, murmurs nothings into her hair.

Both of them are trembling, and Maren lets herself be swept on the tide of Ursa's voice, lifts her hand slowly to Ursa's soft hair, coming loose from its hurried knot, the smooth rope of it like fine cloth between her coarse fingers. She breathes her in, her lips a moment away from Ursa's neck, and as her friend releases her, Maren lets them brush against her, so slight that she could have imagined it.

Ursa gives no sign of noticing as she settles Maren in a chair, begins to brew tea. Her hands shake and clatter the cups. 'You must be careful.'

'I need to speak with him.' Maren voices the thought before it is fully come.

'Who?' says Ursa, and there is a challenge in her voice, as though daring Maren to say.

'Your husband,' Maren pushes on, the idea taking hold. 'I need to tell him he is wrong.'

She rises to her feet and Ursa hurries to her, places her hand on her shoulder to force her back down. Maren lets her. 'That would be a mistake.'

'This is all a mistake.' Maren clenches her fists to stop her fingers shaking. 'It's Kirsten, Ursa.'

Ursa turns away, back to the hearth. 'You must not draw attention to yourself.' Her hands are white birds, fluttering about the pot. 'A trap is set, and I will not have you be the next to walk into it.'

'Then I should not be here,' says Maren, 'in his house.'

Ursa stays her with a look. 'You are perhaps safest here, with me.'

Maren can barely sit still. Her leg jigs beneath the table. 'What will we do for Kirsten?'

'Do you not hear me, Maren? We can do nothing for her but wait.'

'With such a chorus against her?' Maren shakes her head. 'Someone must speak for her.'

'Then it should be me, not you,' says Ursa, bringing cups to the table with shaking fingers. In her distress she has not added leaves, sits with hot water steaming before her. 'Your position is not good, Maren. Even I can see that. You should leave, perhaps, like Diinna.'

Maren looks at her sharply. 'Leave?'

'You could go to Bergen, to my household. My father could keep you safe.'

The terror of leaving Ursa comes harder than that of the arrests. 'How would it look, if I fled? I am guilty of nothing, Ursa.'

'No more than Kirsten and Fru Olufsdatter?' she snaps back. 'And see where their innocence has got them.'

There is sense in what she says, though Maren would wish it different. She would wish it all different.

'They cannot hurt them,' says Ursa. 'Not for nothing.'

'You know they can,' says Maren, her anger flaring at Ursa's suggestion of leaving. 'You are the one married to a witch-hunter.'

Ursa flinches, and Maren wishes she could draw her words back inside her mouth.

'He is as apart from me as Toril or Sigfrid or any of them,' says Ursa. 'You cannot think I knew.'

Maren slumps, ashamed. 'Of course I don't. My mother –' she winces at the sharp pain in her chest – 'oh, God, my mother.'

'She is not herself,' says Ursa. 'Even I can see that. She is taken in by Toril. Toril is the true evil at the heart of it, alongside my husband. And the Lensmann, who sent him. This was his plan all along, to make witches here in the North. He thinks the whole place corrupted.'

'I have been blind,' says Maren, sunk deep inside her own thoughts. 'I did not guess at their hatred of her.'

'Kirsten?'

Maren nods. 'Even Edne—'

'Nonsense. You warned Kirsten, but it did no good.'

'And Fru Olufsdatter,' says Maren. 'Why is she accused? She has done nothing to draw attention to herself.'

'They said she bit them.'

Maren blinks at her, astonished. '*Bit* them? Fru Olufsdatter?'

Ursa gives a shaky laugh, then seems to catch herself. 'I am sorry. It's only . . . it's absurd.' Ursa wraps her hands around her cup. 'The poppets too, and they mentioned the house, how large and well kept it is.'

'Toril always had an envy of it.'

'You think envy enough to cause this?'

Maren doesn't want to say it, though she does think it. 'She is no witch. Those things they said about her, the bite marks. It is all lies.'

'I had thought there was something between you and Fru Olufsdatter?' Ursa is watching her closely.

'Between us?'

'A bad air. A dislike.'

'I have never disliked her,' says Maren. 'She does not like me, that is true.'

'Why?'

Maren sighs. 'Her son, Dag Bjørnsson. He was my betrothed. She did not think me right for him.' She looks to the spot where the bed is now nooked beneath the broad beams, remembers Dag's hands hungry upon her. 'Did not want us to have this house.'

'This house?' Ursa looks aghast, mouth slack. 'You mean, this was to be your home?'

Maren nods.

Ursa covers her face with her hands. 'How stupid I have been. To make you work like a servant in the house you would be mistress of.'

'I thought,' says Maren, 'I was here lately as a friend.'

'You are.' Ursa reaches for her. 'The greatest friend I have ever known.'

Her touch is warm from the cup, and Maren feels as though she is ice pooling into water. Her whole body loosens, and she wants Ursa to hold her as she had when they first entered the house. But Ursa lets go a moment later, looking down at her cup.

'No leaves,' she says, letting out a brief, empty laugh. 'Why did you not tell me?'

'I didn't notice,' lies Maren. 'Besides, I'd rather beer if you have it.'

Ursa shakes her head. 'Nor akevitt.'

Maren rises suddenly, surprising even herself. 'Kirsten has some, at her house.'

Ursa gapes at her. 'You cannot think to go there. Not now.'

'Why not?' says Maren, recklessness making her light-headed. 'She is not at home, after all.'

She lets out a hiccuping laugh, and Ursa stands too, moves quickly around the table and steadies her with a hand on her shoulder. 'Maren—'

'Are you coming?' Maren shrugs her off. Her skin prickles. Her need to see Kirsten's house is urgent as thirst.

'Do you not have any at your house?'

'I'm not going back,' says Maren, with such vehemence Ursa starts. 'Not with that woman there.'

Mamma's pointed finger floats before Maren's eyes, and she rubs her hand roughly across her face, to wipe the vision away.

'The men are all over town . . .' says Ursa.

'So it would be better if I were with the commissioner's wife, surely?'

Maren leaves the second boathouse, not checking to see if Ursa is following. She knows she will. Ursa's footsteps are half a beat behind as Maren strides through the houses. Fru Olufsdatter's door gapes, and Maren can see men moving about inside.

'They are searching,' hisses Ursa. 'They may well be at Kirsten's too.'

Maren knows this is designed to stay her, but she increases her pace, her feet carrying her past Toril's house, which is lit and loud with talk. She wants to push inside and knock a lamp over, spread the embers from the fire beneath their feet, set the whole house aflame. But she hurries on, past the kirke and Sigfrid's house, past the traitor Edne's until she sees the Petersson farm with its reindeer circulating pale as spirits on the fields.

Ursa's breath is coming fast, and Maren can tell she is dropping back, unable to keep up, but she does not stop until she reaches the door set between its two windows, staring blank-faced at the sea. It is still closed up tightly, and Maren peers briefly in. Aside from the loose, foggy light of the burnt-down fire, it is dark and empty.

Ursa catches up, her breathing ragged. 'We must not go in. They will be finished with Fru Olufsdatter's home soon enough.'

'You do not have to,' says Maren, her hand upon the latch.

'What is this about?' Ursa gives a stamp of her foot in frustration. 'You can't have me believe you are so desperate for a drink?'

Maren's heart is hammering, and she realizes the walk has wrung out her breath too. The latch is ice beneath her fingers. 'I want . . .' She searches for the words, how to express the want to see Kirsten's home for herself, the thoughts coming clear even as she speaks them into being. 'I need to be sure there is nothing here. Nothing for them to find.'

Ursa's eyebrows rise. 'You think it possible?'

'I know it is impossible that Kirsten is a witch,' says Maren. She remembers the runestones in Diinna's room, the casting bones and the needle glinting against Toril's lace. 'But they may find things they do not understand, things they can use against her.'

'All right,' says Ursa, nodding slowly. 'We must be quick.'

Maren pushes inside. Ursa follows cautiously, as if stepping onto a boat. 'What are we looking for?'

Maren breaks the bank of the fire, feeds it another square of peat so it sends up a flare of light and heat. 'You will know better than I. Anything that seems out of place to you, that you do not understand.'

'Like those?' She points, and Maren follows her finger to two runestones laid beside the bed.

She crosses quickly and scoops them up. There is the mark of safety on one, smooth sea on another, and she knows that together they are a Sámi remedy for bad dreams. She closes her palms over them, wants to weep at the idea of Kirsten alone in this room, caught on the tide of a nightmare. She always seemed so solid, so strong, but she suffered as much loss as any. Did Kirsten see the whale too? Maren wonders.

'Maren?'

Ursa's voice is soft, and Maren turns to see her holding the trousers Kirsten wore to slaughter in. They are stained with rusty splatters, and by the firelight they look ghoulish. She nods. 'Take those, too.'

'What are we going to do with them?'

Maren eyes the fire. There is not enough fuel to burn the cloth entirely, and whilst it may scorch the stones it would not necessarily obscure the marks fully. She holds out her hand for them. Ursa passes them over. The cloth is soft with wear, and Maren slips the stones into the pockets.

She goes outside, Ursa following, and weights them with more stones from the ground, until the pockets are full. Then she drops them into the sea. They billow for a moment, and then plummet from sight.

'What now?' says Ursa, in a small voice.

Maren rolls her shoulders. They click like the snapping of bones. 'Now we can fetch the beer.'

•

They pass the group of men on their way back to the second boathouse. Maren keeps her head lifted, wishing the flagon of beer and bottle of clear akevitt in her hands were already inside her, giving her strength. The men's gaze feels physical upon her, and she wonders how she ever tolerated being watched in this way when their village was as full of men as it was of women.

Ursa's presence is protection, and a balm. They walk through the village swiftly. Toril's house is still bright and full of chatter, but Maren doesn't torture herself by looking inside. Fru Olufsdatter's house is quiet, and the door has been left ajar, the fire allowed to go out. Maren shivers.

Ursa stays her a few paces from the second boathouse. 'Let me check he is not at home.'

She opens the door cautiously, then gestures Maren inside. 'He must be at Vardøhus. He is like to be a while if so.'

Maren sets the drink down on the table while Ursa coaxes the fire back into full flame, and fetches two cups from the shelf Dag put above the hearth. Maren reaches for the beer, but Ursa points to the akevitt.

'I think it best.' A smile tugs at Ursa's mouth. Her lips are very pink, slightly parted so Maren can see the glint of her teeth. Wordlessly, Maren pours a slug of akevitt into each cup. She has had it only once before, at Erik and Diinna's wedding. Maren had not really enjoyed the burning in her throat, the sudden heaviness of her legs and lids, but now she craves it. She knocks it back, and Ursa, after a moment's hesitation, copies her.

Immediately, she bends over, disappearing below the line of the table, and coughs violently. Maren rises, startled, thinking to fetch a bucket, but Ursa flaps her hand above the table, her head emerging a moment later.

'I'm all right,' she splutters, rubbing her stomach. Her cheeks are flushed pink as her lips. 'That is stronger than I'm used to.' She taps the cup twice on the table, a gesture Maren has seen men make. 'Another.'

Maren laughs, and obeys. Ursa comes to sit beside her as they sip their second cup of akevitt. Maren can already feel the warmth kindling in her limbs. The room feels smaller than usual, and Maren can't stop her gaze drifting to the wall beside the fire, the wall where Dag used to press himself against her. Telling Ursa about him has brought him near again, so she can almost feel his hot breath on her neck.

Ursa is very close beside her, and Maren is not sure if the heat she feels comes from the fire, or her friend's body. She imagines leaning against her, resting her head on Ursa's shoulder. It would not be out of place, not beyond the intimacies they have already shared. But Maren is unsure whether she could rest her head so close to Ursa's, breathe in her sweet smell, feel the brush of Ursa's soft skin against her own dry forehead, and not turn her mouth towards her.

She shakes her head to loosen the thoughts, pinches the skin between thumb and forefinger with her nail. The pain brings her back into her body.

'Perhaps Kirsten will be freed soon,' says Ursa into the silence, and Maren watches her profile, silhouetted against the fire. 'Especially if they do not find anything at her house.'

'Perhaps,' says Maren, but she does not really believe it. She doesn't want to think about it, wants this moment to be a respite from the horrors of the day, the horrors yet to come. She takes another sip of akevitt, and Ursa mirrors her.

Their hands rest on the table, the distance between them so small Maren could brush her little finger against Ursa's wrist if she could only bring herself to stretch it fully out. But it is Ursa who closes the gap, taking Maren's hand easily, and squeezing.

'I will speak with Absalom,' she says decisively. 'We will get Kirsten home.'

Guilt floods Maren's cheeks. She should be thinking on Kirsten's fate, on Kirsten's return and how they can help it come about. But Ursa's hand is so smooth, so tight about hers, and the akevitt is a fire in her belly, her head floating upon her shoulders—

Without warning, the door is thrown open. The two men standing there hesitate. Ursa snatches her hand away and Maren's rests alone, beached on the dark wood.

'Sorry, Mistress Cornet. We thought the house empty.' He is looking at them both, unsure who to address. 'Commissioner Cornet ordered us to begin moving now.'

'Moving?' Ursa stands, and they turn their attention to her. Maren scoops up the bottle of akevitt and places it on the floor by her skirts, out of sight.

'Apologies, mistress. Yes. Most he wants kept, but the bed must be burnt.'

'Bed . . .' says Ursa faintly. 'What are you talking about?'

'The bed at the witch's,' says the other man. 'He wants yours brought instead.'

'You are moving next door, Ursa,' says Maren. She feels sick: her stomach churns about the liquor. 'Is she not?'

'Yes, mistress,' says the first, clearly unsure of how to address her and of who she is. She thinks he is the man Kirsten sent sprawling to the ground: his breeches are smeared with mud. 'To the stabbur. It is only right the commissioner has the finest house.'

'So that is it,' hisses Maren, and Ursa strides forward to detract from it.

'Might I speak with my husband?'

'He is at Vardøhus, Mistress Cornet.' The men are growing bored of explaining themselves, eyes flicking towards the bed, anxious to be on with their duties. 'We have our orders.'

The bed does not fit easily through the door, and they must take it through the store instead, sending the reindeer carcasses swinging. The cherrywood chest and their cases are also removed. When they are gone for the last time, leaving the door open, Ursa reaches at once for the broom, begins to sweep the mud tracked across the floor from their boots. Maren stands to take it from her, but Ursa resists.

'We are moving into Fru Olufsdatter's house. She will not be back.' Her knuckles whiten. She is sweeping the dirt in circles, breaking it apart on the boards and smearing it. 'They mean to murder her, like the Sámi men.'

Maren can't speak. She is thinking not of Fru Olufsdatter, or even Kirsten. She is imagining Diinna and Erik, already lost to the mountains and beyond. *Stay hidden*, she thinks. *Stay safe.*

'How can I live there, Maren? How can he—' Her breath hitches: she holds herself beneath her ribs, leaning on the broom.

'You must,' says Maren simply. 'It is as you say – we must be careful now.'

Ursa straightens. 'I will not spend my days there. We will come here, as before. I cannot live in Fru Olufsdatter's house.'

There is grit to her voice that gives Maren hope. 'Perhaps,' she ventures, 'I could live here?'

Ursa blinks at her, dazed. 'There is no bed.'

'I can't go to my house. I can't sleep near my mother, or in Diinna's room. And then I can be close.' The plan is growing roots. 'You could tell Absalom you will need me nearby, to help in a larger house.'

'It would be a great comfort,' says Ursa. She smooths back her hair. 'I cannot think he will deny me that.'

Even after all this, Maren thinks, Ursa believes herself to have power over him. Witch-hunter or no, Absalom is, after all, still only a man.

Thirty-Three

Though there are only two women missing, and four strange men sit at the back of the kirke, at Sabbath service their company feels entirely diminished. Toril and Sigfrid and Edne sit in the front pew alongside the Cornets, and Maren takes a seat apart from her mother. Maren has already moved to the boathouse, and the mere sight of her sets fury coursing through her blood. Mamma keeps trying to catch Maren's eye, and Maren keeps her face turned determinedly away. The absence of Kirsten stings.

Pastor Kurtsson looks a little thinner than usual. Maren wonders what he makes of the arrests. He should be as pleased as the commissioner, but something in his stance is slumped, his face frowning as he preaches righteousness and mercy.

At the end of the sermon the commissioner stands. Always a large presence, he appears gargantuan, and though she tries to summon hatred Maren feels only dread. Pastor Kurtsson keeps to the shadows.

'As you are no doubt aware, Fru Sørensdatter and Fru Olufsdatter stand accused of witchcraft. I will be compiling evidence against them. If you have suffered at their hands, or know of any malignancy relevant to their charges, come directly to my residence.'

He bows to the wooden cross and strides down the aisle, the men at the back throwing the doors open for him. Maren shrinks from him as he moves past her. Toril follows close behind with her women, and Maren looks up long enough to glare at her.

'That was not wise,' says Ursa under her breath, sliding into the pew beside her.

'Someone should accuse her,' says Maren, furious.

'You are best out of it. I will come to you, as soon as I am sure he is comfortable.'

She leaves the kirke, and Maren waits until it is empty but for Pastor Kurtsson. He starts a little when he turns from blowing out the candles and sees her still sitting in the pew.

'Maren Magnusdatter.' He says her name like it is glass, carefully.

'Pastor Kurtsson.'

They watch each other. The man's throat contracts as he swallows. Maren makes her decision and stands, approaching him down the narrow aisle. He stays quite still, and she stops a few paces from him. Maren is not sure how to begin, but it is he who speaks first.

'You have no charges to lay before our commissioner?'

Maren shakes her head. 'Have you, minister?'

'No.' His pale eyes are weary. There are hollows beneath them.

'You did not tell him of the fishing boats?' Maren can't keep the surprise from her voice.

'There is no sin in feeding yourself,' says Pastor Kurtsson. His hands are limp at his sides, his shoulders slumped.

'But you opposed it.'

'It was not proper,' he agrees. 'But I did not think it ungodly.'

'Our commissioner might, if he hears it.'

'It will not be from me.'

'Will he hear anything from you?'

Something pointed enters Pastor Kurtsson's face. 'What does that mean?'

Maren swallows. 'Will you speak for her? For Kirsten, and Fru Olufsdatter?'

Pastor Kurtsson sighs. 'I can speak only the truth, what I know of it before God. I do not see all of it as He does. He is the ultimate judge.'

'But you are His servant,' says Maren urgently. 'You must have some insight, some sway . . .'

'I know only what He shows me.'

'What has He shown you?'

Pastor Kurtsson brings his palms together, clasps his fingers about themselves. 'He saw fit to save you from the storm, to guide you through the difficult time afterwards. The mercies He bestowed upon you – I cannot think His eye is turned from you.'

Maren wants to push him full in the chest. 'You think it mercy, what has happened here?'

'To think otherwise is a sin,' says Pastor Kurtsson, moving past her. 'I am sorry for your friend. But I cannot judge her innocent. Only God can do that.'

But it is a man who took her, thinks Maren. *A woman who accused her.* Though there is no use in saying it aloud. The minister is already out of the kirke door, and she trails after him, before turning to the second boathouse.

There is a line of women snaking from Fru Olufsdatter's house, and Maren shudders each time one steps into the sun-yellow interior, as though they walk across her grave. She knows Kirsten is damned by many mouths, wonders how many others will follow as accusers, how many will be accused.

•

There is a near-month of uncertainty and silence. The winter draws in and locks about them, and Maren keeps mostly to the house, though her legs long for their walk to the headland, her lungs for air.

Now that the boathouse is hers at last, it has lost all its shine. She sleeps on the floor beneath the hide blanket she made, and enjoys the stiffness she wakes with throughout her body, a punishment she feels she must bear. She dreams of the whale and of Kirsten, her proud form bent into the witches' hole, imagines she takes Kirsten's aches into herself and helps her bear them better.

She wonders how Mamma is coping with the change in weather. She has never borne a winter alone, any more than Maren has. Is she, too, haunted by her own breath coming smoky from her lips, the chill seeping mercilessly into her bones? Maren has managed to avoid her entirely, but she is also tormented – what would Pappa think of Maren leaving Mamma to the midday dark?

Maren tells herself Mamma has new friends. Toril's standing in the village is now higher than any except the commissioner, and Mamma sits alongside the kirke-women at Sabbath. She has not come to visit Maren in the second boathouse, has stopped trying to catch her eye. They are becoming strangers, and Maren feels as though all her family are dead, and only Ursa remains.

Two years since the storm, and a new year begins. No more arrests are made, but the men settle in Kirsten's empty house, circle Vardø like bats. She had forgotten what it was like to live among men, their laughs too loud and stares just as disturbing. There are those who visit the stabbur in the day, and Maren watches them watch Ursa as she crosses the short distance between their houses, grinding her teeth at their leers.

Ursa comes as often as she is able. Absalom is keeping her

close, tethered to his side, and Ursa tells Maren she is worried of bringing attention to her by visiting too often. Despite the sapping cloud of threat that hangs over them all, Maren finds she is still lifted by her presence, still sent spiralling by her touch.

She hates herself for it, for the small pleasure she takes from Ursa without her friend realizing, for taking any pleasure in anything at all while Kirsten languishes a mere mile away in the darkness. But she can't help it. Her feelings are as relentless and powerful as the tides. Sometimes, when Ursa and Maren touch hands or catch eyes, she imagines they are matched in Ursa too. That if she were to speak to them, they would be returned. And then what? What could follow?

Maren tries to prove herself indispensable to the commissioner while keeping from his sight, using the second boathouse as a kitchen and sending stews scented with the musty herbs she discovers in jars. One looks a little like dried nightshade, used in small amounts for fevers, and she fantasizes about upending it into his dinner, his face turning puce, his breath stopped and his tongue swelling black in his throat.

It is a daydream she indulges ever more regularly when, on the first day of the year of our Lord 1620, Ursa arrives with news. Maren is sitting at the scrubbed table when Ursa pushes the door open and sits down opposite her, though she can't look Maren in the face. Maren feels a plummeting in her stomach.

'Fru Olufsdatter has confessed,' Ursa says. 'And is to be sentenced.'

'Confessed?' The word is dissonant inside Maren's head. 'To what?'

'To witchcraft. To the poppets being tools of her witchcraft.' Ursa swallows drily. 'I think they used brands. Absalom said it was hard to bring the confession from her without fire.'

'And Kirsten?' Maren's chest clenches. 'She cannot have . . .'

Ursa shakes her head, meeting her eye at last. Her gaze is so sad it strikes a tender place inside Maren. 'Kirsten would not confess.'

'So they will release her?' says Maren, though she knows it is a fool's hope.

Ursa bites her lip.

'Tell me,' says Maren.

'I wish it was not so. But she is to be ducked.'

'Ducked?' The word sounds comical to her, like a child's game. But Maren knows from Ursa's tone it is no game.

'I did not know the word either. I hoped never to relay it but . . . you must be prepared.' Ursa takes a deep, shaky breath. 'They asked her to confess her crimes, and she wouldn't. So they are to test that she is a witch and should be sentenced as one.'

A feeling of foreboding crosses Maren's neck, like the bird dark at the window before the storm. 'How?'

'They will bind her, and put her in the sea.'

'In the sea?' Maren feels her tongue slow in her mouth. 'It is freezing. She might drown!'

'It may be better if she does.'

Maren gapes at her. 'How can you say such a thing?'

'If she floats, they will say she is a witch. They say water is pure and repels the Devil, and so those who float are witches.'

Maren wants to be sick. 'Who are they? Your husband?'

'He, and the Lensmann. Pastor Kurtsson will be there too, and anyone else who would see it.'

The bile stings Maren's throat. 'It is to be public?'

Ursa nods. 'It must be witnessed.'

'Can you not stop it?' Maren knows she sounds hysterical. 'Can you do nothing?'

A sob grips Ursa's throat. 'What would you have me do? Tell me, and I will do it.'

Maren presses her hand hard against the table, to anchor herself. 'When is this happening?'

'Next week.' Ursa looks at her sharply. 'You cannot think to go?'

'I must,' says Maren. 'She cannot bear it alone.'

'Watching will do nothing,' says Ursa. 'It is better not to see, whatever the outcome.'

'How is this godly?' says Maren, eyes stinging with tears. 'How can they call their work holy?'

Ursa has no answer, and Maren must leave her alone in the house as she goes outside to heave her guts into the mud until she is hollow, full of nothing but her painfully thudding heart.

Thirty-Four

The day of the ducking, the sky is dark and low. As Maren walks to the harbour, she is aware of the stares, the mutters, feels exposed without Ursa's presence to protect her. A small group are already gathered at the joining of land and sea. Ursa is not among them.

'Absalom says it is not for a woman's eyes,' she had said.

'Does he forget it is a woman he means to push into the sea?'

Ursa's brow creased. 'Won't you stay with me? There is nothing to be gained.'

Though Maren knows it would have been best to remain behind too, she could not. Kirsten can't be alone with a group of kirke-women and men, intent on drowning or damning her. She must bear witness, too.

Seeing her resolve, Ursa had sighed and taken her hand. 'Promise me you will do nothing to draw attention to yourself. Stay silent.'

Maren heeds her words now, standing a little apart from the others, careful not to catch the commissioner's eye. Mamma is not there, nor Edne, but Sigfrid and Toril are talking with the minister, whose face is pale as milk. All are lit by meagre lamps laid along the harbour, and it is a lamp that signals Kirsten's arrival too. Maren turns to watch it coming from Vardøhus, swaying with the movement of the cart. When it draws close, Maren sees Kirsten for the first time in months. She must bite down hard on her tongue to keep from crying out.

The shape in the back of the cart is slack as a sack. Kirsten is clad only in a cotton dress, skirt dark with stains. Her eyes are shut even as guards and the commissioner haul her to her feet, wrinkling their noses. Maren can smell her friend too, the wind carrying the rust of old blood and piss towards them. Pastor Kurtsson presses a kerchief to his nose. Maren wants to call out to Kirsten, tell her she is there, but her tongue is pressed hard to the roof of her mouth, and she does not think she can stir it into speech.

Another cart follows close behind, a finer carriage, covered over. Maren recognizes it as the one that collected Ursa to take her to Vardøhus last year. The women murmur as a man steps from it, and Maren takes the measure of their Lensmann. He is short and stocky, dressed in a well-cut fur coat. His face is obscured by a beard thick as Commissioner Cornet's, but it is white as lambswool. He strides to the harbour edge, and though Maren feels a building need to flee, she moves closer to hear what he says.

'Will you confess, Fru Sørensdatter, and save us this business?'

Kirsten is trembling so hard the guards are struggling to keep her upright.

'Will you confess,' he repeats, 'that you are a witch, and did bring down the storm that murdered your husband and many others besides?'

Maren's breath catches in her throat. They cannot think that Kirsten could conjure the weather? She was on the harbour edge same as Maren, same as all of them, screaming as their men were swallowed by the sea. Maren should say so, but her tongue is still latched tight.

Kirsten's hair hangs limp about her face, and Maren wonders if his words can even reach her in her fear.

'Very well,' says the Lensmann, and there is a definite note of excitement in his voice. He nods to the guards, and they pull Kirsten's dress roughly over her head. Pastor Kurtsson averts his eyes, and Toril and the kirke-women peer through their fingers, but Maren cannot look away. The wasted mass of Kirsten's body is pitted with scratches, pressed with bruises and burns. Maren wants to wrap her in her coat, and pulls it tighter to herself.

'The rope.'

Commissioner Cornet fetches rope from the cart, and ties it about Kirsten's waist. It bites at her white and loosened skin. A lump rises in Maren's throat as she realizes this is to haul Kirsten back out, after.

She looks at the sea. It is slate grey and lifts in gently rolling waves. Ice shimmers in small patches upon the surface. Kirsten will freeze to death, and Maren will watch, and not do a thing to stop it. But her promise to Ursa is not all that stays her: Maren is afraid. Terror has her about the heart, and grips her bodily, sticking her in place.

The rope is tested, yanked twice, swaying Kirsten from side to side. She shakes, her whole body twitching, her face downcast. The commissioner takes hold of the rope, as do two more guards. Pastor Kurtsson steps forward and blesses the water. His words are too quiet for Maren to hear, but his hands are clasped tight as they were when Maren spoke to him in kirke.

He steps away, and, so suddenly that Maren could have blinked and missed it, Kirsten is pitched into the water. The small crowd surges as the commissioner and his fellow rope-holders lean back to gain purchase on the frosted ground. Maren runs, forces her way forward.

Kirsten vanishes beneath the water, which is white and churned by her impact. The cold from the waves slaps Maren's face. She is caught between hoping Kirsten will rise, and praying that she will sink as fast as did the runestones in her trouser pockets. But as Kirsten breaks the surface, her eyes wide and rolling, her breath coming fast and desperate from her chest, a keening sound shrill as the terns overhead, Maren knows she is glad Kirsten still lives, though it damns her.

She is hauled to the harbour, her naked body pale as snow. She is so thin Maren can see every one of her ribs jutting, nosing up through her skin like the tracery of roots through dirt. Maren steps towards her, but a hand, cold as the air, grips her wrist. She sees it is Edne, come after all. Edne's eyes are wide, and she shakes her head, almost imperceptibly.

Maren pulls away, looks back at Kirsten. She is being wrapped in a fur and hauled back to the cart. They do not want her to freeze to death before she stands trial. The exposed skin at her throat and wrists is white as bone.

'A witch, as accused,' says the Lensmann, reaching up to clap Commissioner Cornet on the shoulder. The commissioner is panting with the effort of pulling Kirsten up. 'A date shall be set.'

His words ring in Maren's ears like a beaten drum. It takes three men to lift the sodden figure of her friend back up into the cart, and the other watchers begin to drift away before the horses start up. But Maren comes close to the cart, as close as she dares with the guards watching, and must clasp her hands together to keep from reaching out. The horses are ordered into action, and she watches until the lamp disappears back inside the walls of Vardøhus.

Kirsten never even knew she was there. And what help would it have been? Maren's presence was useless as a shredded sail. She had thought she had seen the worst from this harbour, thought nothing could rival the viciousness of the storm. But now she knows she was foolish to believe that evil existed only out there. It was here, among them, walking on two legs, passing judgement with a human tongue.

Pastor Kurtsson is standing still beside the harbour, clutching his cloak about him. Maren remembers Kirsten striding out to him, placing her coat over his shoulders as they waited for Ursa to arrive. He removes his glove and bends to the water, holds his hand over it. He snatches it back immediately, clamps it inside his coat. As he straightens he seems to sense her watching him, and looks at her. His eyes are shining in the dark, though it may be only from the cold.

He turns his back, and she lets him go without challenge. No matter that Pastor Kurtsson believed their survival after the storm to be a miracle: now Maren thinks that the mercies of God would have been better spent drowning them all.

•

The sentencing is agreed for the approaching spring, two months hence. Ursa tells her this is because men will come from all around, other commissioners travelling to witness the sentencing of a witch. The recent trials have centred around Sámi men, but Kirsten and Fru Olufsdatter are the first Norwegian women accused in living memory, and people are coming from as far as Tromsø, perhaps even Scotland.

Maren knows of no one who has been inside Vardøhus but Ursa, and not even she has seen the courthouse. Absalom, Ursa tells her, has refused to say anything about it, though he has been at work there most days, readying himself for the trial.

'It is almost as though he thinks it a treat,' says Ursa, tone bitter with disgust. 'As though he wants to keep it a surprise.'

'It is his hour,' says Maren, kneading black dough with rough punches. 'He wishes to please you.'

She can recognize this because it is something they share, she and the commissioner. How it would hurt him to know of Ursa's disdain for him, she thinks. How delicious Maren would find it for him to notice.

The night before the sentencing Maren scarcely sleeps. Her mind can't go anywhere but to Kirsten in the hole. Does she even know that the day of her sentencing is upon her? Or have they left her so without news that the days have already lost their shape? Is she still suffering from her time in the sea? Maren imagines the chill, can't summon it. They were taught as children that in winter a leg slipped through the ice meant the end. To be thrown bodily as Kirsten had been, finding the air calling you to life, only to be plunged into death at a man's hand – it is monstrous.

She thinks, too, of Diinna and Erik, prays for them to be safe. She wishes she could hold the boy, breathe him in. Can he speak yet? Will Diinna teach him Maren's name? She is glad he is away from this place. Perhaps he will not remember it at all, will forget her. She has no memories so young. The thought is comforting, and terrible.

Ursa must go ahead with her husband to the trial, and so Maren walks unaccompanied in the crowd that pushes through Vardø's haphazard paths to the fortress. Though she has lived with these women all her life, they seem to wear masks of their own faces, made slick by excitement and fear. And as they break from the houses and the stone walls rise ahead of them, Maren sees more and more men, more strangers, all full of the same chatter. She feels herself separate from it, completely alone.

They funnel inside, kept back from the fine squarish house that must be the Lensmann's by a chain of guards wearing a uniform of deep blue, an emblem stitched onto their chests showing a crest of crowns and lions set about a cross.

'King's men.' She hears the mutter go about her. She had never thought much of having a king, felt them here in Vardø to be so far removed from Christiania and Bergen and the other places Ursa speaks of that it is as though their power did not stretch to them, that they were more at the mercy of the sea and wind than King and country. She locks eyes with one of the men and looks quickly away, feeling ignorant as a child.

The courthouse is full already when she reaches it, a mill of people outside churning at the closed door, shouting and barging. Maren stops short of the chaos, cursing her lateness. She should have come last night; she had no sleep as it was. She can't go home to wait for news, and is just looking about for a place to stand when there is a disturbance to her left as two men emerge from a squat, long building, carrying a large bundle.

'Witch!' The shout comes from a cluster of women including Sigfrid and Toril. The bundle lifts its head at the cry, and all of a sudden it is Kirsten, or rather, something like Kirsten. A shadow of her, a mockery. Her friend's face is pale, grime dark against her temples, blonde hair matted to thatch on her head. Maren doubts she has been allowed to wash, shudders as she imagines the salt of the sea still upon her skin after so many weeks.

In another moment they are drawing close, their route taking them past Maren, and as she sees Kirsten's feet go bare and dragging by her she looks up, hopes she has been seen, or not seen, and then she is following in their wake, the crowd pressing all about them, spitting and aiming kicks, those misjudged landing on Maren and the guards holding Kirsten, and always the hiss, the cry, the screech of *Witch! Witch! Witch!* The assembled masses are mostly strangers, shouting at someone they do not know, who never caused them harm. They put Maren in mind of a herd of panicked reindeer.

And then the doors of the courthouse are opening, and Kirsten is inside, and Maren is held back alongside many others, prevented from entering. She finds her breath at last, fills her lungs, cries, 'Kirsten!' and she may imagine the lift of the head, the turn of her friend's face as the doors close and Maren is pushed against the wood, lifted from her feet as those behind surge forward. Maren prays aloud that Kirsten heard her, knew her, felt that she sent her all the hope she can summon.

Thirty-Five

Absalom has made Ursa wear her yellow dress, though she protested it was surely not proper for a courthouse.

'I want you in your finest,' he says. 'The other commissioners will be there.'

He is up early and whistling, helping her with her fastenings, her skin crawling at his touch. The dress is tighter than ever at her waist though she has grown used to the hunger pangs that come constantly.

She prays she isn't pregnant: can't remember, in the disaster of the past few months, whether her bloods have come regularly or not. And her terror at the trial, at what she may witness, means her dreams are full of blood and her mother. She doesn't tell even Maren of these, knowing she has her own horrors to deal with. *Branded. Strangled. Burnt.* And these are the hands that touch her, that may have planted a child inside her.

In some ways, Kirsten's suffering has meant a lessening of her own. Absalom has been distracted by preparations, and made merry by them too. His power has made him stronger, and so he has treated her more kindly. He is happy, and wishes her to share in it. She hates herself for it, but she dissembles, tells him she is proud of him, moans into his ear when he lies upon her. She hates him, but she wants to stay in his good graces. She must protect Maren.

She wonders how Maren can stand to be near her, when Ursa herself is so close to Kirsten's tormentor. But Maren seems to cling to Ursa more than ever, and Ursa finds herself clinging back. It dizzies her, how strongly she feels for Maren. She has never loved anyone so dearly but Agnete, and it seems that their kinship is stronger even than sisterhood.

In the carriage on the way to the courthouse, she lets herself be thrown about on the potholes split wide by winter. There are already people crowded at the castle's gates. They raise bleary faces at the carriage's arrival and she sights the kirke-women at the fore, knows that Absalom has been with them often, praying with them in exchange for testimony. The crowd parts as the carriage pulls up, and she shrinks back into the shadows until the door is opened and she must step onto the slippery flagstones, careful to catch no one's eye.

Absalom guides her into the courthouse beneath the crook of her elbow, as though accompanying her to a dance. It is sparse and clean as a kirke, all angled towards the altar of the Lensmann's seat. A small square demarcated by wooden rails is set before it – this, Absalom tells her, is where the accused will stand. There are rows and rows of seats like pews, and a gallery set elevated to the back of the room where usually the women must go, but as there are mostly women, even with the additional visitors to the island, the rules will be bent this once.

She is led to a smaller gallery up and to the side of the dock, so she will see all in profile and be separate from most of the – what are they? An audience? Witnesses?

'Christin will be here shortly,' he says. 'Perhaps some of the other commissioners' wives.' He kisses her chastely on the cheek, and it feels as if she really were in kirke. 'I must prepare.'

He pauses as though for a response, but what can she say? *Good luck, go well*: these would feel false. She can say nothing that would please him, and so he goes without her blessing.

She doesn't have to wait long for Christin. She is wearing a dress of deep purple that only serves to make Ursa's dress brighter, like contrasting crocuses in a field.

'These seats are so damnably uncomfortable,' she says by way of greeting, after they have curtsied to each other and settled back down on the pew. 'I should have brought a cushion.'

Ursa is saved from making conversation by the arrival of two more women, Fru Mogensdatter and Fru Edisdatter, both older than Christin, who are the wives of Commissioner Danielsson from Kirkenes, and Commissioner Andersson from Kunes. They are introduced but neither seem interested in her. Fru Mogensdatter looks as peaky as Ursa feels, and she wonders briefly if she has found someone as appalled by this as she, but it is only from the travel.

'Why the seat of power must be on an island in the middle of nowhere, I do not know.' She shudders. 'I cannot imagine how you stand it, Christin.'

Christin waves airily. 'We were much away before this business, and intend to be after it is concluded. I never step outside Vardøhus unless I can help it. You grow used to it.'

Below them, the commissioners are assembling. Absalom stands taller than the rest. He is younger too, and Christin points him out to Fru Mogensdatter and Fru Edisdatter.

'That is Commissioner Cornet, who has brought the trial. He is something of a prodigy. I fancy my husband has found him a successor already.' The other women exchange glances, and Ursa wishes she could disappear inside the voluminous skirts of her dress.

From outside, noise builds and at ten of the clock, the doors are thrown open. Instantly women begin to pour in, the few men amongst them led to the front of the room. The crowd fills the remaining seats of the lower pews and upper gallery. They stand pressed against each other, rowdy and hullooing, calling up and down between levels. The men put their heads together and chatter like crows.

There is no sign of Maren anywhere. Perhaps she did not get in, for it sounds as though there are still many outside. Ursa can feel a headache building behind her eyes, a spasming point of pressure that opens and closes in time with her heartbeat. The dress bites into her ribs.

'Are you quite all right?' says Christin, her tone more curious than concerned. Ursa realizes she is breathing raggedly and nods, shifts in her seat.

'It is warm in here.'

'Would you like something to drink?' Christin raises her hand to gesture at the guard stationed at the entrance to their gallery but Ursa shakes her head.

'I'm fine.'

There is the sound of the doors being opened once more, and the noise from outside rushes in. Ursa thinks she hears the name 'Kirsten' shouted, and a moment later two men enter, dragging her with them.

It is worse than Ursa had guessed at. Kirsten is shrunk inside herself, filthy and broken-looking. She looks down at the ground as the hisses start, and so Ursa can't see her face, only her dirty curtain of hair and bound hands, gripping the wooden rail for support. She sways and Ursa can't help but whisper to Christin, 'Will they not give her a stool?'

Christin frowns at her, shakes her head.

'Your husband is here,' says Fru Edisdatter to Christin, and they lean forward as the Lensmann, dressed in long black robes, strides along the centre of the aisle, trailed by a slight man with a thick book beneath his arm. The crowd falls silent as he ascends to his seat, looks about him. He nods to their gallery and Ursa bites her tongue as Christin gives him a small wave. He checks that the court clerk is ready, and Ursa fixes her eyes on Kirsten as Lensmann Cunningham addresses the court.

'I, Lensmann Cunningham, as appointed by our King Christian the Fourth as Lensmann over Vardøhus County and Finnmark, sit in judgement over this court. We are gathered on the twenty-ninth of March sixteen-twenty, in the presence of God and the commissioners of Finnmark, to pass sentence in the case of Fru Kirsten Sørensdatter of Vardø—'

Several people hiss and tut at Kirsten's name, and a ringing starts in Ursa's ears as Lensmann Cunningham continues.

'—for charges brought against her from a period of near three years, with particular notice to the twenty-fourth of December, sixteen-seventeen, and diverse other days and times as well before and after. These certain detestable acts fall beneath the King's Decree against witchcraft and sorcery, enacted in our district on the fifth of January, sixteen-twenty. Commissioner Cornet arrested Fru Sørensdatter on the eighteenth of October of last year.

'She was told she would be spared interrogation if she confessed at once, but pleaded innocence and was ducked on the eighth of January of this year. She has since confessed to several acts of witchcraft. Commissioner Cornet, if you would please rise and read the confession.'

Someone is making low, soft, animal sounds of distress, and Ursa looks to the other gallery before she realizes it is she herself. She searches again for Maren, can't find her.

Her husband stands, back straight, and in his clear, low voice, he reads the charges in his accented Norwegian.

'Fru Kirsten Sørensdatter did confess, on the ninth of

January of this year, her guilt in charges brought against her. She is denounced by Pastor Nils Kurtsson, Toril Knudsdatter, Magda Farrsdatter, Gerda Folnsdatter, Sigfrid Jonsdatter, Edne Gunnsdatter.'

He takes a breath, reads more names, intoning that of nearly every woman of Vardø. She hears Maren's mother's name, even Fru Olufsdatter's, and wonders whether her neighbour has saved herself with this denouncement. Finally the names are at an end, and Absalom takes up a new piece of parchment.

'She confesses that Satan did come to her when she was twenty-two and at work tending a calf, and she did ask him who he was and was told he was the Devil. He did offer her his hand to kiss and said upon it that she would be given power over air and the strength of a man if she forswore God and her baptismal pact. And she did take his hand and kissed it and felt very happy after it. She blew breath on the calf and it did die.'

The story goes on, a litany of such absurdity that Ursa feels herself almost floating above it. It reads like a list of women's gossip, from arguments over fish-drying racks to saying the Lord's Prayer backwards. But the crowd leans forward as one to the swaying woman in the dock, voices held in check only by the Lensmann's admonishments. On more than one occasion Ursa sees someone reach through the rails and pinch her, but Kirsten barely reacts. It is as if she is asleep, her eyes half closed, mouth slack. What more have they done to her, to reduce her so?

Absalom places the first parchment down, picks up another. 'And she confesses that she did, on Christmas Eve sixteen-seventeen, fly to the witches' mountain of Ballvollen and there knot a cloth with five others, and set the storm that drowned forty men, her own husband among them—'

The hissing grows to a sudden cry of rage that echoes about the room, and though the Lensmann shouts for order he must send his guards forward and about the dock to keep Kirsten from being kicked and her hair pulled at. Ursa covers her face with her hands. Christin pats her lap. 'Mark her, Ursula. She is smiling.'

But Ursa sees only a grimace upon Kirsten's face.

'The names!' someone shouts from the gallery. 'Give us their names!'

The Lensmann stands, raises his arms. 'I will have the court emptied!'

A begrudging silence falls. Absalom says, 'If I may speak on the names, Lensmann.' He turns back to the courtroom. 'We asked for the names and she says she couldn't see their faces, that they were shrouded in smoke. But we have established Fru Olufsdatter as one, and have her confession, and are working at her on the rest.' He looks meaningfully out at the crowd, and Ursa shudders as he raises the parchment again. 'And they did raise the storm so they might have property and dominion over their husbands' land.

'And she did steal Mads Petersson's herd which numbered fifty reindeer, and Fru Gunnsdatter was bewitched to row with her and eight others, where they did not lay nets but Fru Sørensdatter called the fish up with her breath. And she did wear trousers and so possessed the strength of a man, and sent terrors to Fru Knudsdatter and did blow upon Fru Jonsdatter and she fell sick with a wasting disease that swelled her belly.'

Ursa looks at the kirke-women. Their faces are rapt, as though her husband were a miracle, awful and beautiful.

Absalom rolls the parchment up. 'Such are the charges confessed to, amongst other sundry acts as are characteristic of a witch. She lay her mark upon them as an "X", and I submit it to the court.'

He places it before the Lensmann with a short bow, and goes grandly back to his seat. There is scattered applause amongst the commissioners, which ripples through the room.

'He has done well,' says Christin. 'You should be proud.'

Ursa gives a tight nod as the Lensmann leans forward in his seat, looks directly to the dock.

'Have you anything to say, Fru Sørensdatter?'

Nothing. One of the guards shoves her, the crowd jeers.

'Have you anything to say?'

The guard moves close to her, wrinkling his nose as he listens.

'"Nobody," she says, Lensmann Cunningham.'

'"Nobody"?'

'She says, "Nobody."'

'Very well then,' says Lensmann Cunningham, sitting back again to address them all. 'Fru Sørensdatter, you have been accused of the grievous crime of malevolent witchcraft and sorcery, and upon receipt of your writ confession I am to follow the rule of the King's Decree that, "If any sorcerer had the sacrifice of God and His holy Word and Christianity, and devoted himself to the Devil, he should be cast down on fire and incineration."'

'She will burn,' says Christin.

The crowd's voice lifts as one, and this time the Lensmann doesn't quiet them, only raises his voice as he sets the date, two days hence. The men take hold of Kirsten, and as they do she at last stirs and lifts her arms.

'May God have mercy upon my soul.' As her unbuttoned sleeves fly back, Ursa sees it isn't dirt patterning her arms, but bruises upon bruises, purple and yellow as Christin's and her skirts, petals pressed into her wasted skin.

•

Ursa excuses herself from the Lensmann's lunch though she knows Absalom will be displeased. She claims a headache, but really it is her whole body that hurts. She changes in Fru

310

Olufsdatter's house, as she can't help but think of it, from her yellow dress into a plainer, looser one, and crosses to the second boathouse. She knocks and, having no answer, lets herself inside Maren's house to wait.

She feels calmer already in that room, amongst Maren's meagre possessions, the noise of the courthouse far away. Now that she no longer lives there it feels more like home than ever. She practises what she will tell Maren, for she is sure she was not inside the courthouse, but when the door opens and Maren enters, the set of her starkly pale face tells her that she already knows what has come to pass.

Ursa reaches out for her, but Maren flinches away.

'Edne told me. They say she caused the storm,' Maren says. 'And she confessed it.'

'She had been beaten, ducked,' says Ursa. 'She would have confessed to anything.'

'Not that,' says Maren, her voice flat. 'Surely not that. You did not see it, Ursa. So sudden, like a hand scooping up the boats, crushing them.' She closes her eyes. 'She would not have confessed to that were it false.'

Ursa does not correct her, does not tell her of the bruises on Kirsten's arms.

'And it is true what they said of the trousers and the fishing,' says Maren. 'She alone among us seemed not to grieve.'

'You cannot believe her a witch,' says Ursa harshly. 'You are not so stupid.'

'You did not see it,' says Maren. 'The storm. It was fast as a breath. And we caught fish easy as that.'

'You had nets, though?' Maren nods and Ursa snaps her hand to the table. 'There, see? They have lied. Edne and Toril, all of them lied. And no one defended her.'

'And you think I should have spoken against it?' Maren doesn't shout, but the ice in her voice makes Ursa flinch.

311

'I did not mean that—'

'You told me not to go to him. You told me not to speak with Cornet, that you would do it, and see what has happened.'

'Maren.' Ursa has lost her words. She feels winded.

'I would wish to be left alone, if I might, mistress.'

'Maren, what are you doing?' Ursa wants to shake her, but can't bring herself to touch her.

'I'll go then,' says Maren, moving to stand.

'No,' says Ursa. 'I'll leave.' She pauses at the door. 'I will go to watch Kirsten's burning, the day after next.' She had decided it as soon as sentence was passed, though no part of her wants to. 'It will be hard, but she will need a friend's face. I hope you will come with me, Maren.'

Maren sits impassive as stone.

'"Nobody",' says Ursa, at last understanding. 'When they asked her for more names, that is how she answered. She wouldn't take another down with her. She is a good woman, and she loves you.'

Maren looks down at her knotted hands.

•

Ursa doesn't go to Fru Olufsdatter's sentencing the next day. She holds her hand to her head and moans softly, so Absalom will insist she rests. He speaks to her more than ever that morning as he dresses. He is happy, and she wishes he were dead. It is a marvel he can't feel the hatred coming from her, like heat as she feels it upon her own skin.

Ursa's anguish keeps her to bed all day, but the exultant, feverish sounds of women returning mid-afternoon tell her that Kirsten will not be sent to the stake alone.

Thirty-Six

Absalom leaves early and Ursa refuses the carriage, claims she needs the fresh air after her day in bed. He presses his hand to her forehead, and she knows he will find her warm – the nerves have set her sweating.

'I hope you are not sickening, wife. Or perhaps . . .' His eyes flick down to her belly. 'I have heard a baby can quicken the blood.'

She pushes his hand away, but gently, forces herself to smile. 'Perhaps, husband.'

He kisses her atop the head as he did the day they married. 'Captain Leifsson arrived on the *Petrsbolli* yesterday. Perhaps we will be able to send happy news to your father when he leaves.'

'Captain Leifsson?' Ursa tries not to let her relief show. 'He is here?'

'Staying at Vardøhus. Did I not tell you of it?'

She shakes her head. The last she heard of his possible arrival was in Father's letter that Absalom read to her. Her thoughts of it had gone up in smoke with that and the other letters. 'The trials knocked it clean from my mind.'

He rubs his beard, blows out air fast through his lips. She

has not seen him nervous before, and it makes her more fearful too. 'I should go,' he says. 'Be sure to stand upwind.'

He dons his hat, and strides out.

She dresses in her yellow again. This time she wants to be seen, wants Kirsten to notice her and know she isn't to go to death without a friend.

She walks to the second boathouse and knocks gently. For a long moment there is no answer, but then Maren is stepping from it, her face blotchy. They do not embrace but Maren slips her arm through Ursa's, and they clamp tight together so their hips bump and Ursa's fingers ache from gripping her.

The executions are to take place on the scrubby patch of grass behind Vardøhus, where they will be shielded from the worst of the wind and where the most people can gather. The crowd is already massive, swelled with visitors. News of the details of Kirsten's confession has spread across Kiberg and Kirkenes, who also lost men and boats, though not so many. Their faces are intent upon the brow of the small hill, but they part when they see Ursa in her yellow dress.

A wooden stake, higher than a man, has been erected at the top of the rise, logs and coarse brushes of shrub placed about its base. The sight of it makes Maren falter, and though Ursa feels a twin twinge of hesitation she pulls her onward until they are almost directly before it, right up against the line of guards marking a boundary about twenty paces short. Past this line are Pastor Kurtsson and the commissioners, her husband fore amongst them, speaking with the Lensmann. The *Petrsbolli* bobs in a calm sea beyond, but Ursa can't see Captain Leifsson in the assembled crowd. Absalom notices her, gives her a brief smile.

Ursa feels outside her body, watching from a great height as the noise of the crowd, dissipated by the wind, laps at her ears. Only Maren is real, solid, an anchor against the unreality of the scene.

314

She considers the stake, hewn from a single trunk, its bark stripped so the pulp stands pale and shining as moonlight. What sort of tree had it been? Was it cut exact for this purpose, brought on her father's ship? Her skin prickles. It must have been sent for months ago. Is that why the *Petrsbolli* came?

She closes her eyes against the horror of the thought, and only opens them when Maren murmurs, 'They are coming.'

An open cart is pulled the short distance from the castle, Fru Olufsdatter and Kirsten bound back to back. A torch burns in the guard's hand, the spark that will start the pyre. Kirsten is facing their direction and Ursa sees that her hair has been combed and her face washed, and she is wearing – there is a clench in Ursa's chest – Ursa's grey wool skirt. It shows her pale bruised ankles and feet. She wears no shoes.

As they come through the crowd, pails of stinking liquid are hurled at them, and there is spitting and shouting, but the sounds are no longer laced with excitement as they were before the sentencing. It is anger, pure and fierce, that hounds them to the stake. The crowd jostles Ursa and Maren, but they stay locked together as the women pass the line of guards and are removed from the cart.

They are lifted onto the narrow platform. Fru Olufsdatter is limp and must be held in place as the rope is tied about their waists. She hangs almost in half against it, but Kirsten is straight-legged. She looks out to the crowd as more wood and kindling are brought to close the gap left for them to reach the platform. Ursa sees some of her old defiance, and stifles a sob.

Maren's fingers dig into her hand, and she is biting her lip so hard the skin is broken and bleeding. Kirsten sees them, and though they make no gesture at each other, her face loosens a little, and she looks up to the sky.

'It is right we came,' whispers Maren, more to herself. 'It is right we came.'

She keeps up the whisper as the torch is brought from the cart. They aren't asked last words, nor prayed over by Father Kurtsson. The torch doesn't blow out in damnation of the event. It is simply lowered to the base of the stake and Ursa can see the bright snake of it slither through the kindling, gathering at the base of the larger logs, striking up and into a full flame.

It spreads in a circle about the women's feet, as though in a dance, and Kirsten begins to shift and roll her head as the smoke starts to wash up and over them in waves, snatched at by the wind. Ursa can't look away now, and the crowd is almost silent about her. Fru Olufsdatter has not moved from her position slumped over the rope, and even as her hair brushes the flames and begins to catch, she doesn't stir. Ursa prays she is unconscious, perhaps dead already, her lungs thick with smoke.

Kirsten, though, seems to be wakened more and more. Her lips are parted and she may be moaning, her words swallowed up by the wind and the guzzling spit of the fire. Flames are licking the platform, and she lifts one foot, then another.

'Breathe deep!'

The call comes from behind them, a solitary woman's voice that Ursa can't place but that is loud enough for Kirsten to hear. She jerks her head towards the sound, her eyes wide and terrified.

'Breathe deep!' it says again, and this time Ursa follows the thread back into a crowd of kirke-women. It cannot be Sigfrid, who only two days previously sat baying as Kirsten was accused of cursing her? But Ursa sees Sigfrid call again, tears on her cheeks, and Toril cries out too. The phrase is repeated, thrown up about them in a growing chant of many voices. Ursa remembers herself telling Agnete the same thing, leaning over the vapours bowl. But that was to clear her lungs. This is so Kirsten will cloud hers with smoke, choke herself before the flames scorch her to death. Ursa joins in. All of them are shouting it, calling it to her, accusers and friends alike.

They see Kirsten's chest begin to heave, the smoke swirling about her head, tears and sweat pouring down her face. She is speaking words they can't hear and Ursa feels choked, as though her own lungs are filling with hot, acrid smoke, and Maren's nail breaks through her skin as Kirsten gives out a strangled cry and breathes and breathes and breathes.

A smell is coming on the wind now, meat and wood and hair, all of it burning, and at last Kirsten falls forward on her ropes and is still. Birds are swirling the air above the stake and there is a release amongst the crowd, a collective swell forwards. Maren loosens her grip then, and Ursa stumbles without her support, has already lost her in the melee when she turns to follow her. She pushes back against the tide, those further back struggling to see the flame-engulfed stake, until at last she breaks from it and is free, and can just spot Maren's narrow body hurrying away.

Thirty-Seven

No one follows them. Ursa falls further and further behind, her dress slipping beneath her shoes, Maren quick-footed and disappearing into the scattering of Vardø's houses.

Instinct tells Ursa to keep going, past the stabbur, past the second boathouse and the strewn remains of the ruined house, to the headland. Ahead there is the cliff and at its edge is Maren. She is bent double and screaming, neck stringy with veins. As Ursa reaches her she retches, spits up thin whitish liquid that is carried away to the sea below, screams again.

Ursa stands next to her, takes her hand to draw her back a pace. She opens her mouth wide and screams too, their voices seized and spun away by the same wind that fed the flames, that climbed high the smoke, taking Kirsten's last words from them.

At last, Maren stops. She sways on her feet, and Ursa pulls her clear of the cliff edge.

'Come away, Maren.'

She allows Ursa to lead her. The village is still empty as a burial yard, and a column of blackish smoke is being swirled about ahead like a flock of storm-thrown birds. Ursa takes her to the second boathouse though it is warmer in the stabbur.

She puts Maren in a chair and breaks the crust of the fire, stokes and feeds it. The heat is harsh on her cold cheek and Ursa shrinks from it. Maren is leaning slightly, barely upright, and so Ursa returns to the stabbur, brings all the blankets she can carry and dumps them on the floor where the bed used to be. From her pocket she takes her last aniseed, holds it out to Maren.

'Come, Maren. Come and lie down.'

Maren's teeth chatter. Ursa comes close to her.

'I smell of her,' whispers Maren. 'She's upon me.'

Out of the wind it is true: they both of them are thick with the smell of smoke and its nauseating edge of sweetness. Ursa can smell it on Maren's hair, on her own skin, greasy as oil.

'Stay here then,' says Ursa, and Maren snatches at her hand. 'Have this.' She gives her the aniseed, places it between her lips like a child taking medicine. 'I'll not be long.'

The washing tub is wooden and heavy, and she leaves long draglines in the gap between their homes. She must do four trips to the well before she has enough water to fill it. Each time she circles back to the second boathouse, Maren has not moved but watches her like something haunted as she sets the pots to boil. Before long the tub is half full of steaming water. In the stabbur she opens her cherrywood chest, removes the lilac water. The bottle is so small and delicate, she worries it will break as she removes the stopper and upends it into the tub.

'Quick then, before it cools.' Her voice grates her throat.

Maren crosses her hands at her lap. 'I cannot.'

'You are not shy of me?' Ursa gives her a gentle smile. 'I have a sister.'

'I am not your sister,' says Maren, sharply.

'I love you as one,' says Ursa, coming close to her and settling her palms upon her shoulders. There is something in Maren's face, a deepening pain, and as Ursa rubs her thumbs along her upper arms she flinches.

Ursa sighs. 'I can go.'

'No,' says Maren. 'Only maybe look away.'

Ursa turns and hears cloth rustling as Maren undresses, her movements quick shadows in her periphery, and then the gentle sound of a body sinking into water.

'All right,' says Maren, and Ursa turns. Her body is curved into itself, knees drawn up, and she has loosened her dark hair so it falls to her waist and covers the nubs of her spine.

'Here,' says Ursa, passing her the tallow soap, and Maren reaches out to take it. 'I can, if you would like.'

Maren nods and Ursa moves aside her hair, begins to soap the narrow stretch of her back, up to her nape. Maren lets out a long breath and her head tips forwards, shoulders dropping. Ursa smells aniseed as she works the soap into Maren's hair and rinses with pails of water until the scent of burning is faded to nothing, masked beneath old lilacs.

'Here,' she says, standing and holding out the soap. Maren's head is still tipped forwards, her hair in long wet strings clinging to her slender body. Her ribcage presses out, clenches in, and Ursa wants suddenly to rest her palm against it, to feel her breath.

'Maren?'

With infinite slowness, Maren looks up. There is something in her face Ursa hasn't seen before, or perhaps only not noticed. A hunger. Ursa's hand is still outstretched, holding the soap, and Maren uncrosses her arms, reaches as if to take it.

But instead, she takes Ursa's wrist in a gentle hold, so light it is almost not there, brings her lips to it, and kisses it. She looks up at Ursa, who can't move, can barely breathe. Maren shifts in the tub, kneels up.

Her body is like nothing Ursa has ever seen, thin and knotted with muscle at her arms and legs, her hipbones sharp against her skin, the hair between her legs and beneath her armpits dark, her breasts small and shining with water. Ursa feels a stab of something low in her belly. Her breath hitches. The want in Maren's face is so naked Ursa knows she cannot deny her. Is this what Ursa has felt, in these past months as they have grown so close? Ursa has not named it, is not even certain she can, but then Maren takes both Ursa's hands, and kisses each wrist with small, light touches. The soap slides from her grip.

Ursa feels caught, at the wrists and at the legs and chest, as Maren lowers her face again and again, and at last lets it rest in Ursa's palms. The gesture sends a tremor through her whole body. She pulls her hands away, holds them to her. Maren stays kneeling, head bowed, as though in prayer. Her thin shoulders are heaving, and despite her height she looks slight as a child.

'Don't be frightened,' she says suddenly, though Ursa thinks it is Maren who looks the more afraid. 'I did not mean to frighten you.'

Their eyes meet, and Ursa reaches out. She lets her hand rest, not upon Maren's skin, but over it, hovering just at the place where her neck and shoulder meet. She can feel the heat from her. Maren tilts her head and guides Ursa's hand up, to cup her cheek. Ursa moves closer, skirts tightening about her knees. She strokes Maren's face, up and down, and Maren brings her own hand up to Ursa's cheek, to match her movement. Ursa turns her head, and takes Maren's thumb in her mouth.

Maren's whole body shudders in answer, and Ursa feels something white hot pass between them as Maren stands and steps from the bath. She helps Ursa to her feet and moves into the circle of her arms, guiding her until Ursa can feel the hard edge of the table at her back.

Maren lifts Ursa's head so their noses touch. Ursa can smell aniseed from her breath, and tallow and lilac from her skin, and something that is only Maren. Her gasp comes sudden, urgent, and she slips her leg between Maren's, presses her hips forward, skirts rustling. Maren brings her own forwards to meet her.

Ursa plucks at her fastenings and Maren steps back. Ursa feels cold air rush at her body where Maren should be, undoes them with trembling fingers. She barely lets her dress drop before they are pushing their bodies together again, only her thin underthings between them now.

They kiss, and though Maren's lips are rough Ursa feels it is the only good and tender thing that she has known for months. The desire in Maren's touch is enough to bring her own rising to meet it, and Ursa slides her hand down to Maren's lower back, to pull her against her more strongly. Maren trembles and Ursa breaks away, her mouth wide and panting, brings her to the blankets, clumsy in her haste, pulling her atop so their bodies can fit more cleanly together.

Maren slides her hand down past the curve of Ursa's waist, the paleness of her belly, and to the light hair between her legs.

Ursa grows very still, suddenly uncertain. Maren begins to pull her fingers away, but Ursa grasps them and says, 'No. Only, slow. Gentle.'

She does not send her mind flying away. She is only her body, and Maren's hand upon her, and in her, and she could weep with the kindness of it, the ache of it. She did not know, she thinks: she did not know it could be like this.

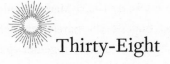

Thirty-Eight

By night-time the haze of Ursa's touch has lifted, and the smell of Kirsten is carried all about her on the air, and Maren can't sleep. The windows of the stabbur are lit, and she wonders if Commissioner Cornet is home again, and the thought of him with Ursa makes Maren press the heels of her hands to her eyes until she sees dots of dancing light.

She starts her usual route to the headland. The nights will soon shrink again, and it will turn warmer, and everything that seemed dead will grow, but Kirsten will still be murdered. She keeps her eyes turned hard from the rise where the stake smokes and glows in the darkness.

But Ursa . . . she can hardly trust it happened. Their lips, finally touching, the moan in Maren's throat returned. Ursa's skin soft as she'd imagined, like the velvety inside of a flower. If not for the throb of want between her legs, Ursa's yellow dress on her floor, she wouldn't believe it.

The villagers are returned and the houses are full of sound. She thinks of Kirsten's home full of guards, and all the reindeer braying in the dark. She had been afraid when she heard her friend's confession, and for a moment wondered at

Kirsten's guilt. That moment of betrayal is a pain she can't yet access, and she feels adrift inside it.

As she passes her mother's house she sees a shape backlit on the porch, the door open.

'Mamma?'

The figure jumps – she had been dozing. Maren moves closer. Her mother is propped against the door frame. The fire is high behind her, and there is an empty bottle of Pappa's akevitt beside her.

'You should not have drunk that. It is years past.'

'We were to drink it at your wedding,' Mamma says, and her voice is low and thick. She lifts her head to Maren and it is obvious she has been crying.

Maren feels a pointed twist of spite. 'You should go to bed, Mamma.' She turns to leave her but her mother lets out a wail.

'Maren. Erik is gone.'

'Yes, Mamma. And if you had not spoken against Diinna perhaps she wouldn't have had to go.'

'No,' says her mother. 'Erik is dead. And your Pappa. And . . .' she breaks off, hand rising to her head. 'And you will be too.'

Maren's breath catches. 'You are drunk.'

'It is true, my girl.' A fresh bout of sobs shakes her. 'Your name . . . it has been mentioned.'

Their house is a ship in the pitching night: the floorboards roll beneath Maren's feet. *The whale*, she thinks. *The whale has come.* It is arching its great back beneath their floor, waiting to break through and swallow her down.

'Kirsten?' says Maren, her voice a whisper. 'Did Kirsten mention me?'

Mamma shakes her head. 'Fru Olufsdatter. Toril says she named you, and Edne. Just before she went to the stake. She says you went with Kirsten to the mountain.'

'What mountain?'

'The low mountain. The witches' mountain.'

'The low mountain,' hisses Maren. 'The mountain Erik would fetch heather from, that you and Pappa walked upon. You think it a witches' hill?'

'No. Yes,' Mamma's words trip out of her mouth, snot runs from her nose. 'Kirsten confessed. Fru Olufsdatter confessed.'

'Do you think me a witch, Mamma?' Maren feels oddly calm. 'Do you think I drowned Erik, and Pappa, and all those poor men?'

Mamma howls, a sound so raw it tears Maren's own throat. 'I do not. We did not know. We did not know, and now see what we have done.' Her voice is muffled as she lowers her head to her hands. 'The way she burnt, Maren. The way her flesh melted. The smell. Oh, God.' She wraps her arms about herself, begins to rock. 'Oh, God have mercy on us. We have begun it, and cannot end it.'

Maren has heard enough. She breaks into a run, Mamma calling to her. 'Maren, my girl, my love. I'm sorry!'

Maren will not wait for them to come for her. She has the money saved from her time working in the second boathouse, can take a boat as Diinna did, find her perhaps in the mountains, or else go to one of the cities she has heard of, where there are so many people you can lose yourself entirely.

But Ursa. How can she leave her, after their time together? She could not ask Ursa to come with her. Maren's breath comes hard through her body, her thoughts chasing her back to the second boathouse, and she hurries inside, closing the door firmly behind.

'Maren,' says Ursa's voice.

She is sitting at the table in a thin cotton nightdress, and beside the fire stands Absalom Cornet, Ursa's yellow dress clenched in his fist.

Thirty-Nine

Maren has walked straight into Absalom's trap, just as Ursa had.

He returned late from Vardøhus smelling of akevitt and meaty smoke, and his hands upon Ursa's skin while the memory of Maren's touch was still bedded into her was too much to bear. She pushed him away and for a moment he watched her in the gloom of their stolen room, so still she hardly dared breathe.

'Why do you not wish to lie with me, Ursula?' She can give him no answer that could keep her safe.

'Do you love me?' He is drunker even than he smells. He sways on his heels.

'Yes.'

He kneels, leans forward until he is in her lap. She lifts her hands away from his head, so she does not have to feel his skin on hers. His broad back rises and falls, and she prays for him to sleep and remember nothing of this. But instead he hauls himself upright, smoothing his stinking tunic.

'I have business I must attend to, and upon my return I expect to find you in a better state of mind.'

She listens, heart thrumming, as he leaves the house. But his steps do not disappear into the distance. Instead, she hears his heavy tread upon the boards of the boathouse, Maren's house. She runs to the window in time to see him open the door, and vanish inside.

He can't know of them. It is impossible, but still a panic sends her flying from the house in her shift, following after him through the unlatched door. Maren isn't there, but her husband stands by the table, staring at the fire.

'What are you doing, Absalom?'

'What are *you* doing, wife?' He turns, looks her up and down. 'You are not decent.'

Ursa clutches her hands to herself. 'Forgive me, but why are you here? Will you not come back to the house with me?'

'I have business here.'

Fear grows hot inside her. 'You are drunk.'

'I am not so drunk.' His voice slurs. 'If you had come with me to dine, you would know it.'

'I am sorry I did not come. Please, let's go to bed.'

She holds out her hands to him, but he does not move.

'I have come to arrest your friend, Ursula. I know you are fond of her, and wished to spare you the embarrassment.'

'Maren?' The room spins as though it were she who is full of spirits. 'She is accused?'

'By the witch Olufsdatter herself. Her last confession. But tell me, wife. Why is your wedding dress on the floor?'

'I had brought it for Maren to clean,' says Ursa. Her hand begins to tremble and she snatches it behind herself. 'See, the tub is set ready.'

His eyes trail to the tub, still half full of grey water. The smell of lilacs is gone, overwhelmed by the ghastly smoke on his clothes. 'Why did you follow me here, wife?'

'Should a wife not follow her husband when he goes at night to another woman's house?'

'Am I to think you jealous of me?' Absalom's teeth glint

327

in the low firelight. 'Because I never have before, and I do not now.'

'Can the arrest not wait, husband? Come to bed.'

'Sit down, Ursula. I want the truth of this.'

'I have told you the truth.'

'Sit.' He picks up the soiled dress. 'Now.'

They don't have to wait long, though to Ursa the minutes seem endless. She prays wordlessly that Maren will not return. Her husband watches her, and the door. Maren sweeps inside, and though Ursa tries to warn her, it is too late.

'Hello, Fru Magnusdatter,' says Absalom smoothly. 'Be seated, please.'

Maren doesn't move. 'Commissioner Cornet—'

He crosses the room in three long strides and pulls back a chair. Maren's knees seem to give way. Ursa can feel Maren looking at her but she dare not return her gaze. Absalom stares down at Maren, as though she is in a dock. She looks small set against him, a wavering candle against a swallowing dark.

'Why is my wife's dress upon your floor, Fru Magnusdatter?'

'I was cleaning it, commissioner.'

'Then why is it upon the floor, and but a little wet?'

'It must have fallen from the chair. I was working upon other laundry.'

'Where is the laundry?'

Maren hesitates and suddenly Absalom's wide hands reach down, and are about her throat.

Ursa jumps up, her chair overbalancing and crashing to the floor. 'Absalom, no!'

'You have bewitched my wife, have you not?' Spit flies from his mouth, and his eyes glitter wildly. Maren is making small crushed noises, like a dying bird. He lifts her from the chair and drags her away from Ursa. 'Tell me!'

'Absalom, she cannot speak!'

Maren's face is turning puce, and her feet are flailing for purchase on the floorboards. Ursa feels as though she moves through mud, slow and useless as she tears at his fingers. Absalom drops Maren roughly to the floor, knocks Ursa with a hard slap to her cheek that sets her head ringing.

'Answer me,' he says, finger pointed to Maren's heaving body. 'Answer me.'

Before Maren can so much as catch her breath Absalom is upon her again. This time he drags her to the tub, and through watering eyes Ursa sees him bend Maren bodily over the water and plunge her in face first. Her legs kick out, and Ursa crawls to them, again tries to break his grip but he is holding grimly, silent now, watching the churning bubbles.

'You will kill her!'

Ursa's mind is full of water. She reaches for her fallen chair, brings it crashing down on his back, but it strikes only a glancing blow before breaking to pieces. Absalom roars and Ursa thinks of going outside and screaming, bringing her neighbours running. But what neighbours are they? None that would take her part over her husband's.

'Please, Absalom,' she cries, pulling at his shoulder with all her strength. 'You cannot kill her.'

He slackens his grip and knocks Ursa back again, sending her head against the shelf beside the fire. Maren comes up, coughing and retching, and Absalom turns to Ursa where she crouches, mind spinning with the impact.

'Ursula,' he says, back on his heels, panting. His voice is bewildered. 'Are you all right?'

She looks up at him, incredulous, her eyes swimming. He reaches out to her; there is tenderness writ over his face, and confusion. She flinches away, grasps for Maren where she lies bucking on the floor, but Absalom stays her with a practised hand on her wrist, and she is forced to look up at him.

Something calm and black settles on his face, and it is exactly the look that comes over him when he pins Ursa to the bed, pushes his way inside. He grabs Maren by the hair, twisting his fingers until she moans, water mottling her breath.

'Do you confess?' says Absalom. 'That you have bewitched my wife, that you brought the storm with Kirsten Sørensdatter?'

'No,' gasps Maren. 'No.'

This time when he dunks her beneath the grey water, Ursa knows all is lost. Her hand reaches for the shelf, closes upon something smooth and cool. She brings it up, arm shaking with the effort, and then lets its weight fall full down upon his head.

The rolling pin smacks at the centre of his skull. It sounds like a bird's egg, cracking, and he lets Maren loose, sways upon his knees. Ursa is dimly aware of Maren scrambling away as she brings it down again and the sound is moister, less crisp, and his black hair is growing wet and he is falling forward into the tub. Ursa brings up the pin again, but Maren grasps at her ankle.

'No.'

Absalom's mouth is beneath the waterline, which is reddening with his blood. The back of his head is split and she can see white and pinkness. His left hand is tremoring, fluttering, reaching.

She pulls Maren clear of it, both of them crawling, backing away into the blankets where they lay only hours before, their bodies bare and warm. Ursa's teeth begin to knock together and Maren cradles her though she is the one half drowned, taking her into her thin body and kissing the top of her head.

'Let go, Ursa.'

Ursa drops the rolling pin and it thumps and spins away. Ursa can't see Absalom but for his back. It is unmoving.

'Of me, too.'

She loosens her grip and Maren crawls forward, moves to the other side of the tub.

'Is he . . .'

'Yes.'

'Oh, God. Oh, God. I did not mean to kill him.' It sounds unconvincing even to herself, though she knows she did not, not really. Only meant to stop him. She had to stop him. 'What will I do?'

Maren does not answer. She coughs up water, then stands unsteadily, staggers to the table. Ursa clasps her knees. She imagines that any moment Absalom will rear up and seize them. The sound of his skull breaking comes in her ear, again and again, and the wet noise as she struck him a second time, the water on his breath as his head fell forward into the tub. She closes her eyes, hugs her legs to her. Her spine is against the hard side of the wall, and she thinks of Agnete, of their backs pressed together as they sleep.

Maren turns to her. Her face is different somehow, smoothed. Ursa reaches for her and she comes, but there is something stiff in the embrace. Maren draws back quickly. Ursa wipes her face – there is blood on her cheeks and it smears over her hand.

'Do you trust me?' says Maren into the unsteady silence.

Ursa looks up at her, at the hard angles of her face. 'Yes.'

'Go back to bed.'

Ursa draws away.

'Go back to bed,' Maren repeats, cupping her face as she had when they kissed.

'What will we do? Can we take the body, hide it beneath the floorboards?'

'No.'

'Drop him in the sea, like Kirsten's runestones?'

'What if we are seen? It will not be easily done.'

Ursa casts about for another answer, but Maren pushes on. 'And when the commissioner is found missing, there will be questions upon questions.'

'Then what?' Ursa's mind is clouded, full of blood and the sound of cracked bone.

Maren's expression is so sad Ursa's own chest aches. 'I am going to go away, Ursa.'

'Go away?'

'Like Diinna. And they will find his body and think I did it.'

'They will kill you.'

'I am mentioned.'

Ursa feels a bloom of pain in her chest. She had forgotten the reason for her husband's visit to the boathouse. 'It's all lies.'

'That didn't save Kirsten.' Maren's eyes flutter shut. Her eyelids are thin and pink and Ursa wants to press her lips to them. 'I can't stay. But you must go now, before anyone sees.'

'I will come with you,' says Ursa, grasping for her hand.

Maren looks her full in the face. 'I do not want you to.'

Ursa could swear her heart stops a moment.

'I want you to go to bed, and to report your husband missing in the morning. I want you to say you saw nothing, heard nothing. Even if it takes them days to find him. And then I want you to go back to Bergen, to your father. That ship in the harbour, it is the one that brought you. It can take you back.'

Ursa knows the truth of it. When Absalom is discovered, there will be nothing to tie her to Vardø. She will be allowed to go home, and Captain Leifsson will ensure her safety. But something has changed, and she tries to put words to it.

'There is nothing there for me without you.'

'There is your sister. Don't you want to see her again?'

Ursa can't answer no. Agnete had been her whole world, but everything is made different since Maren kissed her wrist. Ursa had never dreamt of such a thing until the moment it happened, but now it feels an impossibility that she can live without Maren. It is knowing that all your joy is bound up in another, and to be parted from it would be to live without light for the rest of your days. Ursa closes her eyes against the thought, can feel Maren's sea-grey stare upon her. She meets her gaze, searching for the want that brought them crashing together. 'I will come with you.'

'It will be easier,' says Maren, and now a definite coolness washes into her voice, 'if you do not.'

Ursa kisses her then, desperately, and Maren doesn't return it.

'Maren, please.'

'Go, Ursa. We will lose the night. Burn your nightdress, wash your face.'

'I love you,' says Ursa, the truth of it sudden as a falling star, bright and painful. 'Will you not say it? I love you.'

'I cannot say it,' says Maren. She stands, hauls Ursa to her feet. Sends her weeping into the night.

Forty

There is no time for tears. The morning will be upon them soon enough. Maren waits until Ursa is gone and the door of Fru Olufsdatter's house has been closed. It is easier this way.

Maren looks back at the dead commissioner, his head leaking still. The bloodied pin is at her feet and she picks it up, alongside Ursa's yellow dress. She can leave no clues, nothing that makes it simple. When Ursa raised her hand to strike again, Maren had felt it as though it were her own hand flying down, her fingers closing about the smooth column of stone. It seemed as though they acted together, as they had only hours before in bed.

She closes the door on the second boathouse, taking nothing but the dress, the pin, and her money. She turns, not to the harbour, but to her headland. Hers and Ursa's, hers and Erik's. The yellow dress smells of Kirsten and Fru Olufsdatter's pyre, and she breathes it in. The smell, she knows it from before today. From her dreams of the whale, the whale that came to her the night before the storm.

She remembers lying stretched across it as it was taken to pieces. She remembers its blubber burning in lamps before it even stilled. It feels now like a warning. She will not let herself be caught. She had decided this the moment her mother told her she was mentioned. She will not let herself burn, live long enough to smell her own body blazing.

She is alone as she walks the familiar path between the houses. She knows she is rare in not favouring the months of the midnight sun, but she can never be truly settled in that half-light. It reminds her of the lightning, the greenish bodies of drowned men. Here in the total dark, she feels safe.

Her mother's house is dim and still. She prays for her name to be kept out of the mouths of condemned women, prays for them all – Edne, and Gerda, even Toril and Sigfrid. It is too much death. It will end with her. It must.

She keeps her head down as she passes Baar Ragnvalsson's ruined house and boat, not looking ahead, watching for the changing ground, the lifting wind that means she is where the island stops. The sea slaps against the jagged rocks, and she can taste the salt of it, mingling with the aniseed, sloughing the bitterness of the dirty water the commissioner held her in. Here, where the current carries out to the northernmost places, where Ursa told her there is a black rock that sucks all towards it, she prays even for him.

She sets down the pin, and steps into Ursa's yellow dress, the one she first saw her in, first touched her in, first kissed and knew her to be as much hers as Maren was Ursa's. It is large even over her clothed body, and as she'd run her fingers over Ursa's belly, her breasts, she had felt it and known the reason the fastenings were loosed and loosed again. The hardening of the flesh, the making of space. A baby will protect her. It is another reason she couldn't bring her, nor imagine any end but this.

She throws the pin into the sea. She could follow, easy as a step. She would not float, like poor Kirsten. She would sink, just as in her dream, to the bottom. The sharp rocks that

335

snagged their men would pierce her, and then the sea would take her, and if not the rocks, the sea alone, all the way to the end of the world. She always thought that is all there is, all there was for any of them in this place.

But now she remembers past the whale, past the drowning, to the rising at the end of her dream. The air is cool at the back of her throat. The money is heavy in her pocket. She looks ahead, to where the low mountain looms. As she steps forward, her thoughts are of Ursa, how she was the first and only one to ever know her. How that is enough.

Historical Note

On 24 December 1617, just off the coast of the island of Vardø, Norway's north-easternmost point, a storm lifted so suddenly eyewitnesses said it was as if it were conjured. In a matter of minutes, forty men were drowned. In this already remote and underpopulated place, it was a catastrophic event.

This was a time of great change in the country, then Denmark–Norway. King Christian IV, almost halfway through his fifty-nine-year reign, was growing increasingly desperate to make his mark on the world. He had won some indecisive victories at his borders, but his attention was turning towards what was within his rule, rather than without it. A strict Lutheran, he wanted to establish his Church more fully, and finally drive out the Sámi influence in his country's far northern reaches, especially Finnmark, a vast, wild, largely ungoverned area.

This indigenous population, for whom wind-weaving and spirit-talking were commonly used practices, mostly refused to obey his religious reforms, and King Christian brought in a number of increasingly harsh laws that ultimately amounted to state-sanctioned persecution and massacre. He was aiming at a singular, unified society that conformed to his view of the world, as embodied in his Church.

He turned, particularly, to Scotland. King James VI had recently published his treatise on witchcraft, *Daemonologie*, detailing how to 'spot, prove, and kill a witch', sparking a wave of witch trials throughout the mainland and islands. Hysteria, together with church attendance, was at an all-time high. King Christian brought in sorcery laws in 1618, closely modelled on King James's.

King Christian also had a close personal friendship with a high-ranking Scotsman, John Cunningham, who had served several years in the Danish navy and driven pirates from Spitsbergen. When the King decided that Finnmark must be brought to heel, it was Captain Cunningham who he installed at Vardøhus.

What followed was a reign of unprecedented length and brutality. Though it was not his only duty, Lensmann Cunningham, or Køning as he came to be known, oversaw no fewer than fifty-two witch trials, leading to the deaths of ninety-one people: fourteen men and seventy-seven women. But Cunningham had gone further than the King had planned: of these, the men were all Sámi, but the women were Norwegian. In a region where there had previously been only a handful of such cases, and only two resulting in executions, it was a stark and telling change.

Their alleged crimes ranged from the mundane – arguments over drying racks, mild blasphemy – to the extreme. The first major trial, in 1621, had amongst its accused eight women charged with bringing about the 1617 storm, which had by then taken on a mythic status even in the minds of those who had not seen it.

The panics follow a similar pattern to those repeated around the world, throughout the seventeenth century and beyond. The trials are memorialized by a Peter Zumthor and Louise Bourgeois installation on the island of Vardø, which was the initial touchpaper for this novel. They are documented by scholars such as Dr Liv Helene Willumsen, whose kind support, scrupulous research, and books including *Witchcraft Trials in Finnmark and Northern Norway* (2010), have been invaluable in ensuring a historical foundation to what is ultimately a work of fiction, concerned not with the trials themselves, but with the conditions that make such things possible. Even writing at a distance of four hundred years, I found much to recognize. This story is about people, and how they lived; before why and how they died became what defined them.

Kiran Millwood Hargrave

Acknowledgements

I am full of gratitude. For my mother, Andrea, to whom this book is dedicated, the best of women. For those myriad women who I depend upon to write, and to survive, and most of all when writing and survival feel like the same thing. For Hellie, my agent, who understands this, and without whom this book would not have been written.

For my father, Martyn, my brother, John, for being nothing like the men in this book. For my grandparents, Yvonne and John, for their vivacity. For my family, especially Debby, Dave, Louis, Rina, Sabine, Janis, and Piers.

For my friends, especially those who read this book and held my hand through its journey: Daisy Johnson, Sarvat Hasin, Lucy Ayrton, Laura Theis, Hannah Bond, Katie Webber, Kevin Tsang, Anna James, Louise O'Neill, Cat Doyle, and Elizabeth MacNeal. For my wider writing community, especially Maz Evans, MG Leonard, Rachel Leyshon, Katherine Rundell, and Barry Cunningham.

For Dr Liv Helene Willumsen, who I hope will not be too horrified by the liberties I have taken with history in the name of narrative, but who I hope knows my appreciation and admiration.

For Kirby Kim, and the entire team at Janklow & Nesbit, UK and US. Every book is a labour of love for you all, and I value that deeply.

For Sophie Jonathan, an editor of rare gifts, and enormous grace. You have taught me so much, and I treasure working with you. To Judy Clain, who has shown this book, and me, such generosity and belief, and Carina Guiterman, for her part in shaping this tale. For my team at Picador and Pan Macmillan, the best possible home: Francesca Main, for looking after me and guiding the book in its final stages, Gillian Fitzgerald-Kelly, Paul Baggaley, Kate Green, Katie Bowden, Christine Jones, Emily Bromfield, Laura Ricchetti, Mary Chamberlain, my amazing cover designer Katie Tooke and Nicholas Blake. For Alex Hoopes, Reagan Arthur, and the glorious team at Little, Brown, Hachette.

For you, the reader, for becoming part of the story. For anyone angry, and hopeful, and trying their best.

For the men and women murdered at Vardø.

For Tom, for saving my life, and for helping me to make something of it.

THE
TWISTED
SWORD

WINSTON GRAHAM

THE
TWISTED
SWORD

A NOVEL OF CORNWALL
1815–1816

GUILD PUBLISHING
LONDON · NEW YORK · SYDNEY · TORONTO

This edition published 1991 by Guild Publishing
by arrangement with Chapmans Publishers Ltd

© Winston Graham 1990

CN 1411

Printed and bound in Germany
by Mohndruck Gütersloh

For
MAY

Deliver my soul from the sword;
my darling from the power of the dog.
Psalm 22: verse 20

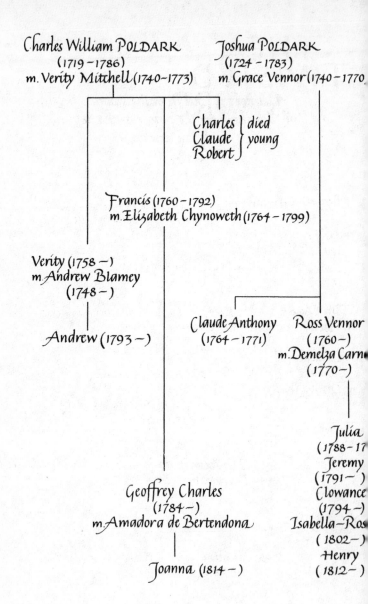

Charles William POLDARK
(1719 – 1786)
m. Verity Mitchell (1740 – 1773)

Joshua POLDARK
(1724 – 1783)
m. Grace Vennor (1740 – 1770)

Charles } died
Claude } young
Robert }

Francis (1760 – 1792)
m. Elizabeth Chynoweth (1764 – 1799)

Verity (1758 –)
m. Andrew Blamey
(1748 –)

Andrew (1793 –)

Claude Anthony
(1764 – 1771)

Ross Vennor
(1760 –)
m. Demelza Carne
(1770 –)

Julia
(1788 – 17
Jeremy
(1791 –)
Clowance
(1794 –)
Isabella-Ros
(1802 –)
Henry
(1812 –)

Geoffrey Charles
(1784 –)
m. Amadora de Bertendona

Joanna (1814 –)

THE
TWISTED
SWORD

Elizabeth CHYNOWETH   Morwenna, her cousin (1776 –)
    (1764 – 1799)   m.(1) Rev. Osborne Whitworth(2) Drake
m.(1) Francis Poldark   (1764 –1799)   Carne
   (2) George Warleggan | (1776–)
                              Conan (1796 –) |
                                              Loveday (1801 –)

Tom CARNE (1740–1794)   Luke WARLEGGAN (1715 – 1800)
m. Demelza Lyon (1752–1777)   m. Bethia Kemp (1716 –1744)
        |
  Demelza (1770 –)
  Samuel (1772 –)   Nicholas [of Cardew] Cary Warleggan
  Drake   (1776 –)   (1735 –1805)   (1740–)
                         m. Mary Lashbrook
                           (1732 – 1812)

                         George (1759 –)
              m. (1) Elizabeth Poldark m.(2) Lady Harriet Carter
              (née Chynoweth) (1764 – 1799)   (1781 –)

                  Valentine   Ursula
                  (1794 –)   (1799 –)

BOOK ONE

One

I

It had been raining without a stop for four days when Demelza Poldark saw a horseman riding down the valley.

Curtains of fine rain had fallen across the land, pushed – though not driven – by a south-westerly wind, bringing the clouds down to the level of the land, masking the sulky sea, converting the narrow lanes into chasms of flatulent mud. Demelza liked the rain when it was this sort of rain, so soft for late January after the storms of December. It didn't matter much for the mines anyway, since most of the work was done underground and the surface workers were used to being wet; but it was bad for the farm. Small though the cultivated area was, its living centre was Nampara House.

Since it was not possible to go out at all without getting wet, one lived in a condition of partial dampness even indoors and in spite of the roaring fires. The stain on the ceiling in the library – which was always going to be looked at but never was – spread some inches more, ill-fitting windows leaked, carpets were damp here and there; but it was not the minor building flaws that mattered so much as the constant procession and presence of human beings: muddy boots standing by doors, dripping stockings hung up to dry, coats and cloaks smelling warmly of damp fur and damp cloth and damp people; you couldn't keep the weather out. You didn't have to worry or fret about the house looking shabby and unkempt. One day soon it would be fine again.

And out of doors it was so mild that primroses were already showing dabs of yellow in the hedges. The rain had a saltiness as it fell on your cheeks stealthily like a moist caress. It was deceitful because you didn't realize you were getting soaked. You drew it into your lungs and it felt good, cleansing, salty and pure.

Deprived of her eldest children – Jeremy being in Brussels with his new wife, still in the army but mercifully out of danger because all the wars had come to an end; and Clowance, married to Stephen Carrington whom she dearly loved – though perhaps no one else loved him quite as much as she did – and living in Penryn – Demelza had spent much time with Isabella-Rose, shortly to be thirteen, and Henry, only just two. Ross had always been at her to take things more easily – 'You're the mistress, let others do the hard work' – but she had found it difficult, partly because of her humble birth, which she still could not forget and which still stood in the way of her telling other people to do something she could do more quickly, and better, herself; and partly because of her abounding energy. But the abounding energy had been intermittent of late, so in some ways she was now obeying orders.

This did not prevent her being constantly active, but in occupations of a relatively unarduous nature. Such as going to see Jud and Prudie Paynter twice a week. Such as going for long walks across the beach or over the cliffs with Isabella-Rose, who chirruped and bubbled with pleasure at most things – of all the children she was the nearest to Demelza in natural ebullience, though sometimes there was a harshness about her that her mother had never shown. Such as walking up to the mine with Ross and meeting him on his way home. Such as picking about in her beloved garden where not much stirred yet but where the soil was too sandy ever to become sticky or to turn to mud. Such as supervising the thrashing and the winnowing of the oats. Such as dosing her black pony, Hollyhock, with an inflammation drench of her own making for a severe cough and cold. Such as visiting Caroline Enys – who refused resolutely to go out of doors when it was raining – and taking tea with her and discussing life in general.

It was a good time with Ross newly home and throwing himself into affairs of the mines and the farm with renewed interest. It would have been a better time without one ugly fact and one momentous decision that hung over her, creating tension in her, especially when waking in the dark of the dawn, listening to the drip of the rain and to Ross's steady breathing beside her.

Before he left London Ross had seen the Prime Minister and they had discussed the possibility of his being sent to Paris as a liaison officer at the British Embassy, with particular regard to the disposition and sentiment of the French armed forces. The matter had been left in abeyance, Lord Liverpool awaiting events before deciding to send him, Ross hesitating whether he was willing to be sent. It had been agreed between them that they should make contact again sometime in late February.

Since then much had happened. America and England had made peace, and the Duke of Wellington would be likely to remain in Paris as British Ambassador, however unpopular he had made himself – or events had made him – in that city. The likelihood of Captain Poldark being *persona grata* with the Duke was fairly remote, for the Duke had objected to his sudden appearance as an observer in Portugal before the battle of Bussaco. The word 'spy' had not actually been mentioned, but the Duke had written to his brother, the Foreign Secretary, complaining of the presence of 'a detached observer' who had been sent, he felt, by members of the Cabinet unfriendly to him. It was not known whether Wellington had ever read Poldark's admirable and admiring account of the Duke's dispositions when he returned to England, but Ross himself certainly had no intention of going on any mission where he would be greeted with suspicion rather than co-operation; so the prospect of a summons to London and then to Paris had receded as the new year broke. And so had receded the dawn apprehensions.

But here was this strange man, formally dressed, clattering across the bridge. In a moment he would have dismounted and, dripping with rain, would be appearing at their front door.

You didn't have to fret about the house looking shabby or unkempt in such weather, provided the people who called to see you knew you and understood the circumstances of a small manorhouse that was also a working farm. With strangers it was different. In the four minutes since she had spotted him Demelza had flown about, gathering up boots and stockings and coats and kerchiefs and scarves, shovelling them into convenient cupboards, had shaken hearthrugs and carpet mats and cleared the table in the parlour by converting the cloth covering it into a handy holdall for everything unnecessary and untidy and stuffed it into yet another cupboard containing Ross's mining books. By this time the faithful Jane Gimlett had appeared at the door of the parlour.

'If ee plaise, ma'am, there's a gentleman come see Captain Poldark. Name of Phillips. Mr Phillips.'

'Ask him in, will you. And send someone to fetch Captain Poldark. I b'lieve he's still at Grace.'

In fact Ross was not at Wheal Grace, though he had been. Yesterday he had ridden to Redruth shopping with Matthew Mark Martin and Cal Trevail. They could have done it all without him, but like Demelza he had a sense of impermanence, of uncertainty, of half-waiting, a feeling that time was not indefinite; and it induced him to take a more personal part in the farm as well as in the mine. Among other things, they had come back with three hundredweight of king potatoes to replenish their dwindling stores, a bag of guano and a bag of nitrate of soda. This last was for a field of early cabbages, and he stopped now to talk to the two men, Ern Lobb and Sephus Billing, who were scattering it and raking it in.

He saw John Gimlett leave the house and make for Wheal Grace, then catch sight of him and veer over in his direction. Messages were exchanged and they walked back to the house together, master and old servant-half friend.

Demelza was in the parlour making conversation with a slight young man in a dark suit of clothes which was even darker, with rain, at cuff and knee. It was not a uniform but Ross guessed his profession by his military stance when he got up.

'Hubert Phillips is my name, sir. Forgive my left hand, I am a little short of equipment in the right.'

Ross saw he had only half a hand, ending in a finger and thumb.

'*Mr* Phillips?' he said.

'Lieutenant to be precise, sir. Lost a few bits at Salamanca, so they won't have me now.'

'What regiment?'

'The 74th. It was a glorious victory.'

'I had a cousin in the 43rd Light Division. And have a son at present in Brussels – in the 52nd.'

Conversation about the late war continued for the space of some three minutes while Demelza moistened her lips and fumbled with her hair and wondered when they would get to the point.

Phillips took out a pouch, and from it a letter.

'I bring you, sir, a despatch from the Prime Minister. There was,

16

he said, a greater degree of urgency about it than could be entrusted to the common delivery, but in faith it has taken me all of three days by post-chaise and latterly by post-horse to reach you!'

Ross took the letter and slid a finger under the seal. 'If you came overland in three days you have driven yourself hard. Some of the roads are bone-shaking. I am glad to see you have a glass. Pray sit down again. Dinner will be in half an hour. You'll join us, I hope.'

'Thank you, sir. In fact . . .' He stopped.

Ross smiled. 'In fact what?'

'I was instructed to wait your reply, which I believe his lordship has requested you to give to me within twenty-four hours.' He turned to Demelza. 'So, ma'am, since this is rather a – an isolated district, it may be that I shall need somewhere to lay my head tonight. As a soldier I am used to simple expedients, so I trust you will not put yourself out on my behalf.'

'I shall not need to do that,' said Demelza. 'You may lie here and gladly. Our house does not lack comforts and I'm only sorry you should see it in such a – such a *damp* condition. Tis not always so.'

'Oh, I'm sure, ma'am. It must be beautiful in the summer.'

She continued polite conversation scarcely aware of what she was saying. At least it was a relief that the visitor's arrival was not in any way connected with Jeremy. Although her elder and most beloved son was no longer in any physical danger from the war, she could not rid herself of ugly apprehensions of another sort on his behalf. From one day to the next you never really knew, you could never be sure.

For she had the suspicion, a suspicion now amounting to certainty, that Jeremy, a couple of years ago, in company with two friends, and operating in some magical fashion no one quite understood, had robbed a stage-coach and – so far – got away with it.

The thought processes by which Demelza's sensitive perceptions, working on clues and little crumbs of information, had come to the conclusion that her son was one of the culprits, had led eventually to a perilous excursion on her part in the early autumn down an old mine shaft called Kellow's Ladder, where in a side tunnel she had found what seemed to be conclusive evidence of what she was seeking but dreading to find. Three sacks bearing initials painted on in black lead: 'J' and 'S' and 'P' or 'B'. And papers. And a

Warleggan seal. And a lady's ring. And a little silver loving cup, with *Amor Gignit Amorem* engraved on the side. This loving cup now stood on the sideboard of the dining-room of Nampara. Jeremy in his last letter had asked her to put it away in a drawer in his room, and she must remember to do that.

Ross of course knew nothing of all this, and never would know if she could help it. For Demelza the discovery had been a profound and dastardly shock. Raised on strong Wesleyan principles – in spite of a drunken bully of a father – she had quickly learned from Ross to treat religion lightly – a visit to Sawle Church twice a year was about his limit. Indeed she had taken to his creed – or lack of it – like a duck to water; it had been no problem to her at all; and brother Sam's pleas to her to consider her Salvation had been politely and kindly set aside.

Well and good. She wanted no different. But when it came to playing the footpad . . . Caught and convicted you hung from a gibbet at Bargus Cross Roads, and when cut down your bones were thrown into an unconsecrated grave. And this was *Jeremy*, her first-born son, inheritor when the time came of Ross's estate: a hundred-odd acres of farmland, two mines, and a distinguished name. Ross was by far the best-known Poldark there had ever been, but those before him, although a fairly randy lot, had been landowners, magistrates, masters of the hunt, patrons of the church, small but fairly worthy notables in the county of Cornwall for over three hundred years.

She so very badly wanted to talk it over with Ross but knew she could not. Instinctively she knew he must never know. But she wanted to say to him: is it something we have done wrong? Have we not taught our children properly? Did they never learn the ten commandments or understand that they must be treated serious? Has it all been too easy for them, too easy-going, come-as-you-please, go-as-you-please, a philosophy of kindly liberty leading to licence? She herself had been dragged up anyhow, strapped whenever he could catch her by her drunken father. According to Ross, *his* father had been insensitive towards his only son, cold and rough most of the time. Compared to his parents, Jeremy had been reared in a hot-house of kindly comfort and gentle caring. And he had seemed a typical product of such an upbringing: artistic, amusing, roused only to anger by cruelty to animals, absenting himself when a pig was to be killed, highly talented in engineering – indeed something more than talent . . . tall, gangling, listless at times but good-tempered, witty, kind. How did such a young man step so utterly out of character?

II

Ross had finished the letter. She brought her mind back to the present, to the lesser apprehensions. He half folded the letter, turned it over, then handed it to her, at which Lieutenant Phillips raised his eyebrows.

She read:

Dear Captain Poldark,

You will remember the conversation of 24th November last when the matter was discussed of your going to Paris on a special mission. It was left between us that you let me know not later than late February whether you would wish to accept this mission, should His Majesty's Government still feel that some proper purpose might be served by it.

Since then events have moved rapidly forward. Peace with America has brought, and will continue to bring, lasting benefits to both countries. But the situation in France has become still more confused.

These are matters on which as you may imagine I am well briefed, but it seems to me that it could be of value to have a detached observer reporting his own personal impressions directly to me. France is her own mistress again – there are no foreign troops anywhere within her frontiers – but how she solves her problems is of the utmost importance to the rest of Europe.

The Duke of Wellington has been appointed to take Viscount Castlereagh's place at the Congress of Vienna, and will stay there as long as the Congress lasts, which may well be a further three months. The Duchess will remain in Paris. Therefore everything will be at the Embassy as it was expected to be when I first put this proposal to you. Our Minister Plenipotentiary will be Wellington's relative and aide-de-camp at Bussaco, Lord Fitzroy Somerset, whom you know and who will welcome you.

Your duties – should you accept them – will be strictly informal. It would help if your wife and family were with you to give the appearance of your taking a three-month holiday – but guided by the advice you receive on the spot you will visit various sections of the French army – suitable excuses can easily be found – and will report directly to me whatever sentiments you feel reflect the prevailing mood. Ample funds will, of course, be supplied for this purpose and for the board and sustenance of yourself and your family in comfortable style.

It may well be that your stay in Paris would not have to be so long – again one can only be guided by results – but I do feel the value of these inquiries lies in their beginning as soon as possible; so I would want you to be in Paris not later than the second week of February.

To this end I am sending this by special messenger, and he has instructions to wait twenty-four hours for your answer. I realize it is shorter notice than was envisaged in November but I trust that in the weeks since you returned home you will have been able to consider the appointment and already have come to some decision.

Believe me to be etc.,

Liverpool

Fife House, 26th January 1815

Two

I

If necessary for a few months the farm would run itself. John Gimlett, though no farmer, knew enough to give the orders and to keep things running on an even keel. And since his drunken bout following Clowance's marriage, Ben Carter had been working to prove himself and was becoming a competent mine manager. Grace was gently fading out; but the yield from Leisure had become regular and of pretty good quality, and the lodes, if unpredictable, were widespread and kindly, particularly in the old Trevorgic workings. Mr Horace Treneglos, long since dead, had said many years ago that he had 'a great respect for the ancients – they knew what they was about.' A mine that had been worked in Roman times, and lost track of altogether more than once since, could still yield its red copper, its zinc and its silver lead.

At least for the next few years, it did not look as if the Poldarks would want for a loaf of bread. Nor the miners either; Ross would see to that. In a county – indeed in a country – where there was as yet nothing to see of the expected post-war boom, Nampara and its surrounding villages were a small enclave living a notch or two above the poverty line.

On the 30th January Demelza waited early upon her closest and dearest friend. The years had not dealt quite so kindly with Caroline Enys as with Demelza, who Lieutenant Phillips had already concluded must be Ross's second wife. Always thin, Caroline had become somewhat gaunt, but the sharp acerbic intelligence of her face compensated for the loss of bloom.

'Oh,' she said, 'so that explains it. I thought from the hectic flush that Hugh Bodrugan had risen from his bed and was pursuing you with lecherous suggestions. And what have you decided?'

'Nothing yet,' said Demelza. 'Or almost nothing. We shall give him the answer at noon.'

'Oh, come. I think it's yes, is it not? Who'd turn down such an offer? The freedom of Paris, at England's expense! A splendid three or four months living in the most sophisticated and brilliant city in the world!'

'That's what I'm afraid of,' said Demelza. 'I do not speak a single word of the language. I should be lost!'

'I've yet to see you lost anywhere, my dear. These apprehensions do you no credit. What does Ross feel?'

'He says he will not go without me.'

'Very proper. So your answer will come soon.'

Demelza moistened her lips. 'Supposing I said I should not go without you.'

There was a pause. Caroline laughed. 'That would be very *improper*. But spoken like a true friend. I fancy Dwight would have a word or two to say about it!'

'Well, last year we talked – you know we did – you *know* we did! – of all going to Paris together when the war was over. Why should you not both come now to keep us company? Dwight has all these scientific friends he wishes to see and while the men were busy we – we could see something of Paris together. It would be lovely!'

Caroline wrinkled her eyebrows at the window panes, which were still glistening with rain. 'I'll not deny it's an enticing prospect. But do you not say you will have to leave very shortly?'

'If we are going – yes . . .'

There was a footstep and the door opened and Dwight came in.

'Demelza!' he said, 'I have just seen Ross and know you are all well, so this is not a call for help. So early in the morning it's a wonder my wife is dressed to receive you.'

Twenty-five years of ministering to sick people had given his always serious face a sombre look, but it lit up in the company of friends. His own health had never been reliable since the ordeal of his internment in France and, as Caroline said tetchily, he was never above catching an infection from the vulgars he attended. He drove himself hard but had long ago in the prison camp become convinced that the mind and the will could overcome many of the weaknesses

22

of the body. Although he had made his life contentedly in this remote corner of the south-west and seldom left it, his reputation had grown, and he corresponded with many of the advanced thinkers of the day.

'Well, it's not a call for help in the normal sense,' said his wife.

He kissed Demelza. She said: 'You have seen . . .?'

'Ross, yes. I was coming back from Mingoose where Agneta was in an epilepsy. Yes, he told me.'

'What?'

'Of your invitation. And that you must reply to it by noon.'

Caroline said: 'They are going, of course! They could not possibly turn down such an opportunity! But Demelza wants us to go too.'

'So does Ross.'

'Dwight!' said Demelza, beaming. 'So you will come? So you will both come?'

Dwight put down his bag, touched his wife's shoulder affectionately as he walked past.

'You're wet,' said Caroline accusingly.

He warmed his hands at the fire. 'It's what we have discussed, isn't it? Promised ourselves . . . But for me it can't be just so immediate. For an absence of perhaps six weeks – two months? – I must find someone more clever than Clotworthy to see to my flock. There is a young man from Exeter who I think might come down, but it cannot be arranged on the instant. I said to Ross we would come at Easter. That is quite early; Good Friday is March the 24th.'

'Easter!' Demelza said in disappointment.

'I know it is not as agreeable as it would be if we all travelled together. But I understand from Ross that if he accepts you must leave next week. That would be impossible for us. Also, Ross will have time to come to terms with his work in Paris and by Easter will probably be much freer of his leisure. And we shall be travelling as private citizens; you will be there in a semi-official capacity. When we come we shall see what we can of you – every moment that we can of you! – and then, for once perhaps, Demelza will be able to show Caroline round!'

There was silence except for the sound of Horace the Third chewing on a bone.

'It is not what I wanted,' said Demelza.

23

Caroline leaned forward and patted her hand. 'It is not what *I* wanted; but for once – just for once – I think Dwight may be right. Easter will be a lovely time for us all!'

Demelza pulled at a twist of dark hair which was still damp from the rain. 'Dwight, is it safe in Paris for children?'

He turned from the window, exchanged a glance with Caroline. 'How am I to answer that? There are hazards everywhere. I do not suppose that Paris is less law-abiding than London.'

'It was not of those hazards that I was most particularly thinking.'

Nor was Dwight but he had been hoping to avoid the thrust of the question. At that moment Mrs Myners came in with the hot chocolate Caroline had ordered, so there was a further breathing space.

When Mrs Myners had gone he said: 'D'you mean as to health? Well, there are hazards everywhere. There has been an outbreak of cholera in Plymouth this month.'

'But not in Nampara,' said Demelza.

There was an uncomfortable silence. It was all very long ago, but Dwight had once attended Demelza and her first daughter for the morbid sore throat which had then been raging through the county, and Julia had died.

'I can't advise you on this, my dear,' he said gently. 'Many thousands of children live and grow up in towns and come to no hurt. Have you discussed it with Ross?'

'No. Nor never could I.' When Caroline looked at her inquiringly Demelza pulled at her drying curl again. ''Tis not for me to shift the responsibility. Or to put a fear in his mind.'

Caroline handed a cup of chocolate to Dwight, who carried it to Demelza.

Caroline said brightly: 'Shall we be taking Sophie and Meliora?'

Caroline too had lost her first child. But it was like her to rush this fence while Demelza was present. It was a measure of her friendship.

Dwight said: 'Of course.'

Ross said: 'My reply to the Earl of Liverpool is confidential, of course, and I do not know how far you are privy to the message you brought me.'

'Nothing as to the content of the message, sir,' said Hubert Phillips. 'I know I must carry back your answer with all speed. I hope to deliver it late on the 3rd.'

'It will be a hard and disagreeable journey for you. The sea passage is usually far more comfortable and just as fast, but contrary winds can sometimes embay a vessel a week and then all the advantage is lost.'

Phillips buckled on his belt. 'This is my first visit to Cornwall. It must be surpassing lovely in the summer.'

'It is nice in the winter,' said Demelza, 'when it is not raining.'

'I had an uncle who had been in these parts as a young man. He talked often of the mines. It is good to see two working. Both on your land, sir?'

'One. But they both belong to me.'

'They are always called Wheal, aren't they? What does it mean?'

'Not always, but usually. It is from the Cornish, *huel*, meaning a hole.'

Phillips bowed over Demelza's hand. 'I'm greatly obliged, ma'am, for your hospitality. And for everything. Even my cloak is beautifully dry.'

''Fraid it won't stay so very long,' she said. 'Though the wind have shifted and there is a break in the cloud. In an hour or two –'

Phillips smiled. 'Alas, I must not wait. But it has been a pleasure and an honour meeting you both. And your two beautiful children.'

One of their two beautiful children was leaning against the panelling near the door, hands behind back, one toe raised so that her heel was on the floor, staring at Hubert Phillips with considerable interest and admiration. During his brief stay Isabella-Rose had been less noisy and boisterous than usual. Now she followed the trio out to the front door and the waiting horse.

Phillips took the reins from Matthew Mark Martin and mounted. He took off his hat, and they raised their hands in farewell as he moved slowly away up the valley.

Demelza had been right. A streak of washed blue sky, almost indistinguishable from cloud, was making its appearance over the sea. Smoke from the newly coaled Wheal Leisure was drifting before the wind, hiding the good news.

They went back into the parlour, leaving Bella still gazing after the horseman as he grew smaller in the distance. Ross crouched, poking up the fire. The new blaze flickered over his strong bony features. Demelza stood beside him, for a moment saying nothing. When he straightened up she was looking at him with her most serious, darkest gaze.

'Well,' he said, 'it is done.'

'It is done.'

He took her hand, which came into his easily. 'In the next week we shall be busy.'

'Have you said a week?'

'I promised I'd wait on him on the 11th or 12th.'

'Oh, there will be that much to arrange! Could I come later with the children?'

'I'd prefer not. I'd be happier if we travelled through France together.'

'So would I! . . . But do you not think you will be several days in London?'

'There was some sense of urgency in Liverpool's message. I'm at a loss to know why.'

She said: 'I am at a loss to know why they will not leave us in peace! Must it not have cost a lot to come from London, post all the way?'

'A shilling a mile. One and threepence, perhaps. At two hundred and eighty miles it adds up, I agree.'

'All the same,' Demelza said after a moment, 'I am proud for you that they would not.'

'Would not what?'

'Leave you in peace.'

'And not at all happy for yourself? Do I take an unwilling woman to Paris?'

'I think when it comes I will enjoy it. It is just the coming that fills me with the mulligrubs. But anyway, is there not that in the Bible: "Whither thou goest I will go"?'

'A dutiful wife, eh?'

'Did you say dutiful or beautiful?'

'Lieutenant Phillips clearly thought the latter. Incidentally, I believe Bella was taken with him too.'

'*I* was not taken with him,' Demelza said. 'His eyes were too close together.'

He put his arm round her. 'Well, we talked around it long enough last night . . . I could have wished we could have left Jeremy here or that Ben could have had longer to prove himself.'

'Well, Zacky's in better health.'

'Yes, Zacky's in better health. And I don't think Ben will go overboard again. We must send word to Clowance. And Verity.'

'I think if I had time I would better prefer to ride over and see them.'

'You saw them both at Christmas . . .'

'But did not mention this possibility to them, as you know. If I am going to France for maybe three months I would like to see Clowance again before I left.'

'I think she should come here. You'll have all your work cut out to pack and be ready for next Monday and for all the preparations and arrangements that will have to be made, without going off for a day visiting Clowance in Penryn.'

'Well, if she can manage it, twould certainly be better. My dear life, my heart is beating already!'

'I hope so, or I shall be sending for Dr Enys.'

'Ross, isn't it a pity that *they* cannot come at the same time!'

Ross saw Isabella-Rose in the doorway of the room and smiled at her. 'Bella, come in. We have plans for your future.'

'Ooh? Goody! What's on? Tell me quick.'

'Mrs Hemple's Academy for Young Ladies. You know of course that it has been arranged that you should start there on the 17th of this month.'

Bella curled her lip. 'Oh yes. A pack of girls . . . But what is changed? I can see by your face that *something* is changed!'

'Something is changed,' said Ross.

27

His face was so sombre that Bella giggled at it. 'Well, Papa, now I know it is good.'

'Only time will tell. But you will not now be going to Mrs Hemple's until September.'

Bella uttered a squeak of joy. For a girl with her powerful vocal chords it showed some deep emotion. 'Pa-pa-a-a! What! Ma-ma! How *delicious*! Do you mean I don't go to a school at *all* – not until September. Glory, glory be!'

'On that we've not yet decided,' said Demelza, 'but it so turns out that your father has been invited to spend the next three months in Paris, and it seems probable that we shall be going with him.'

Isabella-Rose jumped a foot in the air. 'Paris! In France, you mean? Where they have the guillotine! Papa, Mama, how wonderful you both are!'

Half strangled in a wild hug, Demelza looked at Ross and began to laugh. Ross laughed. They all laughed. Teasing her daughter, Demelza flung her arms round Ross's neck and hugged him in the same way. Somehow in Bella's enthusiasm all apprehensions seemed to be dissolved.

'Will you take me to see the guillotine, Ross?' Demelza asked. ''Tis something I've always wished to see!'

'I believe it is still there,' said Ross, 'but has not been so busy of late.'

Bella said: 'Oh, and there will be theatres and exhibitions and dances and balls. And no schooling! I already have a little grounding in French. Think how much better I shall speak it by September!'

Attracted by the noise, little Henry had toddled out of the kitchen, with Mrs Kemp in tow. Seeing their laughing faces, he too began to laugh. Disentangling herself from the others Demelza picked him up and kissed him.

'Harry,' she said; 'Harry, will you come too?'

Mrs Kemp had not advanced beyond the door, but stood wiping her hands on her apron.

'Come too,' said Henry cheerfully. 'Come too. Kempie come too.'

Demelza exchanged a glance with Ross.

Henrietta Kemp – though no one ever dared to call her by her Christian name – was a woman in her mid-sixties. She had originally been with the Teagues as a nursemaid and had first come to Nampara

28

as a casual piano teacher for Demelza who, being still in her teens, had thought of Mrs Kemp even then as an old woman. She had moved in to live in Nampara during Clowance's childhood and had stayed on, with only a few absences, as a sort of general handywoman who could look after the children when necessary, teach them their letters, watch over them in their rare illnesses, and stand in for Demelza when she was not there. She was a tight, ageless, dour little woman, Cornish to the backbone though genteely educated. She came from Mount Ambrose, near Redruth. No one had ever seen or heard of Mr Kemp, but it was rumoured that at a very early stage in their married life he had been 'lost at sea'. She looked and behaved like a natural spinster, was a practising Wesleyan, but did not allow her disapproval for the casual lack of discipline in the Poldark household to sour her love for the children – or for her first pupil.

Her first pupil was thinking 'out of the mouths of babes and sucklings'. She thought, I cannot say anything yet without a private word with Ross first. I cannot saddle him with another person to pay for – and yet, is not the country paying? Is it not natural that the wife of a British envoy should bring a governess to look after the children?

'Yes, my lover,' she said to Henry, who, having enjoyed the embrace, was now wriggling to get down. 'You're coming with us, aren't you? We're going across the sea.'

'The sea!' chanted Isabella-Rose. 'The sea, the glorious sea. Mrs Kemp, we're going to France, to France, to France! *Je suis, tu es, il est. Nous sommes, vous êtes, ils ont!*'

'*Ils sont,*' Mrs Kemp corrected. 'Bella, please do not shout so. Shall I leave Henry with you, Mrs Poldark?'

'Yes, I think so,' said Demelza. 'Ross –'

Ross held up his hand. 'Mrs Kemp,' he said, 'I have been invited to go to Paris for three months. I am taking my wife and children. I feel – we all feel – that it would be most suitable if you came with us.'

Mrs Kemp fumbled with her apron. Although she seldom sullied them with housework, she had gnarled hands which might have spent years scrubbing floors.

'My goodness gracious! *Where?* Paris, did you say?'

'Paris.'

'My blessed life. In France, you mean? That wicked place?'

'That wicked place. Yes. We shall be leaving a week today. Would you kindly think it over? Mrs Poldark will be able to answer your queries. I can give you – we can give you – twenty-four hours to make up your mind.'

Three

I

On the same day in late January that Demelza perceived the young man riding down the rainy valley to disturb her peace of mind, Clowance Carrington, her elder daughter, had a young and disturbing visitor of a different sort.

She had been out for a solitary ride on Nero. Stephen was home – not at sea, that is – but was off on some business of his own. Not that he was secretive about much; he talked to his wife incessantly about his hopes and his plans, so she bore this temporary withdrawal of confidence without any sense of injustice.

She often went riding in the morning. It was not of course the same as Nampara: there was no great beach here edged with grumbling waves; the best you could do was thread your way through the uphill narrow lanes until you got to the moors above Falmouth. Then you could canter along and occasionally gallop with lovely distant views of the cliffs and the sea. Even so – and even if it was the same water and only just round the corner, as it were, from Land's End, facing the English Channel instead of the Atlantic Ocean – it did not look quite like the same sea; there were no beaches here to compare with the north coast beaches, the expanses of sand were shorter and often softer because the runs of the tide were not so great; and the cliffs, though jagged and formidable, were half the height. She missed the suck and sigh of the swell as it moved over the rocks behind Nampara, the hissing roar of the blow-hole when the tide was right, the smell of the sea-wrack, the misty spray, the taste of salt on the lips.

Not that she minded. She was happily married to the man she loved; and this winter they had had splendid times together, hunting at least once a week, sometimes twice. They hunted often with Lady

Harriet Warleggan. Since Stephen had put his affairs in the hands of Warleggan's Bank he had prospered greatly.

They had spent a good deal of money. Hunting was not cheap, and usually once a week after the hunt they supped at Cardew with Harriet Warleggan and played cards and diced afterwards. George's estrangement from his son Valentine had robbed Harriet of the young company he usually gathered round him when he was home, so she had taken to inviting a number of Valentine's friends, such as Anthony Trefusis and Ben Sampson and Percy and Angela Hill and Ruth Smith, to stay on after the hunt and sup and gamble until the early hours. Clowance and Stephen were of this party. George himself sometimes supped with them, but more often than not had a quiet meal in his study, or ate before them with his daughter, Ursula. He never stayed for the cards. Gambling for pleasure was something he totally failed to understand.

But he was always reasonably pleasant to Stephen and to Clow-ance, even though Clowance sensed a steely reserve at the back of it. Stephen was not aware of any such reservations. He believed he was on good terms with one of the most important men in Cornwall, in a small way was becoming a valuable customer of the bank and as such could look forward to a future of continuing prosperity. He acted on this assumption.

Penryn, where Stephen and Clowance lived, was an ancient free borough at the head of the Penryn Creek, a clustering hilly town of about a thousand people. It considered itself far more dignified and mature than its larger upstart neighbour, Falmouth. A charter of privileges had been granted to its burgesses in 1236, four hundred years before Falmouth became a town at all. A fierce rivalry existed between the two, for Falmouth with its deeper harbours and its larger docks had stolen much of Penryn's trade.

Clowance had never lived in a town before, and she found it a strange, secretive little port. Everybody she met was, on the surface, extremely polite, some ingratiating. But she was a stranger – they were both strangers – and didn't belong. Clowance had been too busy for twenty years enjoying life, and taking circumstances and people as they came, to bother about the oddities of class distinction. One of the reasons for her success at Bowood, the Lansdowne seat in Wiltshire, had been her unawareness of having any position in the world to maintain, her absence of pretence, her natural unaffected manner. At Nampara too she treated everyone she met as her equal, and, because everyone there knew who she was, no one had presumed on it.

Penryn was different. They liked their people in recognizable categories, and she didn't quite fit in anywhere. The Poldark name was hardly known as far as this, but she was obviously a lady, and her father, apart from being a mine owner, was a *Member of Parliament*. Stephen, they reckoned, was not quite up to her snuff – and he wasn't even Cornish – but he was jolly, outgoing, generous and prospering. They rented this small house, one of the few overlooking the creek, stabled their horses at the Cambrons', who ran the Pig & Tinker, and they were related to the Blameys of Flushing. They also rode to hounds, which put them on a different footing from their neighbours.

During this winter she had thought often about her beloved brother Jeremy and wondered how he was faring in Brussels with his new and pretty wife, who had been so hard to get and had indeed been willing to reject him and fit in with her family's plans in a most mercenary way that Clowance would not forget. Perhaps it was going to be all right now, but Clowance more than anyone knew something of Jeremy's infatuation for this girl, his moods of utter depression, his vain attempts to seem cheerful and natural when his passion for Cuby was driving him to despair. It had been a kind of madness. Clowance hoped it was over. She thought Cuby might be a difficult person to live with, once the first excitement was past. Certainly Jeremy's letters gave an impression, a real impression of happiness. But not until she saw him again was she prepared to be sure.

It was raining when she clattered into the stables and the nice stable boy, Kimber, came out to take Nero. It had been raining for the best part of a week, but this morning there had been a break and the sun had slanted across the creek. The tide had been in, and the water glistened like an inserted knife among the jetties and the moored ships. Now all that was gone again, the river lost in a damp mist which cut visibility to a hundred yards. Everything seemed mysterious in it, even the familiar cobbles of this now familiar town.

It was a short walk along the terrace to the end house. Next to the Pig & Tinker was a ship's chandler; next to him was Mudd's, a sailors' resthouse of not very good repute; then a house belonging to an anchor smith; then a customs officer; then a genteel lady called Curnow who did dressmaking, and then the Carringtons.

As Clowance reached her house Miss Curnow came out. 'Oh, Mrs Carrington, a young man called to see you about an hour gone. I did not know when you would be home.'

'Did he give his name?' Clowance asked.

'No, I didn't think t'ask. But he said he would come back.'

Miss Curnow had very small screwed-up eyes. Whether it was from doing too much sewing in a poor light or whether they evidenced some specially penetrating talent of inquisitiveness was hard to tell. Clowance favoured the second explanation.

She thanked her neighbour and went in. Theirs was a house with a more than pleasant view, but it was very small. There were four rooms downstairs and four rooms up, but they were all tiny. Nor was there any space at the front of the houses, but each house had a little back garden and earth privy. In the Carrington garden was a pump, which was the only water supply for the seven houses, so it meant that there was not much privacy in the back garden. Clowance had spent most of her time on the interior of the house, utilizing her half-forgotten training in sewing and millinery to make brilliant orange curtains for all the windows to frame the lace.

She felt certain that her neighbours thought them outrageously bright; however, Stephen loved them and that was the important point.

He had said not to wait dinner for him so she had made a pasty for herself. She heated it up in the little cloam oven which was still warm from the early morning cooking, and then, having taken off her riding jacket and boots, sat down to eat it on her own in the front room, cutting the pasty in half and pouring milk into the half she was eating.

She had just finished when she saw a young man walking down the cobbled street. She felt instinctively that he was the young man Miss Curnow had referred to, and now understood the extra quizzicality in the woman's eyes – the sort of look that anticipates discomfiture – because the visitor was almost in rags, and was lightly bearded, which in these days did not so much imply a matter of choice as having no money to pay the barber.

Sure enough the young man stopped in front of their door and knocked. Clowance picked up the remains of her dinner, bore it away, dug her feet into a pair of pattens and opened the door.

He was probably not more than twenty – tall, broad-shouldered, blond-haired with strong features and vividly clear blue eyes. His body looked lean but not over-thin, it was his clothes which were so shabby: a faded shirt which had once probably been royal blue, with a rent at the shoulder and one sleeve short by four inches, a good blue woollen jerkin, newer than the rest, slate-blue coarse drill trousers, much patched with sailcloth and tied at the ankles; and down-at-heel canvas shoes that showed his bare feet.

'Excuse me,' he said, 'be Mr Stephen Carrington in?' A hoarse voice; West Country accent, but not badly spoken.

'I'm sorry he's not. I am expecting him shortly.'

A pause. 'Are you Mrs Carrington, ma'am?'

'Yes.'

He turned and glanced up and down the street as if looking for the man he'd called to see.

Clowance said: 'Is it about one of his vessels?'

'Well . . . only in a manner of speaking . . .' The young man bit at his thumb-nail and eyed Clowance. 'I've just come ashore, y'see. We berthed at dawn. *Annabelle*. Ye see her over there, the brig.'

'Oh yes, I see.'

'From Liverpool. Though she's Bristol owned. We're carr'ing candles, soap and brushes, rope and twine.'

Clowance looked past him farther down the hill. This way a precipitous cobbled alley led to the harbour.

'I think my husband's just coming,' she said. 'I can see his head.' And then: 'From Bristol you say? Did you know him when he was living there?'

The young man flushed as he turned to stare the way she was pointing. 'Well yes, ma'am, in a manner of speaking – though not for some years, like. You see, I'm his son.'

35

II

Stephen said: 'Dear heart, I told you I should not have come to you unshriven. I tried hard just before we was wed, and then again after, but you said leave the past to bury itself; and I was a coward and let it lie. A coward. I make no bones about it now. But just think how I was fixed. I had lost you once already. I'd been without you for more'n the twelvemonth. I was dringed up, not knowing what to do. If I told you that I had been married before, however long ago it all was, and however it had happened, I might well have lost you again. Wouldn't I?'

They were lying together in their bed that night, two candles guttering in the air from an inch-open window. Clowance did not reply to his question. She found it hard to assess her feelings and impossible to convey them to him.

'Or if you did not turn me down . . . If you had the mind to be forgiving, your parents would not have been. Your father asked me once if I had a wife in every port, and I lied to him. He would not have excused that, not ever.'

After a moment she said: 'So you had to deceive me, too.'

'Yes, and I've said why. D'you think if I'd told you about Marion before, you wouldn't have felt compelled to tell your father and mother? Ye are so open and honest. Truly, truly honest. That's the sort of family you've always lived with; I've always admired your family for that and wished I'd been brought up similar. But I wasn't. Life isn't like that where I come from, m'dear.'

Clowance stared up at the low ceiling. 'And after we were married?'

'I was too happy. I reckon I was too happy. And once it was done, I thought, it was done. If I'd done wrong, there was no way of putting it right then. By telling you I might ease me conscience – but at what cost! Making you unhappy. Spoiling our time together. Making a sort of stain where there'd been no stain. So I let sleeping dogs lie . . .'

'Until now . . .'

'Yes, dear heart, until now.'

36

He would have liked to touch her, try to caress her as she lay quietly beside him, her breast rising and falling only just perceptibly. He knew what she was like; he knew every inch of her; he knew what she was like naked; and he knew his ability to rouse her. But with a restraint that he was only just learning he made no move at all.

She said: 'Tell me about Marion.'

He was silent and then let out a long sigh. 'We were both seventeen. She was the daughter of a farrier. Twas a boy and girl thing, light and easy, laughing and joking as a boy and girl will; but there was no more laughing when I got her with child. D'you know about the bastardy laws?'

'A bit.'

'If a girl conceives a child and accuses a young man of being the father and he won't marry her they put him in prison. There's many a good man languishing in prison because of such a law. Well I'd been in prison once and that was enough. We were married. Jason was born the following year. We never properly lived together. Her father was mad at me for spoiling his daughter's chances. She went on living at home. Jason lived with them. I'd visit from time to time, but after the child was born Marion turned against me so I saw little of them indeed. Then I left the district and went into service with Sir Edward Hope. Course I was bound to make the payments and that kept me desperate short of money. Then . . .'

'Then?'

'When Jason was about ten his mother caught the smallpox and died. I left Sir Edward Hope's service and went to sea. I – didn't keep up any more payments. I never saw Jason since he was five until he turned up like a – like . . .'

'A bad penny?'

'Today. God, I was taken aback! I couldn't believe twas him. Look you, m'dear, it has been almost as much a shock to me as it has been to you. Holy Mary, I was dumbstruck!'

'I left you alone,' Clowance said. 'I thought you'd better prefer it. So I don't know what he wants. Is it just to meet you again?'

'No. Some b–, somebody told him I was doing well in Cornwall, so he wants to become a part of it. Somehow. He wants some sort of a job. He's already been to sea, so with your permission I'll take him on one of my ships; push him up the ladder a bit, get him better paid. I don't know yet how much he knows of sailing. He's only eighteen . . . I know, I know, he looks older – that beard – but he's only eighteen and he can't expect too much yet awhile. But at least he might be better paid . . .'

'With my permission?' Clowance said.

'Yes, m'dear. It is up to you. You may not wish to have a – a – my son round and about. Twould be only natural never to wish to set eyes on him again. So you must tell me how you feel.'

Clowance considered the matter. 'I do not think I feel very happy about it *at all*, Stephen. Though perhaps not for just the reasons you suppose. But I do not believe we should take my sadness – my disappointment out on your son. Surely nothing that has happened is his fault, is it?'

'No,' said Stephen uneasily. 'No.'

'I think,' she said, 'you are right in supposing that I do not wish to see a great deal of him, each day and every day; for he will remind me of unhappy things. But surely you owe him something, do you not? You have not been exactly an attentive father, so you can surely do no more than he asks and help him now.'

'Very well,' said Stephen. 'Just so. I'm glad you feel that way, m'dear.'

'Indeed,' said Clowance, 'I was rather surprised when you came into the kitchen and told me he was gone. Was it necessary that he should be sent to spend the night at Mudd's, which we all know is ill-kept and of doubtful repute? He could well have lain here.'

'There again I thought you might not like it. But I'm sure he is well able to see for himself. I gave him money for a bed, and will take care tomorrow that he has better clothes. But I assure you, m'dear, that you need hardly set eyes on him again.'

'But he will exist,' said Clowance.

'Yes . . . he will exist. He will be a constant reminder in my eyes that I have done you wrong.'

It was very quiet outside. A light from somewhere, like a bonfire, reflected briefly flickering on the curtains. Then a gull cried in the night.

Clowance thought, he still doesn't quite understand *what* he has done wrong. If you love someone you love them as they are, totally, virtues and blemishes the same; that's what I learned during my twelve months' separation from him. So if he had told me he had once been married and had a son, would that have been so bad? Would I not have taken it, just as I know he once stabbed a man to death at Plymouth Dock, just as I know that he lied to get himself out of that situation when Andrew Blamey recognized him, just as I know he had girls in Sawle or Grambler before we married, just as I suspect he had an affair with poor Violet Kellow. Being married, as a very young man, hardly more than a boy, was that worse, or even as bad?

What was bad was not telling her, lying by omission, reasoning that with luck it would never come to light. What was bad was the lack of confidence in her, the lack of confidentiality. When people were in love they should tell *everything* to each other. And about other things he had talked so much.

Stephen said: 'Are you still awake?'

'Yes.'

'This has come – him coming – has come on a special bad day.'

'Why?'

'Because I had a surprise for ye. A nice surprise. Something that I reckon should make you very happy. Now . . . Well, now I don't think anything will make you very happy. Not tonight. Not tomorrow neither, I expect. Yet I feel I must tell ye. For it is something I have been busy about all day. For you. Chiefly for you.'

Clowance said: 'I don't know, Stephen. Happiness – is not in this. I can't pretend it is. But if there's something good to say –'

'I think there's something good to say. D'ye know Farmer Chudleigh?'

'Only by name. He has the fields above the town, doesn't he?'

'Aye. Well I went to see him this morning and we spent three hours together, and the upshot is that I have been able to buy me a field of three acres where his land abuts upon the bridle path leading to St Gluvias. And there I propose to build us a house!'

She was silent a few moments. 'Stephen, that does surprise me.'

'And please you?'

'It pleases me very much. You told me nothing of this!'

'I wanted it to be a big surprise. I have also been to the mason's yard at Gluvias – Jago's. He tells me he can begin to lay the foundations next month!'

'Have you – decided on the house, what size, what rooms and so on? Because –'

'Of course I have not. That is for *you* to decide, for us to decide together.'

The excitement of this news was eating at her sickness, but the sickness did not go away.

'There must be room for half a dozen servants,' said Stephen. 'And there must be stables, ample stabling. Of course we shall not have many servants or many horses to begin, but it is right that we should have the room available for later.'

'And who is to pay for this? Can we afford it?'

'My accommodation at Warleggan's Bank was first fixed for two thousand but has recently been increased to three. The *Adolphus* was knocked down to me for 1750 guineas, and repaint and refit will not cost above two hundred. The *Chasse Marée* and the *Clowance* should turn over a modest profit in the next quarter, so I have money to spend on giving my bride a home – a home not worthy of her, for none could be worthy of her, but a home she'll not be ashamed to call her own!'

Go away sickness, rejoice in a loving husband who will do so much for you, lavishing not only pretty words but loving care. A proud husband and a husband to be proud of. A loving husband and a lying husband. Why did the second matter as much as the first?

'Stephen,' she said, 'this is very good of you. I am – *delighted*. *Really*. I – can't say more. This – this strange thing that has happened today. I can't just – just swallow it down like some – some dose of snailwater for the anaemia. It has happened and I am sorry.'

'Me also.'

'But I hope in a day or two it will all look different. As it is, I'll come tomorrow – or whenever you want – to look at plans for the new house. I'll be *happy* to do that – *delighted*.'

They lay there again in silence for a space while the candles burned down. The light from outside was reflecting on the curtains again. Stephen got up and looked out.

'What is it?' she asked.

40

'Only a bonfire on the quay. Wonder anything'll burn this weather.'

He got into bed and blew out the candles.

'Sleep now?'

'How old are you, Stephen?' she asked.

'Thirty-seven.'

'I see.'

He said: 'I just knocked three years off. I felt too old – always I've felt too old for you.'

There was a longer silence.

He said: 'Are you asleep?'

'No.'

He said: 'It has all come about, y'know, from wanting you too much. Since I first thought you loved me I've been scared of losing it, of losing you. I'd have done anything to get you. I'd do anything to keep you.'

'Well you've got me,' she said. 'For better or worse. There's no way out now.'

'Do you wish there might be?'

'No.'

'That makes me the happiest man in the world.'

'Stephen, I'm not the happiest woman, but I can't exactly find the words to say why. Perhaps we should leave it tonight and try to get some sleep.'

'The trouble is', he said, 'that I'm not good enough for you. I've known it since the day we met.'

'You mustn't say that too often.'

'Why not?'

'I might come to believe you.'

He chuckled. 'Now you're like your mother.'

'In what way?'

'Witty. Joking. Even when you don't like me very much.'

Like? Love? Yes, there was a difference. By chance or by perception he had chosen the right word.

'Good-night, Stephen,' she said.

'Good-night, dear heart.'

III

The following afternoon Cal Trevail came with a letter from her mother saying they were all leaving Nampara for Paris on the following Monday. Because of the pressure of time and the many arrangements to be made, it was not possible for any of them to come over to say goodbye. Could she possibly come to Nampara, perhaps Wednesday or Thursday, stay the night so she could be told all their plans? Naturally if Stephen were free they would be delighted to see him too. Cal was delivering a similar note to Aunt Verity and would call back for his answer in an hour.

Clowance said there was no need for Cal to call back, a scribbled note of acceptance was all that was necessary. A hasty word with Stephen confirmed that he would be unable to come.

She left on the Wednesday morning, and by that time had seen no more of Jason Carrington.

Four

I

Belgium was under snow. It had been foul weather ever since
Lieutenant Poldark of the 52nd Oxfordshires had brought his young
bride from Gravesend to Antwerp and thence to Brussels. The
crossing had been none too bad; the sea had been overawed by the
chill density of the grey sky; but there had been, it seemed, light
snow ever since.

They had gone to Jeremy's old quarters, but as soon as possible
had moved to a small but pleasant apartment on the rue Namur.
Jeremy's duties in time of peace were nominal: a few parades, a few
attendances at classes dealing with military strategy, a few duty
visits, waiting on senior officers. For the rest they did themselves
well, attending the not infrequent balls and soirées, getting to know
some of the many other English families which were there because
some member of the family was in uniform, riding in the Forest of
Soignes a few miles to the south of the city, reading and talking and
shopping and making love.

They made love with all the ardour of newly weds – with something added. From the moment Jeremy found himself hiding from
the gaugers and being sheltered by this imperious young girl nearly
four years ago there had been only one woman in the world for him.
Unwaveringly he had been devoted to her, like a man possessed,
wanting never any other. There is a kind of love so destructive in
its preoccupation that it can hardly be borne, and he had borne it,
suffered it unrequited for more than four years. Then, lost to all
real hope, he had accepted his father's eccentric advice and gone to
her for the last time, climbed into the castle where she lived, like a
thief in the night, and had persuaded her somehow – by what
alchemy he still had no real idea – to come away with him. And she

43

had come away with him. They had run away together, as if in some medieval romance, and she had given herself to him wantonly, before even they were married. To him it was a realized dream; sometimes he still stole a look at her to reassure himself that, in a cold and cynical world, it really was true.

As for Cuby, who, after the defection of Valentine had reconciled herself readily enough to the prospect of a long period of maidenhood, had even considered that she might be happiest remaining unmarried permanently, living with her mother and sister and brother and his two young children in the fine castle that was still in process of being completed, and who, suddenly confronted with this tall soldier, abruptly grown older and more authoritative, had found herself driven forward by a rush of strong feeling and sexual emotion which she had never felt before and which she scarcely recognized or had time to give a name to . . . as for Cuby, she had so far suffered no second thoughts, no sense of anti-climax, no rational awakening. She sometimes thought about her family left behind in Caerhays, but only as if they belonged to a former life.

It was as if in her character there had been a log-jam of feeling, of emotion, held up, held back, quite unconsciously, by a cool and rational brain, so that she had remained unstirred at the prospect of marrying Valentine, a charming young man who did not love her – and only marginally stirred by the concentrated devotion of Jeremy who wanted her and no other woman in the world.

The jam had been broken, luckily for Jeremy, by Jeremy, just in time. And it was truly broken; once given way, she had given way with it. She had a beautiful body and she seemed to delight in offering it to her husband whenever he had the fancy, chastely, provocatively, wildly, however her mood took her. They made love together until exhaustion overtook them. But there was no satiety.

They agreed together too, almost too eagerly, happily, without reserve. Nothing she did was wrong in his eyes, nothing he did in hers. Even the appearance twice of Lisa Dupont, his former mistress, cast no cloud. It was an affair that had taken place when he had given up all hope of Cuby. He had no eyes for Lisa now, and after the second meeting she shrugged her shoulders and drifted away. Cuby said: 'A pretty girl, but I think she will get plump. I'm happy that you prefer me.'

They lived well. Jeremy had money in the bank in Brussels – product of an escapade he preferred not to think about – and when that was gone he borrowed more. Cuby, reared on a spendthrift brother, was for making economies, but Jeremy said there was money coming to him at home from the profits of Wheal Leisure, and they could run up bills here in the expectation of settling them when he left the army.

When would that be? Fairly soon, he thought. With all Europe at peace the regiment was likely soon to be disbanded; though he had heard rumours that the Allies were not agreeing well at the Congress in Vienna, and it was likely that the British Government would choose to keep some troops in Europe for the time being. For preference he would like to stay on until October, which would mean he would have served two years. Then, if all went well, he might be able to sell his commission, though it was not a fashionable regiment, and return home to Cornwall for Christmas.

In the meantime, life in Brussels was very good.

In spite of the little thought she gave to what she had left behind, a slight shadow on Cuby's life was that she had heard nothing from Caerhays at all – not a word – so when a letter did eventually come she broke the seal nervously and took the letter to the window to read. It was from her mother.

My dearest daughter,

I do not know what senses you took leave of to induce you to run away in the deceitful and secretive way you did. Your brother and I – not to mention Clemency – were deeply upset, indeed deeply grieved at the circumstances of your Elopement. The letter you left behind really explained nothing – indeed you have expressly said you cannot explain it yourself. And your later letters, though more detailed, have really added little to the first.

I do not believe by anything we did or said that we might suppose we had forfeited your confidence. You gave us all the impression that you were happy at home and contented at the prospect of marriage to Valentine Warleggan. When that fell through, through no fault of ours, it seemed that you were quite content – as we were – until some other equally suitable match presented itself.

Instead you have chosen Mr Jeremy Poldark. A pleasant young man and a Gentleman. He has made himself very agreeable on his visits here, and Clemency, I know, speaks highly of him.

I cannot – we cannot any of us – wish you anything but the utmost Happiness. Shall you make your home in Brussels? We have, as you know, sad memories of Walcheren, where your brother was lost. It is a great cause for relief that the war is over at last, and so long as the Victors do not fall out we may look forward to a period of prolonged Peace.

Augustus is in London still at the Treasury, and I have written to tell him of your marriage. I believe John is to go to London this month, as there are trusts and other business matters to attend to. It has been very wet here almost since Christmas, mild and gloomy with the primroses out and some camellias too.

Your loving Mother,
Frances Bettesworth

After she had read it twice Cuby passed it to Jeremy. He pored over it for a couple of minutes and then handed it back with a smile.

'I think you are already half-way to forgiveness.'

'This came also,' said Cuby, handing him a thin slip of paper. It read:

Dearest darling Cuby, Sweet Jeremy, how I envy you both.
Love, Clemency

II

Henrietta Kemp had apparently overcome her lifelong distrust of the French and her disapproval of the degeneracy of their capital city, for she accepted Ross's invitation within the twenty-four hours, and at dawn on the following Monday they left as a family of five and made the disagreeable muddy jolting journey to London. They put up at Ross's usual lodgings in George Street in the Adelphi. Ross sent word to the Prime Minister that he had arrived, and was invited to call on him at Fife House on Saturday morning at ten o'clock. On the Friday evening Ross took Demelza and Isabella-Rose through a light sprinkling of snow to the theatre in Drury Lane.

They saw Morton's comedy *Town and Country*, with Mr Kean playing Reuben, and after it a musical piece called *Rubies and Diamonds*. Ross privately thought it all rather poor stuff but Demelza enjoyed it, and they were both diverted by Isabella-Rose's enchantment. Her eyes sparkled like the diamonds in the title. She sat rapt, with clasped hands, and came out flushed with a rare joy. She might, like Joan of Arc, have seen a vision, but it was not a holy vision, it was an artificial tinsel-deep theatrical interpretation of life. It served for her. She was lost in the glitter, the candle-lit glamour, the powder, the paint, the perfume, the lines declaimed in unnatural voices, the sheer glorious make-believe of it all.

Just at the end, as they were leaving, a man said: 'Captain Poldark.'

A sturdily built well-dressed young man with a craggy face. Smiling. Then looking at Demelza.

'Mrs Poldark. What an unexpected pleasure. Edward Fitzmaurice. You'll remember . . .'

'Of *course*,' said Demelza. 'How *are* you, Lord Edward? I think you don't know our younger daughter, Isabella-Rose?'

They moved talking through the crowd towards the entrance. As she had not seen him since the morning after Clowance had turned him down, Demelza half expected there might be some constraint – as there certainly was that morning when they left Bowood – but clearly Edward had long since got over his disappointment. Perhaps he had realized, Demelza thought with a pang, that it was all for the best, and the unrestrained, untamed blonde girl from Cornwall would never have settled into the brilliant but restricted social life he was offering her. (So now she was the wife of a young entrepreneurial seaman living in a small terraced house in Penryn and looking, Demelza thought on her last visit to Nampara, dark under the eyes and less buoyant than usual.)

Of course the question soon came up. Eyeing the crush of carriages for his own Edward Fitzmaurice asked how was their elder daughter? She was married? Well, that was hardly surprising, was it? And happy? Good, good. Well, it had been a delightful week they had all spent together in Bowood. A pity you were not there, sir. And another pretty daughter! How old she would be? Fifteen?

Demelza smiled at Bella, who beamed at Edward, and then smiled at her mother for not giving the game away.

How was Lady Isobel? And Lord and Lady Lansdowne? His brother and sister-in-law were very well. They had two sons now, you know. Aunt Isobel had been ill with a gouty infection but was now quite recovered. She had a new ear trumpet which it was claimed magnified the sound more than her previous one, though he had to admit he had not been able to notice the difference. No, he was still unmarried but was much taken up with Parliament and other public affairs.

'Perhaps next week you would come to tea at Lansdowne House with myself and my aunt. Henry and Louisa are in the country but –'

'That's very kind,' said Ross. 'But we are on our way to Paris. We shall expect to leave, I think, on Monday.'

'Paris? I was there in October. A delightful idea. A holiday, I presume?'

'. . . Yes, a holiday.'

'Where are you to stay?'

'It is being arranged for us.'

Fitzmaurice had been aware of Ross's hesitation when answering the earlier question, so he glanced with a half smile at the tall Cornishman and lifted an eyebrow and asked no more.

'You will find it a city of the strangest contrasts, Mrs Poldark. In some ways it is old-fashioned compared to London – as if the long years of war have kept its development back. It is a very rough city, but there are many delightful people there. If you have time on your hands, Captain Poldark, do let me give you the names of one or two of my friends who will, I know, be delighted to meet you and to show you anything in Paris that you wish to see.'

'Thank you. I am greatly obliged.'

'And do not forget to take knives and forks for the journey. They are at a premium in France because of the shortage of steel and other metals.'

After a few minutes they separated, and as soon as they were out of earshot Bella exclaimed: 'What a lovely man!'

Ross said: 'I think Bella is developing a habit of finding all men lovely.'

'Oh, Papa, how beastly you can be! But he *is* a nice man, isn't he?'

'A very nice man,' said Ross. 'I wish there were more like him.'

'So do I,' said Demelza.

III

Ross had seen the Earl of Liverpool in Downing Street last time, but today he went to Fife House, Liverpool's personal residence, which had been built a century or so before in the old private gardens of Whitehall Palace. Punctually as the clock in the hall was striking he was shown in to the Prime Minister's study.

Lord Liverpool, seated before the fire, got up to greet him and said: 'Good of you to come, Poldark. Let me see, you will, of course, know Robert Melville.'

Ross shook hands with a man a bit younger than himself, a tall man, with tight lips and receding hair.

'Yes, of course. How are you, Melville?'

Robert Dundas had been a friend of Pitt's and a firm supporter of Lord Liverpool. In 1811 he had succeeded to his father's title and the following year when Liverpool, following the assassination of Spencer Perceval, had formed his first government, he had appointed Melville First Lord of the Admiralty, and so far as Ross knew he still occupied this position. One could only speculate why he was here . . .

'In case you suppose there is an admiralty interest,' said Liverpool, putting an end to speculation, 'that is not so. But Robert Melville has been assisting me in various ways to do with the situation in France and as an old friend I have called him in to meet you and to hear what we have to say together. This is not, as no doubt you will guess, a Cabinet matter; I am sending you as a personal envoy; but if there should come some situation when you wished to report to me and I was not available, Lord Melville will be able to act as my deputy.'

'I should be happier, my lord,' said Ross, 'if I were more sure of the sort of situation you would wish me to report.'

Liverpool pulled the bell. 'You'll take a glass of brandy to keep out the cold?'

'Thank you.'

'Have you snow in Cornwall?' asked Lord Melville.

'No, just rain – rather a deal of it.'

'Must be a long and wearying journey. Three days?'

'All of that. But it was in my mind to return to London shortly anyhow. The Commons have reassembled, haven't they?'

'Last Thursday,' said Liverpool. 'Not everybody is so assiduous as you are, Poldark.'

'I often am not,' said Ross, 'but I learned there was a Corn Bill in the drafting and I wished to oppose it.'

There was a pause as the servant came in, carrying a tray which he set on a side-table. Ross occupied a few moments admiring the Gobelin tapestries for which this house, and the owner, were celebrated.

Lord Liverpool said: 'No doubt we could discuss the proposed Corn Bill at length sometime. Perhaps this is not the time. I know, of course, that your political sympathies lie in favour of reform . . . Did you know, by the way, that Canning had reached Lisbon safely?'

'Yes, I heard from him two weeks ago. When he wrote he was confined to his bed with gout and had not yet presented his credentials.' Ross eased his aching ankle. 'As for reform, my lord, this, as you say, is perhaps not the time to discuss it, but I have to confess I am disappointed and depressed that since the declaration of peace there has been no improvement in conditions in England.'

Melville said: 'We are proceeding, but slowly.'

'Quite a number of us who supported this administration,' said Ross, 'felt, as I did, that reform in any important degree must wait until the defeat of Bonaparte. It was Wyndham, wasn't it, who said: "Who would repair his house in a typhoon?" And Pitt, of course, stopped his reforms because of the war. But now . . . but now surely they should be resumed. The labourer, whether in the field or in the factory, should be able to live a decent, honest life. Instead one sees starvation in the midst of plenty.'

They sipped their brandy. Ross was aware that his comments were not going down well.

'Believe me,' said Liverpool drily, 'I am not unaware of conditions in the country, and, if later in the session you feel you wish to make your contribution to the House, it might be possible for you to come home for a spell. You can be kept informed. Certainly no Corn Bill will be presented until late March, though I am sure it will figure largely in debate up and down the country. In the meantime, so far as foreign affairs are to be measured, we face another problem.'

'Which means my going to Paris in some haste?'

The Earl of Liverpool blinked his weak eye. 'Not haste. But I think I need you there now.'

'May I ask why, my lord?'

'As I believe I mentioned when we last met, there has recently – that is over the last ten months – returned to France upwards of a hundred and fifty thousand prisoners of war, coming from their camps in Russia, Prussia and England, many of them retaining the most unamiable memories of their captors and eager for any opportunity for revenge. At the same time the arrival of so many aristocratic émigrés has resulted in the enervation, the watering down, of Bonaparte's splendid army by the reinstatement of young men and old men to positions of command which they could never justify except in terms of birth and privilege. All this leads to resentment and unrest.'

Ross inclined his head. 'Yes indeed.'

'What I did not tell you,' said Lord Liverpool, 'is that last October I sent my brother, Colonel Jenkinson, on a mission which might be considered similar to yours, and he attached himself to the 2nd Infantry Corps under Lieutenant-General Count Reille at Valenciennes. His despatches have reported a disturbing degree of disaffection in the French army.'

'Does he describe the disaffection?'

'The army is riddled with secret societies, he says. Many of them are Bonapartist and aim to overthrow Louis – not necessarily to restore Napoleon but to put his son on the throne. Others want the Duc d'Orléans. Many of the higher officers are royalist, he says, but the rank and file cannot abide Louis and what they regard as his corrupt court.'

'In what way do you believe I can be of use?'

'My brother's reports are gloomy in the extreme, and differ

51

noticeably from those of our new minister, Lord Fitzroy Somerset, who speaks more favourably of feeling about the Bourbons. Somerset of course is very young, and while a brave soldier may not be versed in the world of foreign secretaries and diplomacy.'

'Nor am I,' said Ross.

'Once Bonaparte went,' said Liverpool, 'we did, I think, everything possible to bring France back into the comity of nations. One of the most important aims of our foreign policy is to see France stable and strong. Without her, the balance is weighted heavily in favour of the Russians and the Prussians, and at Vienna Talleyrand is negotiating on her behalf to achieve an honourable settlement of the outstanding problems such as the independence of Belgium, and France's frontier on the Rhine. If, while the Congress is in progress, France should collapse into anarchy or civil war it would be a major setback, not merely for him and for our policy but for the future peace of Europe.'

Ross was helped to a second brandy. Melville smiled at him. 'No longer run, Poldark,' he said, holding his own glass towards the light; 'properly imported from Armagnac and all duties paid.'

Ross said: 'I believe you think all Cornishmen are smugglers at heart.'

'Are they not? I was only ever once down there myself and they gave me the impression of a society that admires – unorthodoxy.'

'Is that why you send for me to embark on this – this unorthodox mission?'

'I sent for you,' said Lord Liverpool, 'because of your record of service to the Crown – especially perhaps your last mission to Portugal when you were able to serve your country in more ways than one.'

Ross sipped his duty-paid Armagnac. It looked as if Canning had been talking.

'Do you wish me', he said, 'to link up with your brother, my lord?'

'No. I have sent him south, to sound the feeling in Marseilles and possibly then to go on to Bordeaux. Almost certainly sentiment is more favourable to the King there than in Paris. But I need a second opinion and I need one on a different level. I want someone less obviously related to me and therefore less official. Someone of rank who is on holiday in Paris and can mix with officers in a casual way. The fact that you do not speak French fluently should be an asset. And that you are there with your family will disarm suspicion.'

'It's a wide brief,' said Ross.

'Indeed.'

'And an uneasy one.'

'Do you think so?'

'You will remember, my lord, that General Wellington did not appreciate my presence at Bussaco, saying he felt I had been sent as an observer by certain members of the Cabinet who were unfavourably disposed towards him.'

'I remember it, but you proved the opposite.'

'Nevertheless he has never regarded me with the greatest favour. I should very much regret it if Fitzroy Somerset should feel I was being sent out as an observer of *his* conduct of affairs!'

Lord Melville stretched his legs towards the fire. He was beginning to put on weight. 'Robert tells me you're a friend of Fitzroy Somerset's.'

'Friend would be too much. We have met three times. I think he has friendly feelings towards me – as I have for him.'

'Well, I don't think . . . I hope I'm right in saying this – I don't think you are being in any way asked to report on the judgement of our minister. You are being asked to form your own judgement on the state of affairs in France. We have conflicting reports and we should like another opinion. That is all. Am I right, Robert?'

'Yes,' said the second Robert. 'That is precisely what I want.'

'In fact,' said Melville, 'you are being asked to take a holiday in Paris, like many another rich and titled Englishman at this time. Form your opinion and let us know. That is all. I would have thought it a beguiling prospect.'

'It is,' agreed Ross. 'Before I go, my lord, could you provide me with some of the arguments in *favour* of a Corn Bill. I know – and feel – only those against it, and perhaps it is good to keep an open mind.'

'Gladly,' said Liverpool. 'I can promise you a list of the contentions before you leave. Chiefly perhaps you should realize that if other countries did not protect their farming interests we should not attempt to do so either.'

'It is not so much the owners of farms I am concerned for but the labourers, both in the fields and in the towns.'

'Quite so. Quite so. There are of course many things to be said on both sides . . .'

The clock outside chimed the half-hour, and was almost immediately joined by a smaller, silver one on the mantelpiece. His lordship clearly kept good time.

Ross said: 'When do you wish us to leave?'

Liverpool blinked his eye again. 'Tomorrow evening, I think. The Prince Regent is returning from Brighton in the morning, and I would like you to see him before you go.'

Ross looked his surprise. 'Is he a party to this mission?'

There was silence. Melville again refilled Ross's glass.

'Not exactly a party to it,' said Liverpool. 'But I have asked him to confer a baronetcy on you. I consider it a necessary part of the enterprise.'

IV

'What!' shouted Demelza. 'What, Ross?' Fortunately the children were out with Mrs Kemp, for they would have been startled at their mother's tone. 'You . . . They . . . They want you to . . . Oh, Ross. Oh, Ross.' She gripped his arms and reached up and kissed him. 'But you said *no*! You said you *wouldn't*! In Nampara, that night in Nampara when you first told me about it. You said you had *refused* –'

'I remember very well what I said!' Ross answered in irritation. 'What I said to you and what I said to him! Of course I refused then and of course I refused now! I want no title that I have not earned! He has some damned fool notion that it is of great importance that I shall take it. Melville was the same. They say, they argue, that a mere captain in a Paris which abounds in titles would rate too unimportant for their purpose. Melville had a list of the officers in the French army. Practically everyone is a count or a baron. Even those rating from Bonapartist days had some title to their name – those, that is to say, who had not been created dukes or princes! My God, if I had known this . . .'

54

She kissed him on the side of the mouth. 'You would have refused to come?'

'Yes!'

'But now?'

He disengaged himself roughly from her clasp and went to the window, stared out at a street scene still mantled with light snow, at a woman selling oranges, at another with a wheelbarrow packed with cabbages. For a time he said nothing, but thought of a conversation he had had with Caroline Enys just after Christmas. Caroline had said: 'They tell me you were offered a title.'

'Yes.'

'And refused it?'

'Yes.'

'May I know the reasons why?'

Ross told her. Caroline had listened to him with that loving attention she reserved specially for him, with a glint of humour lurking somewhere in her eye.

'My dear Ross, do you not think you may have been mistaken?'

'If you think my reasons mistaken, then you may think the same of my decision.'

'You live in an ideal world, Ross, and in an ideal world titles would be abolished. But we do not and they are not. And sometimes they are useful. This one, since it is hereditary, could in time to come be very useful to Jeremy, even if you did not want it for yourself.'

'Let him make his own way. People should stand on their own feet.'

'Of course. But shall you not, when you die, bequeath him and the other children the mines, the house, the farm? I do not suppose any money you leave will be distributed to the poor. In what, then, is it distasteful to leave a title behind?'

He grunted. 'You argue like a lawyer.'

'No I don't, because I argue out of love. And think how delighted Demelza would have been.'

'Demelza? What rubbish! She would detest the idea! She has said so.'

'No doubt she said so after she knew you had refused it. But she would adore it – perhaps not being called Lady Poldark, but at least that you should be Sir Ross! Ask any woman, anywhere. *Any* woman. I mean it. I assure you.'

He had thought of that conversation this morning, in Lord Liverpool's study, while hovering on the brink. If he had refused again, would it have meant the cancellation of his mission? He hardly thought so. They implied it, but were they bluffing? In the end he had chosen not to call their bluff.

As he came back from the window he touched Demelza's arm.

'What I have said was not meant in irritation.'

'What if it was?' she said. 'No matter. You have reason to be irritated, Ross.'

'Not with you.'

She pushed a curl out of her eye. 'Why not with me? Yes, you should be irritated with me, for I see small harm in you having this little title. And sir is only a little title, isn't it? Do we need to use it when we go back to Cornwall?'

'I think you may have to,' he said. 'Lady Poldark.'

She put her hands up to her face. 'Judas God! Yes!'

'Those are the first words I ever heard you utter. It must be thirty years ago, isn't it?'

'What words?'

'Judas God. You were complaining that those drunken louts had cut a piece off Garrick's tail!'

'My dear life, and they had! Ross . . .' She stopped.

'Yes, my dear?'

'I have come a long way.'

'We have both come a long way. When I met you I was an inebriate, half bankrupt squireen. You didn't know what a catch you were making!'

'I didn't know I was making *any* catch,' said Demelza.

Ross rubbed his nose. 'I didn't know what sort of a catch *I* was making either. Dear Heaven, that was the luckiest day of my life.'

There was silence again while he watched the cabbage girl. When he turned from the window again he was surprised to see his wife standing there with tears running down her cheeks.

'Demelza, what is it?'

'You don't often pay me compliments, Ross.'

'Good God, of course I do! I do it all the time, but you forget!'

'I don't forget! Perhaps it's not that sort?'

With a sudden tenderness overlaying his frustration and vexation he put his arms around her, fished a handkerchief from her sleeve and wiped the tears away.

'It's all Canning's damned doing,' he said. 'He and Liverpool were at Oxford together and have been thick ever since. When he left to take up the Lisbon appointment George made some sort of a bargain with Liverpool that his supporters in the House of Commons should be rewarded for their loyalty to him. Liverpool told me as much in November! Boringdon was made an earl, Huskisson became Commissioner of Woods and Forests, Leveson-Gower was made a viscount. And they've hung this upon me!'

'Does – does it m-matter?' said Demelza.

'Come on, come on,' he said, as the tears kept falling. 'This will never do. What if the children return?'

'They won't be home yet,' she said. 'They've gone to the Tower.'

'How long will they be?'

'Oh, another hour, I should think.'

'Let me have you.'

She stared at him through big but watery eyes. 'What *can* you mean?'

'What d'you think? I like you when you're crying.'

'Dear love, it isn't *done*, it isn't proper, it isn't decent. In the middle of the day! When we have all night!'

'You sound like Jud.'

'Now don't make me laugh.' She tried not to hiccup.

'Stopped crying now?'

'Yes.'

'Tears of sorrow, no doubt.'

'I know what it is,' she said; 'now you've got this title it has gone to your head and you think to tousle a serving wench. But there's none handy, so you reckon your wife will do.'

'Just so,' said Ross. 'Just so.'

'In fact,' she said, 'I don't care a button for your title. But I still care a little for you.'

'Tell me upstairs,' Ross said.

'Oh,' she said, 'so it's going to be upstairs, is it?'

Five

I

They travelled to Dover on the Sunday afternoon and caught the 10 a.m. packet for Calais. The sea was choppy, the winds contrary and the crossing took six hours. Demelza felt sick, Bella and Mrs Kemp *were* sick, but the newly created baronet and his younger son suffered no ill.

The Prince Regent had said: 'So, Captain Poldark, it is about five years, isn't it?'

'Five exactly, sir, to the month.'

'When you sought to instruct me on the excellence of my military commander in Portugal, and my duties to England.'

'I only answered your questions, sir.'

'That was not the way I remember it. Not the way I remember it at all. Anyway, whether you instructed me or not, you will have observed that England and her Regent Prince kept faith with her mission to deliver Europe from the tyrant!'

'Indeed, sir. And all England was grateful.'

'Except the Whigs, eh? Except the Whigs.'

The five years, Ross thought, had not dealt too badly with the putative George the Fourth. When he had last seen him he had been stertorous, wobbly on his feet, his face and body swollen with an excess of high living, a gross Hanoverian dedicated to pleasure and self-indulgence. Only once or twice had it been possible to detect a keen brain somewhere surfacing through the blubber. Now he looked no worse – if anything slightly better. Perhaps his later mistresses, with their emphasis on a more restrained way of life, had done him some good – or at least prevented further rapid deterioration. The old man, his father, they said, was now so far

58

gone that he had to be lifted everywhere and was only conscious of touch and smell.

'And now I am told you are off to Paris on some new mission. What is it to be?'

Confronted with the direct question, Ross hesitated and then said: 'I believe I am invited to be an observer, sir.'

'As you were in Portugal, eh? Well, there it is. My government – or some group within my government – has its own ideas. I trust your mission of observance will prosper.'

'Thank you, sir.'

The Prince's fingers fumbled with the hilt of his sword.

'It's true, is it not, Poldark, that you have a partiality for duelling.'

Who had been telling tales now? 'Very far from it, Your Highness. I have only been involved in one duel in my life, and I derived no satisfaction from the outcome.'

'Well, let me tell you, my friend, let me give you a word of warning. All Parisians at present are duelling mad. Whether it is because they can no longer fight a war and have to express their spirits in some other way I know not. They look for an insult anywhere, and if they detect one you will be out on some draughty heath at six o'clock of the morning with pistols and seconds and the rest of the paraphernalia before you can say knife. Are you a good shot?'

'Fair, I suppose. Not more.'

'Well, step lightly and avoid corns. I have no patience with the custom meself and neither does the law of England, but those Frenchies please themselves.'

'I appreciate your warning, Your Highness.'

The Prince grunted. 'French are a strange race, eh? No sense of moderation, no sense of humour. Remember the Gordon riots?'

'I think I was abroad at the time.'

'Maybe. Twould be thirty-five years ago, I suppose, give or take a year. A good nine years before the Bastille nonsense. Can't remember what started it now.'

The Prince seemed so lost in thought that Ross wondered if he had forgotten what the purpose of the meeting was.

'Must have been something to do with a man called Gordon, I suppose. Anyway all London ran amok. Populace went mad. All the prisons were broke open: the Fleet, the Marshalsea, the King's

Bench. Prisoners were freed, just like at the Bastille. Some distillery
– Langdale's, I think – was set afire and gin was handed out to
everyone. They say folk lay in the gutters drinking it as it flowed
away. Then looting and burning everywhere. My father – you know
he is no tyrant – nor no milksop neither – finally he ordered out the
Horse Guards. They charged the crowds with swords and bayonets.
Some two hundred and eighty-odd people killed. About thirty
hanged. All over in no time. Dead weren't found – their bodies
were dumped in the Fleet. Scarred houses were plastered up before
dawn – blood-splashed walls of the Bank of England even white-
washed too. Next morning all peaceful. No inquiry called for, not
by MPs, not by the mob. An incident – much more bloody than
the Bastille. But did it lead to twenty years of revolution and a
war-thirsty dictator? It did not. Twas over and done with in a single
night. I suppose the English have more sense.'

'It seems so,' said Ross.

The Prince weighed the sword in his hands again and yawned.

'Well, I suppose you'd best kneel, sir. That's the custom, y'know.
That's if your back is not too stiff . . . Have no fear, I do not intend
to decapitate you.'

II

When the crowded packet reached Calais all was confusion and
bustle. The Poldarks had accommodation reserved at the best-
known and largest inn, M Dessein's famous hostelry, which claimed
to have a hundred and thirty beds and sixty servants, and presently,
though so late, they assembled in their sitting-room and ate a
breakfast of fresh mackerel, roast veal and gulls' eggs and drank
between them a flagon of red wine. Then everyone tumbled into
bed and slept heavily but fitfully amid the shouts and the tramp of
feet and the movements of other travellers coming and going.

The next morning it was necessary to apply for fresh passports,
and by the time this was done and the bill paid it was ten o'clock
and the diligence was waiting for them. Two shabby moth-eaten
coaches were drawn in tandem by three great carthorses which
proceeded at a walking pace over the broken rutted streets. The

driver was a dark little man in a ragged army-blue uniform wearing brass earrings and a heavy moustache; the postilion, in a long blue blouse, sheepskin apron and enormous muddy boots, looked as if he had been wading in the harbour. At a lumbering crawl they moved out into the open country with a thin snow still falling. There was no proper stop for several hours except to change horses, and they passed through Boulogne, Samer, Cormont and reached Montreuil where they spent a second night and where both Bella and Henry were bitten by bed bugs.

Henry – or Harry as he was more frequently called – was the most placid of children, and, to Demelza, most nearly resembled Clowance in babyhood. He had none of the nervous tensions of Jeremy, nor the constant rebellious self-assertion of Bella. But he didn't like itchy red spots and whimpered through most of the next day's journey, which began at six in the morning and ended at five in the afternoon at Amiens. Here the hostelry was cleaner and the host offered them some lotion which helped to soothe their wounds.

Demelza had stayed awake throughout all the bumpy lurching journeys, staring out of the window beside Ross, watching and listening, and occasionally, hands under armpits, shivering with excitement.

She said: 'I can't follow a *word*, Ross. Tis worse than double Dutch. And they are all so shabby! The war must have cost them dear. But the country! It is just like England, is it not! Little difference at all!'

'Did you expect one?'

'Oh yes! This is France. You have been here before and you know what it looks like. But I expected the countryside to be *different* – like a foreign country.'

'It *is* a foreign country.'

'But you could close your ears and think this is England – except it is a poor part of England, a shabby part. The trees look the same, except thinner, the cows look the same, except thinner, the dogs look the same.'

'Except thinner?'

'Well yes, I suppose that too. And everywhere more dirt. When shall we reach Paris?'

'About four, I think.'

They were in Chantilly, a pleasanter village, with tall trees lining the roadside and châteaux visible here and there among the massive darkness of winter woodland. As they rattled and rumbled on they passed between acreages of small stunted shrubs, no more than two feet high, which Ross said were vineyards, and came to St Denis and stopped for refreshments and just before dark sighted the formidable gates of Paris.

Tall wooden palisades flanked the gates, which were guarded by soldiers; urchins and ragged hangers-on stared inquisitively at the newcomers, and dirty women stood and shouted in the doorways of mud huts and wooden shanties.

Here passports were scrutinized, and they had to change to a smaller private carriage as the diligence was going on to Notre-Dame. So off again and through narrow crowded streets that made London almost spacious by comparison. Traffic confusion and noise and struggling crowds all pressed between crumbling medieval houses which shut out the darkening sky. Children ran begging beside the coach, and horses reared and slithered on the melting snow, and upturned carts and fighting, brawling men and crowded taverns, open sewers and villainous soldiery and beggars, beggars everywhere, until quite suddenly their coach was through the worst of the old town and rattling out into a great open space which was the Place de la Concorde.

'Bella,' said Ross, 'this is where the guillotine was. See that railing, surrounding that small square. That is where the King died – the former king – and all the aristocrats, and Danton and Robespierre in their turn and many thousand more. I am sorry it has been removed, but that at least is one good thing Napoleon did.'

'Oh what a shame!' said Bella. 'I'd've loved to've seen it working.'

'And by God he has done more than one good thing,' added Ross, looking around him after twelve years. 'This is almost a new city! All this part. Dwight will be surprised when he sees it.'

III

The British Embassy was in the rue du Faubourg St Honoré. A huge handsome building originally belonging to the Princess Pauline

Borghese, it had only recently come into British hands, Wellington having taken it on himself to buy the mansion on behalf of the British Government. It was said he had paid nearly a million old francs for it.

They turned in through high open portals, the driver spoke to a guard, then they clattered into the courtyard, with stables on the right, and what looked like kitchens on the left, drew up in front of a handsome curved stone staircase leading to the front door.

Travel-stained and tired, with a maid and two children in attendance, feeling shabby and dirty and uncouth, greeted by a smartly dressed secretary called McKenzie, and with two liveried footmen in scarlet cloaks and white wigs to escort them upstairs to their rooms and to carry their baggage, Demelza felt as out of place as at any time in her life. On the other hand Mrs Kemp, having clearly wished for the last three days that she had never taken a single step beyond the Tamar, was impressed and encouraged by the magnificence. This was what she had hoped for, and perhaps some of the discomforts and fatigues of the last two weeks would eventually be forgotten. Two large rooms had been put at their disposal on the second floor, with an extra dressing-room if needed, and while they were going about the first motions of unpacking valises and boxes and another footman was making up the fires, a slim pretty girl of about twenty-one came in and greeted them. This was Fitzroy's wife, Emily, who had been a Wellesley-Pole and therefore a niece of the Duke. On her heels came the acting British Ambassador himself. Fitzroy Somerset was young, handsome, fresh-complexioned, with penetrating eyes and the high-beaked nose of his Boscawen mother.

Later they supped together and met the Duchess of Wellington, a plain, grey-faced, spinster-like lady who was probably no older than Demelza but looked a generation away. It seemed that only yesterday she had received news of the death of her favourite brother in the unnecessary battle for New Orleans, fought after peace was agreed, and this was reason enough for her to take little part in the conversation. The Minister's second man, a Mr Charles Bagot, was also at the table.

Fitzroy Somerset exchanged pleasantries with his guests about Tregothnan and the Falmouths, assured Ross he was quite recovered from his wound at Bussaco, told them he was giving a reception on the following night, when there would be various people present it would be useful to meet, while Lady Fitzroy Somerset advised Demelza that they had taken an apartment for them on the rue de la Ville l'Evêque, which was not very far from the Embassy, but suggested they should spend a second night at the Embassy to give themselves time to settle in.

The ladies soon left, and the three men took to the port.

After a few moments Somerset abruptly said: 'I know roughly the purpose of your visit, Poldark, and I will help in any way I can.'

'Thank you. I'm relieved to know it.'

'Relieved?'

'Yes. If the Government sends over a special envoy to report personally, it might be taken by some ambassadors as a sign of a lack of confidence in their own despatches.' He thought it better to clear the air.

Somerset smiled, but rather thinly. 'Jenky is an old woman and sees bogies round every corner. He does in England, let alone here. Hence his unnecessarily repressive measures where discontent has shown.'

'Oh, agreed. And as for France?'

'As for France, of course the Bourbons rule uneasily. How could it be otherwise? For a country as dynamic as this has been, it must seem a come-down to be ruled by a gouty old man who has been imposed upon them from outside. But my feeling is that the solid middle classes of France, particularly in the provinces, have had enough of war and bloodshed and welcome the peace and the return to a peaceful commerce in which they can settle down to live their lives. It is barely a year yet! Give them time!'

'Was that the Duke's opinion too?'

'The Duke became very unpopular before he left, and I think his leaving has done nothing but good. Not that much of the unpopularity was his fault – except a certain arrogance, dare I say? – but as the military representative of the victorious powers he was the suitable target for any complaints, any discontent that could be laid, however unreasonably, at his door. I know my own tenure is temporary, but I rather hope he does not return when the Congress is over. I believe someone quite new, without the trappings of being

64

an eminent and victorious general, would be a far more tactful appointment.'

Ross said: 'And do you feel the army – the French army – is loyal to the King?'

Somerset reached over for the port.

'Allow me, sir,' said Charles Bagot, getting up.

'You will know', said Somerset, 'that Liverpool has never relied on Embassy despatches for his information. He has developed an army of informants who add to the confidential reports sent from here. I do not know if one should criticize this. Jenky looks on it as a necessary arm of government; but as a result I have no doubt he already receives too many reports on what the French are thinking. It could not be other, because there are almost as many French opinions as there are Frenchmen! Late last year a Colonel Jenkinson – a brother of the Earl – came to the capital and has visited various parts of France; and, although I have not seen his reports, I believe they have been alarmist.'

'Unduly so?'

'In my opinion, yes. And in the Duke's opinion too. There is much talk of Bonapartism. But really it is a word used as an instrument of opposition. Many people who use it would not have Napoleon back for the world. But Lord Liverpool, as I have said, sees a revolutionary behind every bush, and I suspect his brother is of the same persuasion.'

Ross reflected that in London he had drunk brandy from France and in Paris he was drinking port from Portugal. What, he wondered, was Canning drinking in Lisbon?

'This reception you are giving tomorrow night . . .'

'Ah, yes. I would tell you, my friend, in Paris there is nothing but receptions, dances, operas, theatres, one long round of entertainment, ignoring the poverty that sprawls all around. And this reception tomorrow night is just one of many. But I am holding it chiefly so that you and Lady Poldark may meet a number of people who will be valuable to you socially or for your other objective of seeing and understanding something of the stirrings in the political undergrowth.'

Bagot said: 'There is one man who says he knows you, a Colonel de la Blache, who wishes to see you again.'

Ross looked blank. 'I don't think I recollect –'

'I'm not sure if he knows you but I believe you knew his sister – or his sister's fiancé, the Comte de Sombreuil.'

'Oh yes indeed! I shall be happy to meet him. When I was in Paris last, fourteen years ago, I tried to find Mlle de la Blache but could not.'

'What happened to de Sombreuil?' Fitzroy Somerset asked. 'I suffer from the disadvantage of being young.'

'De Sombreuil and I and many others took part in an Anglo-French landing on the Brittany coast – near Quiberon – that was in '95. It was a big affair with a strong escort of British warships and was intended to rouse the Chouans, who had been carrying on a desultory war against the Jacobins for years. A large party of Frenchmen was landed and the King's flag raised, but the invasion fell apart from lack of direction and organization. General Lazare Hoche led a Republican army against us and gained a victory. Hoche gave his word that the lives of all those who surrendered should be spared, but the Revolutionary Convention overruled him and about seven hundred men, most of them gentlemen, were shot to death. The leaders, like Charles de Sombreuil, were executed later.'

There was a brief silence.

Ross added: 'It was really the very last hope the Bourbons ever had, until Napoleon abdicated last year. If the invasion had succeeded . . . Instead we have had to slog it out.'

Bagot said: 'I often wonder why the French have the face to speak of "*Perfide Albion*". No one could be more perfidious than the French, especially when dealing with each other!'

IV

Demelza was not asleep when Ross came in, and they lay a time in bed in desultory talk.

He told her what had passed downstairs.

Demelza said: 'Lady Fitzroy Somerset is a nice, easy person, isn't she. The Duchess I'm not so sure about. Very tight. She adores the Duke. But of course the loss of her brother . . . Did you think Harry was a thought feverish this evening?'

'I'd not be surprised after all this travelling. Have you a draught you can give him?'

'I have given him one. Mrs Kemp thinks it may still be his teeth.'

'Bella was very good at supper.'

'Ross, I did not know whether it was proper to bring her in, but she is so grown-up looking – that is when she restrains her high spirits. Lady Fitzroy Somerset thought she was sixteen!'

'So did Edward Fitzmaurice.'

Demelza yawned and stretched. 'Well, we are in Paris at last! Amid all these lords and ladies I am quite overcome.'

'You are one yourself now.'

'Do you know,' she said, pushing her hand up through the hair curling on her forehead. 'Do you know, I cannot at all begin to see myself as such; but here – in Paris – it does not matter! Here we live in a world of make-believe. I can easy pretend to be Lady Poldark; twill be great fun! I shall put on airs if I like to and pretend I am used to the high life. But it will be when we go *home* . . .'

'What then?'

'Then – there – I will always be – will always be Demelza Poldark – *Mrs* Ross Poldark, same as I have always been. I want nothing more.'

'You'll find in the end it will be just the same thing.'

'Hope so.'

Outside a clock was striking midnight.

After they had counted together Ross said: 'I wonder if I am here on a fool's errand.'

'Why should you be?'

'Fitzroy Somerset is astute enough, though so young. Although he is very gracious about it – and friendly towards us because we were already his friends – I think he feels exasperated that Liverpool should keep adding to his reporters and advisers. And I don't blame him. Anyway, he thinks that fears of an insurrection in France are overdone. So apparently did Wellington, who has only been gone a month. His reassuring reports to Liverpool failed to convince; but Liverpool, I know, is full of apprehensions about Jacobins, whether in England or in France. I feel I should have made something more than a token protest about conditions in England before I came on this mission. For it is much more conditions than principles that

67

make the revolutionary. Do you know, for instance, that the Treasonable Practices Act is still in force in England? This forbids public meetings and makes writing, printing and speaking against the Government a punishable offence.'

She looked at him gravely for a moment. 'I am not sure as to your meaning, Ross.'

'Of course I know that Liverpool would say the Act, though still in force, is seldom used. But its existence is a constant threat to the expression of free opinion. And now comes the Corn Bill! What I am asking you is what I am doing receiving a title and a handsomely paid holiday in Paris just to inquire into the Jacobin and Bonapartist tendencies of the French army? If I were more important . . .'

'Yes?'

'If I were more important I would think I might be being bought off. Since that is ridiculous – the amount my influence would sway opinion inside Parliament or out is so small as to be ludicrous – I can only suppose that he was sincere in inviting me to make this excursion. But God knows whether there will be a worthwhile outcome.'

'This is the first day,' said Demelza. 'We have only been here a few hours. Let us wait and see.'

Six

They slept late and were not wakened. They breakfasted in their rooms, with views over wide lawns to a large boulevard full of traffic, and then a servant took them across to their apartment in the rue de la Ville l'Evêque. It was on the third floor of four, spacious, light, with shutters to keep out the absent sun, sparsely furnished, draughty, though fires burned in the grates and two menservants went with the apartment to stoke them. Fitzroy Somerset had warned Demelza the night before 'the French do not quite understand the idea of an English fireside'.

The silken hangings needed washing and there was dust and an occasional web in a corner, also there were far too many gilt mirrors. But the kitchen looked clean, the beds were fairly clean and certainly there was ample room for all. Bella went dancing round the apartment, hopping from rugs to tiled parquet and back again and singing 'Ripe Sparrergras', but fortunately only at half power. Henry kept slipping on the rugs and ended up banging his head on a massive stool which he henceforward claimed as his own.

They dined at the Embassy and changed there for the reception, which began at five.

Demelza was glad that she had spent so much money on new gowns for her stay at Bowood a few years ago. What she was wearing might not be the height of fashion, but it reflected the big change there had been in general styles at that time and had not become so outmoded in the last three years.

By the time the reception was in full swing it was a glittering company. Ross early on met a youngish officer of artillery called Brigadier Gaston Rougiet, whom he took a liking to. He was a buoyant, frank, engaging man with a duelling scar that made Ross's old cicatrice look like a pin scratch. He was stationed at Auxerre, and he invited Ross to visit his unit 'any day next week when I am back' to sup with his fellow officers and to spend a couple of nights. He had been very much a Napoleon man until the last grim battles of last year, when he had sided with Ney and the other generals. However, from one or two half laughing asides, he gave the impression that he found the Bourbon regime not easy to accept. He told Ross that his father had been a tradesman and that he had begun life as clerk to an attorney. He had gone into the army at nineteen and at thirty-eight was the hardened veteran of fifty battles.

He seemed exactly the sort of man Ross, in his dubious capacity as an agent for the Earl of Liverpool, should get to know, so he accepted the invitation. Rougiet asked him if they were going to the opera tomorrow evening; if so he hoped that they would share his box.

Demelza had stood near her husband for a time in the *chambre de parade*, listening as far as she could and admiring, without appearing to admire, the lavish decorations and ornaments of these reception rooms, one leading out of another. It was indeed a palace, not so great a mansion as Bowood, but excelling it in magnificence. Dozens of candles already burned in sconces – though it was not yet dark – illuminating the carvings, the statues, the gilded chairs, the paintings; and the bare shoulders and elegant gowns of the women, the brilliant uniforms of the men.

But presently the precocious Bella urged her to take her into the *grand salon* where ice-creams were being served. Demelza had been exercised of mind whether to allow Isabella-Rose to accompany them tonight; she was just at that awkward age, half child, half woman, when there seemed no sure dividing line. It was Emily Fitzroy Somerset who had suggested she should come – there would be other young people there – and indeed Bella was already tall and well grown, tremendously vivacious and, when she could keep her vivacity within bounds, a very attractive girl. She had behaved herself so well at supper last night and at dinner today that she deserved the favour.

But it was awful to find oneself an island in a sea of French speakers. True, most of them, when they found Demelza uncomprehending, could produce a few words of English and smiled and nodded and were very gracious. Before she was pulled away by Bella she had heard Ross speaking his halting French to Brigadier Rougiet and had resolved that somehow she must make head and tail of the language or perish. Tomorrow morning first thing a teacher should be engaged to teach both her and Isabella-Rose, and if this did not please Mrs Kemp (who had a smattering and thought she had more) it was just too bad.

She had been at the party for quite a time and was wondering how soon she should escape when someone behind her said: 'Lady Poldark?'

She turned and saw a slim young man with long fair hair down to his shoulders and a drooping moustache. He was dressed in a brilliant royal-blue velvet coat, a green embroidered waistcoat, yellow nankeen trousers and was smiling at her as if she ought to know him. She was sure she'd never seen him before in her life.

She swallowed the lump that always came in her throat when anyone called her by her new title.

'Yes?'

'My name is Havergal. Christopher Havergal. Emily told me you were here, and I felt sure – it is such an unusual name – that you must be related to Major Geoffrey Poldark of the 43rd Monmouthshires. If I am wrong pray forgive me.' He looked at Isabella-Rose and smiled.

'Geoffrey Charles is my cousin's son,' said Demelza. 'My husband's cousin's son. He's in the next room. My husband, I mean. You are – *Mr* Havergal?'

'Lieutenant Havergal, ma'am. I had the honour of serving under Major Geoffrey Poldark at the Battle of Toulouse – the last battle of the war. Soon afterwards, alas, Major Poldark resigned his commission.'

Isabella-Rose looked at Lieutenant Havergal and smiled.

'Are you still in the army?' Demelza asked.

'I transferred out of the 43rd before they left for America, and am now in the 95th Rifles. On leave, of course. And since there is no war at present, enjoying an extended vacation in Paris. Is this young lady your daughter, ma'am, may I ask?'

'Yes. This is Isabella-Rose, our second – third daughter.'

Lieutenant Havergal bowed. 'What a beautiful girl!'

'Thank you,' said Demelza, while Bella glinted back at him, not at all embarrassed.

'But of course,' said Havergal, 'what else could one expect? If you will pardon the familiarity.' He looked as if he expected the familiarity to be pardoned.

Demelza decided if he didn't have so much hair he would look very young. Perhaps that excused the familiarity. She said: 'I'm sure Ross will wish to meet you.'

'Thank you, ma'am. I believe Major Poldark married a Spanish lady, didn't he? Is he in Paris, do you know?'

'I do not think so. The last I heard, he was in Spain. They have a child, a daughter, born late last year.'

'How delightful. Are you staying long, Lady Poldark? In Paris, I mean?'

'Well, yes, we've only just arrived. We have an apartment on the rue – rue, what is it, Bella?'

'Rue de la Ville l'Evêque,' said Bella, already getting the accent right.

'I shall be here another two weeks.' Havergal twisted the end of his moustache, which was smooth and silky. 'Perhaps I may be permitted to call on you? It would be a great honour.'

Demelza's attention had been temporarily diverted by the arrival of two extraordinary men, just walking in from the *antichambre*.

'Of course,' said Bella, deputizing for her absent mother.

Both newcomers were of medium height and of middle age. The first was dressed in a silk coat and breeches of clerical black; the white stock cut low added to the impression that he might be of the church; but no recognizable brand of Christianity was observable on his face, which was thin and of a ruddy complexion and simian in expression. He was clean shaven, wore his own greying hair, which had a reddish tinge; his eyes were small and of a deep bloodshot brown.

The second man was in a pale blue coat and breeches with a white fur waistcoat. He had a long pendulous nose and sensuous lips. His skin was the colour of a man who has had yellow fever, and he wore an eye-patch. He seemed to be attendant upon the first, not as a servant but as a lesser light of the same order. Both were looking about the room to see who was there.

72

A flow of French conversation washed over Demelza. She said: 'Where is your regiment stationed?'

'Outside Brussels, ma'am.'

'My son is in the army,' she said. 'Jeremy Poldark. He too is in Brussels. Perhaps you know him?'

'What regiment?'

'The 52nd Oxfordshires.'

'I shall make a point of seeking his acquaintance when I return.'

Brigadier Rougiet was introducing Ross to three other French officers, brilliant in their greens and golds, and for a while Ross was content to join in the conversation and listen. Sometimes his knowledge of French failed and the sentences slipped by before he could catch them, but he realized that all these high-ranking officers had been in Napoleon's army until last year. One had been at the occupation of Moscow and the disastrous retreat, another called Marchand had been at Bussaco under Masséna. But that was all over and past. They showed no signs of bitterness or resentment at their defeat – Liverpool had said this was a rampant sentiment – but perhaps it was their natural good manners which did not allow them to betray their feelings to an Englishman.

Some ten minutes later he glanced through the big open doors and saw two strange middle-aged men talking to Demelza, one in black silk, the other in blue, with an eye-patch. She was smiling at them and answering back but clearly not at all comfortable in their presence.

In a gap in the conversation Ross said in an aside to Rougiet: 'Who are the two men talking to my wife?'

A sardonic expression crossed Rougiet's scarred face. 'The one in black is the Duke of Otranto, the other is M Tallien.' After a moment he added: 'Both survivals of the revolutionary days.'

'Indeed.'

'M Tallien was responsible for sending Robespierre to the guillotine. The Duke of Otranto has been all things to all men for so long that one does not know *what* he believes in, except himself.'

'It is hard to remember that the worst excesses of the revolution are not so long ago. What is it – twenty-three years since Robespierre's death?'

'Twenty-one.'

'But surely – a duke in a revolutionary council?'

'He was Joseph Fouché. You may know his name. For many years he was Minister of Police under Bonaparte. Indeed, was so until last year.'

'And how is it that he – that they – are welcome guests at this reception?'

Rougiet smiled. 'Perhaps not welcome but accepted. It is impossible for a simple soldier such as myself to understand all the ramifications of French politics. So perhaps even less so for you, sir, as an Englishman. Fouché was one of the signatories of the death warrant of Louis the Sixteenth, yet when his brother ascends the throne Otranto is forgiven and allowed his freedom and his influence. Influence, I suppose, is the word. He always seems to have influence, and the King has made use of him. In any devil's brew, in any cauldron of muddy political intrigue, Fouché can be relied on to swim to the top.'

Ross stared across the room. 'I wonder who introduced them to my wife.'

'I do not suppose they waited for an introduction. Tallien is a great ladies' man. Indeed all his life he has been a great lecher. And your wife, sir, if I may say so, is a beautiful woman.'

'I have often thought so,' said Ross, nevertheless looking across at Demelza with new eyes.

'She has such freshness, such a lack of artificiality, of pretence. I mean, of course, as to her physical appearance, for I hardly know her; but I would suppose she is equally untrammelled by affectation in her personal life.'

'You are entirely correct, sir,' said Ross.

Lady Poldark being much preoccupied with her two middle-aged revolutionaries, Lieutenant Havergal had been able to draw Isabella-Rose aside.

'I hope, Miss Poldark, your mother will permit me to show you something of Paris while you are here.'

'Curse me,' said Bella, who had never been called Miss Poldark before. 'That would be enjoyable, but I do not think my mother would allow it! For is not Paris a very wicked place?'

'Wicked, yes. But also exciting and beautiful. Perhaps your mother would consent to come with us and then we could go to the

Tivoli Gardens together? There is great entertainment to be had there.'

'It would be enjoyable,' said Bella again, looking at his moustache and wondering if it tickled. 'You must ask Mama, for if *you* asked she would be far more likely to agree than if I did.'

There was a silence between them for a moment.

'Have you seen the *boudoir rose*?' asked Havergal. 'See, it is just through here . . .' He led her off, a finger on her arm. 'That is the Princess Borghese's bed. She was Napoleon's sister, you know. She used to recline on this bed all morning, entertaining visitors.'

Bella stared round the room, with its elegant draperies, and at the blue silk and satin bed. Then she glanced up at Havergal, who was regarding her with frank admiration. She looked back at him for a few seconds with equal frankness and then dimpled at him and had the grace to lower her eyes.

They walked back slowly into the *grand salon*.

'I was damn near involved in a duel this morning,' said Havergal. 'There's always duels about in this town. But it was Charlie Cranfield – Lord Cranfield, that is – who provoked it. We'd been out together, the four of us . . .' He paused. 'Perhaps this is not a suitable story for a young lady's ears.'

'You must tell me at once,' said Bella, 'or I shall explode with frustration.'

He laughed. 'Well, twas all a storm in a teacup, believe me. You see we had all been dining at Very's, which is a famous restaurant near the Palais Royal, and had been looking upon the wine when it was red, if you follow. In coming out there were some mendicants trying to sell us a variety of nasty trinkets, and Cranfield kicked their merchandise into the gutter. A Frenchman stopped to protest, and Cranfield pushed *him* into the gutter. Alas, the Frenchman was a captain in the 3rd Chasseurs, so after an angry scene cards were exchanged for a meeting this morning.'

'Oh,' said Bella.

'Well, d'ye know, my dear Miss Poldark, when I got to my lodgings last night it was very late and they were all bolted and barred, so Charlie Cranfield says come home with us, Christopher, he says. So home I go with them and bed down on a sofa in front

75

of a crackling fire. Next thing I know it is early in the morning and a hammering on the door and who should be there but our chasseur and his two friends all anxious to proceed with the duel! Now out of the bedroom appears Charlie Cranfield himself wearing nothing but a baggy pair of trousers and a nightcap full of holes. Ye see, he is so particular to have it aired that it has got many times singed in the process. And following him comes Captain Merriman of the Leicestershires wrapped in a huge blanket and wearing his army trousers and no more; and then the other chap whose name escapes me, rubbing his eyes and whistling through the hole in his teeth that he has had bored to imitate the coachmen, and not one of the three can understand a word of what the chasseur and his seconds are saying!'

'Oh,' said Bella, clasping her hands.

'Well, you may imagine I was much in demand as an interpreter, since I was the only one in the room with any pretensions to be bi-lingual, and I am none too fluent. But I was able to convey to Charlie Cranfield that M le Chasseur wished him to choose his weapons. Now Charlie has quite forgotten all about the quarrel and what offence he gave, but he is ever ready for a bit of a fight so he says *fusils*. He thinks it means a duel with pistols, my dear, dear Miss Poldark, but *fusil* means a musket or a fowling piece, which at twenty paces would be certain Kingdom Come for the one who was slowest at pulling the trigger. Our French friends are much taken aback, but I believe are about to agree when Merriman, standing with his back to the fire, which is still glowing hot, lets go his hand upon his belt, whereupon his trousers slip down over his ankles!'

'Oh,' said Bella, giggling.

'That is exactly what happened! Everyone bursts out laughing at such a frightful sight, even the Frenchmen, and in next to no time everyone has forgiven everyone else and we all sit down with a bottle of wine that by some fortunate chance has been overlooked last night! But this is what can happen in Paris all the time! Do allow me to fetch you another ice.'

Jean-Lambert Tallien said: 'Madame, I was in your country in 1801, as a *prisonnier*, but a much-honoured one. I was returning from Egypt, where I had been editor of the newspaper *officiel*, and my vessel was captured by a British cruiser and I was taken to England.'

'I'm glad you were well treated, sir,' said Demelza.

'But indeed. I was, of course, a non-combatant, you understand. But as a former President of the Convention I was entertained most generously by Mr Charles James Fox and members of his famous circle.'

In spite of his eye-patch he was not without attraction. Yet it was a disagreeable attraction. His one eye was dark brown and bright and twinkling. His long red nose was sensitive and fastidious. He had a full sensuous bottom lip with a deep cleft in it. Although probably about fifty years of age, he was still on the hunt. He smelt of lavender.

'I gather that you are visiting Paris with your husband, madame. He is here tonight?'

'Yes, in the other room. Captain – I mean Sir Ross Poldark.'

'Lady Poldark. It could be a French name, eh? Are you part French?'

'No, Cornish.'

'Ah, *Cornouailles*. There I have never been to visit. It is like our Brittany, eh? I know Brittany ver' well. And how long do you stay in Paris?'

'Some weeks.'

'It is all *vacances*? Holiday?'

'Er – yes. I have never been before. My husband came in 1803.'

'Then I trust we shall meet again, madame. Many times. Paris is very big, but Paris is very small. You understand?'

'I am afraid not.'

'It has a larger populace of – of *les vins ordinaires*. A small populace of those who are important in the life of the state. So this smaller group meets again and again – meeting, dissolving, re-meeting in other surroundings, the *mélange* not always the same but similar.'

During this exchange the Duke of Otranto had been eyeing her and then glancing round the assembled company with the same chilly, assessing gaze as he would no doubt have looked out upon a hard-working guillotine. Demelza thought that her hesitation when asked if they were here on holiday had been carefully noted and filed away in a cold, calculating mind. She had no idea who the

Duke of Otranto was or where his interests lay; all she knew was that she didn't like him or trust him. Indeed, if circumstances ever ran against her, she would be scared of him.

Ross, intent on rescuing her from the attentions of her two strange men, was stopped half-way across the room by John McKenzie, the under secretary, and told that Colonel de la Blache wished to meet him. A dapper youngish man was standing beside McKenzie and he came forward and grasped Ross's hand.

'My dear friend,' he said, 'if it is not too much to call you that on first acquaintance; but I believe you met my sister Jodie in Cornwall many years ago.'

'Oh,' said Ross. 'Yes, I did. She was engaged to marry Charles de Sombreuil, and we met at a house called Trelissick overlooking the River Fal. That was many years ago. Twenty, I think? I believe it was the summer of '95.'

'Alas, poor Charles. I was only eleven at the time . . . A noble and kindly man. He was the last de Sombreuil. The restored estates have now gone to a cousin of another name. Did I not hear you were involved in the tragic landing at Quiberon?'

'Yes. I was with him until nearly the end.'

'Mlle de la Blache heard that you were here and would very much like to meet you both again. Perhaps we can arrange something?'

'Willingly. Your sister never married, then?'

'Yes, she married an Austrian but is now a widow. When the King returned she reverted to her original name. She is now head of the family. Both our parents, of course, went to the guillotine. But she will tell you all about it when you meet. Is your wife here?'

'Yes. Come with me. I will take you to meet her.'

Seven

I

Late in February Clowance went to spend the night with the Enyses. Easter was early this year so they would soon be making preparations to join their friends in Paris.

After the storms of December the winter had been mild and wet in Cornwall, the endless days of drifting rain interspersed with springlike hours of sudden sunshine. But in late February a cold spell set in and as she rode up to Killewarren flakes of snow were drifting in the wind. The shabby old house, which in twenty years had received only marginal improvements – since both Enyses preferred it as it was – looked speckled and damp in the shifting morning light.

To her surprise Music Thomas was there to take her horse and lead it away, and when Dwight opened the door he explained that Myners had sprained his ankle and Bone was a-bed with influenza so they had borrowed Thomas from Place House. Since Valentine Warleggan and Selina were in Cambridge, it seemed he could easily be spared; in fact Saul Grieves, who was in charge of the house while they were away, had given Dwight to understand he would not be upset if Music never came back.

They went upstairs into the drawing-room and Caroline embraced her and gave her a glass of canary to whet her appetite for dinner. After they had talked in a jolly way for a few minutes Dwight handed her a cutting from *The Times*, wondering if she had seen it.

Clowance squealed with utter surprise.

'Heavens *above*! My dear, dear life and body! Mama told me he had been offered it before Christmas but she said he had definitely and absolutely *refused*!'

'So he did. I cannot imagine what can have persuaded him to think better of it – some sort of extra pressure *must* have been applied. He would never take it willingly.'

'And why ever not?' demanded Caroline. 'He has done so much in one way and another for the Government, for the country, over the last ten years – entirely without reward. He's been a Member of Parliament for much longer than that. Sometimes he has neglected his own affairs – think of the tin scandal; that was when you were very young, darling – but there have been other, lesser things. So it's only right – very meet, right and proper – that he should get some recognition now!'

'It's very meet and right,' Dwight agreed. 'I'm delighted that he's accepted, but still astounded.'

'A baronetcy,' said Clowance, staring at the cutting. 'That means, doesn't it, that it will go on? Golly! So one day there will be a Sir Jeremy. Crikey – what fun! And *Mama*! That I cannot believe. *Lady* Poldark! I do not suppose it will make one whit of difference to her. Oh, I am so delighted!'

'You must not ever tease her about it,' said Caroline. 'When she comes home among her own people it will be troublesome for a few months, but then everyone will accept it and forget it has ever been any different.'

'I have been expecting a letter,' said Clowance, 'but I suppose they will have been travelling all the time. I wonder if they are in Paris by now.'

At dinner Clowance chatted brightly about herself and about Stephen and the way he was prospering in his coastal trade, and the new house he was proposing to build and the furniture they intended to buy when they could afford it, and their occasional evening at Cardew and Stephen's ambition to find himself a good hunter to partner Nero instead of hiring a hack or depending on Lady Harriet for a loan; and what a pity Caroline rode with the Forbra for it would be lovely if they were able all to go together.

Last week, Clowance said, an American privateer had come in to Falmouth for a refit and repairs; the rules of the sea were strange that he was given this facility even though he might afterward prey on our ships in the open Channel. And another frigate had just come in with news of the casualties of the last battle of the American war – at New Orleans – and those who had seen the lists had said they were frightful. What news of Jeremy? Caroline asked.

'I had a letter only last week. Being in the army for him has been not at all unagreeable. He seems to spend little or no time soldiering and most of his time taking Cuby to balls and soirées and tea parties. They do seem so happy, so very, very happy.'

Caroline thought Clowance was talking too much and too brightly; it was not in her nature to chatter. What impression was she making an effort to give? What was she trying *not* to say? Was she already missing her parents? Or was it because she was not having a baby? Or was her marriage to Stephen less of a success than she had romantically pictured it would be?

Caroline put these questions to Dwight when they retired that night.

Dwight said: 'The trouble with Clowance is that she doesn't know how to dissemble, so when she tries she makes a hash of it . . . But we are only guessing. Perhaps she is well enough and married life is just effecting a change.'

Next morning in a fine spell Clowance went over to see Jud and Prudie, but about midday the snowflakes fell thicker, black spots drifting down from the pewter sky, and she decided to leave for home.

Having failed to persuade her to spend another night with them, Caroline said: 'You shall not go alone. In any case it is not safe to be a solitary lady with so much distress about.'

'You can hardly lecture me,' Clowance said, 'since you ride so much alone yourself. I'm well able to look after myself.'

'On the contrary, I scarcely ever ride alone since the end of the war. With so many discharged and destitute soldiers about it is no longer safe.'

'Music will go with you,' said Dwight.

Clowance laughed. 'Would I not be safer on my own?'

'Oh, he rides very well. And he is much underrated. Having once been dubbed the village butt, people laugh at his attempts to escape from that derogatory pigeon-hole.'

'Dwight has been trying to help him for long enough,' said Caroline, wrinkling her nose.

'Because he came to me for help in the first place! In some respects

81

he is very slow – almost half-witted, I agree – but in others he is quite quick and able and willing to learn. And he has learned. I have a mind to offer him permanent work here – we could do with another man. But I know he would be likely to refuse.'

'Why?'

'Because he has this hopeless passion for Katie Carter, who is now head housemaid at Place House.'

'Katie Carter? Ben's sister? I didn't know. I thought I knew everything that went on in Grambler and Sawle!' Clowance spoke with slight embarrassment, because of Ben's hopeless passion for her. It was Ben who, by his fight with Stephen, had been instrumental in delaying their wedding by more than a year. 'And why is it hopeless?'

'Katie tends to the general view, that he is a simpleton. Also, there is a rumour that she is taking up with Saul Grieves. After all, it is a more natural union.'

'Dwight doesn't care for Saul Grieves,' said Caroline, picking Horace the Third up from the rug and rubbing his little pug nose.

'Oh, it's no more than a feeling,' said Dwight, as always anxious to be fair. 'I've never attended him. But he has two faces, one, ingratiating, which he turns on to the gentry, another, intimidating, which he turns on those he considers less important than himself.'

'And Valentine and Selina are likely to be absent for some time?'

'They should be back for the Easter holidays.'

II

Clowance and her tall gangling smiling escort left at 12.30. Music rode one of Dwight's older horses, and had difficulty at first in keeping up with Nero who was full of spirit after a night in strange stables. But after Nero had exhausted his first energies Music caught up. Then he remained, respectfully, a horse's length behind, following at a steady pace, adjusting himself to Clowance's.

The snow was lying, which was unusual for Cornwall. Often a fall of snow was followed by brilliant sunshine which melted it away. Today there was a thick misty pall of cloud, low lying, steamy, cold.

After leaving the wooded area around Killewarren they climbed to the moorland where the bleakness of the day was accentuated by the bleakness of the scene. The few mining cottages crouched more closely among the ruined mine houses and the working mines. Piles of dead stuff stood like hills everywhere. A mule train threaded its way among the excavations and the pits and the rubble. Children, grey-faced and ragged, were still at work stirring the water round and round with their bare feet. Clowance shivered and urged Nero into a trot.

Once they were past the worst she slowed again, and when Music slowed she stopped and beckoned him to catch up.

'Have you ever been this way before, Music?'

'Nay, ma'am, I not been gwan this way afore. Tes all stra-ange, you.'

Clowance noticed that his voice had deepened from the reedy alto she remembered. He'd filled out too, was not so gangling and stooping as she remembered; and on a horse his peculiar prancing walk did not show.

'I hope you will be able to find your way back.'

Music turned and looked behind him as if to reassure himself. 'Oh, ais. I d'reckon I can always find me way 'ome.'

'Well, I'm quite safe now. It is only a few miles further, down among these woods. The snow is getting worse. You can safely leave me here.'

His face showed doubt, almost dismay, as it always did when confused by new directions. Then it cleared. 'Oh, no, ma'am. Surgeon told me. I always d'do what Surgeon tell me. I see ee right 'ome to yer door. That's what Surgeon d'say.'

'Do you like working for Dr Enys?'

'Oh, ais, ma'am. He done a lot for me. See ee right 'ome to yer door. That's what he d'say.'

They proceeded downhill. Now they were out of the mining district it was very quiet, the world an empty bowl of silence; there was just the click and creak of harness, the scrape of a hoof on a stone, breath rising like steam from horses and riders, distantly now and then the desolate squawk of a bird.

Music still tried to keep a respectful distance behind, but Clowance kept waiting for him and some talk resulted. She could

83

see what Dwight meant. Somewhere at the back of the stupidity there was a reasoning brain.

He was reluctantly telling her a little about his work at Place House when he broke off and half checked his horse.

'What be that?'

'What? I didn't hear anything.'

'Hark! Wait now! Hark!'

They both stopped. The sighing wind blew the snow dove-soft against her face.

'Hark!' he said again. 'There!'

She heard it now. It was a wail, a howl, over to their left, a distance over to their left. It was still rough ground here but improving: gorse and hawthorn and bramble, but coppices of elm and mixed wood not far away.

'It sounds like a dog.'

'Ais. Or a caow. Go see, shall I?'

'I'll come with you.'

They broke away from the track they were on and made a diagonal approach to the woods.

'Wait,' she said. 'It's someone's property. This fencing is new. Where would we be? The back of Lord Devoran's? No, he'd be farther down the valley. It might be the Hills' place. Can you see any house, Music?'

'Nay, ma'am.'

A small gate with a loop of wire over the post to fasten it. The howl came again, much nearer this time. She slid down off Nero and opened the gate.

'We'll leave the horses here,' she said. 'It's too rough for them.'

'Leave me go see, ma'am. Tedn't right for ee neither. Leave me go see.'

She took no notice of this, and pursued the overgrown path, which was scarcely two feet wide, leading from the gate. The snow was sticky, heavy on the branches, cascaded over them when they disturbed it. Her fur hat was soon white, the hem of her skirt embroidered with it.

Although still early afternoon the woods winnowed the light, and shadows frowned from the overhanging snow. Music stumbled twice. But she noticed he no longer walked on his toes.

The sound had stopped. They waited and nothing happened, except that a stoat fled across their path and a pheasant stirred in a nearby tree. The path had run into a clearing about ten yards in diameter, but here it seemed to end.

'What now?' she said to Music.

'Reckon twas this way. Reckon twas this way somewhere. He've gone quiet. Maybe we'd best be going back.'

'Wait a bit.'

Silence. The quietness of the snow ate into their ears.

'Who-eee,' called Clowance. 'Is anyone there?'

It did the trick. The howl came almost immediately from a few dozen yards to their left. Music pushed through the undergrowth, getting snow-smothered. Clowance followed and presently stopped.

It was a dog, caught in some sort of a trap. A very big dog, the size of a young calf but much thinner. Lean-flanked, grey-flanked, great head, sharp-eared, red tongue lolling. Clowance had seen it often before – at the Warleggan fireside – frequently to George's distaste but tolerated for Harriet's pleasure. The dog had been caught in an iron trap; one leg was held by a spring device with short iron teeth.

'My dear life,' said Music. 'Tes a mantrap, you. God save us all!'

There were two of these boarhounds. Castor and Pollux. Which was this? The creature had obviously been in the trap for some hours and had torn its leg trying to pull free. But there was no chance of pulling free for the trap was attached to a steel chain which itself was fixed to a concrete stone sunk in the ground. The dog was panting but had its eyes closed.

'Castor,' said Clowance.

One eye opened; a gleam of quick intelligence. It seemed she had guessed right first time.

'Castor. You poor, poor dog. Oh, my dear, it makes me sick to see you. Music!'

'Ais, 'm?'

'Can you spring the trap?'

'Oh, ais. Tes like most traps only biggerer. Ye d'pull them two levers back.'

'But are you strong enough? The springs must be so strong to prevent a man opening them.'

'Oh, ais. But he couldn't get at 'em, see? Tis strength and knack. Strength and knack . . . Twill 'urt the 'ound some awful. 'E's like to leap and bite.'

'I don't think so. He knows me, don't you, Castor? Don't you, boy? He'll know we're trying to help him, and he's quite weak, I think. He's lost a lot of blood. I think we must try. I will put my arm around his shoulders when you begin. You can open it quick?'

'Oh, ais, I can open of 'n quick.'

III

George Warleggan was in a bad temper. Although normally tight-lipped and taciturn, it was seldom that he allowed himself the luxury of anger. He seldom had to. The mere sight of his annoyance was enough to send most people scurrying. (But not his wife.) But today his mood was of the blackest.

He told himself it didn't matter. It was no longer of the slightest importance to him what any of the shabby, pretentious Poldarks were up to. All rivalry had properly died with the death of Elizabeth. Chance encounters since then had been few and, if tautly hostile – particularly that encounter at Trenwith when Geoffrey Charles was showing off his Spanish wife – had led to nothing, could lead to nothing. It was a chapter ended, a door banged shut. So why this black anger at an entry in *The Times*?

He seldom glanced at the Court news. He read the parliamentary reports thoroughly to keep himself up to date – it was easier than going up to the House himself: the tiresome trip to Westminster was one he was becoming less and less inclined to undertake. Then he would read the shipping news; then the foreign news, and would glance at the rest of the paper to see if there was anything on the movements of the markets. But just by chance; his eyes glimpsed a name; then he read it. 'The Prince Regent has graciously bestowed a baronetcy upon Captain Ross Vennor Poldark, of Nampara in the county of Cornwall.' Just that. Just three lines.

It was the baronetcy that stuck in George's crop most, elevating his old enemy above the mere knights, ensuring that the title would go on. There had been a time not so long ago when George himself had thought to pull what parliamentary strings he could to gain the same title for himself; but since his bitter, irreconcilable quarrel with Valentine he had lost interest. The thought of Valentine inheriting *anything* from him would have made him sick. If only little Ursula could have come in for it . . . Ursula should have all.

He wondered savagely what influence Ross had been able to exert on Liverpool. Those trumpery little trips he took abroad might look good on paper but were in fact of minimal importance. No government in its right mind would pretend they deserved any recognition.

Of course Ross had for a long time been a toady to Canning, and though Canning was now a thousand miles away lording it over the Portuguese in Lisbon, he probably still had influence in the right places. Two or three of his cronies had received awards and sinecures last year.

Anyway it was done and one had to live with it. But George knew from his own experience what a title meant to ordinary folk, especially in Cornwall, and it was gall and wormwood to think of that arrogant, prejudiced squireen returning here with his servant-girl wife. Insufferable.

At this time of year Harriet hardly opened *The Times*, and he did not feel inclined to tell her. Let her find out in due course. In any case if he told her she would only laugh. She might even have the lack of taste and tact to show her pleasure. He had married Harriet long years after Elizabeth's death, and she had never become involved in the feud. She pretended to like Ross Poldark – she had said once, 'He looks the sort of man who if he ever draws his sword will throw away the scabbard' – but this was probably chiefly to annoy her husband. She had even danced with Poldark at that Trenwith party. She refused to accept her husband's judgement, never attempted to put herself in his place, to try to understand the causes of the enduring enmity.

Of course she might well pick up *The Times* today, for it was snowing and hunting was off. No doubt she would have done so, but she was distracted to a ludicrous degree because one of her boarhounds was missing. Pollux – he thought it was Pollux – had come home yesterday, dirty and dishevelled and scratched about the mouth and paws as if he had been trying to get through wire.

87

But Castor had not come home at all. It was very rare for the dogs to stray far from the house – they were gentle creatures in spite of their great size – and although given full liberty hardly ever took advantage of it. But – and this was the only circumstance which gave George a twist of amusement – there had been a bitch on heat somewhere and they had gone off on a long chase. Forgetting their duties, their fealty to their indulgent mistress. Ha, thought George, and would have laughed in her face if he had dared: so much for loyalty when a bitch is loose.

His relationship with his wife had not improved over the last year. It was not so much that they outwardly quarrelled but that she took less notice than ever of what he said. Of course this had been true in a sense ever since their marriage but she was becoming, he thought, less and less concerned to put a pleasant and humorous face on it. She lived in his house, took his money – for she had none of her own (three hundred pounds a year he had discovered by devious means) – and did precisely what she liked. She still accepted him into her bed occasionally, and this was still an earth-stirring experience for him; he would come down next morning ready in his grudging way to forgive and forget a lot, and she would have slipped back into her detached, impersonal, aristocratic indifference. The woman of the night was gone – a woman to whom he would have given a great deal – and in her place was the sister of the Duke of Leeds.

Indeed, he thought with mounting annoyance today, she would probably have betrayed less anxiety if *he* had gone missing, not a damned dribbling lolloping great boarhound.

She had been out all morning with a search party but condescended to come in to dinner and swallow a few moody mouthfuls. They had gone down to the River Fal, she said, and as far as Restronguet Creek. Another party had covered the area of Kea, a third Perranwell. (George realized why the house had seemed so empty of servants and the dinner half cold.) Pollux, she said, had been completely useless; dogs couldn't follow a scent in snow.

'It should thaw by tomorrow,' George said.

'Tomorrow is likely to be too late.'

He saw she was in no mood to be consoled so gave up his attempt at consolation. Instead, eating his venison pie with sweet sauce, he occupied his mind with matters nearer to his heart such as a possible change in one of the parliamentary members in his rotten borough of St Michael – Colleton had become impossible and pressure must be put upon him to resign; such as the knowledge of the figures for Wheal Spinster where, after a lean two years when part of the mine had been closed, a fine new lode had been sprung, promising high grade copper; such as the fact that his granite quarries above Penryn were turning in a handy profit; such as the fact that he greatly missed little Ursula who was in her first term at Mrs Hemple's; he would have been in Truro today to greet her when she came home from school, but for the snow.

'If you please, ma'am,' said Smallwood, appearing suddenly in the doorway.

Smallwood was a groom and it was on George's tongue to order him out of a room in which he was not normally permitted to appear; but clearly this was a moment of some special importance. Smallwood's ginger hair was speckled with unmelted snow, and he was not addressing his master.

'Yes?' snapped Harriet. 'Is there news?'

'I think he've been found, ma'am.'

'What? Where?' Getting up, her chair rocked back on its legs.

'They've brought 'im to the side door, ma'am. A lady and a servant. I think he's . . .'

Harriet was out and striding through the rooms to the kitchen. At the door, surrounded by other servants, were two horses. Dismounting from one was Clowance, scarcely recognizable among the mud and snow and bloodstains. Slung over the other horse, which Music had been leading, was the great dog, half open bloodshot eyes, very crestfallen and sorry for himself, tongue lolling, a front leg tied and bandaged.

'Careful!' Clowance was saying. 'Easy now. Don't let him fall. Two come this side, two the other . . . Oh, good-day to you, Harriet. We have brought back Castor. It is Castor, I think? We found him in a trap in the woods some miles up the valley. I think he will be well enough if he gets a good meal.'

Eight

I

They had been in Paris two weeks. To the opera with Brigadier and Mme Rougiet, to the Tivoli Gardens with Lieutenant Havergal, to a soirée at the Duchess of Orléans', and to a ball given by the Duc de Gramont, who spoke English without an accent and was a captain in the 10th Hussars. They had been to the Louvre, admiring the many masterpieces that Napoleon had brought there. They had ridden up the Avenue des Tuileries as far as the Place du Carrousel and seen the bronze horses stolen from St Mark's, Venice, still waiting to be placed on top of the unfinished Arc de Triomphe. Ross had spent two nights with the 2nd Army Corps at Auxerre as a guest of Brigadier Rougiet and had twice written despatches home. They had met Mlle de la Blache and supped with her and her brother at Tortoni's. Uncertain whether to open old wounds, but feeling the moral compulsion of that long-made promise, Ross had given her the ring Charles de Sombreuil had left him to give to her twenty years ago. Jodie's eyes had filled with tears but she thanked him and put it on her finger where it was dwarfed by other rings.

'After I had heard about Charles I am badly broken. I stayed in England two more years. Then I left my brother at school in England and went to stay with an aunt in Vienna. There I met Baron Ettmayer and a year later I married him. He is attached to the court. When he died in 1806 I moved back to Paris but as Baroness Ettmayer and made no attempt to claim my family's property. For eight years . . . I suppose I can tell them now, Henri?'

'Assuredly.'

'For eight years I have acted as *une espionne*. Reporting to King Louis in England, and sometimes to members of your government, events in Paris, sentiment in Paris, and what military and naval information I could glean.'

'Often I trembled for her,' said Colonel de la Blache. 'For if she had been discovered she would have been shot. Do you know what *espionne* means, Lady Poldark?'

'I can guess,' said Demelza.

'If you say you wish to learn French,' said Mlle de la Blache, 'pray come and visit me often. I have a very easy way, by talk, by conversation, much better than any teacher!'

'Thank you.'

She had changed a lot from the day of that one meeting at Trelissick. She was now red-haired instead of dark and was more brittle in manner; she had tired eyelids and the lines of living. It was said she had been the mistress of one of Napoleon's most gifted generals. Yet she was so open and frank that it was hard to see her in a world of concealment and deception.

'When Bonaparte was deposed, and there is a chance of some of our property to be restored I return to my *nom de demoiselle*, for it is then the family name which matters. And so I have become unmarried again! And now we have about half our property restored, which is more than the King has managed for many of his subjects. Bless him!'

'Amen,' said Henri.

Demelza said: 'Did you stay in England, Colonel? Your accent is – is *parfait*.'

They all laughed.

'I stayed in England for ten years, Lady Poldark. I stayed for ten years, but then I too went to Austria and later fought in the Netherlands – on the side of England, believe it or not! – but for three years, the last three years, I remained at Hartwell with the King, and came over with him as part of his personal bodyguard. It was, for me, a very frustrating time, for there was so little to do. I was young and ambitious. Dancing attendance at a non-existent Court is not an ideal way to occupy one's most vigorous years.'

'And now?' said Ross, knowing pretty well already.

'I am still one of the *Garde du Corps* to the King; when not on duty in the palace I am an artillery colonel at the barracks. When the King returned to his throne he wished to make me a general but there were many other and older men expecting favours and I chose to refuse. That of course is part of the ill-feeling in Paris today. The King has so many obligations to repay, often to men who have spent the whole of twenty years in exile with him, and seen little of war; yet he owes them much and must promote them to positions of authority while much of Bonaparte's great Imperial Guard is disbanded. One cannot be surprised at disaffection.'

'It will pass,' said Jodie. 'Time will allow the passions and the jealousies to cool.' She smiled at Demelza.

Ross thought of the conversation he had had with Brigadier Rougiet and two other officers at Auxerre.

The second of these men, a grizzled colonel, had said: 'These people who have come to take over now, sir, they are attempting to dig up a corpse buried for a quarter of a century! They expect to live as they lived in 1790! They have learned nothing and forgotten nothing. The revolution might not have taken place. Very well, accepted, there were many cruel outrages committed in the name of liberty, equality and fraternity, but there was a great new ideal born with it all. When Bonaparte became Emperor he did not try to put the clock back – rather he built on what was good, established his own code of justice, stabilized a rule of law and common fealty – that was why we fought for him so well and so long! But these royalists, with their endless train of rouged and powdered countesses and duchesses and little princelings – they are arrogant, insolent, self-seeking! Wherever they go they make themselves hated. They are no longer France! They died with Louis the Sixteenth!'

The other was a quieter man but a general. He said: 'Last month I was at a reception given by the King. Marshal Ney was present, with his wife – who is now herself a duchess because the marshal was created a duke. But I saw her deliberately snubbed and cold-shouldered by these old aristocrats. I think Mme Ney was almost in tears!'

After a silence Ross had said almost what Jodie de la Blache said three days later: 'Perhaps it is all too new. There have been rights and wrongs on both sides. Time may help everyone to adjust to the new circumstances.'

No one replied to this. Then Rougiet made an effort and said: 'I believe the King is doing his best for the army. Arrears of pay have been made up. Most of the cavalry regiments have been remounted. Fresh supplies of clothing and arms are being issued. He said only the other day to a group of generals – "It is on you, gentlemen, that I must lean." I think we must give him his due.'

'There was hope at one time', said the Colonel, 'that he would attempt to retake Belgium. It is after all our natural possession. But no. He is peace-loving, flabby, weak. The army remembers the old glories but cannot add to them.'

All this and more had been said. When they returned to their apartment after their supper with the de la Blaches it was late but Bella was sitting up in bed reading. When Demelza looked at the book she saw it was an illustrated French book called '*La Cigale et la Fourmi*'.

'Christopher gave it to me,' she said.

Demelza exchanged a glance with Ross but kissed her daughter good-night without comment.

They had been rather much together, Christopher and Bella during the last two weeks, too much together, but it all seemed so light-hearted, so jolly that Demelza did not want to become the heavy parent. He was like an older brother. In fact he was younger than Jeremy. Far more sophisticated than Jeremy, and enlarging Bella's experience enormously, yet boyishly scrupulous over just what he said and how he behaved to her.

Another, though far less important, influence in Bella's life in Paris was her friendship with Etienne, one of the menservants. He was not a particularly good servant, but he knew a little English and was happy to prattle away to Bella, teaching her French. He was also a passionate Bonapartist and impressed on Bella the idea that Napoleon had never been defeated, only betrayed by his generals. He also taught her a new song.

'What is that you are singing?' Demelza asked one day.

'The "Marseillaise", Mama. *Aux armes, citoyens! Formez vos battaillons!* Is it not a lovely tune?'

Ross had no objection to revolutionary songs, but he was less inclined than Demelza to view Christopher Havergal's friendship with his younger daughter in such an easy light. Havergal was an army officer; a hardened campaigner though still so young. Bella was a child, yet no longer a child. She certainly didn't look one.

Under Havergal's admiring attentions she had suddenly become much prettier. Little spots on her face, just where the chubbiness of her cheeks joined her mouth, disappeared as if by magic. Her hair seemed to grow more exuberantly. Her eyes, so often alight, glinted from a deeper fire. Of course it couldn't mean anything at her age. Did Havergal even know her age?

Talking of ages, Ross looked not infrequently at his wife and wondered if the men who made such a great fuss of her knew how old *she* really was. It was Bella's situation in reverse. If Bella sometimes looked nearly ten years older, Demelza looked ten years younger. Ross wondered what he had fathered, what he had fostered, what he had wed. In spite of the language barrier Demelza was enjoying herself. A Cornish housewife for most of the last ten years – with the brief interlude at Bowood excepted – she had happily settled into her life as the wife of Captain Poldark and the mistress of Nampara, not so much considering her looks so long as her most beloved husband contrived to be pleased by them. That was life; that was the way it went. She was the wife of one of the most distinguished of Cornishmen whom she loved dearly and who loved her with equal devotion, mother of five children, four living; worrying for them, caring for them, loving them and him, the mother and wife of a happy family. What more could she want?

Certainly not to be sharply translated to a strange capital city with no knowledge at all of the outlandish language they all talked. Not understanding a word, coming to grasp a word here and there, making do with the many sentences of halting English her friends and hosts and neighbours spoke, somehow surviving and surmounting the barriers of communication. But out of the blue, as it were, suddenly, as it were, without the least intention or design, as it were, finding herself the centre of so much male admiration as to take her breath away.

All right, perhaps all foreigners were like this, perhaps it was a sort of hot-bed society in which attractions and repulsions sharply flourished, but she was overcome – and as the Lord was her witness she could not say unpleasantly overcome – by this wave of sexual attention. She had no thought in her mind of being unfaithful to Ross; but one simply could not fail to be inspirited, laughingly diverted, occasionally thrilled and excited by it all.

There was a belief abroad that she really knew more French than she pretended, and that her stumbling attempts were a sort of conspiracy on her part to make fun of the language and of them. Her frank replies to subtle compliments were looked on as witty. Her company was sought by women too – much older women who looked on themselves with confidence as still being in the prime of life.

She *had* to do some shopping – for the Bowood purchases were simply not enough – and Jodie de la Blache went with her, acting as interpreter and consultant. Not only did she take her to the right shops, she insisted the merchandise should be at the right price, denigrating some beautiful material or costume in a way which would have deeply offended Demelza had she been the milliner, until it was bought and paid for and they were on their way home; then she was full of admiration. Jodie was a very feminine woman in a very French way, and Demelza had never met anyone like her.

With Ross's tacit acceptance as to expense they bought two new gowns, one for evening, one for afternoon, and two outdoor habits. The afternoon frock was of jade-green gauze over a grey sheath of silk marocain, the evening one a rich plum-purple velvet, much off the shoulders but with a wide necklace of silver tulle. And there had to be sandals – much in vogue – and stockings and fans and reticules. Demelza died at the thought of the expense but died with pleasure at the thought of wearing them. And like many of the men, Ross approved of the result, and unlike the other men, was able to prove his approval when he got her home at night or most often early in the morning. It was many years since he had been out of love with his wife, but now he fell in love with her over again.

He even, wonder of wonders, allowed himself to be persuaded to order a new suit for himself, from Staub in the rue de Richelieu, for his evening clothes were horribly out of date. Knee breeches and stockings had altogether gone except when royalty was present. The young men in particular wore bright coats and embroidered waistcoats but tight ankle-button trousers with low shoes.

Jodie tried to persuade Demelza to have her hair cut *à la Titus*, which meant a short cut curling round the head: it made the new hats so much easier to wear and was all the rage; but the most Demelza would agree to was a shortening. She was reluctant to lose too much of her hair which for so long had been a part of her, and she was scared to face Ross. But when he *was* faced, albeit with a compromise, he approved it.

Sometimes she would watch Jodie making up her face. Jodie would put rouge on her bare ears, on her temples, under her eyebrows. It was extraordinary. Demelza wouldn't let Jodie touch her own face, but, left alone, she experimented a bit and the result was interesting.

Of course there was much that was surprising in this strange city. Everyone spat, women as well as men, in church and in shops, rubbing out the spittle with their heels. The streets had no pavements for pedestrians to use, and you had to be careful lest a window should open and slops be emptied on you. All the ordinary people wore sabots, which made the noisy streets even noisier. The air was much cleaner than London, but the litter even greater. The food was strange, often poor in quality but rich in flavour.

It was embarrassing to be picked out as English and followed by a crowd of urchins, dancing and jeering; nor were some of their elders so much better behaved, making loud and unflattering observations about hats or clothes as they passed. On the other hand, you scarcely ever saw a drunken person in the street, or a badly treated horse, and those pedestrians who didn't choose to be insulting were notably polite. Bella on one occasion was immensely diverted by seeing a man arrested for urinating against a wall.

It was all heady fun.

Or almost all fun. The persistence of Jean-Lambert Tallien, who absolutely refused to be put off by competition from younger and better-looking men and by Demelza's distaste for him, which in the interests of good relations she tried to disguise but which a less thick-skinned man would soon have perceived, led to the first unpleasant scene of their stay.

No more tolerant of people he did not like than he had ever been, Ross pursued his chosen policy of listening to everyone and being superficially agreeable to everyone, so M Tallien was accepted with a degree of patient, cold courtesy that he may have mistaken for friendship. Or perhaps he thought nothing of Ross's feelings either way, being certain that no wife long married to one man could continue to care for him and that this ingenuous Englishwoman with such a pretty face and engaging manners could not fail to fall for him who had had so many agreeable conquests in the past.

It came to a head when Ross returned from Compiègne, where he had been to spend a night at the Palace there as a guest of a M Vendôme, a friend of the de la Blaches. When he returned Tallien had called at their flat and found Demelza alone except for the two servants, Mrs Kemp being out with Isabella-Rose and little Henry.

It was midday, and Ross was dusty and tired after an early start, his horse having just been taken round to the stables by a groom. M Tallien and Lady Poldark were sipping coffee, Lady Poldark very much on the edge of her chair and preparing to retreat from the Frenchman's advances.

'Ah, Sir Ross, is it not,' said Tallien, putting down his cup and rising. 'I have called to invite you both to a supper party I am giving, with the Duke of Otranto, at the house of a good friend – Mme de Brune – who will play the hostess on our behalf. There will be supper and a little gaming. A very fashionable evening.'

'Ah, M Tallien, is it not,' said Ross. 'I regret we shall not be able to accept your invitation.'

Tallien adjusted his eye-patch and smiled at Demelza. 'But you do not know the date yet! I am sure madame will enjoy the company in which she will find herself.'

'I am sure', said Ross, 'that madame is not enjoying the company in which she finds herself at present. Do I make myself clear?'

'In what way is he clear?' The Frenchman still addressed Demelza. 'We were very happy, were we not, in simple conversation. Tell your husband, pray, that he is mistaken.'

Ross did not wait for Demelza to reply. 'All I can say, sir, is that I am not happy to see you here. Nor is my wife. Nor shall we expect any sort of meeting with you again.'

Tallien bent and finished the rest of his coffee. 'We do not take kindly to insults in this country, monsieur. Unfortunately I am somewhat handicapped in the matter of demanding satisfaction, since the absence of an eye puts one at a disadvantage. Perhaps you had counted on that before offering me such offence.'

'If you wish me to,' said Ross, 'I will meet you with a patch over one of my own eyes so that the contest can be fair. It would give me the greatest pleasure and satisfaction to rid the world of such scum as you.'

There was a change of colour in Tallien's face as he bent over Demelza's hand.

'I will take my leave of you, madame. It grieves me that you should be afflicted with such a husband.'

Ross took him by the collar. A coffee cup rolled and smashed.

'Get out,' he said.

Tallien struck at the hand as Ross thrust him towards the door.

'You shall hear more of this!'

'Get out!' said Ross. 'Before I kill you now!'

II

Bella said: 'Where was you yesterday?'

'Oh . . . out with some friends.'

'Drinking and wenching, I suppose.'

Havergal laughed. 'My beautiful girl, it is not proper for such words to pass your lips!'

'I have lived on a farm,' said Bella. 'I am not ignorant of life.'

'And you would rate me among your farm animals? Shame on you! Do you not admit that I am a human being with all the feelings of sentiment and attraction that a young man can feel? It is not animal, I assure you.'

'What is it, then?'

'Avuncular.'

They both burst out laughing, as Mrs Kemp came back holding the reluctant hand of Harry, who had been toddling off.

They were in the Boulevard du Temple where Punch and Judy shows were daily performed and run by a man called M Guignol.

Mrs Kemp was a great one for taking the children walks – or, in the case of Henry, partly rides – 'for the good of their health'; and after a week, during which she had gradually become reassured that there was no particular hazard in the Paris streets in daylight, she had gone farther and farther, keeping chiefly to the wide, tree-lined boulevards of Madeleine, Italiens and Poissonnière. They had made a longer than usual trip this time to du Temple because she thought this would prove good entertainment for both children. By some mysterious means of his own, Lieutenant Havergal had discovered them. He could of course have been mischievously following them from a distance.

'Why, Lieutenant Havergal!' said Mrs Kemp, more than half disapproving. 'How strange you should meet us here!'

'Isn't it?' said Christopher, uncovering to her with elegance and a slight bow. 'It is a popular place, and I ventured a guess that just possibly you might come this way. So this way I came, and on the way ventured to buy you a posy.'

'For me?' said Mrs Kemp, staring at the violets with suspicion. 'Well, you know, I didn't ought to accept that sort of thing. A kindly thought, no doubt, but –'

'And kindly accepted,' said Christopher, handing the posy to her.

'Judy,' said Henry. 'Judy. Kempie, where's Judy?'

'In a moment. Any moment now,' said Havergal. 'See I have kept you a seat next to me, Henry. Up you get. There! And while we are waiting I have bought you a toffee-apple. How's that?'

'Kyou,' said Henry, grasping the stick firmly and beginning to lick at the toffee.

'And for Miss Poldark,' said Christopher, handing her a packet, 'a little box of sweetmeats, specially chosen for a songbird.'

'Oh, thank you, Christopher. I do call that very genteel of you.'

Sitting in this formation with Henry between them and Mrs Kemp, they were able to mutter asides to each other which she could not hear. Havergal had soon noticed that she was a little deaf and took advantage of it. He had even worked out which was the deaf ear.

Presently a man dressed as Punch came out onto the little stage and addressed the audience in harsh nasal French. It was a monologue which went on and on.

'Can you follow this?' Christopher asked.

'Not at all.'

'He reminds me of my riding instructor back in England. You could not understand a word he said and he was talking English.'

Bella giggled.

'Do you hunt, Bella?'

'Very little. My parents do not hunt at all but I have an aunt – a sort of aunt – who sometimes takes me.'

'Foxes?'

'What else?'

'Oh, I hunt everything. Rabbits, stoats, wild boars, geese, ducks, fieldmice, moles, voles, anything that hides in holes . . .'

'I have never met so comical a person as you.'

'. . . I even hunt men sometimes. And little girls . . .'

'I'm *not* a little girl!'

'As you say, I am being comical. And I would never hunt you, Bella. You are only to be wooed.'

'With sweetmeats?'

'Yes indeed. But notice I give the posy to Mrs Kemp. Did you not know it is really Mrs Kemp I come to see?'

She giggled again and they chewed contentedly together as the Frenchman at last finished his introduction and the performance began.

Unfortunately they had to leave – much to Henry's disgust – well before it was over, as Mrs Kemp, not without reason, judged the show to be obscene.

III

Demelza said: 'I am still upset for you. Even if he does not challenge you himself he can so easy get one of his officer friends to pick a quarrel with you. One hears of duels all the time.'

Ross shrugged. 'It could happen. I will be scrupulously polite to everyone.'

'I shall believe that when I see it!'

They were lying in bed together. She had herself been offended at Ross's brusqueness.

Demelza said: 'It is the 1st of March, isn't it. In three weeks Dwight and Caroline will be here. I wish they would hurry.'

'You think they might look after us?'

'Not so. But they are such old friends. You can talk to them in a way, in such a way.'

'By the time they come a lot may be clearer.'

'A lot of what?'

He did not reply, wondering why he had not told Demelza the rest.

After a while she said: 'Mrs Kemp tells me Lieutenant Havergal was with them again this afternoon. He is such a nice young man and such jolly company . . .'

'I'll have to warn him off.'

Demelza turned on to her side where she could see Ross's profile in the candlelight.

'I think he is just – lightly taken with her, as she is lightly taken with him. It cannot be serious. She's only thirteen.'

'Juliet was fourteen.'

'Who's Juliet?'

'Romeo and Juliet.'

'Oh.'

'Some girls grow up very young. Shakespeare knew well enough.'

She put her hand over his. 'Give it until the end of this week. I think his leave is nearly up.'

The candle was guttering but he delayed to put it out.

'Demelza, you may as well hear. I have not been quite frank with you, and God knows why, for there is nothing I need keep from you. About Tallien . . . I know too much of Tallien. Otherwise of course I should not have said what I did say.'

'What?'

'On our second visit to the de la Blaches, I told Jodie the purpose of my visit to France. There seemed no reason why I should not. It was quite clear from what she had been saying that, although her mission in Paris as an agent of the Bourbons has ceased, since there is no more need of her; yet she has continued to remain in touch with the many sources that she had dealings with until Napoleon fell. I felt that she might help me, and she has done. Last night in Compiègne I supped with a M Vendôme, who had many interesting things to tell me about the disposition of the army. Among other things that the Duke of Otranto – Fouché – and his creature Tallien are conspiring to start an insurrection to depose Louis and to put Bonaparte's son, the King of Rome, on the throne (under a Regency, since the boy is only four). Jodie said she had heard that the revolt was planned to start under a general of the 6th Army Corps, from

Lille in about two weeks' time, and this Vendôme confirms.'

'So Fouché and Tallien are traitors. Can they not be arrested?'

'So far it is all confidences behind the hand. No solid proof. At the moment Fouché is apparently advising the King!'

'My mind spins. What shall you do?'

'Nothing except report it to Liverpool. But in truth it is not *that* I wanted especially to explain to you – to explain my particular animosity for Tallien. Of course I resent his insolence, his arrogant attempt to seduce you under my nose. But it is something more. Something much more. Jodie has told me . . . You remember of course the landings in Brittany in 1795, in which I took part, when Jodie's fiancé, Charles de Sombreuil and many others lost their lives . . . It was an ill-wished adventure from the start, and it was crushed by General Hoche – as brilliant a soldier as Napoleon. At the last, only de Sombreuil remained with about eleven hundred men, in a strong defensive position until they ran out of ammunition. Then he entered into a parley with General Hoche, who agreed that they could surrender with honour and that their lives could be spared. But a man came down from the Convention in Paris and ordered that this promise should be betrayed – so, after they had surrendered, eight hundred men – most of them gentry and aristocrats – were shot to death in a field outside Autry. The others, the leaders, were taken out on to the promenade of the Garenne at Vannes – including Charles de Sombreuil – and executed. Personally supervising the execution to make sure that none should escape was the representative of the Convention from Paris. His name was Jean-Lambert Tallien.'

IV

In the afternoon of that day, on the south coast of France, in the gulf of St Juan near Fréjus, a flotilla of seven small vessels began to land men on the sandy beach in the bright spring sunshine. They consisted of six hundred and fifty officers and men of the Old Guard. With them were a hundred and eight Polish lancers, unmounted but carrying their saddles, about three hundred motley volunteers, and wives and children of members of the former Imperial General

Staff; something over eleven hundred in all, with arms and some scanty baggage.

Leading them was a stocky figure, grown portly, wearing a grey overcoat – for the air was chill – and the familiar battered tricorn hat decorated, since midday, with the famous red, white and blue cockade. There was no one to oppose the landing, scarcely anyone to witness it. As he stepped ashore a thin but hearty cheer from his supporters was almost lost in the wide, open air. Then some of the vessels fired off their guns in salute.

It was the man who only two years before had been the master of Europe, come to reclaim his rightful kingdom.

Nine

The medical fashion of the day, which catalogued people according to their humours, would have listed Stephen Carrington as sanguine. He felt himself at present to be on a wave of success, and he had no doubt he could continue to ride it until he had made his fortune.

Ever since he married Clowance things had been running his way. In years it was no time at all since he was picked up off Nampara Cove, a penniless starving seaman; yet now he was married to a beautiful, well-bred and well-connected girl, financed by the most influential bank in Cornwall, and owner of three vessels – *three*, mind you – which were in service earning him money in the coastal and cross-Channel trade. And he was building his own substantial house overlooking the harbour of Penryn. Everything was coming right.

Because his nature was what it was he disregarded the problems he had to surmount in making his three ships pay. Ever since he married he had spent more than he earned, and building the house would add to his indebtedness. But these were all natural developments in the life of a man still only feeling his way in the maritime world. His principal difficulty was in keeping his ships fully employed. The trade was there but it had to be fitted in. A vessel idle for two weeks cost almost as much as one employed. Even 'light passages', as they were called, when a vessel sailed out or home half full, usually meant a loss.

The *Lady Clowance*, under Sid Bunt, was slipping nicely into a routine. She would take on tin at Truro or copper at Gweek and carry them to London, bringing back a miscellaneous cargo for the small ports around the Cornish coast: groceries for Devoran and Port Navas, pipe clay and salt for Gunwalloe and Porthleven, ironware and maybe a 'passel' of books for Penzance. Because the *Lady Clowance* had a shallow draught she could venture up almost any creek, and Sid Bunt, the best navigator among them, could edge her in and out with the tides. He knew just how to handle her. Well and good.

But the *Chasse Marée*, though fir built and with fine raking lines, was what was known as a slopped ship: corners had been cut in her construction and she had been inefficiently fastened; so that there was a bit of trouble on most voyages. Moreover Andrew Blamey, who was in charge, though a good enough seaman, didn't understand the coastal trade. Bred into the Packet Service, which was only a step down from the navy, he never seemed to accommodate himself to his new role as master of a casual tramp. Nor was the money good enough for him.

Andrew was something of a thorn in Stephen's side; a jolly character in his way, but attracting trouble (either with men or with wind and water) as a magnet attracts iron filings. And in his new-found respectability and settled married state Stephen was keen to side-step trouble if he could – at least relating to his past life. (The sudden appearance of his son was bad enough.) Andrew, though mercifully ignorant of Stephen's involvement in the coach robbery, knew enough about his past life to hang him.

Not that Andrew for a second would mean to give him away; his cousinship with Clowance was surety against that; but Andrew in his cups was not a safe person to know anything. An incautious word at a wrong time might fall on a receptive ear.

So cargoes for, and maintenance of, Stephen's two larger vessels still had to be constantly seen to and negotiated. For some time he had been angling with George for a share of the trade carrying granite from the quarries above Penryn. This regular trade – at least outward – would almost certainly lead to reciprocal cargoes in London and Hull and Newcastle, and once established would mean a constantly profitable line. *Chasse Marée*, though built for fishing – or privateering – would well adapt for that if the chance came along.

That left his flagship, *Adolphus*, in which so far he had been chiefly trading with Brittany. Since the end of the war a flourishing – and now legal – trade had grown up. The French were eager for all the manufactures of England, of which they had so long been starved, the English for the silks and wines and fruits which until now had only come in under cover of darkness and under threat of seizure. It was a fairly easy trade, the easiest to negotiate though not the easiest to exact payment for, since the French were slow to part with their gold. And of course the profit was only a modest one on each trip, eaten into by maintenance, seamen's wages, and the like. Nothing to compare with a cargo run at night and shipped in duty free. There was also tin to be had – if one chose to carry it – on which poundage duty had not been paid, and this, shipped illicitly, doubled the profit.

So far, with Warleggan backing, Stephen had chosen to live within the law, but at times he grew restive.

It was on a fine early-March morning that they walked together – Stephen and Clowance – over to the site where their new house was to be built. In fact it was already in the process of being built, the first sods having been cut, some of the foundations already laid. Mr Jago, the master mason, had gone over it with them, pacing out the size of the rooms.

'They mayn't look so very big when ye just see the foundations,' said Stephen, 'but Jack Jago says rooms always look smaller when they're only planned out, and I believe he's right.'

'They're big enough for us,' said Clowance. 'Heavens, there are only the two of us, as yet – and did you say two servants?'

'To begin. But there's more bedrooms to spare in the space over the stables.'

'Can we afford even two?'

'This'll be my office,' he said. 'Clowance, I been thinking a long time – when we move in here and I'm away, could ye bring yourself to see to things for me?'

'See to things? You mean – the ships?'

'Just the business side. Just while I'm away.'

'Of course,' said Clowance instantly. 'I'd be delighted.'

'Ye would, my dear heart? Ye would? Not find it – unwomanly . . . demeaning?'

'Heavens, why should I? A woman is allowed to look after her husband's affairs! If anyone is so stupid as to think different, they can take their thoughts elsewhere!'

He squeezed her arm. 'It would be a great help to me. I try to deal with agents as little as possible, for they eat into your profit. But I have to tell you I get real frustrated sometimes – the paperwork is not what I like, and now Warleggans finance me I've always got to write things out to satisfy 'em. And then I get held up with mastmakers, ropemakers, chandlers and the like. Even if I miss one tide it costs money.'

Clowance was flattered by his invitation and squeezed his arm back.

'Talking of costing money. This house . . .'

'It is a question of planning for the future,' said Stephen, 'and not being afraid to expand. As things are going at the moment I reckon in a few years we shall be rich, and it's right that we should be living in a suitable house, like. Why, in a few years' time your father'll be talking about his son-in-law, the ship owner!'

Clowance somehow could not see her father expressing himself in those terms but she held her peace. Presently Stephen was called away and she paced round the perimeter of the new house, trying to visualize it when it was completed. From this site you could not see the creek, but you had a fine view of the bay of Falmouth. Today the sun glinted on a score of coloured sails bending before the breeze; there were brigs, schooners, snows, luggers, smacks. The water drifted and shaded into bottle-greens and kingfisher-blues and muddy browns about the vessels and the piers and the headlands of the Roseland peninsula.

She was happy at his new suggestion and appreciated again the zest with which he tackled any new enterprise. This was the first time he had had a business of his own – and a home of his own. If he was over-stretching himself out of sheer hubris, out of the pleasure of his new situation, well and good; should unexpected obstacles arise he would have the determination and the enterprise to surmount them. He was that sort of man.

Last night Verity had told her that she and Andrew senior were going to spend a month with James Blamey – Andrew's son – and his family in Portsmouth, and she, Clowance, was feeling isolated. For Easter her family would be in Paris, the Enyses in Paris, Jeremy and Cuby in Brussels, and the Blameys in Portsmouth. It was a notable exodus at a time when she would have liked to see her family or old friends. Not that Stephen must be allowed to notice this. She could not help but wonder whether his latest suggestion had come partly because no child was yet on the way. It was logical enough.

A step behind her and she turned to smile at Stephen brilliantly. But instead it was Jason.

Washed and shaven, in good clean workaday clothes, with the same blue woollen jerkin, fuller in the face, his blond hair brushed, his face smiling.

'Mornin', ma'am. Handsome, handsome mornin'. I thought as my father was here . . .'

'So he was but he has just gone to see Mr Jago.'

They stood in the sunshine, looking over the scene. Turning away from the sea, you could see part of the town, the parchment works, the gunpowder factory.

'Are you settling down, Jason?'

'Oh, aye, ma'am. This be the best thing that've ever happened to me. Tomorrow I leave for Cork in the *Chasse Marée*, carr'ing slate and bark and tin stuff. Mr Blamey in command. My father have made me second man.'

'Where have you been living? In Penryn, I mean.'

'There's a room at Widow Cardew's. But I've been to Liverpool and Glasgow since I seen you last.'

For him to keep calling her ma'am seemed too respectful, but her Christian name was too familiar and she felt Stephen would not like it. Officially she knew he had been introduced into the town as Stephen's nephew, but how long that story would hold she wasn't sure.

'They're ploughing over there,' said Jason. 'Bit late, but I suppose tis all this wet weather.'

'Of course, I'd forgotten. You were brought up on a farm, weren't you?'

'Sort of, yes. But before ever I seen the sea I wished to venture upon it.'

'Like your father,' said Clowance, smiling.

'Oh, I suppose. Twas my grannie's sister learned me to read an' write. She lived in a cottage two mile from us; twas a tiny shop they kept; and Uncle Zed had a pair of millstones that he worked wi' a horse, grinding barley and wheat for the folk around. But he died quite sudden and Aunt Loe couldn't manage by herself. But they was better than us, had been school themselves, better'n my grandfather, who seemed to know naught or care for naught except horses. They was his life. But I used often to go help Aunt Loe, and she give me books to read; there was only seven, I remember, extra to the Bible, but the four of 'em was about the sea. Two of 'em was books called *Voyages*. Somebody's *Voyages*. Hak – Hak-something. I read 'em over and over and I s'pose that started me off. That was before ever I seen the sea. I only seen rivers until I was a ten-year-old.'

'I expect you helped your mother as well,' said Clowance.

'Oh, yes. My grandfather kept two cows and a donkey and did cartage work t'make ends meet. I used to milk the cows and drive the donkey and help load the cart. Gran had rheumatism so bad she couldn't bend to get her shoes and stockings off. When one of us was about we'd do it for her, but sometimes I'd come in and see her sitting on the floor trying to get undressed for bed and pushing her stockings down with the kitchen poker. Mam did most of the work about the house, see, and of course helped Granfer wi' all manner of things.'

'Do you not have any real uncles and aunts?' Clowance asked.

Jason blinked. 'Real ones?'

'Well, you're speaking of your grandmother's sister, aren't you? Did your mother have any brothers and sisters?'

He blinked again. Perhaps the sun was too bright. 'Oh, aye, two, but they left home when I was young.'

He stopped there. A man was climbing the gate back into the field where shortly his fine new house was to be built. He wore a blue coat with a yellow swansdown waistcoat, dark kersey small-clothes, brown top-boots. His mane of yellow leonine hair was ruffling in the wind. The coat was becoming too tight to fasten comfortably. (They laughed together that he had put on weight since their marriage.)

But he did not look over-pleased to see his son.

'Well, Jason?'

'I hoped to find ee here, Father,' Jason said. 'Mr Blount sent me t'ask about the replacement bower anchor. I know tis off the schooner *Ferris* but Blount says it is not the weight Barker's promised. *Lady Clowance* catches the morning tide and he'd like a word . . .'

Stephen put his arm round Clowance. 'Tell Blount to go to Barker himself. Tell him if there's anything not to *his* requirements we'll trade elsewhere. I'm for Truro myself and shall not be back till the morning.'

When the boy had gone Stephen said: 'I intended to tell you, dear heart, but there's a consignment of carpets and rugs from Calvert's not yet agreed and it will be to my advantage to see them personally. Calvert thinks he can strike a hard bargain, but two can play at that game. Also I wish to see Sir George, for there's the deeds of the land to be transferred and other associated matters.'

'Will he be in Truro?'

'Yes. I hope Jason was not bothering you.'

'No. Oh no.'

'I'll do my best by him. But him being here, it's a reminder of what I did wrong by not telling you about him, and that makes him uncomfortable company.'

He went to Truro by dinghy, sailing up the river and mooring at Town Quay: with a decent breeze it was quicker than by road, and he still lacked what he called a first-class horse. On the way he wished he had brought Jason. Honest truth was, he *liked* the boy. Maybe it was natural, finding a full-grown son – reminding you of yourself – where you had left a squalling child.

There was no trace of resentment in Jason's manner at having been deserted, only pleasure at having found his father again. And admiration. He was *full* of admiration for Stephen, and this warmed Stephen like the summer sun. Jason was more romantic than Stephen had ever been. The books he had read – Somebody's *Voyages, Piracy on the High Seas, The Corsairs of the Barbary Coast* – had all given him an unduly romantic picture of what it was like to make a living at sea. Stephen, who had begun his short commercial career by taking all the unorthodox risks, who had broken the law on so many occasions, found himself taking the orthodox, law-abiding view against the eager questions of his son, who thought privateering the natural aim of any daring and ambitious man, who saw smuggling as a suitable side-line and expected his new-found father to know all about it.

His new father did. It was a paradox. The war had ended too soon.

There being as yet no children between himself and Clowance had not become an issue – nature was taking its time, no need to fuss or worry. But the absence of that issue was partly filled by the arrival of Jason.

Clowance had been very good about it, bless her. But he walked on a high wire; an incautious word would tip him off.

He saw the Calvert brothers that evening, drove a hard bargain with them, which ended with an equally hard handshake accepting the terms, and ate a hearty meal and slept at the Fighting Cocks Inn. He was up early and waited on George at nine.

George had slept well too, and all his interests were prospering. Ursula had been bright and affectionate last evening and she had hugged and kissed him before going off this morning. So he greeted Stephen without evidence of distaste. One could not put it higher than that, for his association with the young man had frayed and irked him since he had allowed it to begin. Apart from the fact that Carrington was married to a Poldark, the man was too free in his manner – had no real *manners* as such – thought too highly of his own abilities, was over-confident, with the slightest encouragement would get above himself. Harriet – *naturally* – pretended to like him.

Yet he, George, was really responsible for bringing the fellow forward and helping him to establish himself as a small-time but potentially prosperous merchant.

That first morning when they had met in the chamber above the bank George had just been fresh from the bitter, searing quarrel he had had with his own son over his marriage to Selina Pope; and the idea of putting this young man on his feet instead had had a cynical appeal. Now he kept Carrington at a grudging distance; so far he had been a good investment, and was likely to remain so. But if in any way he overstepped such marks as George had mentally laid down for him, he could be very quickly brought to heel.

That morning there were several legal documents to be signed, so Hector Trembath had been called in. Trembath was the tall thin still youngish mincing solicitor who fifteen years ago had taken over the remnants of old Nat Pearce's business and had since become very much a Warleggan man. (Ross now used Barrington Burdett.) He was a man of good education and genteel manners who had served George well.

The documents were signed and witnessed. Stephen Carrington became the official owner of four acres of Penryn farmland and of the house which Warleggan & Willyams Bank were going to finance him to build on it. They drank a glass of canary wine, and Stephen spoke of the hopes he had of getting one of his vessels into the granite trade. He knew well enough that George could put this business in his way with the stroke of a pen; but George, knowing Stephen knew, would not be drawn.

After it was over, Stephen shook hands with the two men and left.

'A forthright young man, sir,' said Trembath deferentially.

He would please me more if he were as deferential as you, George thought. But he only grunted and turned over the papers on his desk.

'One thing did strike me, if I may say so,' said Trembath. 'It was just a thought that occurred to me but . . .'

'Well, go on, go on.'

'You'll remember, Sir George, the mission you sent me on to see Mr Rose, to bring him from Liskeard for the purposes of – of identifying if he could the – the –'

'Of course I remember, man! My memory is not so defective as to forget something of such importance! What are you on about?'

Trembath's bony Adam's apple jerked as he swallowed nervously.

'I never told you, Sir George, it seemed then to be of little import at the time, for Mr Rose was coming in *person* to see if he could identify any of the men concerned in the coach robbery. And after he died, the matter went quite out of my head. While we were in the coach proceeding from St Austell towards Grampound – this was before he was attacked by the gouty pain in the head – he was talking about the men with whom he shared the coach on that fateful day. And he said – he said he particularly remembered that the naval lieutenant – what was his name? – Lieutenant Morgan Lean – that was it – Lieutenant Lean. Mr Rose said he particularly remembered that Lieutenant Morgan Lean lacked an eye-tooth. You'll forgive me if I am making too much of nothing at all, but this morning, talking to Mr Carrington, it was clear, was it not. I mean, it is clear, if you take my meaning, that he – that he –'

'Lacks an eye-tooth,' said George. 'I had noticed it.'

'Oh, so then there is no need for me to have brought it up!' said Trembath, in relief. 'I do beg your pardon.'

'I *had* noticed it on Mr Carrington,' said George quietly. 'I did *not* know until this moment that Mr Rose had noticed it on Lieutenant Morgan Lean.'

'Oh. I see. Well, then.'

'Well, then,' said George, 'may I put a suggestion to you, Trembath. If you wish to retain the business that I put in your way from time to time, pray never again forget to keep me informed of such things. Do not allow them to go out of your head. It is not a suitable characteristic in a solicitor. Indeed if it were to occur again I should look elsewhere for my legal assistance.'

'Yes, sir,' said Trembath, sweating. 'I'm sorry.'

'Did Mr Rose, if you recollect, say whether it was the left or the right eye-tooth that was missing?'

Trembath thought. 'I believe it was the left.'

'And Mr Carrington's missing tooth is on the left also.'

'That is so,' said Hector Trembath, rubbing his fingers nervously together. 'That is so.'

Ten

It was Cuby's birthday. She was twenty-three; ten months younger than her husband.

Jeremy planned a party for her. When she asked if they could afford it he said that they could always afford the necessities of life, and celebrating the birth of his beloved wife was the most necessary thing in the world.

He planned a supper for ten at one of their favourite restaurants, the D'Angleterre, and invited the best of the friends they had made while in Brussels. There was his first special friend, Frederick Barton, from Tiverton, a lieutenant like himself. There was John Peters, the farmer's son, who had recently married a Belgian girl with a very difficult first name, which had been simplified into Denke. And David Lake, who had known Valentine at Eton. Three other men and two girls made up the party, which began in lively fashion and never lost its zest.

Jeremy, by now knowing his wife's taste in food, had been along to the restaurant to order it in advance. They had soft-boiled eggs on shrimps in little pastry tartlets; lamb cutlets garnished with cock's combs and chicken livers; then pigeon pie with creamed spinach; and French open apple tart. A good Rhenish wine went down bottle after bottle. And then they called for nuts and sweet tarts and cheese. They were at the table from eight until midnight, talking, laughing, arguing, gossiping. At ten Jeremy rose and proposed the toast of the evening: to Cuby, who had won his heart four years ago and who, four months ago, had brought joy into his life by giving him hers.

Demelza might have been surprised at the warmth and emotion with which her son spoke, considering that it had always been his habit to disguise his feelings in an amiable easy-going flippancy.

But perhaps the Trevanions would have been equally surprised when Cuby, being pressed and pressed and pressed to reply, got up and pushed back her hair and quietly said: 'In December Jeremy made me part of him. There is no other way in which I ever want to live.'

Of course there was a present. It was a star ruby brooch set with small diamonds. 'Madness,' Cuby said under her breath to him, knowing they were already in debt. 'But sweet madness. I so love you, Jeremy.'

He put his fingers over hers, one finger over another, like playing a piano. It was a sexual caress.

'Later you shall tell me.'

By eleven most of them were become hilarious and a little fuddled. They had discussed the vulgarity of the Prussians, the inefficiency of the Belgians, the perfidy of the French, the ruthlessness of the Russians, the unreliability of the Austrians, the treachery of the Irish, the boastfulness of the Americans, and over and above all the total awfulness of the English.

Each member of the party was drawing on some reminiscence to confirm these opinions, and each one seemed to be funnier than the last. The laughter was getting more continuous, when a young officer called Carleton was seen to come into the restaurant with a girl they did not know. He waved and they all waved back. David Lake, who knew him best, called to him to come over. Just then the restaurateur showed them to a table at the other end of the restaurant. Carleton saw the girl to her seat, excused himself to her and came across.

The group exchanged quipperies with him and he wished Cuby many happy returns.

Then he said: 'Oh, had you heard? No, I don't suppose you will have. Word has just come through that Bonaparte has landed in France.'

This news sobered two or three men at the table, the others were too fuddled to find it anything but amusing.

No, Carleton had no details. Just that it was somewhere in the south. They'd sent the news by this new semaphore telegraph. Got away from Elba somehow. He'd always promised he'd come back when the violets were in bloom. Well, well, pardon me now, I must rejoin my pretty Clotilde.

When he had gone talk quickly broke out again, but a little of the spontaneity had gone from it.

'Imagine,' said David Lake. 'Old Boney back again. That's going to be a trifle of a nuisance. Wonder what he hopes to do.'

'Little he *can* do,' said Barton. 'It's not twelve months since he was turned out. They say on his way to Elba he had to travel in a closed cab; people, his own people, were hissing and spitting after him. Even his own generals repudiated him.'

'It might mean civil war in France,' said John Peters.

'Doubt it. He hasn't got the following. Where's Nosey these days? Isn't he Ambassador in Paris?'

'No, he's in Vienna,' said Jeremy. 'At the Congress. With Talleyrand and Metternich and the rest. My father and mother are in Paris at present. I've applied for leave to join them for Easter.'

'Might put that plan out of joint, my boy. There's sure to be a bit of edginess with old Boney on the loose. Unless he's caught soon and taken back to Elba with a halter round his neck.'

'Halter should have been put round his neck and tightened!' said one of the other men. 'Last year when we had him. Or stuck under the old mincing machine, what? Put him out of mischief for good.'

After the supper they all went on to a dance hall and danced till three. When Jeremy and Cuby reached their room it was twelve minutes to four. The fire had nearly gone out in their bedroom, but Jeremy went downstairs and brought up more faggots to set it to a new blaze.

'Don't undo a single button,' he said to Cuby. 'I want to do it all.'

Which he did, by the flickering light of the fire. When they were naked she moved to the bed and lay on it while he stroked and kissed her. The only light then seemed to come from her dark fringed eyes.

He said: 'This is not lust. It's love.'

'Just love,' she said, and put up her hands to his face.

Eleven

I

The news was slow in reaching Paris, and when it came at first it seemed to have no impact. The King was on his throne. The Bourbons controlled France. Outside their frontiers powerful armies possessed by powerful kingdoms ensured that the world should not be turned upside down again. The Palace heard first only that Bonaparte had left Elba; many people thought he would go to Africa or seek asylum in Egypt. Not until the 4th March did the semaphore telegraph confirm that he was in France and moving up from the coast making proclamations as he came.

The 5th was Lieutenant Havergal's last day in Paris before he rejoined his regiment in Louvain. He invited Mrs Kemp and Isabella-Rose and Henry to visit the Jardin des Plantes. Demelza had persuaded Ross to say nothing to the young man, and, as this was his last day, she let them go.

The garden – a long way over on the other side of the Seine, Havergal having hired a carriage for the morning – was much more than a botanical garden, it was a sizeable zoo, which was much to Henry's liking, and Bella's also, for she had never seen a live elephant before – nor in fact many of the strange creatures on display. There were wolves, panthers, hyenas, porcupines, deer, gazelle, elks, and no less than six lions, one of which kept a dog as a pet. Wherever the great beast strolled the little mongrel terrier would follow faithfully after him, and sometimes a long tongue would come out and lick the terrier's head, whereupon the dog would roll over and bark with delight.

With Henry off on determined treks of his own, Mrs Kemp was kept busy and gave Christopher plenty of time to talk with his little songbird.

'You see that bear,' he said, 'the one with the white on his snout. He's called M Bertrand.'

'How do you know? And why?'

'A few years ago, they say, M Bertrand was his keeper, and one day someone threw some francs into the cage. Bertrand decided to go and recover them, but the bear was waiting and caught the keeper and gave him such a bear hug that he died. So ever after the bear has borne his name.'

'Ugh!' said Bella. 'What a spookish story. You are full of spookish stories. Do the French find that amusing? What a strange race they are!'

'No stranger than us, surely, since we glory in bear-baiting.'

'But *are* they not strange, Christopher, are they not? Look at them. Look at those two men over there, with their tight brown trousers and their thin legs and their swollen bellies. Do they not look like frogs? One expects them to go jump, jump!'

'Some people do call them frogs,' said Christopher. 'They use the name Frog for a Frenchman. I thought it was because they ate them, but perhaps you are right and it is because they are like them!'

They strolled on. Bella hummed to herself.

'What is that? Tell me the words.'

> *'Entendez-vous, dans les compagnes*
> *Mugir ces farouches soldats.*
> *Ils viennent jusque dans nos bras*
> *Egorger vos fils, vos campagnes.'*

'I never knew the words before.'

'Etienne, our manservant, taught me them.'

'That song is almost treasonable, little love.'

'That is why I am singing under my breath.'

They both laughed.

'Talking of frogs,' said Christopher, 'reminds me of my old headmaster at the Charterhouse. Frogmore. Naturally he was called Frog. Or Flog, for he flogged his pupils for the slightest misdoing. He was much hated, for he followed a man called Green who was a learned, gentle, understanding soul. But we got back at Old Frog on one occasion. Let us go look at these wonderful birds.'

'No, tell me what happened, Christopher. I want to know.'

'How much d'you want to know? This much?' Havergal held up an inch gap between finger and thumb.

'This much,' said Bella, opening her arms.

He looked at her in admiration. 'Yes, you would, wouldn't you. It is in your character, my little one. My not so little one. I think you are adorable.'

'Hush,' said Bella. 'Mrs Kemp is near.'

But she took his arm as they strolled towards the parrots.

'Well,' said Christopher. 'I and a man called Flanders, we thought we should get our own back on the Frog. The headmaster on his way from his own chambers into the upper schoolroom has to come through his private door to which only he has the key. But this day when he came to the door he couldn't get his key into the lock, and he found that a piece of a bullet had been forced into it. The horrid man then had to retreat and go down his private stairs and up another flight eventually to reach the upper schoolroom by a long detour – which he did, and by the time he reached it he was breathing like a dragon. With all the upper school watching, he marched across the room and went up the stairs to the pulpit, where he found that door screwed up and he was unable to enter.'

'How very droll,' said Bella, laughing.

'However, not to be outdone, he takes two steps backward and puts a hand on the door and vaults over it and into his sanctum. He glares around the room and says: "The insolent puppies who prepared this surprise will suffer the severest beating it is in my power to administer." Whereupon he sits down, and finds he cannot get up without tearing his silk breeches, which have become glued to the chair.'

'Isabella-Rose!' said Mrs Kemp reprovingly, 'you must not laugh so loudly. It is not ladylike.'

Bella bubbled and crowed and choked. 'Sorry, Mrs Kemp, but Lieutenant Havergal does tell the most comical stories!'

Later, when they had another moment alone as they were about to leave the gardens, Christopher said: 'Tomorrow I shall be on my way to Louvain. It is a sad parting. But believe me I shall find you again, even if it means coming to Devon to seek you out.'

'Cornwall!' said Bella, not as indignantly as she would have done if anyone else had made such a mistake.

'Cornwall, then, or the ends of the earth. That *is* the end of the earth, isn't it? What do they mine down there? Is it diamonds?'

'Copper and tin.'

'I think it is diamonds also.'

II

On the 7th, which was a chill, foggy day in Paris, the French newspaper *Moniteur* published the news of Napoleon's arrival in France, and the general public of Paris learned of it for the first time, though rumours had been circulating. Not much changed. Life went on as usual. The theatres were full, the cafés busy, the traffic in the streets as crowded as ever. There was some extra surreptitious activity at places like the Café Montansier, near the Palais Royal, but these disaffected minorities were disregarded. The ogre would soon be rounded up and put back on his little island.

That evening the Poldarks and the de la Blaches dined together at Hardi's and then went to the French Opera in the rue de Richelieu, to see *Castor and Pollux*. Afterwards they went to the Ice Caffé on the Boulevard des Italiens, which as usual was crowded with well-dressed people, chattering and drinking and laughing.

Henri had been with the King part of the day and said that, in spite of a general lack of apprehension, he and his ministers were leaving nothing to chance. At a council that morning Marshal Soult, the Minister of War, though long one of Bonaparte's most notable generals, proposed to put an army of thirty thousand men into the southern provinces to confront any advance by the usurper. The Comte d'Artois, brother of the King, would command them, and under him would be the three Marshals of France, Macdonald, Saint-Cyr and Ney. Ney had had a personal audience of His Majesty, in which he had promised to bring Bonaparte back as a prisoner in an iron cage. Word had also been sent to the Duc d'Angoulême, who was in Bordeaux, ordering him to proceed at once to Nîmes.

All the same the de la Blaches were not without their doubts. If once Bonaparte collected an army about him it would mean civil war. Most of the officers were loyal to Louis but one could not rely on the ordinary soldiery. So many forgot the bad times of Bonaparte's reign and remembered only the good. Henri was confident but anxious, Jodie just anxious.

'And you, Ross?' she said, half smiling, but with wide open, deserted eyes. 'How will you report this to your Prime Minister?'

'I am not too certain even of some of the officers. Gaston Rougiet would never, I'm sure, betray his King, but there are others I have spoken to I'd hardly be so sure of.'

Henri said: 'Have you seen more of Fouché and Tallien?'

'Twice at receptions,' said Ross, 'but we have avoided each other.'

'Be careful, my friend,' Jodie said. 'They are enemies to beware of.'

'But are they Bonapartists?'

'They began as Jacobins. Now they bend with every wind. But Fouché would come to have a greater influence under Bonaparte than he has done under the King, and he knows now how I fought him and his kind during the long years of Napoleon's greatness. He did not then, otherwise I should not be alive. But under the King he is powerless.'

'Except to begin new revolutions in Lille to put the Bonaparte child on the throne.'

'I have to tell you that the authorities have now been fully informed of this. The revolt is due to begin this week. I do not know whether Napoleon's reappearance will have altered their plan or whether it was part of it.'

Demelza had been trying to follow this conversation, which had been partly in English and partly in French. 'But if the King knows of this plot, why are they not arrested?'

'Because, my dear, until they move we have no proof against them, and because Fouché is too powerful a man to arrest on suspicion.'

Ross said: 'Rougiet has invited me to visit him at his corps headquarters at Auxerre next week. I was there, as you know, in February, and learned a lot from the officers I met there then.'

Jodie shrugged. 'By next week we shall know it all.'

'I hope this fog clears,' said Henri. 'Today the telegraph cannot work, and it is important to know what is happening in the south.'

III

Unlike France, the day had been fine in Cornwall and visibility was at its most startling. The heavy rains which had washed the snows away had so drenched the atmosphere that no dirt or smoke or steam remained. Everything could be seen for miles. Not that this greatly affected the interior of Warleggan & Willyams Bank in Truro. Windows as usual were scrupulously clean but, as befitted a building in which security was paramount, they were small and the cross frames were reinforced with iron bars. The sun thieved its way in but received no priority treatment.

Frederick Lander, the chief clerk, came quickly to his feet when at about five in the afternoon his employer entered the little office behind the main counter. Lander was a man of forty-six, who had the misfortune to have bad teeth and disagreeable breath, but George bore with him, overcoming his distaste for the sake of the man's acute financial brain.

'Sir?'

George turned over the guineas in his fob and stared at the clerk, not quite sure how to announce his purpose.

'Mr Stephen Carrington is one of our clients.'

'Yes, sir. And doing pretty well for himself, I rather fancy.'

'No doubt. And largely thanks to us. He came to us, as you know, about six months ago, putting his affairs in our hands. Since then he has prospered.'

Lander sucked some of the tartar off his teeth. 'Yes, sir.'

'When he came,' said George, 'you will recall that his attempts to keep a record of the financial transactions in which he was engaged were primitive, minimal.'

'They were, sir. I helped him to go through them, at your request. Really they were just entries in a notebook, and none too many of those. No attempt, of course, to strike any balance or keep a detailed log. Since then, with our help, all that has been changed.'

Sunlight was reflected from the top of a deed box and a ray struck George's grey cheek. He turned away.

'I would like you to go carefully into his books. Such as they were before he joined us, but more particularly since. I would wish you to scrutinize each entry for its accuracy and for any discrepancies which may appear.'

'Yes, sir.'

'If there are any I would like you to find them.'

'Of course, sir.'

There was a pause.

'Mr Carrington does not have, I would imagine, a good head for figures.'

'Well, sir, average, I suppose. He is very – alert, as you might say; has quite an instinct for making money. But, of course, I have been helping and advising him, at your request, sir, so it may be that all his later book-keeping will be free of serious error. I thought that was your intention, sir.'

'So it is. So it was. But are you sure that all the information with which he has furnished you is as accurate as it might be?'

'Not that, certainly, no sir. But I have never found him out to be untruthful deliberate. He does not have much patience, like, hasn't really time for detail. Putting it down in black and white and red, so to say. Could do with a full-time clerk, I would advise.'

'See that this matter is looked into, will you. I should like you to spend some time on it.'

'Only last week,' said Lander, 'he accepted a contract by word of mouth and a shake of the hand. He's willing to do the sums later. Would you like –'

'See what you can *find*,' said George impatiently. It was better after all that there should be no misunderstanding.

IV

French society – or more properly Anglo-French society – or that part of it which in some way had connections with the Court – found Ross and Demelza an attractive couple, and there was a round of events in which they became involved, sometimes together, sometimes apart. Demelza went on her own, that is, with Emily Fitzroy Somerset, to meet the fearsome and formidable Mme de Staël. The company was altogether brilliant, and included her secret husband, Albert de Rocca, and her daughter, Albertine. Demelza was terrified, but the conversation of the entire afternoon was conducted in English for her benefit, and Germaine, as her closest friends called her, seemed to take a fancy to the alert, humorous Cornishwoman.

Mme de Staël gave it as her opinion that if by any frightful mischance Napoleon ever came back to control France again it would be the end of all liberty.

The same evening Ross went with Charles Bagot to the Palais Royal. This enormous building, erected round five courtyards and formerly the home of the Dukes of Orléans, had for the last quarter century been given over to the lower pleasures of Parisian life. Although close to the Louvre, it was surrounded by a labyrinth of narrow streets and alleys and was considered to be the very centre of the city's dissipation and depravity. No decent woman would be seen there, but Bagot said a man could not possibly visit Paris, even on the soberest of missions, without spending an evening in the place.

The ground floor had neatly arcaded shops and booths, and an uncountable number of restaurants and cafés and drinking dens; below were the vast wine cellars, gaming houses, billiard and hazard tables, dance halls and beer parlours; on the first floor, vastly larger gambling rooms, and bawdy houses so public as to be exhibitions in themselves. The top floor was chiefly for prostitutes, but in fact they were everywhere. Noise and quarrels and semi-nudity and sweating clowns and drunken soldiers and beggars and pickpockets abounded. Not surprisingly, the present Duke of Orléans had not attempted to reclaim it as his own.

The only incident of note on this particular evening was when a drunken Grenadier fell over Ross's foot and accused him of having stretched out his leg deliberately. It seemed inevitable that cards would be exchanged and seconds appointed, but Ross, contrary to the habits of a lifetime, apologized profusely and insisted on buying the Frenchman an expensive drink, whereupon the incident ended peacefully. They left the Frenchman laughing but talking loudly of *le sale Anglais*.

When they were out of earshot Charles Bagot said with an inflexion of criticism in his voice: 'You were well quit of that. These out-of-work officers have little better to do than pick quarrels and shoot each other.'

'It's a new policy I have,' said Ross.

On the Sunday they were invited to sup with a Countess de Jordan at her apartment in the rue de Clichy. Ross had referred the invitation to Jodie de la Blache – as he was coming to refer many things – and she said: 'I know this one by repute but I have never met her. There are a number such in Paris. She has no title: it is just assumed to give her the importance. As you will have seen, titles are held in esteem in Paris today and one can hardly afford to be without one.'

'Yet you abandoned yours.'

Jodie fingered the ring de Sombreuil had left her. 'It was an Austrian title. And the de la Blaches do not need one in Paris.'

Ross inclined his head. 'Is there anything against one going to take supper with the lady – apart from the fact that she is presumably a parvenue?'

'She is not so much a parvenue as an adventuress, employed by other adventurers to entice the unwary. After supper you will be invited to gamble, and the tables are always crooked.'

Ross looked at Demelza. 'We have accepted, but can make an excuse . . .' To Jodie he said: 'There will be army officers there?'

'Oh, of a certainty.'

'So it's likely that much will be said about Bonaparte . . . I am trying to gain all the information I can . . . Would it be better if I went without Demelza?'

'No,' said Demelza.

So they went together.

V

Their hostess was elegant in a slim-fitting gown with black sequins and ostrich feathers. She was gracious to all, and her guests, though not of the group with which the Poldarks had previously mingled, were titled and rich and from both the army and the navy.

Another fine house, this, with two rooms adjoining, one for supper, one for gaming. Silver candelabra lighted each end of the dining-table, which was laid with a damask cloth, Limoges china, antique silver. A sirloin of beef was flanked by game, poultry, ham, tongue, lobster, salads; preserves and confections, creams, jellies, fruits. The rooms were made to look larger by the use of carefully sited mirrors and mirror branches candle-lit; the chimney pieces were hung in crimson and gold velvet; chandeliers suspended from the ceiling seemed to glisten as much from the cut glass as from the lights they carried.

Before supper and through supper, as Ross had hoped, the topic was Bonaparte. He could now no longer be ignored, but as the foggy weather had persisted accurate information was impossible to come by. It was said that he had reached Grenoble, marching two hundred miles in a week, and not a shot had been fired. At the gates of Grenoble, confronted by troops under hostile officers, who were ordering them to fire, he had walked forward calling, 'Soldiers of the Fifth, do you recognize me?' and when it was clear that they did he had opened his greatcoat and walked towards them smiling and inviting them to shoot their Emperor. They had unanimously thrown down their arms and joined him.

Some said Bonaparte now had four thousand troops at his disposal, others eight thousand. But in any case, this was all several days ago. What of Lyon, the capital city of the Rhône, only eighty miles north of Grenoble, where the Royalists were in force, under the command of the Comte d'Artois, the King's brother? It was said that Napoleon had met with resistance on the way and had turned back towards the south.

There was also talk of a revolt that had broken out in Lille and, led by General Desnouettes, was now heading for the capital . . .

But overall the mood was jolly, not unaided by the dry, cool, tingling champagne served before, during and after the meal. Soon after supper people drifted towards the gaming room where a long oval hazard table occupied the centre of the room, with rouge-et-noir on one side of it and roulette on the other. A very pretty French girl approached Ross, and he allowed himself to be steered in the direction of the tables. (It had been planned before between himself and Demelza that he should allow himself to be treated as a dupe; but she could have wished that the girl might have been less obviously ravishing.)

Early on they had seen the Duke of Otranto was present – though this time not accompanied by Tallien. So far they had avoided him, but going into the gaming room they came face to face.

'Sir Ross,' said the Duke, in his even, clerical voice. 'So you are still in Paris?'

'Did you suppose I should be elsewhere?' It was only the second time they had ever spoken. Ross looked restlessly over this priestly regicide, this one-time leader of the Jacobins, who by sheer manipulative skill had ridden all the storms of revolution, dictatorship and restoration and still remained a power in the French establishment.

'My inquiry was a solicitous one,' Fouché said, bowing to Demelza. 'Reports have it that many English are making preparations to leave Paris, or have already left. I understand that the Duchess of Wellington plans to leave tomorrow.'

'Are you suggesting that it is dangerous for the English to remain in Paris?'

'I am suggesting nothing, sir. I am simply observing – observing not so much a migration as an emigration. I suppose it is always possible that if Napoleon should reconquer France – which Heaven forbid! – the British might suffer at his hands in the way they did before. That must be the opinion of your Minister Plenipotentiary, who, when consulted, is advising your countrymen to leave.'

'And what if the other revolt should succeed?'

'The other?' Fouché's eyes, which Demelza thought were like a fox's, clouded. 'Oh, that uprising led by General Desnouettes? If the King of Rome is put on the throne, there will clearly have to be a regency, of which I shall hope to be a member; and I can assure you in that case that the English will have *nothing* to fear!'

'Nor the French?' Ross asked. 'The loyalist French?'

'Oh,' Fouché shrugged; 'I have lived in every climate; why should not they?'

'Perhaps they do not all have your ability to trim your sails to differing winds.' After Fouché had looked his dislike at the remark, Ross added: 'Many were not given the opportunity.'

'I don't think I follow you.'

'Courtesy forbids me to remind you of the massacres in Brittany, the countless women and children murdered on the guillotine.'

Fouché smiled. 'It is a strange kind of courtesy, sir, which seeks to offend while pretending the opposite. This is an English custom, no doubt?'

'It is an English custom', said Ross, 'to dislike regicides.' And passed on.

'*Ross*,' whispered Demelza, 'you should *not* have said that! You *promised*! He is still a dangerous man.'

'Who should be in prison,' said Ross, wiping his hands, which had become damp with anger. 'And surely will be if the Bourbons stand firm and his insurrection fails.'

'And if it succeeds?' Demelza said; but the ravishing French girl was plucking at his sleeve.

They gambled for a while, but Ross was too old a hand to allow himself to be drawn in deep. He had two soldiers as his neighbours, and between hands they exchanged news and speculations which he was careful to take note of.

For a while Demelza stood watching, then she moved to a table where coffee was served. She enjoyed champagne – unlike most wines it uplifted instead of making you heavy in the head – but after a time it dried the mouth and one became thirstier than before. (As thirsty as a goose with one eye shut, as Prudie would say.) So she took coffee. One thing the French could do was make coffee. They seldom drank it in Cornwall; henceforward it would be much more used at Nampara.

She thought of Henry, who was ailing. So far the change of food and surroundings had affected him not at all, but today he had been fractious and queasy. Demelza had brought a variety of Dwight's powders and syrups for just such an eventuality, and she hoped they would put him right again. Thank Heaven for Mrs Kemp, who had been an absolute rock all through the visit, disapproving of everything French but adapting herself to whatever she found she could not change. She provided a sturdy English-Cornish basis on which you could rely or refer back to.

She had been helpful too dealing with Isabella-Rose's recent moods. Isabella-Rose, you might conclude, had also been ailing.

For two days after Lieutenant Havergal left she had hardly eaten a thing, picking at her food, complaining of headaches, ready to burst into tears at the least excuse. Ross did not have the greatest patience with moody children, so it was lucky he had been away with Henri de la Blache at the Paris barracks for most of the time.

It was young love, of course. Demelza knew the signs all too well. It was sad that it had come to Bella so early, because at that age there was no hope of a favourable outcome. Yet maybe it was salutary. The first time was the most awful for any girl – or any young man; after that it was never perhaps quite so terrible, and Isabella-Rose would get over it, and the inoculation would have worked.

In fact she was already getting over it; Demelza had heard her humming today; surprising how one missed it when it was not there, like a flower garden from which the bumble bee has fled.

They had seen King Louis this morning when they had attended mass in the chapel of the Tuileries. Distinguished visitors were permitted to sit in the *Salle des Maréchaux* and see him walk into the chapel. He had lumbered in, one foot swathed in bandages, helped by a page; but he had looked cheerful and well and happy, and he had bowed to the English and other guests as he passed. How could he be suddenly unseated by a defeated and discredited usurper?

And what of Dwight and Caroline? If they heard of Bonaparte's escape, would it prevent them from leaving England? Had not Bonaparte been particularly gracious to English scientists like Sir Humphry Davy, inviting him to come over and meet the French scientists, right in the middle of the bitterest part of the war? So even if the unthinkable happened . . .

Demelza got into conversation with two handsome young Frenchmen whose names she never knew. She was learning a little French and could make herself understood by the two servants who looked after them in the flat, but when it came to a social occasion such as this her new tongue completely deserted her and she had to help them struggling with broken English.

However, they made do very well, and somehow it turned into a laughing interchange about the Palais Royal, which both of them assured her was not nearly so shocking as it was rumoured to be, and they would together be altogether enchanted to show her round any evening after five.

There was a stirring by the double doors which led from the large lobby to the gaming salon. A man unsuitably dressed for such a smart occasion had just come in, his face sombre, his leather jacket and riding breeches and boots spattered with dust and mud.

A flood of French which she could not follow, and then the taller of her two young escorts bent to explain to her.

'Lyon has fallen.'

Twelve

I

Fitzroy Somerset said: 'Yes, the Duchess is leaving this morning. A precautionary move – no more – but if there is fighting, as there surely will be if Bonaparte continues to advance, Paris is no place for the wife of the Duke of Wellington. She would be too important a capture if anything went wrong. As for the ordinary individual holidaying in Paris, it is a personal choice. Ney and an army of twenty thousand are blocking Napoleon's advance. There is another whole army corps at Sens.'

Ross said: 'It seems that the garrison at Lyon and all the troops in the vicinity surrendered without firing a shot.'

'They didn't surrender, they just changed sides. What are your plans, Poldark?'

'To stay, of course. I believe I have been able to send home a few despatches which may have been useful. And now there is this emergency, it seems there is at last a good reason for my being here.'

'And your family?'

'Will stay with me for the present.'

Fitzroy Somerset plucked at his lip. 'I am undecided about Emily. You know she is with child?'

'No, I didn't. My congratulations.'

'Thank you. But in those circumstances I may decide to send her home. If one errs, it should be on the side of safety.'

'Of course. Have you news of the other rebellion?'

'What? Oh, the one from Lille? It has collapsed. Part of an army corps set out on Sunday from Lille, led by General Desnouettes and proclaiming the King of Rome; but it met with so little enthusiasm that by yesterday evening hardly a brigade was left. That dispersed at Fontainebleau. At least one crisis is over.'

'And Fouché?' said Ross.

'Fouché?' Somerset raised his eyebrows.

'Was he not behind the revolt?'

'I hadn't heard so. Had you?'

'Yes.'

'I wonder if the King knows.'

'I think he may by now.'

Somerset looked at Ross. 'Your mission has led you into strange company . . .'

Ross did not answer.

'In any event,' said the young diplomat, 'I doubt if Fouché could be moved against. Proof would probably be hard to come by, and at the moment it is unlikely that the King, needing all the popular support he can get, would touch him for fear of alienating the Jacobins. Do not forget that under the Bourbons they have found a much greater freedom to operate than they were allowed under Bonaparte.'

'You know, do you, that I am invited to Auxerre again on Thursday.'

'You'll not go?'

'Oh, I may do. In two days, of course, the major battle may have been fought. But it is a long way from Lyon to Auxerre. I have been studying the map. Near on two hundred miles. An army can't move at that speed, even without obstruction.'

'Well,' said Fitzroy Somerset, 'now the weather has cleared we shall get our news more quickly. How long do you plan to be away?'

'If I leave on Thursday I can be in Auxerre before dark on Friday. Friday evening as a guest again of Brigadier Rougiet. I think there are some cavalry exercises he wants me to see on Saturday morning – I can leave late on Saturday and be back on Sunday evening.'

'The stables I recommended: did you get a good mount?'

'Excellent, thank you.' Ross got up. 'I realize that there may *be* no cavalry manoeuvres when I get there. Or they may have become manoeuvres in earnest.'

When he returned to the rue de la Ville l'Evêque he bore with him two letters Fitzroy Somerset had handed him which had come in the diplomatic bags. One was from each of their grown-up children.

Jeremy wrote:

Dear Absent Parents,

I trust you are both well and happy and are preserving a decent moral dignity among the depravities of Paris. We are well and very, very happy. This time last year I would not have conceived it possible.

Yesterday was Cuby's Birthday and I gave a party for a few friends, which ended in the small hours and was much enjoyed. She is a wonderful wife, and I still count my good fortune that – partly thanks to the encouragement of my mother and the urgings of my outrageous father – I was able to bully her into coming away with me. I want very much that you shall meet her properly very soon, and I am delighted that you will have room to accommodate us in your apartment in Paris, for we have been overspending of late – or rather I have been overspending and Cuby has been clinging to my coat-tails to deter me. We shall all be together for at least a week and I can see my big brother again and pull Bella's hair. Know you when the Enyses are arriving? It would be even more pleasure still if they were in Paris for Easter too.

News reached us last night that old Bony Part has slipped away from Elba and is in France again. Some Belgians are whispering that the English deliberately let him go. Can you imagine anything more stupid than that? Others think he will come heading straight for Brussels, and a few English are leaving. I'm sure you have more recent reports than we do, but he could make a Nuisance of himself. Perhaps by now he will have been re-netted and will not be casting shadows over our Easter holiday.

Did you before you left have any advance information as to the likely profits of Wheal Leisure? When I was home the 30, 45 and 80 levels were all yielding well, so I am hoping for a bumper share-out to see me free of my debts. I am hungry to be home long enough sometime to get the engine house thoroughly cleaned – apart from the engine which of course is spotless. It is a curious habit of mining engineers that they are only concerned for the working parts.

By the way, did you see about the disaster that occurred at Newcastle Colliery, Durham? A great many people assembled to witness the opening of the new steam railroad to carry the coal in wagons to the dockside. The engine burst and killed ten, with another fifty badly scalded. Perhaps I am safer in the army! Seriously, some people will never learn. I am comforted to hear that the London Times *newspaper will shortly be printed by steam. Perhaps their editorials will become more explosive!*

Cuby is beside me and sends you her love to join with mine.

Your loving son,

Jeremy

Clowance's letter ran:

Dearest Mama and Papa,

It was more than good to receive your letter and to learn you were safely installed in a comfortable home. How lucky you are to be there. I so very much envy you, and especially I envy Bella the opportunity to learn French. And the opportunity to see Paris after all these years of War!

I trust you had my earlier letter telling you of my joy that Papa had decided to accept a title. It is so right that he should have done so. I trust you are now getting used to being so addressed. Stephen says he walks three inches taller for having a baronet for his father-in-law!

We are beginning the building of our new house! It is very exciting and I believe will be wonderful when finished. Stephen is away at times but less than he used to be. Bert Blount is permanently in charge of the Lady Clowance, *and Andrew of the* Chasse Marée. *Stephen is so proud of* Adolphus *that he is at present using her for quick trips to France and back only and commanding her himself. He can't bear to be away from Falmouth for long; but he has asked me if I can Deputize for him when he is away and maybe help with the office work even when he is home. Of course I shall love to do this, and in no time will be making out Bills of Lading in triplicate form!*

Long before all this you will be home from your stay in Paris and will have told me all your adventures. Dwight and Caroline were much looking forward to joining you, and I only so much wish that Stephen and I could grow wings and make up the family party.

Lady Harriet (Warleggan) has been in a great taking because someone in the woods above Cardew has been setting mantraps to deter poachers, and one of her great boarhounds wandered off a couple of weeks ago and was caught in the trap. By chance I found him – returning from the Enyses accompanied by Music Thomas – and we bore him home. He has his leg in a splint but I think will have come to no hurt. Harriet's fury knows no bounds. She is still trying to find who is responsible, and has narrowed the search to the Devorans and the Hills. (Lord Devoran, of course, wouldn't harm a rabbit, but Betty is capable of anything!) I incline to think she is to blame.

In any event, Music profited by it, for Harriet gave him five guineas and a new suit of clothes. I do not believe he had ever seen so much money, and I am sure he went lollopping off in the snow singing all the way at the top of his voice. He is a much improved person since Dwight took him in hand. He was wonderful with the hound.

The weather is brilliant now, but with a chill wind. The daffodils are in full bloom, and I'm sure the garden at Nampara looks its best. I am hoping to have a garden. We shall be exposed to the east winds, but look what a wall has done for Nampara!

We hunted twice with the Stithians pack last week. Nero is fine, but Stephen is still looking out for a hunter for himself. It is expensive to hire them and we cannot for ever be borrowing from Harriet. I saw Paul Kellow in Truro last week looking very smart – the coaching business is strangely prospering for him – and with a new inamorata, one I had not met before, called Mary Temple. Someone says she is a daughter of the Temples of Tregony, who are supposed to be rich, aren't they?

All my love,
Clowance

'It does not look as if Jeremy yet knows about you,' said Demelza, turning the letter over. 'It is addressed to Captain and Mrs Poldark. You did say you had written to him?'

'Yes. I believe I omitted to mention it.'

'You . . .? Oh, really, Ross! I cannot *believe* you! That you should not tell him the most important thing! I wish I had written myself!'

Ross said: 'What would you have had me say? "Dear Jeremy, you will be shocked to know that your father's egoism has triumphed over his honesty and he has allowed himself to be pushed – not quite resisting every step, protesting loudly but insincerely – into accepting a title which he neither needs nor deserves. Furthermore, this absurd appendage which will now forever more be hung at the front and back of his name like a rosette on a donkey's head and a ribbon on his tail, will on his decease – which may occur any day –

135

be transferred to you. This blot, this scar, this appendage, can never more be discarded –" Whatever's the matter?'

He could not go on for Demelza was crowing with laughter.

'Stop it!' he said angrily. 'You sound like Bella!'

'My lover,' she gasped. 'My dear, dear Ross. I did not know you could express – express yourself so well! You have said you are no House of Commons man, but I am sure the – the chamber, is it? – would – would listen spellbound.' She sobered suddenly, dabbing her eyes. 'At heart, my lover, is it not now that *you* are being insincere? Not for accepting the title but for even pretending that Jeremy will look on it that way. Or that anyone else in the whole world over would, my dearest. *Would* they? Would any of your radical friends, even? They would say, if we have a friend called Sir Ross Poldark, is he not more valuable as a helper than *Captain* Poldark?'

'You don't understand at all –'

She went up to him and squeezed his arm. 'I think maybe I do a little. You are too proud to *need* a title, is that not it? Your name is good enough anywhere in the world. Well, nobody has ever been prouder of the name of Poldark than I have since you gave it me. But this is just – just a little icing on the cake, is it not? Not to be taken serious. Not to grow larger in the head and more proudful for it. Not to expect folk to bow and scrape because you are a baronet. Not to let it make one scrap of difference how you think and feel about people or people's rights, or justice or freedom. You are the same as you ever were, and if the world thinks different it will soon discover its mistake.'

'Your hand's cold,' he said.

'Tis your arm that's hot,' she said. 'Hot with annoyance because somebody has persuaded you to take what you do not want to take. So now you must sit down and write to your son today. Or else I will write.'

'That is someone at the door,' he said.

'Let 'em wait, Cap'n Poldark.' She slipped her hand down to his. 'See how your heat is warming my hand, Cap'n Poldark. It would warm my heart too if I thought you were as happy as I am about it.'

'*Are* you happy about it? About *that*?'

'Of *course*. It is just what I said – a little icing on the cake.'

'Caroline thought you would be.'

'*Caroline?* You haven't *seen* her!'

'After Christmas. I saw her one afternoon. She said you would have wanted me to take it.'

'I believe you take more notice of her than you do of me!'

'Sometimes. On some subjects. Yes. That *is* someone at the door.'

'If we wait long enough they will go away.'

'Jodie said she was coming round this afternoon to take you shopping. But it would be early for her.'

'I don't know what I can possibly want. Only perhaps shoes. Is Jeremy right, Ross? Is Leisure doing well?'

'Very well. We shall not want for a loaf of bread.'

'I dearly hope Jeremy does not get into the hands of money-lenders. I have always felt he was so good about money. Now I am not so sure.'

'Why? What has he done?'

'It says in the letter,' Demelza corrected herself hastily, 'that he is in debt. I just worry when I think of any of my children in debt.'

'No one is going to the door,' said Ross. 'Meurice is a lazy skunk and Etienne little better.' He detached himself from his wife.

'Ross,' she said.

'Yes?'

'If you hate a title so much why did you allow yourself to be called Captain? Should not plain Mister have been enough?'

He considered her. Then he reached forward and tweaked her nose.

'Ow!' she said.

He kissed her nose and patted her hand as he went towards the door.

'You should be in Parliament,' he said, 'not I.'

II

It was Jodie, and she was just turning away.

'Oh, I thought you were from home. I came early for I may not have time this afternoon. Can you come with me this morning, Demelza?'

She was looking very smart in her scarlet merino coat and white silk hat trimmed with striped ribbons. But her face was colourless and her dark eyes at their most desolate.

'Well, I can't go in this!' said Demelza. 'Give me five minutes to change. Have you brought your *coucou*?'

'Yes. It is quite a long way to walk.'

'I delight to drive in it.'

'Wrap up. The wind is cold.'

When Demelza had gone Ross walked to look out of the window at the trim little carriage with its single roan pony and the waiting groom.

'Do you have further bad news for us?'

'. . . Perhaps it is the news we do not have which is worrying.'

'Tell me.'

'Well, we have reports of Bonaparte's proclamations. He proclaims himself the liberator of his faithful subjects from a foreign-imposed Bourbon tyranny. He says his eagles are on the wing and will perch from spire to spire until they reach Notre-Dame. He proclaims that he was permitted to leave Elba by the British (who control the Mediterranean), that he is to be joined en route by the Empress and by her son, the King of Rome, and that they will shortly be crowned in Paris. (Thus implying that Austria also favours his return.) He has already named part of his cabinet: Cambecérès as Minister of Justice, Carnot of the Interior. Fouché's back to his old position as Chief of the Police. He promises free elections, a free press . . . Above all he asserts that he comes in peace and wishes peace with all nations. He is here to re-establish the Empire and the self-respect and dignity of France.'

After a minute Ross said: 'Part of it is lies, but it will appeal to many people.'

'Free press!' exclaimed Jodie. 'Four newspapers are published in Paris when Bonaparte rules, and all are in strictest government control.'

'What else do we know?'

'They say his route will be by Mâcon and Chalon, making for Dijon. But before he gets there he must meet and defeat Ney's army.'

'Do you rely on Ney?'

'I know him well, my friend. He has lived a dissolute, a vivid life. He is impulsive, generous, brave to a fault, warmly fond of his wife in spite of all his infidelities, indiscreet, quick-tempered, emotional. He has quarrelled bitterly with Bonaparte but I suspect, yes, I suspect secretly loves him. He has two very loyal generals under him, Bourmont and Lecourbe, who will certainly keep him faithful to the King, even if he were to waver. But I do not think he can possibly waver – after such promises.'

Ross kicked at the fire. It was a cold day, and when there was a north wind this room was always chill.

'Well, the other insurrection has collapsed. The march from Lille. Fitzroy Somerset told me.'

'I have not seen Henri today. He has been working day and night to bring all our forces up to the maximum strength – just in case they are needed. The King's Bodyguard has been almost doubled by the enlistment of new Royalist volunteers. There is every sign of high spirits and warm affection in the Palace. This second army is to be concentrated before Melun.'

Demelza returned wrapped in a grey suede coat with fox fur at collar and cuffs. Her hat was of green suede with a small brilliant feather. Jodie smiled at her.

'We shall not be so long, Ross, for I have urgent work this afternoon.'

'And Fouché?' said Ross.

'Fouché. Ah yes. A strange thing has happened. The King sent for him this morning. He knew of his involvement with Desnouettes, but was not intending to face him with it. The King wished that he might ask for his advice, on the assumption that Fouché would be useful in this crisis. But when they send round they learn that the Duke of Otranto has gone away for a few days . . . This is clearly a diplomatic absence. He is somewhere in Paris – with Tallien, no doubt – waiting the events of the next few days before he emerges again from his sty.'

'Bonaparte has already said he wants him to serve as his next Chief of Police.'

'So our agents report. Of course if that ever happened . . .' Jodie opened the door and waited for Demelza.

Demelza said: 'If that ever happened?'

'I should be arrested at once. Fouché would never miss a chance like that.'

Thirteen

I

But on the 16th all was changed. The *Moniteur* published an official despatch received by telegraph that morning, stating that although some troubles had been reported in Mâcon, Chalon and Dijon, it was only among the dregs of the population. Napoleon with a harassed force of four thousand men and a few cavalry was now retreating upon Lyon and his troops were deserting in masses. He was isolated in the middle of France, and Marshal Ney was advancing on him.

It looked like a repetition of the collapse of the revolt from Lille.

The Minister of War entered the officers' guard-room at the Paris Barracks and said: 'Well, gentlemen, you may take off your boots. The commandant of Napoleon's advance has been taken prisoner and is at this moment in my apartment. Desnouettes is in a place of safety with his accomplices. General Marchand is in the rear of Napoleon. All is working quickly and well. The emergency is over.'

The *Moniteur* also reported messages of loyalty pouring into the Tuileries from the heads of departments all over France. The King attended the sitting of the Chamber of Deputies and made a moving speech which was loudly applauded. He announced he would review the garrison troops of Paris, six thousand in number, the following day in the Champ-de-Mars.

With the main struggle now over, Ross left for Auxerre as arranged. He had had no communication with Brigadier Rougiet for more than a week, but reasoned that if he arrived in Auxerre and Rougiet, because of the crisis, had had to change his plans, it would not so much matter. Ross felt he could gain a better idea of the swaying sympathies of the army by visiting them at their base.

To his surprise he found it hard this time to hire a good horse.

In a month prices had doubled and quality halved. Too many people had recently decided to leave Paris. He wondered if Fouché and Tallien had really left or, as Jodie supposed, simply gone to ground. He would have felt slightly happier leaving Demelza for three days if Tallien were under lock and key. Though, Heaven knew, if Tallien turned up again and tried to take any liberties he would find himself faced by a spitting cat. (And two menservants, and an outraged Cornish Wesleyan.)

It was strange, he thought to himself, that he had heard Tallien's name, as the man who had betrayed General Hoche's promise of safe conduct, all those years ago – twenty years this coming autumn – he had heard it and execrated it and then almost forgotten it. It had never crossed his mind that one day he would meet this evil man. Somehow he had thought all those monsters, like Robespierre, had ended up on the guillotine to which they had condemned so many others. Not so.

The best horse Ross could find was an elderly grey gelding called Bayonne; it was brought round for him on the Thursday morning, and after a loving parting from his family he made his way out of Paris and headed south for Melun. Because his horse was so slow, and soon slightly lame, it was late in the evening when he reached Sens and found lodgings in an inn by the river. On the 17th he was off early but constant rain made the trip disagreeable.

II

The morning that Ross left Sens, news reached Paris that Marshal Ney, far from capturing the Emperor, had changed sides at Lons-le-Saunier three days ago and, except for a few loyalist officers, had taken the whole of his army with him. The King when he heard said: 'Is there no more honour?' Nevertheless, as planned, he reviewed his troops at the Champ-de-Mars and went through the ordinary duties of the day.

It also became clear that as he advanced Bonaparte had seized the semaphore stations and had had them send out the falsely reassuring news of yesterday. Nothing is more calculated to create panic than optimistic information that is found to be based on lies.

In the afternoon a grim and subdued Henri de la Blache called to see Demelza.

'Jodie tells me that Ross has gone to Auxerre. He is sure to receive intelligence on the way about the manner of Ney's treachery and Napoleon's approach. So he'll turn back. In any case he is an Englishman and a non-combatant so he is not likely to be at risk. All the same, and Jodie agrees with me, I think it is time you all obtained passports to leave France. I shall stay here, of course, for my place is with the King; but Jodie will leave also – for her own safety. Tomorrow morning early she will call for you and take you to M le Comte de Joucourt, who will provide them.'

'D'you think Napoleon will reach Paris, then?'

'I think so – after today's news. Yes.'

'When?'

'When? Well, we are not sure where his forces are. Probably already north of Dijon. He still has to confront the army of Melun. There is a stronger stiffening in it of the older aristocracy, but after the tidal wave of sentiment which has engulfed the other armies . . . I think we should be certain only of about a week.'

'I dearly wish Ross had not gone.'

'So do I. But never forget if this comes to war, it is civil war, between Louis Bourbon and Napoleon Bonaparte. Whatever might happen in the future, France is not now at war with England or Austria or Russia or Prussia. Ross is a civilian foreigner. And I have a strong feeling that Bonaparte will go out of his way to placate foreign opinion.'

'He did not do so last time.'

'You mean twelve years ago? But then he was at the height of his powers, and he knew, having gained all the concessions from England that he could, that his next move was to resume the war. At the moment, if he comes to power again in France, he must have at least a year's peace to consolidate himself.'

Demelza looked out at the rain beating on the windows. 'Lady Fitzroy Somerset sent a note this morning advising us to leave. She says she is leaving tomorrow.'

'Jodie will call for you in the morning.'

'I would not go without Ross,' said Demelza.

'Of course not. When he hears the latest news, he's sure to return tomorrow. But to have the passports will be a help.'

'Twill be nasty for him riding a long way in this weather.'

III

To follow the road from Sens to Auxerre you kept within sight of the River Yonne all the way. It was flat rich country but sparsely populated, and what people there were lived in hovels. About ten o'clock the rain cleared and the sun peered out with a watery, etiolated eye. To balance this benefit Bayonne's lameness became worse. Ross dismounted to see if he could find what was wrong. The animal was perfectly docile, and held his head in a dejected way as if ashamed of his shortcomings. There seemed nothing wrong with his shoes. It was the right hind leg and after a careful and discreet prodding Ross came to the conclusion that the trouble was probably rheumatism made worse by the cold and damp.

They were already through Joigny, but he found a farrier in the next village. The ragged little Frenchman shrugged his shoulders and said: 'C'est vieux.' True enough. With the sun warming his damp shoulders Ross thought the description applied to him as well. He asked the farrier about the prospect of hiring or buying a mount of some sort, but there was apparently nothing to be had this side of Auxerre.

Ross went on, riding half a mile on the limping horse, then dismounting and limping the next half-mile on foot. The camp where the Sixth Corps was stationed was north of Auxerre so the distance now could not be great.

The previous time he had visited this camp he had remarked to himself on the casual attitude of the guard, the general untidiness of the soldiers. He had discussed with Rougiet the difficulty of maintaining proper discipline in any body of troops during a period of prolonged peace; and this more particularly the case with France whose army was still swollen beyond any necessary peacetime needs.

A difference this time: the sentries were smartly at attention and brusque to the point of discourtesy. He had to produce the letter he had had from Brigadier Rougiet before he was allowed beyond

143

the guard-room. Then it was half an hour before an orderly came for him.

At least there was little difference in the warmth of Gaston Rougiet's welcome, though perhaps it carried an overtone of anxiety.

'Welcome, welcome, my friend. You are too good to have come again. Was the weather atrocious? Pray sit down and take a glass of champagne and tell me all the news of Paris.'

This was a permanent camp, the officers' quarters brick built, and comfortable chairs, and fires burning.

They talked a few minutes; Ross told him that his horse had gone lame, and Rougiet sent an orderly to get an army farrier's expert report. But it could not be long before the one subject uppermost in both their minds was spoken of.

Rougiet said: 'Believe it or not, do you know where his advance forces had reached by this morning? Avallon.'

'Is that far from here?'

'Fifty kilometres. And do you know where Marshal Ney's troops are now? Tonnerre. That is thirty-five. They could be here tonight, if they wished to be!'

'Then I must not stay.'

'I have heard they have arranged to meet here in the morning. It will be a grand moment. No doubt, in spite of past disagreements, they will embrace as brothers. You can lie easy here tonight.'

'And this camp?'

Rougiet shrugged. 'There are only two brigades here at present – mine and Baron Novry's – and the 14th Regiment of Lancers – and two batteries of artillery and a few engineers. About seven thousand all told.'

'And their sentiments?'

'Bonapartist to a man.'

Rougiet was watching him intently.

'And yourself?' said Ross. 'Or need I ask?'

'You have known since we first met of my dislike of what the Bourbons have brought to France.'

'You also admitted your dislike of what Bonaparte had brought France to.'

'Indeed. But he is too great a man not to have learned by his mistakes. I believe the government he will set up in Paris will be a

144

better one in all respects than the one he left behind twelve months ago. At least it cannot fail to be better than the one we have now!'

Ross tried to ease his aching ankle. He had walked farther today than he had done for years.

'I can see your point of view. Though from what I have seen I cannot fault the King so much as his relatives. And has he not had an impossible task, trying to reconcile the old with the new – bringing back the kingship and the courtiers of twenty-odd years ago, trying to form some sort of an accommodation between an old and a new regime?'

'You cannot turn the clock back,' said Rougiet. The light showed up the vivid scar across his face – a relic of Jena, he had told Ross. 'The Jacobins turned equality into a blood bath, but Bonaparte stopped that, and under him an element of equality, a degree of fairness and even-handedness and justice within the law was established. But the evil stupidity of these émigrés who have returned, claiming their old rights, their old estates, without an idea or a principle in their heads which did not exist before 1793 . . .'

Ross accepted another glass of champagne. 'And if the return of Bonaparte leads to a resumption of war?'

'It should not, my friend. Bonaparte will not be seeking war with anyone this time. But if war is forced upon us we shall show that we can still fight!'

'No one surely has ever doubted that.'

'I trust we shall never again be on opposite sides.' Rougiet's brooding face suddenly lightened into a smile. 'If we are, I trust we shall avoid each other. I think you would be a brave enemy, but I prefer you as my friend.'

'Amen,' said Ross.

IV

They dined and wined and grew more expansive towards each other.

'This injury of yours, this ankle – you got it fighting us?'

'No, the Americans. Almost before you were born.'

'Rubbish. I am thirty-eight. But it lames you?'

'Not seriously. The wet weather does not suit it. Nor does a lame horse.'

'Understood. Well, Martin tells me the report on your horse is not good. He is very old – he should be put out to grass – or just put out. If you hired him you were cheated.'

'There was no other.'

'Ah. In this crisis horses have become the new gold of France. You will scarcely find a nag. As for the countryside, where it lies in the path of the Emperor – everyone knows that he will pay for any useful mount. And we who are already mounted know that it would be treasonable to lend or give a horse away at this time.'

Ross continued to eat his supper with a disregard for what he was being told. But when it was finished he said: 'Does this mean you are expecting me to walk back to Paris tomorrow?'

Rougiet laughed heartily but with a heartiness that hid embarrassment. 'No, my good friend, that will not happen, I assure you. But I trust you understand my plight – as I understand yours. You came in answer to my invitation; but in the course of a week the universe has changed! Could you bear to return by diligence?'

'How?'

'There is one leaving here at nine tomorrow. You would be a fifth passenger. There are two ladies and two gentlemen – all non-combatants – one a priest. They all – for sentimental rather than political reasons – wish to leave Auxerre before Bonaparte arrives – like you, in fact. It will be slow, the diligence, but it should be sure.'

'How slow?'

'First night in Sens. Then an early rise and you should be in Paris Sunday afternoon.'

Ross glanced out of the window. It was going dark but you could see the rain beating on the window panes. His ankle nagged.

'Very well,' he said.

V

There had been no difficulty about the passports. Jodie had gone with her and had got one for herself under the name of Mme Josephine Ettmayer.

146

'If it becomes necessary to travel, then it will be safer to travel under my married name. We have perhaps another week; I do not think we can rely on more.'

'And the King?'

'Is staying. That means Henri and his regiment are to stay. I fear greatly for his life, for he and his kind will resist to the end. Do not forget that the Palace of the Tuileries is still marked with cannon shot from the massacre of the Swiss Guard only twenty-odd years ago.'

Demelza stared at the rainy street. It all looked so ordinary, so matter-of-fact. People were about their normal business as if nothing had happened and nothing was expected to happen. Could all this casual busy life be destroyed in a few days by civil war in the street, by corpses sprawled on the cobbles, by blood running in the gutters, by children caught in a cross-fire and running and falling . . . ? She shivered.

Jodie said: 'Shall the Embassy provide you with transport out of the city?'

'We have no plans. When Ross left on Thursday the emergency seemed to be over! We expect friends coming from England for Easter! My son and his wife should come also from Brussels. I have no idea at all what Ross will do!'

Jodie said: 'I think your friends and your son may be turned back – even if they should leave. It will be a miracle if by Good Friday Bonaparte is not back in his place . . . Demelza, I have been wondering.'

'Yes?'

They walked on a few paces, Jodie a little ahead, holding her yellow silk scarf more closely to her throat. Then she stopped.

'Carriages are at a premium. I do not think the Embassy will have enough transport to evacuate itself if the emergency should come to that. All my closest friends they are in a panic today, and I do not think I can rely on any one of them to lend *anything* on wheels! But I have a carriage. I shall be leaving tomorrow – not later than tomorrow evening. At a pinch it can convey six. I can leave my personal maid behind, and then there will be room for you all! Ross is a big man but Henry is a small one.'

Demelza's troubled eyes considered her friend. 'That is some kind. I think Ross will be only too happy to – to leave Paris. I shall because of my children. Twill depend on what he says, but thank you, Jodie, if you really think you can take *five* of us.'

'It will be better and safer for us all,' said Jodie.

They returned to the rue de la Ville l'Evêque, but Ross was not home, nor did he come back all that rainy day. The wind was gusting among the tall narrow houses and the torn clouds seemed to clutch at the chimney pots. Although companioned by her two younger children and the sturdy Mrs Kemp, and waited on by the two French servants, Demelza had never felt so much alone. In almost all the crises in which she had found herself in her life she had discovered some native commonsense to help her make choices, to arrive at decisions; and usually, it seemed, what she had done had worked out well enough in the end. Here in a strange city, whose language she was only groping to speak, a city in the grip of a revolutionary change, surrounded by people whom she trusted and distrusted in equal parts, bereft of her husband on whom during this visit she had relied for all guidance, she was lost. For once her children, kept in by the rain and at a loose end to entertain themselves, irritated and vexed her. She blamed herself, but knew that under the irritation with them was an irritation, laced with worry, for Ross.

She blamed him for leaving her here like this. The world was going topsy-turvy: the King, King Louis Stanislav Xavier the Eighteenth, the monarch of all France, was about to be deposed, it seemed, and the usurper, adventurer, supreme soldier and traditional nightmare enemy of England was driving up from the south to take his place. Almost all her adult life – or at least for the last twenty years of it – Napoleon Bonaparte had been the one menacing enemy. For years England had lived under threat of an invasion from him. Nelson had died defeating him. So had Geoffrey Charles's idol, Sir John Moore. So had thousands and thousands of other ordinary decent Englishmen, fighting on the sea or in Holland or Spain or in India or Egypt or Italy or the West Indies, always, always fighting this great but wicked Frenchman.

And last year he had been finally, ultimately vanquished, and all the world had rejoiced. And the great shadow had lifted off their lives. And no longer could nursemaids frighten their children into obedience by threatening that Boney would get them. And it did not matter that Jeremy was still in the army, for once the peace was signed with America there was no one else to fight.

Now this. And he would be here within a week. And somewhere – more or less in his path – Ross was risking his life by merely being an observer. Why did he? What was he doing, standing in the way of an approaching army? What good would it do the Government or this mission they had sent him on if he should end up as another dead body trampled into the mud? Why did he not think more about his wife and children? Where *was* he? It was *Saturday* now and he had left on *Thursday*.

She left the flat, putting on a purple cloak with a heavy hood and walked through the rain to the Embassy.

Charles Bagot saw her first. 'My dear Lady Poldark, come in. Come in and dry yourself. A large contingent of the King's Bodyguard has just left the Palace for Melun under the Duc de Luxembourg. Colonel de la Blache is with it. This should raise the army protecting Melun to over twenty thousand men. There will be a battle there. I think your husband is likely to be home at any time now. When he comes I urge you all to leave. We are here simply as a skeleton staff – Lord Fitzroy Somerset, myself, Mr McKenzie and two secretaries. Fortunately the Duchess got away in good time.'

Demelza said: 'Is there any way we *can* leave, Mr Bagot?'

Bagot frowned and bit at his finger. 'It's unfortunately impossible for us to provide transport. The two carriages that we had have both gone. Perhaps –'

'Mlle de la Blache has offered us room in her coach. She is leaving tomorrow.'

His face cleared. 'Then take it by all means. She is, of course, very much a Bourbon, and I think should not be here if power changes hands. But if she leaves tomorrow she will be safe – and you should be safe with her.'

'Provided my husband returns in time.'

'Oh, I would think that a certainty! He can only have been delayed by the confusion in the countryside which must result from a situation like this. But even if he were not to come . . .'

'What then?'

149

'You should still go. I think he would wish you to. After all he is a distinguished man and a soldier and well used to looking after himself. I think you were better out of Paris, if not for your own sake, Lady Poldark, then for the sake of your children.'

Fourteen

I

Bella had been out in the rain yesterday with Mrs Kemp and had succeeded in finding a shop where they sold music. She had bought a book of simple songs but of course had no musical instrument to play them on, nor could she read music well enough to pitch the correct notes. So Demelza found herself trying to sing the simple tunes for her daughter so that she could learn them. It wasn't easy, for Demelza was no expert, and it needed Mrs Kemp to tell her when she went off the note. In the end Bella memorized three, and this contented her for the time being. It was a change from the 'Marseillaise', which she had rather done to death. One, which was probably based on some fable, ran:

> *Autre Fois le Rat de ville*
> *Invita le Rat des champs*
> *D'une Façon Fort civile*
> *A des reliefs d'Ortolans.*

Demelza never thought of that time without thinking of the simple tune and the words – there were other verses but she forgot them – and, later on, if Bella even began to hum it she was sharply told to stop.

Normally on the Sundays when they were in Paris they went to church, in the chapel in the Tuileries, but of course today that was out of the question. Under no circumstances could she leave the rue de la Ville l'Evêque until Ross arrived.

Often in her life she had considered herself the luckiest of women – even more so recently, in their last few days in London, the first two weeks in France. Now she wondered if in one respect she was not among the unluckiest. Over and over again in their life he had been gone away – not just to London which did not so much matter – but on some diplomatic or semi-secret mission abroad, and usually there had been no letters, or if one were received it was two weeks out of date. And then at any given moment of the night or day she had not known whether he was dead on some barren hillside, or sick in a foreign hospital or enjoying supper with some beautiful girl in Portugal, or being tossed in a Biscay gale . . . or just coming over the moors twenty minutes from home; and in half an hour would be drawing off his boots and smiling at her and all would be well again.

Other women no doubt suffered the same sort of uncertainty, the same sort of deprivation. But perhaps, she thought, other women were able to grow a protective shell as the years went by. Or else they just did not care as much. The Duchess of Wellington must have had an anxious life with the Duke, but although Demelza had never seen them together, from what she heard their lives had in no way resembled hers and Ross's.

Gaston Rougiet was known for his Bonapartist sympathies. What would his attitude be towards this intrusive Englishman? There had been warm smiles and impulsive invitations and visits to the opera – Demelza still remembered the brigadier's admiring glances, his extreme courtesy towards her, his halting attempts to be complimentary to her in a language of which he could only speak a few words. And Mme Rougiet had been almost equally charming. But in the present crisis? *Vive l'Empereur!*

'*Autre Fois le Rat de ville,*' sang Bella. '*Invita le Rat des champs.*'

Was Ross or Rougiet the town or the country rat?

And where was the ominous Duke of Otranto and his creature Tallien? What would she do if they called on her at her apartment today?

At last now there were differences in the streets outside. Normally they hummed with life on a Sunday. Today, though it had stopped raining, nothing stirred. The pools and puddles reflected only hurrying clouds and patches of blue sky, winking, basilisk, cold, lizard-like. Paris was waiting.

Demelza let the curtain fall and moved away from the window, stiff with standing and watching for the man who did not come. She made a half-hearted attempt to play with Henry, who had been clutching at her skirts half an hour ago but had finally abandoned her in disgust. She had asked Mrs Kemp to begin packing – strange, how in so short a time they had already accumulated so many things. There were the clothes she had bought, and the shoes; and skirts and cloaks for Bella; and toys for Harry and Ross's new suit. At any moment a tired horse would come clopping over the cobbles and Ross would be in the room saying: 'I have a carriage, pack what you can, we leave at four.' Or: 'No, there is no reason to panic: we shall sit it out here. Dwight and Caroline will probably be a couple of weeks late, that's all.'

The bell rang. Demelza flew to the window: no horse. Etienne opened the door. Jodie. She had come in her little carriage but had left it round the corner.

She threw off her hat and sank into a chair. Her dyed auburn hair was ruffled and looked as if it had not been brushed today. But even in distress she was an elegant woman.

'Ross?'

'Not yet.'

'No news? Of course there will be no news until he turns up . . . Demelza, things go worse. I have been round to some of my friends – they all leave: some with just enough to last them three days, certain that by then the crisis will be past and they can return. Others are taking whatever they can, anticipating a new exile. But some have no transport or are too feeble to remove again – they must remain here and depend on the tyrant's mercy. The King swears he will stay to the end, but I do not know. They found Fouché yesterday and tried to arrest him.'

'Tried to?'

'He was recognized in the street not far from his house. Two of the men I used to employ have been watching the district. They send a messenger to the King, who orders his arrest. He is stopped in the street by the police but he insists that a man of his importance must be formally charged in his own house. This they proceeded to do, whereupon he raises a host of technical objections, and while they are arguing these a servant faints, by design. With attention briefly diverted, the good Duke glides inside a moving panel, and when they break it down they find he has gone down a ladder into the garden, climbed a wall and is gone.'

'So what is to happen now?'

'. . . Will you do something for me, Demelza?'

'Of course.'

Mlle de la Blache smiled. 'My dear, you are too generous with your promises. First hear what it is. When I leave this evening it will be in a coach. But it is not a recognizable coach, and it will be driven by Benoir, who has been my man for ten years and is incorruptible. I will like it to appear to be *your* coach and for me to travel as your companion, as Mme Ettmayer. I do not know how far pickets will be out to arrest such people as myself, but it is likely there will be some. As an Englishwoman travelling with her family – or as an Englishman if Ross returns – you will not be molested. But the de la Blaches are known for their sympathies. And with my record in Paris, I am a special target.'

Demelza was at the window again. 'To look at the Duke of Otranto you would not think he could be so active as that.'

'He is fifty-two. Self-preservation is a vital spur.'

Demelza said: 'I will leave with you as you suggest. Mr Bagot said at the Embassy that the safety of my children must be the first consideration. And that's true . . . Perhaps even yet Ross will come.'

Jodie said: 'Thank you. I pray he will. Have you paid your servants?'

'No. I do not have much French money – and only a few guineas in English.'

'I'll pay them now. Money is no obstacle. Could I ask you to tell them you are leaving this evening and tell them to go home? I will come for you but I would prefer they did not see me leave with you.'

'Very well.'

'We shall not go until dark. I will send word. I am waiting to hear from Henri.'

The door opened and Bella burst in, holding Henry's hand.

'Has Papa not come yet? *Bonne après-midi, ma'mselle. Comment allez-vous?*'

'Bella,' Demelza said, 'we are leaving Paris this evening. I have

154

told you of the crisis. We will be safer now in England. We are just waiting for Papa.'

'Papa,' said Henry. 'Papa not come yet? No Papa yet? Why is he so long?'

'I wish I knew, my lover,' said his mother. She looked at the gilt clock wagging its admonishing finger on the wall. 'It is dark by seven. I want to delay just so long as possible in case he comes.'

'I will send the word. But – alas – bring only a small bag – as I shall – just your most valued things. What is left should be safe here – though I do not know the mood that will prevail. Perhaps you could leave some things at the Embassy . . .'

Demelza nodded. 'I'll do that as soon as you go . . . Though it is not important – clothes and things – they are not important.'

'One other point, my dear.' Jodie got up. 'If I may ask this of you. If Ross should not turn up, do not leave a note for him telling him what you have done. Just put: *Please go to the Embassy*. Then leave your note of explanation there. It will be safer if no one here could pick it up.'

II

At eight Demelza received the note from Jodie. 'I have just come from the Palace. Bonaparte is forty miles from Paris. I will call for you at 9.30. Give the children a good meal before they leave and make them wear their warmest clothes. Eat something yourself if you can, for it may be a long night. Do not forget that I am your companion, not your friend; it is *your* coach. I trust Ross is with you by now. Ministers are packing up and preparing to leave, but as yet the King remains adamant. When we arrive I will not come up myself but will send Benoir. Be ready if you can.'

Demelza had been to the Embassy again and spoken with Fitzroy Somerset. The distinguished young soldier looked ill at ease. Known for his liking for hunting and shooting and good food and pretty women – and the stark choices of battle – he gave the impression of being tired of diplomacy and trying to think for the British nationals still left in Paris – several hundred only out of the twenty-one thousand who had been here at the beginning of the month.

'Of course I will give your message to Ross personally. Try not to worry about him; I have a great respect for his judgement and skill and I'm convinced that you yourself are being wise and prudent to leave while you can.' He offered her a glass of wine, which she reluctantly accepted. 'What a man!'

'Please?'

'I mean our enemy – Napoleon Bonaparte. One dislikes and detests so much of what the man stands for, but indeed he works miracles. He has been in France only nineteen days and has travelled a distance which would take an ordinary traveller five weeks. They tell me he rides ahead of his troops in a carriage now – well ahead of them and arrives in villages with scarcely more than a half-dozen for escort, and *everyone* welcomes him. Not a shot has been fired, not a spot of blood spilled, and he has reached Fontainebleau! By merely arriving he has electrified the nation, and they worship him.'

'And the King?' said Demelza.

'Louis has only meant well. His is the better case. But Corporal Violet has returned, and there is no stopping him.' Fitzroy Somerset put down his glass and passed a finger over his bottom lip. 'Unless we stop him.'

'That – that will mean war.'

'Let us hope not, but . . .' He smiled suddenly as if the prospect of action were more welcome to him than the vacillations of diplomacy. 'We can only see. Be sure Ross will get your message . . .'

She had written:

Sunday evening

Dearest Ross,

I am still hoping and praying that you'll not ever have to read this letter, as you will have turned up before I have to go, but in case you do not then this is to say I have been pressed to leave Paris by everyone – by Jodie and Henri, by Fitzroy Somerset and Charles Bagot, by the Daulnay sisters and by Captain Bernard – and I am going for the sake of the children. I have been some worried these last days when you did not return, but if it wasn't for Bella and Henry I would stay on and on and never go, wishing only to be near you and know you were safe.

But Jodie has offered us a lift in her coach and I have accepted, so if all goes well, as I pray it will, we shall be in Calais by Wednesday and safely in England sometime on Thursday.

If I hear nothing from you before, I shall go to London and wait news of you there. Jodie says she will lend me money if I need it, but if need be I shall not be afraid to appeal to Lord Liverpool for help.

I have paid off Meurice and Etienne and so I think there are no serious debts in Paris. I have left a few things at the British Embassy that we could not bear home – perhaps someday we shall be able to retreeve them. But have no fear for us. Only take care for yourself. We shall wait in London for you.

Your loving Demelza

In the flat when she returned she left a large printed notice and tacked it on their bedroom door: *Please go to Embassy. All information there.*

III

It was twenty minutes to ten when the coach arrived. There were too many horses clopping for it possibly to be Ross. Benoir was a stocky built middle-aged man with tight-cropped hair and the fanatical black eyes of a Breton. Demelza had seen him about Jodie's house, and he smiled and took the one case they had packed and offered Harry his hand to go down the stairs. Well-fed and thickly clothed, the two children did not seem to mind the new adventure, once they had been reassured that Papa was safe and would soon be following.

The coach was a large black berlin, with two postilions as well as the driver to command the four horses. In spite of its size there would not be much room inside, and Demelza was surprised when she climbed in to find a small elderly tight-faced man sitting beside Jodie.

'This is Sieur Menieres,' said Jodie. 'It was necessary – we thought it necessary – the Palace thought it necessary that he should leave tonight. Unfortunately he speaks no English so I can only translate his apologies for the inconvenience.'

M Menieres broke into a flood of quietly spoken French. He

carried in his lap a small black deed box with a heavy padlock. He bowed as well as he could to Demelza and Demelza smiled back, wondering how they could have accommodated her tall bony husband in this confined space.

'We are lucky to have this transport,' Jodie whispered to her. 'The government have put all horses in requisition. We should be out of Paris before midnight. Mme Kemp, are you comfortable? Please, there is more room than this. Bella, come and sit by me and sing to me. It will be perhaps quite a long night. Are you cold, my dear?'

Demelza had shuddered. 'No, not cold.' She held on to her arms inside her cloak to stop the shivering.

The coach creaked into motion, moving slowly out of their street, past the great pillared temple and then along the treed boulevards where Mrs Kemp had so regularly walked the children; then they turned north up the rue du Faubourg Poissonnière towards the St Denis Gate. There was little street lighting at the best of times – comparing unfavourably with London. Specks of cold rain in the wind were falling from full-bellied clouds.

But by this route they avoided most of the narrow streets and tangled alleys of the old town.

'The King is leaving after all,' said Jodie, breaking the silence that had fallen inside the coach. 'He must go within the next few hours if he wishes to escape. He will have with him four companies of bodyguards. They will be commanded by the Prince de Poix. I do not know yet whether Henri has been instructed to go or to stay.'

'Is Papa really safe?' asked Isabella-Rose. 'Have you heard from him? Really heard from him?'

'No, my lover. We do not know.'

'Then I cannot sing if he is in danger.'

IV

Once out of the city the land was drenched in darkness. The berlin with its two carriage lamps outside and its one small lantern within seemed an oasis of civilization and luxury in a barren and alien land.

They lurched and jolted over the cobbled road and through dark empty villages at a pace not much faster than a walk.

'We shall spend the night at Bourget,' said Jodie, pulling her cloak around her. 'I have made arrangements for Henri to send a message there. We could go further but we could not expect to change horses at this hour. Besides, I wait instructions.'

'Instructions?'

'Yes. What road to take and how to proceed.'

'From?'

'From the Court. We have to consider M Menieres. But now we are out of Paris I think we shall be safe.'

They reached Bourget two hours later, a long straggling village in impenetrable darkness. They stopped at the first inn and Benoir hammered at the door. There was no answer. They waited fifteen minutes, and at the fifteenth summons a sleepy stable man came out to say they did not have a single room vacant, but he recommended Le Lion d'Or farther along the street. Jodie was furious, for she had sent word ahead to reserve rooms. The stable man shrugged and shook his head and said everyone was leaving Paris; they had people sleeping on the floor.

Le Lion d'Or was no better, nor La Voile Verte at the end of the village. A fourth ramshackle inn called simply Norbert could offer them one room only with four beds. They took it, and M Menieres and the coachmen agreed to sleep on mattresses in the kitchen.

By now the dozing Henry was fully awake and fretful, as was his older sister. But a magnificent hot soup was conjured up out of nothing and everyone ate of it round a scrubbed white circular kitchen table, and drank comforting red wine. Even the children had a glass or two.

Demelza longed for port, but she drank as much wine as she could to dull the pain of the flight and her worries for Ross. And presently she was dozing off, with Jodie in one bed and Mrs Kemp in the far one and Bella next to her and Harry curled up in a warm ball beside her.

The messenger arrived at seven, having spent an hour searching for them at the other inns. Jodie read the letter he brought.

'The King has got away,' she said. 'He left three hours after we did. He is making for Arras. Then Lille. Some of his ministers remain in Paris. We are directed to make also for the Belgian frontier.'

'But that is not England!' cried Demelza. 'I told Ross we were going direct to England!'

Jodie looked haggard in the morning light; it was as if years of tension were catching up with her. 'I *am* so sorry. I did not know when we leave. I am not altogether my own mistress in this matter. I thought we should make directly for Calais until Sieur Menieres joined us. But it will only be a delay of a day or two. And do you not have a son in Brussels?'

Demelza's knowledge of the relative positions of these French and Belgian towns was not detailed. 'Is that near Lille? I would like to see Jeremy, but the most important thing is that I should be able to get in touch with Ross and he with me. Maybe I could get a coach from Lille to Calais?'

'Let us first see to our present movements.' Mlle de la Blache screwed up her eyes to peer out at the grey daylight. 'I think the rain has stopped. We are much too near Paris as yet. This letter also warns me that some of Bonaparte's Polish lancers are abroad north and east of Paris. I do not know if they have orders to cut off the King, but it would be bad for us if we were stopped by them. Particularly is it important that M Menieres should not fall into their hands.'

Demelza looked at her two children who were still sleeping. Mrs Kemp had gone downstairs to see if she could find hot water for washing.

'Who is he?' she asked. 'Who is this – this what do you call him – Sieur Menieres?'

Jodie put a hand through her hair. 'He is a lawyer, my dear. Sieur is a legal term. But also – and I suppose you may as well know this since you have been in my confidence in all else – but also he is the King's jeweller.'

Demelza began to fasten her bodice. It was cold in the room; a draught blew under the door, and the windows, though closed, let in the chill air. 'That box he carries and tends so carefully? Is that of special value?'

Jodie sighed. 'It contains most of the crown jewels.'

Fifteen

I

Ross arrived at Sens at six o'clock on Friday evening, and slept at the inn there. Sens is less than a hundred and twenty kilometres from Paris. This distance took him thirty-two hours to travel.

The heavy rains had turned the roads into a sea of mud; there was an army of twenty thousand men gathered at Melun to bar the progress of the Emperor Napoleon; the countryside was in a state of extreme unrest, undecided how to declare its allegiances; and the diligence broke an axle ten kilometres outside Sens, far, it seemed, from any sort of help or repair. The rain beat relentlessly down.

Everyone waited patiently for two hours, while the coachmen went in search of a replacement axle. One of the coachmen came back to say they had gone as far as Bray and help was promised within the hour. In the meantime they had found a farm only a mile down the road where rest and refreshment could be had while they waited. It was a wet and muddy walk and the two ladies, who were both elderly, made slow and sedentary progress. The priest complained incessantly and the third man, a distinguished-looking lawyer called Hassard, helped Ross to help the women. The farmhouse was huge and draughty and in poor repair, but they had bread and cheese and pots of strong steaming coffee and presently a bottle of plum brandy. So morning turned to afternoon and no coach appeared. The ladies dozed in front of the fire and the priest read his breviary. Hassard paced up and down, stroking his thin silvery imperial.

Ross had no knowledge of the urgencies that beset Paris but he knew that yesterday, soon after he left, Bonaparte would have reached Auxerre and presumably been united with Marshal Ney; and, such had been the speed of his advance so far, that one could

161

not rely on his taking time off to admire the cathedral or the abbey of St Germain. The chances were strongly on his spending the night in the camp at Auxerre – recently vacated by intruders like the Englishman Poldark – and that today he would be on the move again. Which meant that – assuming not unreasonably that the axles of his coach would be in a better state to withstand the jolting of the roads – he might by now not be far behind.

In the early afternoon, seeing an old wagon draw up outside the farm, Ross went out to the driver and found that the man was an itinerant pedlar who called this way monthly, offering for sale almost everything: tinder-boxes and metal flints, iron hoops, faggot twigs, skimming pans and sabots, tippets made of rabbit skin, and woollen stockings. His accent was so thick Ross could hardly understand him, but he eventually worked it out that the man lived in Melun and hoped to reach there before nightfall. There was just room on the front seat beside the driver, and the hood over the front of the wagon like a woman's bonnet gave protection from the rain. When the wagon left Ross left with it.

A dismal journey and a cold one, for the rain came from the north. From Angleterre, as Joseph ironically pointed out. In taking the lift Ross had known that this would not be a direct journey; other farmhouses had to be serviced; but he hadn't estimated the length of each visit and the bargaining that went on before the smallest piece of merchandise changed hands. But having accepted this form of travel he had no chance of changing it. What did buoy him up was Joseph's cautious statement that he could find him somewhere to sleep tonight and that Joseph's son had a horse he would be prepared to hire out or sell.

Dusk was not far away as they neared Melun, and here the roads were crowded with troops, many of them bivouacked beside the roads, some still plodding through the mud or trying to cook in the shelter of leafless trees; others with horses pulling artillery into position; officers riding up and down, or more often clustered in anxious consultation wherever rising ground gave them a better view of the way ahead. Regimental bands were playing. This was the last line of defence. Tomorrow would decide the battle for the soul of France.

Full dark by the time they reached Joseph's cottage, where his ·

162

slovenly wife was not pleased to see a guest. However, Joseph said he had a cousin in the next lane who could provide a meal and a bed, and if he came round in the morning he would find him a horse.

Ross was escorted to a slightly larger cottage where Joseph's cousin, evil smelling and pock marked, leered an insincere welcome. But the food was passable and the bed smelt only of mice. Ross dozed throughout the night. His ankle was paining again and he lay with his purse looped under his arm where it could not be detached.

In the morning the rain had stopped. Joseph greeted him with the news that Bonaparte was at Fontainebleau – eighteen kilometres distant – so the battle was imminent. Unfortunately, his son had gone into Nangis yesterday and had not yet returned; so no horse was available. But he could be returning at any moment. This emergency, this crisis, the return of the Emperor, the little corporal, the father of them all – it was to be expected that life should be disorganized. Joseph had fought in the early campaigns, the great, the victorious campaigns of Marengo and Austerlitz, been invalided out, had this comfortable little living in Melun. His work took him away from home just enough not to be under the thumb of his wife – it was not as good as being in the Grande Armée, but it was agreeable.

The son did not return until midday. He was a shabby but good-looking young man, his face hectic with excitement.

'There is no battle! All was prepared, all the artillery at the ready, all the cavalry waiting to charge, and suddenly before them appeared an open carriage, with Bonaparte sitting in it and a small escort of cavalry. And the cavalry dismounted and embraced their old friends in the waiting army, and then it was all *Vive Napoleon! Vive Napoleon!* The whole army has gone over to him!'

It was an old moth-eaten nag, but it bore Ross towards Paris. Nothing now stood between the Emperor and his capital except a few hours of waiting. Ross knew what he had to do: pick up his wife and children and, as Bonaparte entered Paris by one gate, leave by another. He had discharged his mission as far as he had been able, and it was no fault of his if events had cut his visit short.

It was a pity, for he had been enjoying his time: the stimulus of meeting so many people, most of them French officers, the struggle with the unfamiliar language at which he was every day becoming more adept, the challenge of fresh minds and outlooks, the trips out of Paris and the social life of Paris, they had all suited his restless inquiring nature. And Demelza, he knew, had also been relishing the experience. He enjoyed seeing her admired – especially for her liveliness and freshness and naturalness – by women as well as men. And the new gowns they had bought brought out her charm and good looks. It amused him when people thought her his second wife. And Bella had got over her calf-love affair with Havergal and was learning all the time from her stay. And Mrs Kemp and Henry had come to no harm at all.

A great disappointment not to spend Easter in Paris with the Enyses and Jeremy and Cuby. It would have been a lovely week for them all. But the one-time master of Europe was loose again, and all other plans had to be shelved until he was put back on Elba.

He crossed the Seine and entered Paris from the direction of Charenton. It meant traversing some of the old part of the city, and he noticed how quiet it was for a Monday afternoon. Shops were shuttered but cafés were crowded. Already a few tricolour flags were out; in several places he saw tradesmen taking down the royal signs and putting up the bees and eagles of the Empire. In the squares men stood on tables haranguing the people who passed by. A group of workmen were sitting on benches chanting '*Vive l'Empereur*'.

Demelza must be worried by his late return, and though he had eaten nothing since breakfast he pressed on and reached the rue de la Ville l'Evêque at four. He looped the reins of his tired horse over a hitching post and went up the stairs three at a time. The door of the apartment was locked and no one came in answer to his knocking. Half irritably, half anxiously, he fumbled his key out of his purse and let himself in.

The windows were shuttered and no fires burned. He saw the notice.

Downstairs. 'Sorry, my friend,' he said to the old horse grimly. 'A few streets more.'

The tall outer doors of the Embassy leading to the courtyard were shut and bolted and looked as if they could repel all strangers; but after he had dismounted he detected a movement in a curtain at an upper window above the stables. He was not in a mood for the delicate approach and presently, in answer to his vigorous pealing of the bell, one of the doors was reluctantly opened. The guard led him across to the front door of the Embassy and an under-secretary let him in. He read Demelza's letter while he was taking some soup and a glass of wine, and Fitzroy Somerset stood back to fire watching him.

'I advised her to go. Everyone advised her to go. The attitude of Bonaparte to aliens, particularly to the English, is unpredictable. It would have been an impossible situation had your family been interned.'

Ross nodded, reading the letter through again. 'What time did they leave?'

'Late last night. Or it may have been early this morning. The other consideration was transport. We have no horses here, and if Demelza had not gone with Mlle de la Blache she might have been stranded until too late.'

'Yes, I see.'

'And you?'

'I? I have a flea-bitten nag which may carry me a few miles more.'

'And money to buy a change when you need one?'

'Enough.'

'Then I'd advise you to go. Tonight if possible. Napoleon can enter now in his own good time. If the worst comes to the worst we could offer you sanctuary here. But if you have a horse and it will carry you I would advise you to use it.'

Ross finished his wine. 'The nag must be fed. That will take more than an hour. Did Mlle de la Blache give any idea of the route she would be taking?'

'I did not see her. Probably the ordinary coach road to Calais.'

'I might catch them up. Though not, I think, on this nag.'

Fitzroy Somerset came away from the fire. 'It's a sorry situation. I wonder what the Duke will think of it.'

'That he has his war to fight over again,' said Ross.

'I cannot imagine him staying long in Vienna. You know that the Allied Powers have declared Napoleon an outlaw? Unless he can persuade them to rescind that declaration it must mean war . . . But all his – all the Duke's great Peninsular army is dispersed – some of it in America, much of it disbanded! If it comes to a battle he can only command a motley collection of armies and men.'

'What shall you do?'

'I?' said Somerset. 'I shall get out of here as soon as I diplomatically can. I want no more ambassadorial tasks! I shall rejoin the army wherever it is and whenever I am permitted.'

II

Ross took the horse back to the mews behind his apartment and left it to be fed and watered and rested. He could not decently expect the beast to be ready for another couple of hours.

Then he went upstairs, but the rooms were cold and empty. He opened one or two drawers, seeing that most of his own clothes had been left and quite a few things belonging to Demelza and the children. So they had been travelling light. Then, unable to contain his patience, he went out again and walked to the de la Blache residence, which was only about half a mile away, on the rue d'Antin.

The door of the *porte cochère* was ajar, and he strode in, crossed the courtyard and knocked at the inner door. It took some minutes of perseverance before there was movement, and then the door opened two inches, clacking on the chain.

'Mme Victoire.' It was Jodie's rather saturnine housekeeper.

'*Oui, monsieur?*' She recognized him, of course.

'Your mistress, Mlle de la Blache – she has gone?'

'Oh, yes, monsieur. *Hier soir.*'

'At what time did she leave?'

The housekeeper shrugged. '*Neuf heures – neuf heures et demi.* I do not remember exact.' As he still stood there she reluctantly unhooked the chain and he followed her into the hall. The place was in great disorder.

'Has someone else been here since she left?'

'Three men from the *Service de Sûreté*. I am here alone now except for Marcel, who is nearly blind.'

'What did the men want?'

'They would not say, except that they wished to interview Mlle de la Blache.'

Ross glanced around. 'My wife and children, as I'm sure you know, travelled with Mlle de la Blache when she left. Did she give you any details of the route they would take?'

Victoire's sullen face showed a glint of surprise. 'Monsieur? Oh no, monsieur. Lady Poldark and her children were not in the coach. Madame left with one gentleman only.'

Ross stared. 'But I have my wife's letter here saying Mlle de la Blache was taking her with her! And the children.'

'I heard nothing of this, monsieur. And it was talked of freely in my presence. I saw them go. They left, just the two of them, in madame's berlin. I watched them to the end of the street and then came in and locked up and went to bed.'

Ross continued to stare at Victoire. She had no charm but her honesty was evident.

'Who was this man who went with your mistress?'

'Sieur Menieres. He is a known figure at Court and I have seen him here before. It was decided only a few hours before they left. A message came from the Palace requesting that madame should take Sieur Menieres with her. Perhaps that led to a change of plan. But I never heard Lady Poldark's name mentioned. Perhaps some friend of madame's was able to oblige her. Madame de Maisonneuve perhaps, or Madame d'Henin. Everyone has left who could leave. Those remaining must look forward to resigning themselves to submission to the tyrant.'

'But I have it in my letter . . .' Ross stopped. There was no point in continuing to argue. 'Did these men – these men from the police – ask you where Mlle de la Blache had gone?'

'Naturally. I said she had left Paris. I did not know how or with whom or where she was going. I said I was not in madame's confidence.'

Outside darkness was falling. Ross began to walk back to the apartment. His ankle was not as painful as yesterday. Perhaps it meant the wet weather was over.

So if he picked up his horse and went off, what then? Demelza and the children must have left somehow, otherwise they would be in the apartment. There could have been some sudden change of plan. Ross knew Madame d'Henin slightly but had never heard of Madame de Maisonneuve. Useless to return to the Embassy. What of Henri de la Blache? With the King gone and the resistance before Melun a débâcle, Henri might well be back in the Tuileries, superintending the evacuation of the Palace. Worth a try? It was no more than half a mile out of the way.

Ross approached the Palace from the rue de Richelieu. The streets were still very quiet and deserted, but as he neared the courtyard of the Carrousel he could hear the murmur of voices, and soon he was threading his way through a great throng of people, many of them soldiers, who talked and muttered and stamped their feet and stood in groups smoking.

He got virtually to the steps of the Palace before he realized what they were waiting for. A great shout went up in the distance and travelled towards him in diminishing waves like a Cornish sea. The cause of the shouting was coming nearer, bringing the sound with him. There were lights all over the Palace now, windows thrown up and candles guttering.

An open coach was approaching. Surrounding it was a glittering cavalcade of mounted men but not proceeding in the dignity of a formal cavalry procession; most of them had drawn swords and were waving them triumphantly in the air, and they were all shouting at the top of their voices. It was quite clear what they were shouting.

The carriage creaked to a stop. The coachmen jumped down. People appeared in the doorway of the Palace, waving and bowing. A score of the mounted men jumped from their horses and rushed towards the carriage. A small stocky man stood up in the carriage and raised his arm in languid welcome. He was engulfed, and after a few seconds reappeared on the shoulders of his followers. Everyone round Ross was shouting as if demented.

The stocky man was carried across the courtyard to the open door of the Palace. He was put down and assisted up the steps and, after waving a couple of times, disappeared inside. He seemed to Ross to be quietly, confidently smiling.

Sixteen

I

The berlin left Bourget at eight on the morning of the 20th and took the road for Senlis. They hoped to be in St Quentin before dark.

Jodie said: 'I do not think Ross will ever forgive me for allowing his wife and children to become involved in French politics, but believe me when I ask you to come with me I have your good at heart.'

'Well, yes.'

'Your good but also my safety – I have to admit that. But I had no idea in the world that I shall be asked to take M Menieres.'

Demelza peered out at the slow-moving countryside. A sword of sun lit up the muffled clouds, promising at last a fine day. Bella was playing snap with Henry. M Menieres sat upright in his corner, his deed box on his knee. Mrs Kemp, who said she had not slept a wink, dozed in her corner and was unlikely to pick up the whispered conversation of the women opposite.

'When it was realized at last that Bonaparte was likely to take Paris, there were two objects it seemed essential he should not capture – the King and the crown jewels. King Louis might well be used as a hostage, though there are some who think he might also be an embarrassment. But there are no two opinions about the value to Bonaparte of the crown jewels. Once before he pledged them to finance a campaign: he could do so again.'

'*Autre Fois le Rat de ville*,' Bella hummed, forgetting her depression about her father, '*Invita le Rat des champs.*'

'This', said Jodie, 'is what you may call the meditated risk. If the King is betrayed and captured, the jewels will have fallen into Bonaparte's hands as well. We still do not know and shall not know if the King is safe yet, but it seemed to Henri and others that it was wiser to slip the jewels out unobtrusively and so divide the hazard. Time will show if this is wise.'

Silence then in the coach except for Bella and Henry in their corner. The countryside looked desolate and cold and deserted. The houses they passed were shuttered and silent, no one worked in the fields. Jodie said: 'Everyone who is loyal has fled to save their loyalty. Those who favour the Emperor have rushed in to Paris to greet him. I wish these horses would go faster!'

They reached Senlis in the middle of the morning and all got down and stretched their legs and took light refreshment while the horses were changed. At least the innkeeper was there – a sullen man with the inevitable pock marks – and one ostler who saw to the horses. Here the pretence was kept up of this being Lady Poldark's coach and Mme Ettmayer her companion, M Reynard her clerk. The innkeeper waited on them himself and disclaimed knowledge of where the rest of his staff had gone. Pretending that the inquiries were coming from her mistress, Jodie asked after the health and whereabouts of three friends of hers who lived in substantial houses in Senlis, but they were all gone. The houses were shuttered and empty. The coach set out again on its next stage, to Estrées-St-Denis, where they had dinner and the horses were changed again.

Soon after leaving this little town the carriage creaked to a stop and Benoir jumped down and tapped on the window.

'A troop of cavalry is approaching, madame. Do not draw the blinds for that will attract attention. But I would suggest that the children are given prominence at the windows.'

'Can you not see who they are?'

'Not yet. But I have a suspicion they are the Emperor's men.' He was gone.

The coach went on its way. Above all the customary noises of their own horses, the clink and rattle of the coach, the rumble of the wheels, there could presently be heard the peculiar multiple sounds of many horses approaching. It was a bobbling, gurgling, clopping sound, and the children needed no urging to press their faces to the windows. Sieur Menieres drew back, trying to persuade the shadows to swallow him. The berlin slowed to a stop and drew in at the side of the road. A company of horsemen went past – about twenty – overtaking them, going the same way as themselves. The fleeting sun glinted on helmets and breastplates and sabre hilts. The leader called something to Benoir and he replied, but they did not stop. Bella lowered the window and put her head out to watch them go.

After a minute Sieur Menieres came out of the shadows and said something to Jodie. Jodie said to Demelza: 'Polish lancers from Napoleon's guard.'

II

They did not reach St Quentin as planned but spent the night at Roye. When they stopped for refreshments about five, a traveller coming from the other direction told them that all persons attempting to enter St Quentin had their passports scrutinized, and there were long delays because the police were not accepting as valid passports issued by the royalist government of Paris: a new permission had to be obtained.

One advantage of Roye was that Jodie knew the *maire* and when he was finally located he proved overwhelmingly helpful. Bedrooms with an adjoining sitting-room were found at the leading inn and M Sujet said that if they would stay there he would obtain valid passports for them by the morning. The innkeeper too was an ardent royalist and soon saw through the pretence of Lady Poldark being the owner of the coach, though with great delicacy he asked nothing except to give them the best meal his hostel could provide.

They had not been in the inn ten minutes before Isabella-Rose discovered a small dusty harpsichord in one of the downstairs rooms. She had not been able to touch a musical instrument for more than two months, and she besought her mother to ask permission that she should try it. Demelza was very tired with the journey, and tired too of facing the endless self-criticism as to whether she had done the right thing leaving Paris without Ross. She said impatiently: 'In the morning, in the morning,' but Bella the irrepressible went down and by means of sign language and a few halting words got the innkeeper's agreement. Soon the sounds of the old harpsichord, played to Demelza's surprise with becoming delicacy, floated up from below.

Supper was served upstairs in their sitting-room – so many flavours that Demelza although she was not hungry found herself eating everything that was put before her, so that her stays grew tight. It was still only nine o'clock but everyone was ready for bed. And then there was a peculiar noise outside the inn and M Menieres moved quickly to the window. Jodie followed him.

'It is the lancers,' she said.

A maid came in to clear the supper table and another to make up the fire. Among the clink of dishes and the rattle of coals new voices could be heard. As the maids left, the second one leaving the door ajar, heavy footsteps sounded on the stairs. There was a polite tap on the door.

'*Oui?*' said Demelza.

The innkeeper half entered with an apologetic bow. Behind him two men in scarlet uniforms with silver breastplates were made to look even more formidable by the tall brimless sheepskin hats they wore. One, the senior officer, was very blond with the palest blue eyes Demelza had ever seen and a pallid complexion; the second was brown haired and moustached and dark eyed and alert.

The senior officer bowed to Demelza in a manner that suggested he appreciated her good looks and spoke to her in rapid but halting French.

She turned to Jodie, who said respectfully: 'The officer, ma'am, says he is under the command of Colonel Baron Termanovski. He requests that you tell him the purpose of your journey and where you are bound for.'

Demelza said: 'Tell him I am English, my name is Lady Poldark and that I am returning with my children and servants to England.'

Another interchange. 'The officer asks if you have a husband?'

'Tell him my husband has – has remained in Paris but he thought I should return to England.'

'He asks why?'

'Tell him that with a new regime in France he thought it safer for us.'

'The officer says you are in no danger. Bonaparte does not make war on women and children.'

'Pray thank him. But does he not sometimes intern them?'

'I'll not pass that on,' said Jodie. '*Nous vous remercions, monsieur. Pour tout.*'

The Polish officer was still appreciating Demelza. He looked as if he would not have minded breaking Bonaparte's undertaking. After a moment the dark man said something to the officer, who spoke again.

'He asks to see our passports, madame.'

'Do we tell him the truth?'

'Yes.'

'Tell the officer that they were – they have been issued – been made out of date by the changes in France and that the Mayor of Roye has taken them away to get them reissued.'

'Very good,' said Jodie before she passed on the message.

The fair man was looking round the room. Mrs Kemp was perched stiffly in a corner with the sleepy Henry on her knee. Sieur Menieres was sitting in front of the fire reading an old copy of *Moniteur*. A corner of one of the pages was shaking slightly. Bella was nowhere to be seen.

'*Qui est-ce?*' asked the Pole, pointing at Menieres.

Demelza did not wait for the next translation. 'He is M Reynard, my husband's secretary, who is accompanying us to England.'

After translating this Jodie took up the next question.

'He asks why we have come as far east as Roye if we are going to England. May I suggest, madame, that I tell him we are taking this route to avoid all the other coaches making for Calais?'

'Please do.'

The Pole laughed, showing white, wolfish teeth, and said something in his own language to his companion who shrugged his shoulders and did not join in the joke. The officer strolled slowly round the room and peered at the dozing Henry. By pointing he asked if he were Demelza's child. Demelza nodded and permitted herself a slight smile.

'*Mes compliments.*' He went round and looked at Menieres, who was still pretending to read the paper, then pointed to the small black deed box.

'What is that?'

Sieur Menieres did not move.

Demelza said: 'Tell him it belongs to my husband – just some of his private papers and small personal belongings.'

'It is locked. Pray unlock it.'

Menieres turned over his newspaper.

Demelza said: 'Tell him I do not have a key. Only my husband has the key.'

'Surely your secretary has a key.'

'Tell him no. Only my husband has the key.'

The fair Pole hesitated. He was clearly debating whether to break the padlock but he was not willing to risk damaging the point of his sword. He said something to the sergeant, who turned to the fireplace and picked up the poker. He tried it on the padlock but the end was too blunt to go in and give him leverage.

Demelza said: 'Pray ask the officer what right he has to break into my husband's private property? Did he not say that women and children had nothing to fear?'

The officer looked at her with his pale eyes and half smiled, licked his lips lasciviously. He shrugged and smiled again while the other man tried to get the end of the fire tongs into the padlock.

Just then, through the open door, came the sound of music from downstairs. But it was not being played with the restraint and tentative touch noticeable before supper. So far as any weight could be brought to bear on the poor old instrument it was being applied. And then a girl began to sing – in the powerful musical-unmusical voice that only Isabella-Rose could produce.

But what was she singing? Not the genteel cadences of the little song about the country rat and the town rat. It was the song first called *Chant de l'Armée du Rhin* but long since adopted as the national anthem of revolution and republicanism, the song that Etienne, the unrepentant Jacobin, had taught her.

> *Aux armes, citoyens!*
> *Formez vos bataillons!*
> *Marchons! marchons,*
> *Qu'un sang impur*
> *Abreuve nos sillons.*

The two Poles had stopped to listen, and an appreciative grin crossed their faces when they heard men's voices joining in. They talked together in their own language. It seemed there was a difference of opinion between them. Then the fair officer spoke curtly to his subordinate, ending the matter. He turned again and looked at the two women standing in a defensive attitude before him. The dark man put down the fire tongs, brushed his uniform, and left the room.

The officer said something to Jodie but it was in Polish. Then he bowed to Demelza once again and followed the other man out, shutting the door behind him.

III

In the room when they had gone no one spoke. Then Sieur Menieres put down his paper and began to shiver as if with a shaking palsy. Jodie sharply rounded on him, hissing at him to pull himself together. Then she turned to Demelza.

'You were *magnifique* – superb!'

Demelza brushed the compliment aside. 'Bella!' she said. 'She's down there. Judas God, what a thing for her to do! The *danger* –'

'Heaven bless her,' said Jodie. 'I think she may have saved us! Leave her, my dear. So long as she continues to play the *clavecin* –'

'No! Those are *soldiers*! And Poles! How do I *know*?' Dreadful possibilities were raging through Demelza's mind. She tore herself away from Jodie's hands, grabbed the poker and went to the door, flinging it open. Jodie ran after her, grasping her arm again.

'Pray go slow. If we draw their attention again . . .'

She could have saved her breath. Demelza was out on the landing. There she stopped and knelt, peering through the bars of the bannister. From here you could just see into the room where the harpsichord was and Bella sitting at it. At least you could see a curl of black hair, a bow of ribbon, part of a slim adolescent back -- all the rest was blocked off by the broad shoulders of soldiers.

Jodie came and knelt beside Demelza, put a restraining hand on her hand again.

The singing went on for about five minutes which to the watcher upstairs seemed an hour. Then the pale-eyed officer issued a sharp order and the men round the harpsichord broke up and a smiling Bella emerged from among the group, as yet unscathed.

The men chatted among themselves and one or two said suggestive things that made the others laugh. But one by one they downed their mugs and put on their tall hats, hitched up their belts and moved away. Outside presently there was the clatter and clink of horses as they swung up into their saddles. At a word of command silence fell, and at another word the cavalcade of twenty horsemen moved slowly off, clopping and stumbling over the pebbled street in the direction of Amiens.

Bella made a move back to the harpsichord and then, startled, saw her mother's fiery face peering over the bannisters. She bounced lightly up, three steps at a time. Demelza resisted a temptation to hit her.

'Wasn't that fun, Mama! Wasn't that fun! And – and d'ye know – they all kissed me!'

'I noticed it,' said Demelza.

Seventeen

I

After witnessing the arrival at the Tuileries Ross walked back to the apartment. Last night he had spent dozing and starting awake, aware of the armies behind him, anxious to get back to Paris. It had been rest more than sleep. Despite his strong frame and physically good constitution, he was heavy with fatigue and thwarted by a fierce perplexity.

It seemed unlikely that Demelza could have left in Jodie's carriage without Victoire having some knowledge of it. Yet if she had gone with someone else, why had she not left a later note in the apartment? They were not here, they were gone, that was the only concrete fact. By what gate, by what route, in whose carriage there was no way of knowing.

And no one to ask. The doors of the British Embassy were bolted and barred as if expecting a siege. What purpose to trek back there and rouse everybody to be told over again: 'We are sure they are safely away. Go you likewise.'

Henri de la Blache had also disappeared. Hopeless to march into the Palace – even if one were allowed – looking for one of the most ardent of the Bourbon camp. Perhaps he was dead, making a last defiant gesture. Though there had been virtually no fighting. The revolution had taken place like a change of wind, like an act outside human control. Henri could well be under arrest; or perhaps he was just mingling unnoticed with the crowd. How pick out culprits when half Paris was in the streets?

In a few days, when things were settling down, when the new regime had gathered up the reins of office, then might come the reckoning.

Certainly nobody would be interested at present in the

whereabouts of Sir Ross Poldark, a Cornish mine owner and mine captain elevated above his true importance and much against his inclinations.

Apart from the soup at the Embassy, he had eaten nothing since breakfast, and he was hungry as well as tired.

There was not much to eat in the apartment, but he found a *flûte* of bread, some butter and a piece of Brie, and began to wolf them down. The bread, being yesterday's, had lost all that crisp lightness which makes it the best bread in the world to eat new, but the cheese was just coming ripe and beginning to run. A bottle of red wine was unopened, and he drank it in thirsty gulps.

He thought again of the undeserved importance people had tried to thrust upon him. They had tried to persuade him to become a magistrate years and years ago. That chap Ralph-Allen Daniel at Trelissick, back in about '94. He had refused – one of the few sensible decisions of his life: said he wasn't prepared to sit in judgement on his fellow men – so they'd given the job to George Warleggan, who had relished it, no doubt still did. Sending lads to be transported for stealing a rabbit. It suited him.

Then no sooner had he turned that down than they were inviting him to stand for Parliament. First Sir Francis Basset, then Lord Falmouth. Falmouth hadn't chosen him for his high abilities or beautiful nature. It had suited his book because in a petty revolution in the rotten borough of Truro George Warleggan had succeeded in ousting his candidate, and Falmouth, bent on the earliest possible retaliations, had seen Ross as the only man with sufficient popularity among the twenty electors likely to succeed in regaining the seat.

So, that was one side. (Ross drank the last of the wine and reached for a half-used bottle on the next table.) The other side was, having refused to be made a *J*P, why had he been willing to be elected an *M*P? Chiefly because of Demelza's defection, her infatuation with the young sailor-poet Hugh Armitage, her unfaithfulness, in thought – and he suspected deed – her straying away from him in sympathy and understanding and compassion and love. God, how it had hurt at the time! It had burned in him like an acid, corroding the linings of his stomach and heart. The effects of it, even after Hugh's death, had gone on for years.

Perhaps it had been salutary in a way to discover how much,

among all the thousands of women in the world, he depended upon one woman for his happiness – and she something he had picked up casually as a starving brat, barefoot and ragged and with lice in her hair, to work in his house and kitchen. And for so long the other shadow on their lives had been the existence of his first love, Elizabeth, to whom once he had been deeply, it seemed irretrievably, attached. Now she was indeed a shadow, a shade, like Hugh Armitage, long gone, long dead; yet thoughts of them both still brought pain, a dull reminiscent glow among the ashes.

He finished the cheese and looked around. There was nothing more. He yawned, with a terrible sense of lassitude. If he left now, where would he go? He did not feel like another night in a cottage with his purse wedged under his arm. At least Demelza and the children must now be safely out of Paris and therefore out of any danger from civil war or Bonaparte's malice. He could not help them by following, because he could only guess at their route. The sun rose about six. Day would be breaking soon after five. If he slept now, rose at four, it would give his nag a longer rest as well as himself. There was no knowing how scarce horses would be on the routes to Calais, but if this animal were cosseted and conserved it might even see him all the way. Once Napoleon was in command of Paris his first task would be to appoint a cabinet, and it would take days to draw up the new Constitution he had promised. Then there would be plenty of provincial problems to deal with. Bordeaux was traditionally royalist, and others of the smaller cities. North of Paris, apart from Lille to the east, there was no town of importance, certainly nothing to demand his early attention.

Ross went into their bedroom and took off his clothes for the first time for two days. They had been wet and had dried and been wet and had dried again. He put on an old dressing-gown and lay down on the bed.

For a few moments his thoughts continued on the lines they had been following over supper. After he became an MP he had gone on a number of overseas missions, some of minor importance, some, it seemed to him in retrospect, of no importance at all. He had neglected his mines and his farm, and to some extent his wife and family. Had he stayed in Cornwall all the time, with his banking and mining connections, he would by now have been a rich man.

Finally – or finally so far – he had been over-cajoled into taking a title he didn't want and didn't deserve.

What would his father have said? 'What are you taking that for, boy? Poldarks don't need handles. We're as good as any just as we are.'

And his mother? His beloved, dark-haired mother who had died so young that even his memory of her face had faded. She might have said different. Like Demelza, she might have been glad he had taken it. But women, as Caroline had said, were like that.

But now, finally, his mission, though it had been developing well, had been aborted by events. Who wanted to know the temper and inclinations of the French army when in three weeks they had made their temper and their inclinations brilliantly, abundantly clear?

Suppose he went to see Prinny and said: 'The purposes for which I accepted this title just haven't come to any good, Your Highness. How about taking it back?'

At this stage he went to sleep.

II

He was normally a good but a very light sleeper. If he set himself to sleep for five or six hours he would waken easily within the time. But he had reckoned without the long dragging fatigue of the last few days and the effect of a bottle and a half of wine.

When he woke it was full daylight and someone was knocking on the door.

He got up, stopped to pull on his breeches and a shirt, redonned his dressing-gown and went to the door.

Two gendarmes stood there and behind them a man in a civilian suit.

'Sir Ross Poldark?' this man said.

'Yes?'

'May we enter?' This in English.

Ross stood aside without comment. He was afraid it was something to do with Demelza. They came in.

Then the civilian produced a document. 'We have a warrant for your arrest.'

There was another man on the landing but he was holding back.

Ross looked out of the window. It was a fine day, with a hint of cold sun.

'On what grounds?'

'On spying for the Bourbon cause.'

'This is nonsense. I am an English soldier attached to the Embassy.'

'I know, sir, what you pretend to be. If we are wrong no doubt there will be a full apology for our mistake. But that can all come out before an examining magistrate.'

Ross rubbed his chin, which had not been shaved for two days.

'I am attached to the Embassy. I claim diplomatic immunity.'

'Well, sir, if you were in the Embassy it would be an arguable case. But here you are on French soil.'

Ross cursed his own lack of sense in yielding to fatigue last night. But this could not be much. An attendance in some court – the matter would soon be disposed of.

'Allow me to dress.'

'Certainly, sir.'

There was another step at the door. It was the fourth man. Jean-Lambert Tallien. In the morning light he looked as yellow as a well-worn guinea. He had taken off his eye-patch, and the defective eye looked downcast at the floor.

'Good morning, Sir Ross.'

'M Tallien.'

'I am sorry to find you in this situation.'

'I am sorry that I had forgotten you,' said Ross.

'Yes.' Tallien nodded. 'Quite so. To forget me was not wisely done.'

BOOK TWO

BOOK IV

One

I

April is a wayward month – so often all the burgeoning blossoming greenery is savaged by cold and angry winds – but April 1815 turned out to be a pleasant gentle time in Cornwall, with sighing breezes and rare warm showers. All the countryside was benign. Most of the trees were still black, unwilling to expose their foliage before it was safe, but the hedgerows were rampant. The Cornish hedge which was going to surround the new Carrington house was multi-coloured with tiny flowers, and the fields were yellow with celandines and dandelions.

The house was to be built of granite and killas and roofed with Delabole slate. It was to be of an unusual shape, worked out between Clowance and Stephen with Mr Jago's co-operation. You would go in at the side, through a porch with granite pillars and a slate roof, into a longish hall with stairs leading up to the bedrooms. Off to the left would be two doors, to the parlour and to the dining-room; both of these would be square lofty rooms with bow windows, so that from both rooms you had the best possible view over the sloping fields and the clustered elms, to Falmouth Bay. When they could afford it they would have a terrace built with a balustrade so that on fine evenings they could stroll out and watch the gulls circling and the ships dressing and undressing their sails.

In the fine weather Clowance divided her time between the house, which was now waist high, and the boats. With three vessels in service, there was nearly always one in the harbour, loading or unloading or receiving orders or in for some minor repair. In April she had gone across twice with Stephen in the *Adolphus* with a cargo of slate to Dieppe, and as the summer advanced she was looking forward to more such trips, which were exciting and stimulating.

Like her mother, she had never been to France before, and like her mother had begun taking lessons in French. This was so much more fun than the social life of Penryn and Flushing, sewing and needlework, quadrille parties, or reading a borrowed copy of the *Spectator*.

But events had taken an ugly turn. In mid-March Harriet had shown her a leader in *The Times* which began: 'Early yesterday morning we received by express from Dover the important but lamentable intelligence of a civil war having again been kindled in France by that wretch Bonaparte, whose life was so impolitically spared by the Allied sovereigns. It now appears that the hypocritical villain, who, at the time of his cowardly abdication, affected an aversion to the shedding of blood in a civil warfare, has been employed during the whole time of his residence at Elba, in carrying on secret and treasonable intrigues to facilitate his own escape and return to claim the Empire that once was his.'

Local papers soon became more explicit, and Clowance began to worry about the safety of her family. The Enyses, she knew, had gone also. It was not until mid-April that a letter from her mother reached her.

Dearest Clowance,

Alas I have poor news for you. As you will know, Napoleon took over Paris and most of France on the 20th and 21st of March. Your father was visiting an army camp in Auxerre and appears to have been taken prisoner by the French, though on what pretext we know not. I left Paris, very reluctant, but because of Bella and Harry. I was offered a lift in one of the last coaches to leave, all the ladies had left the embassy a week before and it was nigh impossible to find horses. I thought my coach, which belonged to Mlle de la Blache – I suppose you will remember us speaking of Charles de Sombreuil, they were engaged to marry at one time. But I thought she was going to Calais, and I was intending to wait for your father in London. Instead, after many scares and trials, we have reached Brussels, and I write from there now.

Jeremy and Cuby have been real good and for the first night we all five slept in their tiny apartment. Now we are staying at the Hotel des Anglais. I wrote to the Cornish Bank and they will send a draft.

I know nothing of your father – where he is or how he fares, and you may understand how worried to death I am. Jeremy and Cuby have been trying to encourage me to go out with them and mix in some of their society – it is a lot English – but I have not the heart. Bella sometimes goes.

The Duke of Wellington is expected here shortly; I think next Tuesday or Wednesday. We have seen nothing of Jeremy for the last three days as he has been away at a place called Ninove, where some of the army is stationed. It is said that the Duke of Wellington does not think there will be a war – instead a sort of compromise – is that the word? – since Bonaparte has come back preaching peace and liberalism. Pray Heaven his liberalism will result in him releesing your father.

I have not heard of Dwight and Caroline and their children, I do not know if they had already reached France before the change of government, it was a sorry Easter, when it should have been such a happy one. At least I have seen Jeremy and got to know Cuby better. That, at least, is something that has gone well. They live for each other, and they are both worth living for.

The Bourbons are not at all popular in Belgium, nor is their new ruler, the Prince of Orange. Jeremy says many of them would prefer to be under the rule of the French!

Next week we shall leave for London. I feel I shall hear any news more quickly there, and I can knock on Lord Liverpool's door and ask him how he can get a prisoner releesed!

My dearest love to you both from Jeremy, Cuby, Isabella-Rose, Henry, and your loving Mother, D. Love from Mrs Kemp too. She has been stalwart and steadfast in all things.

PS Monday. Have just heard from Lord Fitzroy Somerset, who was not permitted to leave Paris until the 26th. He writes me from Ostend on the 30th to say that news of your father reached him through the Duke of Otranto, who says he is being 'temporarily detained and questioned', but that he is not in prison, simply in 'guarded custody'. I hope for the best but the Duke is an evil man whom your father did not hide his dislike of, and he is now the Chief of Police. But your father has done nothing wrong, and I do not see on what grounds they can hold him.

PPS Can you send this letter to Nampara so that the Gimletts may see it? Or go yourself if that is convenient. I am writing to them separately in a day or so, but my pen runs quickly dry on such a subject.

When she put it to Stephen he said: 'Go if ye have the mind. Why not?'

'Tomorrow, then? I'll see there's plenty of food in before I leave.'

'Tis of no consequence. I can eat at the inn.' Stephen was in a good mood because he had just contracted for a cargo of clay to be shipped from Par to Oslo in the *Chasse Marée*. It had been a coup to make the deal, and resented by some of his competitors; he had pared his profit to the bone to break into a useful market. Moreover, he hoped the return cargo, which was mainly to be timber, would contain some high-quality pine for the floors of the new house. But his mood did not prevent him saying: 'Don't you see anything of that Ben Carter, will you.'

'Stephen,' said Clowance; 'I am *married* to you. However, if you do not trust me I will not go. Your son can carry the letter.'

Stephen winced. 'I know, dear heart. I'm sorry. It was half in jest. Soon we shall be able to joke about it all.' Later he added: 'I'm not sure I like ye riding all that way on your own. You are crossing lonely moors and the tin mining of Gwennap and St Day. The Enyses would not let you return on your own in February.'

'That was because of the snow. And although there are lonely moors you are never out of sight of a house in Cornwall. So long as it is daylight there is no risk. But if you feel anxious for me, why do you not come too?'

'I'm off to Truro. I'm seeing the bank again. They want to see me.' Stephen hitched his coat. 'Anyway I do not take kindly to Nampara. It recalls things I better prefer to forget. Chiefly my fight wi' Ben – but other things too. Y'know . . .'

'So be it,' said Clowance. 'I'll leave tomorrow and be back on Friday.'

On the way over she made a detour to pass through Grambler village and call on Jud and Prudie. It was pretty certain that in the nature of things Jud would shortly topple off his stool for the last time, calling down the wrath of God on everybody as he did so; but it hadn't happened yet. He seemed to have achieved a condition of stasis in which there was virtually no sign of progression or regression from one year to the next. He could still smoke his pipe – which he did continually – and drink his gin – which he did continually – so that one imagined his organs as continuing to function though black

188

with nicotine and pickled in alcohol. His voice was still strong so that his complaints could be heard far beyond the confines of his cottage. His pessimism was unimpaired. His dislike of his wife did not waver. His legs, he said, were like jelly. If anyone was patient enough to listen he would describe the condition of his legs. The bones, he said, were festerated. His kneecaps were diseased and soggy and burned all the time like apple-ginger jam. His feet, he said – well, his feet were petrified puddings of swollen matter best chopped off and had done with. Best chopped off with a carving knife and wooden feet fitted so that he could have some peace and comfort in his last days.

Under the strain of keeping up with Jud's drinking, glass for glass, Prudie had aged noticeably, and the lank black hair which had stayed well into her sixties was now a white horse's tail that has been stained with tar. Her face was as red as ever, her nose as often as ever adrip. But under the competition of Jud's trumpeted complaints she said less about her own feet than in the days when she had worked at Nampara. Perhaps it was because she was on them so seldom. She now occupied permanently the one comfortable chair in the cottage and apart from stirring to prepare a sparse meal or to go for another jar of gin, she stayed there all day.

It crossed her mind not infrequently to think that her lamentations on Jud's apparent death twenty-five years ago had been much overdone, and when it crossed her mind she told him about it. However, having climbed unaided out of a coffin once, Jud was in no hurry to be lifted into another one.

In spite of their complaints, and the dirt and the smell when she visited them, Clowance had inherited some of Demelza's sense of responsibility towards them, and when she went on her way, drawing deep clean breaths of air into her lungs she felt a sense of duty fulfilled.

Nampara was woefully empty. The Gimletts were glad to see her but upset by her news. She had dinner all on her own in the dining-room, feeling like an old lady. After dinner she walked up to Wheal Leisure and found Ben. His grim face lit up when he saw her, his eyes glancing swiftly behind her to see that Stephen was not there, then focussing gratefully on her face and what she had to say. Like the Gimletts he was sorry to hear of her father's imprisonment but his faith in 'Cap'n Poldark's' ability to get himself out of tight corners was such that Clowance was cheered by his reaction. In the purser's office, which was no more than a large lean-to shed with a few chairs and a table, he unfurled and spread out a plan of the mine workings and explained to her where development was taking place and how the lodes were yielding.

'She's a keenly mine now,' he said. 'Never like Grace – she'll never pour riches into your pockets the way Grace done – but she's yielding all the time, and if the copper price will but keep up we shall do nicely.'

'Are doing nicely,' said Clowance.

'Are doing nicely,' said Ben, and straightened up sharply.

Their heads had been close together and her nearness was unsettling. For the first time Clowance felt a stirring of attraction. That night lying in bed – in her own bed – and listening to the hollow jarring of the distant steam engines – she wondered about it. Her sexual feelings had been almost dormant when she was young. Too dormant. She had larked about with Ben and Matthew Mark Martin and never thought of them in any physical way at all. Until Stephen was washed ashore she had hardly known what sexual urges were. Then they had come on her fast enough.

Now, as an experienced young married woman, she found Ben attractive in a way she had never done before. She could well understand what the girls of the village thought about him. Why *didn't* he marry one of them? It was no contribution to her happiness to feel that because she was ineligible he would make do with no one else. It was such a *waste*. She wondered that her mother, who was so gifted in such matters, had not contrived to find someone for him.

But tonight she had something else to think about. There had been trouble at Place House.

''Tis that Saul Grieves,' said Ben. 'He've been friendly along with Katie, I reckon she thought twould be a wedding. She brought him home t'see Mother an' all. A bit up in the world was Saul Grieves. Was at the King's Head at R'druth before he come here. Thinks himself up in the world. Never took t'im greatly meself. Now he's gone.'

'Gone where?'

'Gone sacked. When Mr Valentine Warleggan and Mrs went to Cambridge in January they left Saul Grieves in charge of the house. When they come back in March they found 'e'd been thieving things. Lucky he were not sent to gaol.'

'Thieving things? Stealing? From the house?'

'Oh yes. Oh yes. Seems he've been gambling, taking time off to go gaming in R'druth, got his self into debt, started taking things, selling 'em, small things, which he thought they mightn't notice. But the worst thing to befall was that Katie got drawn in.'

'Katie? But she wouldn't –'

'Not knowing, like. But this Saul Grieves gives her a scarf, a scarf the hue of an orange, says he have bought'n for she at R'druth Fair. Not so. Twas one belonging to Mrs Warleggan he'd thieved out of a drawer.'

'Have they accepted her explanation?'

'It seems so. But Katie cann't forgive herself. She say she should've known. An' she think Mrs Warleggan still d'hold it against her.'

'I'm sorry, Ben.'

'Yes. An' tis not just that, y'see. Katie was much taken wi' Saul Grieves. She d'think she've been let down, betrayed both ways. I never seen her like it! She come home last week beside herself wi' distress and weepin'.'

He was scowling out at the sea, which was flat and grey today. Only the currents made scrawling patterns on it like a child's first experiments on a slate.

'There's no way you can help, Ben. But maybe I could go and see young Mr Warleggan, make sure if I can that Katie isn't being blamed.'

Ben did not look at her. 'That'd be a rare kindness. D'ye mean on this visit?'

'I can call in tomorrow morning on my way home. It is scarcely out of my way, and he *is* my cousin.'

'If,' said Ben, 'if you did so happen to see Katie, twould be another kindness just t'ave a word with she. She seem to bamfer herself with vain regrets.'

II

Since the Enyses were away she had had it half in mind that she might call and see Valentine and Selina anyway.

The grey mild moody weather of yesterday had been dismissed by a fresh westerly breeze, hurrying cloud and sun across with an occasional freckle of rain. It was just such a day when Clowance's mother had ridden this way years before Clowance was born to make the acquaintance of Sir John Trevaunance on behalf of Ross, who was shortly to stand trial for his life.

Not much had changed in the appearance of the house since then, except that the scars of the long abandoned copper smelting works were almost healed over and a new excavation, only recently begun and nearer the house, showed raw earth in piles, and brick and stone and a dozen men toiling.

When she reached the pillared porch she was about to slide down from her saddle when the doors opened and Valentine came quickly out to hand her down.

'Well, well, Clowance it is! We saw you coming along the valley. I said to Tom, can it really be, and alone and unescorted, my very own cousin? And look who is here to greet you!'

In the doorway Tom Guildford was standing. He came forward smiling his sweet smile, and kissed her on the lips in uninhibited fashion. She felt herself flushing.

'Clowance! *What* a pleasure! And the more joyous for being so unexpected. Have you been visiting your old home?'

They went in. Selina was not about. Tom, whom Clowance had first met through Valentine, was staying a few days with the young Warleggans, and they exchanged news. They knew nothing of Demelza's scares and trials or presence in Brussels nor of Ross's internment. It was a sorry business, said Valentine, but there was a strong peace party in England. 'I'm told the officers of the 51st at Portsmouth drank a toast to Old Nap last week; and Whitbread in the Commons has said that Bonaparte has been welcomed back to France as a liberator, and that it would be monstrous to declare war on a people in order to impose a government they didn't want.

D'you know, I believe he's right. They say there's going to be an entirely new constitution in France which will effectively hobble Old Nap if he becomes too warlike. I wish 'em luck and predict there will be no war.'

'All the nations of Europe', Tom said, 'have pledged themselves to depose him. I do not see how they can break such an undertaking.'

'You do not?' said Valentine, and laughed. 'Don't you remember it's only a couple of years ago since they broke all their previous treaties – with Bonaparte! One fraud is no greater than another. They would change sides and drop their arms tomorrow if it should suit their interests!'

Selina came downstairs, as willowy and as ash-blonde as ever, with her sleepy Siamese cat's eyes and contained manner. She insisted Clowance should stay to an early dinner. They talked and laughed until the meal was ready. Clowance thought she detected a coolness between husband and wife. It would not be surprising, she imagined, since Valentine took a delight in teasing people and Selina perceptibly lacked a sense of humour.

They were starting a new mining venture not far from the house – perhaps she had noticed it? – on the strength of some old maps and some new samples. It was all thought up first by Unwin Trevaunance and a man called Chenhalls, but they'd been sent packing. It was their own venture now and they had high hopes. Copper price was good at present. Wheal Leisure a few miles along the coast was doing very nicely. Wheal Elizabeth, she was to be called.

After dinner, when the servants were out of the room, Clowance told them she had heard about Saul Grieves. It was easier this way, with Tom Guildford present, rather than mentioning it privately to Selina. Valentine said he wished now he'd brought the lazy rogue up in court; he deserved to be hanged or sent to the hulks; but Selina who was partial to the man's good looks, had said just turn him out, get rid of him, the loss is small.

After Selina had made her ritual indignant protest, Clowance said: 'And Katie?'

Selina looked obliquely at her. 'Oh, the scarf. That was indeed ill done. She should have known better.'

'Perhaps she did know better,' said Valentine. 'She was completely under his thumb – and maybe not only his thumb!'

'Ben Carter, her brother, is worried about her,' said Clowance.

'Rightly so,' said Valentine. 'She should have gone too.'

'On the whole I think not,' said Selina, as if it pleased her to disagree. 'Katie has been with us since we came here – in 1808. She is a clumsy, simple girl but very loyal. I do not think she would willingly have connived with theft.'

'Is she still with you, then?' asked Clowance innocently. 'I have not seen her today.'

'She's in the kitchen. At the moment I have put her back in the kitchen, just as a punishment. But if all goes well I'll restore her as a parlourmaid when we return for the summer.'

'Do you think', Clowance said, 'I might have a word with her before I leave?' At Selina's surprised look she added: 'Ben asked me to see her. I am told she is taking this very much to heart.'

Selina glanced at Valentine, who looked down his long thin nose and said: 'Little cousin, you may do so if it pleases you. I beg you not to remove altogether her sense of guilt.'

Tom said: 'When you leave, Clowance, I'll come with you.'

'Oh, Tom, no, please! There is no danger in riding alone.'

'No danger, but is there pleasure? At least afford *me* the pleasure. I shall come with you to the verges of Penryn and leave before your husband sees me . . . Is he at home or sailing the seas?'

'He's at home.'

'Anyway, I have to visit my uncle, and today would be exactly right, in the middle of my stay. If you don't want to talk to me I promise to follow behind.'

'Oh Tom,' said Clowance, laughing, 'of course you may come if you wish. So long as you are not coming out of your way.'

'I assure you, I am not coming out of my way.'

Two

I

They left just before three. The wind had slackened and backed, and thin cloud like a gauze scarf had drifted up to wreathe the sun. But it did not indicate real rain until tomorrow. As they left, as they reached the top of the rise before they turned inland, Clowance cast a backward glance.

'Do you miss it?' Tom asked.

'What? The sea? No, I have it on my own doorstep! But yes, well, it is a somewhat different sea – by no means docile but – different. I suppose I miss the cliffs and the surf and something of the wildness.'

'But you are happy?'

'Yes. Oh yes. And we are building a house!'

She told him of it as they jogged along, horses at walking pace, all the afternoon to spend. He told her of an offer he had had from the East India Company, to go out to Bengal as a legal adviser.

'Shall you take it?'

'It's the place to make money. I should probably come back at forty a nabob. And I have no family ties, as you know.'

'Then?'

He checked his horse, which, encouraged by the slow progress, had wanted to stop and tear off some grass.

'I have a fancy for the English bar. And if mere vulgar money were being considered, that is not an ill-paid profession – for the successful!'

'How long have you to decide?'

'Some months. The man I would be replacing is not due to leave Calcutta until September. They would probably need an answer by July.'

'And what shall decide you?'

'Probably my feelings for a young lady called Parthesia. Better known as Patty.'

Clowance also checked her horse. 'Oh? Oh . . .' She looked across at a smoking mine chimney. 'Do you love her?'

'No.'

'Does she love you?'

'She affects to. It would suit her to marry me. And we like each other. I think it would be an agreeable match.'

'Is she pretty?'

'Not as pretty as you.'

By accident or design Nero moved ahead of the other horse so that there was no conversation for a minute or two.

Then Clowance said: 'I'm sorry, Tom. I shouldn't have said that.'

'Perhaps I should not have said that either. But surely what has long been acknowledged between us need not be hidden for the sake of circumspection because you are now married. We are both grown up enough to see facts as they are, without embarrassment.'

They rode on a while in silence.

Clowance said: 'So that is another decision you will have to make shortly.'

'Indeed.' Tom added with a glint of humour: 'Probably by the beginning of the Michaelmas term.'

Later he told her of the riots there had been in London last month, as a result of the proposed Corn Bill. There had been sixty thousand signatories against it and a mob had gained entrance to the house of F. J. Robinson, in Burlington Street, the mover of the Bill, and systematically wrecked it. The Earl of Pembroke, on his way to the Lords, had had his carriage broken to pieces. Lord Darnley's house in Berkeley Square and Mr Wellesley-Pole's in Savile Row had been severely damaged and the military had had to be called out.

'Your father should have been there,' said Tom. 'He was telling me that day when I called to see you that his Radical friends trusted above all in *peaceful* reform; but I suppose they can be goaded beyond the breaking point.'

'The crowd can,' said Clowance.

'Yes, and with a pretty good reason. The price of a quartern-loaf in London is already three times what it is in Paris. Mr Baring made a splendid remark in the Commons against the Bill, which as you know would prohibit imported corn. He said – if I can remember it, he said – that the theory behind the Bill was that you must cut your population to suit your supplies of home-grown corn, instead of regulating the supply of corn by the needs of the population. This, he said, is not lengthening the bed to fit the man but shortening the man to fit the bed!'

The sun was fading altogether now and the backing wind was bringing up its own supplies of herringbone cloud.

'Perhaps you will go into Parliament, Tom.'

'The law is often a way in. But the difficulty I have is that I sway between one view and another. I should not know whom to attach myself to.'

Just before they separated Clowance told him of Katie. It was in strict confidence, she said.

'You may wonder why I concern myself so much, but Ben and Katie's mother used to work for us at one time. And before that their father, Jim Carter, worked for my father, and he was caught poaching and went to prison, and my father heard he was ill and went to Launceston prison and got him out. But Jim was too ill with fever and died. My father was godfather to Ben – or Benjy Ross, as he was called then. Jinny remarried – a man called Scoble. But these two, Ben and Katie, seem to have been a part of the Poldark family. I know my mother would be concerned.'

'But in what way concerned?' asked Tom. 'From what I heard it sounded as if it was all over.'

'Not quite, alas. I went to see Katie, as you know, to tell her that she was forgiven and that she'd be put back on her parlourmaid duties in a few months. But she tells me she's with child.'

'Ah,' said Tom and flicked at the tall grass on the hedge. 'More or less inevitable, isn't it? Do Valentine and Selina know?'

'No one knows yet. I am the first person she's told. She has only become sure this week.'

'And Grieves is the father?'

'Oh yes. She is not a light girl. Indeed strictly brought up. I was quite astonished. Jinny is a stern Methodist. Katie told me in February that – does this weary you?'

'Not in the least.'

'She told me that she and Grieves were alone in the house one evening and he teased her into taking a glass of wine. Like her brother, she had never tasted liquor. One glass led to another, I suppose, and then . . .'

'It does,' agreed Tom. 'So where is Grieves?'

'Gone near a month. No one knows where. Perhaps he could be found, but she swears she would not marry him at any price. She hates that he cheated her over the scarf and is a proven thief. She says she hates him now for having seduced her.'

'What will happen when the Warleggans find out? I'm sure Valentine wouldn't flicker an eyelid.'

'Selina is rather strait-laced, but perhaps I can get round her . . . Katie feels the personal disgrace.'

'She cannot be the first in your village.'

'Oh no! Near half, I'd guess, become pregnant before they marry. But they *do* marry, that's the difference. I hope she will not do anything silly.'

'You told her not to.'

'I told her not to.'

They had come to the parting of the ways.

'How is Betty?' Clowance asked. Betty was Lord Devoran's wayward randy daughter. It was curious that one never asked about Lady Devoran, who still lived, but in complete seclusion; if you called you might see her peering round a corner at you.

'I've yet to find out. I chose to stay with Valentine this time because the company is better. I'm not sure how my uncle will regard this neglect.'

'Ask him,' said Clowance, 'if he ever sets mantraps on his property.'

'Why?'

'No matter. It was just a thought.'

To separate they did not dismount, but Tom somehow manoeuvred his horse into a proximity that enabled him to give Clowance a smacking kiss.

Clowance nearly lost her hat. She said: 'Tom, you *are* nice. It has been good to meet you again.'

'Let us make this a twice yearly assignation. It will keep our friendship warm.'

II

Going home in a degree of personal contentment only discomfortable because of concern for her father, Clowance was surprised to find Andrew Blamey waiting on her doorstep. She kissed him and welcomed him in and made him a pot of tea and they drank it in friendly talk together.

'I put in just to say goodbye, little cousin. Off tomorrow by the noon tide, loading at Par and carrying to Norway. We'll be more than a month away, I suspicion, even if all goes well, which it seldom does with the *Chasse Marée*. Damned Frenchies can build well when they want to, but not when they knocked the old *Chasse* together. Last trip even just from Swansea . . . "A leaky ship with her anchor down, Hurrah, me boys, Hurrah!"'

'I think perhaps that's where Bella gets her aptitude from.'

'What aptitude?'

'Liking to sing comic songs, not always in tune.'

'Thank you, Clowance. You are too kind.' He stirred his tea and stretched his sturdy legs towards the fire.

Clowance said: 'Do you ever regret leaving the Packet Service, Andrew?'

'No choice, little cousin. The bailiffs were after me.'

'That doesn't answer my question, big cousin.'

His heavy sandy eyebrows wrinkled. 'I sent Jason and Fred Barton up to furl the mainsail, and the strap supporting the upper block gave way. Down they came, yard and all. It was the greatest good fortune no one was *crippled*. That shouldn't happen on any vessel decently crafted . . . We were off Land's End. Luckily the wind was taking off and the sea was light.'

'You told Stephen?'

'Oh, yes. He pays the bills, doesn't he? Not too pleased about it neither . . . Clowance.'

'Yes?'

'What do you think of young Jason?'

'I've . . . hardly met him.'

'D'you like him?'

'So far as I know him. Don't you?'

'Not much. A bit above himself, you might say. Stephen's pushing him up the ladder, wanted to make him mate under me for the next voyage. He hasn't the experience. A lad of that age should be the ship's boy. It's the way things go, always have gone, at sea; begin at the bottom, cooking, cleaning, brass-polishing, scrubbing. There's six of us on the *Chasse Marée*, and there was some grumbling on the last trip. The older men don't like it.'

'I suppose Stephen wants to do the best for his nephew.'

'Dear yes, my handsome. But I don't think it will do. Heigh-ho, I mustn't bother you with my troubles. Where is Stephen now?'

'I don't know. Still in Truro perhaps.'

'Oh no, I caught a glimpse of his jib this morning coming out of the chandlers – Priors, that is – he was luffing up towards the Royal Standard, but he was wearing a grim face, and we've not been seeing quite eye to eye recently, so I did not hail him.'

Clowance poked the fire and put on some coal. 'Why have you not been seeing eye to eye?'

'Well, chiefly over Jason. I told him last Monday what I thought, so he's taken Jason off the *Chasse Marée*. I'm sailing one crewman short, will pick one up in Par. I've made Fred Barton mate. He's forty-eight, married with two children; he's been at sea since he was sixteen. He deserves the extra money.'

Clowance thought Stephen might well have wanted Jason to sail with Andrew to keep him from being too much in evidence when she was about.

Andrew had been watching her expression. He suddenly laughed. 'You're a dear, good girl. I wish you had fallen in love with me.'

'I always thought that was a joke.' She smiled wide-eyed at him. 'Wasn't it? About it not mattering us being cousins . . .'

'Truth and jest – you can't always separate 'em, can you? Anyway . . . What's the time? I must weigh anchor.'

'Stay till Stephen comes.'

'I still have to take leave of my parents. My dear mama continues to extend all her usual indulgence towards her one ewe lamb.' He got up.

'What were you going to say, Andrew?'

'When?'

'A moment ago. You broke off.'

'Did I? So I did. But you should not have noticed. Ah well . . .'

'Well what?'

'Little cousin, you are very persistent. Well, to tell the truth –' He broke off. 'Have you noticed when folk say "to tell the truth" it means they are going to tell a big lie – or else that they have been lying before? To tell the truth then, really the truth, since I know you are happy wed to Stephen, and lost to all your other suitors including me, my eyes and my fancies are straying elsewhere.'

'Oh?' Clowance looked pleased. 'In a particular direction?'

'In a particular direction.'

'May I know the fortunate young lady?'

'You may. You do. But slightly. Whether you consider her or me fortunate in this matter is another kettle of fish.'

'Come *along*,' said Clowance, getting up. 'Who is it?'

'Thomasine Trevethan, George's younger sister. You've seen her once or twice at Cardew. George Trevethan is twenty-six. Tamsin is twenty.'

'But how lovely, Andrew! What should be wrong with it? Does she not care for you?'

'I believe she cares. Yes, I know she does. But her father owns the gunpowder mills up the valley. They're a family with money. I have reason to know they do not think the master of a tramp schooner that he's got no interest in – no financial interest in and no money outside his meagre pay, is any sort of catch for their only daughter.'

She went with him to the door in the half dark of evening and watched him tramp off towards the steep steps that led to the harbour. He had borrowed a skiff which would take him down the creek and across to Flushing.

There was a moon somewhere but the gathering cloud and mists off the sea had so far obscured it. 'And like a dying lady lean and pale,' Clowance had read somewhere, 'who totters forth wrapped in a gauzy veil.' That was what the moon would be like tonight, rising slowly, overlooking the dulled silver platter of the bay, the tendrils of smoke climbing up from the roofs of the town. Lights winking here and there. When the evening comes and the busy world is hushed. Even footsteps, voices, the barking of a dog were absorbed into the empty air.

Where was Stephen? Of course she should have known he was home because the fire had been in, though smouldering on its last embers when she returned. What was there to eat in the house? Eggs, bread, butter, milk, the remains of a flitch of bacon. Should she go down to the quay, buy some mackerel or a piece of hake? She was not hungry and he might have eaten out. Better to wait until he came. He must have expected her today, but there was no note.

Somehow she must persuade him to be more generous towards Andrew. He was not at all an ungenerous man but perhaps possessive, reluctant to share any power he had come by. It would not help that they had had words over Jason.

But she could see how the Trevethans would feel. A young man, son of one of the most respected of the packet captains – though at one time there had been ugly stories about *him* – a young man in the service but suddenly giving it up for a less esteemed position as master of a tramp schooner – with some reputation in the town for drunkenness and debt. Not quite the best catch for the only daughter of a well-to-do middle-class family with social ambitions. Clowance did not very much care for George Trevethan who, she thought, rather sucked up to the Warleggans and laughed at everything he said himself as if there were a hidden joke. Thomasine she only remembered as small and fair and rather pretty, with a retroussé nose.

But she must work on Stephen. Andrew would be away at least a month; lovely if something better could be arranged for his return.

She made herself another cup of tea, nibbled a biscuit and read the *Cornwall Gazette*. But it was getting late, and she was tired after a long day. The candle flickered in some draught she could not locate, and her eyes pricked. She undressed and lay on the bed in her nightgown and dressing-gown, sure that she would keep awake if she didn't actually get into bed. But almost at once she drifted into a deep dreamless sleep.

She woke with a start to hear someone moving cautiously about the room. She sat up instantly.

'Who is it? Stephen?'

'Aye,' he said, 'I thought not to wake you. These floorboards creak like old bones. Go back to sleep.'

She knew at once he had been drinking. No one else would have known, for he had far too hard a head to show the obvious signs.

'You're late. Is everything all right?'

'Late!' he said. 'You're a fine one to talk! Where've you been all day?'

'At Nampara, of course. I said I'd be home for supper – I had dinner with Valentine and Selina, that's all.'

'I was waiting for ye! Then I went out again.'

'Is something the matter? Make a light, will you.'

'Nay, go to sleep. Twill keep till morning.'

She had a box by the bed so she scraped the tinder and presently lit the stub of candle. As the light grew he was standing by the dressing-table in his shirt sleeves. His jacket was on the floor. He looked ill.

She got quickly out of bed. 'Let me get you something to eat.'

'I've eaten,' he said roughly. 'Had a bite at the Royal Standard wi' one or two lads. Stopped on for a game of billiards.'

It was not only a bite he had had.

'Stephen. Come and sit on the bed beside me. I'm sorry I was late but I really did say I'd be home for supper. Has there been some trouble while I've been away?'

'Aye, ye could call it so.' He would not let her lead him to the bed but sat in the tall wooden armchair which stood between the bed and the window. She sat on the bed and knelt up, looking at him.

'Is it one of the ships?'

'Not so easy as that. It all happened yesterday afternoon. I could've done with ye when I came home. But you were off at Nampara!'

She waited, knowing he was trying to lay some blame on her for whatever had happened but carefully not rising to the bait.

'Something happened in Truro?'

'That's it. Good guess.'

'Then *tell* me, Stephen! What can I say until I know?'

His hand bristled as he rubbed his chin. 'It was yesterday

afternoon. The bank'd asked me to call. When I went in, there was Warleggan himself and that fellow Lander, his chief clerk or whatever he is. They said they wanted to see me because they had been going through me ledgers and books, et cetera, et cetera, and found discrepancies in 'em. Discrepancies! Why, most o' me books and accounts since I joined 'em had been under Lander's sharp eye! I told 'em so. But they said they had only worked on the figures I gave 'em and that some of the figures they had found were false. False! What the hell was I to say to that? Inaccurate by a pound or two, maybe. But genuine mistakes – and all small things! They wouldn't find one to get that hot about. Twasn't even as if they were all in my favour! Small things one way, small things the other. Ye know I'm not one for cheeseparing, for counting the pennies. But I might've been cheating the bank – deliberately cheating them of hundreds of pounds! Their faces! Holy Mary, their faces! Like I was a criminal. Clowance, I can't tell ye what twas like . . .'

'So what happened then? Does it mean you will have to employ a clerk in future? Because if so –'

'Future? There isn't one! Not in Warleggan's. They've said, they told me they're going to withdraw all the accommodation they've offered me and invite me to find another bank! They've given me two weeks. Two weeks!'

Clowance drew her feet under her. But it was her heart that was cold.

'And can you?'

'Find another bank? What hope? Twill soon get known that Warleggan's have withdrawn and're calling in their notes. And when they hear why – and Warleggan's are sure to make it sound as bad as they can – who'll want to take on someone who's been found out a swindler?'

Clowance got up and ran down the stairs, brought up a half-used bottle of brandy and two glasses. He might have already had too much, but she needed it. She was feeling sick. They sipped together. The spirit took her breath away.

'If that happens . . .'

'Bankruptcy.' He put his head back against the chair. 'Bankruptcy. I can't cover me debts. Can't begin to.'

204

'Three ships.'

'Buying and selling are different things. Specially if it is under pressure.'

'How much – do we owe?'

'There's a permanent three-thousand-pound overdraft on the security of the ships. And I've also taken out a tidy number of accommodation bills – these aren't secured by a commercial transaction but are just – credit.'

'How much would that be?'

He made an irritable gesture. 'Can't be sure. Mebbe eight hundred pounds.'

She finished her drink and nearly choked.

'But they cannot *do* such a thing, Stephen! We have been friends of theirs. We go to their home! We hunt with Harriet! Surely – aren't you making too much of this threat? Perhaps George was angry, said more than he meant, will cool off in a few days . . .'

'Strange thing is,' said Stephen, 'through it all – and Lander did most of the talking – twas as if George sort of liked doing what he was doing. Once or twice I caught his eye and ye could see as if there was malice there. I been wondering – d'ye think he led me into this, encouraging me to borrow from him so that one day he could ruin me? D'ye think tis a way of getting revenge on you and your father? The old Warleggan-Poldark feud?'

Clowance shook her head. 'George has always been specially nice to me – before ever I met you. I don't think even he could be as devious as that . . . But it always has been a danger, hasn't it. So many people warned us when we first went to him.'

'When *I* first went to him,' Stephen said bitterly. '*You* warned me. But I didn't expect to suffer for an old feud!'

'Are you trying to blame me now?'

'No, of course not.' But he was a little, trying to offset some of the responsibility.

'What will you do now?'

'What I've been trying to do last night and all day today. Find somebody, someone who might help give me a breathing space!'

'And is there anyone?'

'Never in this world. Of course today I went back to Carne's, where I was banking before – before Warleggan's – but they were not interested. I might get eight hundred pounds from 'em but they'd want one – or maybe two – of me ships. I've tried – these two evenings I've tried at the Royal Standard – ye know most of the Packet captains, the agents, the merchants, the chandlers, meet there. Often when ye launch a new vessel, whether for trade or – other work, folk will take a share, not unlike opening a mine – like the two shares I own in Wheal Leisure – they'll take a share in a ship or ships. I thought maybe if I could divide up into, say, sixty-four parts of, say, a hundred pounds a part, it would take care of all our troubles. Maybe even fifty pounds a share would see us through. But d'ye know what I got? Captain Buller said he might take one share. And Jim Prior said he'd take two shares if I could get a bank to guarantee ten.' Stephen poured himself another drink. 'It's different ye see than if you are just starting. Like laying foundations; people will come in. But they all know I've got the backing of Warleggan's – why do I need their money now?'

'What will you do next?'

'There's little enough *to* do. George Warleggan has got me in a trap and it will not be easy to get out. I might likely go to prison!'

'There's the Cornish Bank in Truro,' said Clowance.

'Ye mean your father's bank?'

'It is not his bank, Stephen, or all would be well. He is but a small shareholder. But I am sure they would step in if – if there was any danger of – of prison. If my father were here . . .'

'That would not be easy neither,' said Stephen. 'I can't just go up to my father-in-law and say kindly lend me four thousand pounds to keep me out of gaol!'

There was silence for a long time. Clowance said: 'Come to bed, my dear. Perhaps things will look better in the morning.'

Stephen half laughed. 'Don't believe it. Warleggan's are the power around here. If they draw back, repudiate me, there'll be no one willing to take me on. If I sell my three ships and am still five hundred pounds short, maybe the Cornish Bank will step in to see me clear of the worst. With you my wife they could do no other. But aside from that I reckon all is lost.'

III

Tallien said: 'You have already denied, Poldark, that you know anything of Mlle de la Blache's work as a spy. We find that hard to believe.'

'Why should you? I met her only when I first arrived in Paris in February.'

Tallien fingered his eye-shade. He was less sinister with the downcast eye hidden.

'That we know to be untrue. You knew her in England before you landed in France with the Bourbon uprising of '95. We have reason to suppose you met in Paris in '03. As you have frequently been used as an agent by the British Government, it is likely that you have been in touch with her ever since.'

Ross got up and walked to the barred window. It was a room, not a cell, but it was a small room.

'I came to Paris in 1803 with a doctor friend and made an effort to trace Mlle de la Blache, because I had a ring given me by her fiancé, Charles de Sombreuil, before he was murdered by your jackals and at your express command. I failed to find Mlle de la Blache because she was not then in Paris. She was married to Baron Ettmayer and living in Vienna. Are there any more charges you can trump up?'

'Oh, any number,' said Tallien. 'One merely of common assault, which you may have forgotten.'

'Clearly you have not,' said Ross.

Tallien looked at the guard by the door. They were alone except for him.

'The guillotine disposed of many people better than you, Sir Ross. More worthy than you, Sir Ross. Who were a greater loss to the world than you would be, Sir Ross. Unfortunately the Old Lady has gone out of fashion. In the end she became too greedy. You will be surprised to know that towards the end I spared many lives. Many lives I spared, especially women. Now Mme la Guillotine is reserved for thieves and criminals. The firing squad has returned to deal with the traitor and the spy.'

His eyelids at their heaviest, Ross looked at the man sitting in the one comfortable chair. You could smell his lavender scent. 'Has this conversation any purpose?'

'Yes, it is to ask you for the names and descriptions of all the people you met at the de la Blache house.'

'I know of none. My wife and I went there as friends, spent a few evenings together, remembering old times when Charles de Sombreuil was alive. I do not know if she was a spy, but if so she gave me none of her confidences.'

'Come, think again. Two acknowledged spies meet together and discuss what – the weather, in typical British fashion – or perhaps the performances at the opera? Is that it, eh?'

'Something like that. Mlle de la Blache also helped my wife with her shopping.'

'And no doubt to leave Paris before you returned?'

'On that,' said Ross, 'you are better informed than I am. I only know my wife and family left Paris about the 19th – fortunately, it seems.'

'Oh I am sure we would have allowed *her* to go free. Such a pretty woman.'

'So by what right do you prevent me from going free?'

'Monsieur, we know you to be a spy!'

'I have repeatedly asked your guard to allow me to see my Ambassador.'

'Alas, he fled from Paris at the end of last month with his tail between his legs. No doubt he has rejoined ex-King Louis. England has not recognized the Emperor, so is not represented in France now. Your Embassy is closed.'

'Then I request to see the Emperor.'

'Alas, he is too busy attending to affairs of state and attempting to create some order out of the chaos left by eleven months of Bourbon misrule.'

'Does he know I am being detained here without trial?'

'I have no idea, monsieur.'

'I think he must be aware – and you must be aware – that if he wishes to maintain friendly relations with England it is impolitic to imprison one of their nationals, especially one attached to the Embassy.'

'I do not think the Emperor would wish to be bothered with such trifles.'

'All the same I do not think he would approve of his minor officials – such as Fouché and yourself – keeping a British national in internment out of petty spite.'

Tallien lit a cigarillo. He did not offer one to Ross.

When the smoke had cleared he said: 'Do you complain of your treatment here?'

'I complain of my imprisonment!'

'But you are housed and fed, provided with an hour's exercise a day and the Paris newspapers.'

'I complain of my imprisonment.'

'Do you want a woman? One can be supplied if you wish.'

'Thank you, no.'

'Well, I can understand anyone would be a trifle hard to please who had had Lady Poldark in his bed.'

Ross did not reply. He took a couple of gentle breaths to keep his temper. He heard Tallien get up but did not look round. Presumably this sally was the end of the interview.

At the door Tallien said: 'You realize, monsieur, that you have only to tell us everything you know of Mlle de la Blache and you will be set free.'

'May I ask what has happened to Colonel de la Blache?'

'Like his sister, he has escaped – leaving lesser men to pay the bill.'

Ross sighed. 'I have told you repeatedly what little I know of the de la Blaches. If I told you more I would have to invent it. This condition you make is really a ruse on your part to exact a cheap and stupid revenge. I would have thought any honest Frenchman would have been ashamed of it.'

Tallien blew smoke. Suddenly Ross would have liked his pipe but he would not say so.

'I have consulted with my colleagues,' Tallien said. 'The feeling is that if you refuse to co-operate you should be moved from Paris. The proper sort of accommodation is not available here. You will be moved next week. But of course you know,' he added with a sly smile, 'freedom is always open to you.'

'You know it is not,' Ross said.

Three

I

Demelza returned with her family to England in April. She had wanted to leave before, but Jeremy and Cuby pressed her to stay, arguing that they stood as good a chance of learning something of Ross's situation in Brussels as in London. She might have heeded their opinions if conditions had been less confused, but everything had been thrown into the melting pot. King Louis was at Ghent, some new man called Stewart had been appointed British Ambassador at his depleted Court. And it was indeed depleted, for of the four thousand French men and women who had accompanied him in flight only two hundred had been allowed into the Belgian Netherlands.

The single berlin containing so much valuable human and jewelled cargo had been held up for three hours and had eventually only been allowed into Belgium after an interview between Jodie and the commandant of the frontier post.

As soon as she had seen Demelza and the children safely installed with Jeremy, Jodie, not knowing of her brother's whereabouts or survival, had left with Sieur Menieres for Ghent.

Fitzroy Somerset, relieved of his diplomatic duties, had been appointed military secretary to Wellington, who was trying to make something of his polyglot army. Somerset had a longish talk with Demelza in which he sought to reassure her that, as soon as things had settled down, Ross would, like him, be allowed home. It didn't altogether convince her, but she could do no more than hope, and eventually head for England.

On their one brief meeting at Geoffrey Charles's party Demelza and Cuby had established a sort of half-friendly, half-hostile understanding. At the time Demelza was offended that Cuby should be preparing to marry Valentine Warleggan for the money involved, and so was refusing her own son Jeremy whom she appeared to have bewitched. Demelza had expected to meet a calculating little gold digger; but the first sight of her at that party had shown her to be very different from such an image. She registered at once as a girl of quality, not just social quality, but a personality, a character, a strong character, a charming young woman. Demelza could see what Jeremy saw in her. She still disliked her for causing her son such bitter unhappiness, but recognized her worth.

They had not met since then. And since then Cuby had by fortunate mischance lost Valentine and been persuaded by Jeremy to elope with him, and now had been Jeremy's wife for about four months.

It was a situation which could have been fraught with constraint but the circumstances salved it. Demelza was too concerned about the wisdom of her flight and about Ross's safety to worry over smaller things, and Cuby was just beginning to be sick in the mornings, which fact created a bond. Cuby said to Demelza one day: 'I want you to know how lucky I feel myself that things have turned out as they are for me, and how very proud I am to be Jeremy's wife.'

The further threat that hung over all their heads was the imminent prospect of war. Jeremy had been promoted to lieutenant and was much away, though he contrived to be home most nights. He reported that the Bourbons were generally unpopular and that if it came to a battle against their old leader he doubted whether the Belgian and Dutch troops would stand and fight. The other nations – Russia, Prussia, Austria – had promised troops, but they had problems of their own keeping down various territories they had conquered. It was not even sure yet that the Duke would be put in full command of the armies. Prince William of Orange was still titular head, and if he remained so we didn't stand a chance.

And England, he said, was wickedly tardy in sending troops. So many regiments had been disbanded, so many were still in America and Canada, and the English were being very slow to be persuaded that their short peace might not last. How lucky he was, Jeremy said, to be with a British regiment already in being, and the famous 52nd 'Light Bobs' at that.

Demelza wondered at her son's good spirits. She had known Jeremy longer than anyone else and she knew him to be imaginative and not particularly brave. Yet his interest and eagerness were not assumed. Perhaps it was the company he was keeping, turning his thoughts away from the bloodshed to the possibility of glory. She watched Cuby when she looked at Jeremy and saw that she was certainly not the instigator of any enthusiasm for war.

The family was leaving via Antwerp and the long sea crossing to Dover. When they assembled to take the coach Jeremy and Cuby were there to see them all off. Demelza's younger son had stood all the changes of scene, of room, of food and of temperature with the imperturbability that was to be a feature of his later life. His occasional bouts of tetchiness had come from boredom rather than any physical malaise, and the relentless, invaluable Mrs Kemp had been helped by Isabella-Rose in keeping him interested and amused. After her adventure with the Polish soldiers Bella had been quite circumspect; and she had never understood why the rather formidable Mlle de la Blache had hugged and kissed her and thanked her when taking her leave.

Now another leave had to be taken. There were embraces all round. Never having had to take so many decisions without Ross, and now about to part from her elder son who might, too, at any time find himself in dire danger, Demelza was feeling lonely and emotional. But she hid it – most of it – and Jeremy, also moved, as usual joked about it; and Cuby smiled at them with her dimpled, hazel-eyed smile and Harry shouted and Bella waved and they rumbled away down the narrow street and were lost to sight.

II

It was Ibbetson's Hotel to begin, but this was expensive, and after a few days they moved into Ross's old lodgings in George Street. Almost the first person to call on them was Caroline Enys.

'My dear!' she exclaimed as they embraced, 'I had so *hoped* I might find you! And Ross? Is he safe?' She listened. '*Damn* them! They have no business to detain anyone. It is outrageous! You must go to the Prime Minister or the Prince Regent! It can only be a matter of days surely.'

'It has been nearly a month already!'

'I cannot believe they would have had the audacity. Everyone else has been allowed to leave, so far as I know . . . No, we never crossed the Channel. We had just arrived in London when the news reached us that the infamous wretch had escaped. I was for going whether or no, but Dwight said let us wait a week, and of course we had the children with us, so it was as well we did. He's gone home – there was no point in his staying – and taken Sophie and Meliora. The little brats were bitter disappointed. I am staying with Aunt Sarah, partly out of self-indulgence, partly so that I could learn as soon as possible what had happened to my dearest friends.'

'Caroline, I try to preserve a calm front for the sake of Bella and Harry, but I am some sore inside. I ask myself, did I do the right thing to leave, might it not have been better if he was to be interned if we had not been interned with him? It was a monstrous strange journey I took from Paris to Brussels; someday I will tell you of it, but all the way I regretted leaving the apartment empty for him to come back to. I have the most disagreeable forebodings. While in Paris Ross, as is his way, did not hide his dislike of two evil men who have now come to power again and I believe can do him ill – even if it only means internment, but for how long? It might be for years . . .'

Caroline patted her hand. 'Come, come, this will not do. I am not accustomed to see you so near tears. Look, where are the children now?'

'Out with Mrs Kemp.'

'They will be happy enough on their own tonight. Do you come to sup at Hatton Garden this evening with my aunt and with me; and I believe there will be one or two other people there –'

'Caroline, I am in no mood for jollity. It is real kind of you –'

'All the more reason for you to come! From that letter I received from you after you had been in Paris a sennight I took the impression that you were greatly enjoying yourself. I suspect that you had a fair round of gaiety in Paris until the monster escaped, and I suspect that for the last month, ever since you left, you have been moping in your lodgings, worrying about Ross and criticizing yourself unnecessarily. This has to stop. You will make yourself ill. It shall stop tonight. A chair will come for you at seven. You will be brought home at eleven. You know how Mrs Pelham enjoys your company. Do not spoil her pleasure.'

Demelza laughed. 'Ross says you are the most strong-willed woman he knows.'

'After you,' said Caroline. 'But I combine my will with arrogance, which makes it more overt.'

Demelza wondered if there were ever a night at the house in Hatton Garden on which a party did not take place. Mrs Pelham was one of the most hospitable of women and had the means to indulge her fancy. Tonight was very small, a mere eight, but as usual elegant and enjoyable. That is, it would have been enjoyable if Demelza had not been the object of so much sympathy and kindness. She was encouraged to tell her story, which she had done so many times that she had come to hate it, and the observations on it had all been made, with suitable variations, before. It was so good of everyone to want to help her with comment and comforting advice, but what she wanted was to see Ross come in at the door. Old Colonel Webb, taller, it seemed, and more ramshackle than ever, was there, and Miss Florence Hastings, whom Demelza had met at Bowood, and Lord Edward Petty-Fitzmaurice, whom the Poldarks had last seen at Drury Lane Theatre. Demelza thought these two had come together and that perhaps there was to be a match; but in this she saw herself to be mistaken. Another man called Henry Crediton, another Member of Parliament, was in attendance on Miss Hastings.

Conversation for a while was exclusively about the situation in France and the prospect of peace or war. Most of it went over Demelza's head: Bonaparte's abolition of the slave trade, which the Bourbons had not been willing to accede to – was this not a stratagem to ingratiate himself with the British? Bonaparte's schemes to re-cover his wife Marie-Louise and their son from their custody in Austria. The power that the two old Jacobins Carnot and Fouché now exercised. (Demelza listened sharply and painfully to this.)

Lord Edward was touching her hand. 'Lady Poldark, my aunt would much like to meet you again. Would you be able to take tea with us tomorrow afternoon? And bring your daughter – your younger daughter, that is. So different in colouring and looks, isn't she, from Clowance? . . . How is Clowance? I would like to see her again.'

'She's married – as of course you know.'

'Yes, you told me. A disappointment for me.'

It was the first time he had ever mentioned his proposal to Demelza.

'I'm sorry.'

'So am I. Clowance has a very special quality which many of us lack. I know she would have been very good for me. At least I would have been very good *to* her.'

'I'm sure you would, Lord Edward. Perhaps I should explain . . .'

'What?'

Demelza nervously crumbled a piece of bread. 'She told me of your – interest. We did not, of course, know it was more than that. My husband and I have never tried to influence our children – those who are old enough – in their – their choices. It is perhaps an unusual way to behave but it is the way we thought right. When Clowance told me, I said to her that she must be altogether free to come to a decision without giving special thought to your position in life and the – the privileges that would come to her. Perhaps I was wrong.'

'No, I'm sure you were right, Lady Poldark. I'm only sorry that my offer was turned down, and I hope she is very happy now in her new married life.'

'Thank you.'

'Are there children yet?'

'No, they have only been married – what is it? – about eleven months.'

'I see. Well, I trust you can come to tea tomorrow? I know it would give Aunt Isabel great pleasure.'

III

The Earl of Liverpool said: 'I am sorry to have kept you waiting for an interview, Lady Poldark, but Government business is so pressing and I specially wanted to see you myself.'

'It does not matter,' said Demelza. 'I have nothing to do in London – except wait for news.'

'Quite so. Well I much wish I had more definite information, but you will appreciate our present difficulty. We do not recognize Bonaparte, so we have no representative to put through the necessary inquiries. Virtually all the other embassies and legations have been closed, so we cannot ask anyone else to intervene. Agents are our only source of information and they tell us that Sir Ross has now been moved to Verdun.'

'Verdun? Where is that?'

'About a hundred and sixty miles east of Paris. There is a famous fortress there, but also a camp, where many English were interned when war broke out again in 1803. Apparently he is being treated well, though in fairly close confinement. I am totally at a loss to know why he is being imprisoned in this way when almost all the foreigners who wished to leave France have been allowed to go.'

'Mlle de la Blache, who aided me to leave the country, said that they might make the excuse of treating him as a spy.'

Lord Liverpool blinked several times. 'His mission was – confidential, I agree, but scarcely more. But why should they seek the excuse?'

Demelza told him.

'I see. And Fouché is now Chief of Police again . . . I think an appeal to the Emperor himself would be the only way of circumventing that. It will be difficult to attempt at this juncture because very recently Bonaparte sent a personal letter to the Prince Regent declaring his peaceful aims, and the letter was returned to him with a stern note from Lord Castlereagh . . . But we will try our best, Lady Poldark, I assure you. In the meantime I can only ask you to be patient, in the knowledge that although your husband is not a free man he is not coming to any physical harm.'

'Imprisonment, my lord, for someone like my husband, is a sort of physical harm.'

'Yes, that too I understand. Well, be assured we will do our best. In the meantime what are your plans?'

'I will hope to stay in London perhaps another two weeks, just hoping, hoping for some more news. Then, if there is none, I suppose I shall take the children back to Cornwall.'

Lord Liverpool got up. 'I do not know how you are circumstanced, but while your husband is interned I shall personally see that the monthly payment he has been receiving while on this mission will continue to be paid into his account at Messrs Coutts who I believe are the London correspondents of the Cornish Bank, of which he is a partner. There should be no difficulty in your being able to draw ample funds.'

'Thank you, my lord. And d'you think an appeal *will* be made?'

'Appeal?'

'To the Emperor.'

'Lord Castlereagh, as you know, is the Foreign Secretary. I will consult with him and see how we may best go about it.'

This sounded to Demelza like a diplomatic evasion. She said: 'D'you think the – the Prince Regent might help?' When Liverpool stared she stumbled on: 'I mean by letter. Ross said he was very interested in his mission when they met, when Ross was knighted.'

Liverpool fingered the back of his chair, frowned, then half smiled at his visitor.

'I don't think at the present time it would be diplomatically possible, my dear. All the crowned heads of Europe have taken this united stand not to enter into any correspondence with the usurper. It would be impossible to ask his Royal Highness to break that undertaking, however worthy the object.'

Four

I

The first week living under the threat of imminent bankruptcy had almost gone, and Stephen was no farther out of the wood. Over the last year he had made a number of business friends in the area and a host of acquaintances, and he had tried them all out; but although he was liked by most people it went no farther than that.

A difficulty was that he did not dare to state that Warleggan's Bank was withdrawing all credit at short notice, for, once the news got around, his creditors – of whom there were not a few – would be waiting on his doorstep. His approach was to say that he found the Warleggan banking methods too restrictive and he was looking for alternative finance. Whether that convinced his hearers or not, it did not open their purses. Clowance had had the idea of approaching Valentine – he had always been friendly with Stephen and so hated his father that he might take on the loan to spite him – but no sooner did the idea occur to her than she met Tom Guildford in Falmouth, who told her that the young Warleggans had left for Cambridge yesterday.

The only constructive move was from a man called Jack Pender – the son of the Mayor – who, being told by Stephen that he was thinking of selling one of his fleet, offered four hundred guineas for *Chasse Marée*. It was a poor price but better than it might have been. Pender had a couple of three-masted luggers that fished and trawled in the Channel, and he was looking for something a bit bigger and faster. *Chasse Marée* had originally been designed for fishing and would fit well into his plans for expansion. The vessel in question was at present somewhere in the North Sea, but after a token show of reluctance to try to get the price up, Stephen shook hands on the sale. Unfortunately the money would not be paid over until the brig returned.

Nor could the *Adolphus* sail next week with a third cargo of slate for Dieppe while its captain struggled for solvency. More than half of the cargo was already loaded and by Saturday she would be ready to leave. An excuse could be found for the delay, but such delay would cost him half his profit, and if she had to be unloaded in Penryn it would be another stone round his neck to sink him.

During this period Clowance had not seen Harriet at all, but a month ago Harriet had lent them two books on architecture belonging to George. (George had come by them accidentally at a sale while buying some mining books, and although he had no intention of ever reading them he was too thrifty to throw them away.) It was when the new house was being planned and the two books had been the subject of much study and discussion over the table in the Carrington home with the candlelight flickering. It was time to return them. In any case building on the new house had to come to a stop.

Stephen was in Falmouth. He had contrived a meeting with the manager of the Cornish Naval Bank. After all, what purpose, he said to Clowance, could a Cornish Naval Bank have other than to finance respectable seagoing ventures such as his own?

Clowance decided to ride to Cardew and leave the books with a footman. The sooner they were out of her possession the better. Nero was headstrong for lack of exercise and she galloped and trotted and galloped again until at length, climbing the steep hill to Cardew he consented to fall into a dignified snorting walk.

Harriet was on the steps. It was the last thing Clowance wanted. Harriet raised an arm and smiled.

'Welcome. I am just about to feed the hounds. Come in and join me.'

'I was only returning these books,' said Clowance, not dismounting. 'I ought to get back.'

Harriet raised her eyebrows. 'Something amiss?'

Faced with the blunt challenge, Clowance said: 'Oh? . . . Er – no. I just thought I would bring these books back. We have – no further use for them.'

'You weren't out with us yesterday. It was very good for the last day of the season.'

'Yes,' said Clowance. 'Well, we really could not manage it.'

Harriet pushed her hair away from her face. 'My dear, are you coming or going?'

'Going,' said Clowance.

'In that case something *is* amiss. Are you willing to come with me to meat the hounds and make me a party to it? Or do you wish to go away and sulk in silence?'

Their eyes clashed. Clowance hesitated. She had no quarrel with Harriet, except for the company she kept.

She said: 'I'll come and help you feed the hounds.'

II

Harriet said: 'You have to watch 'em. Some are greedy, some pick and choose. It is no good offering them a free for all.'

The oatmeal pudding had been made in huge coppers, with the grooms stirring the mixture for the best part of an hour over the fire. Once it was stiff enough the fire was kicked out and the pudding taken in buckets and turned out on a slate slab to cool. Volcanoes of oatmeal stood smoking until they were ready for the hounds to eat them. Then the hounds were released by the grooms by name, so that the greedy ones should not gobble up more than their share.

'Well,' said Harriet presently. 'I do not suppose you to be the sort of young woman to get some bee in your bonnet without good reason. If you are, then I think less of you, and you can be gone.'

Clowance told her.

For a while Harriet watched the hounds in silence. 'I know nothing of this.'

Clowance smiled in a wintry way. 'I did not suppose you would.'

'And what has Stephen done so far?'

'All he can. He is trying the Cornish Naval Bank this morning, but I do not suppose their answer will be any different from the others. If Warleggan's are withdrawing credit, who wants to take their place?'

'True, I suppose, so far as Cornwall goes.'

'Carne's, whom he was with before, are not interested. My father's bank have offered to step in if there's a risk of Stephen going to prison. That at least we have to be thankful for. But of course it would only be a – a salvage operation. Recently he's been trying to organize a joint stock company: but there's simply no time! If Sir George keeps to his threat we have eight days more only.'

Harriet scratched inelegantly under her arm. 'And in your view Stephen has done nothing to deserve this disgrace?'

Clowance said: 'I try to take an impartial view of Stephen. He is a strange man, and because I love him I may be blind to some of his failings. But . . . I do *not* believe him to be dishonest deliberate. I do *not* think he has in any way attempted to cheat Warleggan's Bank. When he came home, only six or seven months ago, saying that your husband was prepared to finance him to buy the *Adolphus*, he was so full of pleasure and pride that I cannot believe he would – would do anything to destroy his own position, to risk destroying his new relationship with Warleggan's Bank for some petty small profit! I just do *not*, Harriet, and therefore I take his part.'

There was silence for a while, except for the salivatory noises of the hounds.

'They like fish,' said Harriet. 'It seems to suit 'em, though we mix it with a good proportion of old cow. These damned beasts run a long way in seven months and they need good food. Now of course they are just beginning their hols. Not that they'll be allowed to slack, you know. They've trotted a couple of miles this morning, and will go another half-mile now before being allowed to snore off their dinner in the straw. Forty couple of 'em need a lot of feeding. And three huntsmen and nine horses. Although John Devoran is the official master, George foots almost all the bill, and that's entirely on my account as he never hunts himself. By the way, we shall be having a little mock-hunt tomorrow, just exercising the horses. Why don't you come along!'

Clowance smiled wryly. 'I couldn't, Harriet. How could I?'

'George is in Truro,' said Harriet. 'Still, I see what you mean. Very well, go home and nurse your grievance. But when I see George, which should be Friday, I will ask for his side of the story.

Very difficult for me to judge until I hear what he has to say. It is a pity it has come to this.'

'Yes,' said Clowance, 'a great pity.'

III

George said: 'Who has told you this?'

'Clowance, of course. Who else? She came on Wednesday, clearly with some disturbance on her mind. I persuaded her to disburse it.'

'No doubt Carrington sent her.'

'I do not suppose so. Anyway, open my mind to what it is that you have discovered against him.'

'It is chiefly my head clerk, Lander,' said George, and blew his nose. 'He finds Carrington's devious book-keeping impossible to deal with. Carrington is incapable, it seems, of making an honest entry. We cannot continue to conduct business with or for such a person.'

'Why did Lander not find this out at an earlier stage before Stephen had so much committed himself?'

'Carrington came one day last autumn blustering into my office, and I allowed myself to be taken in by his self-confident manner. He agreed to hand over the financial conduct of his affairs to us, and he has not done so.'

'Clowance tells me that since he was taken on by your bank he has virtually done nothing without Mr Lander's approval. Surely Lander is also to blame. In any event I would have thought this an occasion for a severe reprimand not a withdrawal of credit and a calling in of bills which will force him into bankruptcy!'

George said irritably: 'My dear, you do not understand these things. Kindly change the subject. Ursula will be home this weekend, and her pony is sick. I want your advice as to the horse we should mount her on tomorrow. She's tall enough now to merit a sensible horse, but not a wayward one. There's no need to take risks.'

Harriet was brushing her shoulder-length hair. Her brilliant dark eyes watched George through the mirror.

'Is this – this change of mind towards Stephen – has it anything to do with the old feud?'

'What old feud? You mean, because Clowance is a Poldark? Certainly not.'

'Do you mean it never entered your head?'

'Certainly *not*. I do not run the most prosperous bank in Cornwall by allowing such petty quarrels to influence me.'

Harriet resumed her brushing. Her hair gleamed like patent leather. When she had done she put down her brush.

'I think it was more than a petty quarrel, wasn't it? From all one hears; even what one hears from you. And it was not improved by the abrasive meeting last summer at Trenwith, was it. I am relieved to know that this is not at all in your mind, for it will be much easier to reconsider your decision.'

George put on his coat. The collar did not fit as it should. After years of having been dressed by a London tailor he had recently gone to a local man of good repute – he was so much less expensive. But it did not do. It would have to go back.

'Reconsider what decision, my dear?'

'Your decision to bankrupt Carrington.'

George looked at his wife sharply. She shook her head at him. 'It won't do, George. It won't do.'

'What on earth are you talking about?'

'This cannot be allowed to happen, on what is really a very small excuse. I find Stephen Carrington an interesting man, and in some ways I rather admire his – roughness, his maleness, his self-confidence. Yes, I admire all those qualities. But I would not care a button really for Stephen. It is Clowance I will not see dragged down in such a degrading fashion. I am fond of her and wish to keep her as my friend.'

'This no doubt you will be able to do.'

'No, I shall not. And I have to remind you that she saved Castor's life when he became caught in that devilish mantrap in February.'

George finished criticizing the set of his coat and looked at Harriet.

'You cannot be serious that I should change the board's decision.'

'Never more so, my dear.'

George took out his watch. 'The Vivians will be here in ten

minutes. They are never late. As you know I want to talk business with him after dinner, so –'

'So I shall be saddled with the tedious Betsey, who at heart, I am sure, has the instincts and interests of a washerwoman . . . Then let this matter lie until this evening – or even tomorrow, so long as you will admit to second thoughts on the matter.'

'Second thoughts?'

'On the matter of bankrupting Stephen Carrington.'

'Quite out of the question! The matter has been decided. There is nothing more to say.'

'There is only one thing more to say, dear George,' said Harriet, 'and that is that it cannot be.'

IV

The argument was resumed in her bedroom late that night. The Vivians had been and gone – he the impoverished younger son of a peer with certain land and mining rights he could be persuaded to sell. Ursula had come and gone, arriving from school an inch taller in six months, still too fat but shedding the worst of it, bursting with talk of school and other irrelevances, unlike most girls not really interested in horses but trooping dutifully after her step-mother – at her father's behest – to choose a mount for tomorrow's ride; then staying on, staying up much too late, indulging herself and being indulged by George because it was the weekend.

Harriet had various ways of managing George, but this was not an occasion when any of the usual methods would serve. Usually she avoided a confrontation: after the terrible storms of her marriage to Toby Carter it had amused her lazy good temper to get her own way with George by elegant manoeuvre and a bare-faced tolerant insolence. The success of these methods she knew stemmed equally from her good looks and her blue blood. Not to mention her ability to bemuse and excite him sexually when she was in the mood. In business she knew him to be a hard and sometimes vindictive man; as a husband he was not half bad. She had never had so much money and so much freedom to spend it. But there were limits to her good temper.

She began almost as she had left off, quite casually, asking him if he were not really deceiving her and that this decision to jettison the Carringtons did not spring from the old feud, as she had suggested before dinner.

'Not at all. Not in any way at all!'

'Then I fear, dear George, that you will have to produce some better reason for your decision than you have already given! After all, they have been to this house many times – and two or three times at least at your invitation! They are more than casual acquaintances. You cannot tip them into the ditch and walk away as casually as you propose! Has Stephen insulted you in some way? Or Clowance? I seek an explanation that I can believe.'

George's bull neck showed as he lowered his head, much as if someone had held up a red flag. 'Harriet, it is no business of yours!'

'Of course it is business of mine! Don't be so silly.'

'I have told you my reasons!'

'And I don't believe them.'

'Accept that I *have* good reasons!'

'Certainly I shall not unless you tell me them.'

George took a handkerchief out of his pocket and blew his nose.

'I think I am developing a cold.'

'Don't change the subject.'

'I shall take some tisane tonight. It is a good opening medicine.'

'And what of the Carringtons?'

'They are to be jettisoned, as you put it. Or he is. I am sorry if his wife has to be included, but there you are. It is not my fault that she married him. No doubt they will make out. A scoundrel like him will turn a penny somewhere.'

Harriet got up, grabbed George by the arm.

'Tell me the truth.'

George shook his arm free. It was not often they were in physical contact with each other except in their rare sexual encounters. A contact which represented hostility was unknown.

'Very well,' he said roughly, 'if you will have the whole truth, sit down and listen.'

She moved a pace away from him, sat on the end of the bed, pushing the curtains aside and holding them against her cheek.

He sat astride a chair, looking more than ever like the Emperor

225

Vespasian. 'Do you recall – perhaps you do not – that in the year after our wedding, in the following January to be exact, there was a coach robbery and a large amount of securities, bank notes, bullion and jewellery were stolen from the Self Reliance coach?'

'Of course I remember. You were very angry. And did not my Aunt Darcy lose some trinket? A loving cup?'

'Yes, a loving cup. It was of small value, I remember, but she seemed to hold me responsible for having allowed it to be stolen! However, the total loss was indeed considerable – near on six thousand pounds when all was added up. *Listen to me!*' he said sharply when she was about to interrupt. 'The scheme was a very clever one, carried out with audacity and cool nerve which only educated people could have achieved. All four inside seats were booked ahead from Plymouth to Truro, and three were occupied. Whether a fourth ever intended to join them we do not know; he did not turn up. Somewhere on that journey from Plymouth to Truro they pulled back the felt lining and cut a hole by drilling through the mahogany framework of the coach into the box seat where the two bank boxes were stowed; they pulled these down into the coach, broke them open, put the contents into some receptacles of their own and replaced the empty boxes in the box seat. They then roughly replaced the large piece they had taken out of the woodwork of the coach and tacked the lining back into place. We have reason to suppose the thieves made good their escape at Lostwithiel.

'*Now,*' said George, 'we have some description of the three thieves. Two people pretended to be the Revd and Mrs Arthur May. No such persons exist. The third was a Lieutenant Morgan Lean, who claimed to be in His Majesty's navy. No such person exists. The false clergyman and his wife were both tall, he with greying hair and heavy steel spectacles; she was dark-skinned, had little to say to anyone, and pretended she was ill, so that they might draw the blinds. Lieutenant Morgan Lean was not so tall but broadly built and younger, with a white wig and heavy black eyebrows. They were all to some extent disguised, but clearly could not wear anything too obvious, or they would have drawn attention to themselves. Neither the coachmen nor the guards were observant enough to give anything more than the vaguest of descriptions. We offered a reward, as you know, of a thousand pounds but no one came forward. It seemed that the thieves had got away.'

'Did you not advertise the numbers of the notes?' asked Harriet.

'We did. But we laid a trap. By no means all the numbers of the notes were known. Only twelve, in fact. We advertised the numbers of seven and kept five back. None of the seven has ever come to light, but one of the other five did. It was paid into our bank at Truro. It was the first break we had made, the first clue, the first advance. And do you know who paid it in?'

Harriet shook her head.

'You, my dear.'

'*What?* What on earth do you mean?'

'I mean that it followed one of those gaming evenings when you were entertaining your young gentlemen friends, and someone clearly had lost money to you and paid you with this note.'

'I'm damned!' said Harriet after a moment, and rubbed the curtain against her cheek.

'The names of all the young men who had been gaming at our house that week were therefore carefully noted. There was Anthony Trefusis, Ben Sampson, Stephen Carrington, Andrew Blamey, Percy Hill, George Trevethan, Michael Smith. When I asked you casually how the games had gone you told me that the chief losers had been Anthony Trefusis, Andrew Blamey and Stephen Carrington. So I set in train a number of inquiries which suggested to me that the likeliest of these was Stephen Carrington.'

'So that is how the wind is blowing,' said Harriet, staring at him. 'But hold hard. Bank notes change hands. Stephen has been in trade for some time. He could well have received the note from someone else that morning!'

'There was clearly no proof. But there was good reason for suspicion.'

'And what has happened since? Supposedly something to foster it.'

George did not like his wife's tone.

'On the day of the robbery the coach was joined at Liskeard by a Mr Arthur Rose, an elderly lawyer, who insisted on travelling inside, since there was a spare seat. Whether the robbery was in process at the time I know not – possibly it was interrupted by him – but he noticed nothing untoward and left again at Dobwalls. But, unlike everyone else, he had an opportunity of observing the other three passengers at close quarters; also being a lawyer he was a keen observer; and later, when the robbery became known, he stated that he would be likely to recognize the thieves if he were confronted with them.'

'Was he the –'

'After the discovery of the bank note which had come to light as a result of the gambling here, I arranged an invitation for all the young men who had been present at our house during that particular week, and invited Mr Rose to come to see me on some other business. I thought this might help to solve the identity of one or more of the thieves.'

'And he died on you!' exclaimed Harriet. 'I remember the party! You were expecting this mysterious Mr Rose and he never turned up!'

'He was taken ill in the coach while being accompanied here by Hector Trembath. He died in Truro,' George added bitterly.

Harriet laughed her low contralto chuckling laugh. 'I often wondered about that night. You were in quite a taking. So it all ended in failure? But something, I suspicion, has come about more recently?'

'Indeed. Something has come about. Last month Carrington was in my office, and as a legal document had to be attested Trembath was present. After Carrington had gone Trembath told me that in the coach Mr Rose said he had noticed that Lieutenant Morgan Lean had lacked an eye-tooth – on the left side of his mouth. Stephen Carrington, as I am sure you will have observed, lacks an eye-tooth – on the left side of his mouth.'

The fire in the grate was burning low, and Harriet got up from the bed and put on a silk dressing-gown. Although early May, there was a chill in the house.

'And so? What else?'

'Nothing else. The fool never told me before. But it is enough.'

'You would get no conviction in a court of law.'

'Of course I could not! I am not seeking one!' George said in irritation: 'I know we shall never bring these men to justice now. Not, that is, without some singular piece of good fortune. But the evidence against Carrington is enough to convince me beyond the shadow of a doubt. There is the general description of the man, his age, his build, his colouring – eyebrows are easily dyed – the appearance of the bank note, and now the identification of the tooth. And finally the fact that he found money from somewhere to set up in trade and buy two trading vessels. I am utterly convinced – and that is enough.'

Harriet reseated herself on the bed. Her face wore its most non-committal expression; George looked at it and could read nothing there.

'I have tried to be perfectly frank with you, my dear,' he said, in a grudgingly gentle voice. 'You asked for my reasons. Now that I have given them I'm sure you will fully endorse them.'

Harriet said: 'You suspected Carrington almost as soon as the bank note came to light.'

'I thought him far the most likely. Also, unlike most of the others, his movements were not accounted for on the days in question.'

'But if you have been suspecting him all this time, why did you agree to help him when he came to see you last autumn?'

George bit his lip. With women it was usually unwise to be too frank.

'I was taken in by him. I had just quarrelled with Valentine. The robbery was in the background. I thought, there can be no proof, so let him be given the benefit of the doubt.'

'And an eye-tooth makes all the difference?'

'An eye-tooth makes all the difference. It may seem less than conclusive to you. To me it is as if everything, all the facts, have fallen into place –'

'If this is what you suspect, why do you not tell him so to his face?'

George hunched his shoulders in irritation. 'Impossible.' It had never occurred to him and he considered the suggestion outrageous. 'You cannot accuse a man of such a thing! Had Rose lived it would have been quite different!' He sneezed. 'I *have* caught a cold. This weather is treacherous.'

'But you condemn him unheard.' Harriet still rubbed her cheek up and down the curtain. It was a silly gesture, he thought. 'Really, George, it won't do. It won't do.'

'What won't do? I have already told you it is done! Now I wish you good-night.'

'And I have already told you,' said Harriet, 'that so far as Stephen is concerned you may do what you will with him for all I care – or could do so were it not that he is married to Clowance. And her I will not see bankrupted and deprived of her new house and made destitute, all for the sake of an eye-tooth! As I have told you –'

'Pray do not mention that dog again!'

'Castor. That's his name. He has a name, George, and do not forget it. He is nine years old and I have had him since he was nine weeks, and I am indebted to Mrs Carrington for the fact that he is still alive!'

'And I have told you it is done. Carrington receives no further accommodation from my bank. Good-night!'

'George,' said Harriet.

Something in her voice stopped him at the door.

She said: 'I have an obligation towards Clowance. It must be discharged.'

'Then discharge it in some other way.'

'There is no other way. You must do this for me.'

'I cannot and will not!'

'Then you must humour me.'

'*Humour* you?' George stared at her, scandalized. Whatever did she mean? He had never been asked such a thing before. 'I have to tell you once and for all that my mind is made up! There is no going back on what I have decided! If the young man cannot be hanged – as he well deserves to be – he shall certainly not be allowed to live comfortably subsidized by the man he has robbed! Alas, he will not starve in the gutter or go to prison for debt, as I had hoped. I had forgot their connection with the Cornish Bank. More's the pity. But he'll have to sell up! Seeing him sell up will repay me in a small way for all the money he stole. And I shall make sure – as I can make sure – that he will never work in Cornwall again!'

Harriet looked at her husband's grey, hard face with some distaste. 'And have you no concern for me?'

'You? What do you mean? Of *course*, I have. But not to the point of allowing that gallows-bird to flourish, if I can clip his wings!'

'But I have to be humoured, George.'

He thumped the open door with the flat of his hand and shouted: 'Humoured? Humoured? Such a damned stupid silly word! I do not know what you are about.'

'What I am about,' said Harriet, 'is to give birth.'

George sniffed and dabbed his nose. 'Well, I do not know what your idea may be, but you may tell me of it in the morning. So long as it is not –'

'My idea', said Harriet in her most austere voice, 'is that I am enceinte, gravid, pregnant, in pup, call it what you will. No doubt there are as many names for the production of a child as for the act which initiates it. If you –'

'Is this some *joke?*' George shouted again, thoroughly angry, and peering at her as if he were becoming short-sighted.

'Perhaps you may think it so. I do not. It has come as surprising to me since I have not conceived before. But after all it is a natural consequence of coupling. My age is against me for a first child – I am thirty-four – but older women have done as much as I shall be expected to do. What I am most furious and frustrated about is that it will play the devil with the hunting season. A Christmas child, I suppose. That will be a great bore.'

The door shook a little in George's hand. 'You are not *joking?*'

'Indeed not. I only wish I were.'

A rather long silence ensued. Harriet eventually got up and bent to throw a couple of pieces of wood on the fire.

'That,' said George, almost in a whisper now. 'That was the meaning of that word?'

'What word?'

'Humouring.'

Harriet smiled bleakly. 'Yes, George. I rather suppose it was.'

Five

I

From Lady Poldark in London to her elder daughter in Falmouth.

Dearest Clowance,

I have had a letter from your Father!!! It has come in care of the Prime Minister and is writ from Verdun, he says he is well and suffering no great hardship, I would send you the letter but I cannot bear to part from it. Of course he would say he was well just to reassure me, but I believe there is something about the letter that makes me believe him. In his nature being confined will greatly irk him but perhaps that is all, I pray that is all, he says he is getting used to French food and will be all the harder to please when he returns to Nampara! There is no term he says as yet to his internment and this deeply frets me, but at least I have a letter and that is important and he sends his love to you and all!!! It seems he reached Paris he says only a few hours after we left I cannot forgive myself for not staying on.

I remain in London for a few more weeks but Isabella-Rose and Henry will go home when Caroline goes home. Travelling with her. Perhaps I should do the same, but I feel just at present I am a little matter nearer to your Father than if I was in Cornwall. It is not at all the same as when he was away on some Mission, then I could settle to look after the house and the mines and the children and the farm and everything knowing that he would come home as soon as he could, this is not at all the same, but at least I know he has so far come to no harm.

In the end I may have to return home without him. Things look ill between us and France and you cannot see into the future, I am anxious for Jeremy.

What do you think? At a dinner at Mrs Pelham's (Caroline her aunt) I met Edward Fitzmaurice, and he invited us to tea at

232

Lansdowne House to meet Aunt Isabel again. She was some kind – I cannot tell you – and has invited me, when the children return home, to spend a few weeks with her at Lansdowne House, as the Lansdownes are at Bowood, and she says she is lonely! So I have accepted.

Dear life, you must think my nature has changed to accept such an invitation, but I too am lonely and I welcome the thought to be with friends – even such high-bred friends – instead of the emptiness of your Father's rooms in George Street, also I look for all means to aid your Father, and if Lord Lansdowne comes back while I am there he may be able to help in some way.

One thing which is irking me a great deal is that, although post can be received in England from France, no postal communication is permitted to France from England. This is because Bonaparte is being treated as an outlaw, and while he controls France France too is being treated the same. I have spoke to Lord Liverpool and he says he will do his most to circumvant – I believe that was the word – these regulations, I have writ a very long letter to your Father and it is urgent that he know we are safe and well.

I did not tell you in my letter from Paris for it seemed so trivial but Bella met a young Englishman at an Embassy party and they were much taken with each other. He is a Lieutenant Christopher Havergal who says he served under Geoffrey Charles in Spain. He is about 21 and of course much too old for Bella, but Bella is so tall and well grown for her age that many folk in Paris took her for seventeen. We both know that Bella is too young for anything yet but that is not how she regards herself. Well, we let the flirtation run its course, for he was there but two weeks and then he was returning to Belgium, when he left Bella was full of the mopes for a few days – and you know how once in a while she can be like that – but then it all passed away and was seemingly forgot. But now he has turned up in London! Again it is for scarcely more than a week but he calls regularly asking if he may take Bella out and I sometimes let her go, though I make certain sure that Mrs Kemp goes with them. It is another good reason for Bella to return to Cornwall with Caroline. It is all some silly, and I fear Lieutenant Havergal though seeming so charming is really trifling with a child's affections. He is good-looking in a somewhat dashing way and would be much better occupied with some young lady of his own age. I do not really understand him at all.

This is all about me and about us and not about you but that is what a letter is for isn't it. Pray tell me in reply all your news even the smallest part of it. Did you go to Nampara and how did you find them and how is Stephen and how do you fare yourself? Although so far apart we are thanks be in the same country and there is nothing to restrict a letter or as many letters as we have the time and the patience to write.

Mrs Kemp is of course to return with Caroline and the children and until I come home she will be in charge of them with the Enyses to keep an eye on them as often as they may. I do not need to ask you to go over to see them, and they will tell you far more of our experiences than ever I have been able to squeeze into a letter. Perhaps if your Father return quickly and there is no war I shall feel different, but for now I do not think I ever want to journey out of England again.

> *My dearest love to you both.*
> *Mother*

II

On a morning in early May Ross had a visitor. It was a brilliant day and having spent nearly half an hour looking out of his window at the sun glinting on the trees and the river, Ross turned and could not for a moment adjust his eyes to recognize the bulky figure in the doorway.

Then he exclaimed: 'Gaston!'

Brigadier Rougiet stepped into the room and the soldier closed the door behind him. He walked over and clasped Ross's hand.

'My friend, this is a pretty pass I find you in! I had no idea! I thought you were safely home in England long ago, *long* ago! How has this happened? Pray tell me.'

Ross told him. Rougiet rubbed at his long livid scar.

'But this is disgraceful! I still do not understand. You accepted my hospitality, that was all! Did you go elsewhere in France?'

Ross told him. He had never been entirely frank with Rougiet as to the mission Liverpool had sent him on, and he thought it was perhaps a bad time to confess it now. In any event there could hardly be proof of the despatches he had sent and nothing detrimental to the safety of the new France even if they were intercepted. The last of them had been in the Embassy post-bag while Napoleon was still in Lyon.

Rougiet scowled round the room. 'Are you comfortable here? You cannot be comfortable here! I am amazed. I know there is trouble between your country and mine – indeed between France and all the European powers. They seek to oppress us, they seek to dictate who shall lead us, they seek to turn back the clock. But no *war* has been declared. There is neither reason nor excuse for detaining a British citizen just because while he was on holiday in France he accepted an invitation to visit one of the army groups stationed near Paris! Your Embassy staff has gone long ago. I do not believe many if any of the citizens of your country who were surprised in Paris or in other parts of France have been detained; though I believe their exits were sometimes delayed by passport formalities. Why, therefore, you? I must find out.'

Ross was about to reply but Rougiet got up and strode back to the door. When the soldier came Rougiet said: 'Bring some cognac. And some sweet biscuits . . . Well, find some.' He grimaced at Ross. 'I will make further inquiries. In the meantime help yourself, and I will return as soon as I am able.'

Ross was on his third cognac and feeling rather less discontented with life when Rougiet returned. But his friend was not beaming with triumph. He helped himself to a small glass of cognac, drained it and looked at Ross with a puzzled expression.

'This is not a military matter, my friend, it is a police matter. You have met General Wirion?'

'When I first came here, yes.'

'He says he simply obeys orders from Paris. He showed me the order. It is headed "The Minister of General Police to His Majesty the Emperor" and it is signed "The Duke of Otranto". Formal detention. Not even parole.'

'It was offered me,' said Ross. 'I refused it.'

'But such a pity! You would have been far freer, more comfortable.'

'I have hoped to be able to escape. No opportunity has presented itself so far.'

'I can see they are being very careful . . . But have you not been *charged*?'

'Presumably they can find nothing to charge me with.'

'All this is on the direct orders of Fouché. Have you met him?'

'I have met him.'

'He is acknowledged to be the cleverest policeman in Europe. Did you have some quarrel with him?'

'I did not hide my dislike.'

'Ah.' The big Frenchman refilled both glasses. He held the dark amber liquid up to the light. 'If it is some personal vendetta it will be more difficult, for he is, at present, a very powerful man. If one could get to the Emperor . . .'

'Gaston,' Ross said, 'I am greatly obliged for your interest in my comfort and welfare. But I charge you not to endanger your own position on my behalf. This is a misfortune that has happened to me and is in no way your responsibility. So leave it be; I am sure I shall be freed in due course.'

'Of course you will. But I am your friend – even though our countries are at loggerheads – and I must do what I can. Do not fear for *my* position. France has need of her soldiers, particularly her artillery, and no police chief is likely to do me any hurt.' Rougiet smiled as he sipped. 'I believe I have frightened the guard into bringing General Wirion's own brandy.'

They sipped in silence.

Rougiet said: 'Have you been questioned?'

'Oh yes. Twice. For six hours at a time.'

'Was any ill treatment shown you?'

'No.'

'These police. You cannot always be sure. What did they ask you?'

'While we were in Paris I became friendly with a Mlle de la Blache. I had met her once in England many years ago.'

'Oh yes, I know her. She was formerly Baroness Ettmayer. For a time she was the mistress of Marshal Ney.'

Ross raised his eyebrows. 'I didn't know that.'

'For two or three years at least. Whenever he was in Paris they were seen everywhere together.'

'They now suspect her of having been a spy working on behalf of the Bourbons. She left Paris just before Napoleon arrived.'

'In that case I would not blame her! Fouché would have been swooping on her as soon as he had the authority.'

'Apparently my wife and children left Paris with Mlle de la Blache. This seems to have bred the suspicion that I was in some way involved in her activities.'

'These police,' Rougiet said again. 'They have strange and tortuous minds. If they try they can believe anything. I must somehow get word to the Emperor about this . . .'

'I saw him arrive in Paris,' Ross said.

'*Did* you? *Did* you? That must have been a great moment.' Rougiet passed a hand over his hair. 'Yet all Europe is against him. Even some parts of France murmur and are disaffected. But if it comes to war Bonaparte will prevail.'

'I trust it will not come to that.'

'So do I! So do we all! No one is more ardent for peace than the ordinary Frenchman. But everyone is against us.'

'Against Bonaparte.'

'Yes, but he arrived with a few hundred men on the south coast of France and in three weeks totally repossessed the country without a shot being fired! If that is not your democracy I don't know what is! It was the overwhelming will of the people! And he too now only wants peace. You will have heard, perhaps, that the Empress and his son, the King of Rome, have been forcibly prevented from joining him. It has been a great distress to him. He has left the Tuileries now, except for great occasions, and lives quietly in the Elysée, surrounded by his relations, his friends and his personal advisers.'

'And Fouché?' said Ross.

'Ah, Fouché, no. He keeps to his office and weaves his own spider's webs. Do you know it is said that when the Emperor arrived on the evening of the 20th and made his appointments, Fouché was at his desk by 2 a.m. the next morning. Your Mlle de la Blache did not leave a moment too soon! . . . Pah, I would not trust him an ell. He would as easily betray the Emperor as he did the King. He should have been guillotined years ago!'

The lovely spring morning was becoming tarnished by drifting cloud. It reminded Ross of the weather in Cornwall, light, frivolous, changeable. He wondered what Nampara would be like today. An azure sea hemmed in with surf, thundering over the sand? His house, the chimney's smoke blowing eccentrically in the breeze, grass whispering, a horse neighing in the stables, men working in the fields? And his mine? His two mines? Why had he ever been such a fool as to leave it on this bizarre mission which had served no good purpose and ended in disaster? Was it ambition? But he had no ambition. Was it a sense of duty? But to whom did he owe any duty? Was it something in his perverse nature that hankered after a new and an unusual adventure?

But it had all gone so *well* for a time; it truly had. He knew that his strange pretty Cornish wife with all her earthiness and all her high-strung perceptions had enormously enjoyed the early weeks in Paris. It had renewed her. The heady entertainment, and the admiration that had come her way had brought her to bloom all over again.

If he had not taken that last trip to Auxerre . . .

Rougiet was eyeing him. 'You are far away, my friend.'

'Yes.'

'I was saying . . . But what does it matter? Maybe it is better unsaid.'

'Pray tell me.'

'I was saying to you – and it is a sombre thought – that the arsenals and factories of France are working at high pressure, the armourers have been called up, the National Guard likewise throughout the country, thousands of extra horses commandeered; arms are arriving from across the Rhine smuggled in barges and small boats, the Imperial Guard brought up to full strength. I need not explain to you that these preparations are not being undertaken with peace in mind – but they will only come into operation if the Germans and the English oppose us in Belgium.'

'Why must you have Belgium?'

'It has been ours for too long. We are almost the same people.'

Ross said after a moment: 'I do not feel that England would fight so hard just to replace Louis. But there is strong feeling about the independence of Belgium – even among the Whigs, who generally favour Napoleon.'

'It is too bad,' said Rougiet, cracking the knuckles of his big hands. 'But I have to tell you we shall very shortly have a hundred and fifty thousand picked troops in the Army of the North. There will be no chance for Wellington with the mixed and unreliable army he now commands . . . Still, there may yet be some chance of an accommodation, a compromise. I pray so.'

'Amen. But if you had to fight such a battle how would you go about it?'

'Oh . . . At the present we are making a few early concentrations in the area of Philippeville and Beaumont. But I must not disclose more to you. Nor could I, for I am not in the Emperor's confidence.'

Ross saw that the brandy bottle, half full when it came in, was now empty.

'There is also in this', he said, 'a man called Tallien. He was at that Embassy party where I first met you. Fouché was there too, you will remember.'

'Tallien, oh yes. Fouché's jackal.'

'When I was arrested Tallien accompanied the gendarmes. He may be the cause of my imprisonment. I shook him up on one occasion because he was paying unwelcome attentions to my wife.'

'So? An odious little lecher. He counts for nothing, of course, compared to Fouché. But Fouché protects him. Long ago the rôles were quite reversed. For a time, in those wild days of the nineties, Tallien was President of the Convention. I am told that he protected Fouché then – that he saved him from the guillotine. Fouché, it is said, never forgets a favour and never forgets an injury.'

'I can believe that.'

'It is strange to think that Tallien cannot be more than eight or nine years older than I am, yet I was a mere youth at the time. Well . . .' Rougiet stretched his legs. 'Let us talk of happier things, eh? Your wife is safe and well? And your children? That is good. That is something . . . But we must spring you from this trap, my friend. Have a little patience and we will get you out.'

Six

I

On a fine Thursday, a week before Demelza left for Cornwall, Lieutenant Christopher Havergal called on her at Lansdowne House and asked her permission to pay his attentions to Isabella-Rose.

Demelza, who had been trying to concentrate on reading a book – a novel – recommended by Lady Isabel Fitzmaurice, picked the book up again, found a spill to mark her place, and then put it back on the table.

'Your attentions, Lieutenant Havergal? I'm not sure what that . . . It can't mean what I think it mean.'

'It means that eventually I wish to ask Isabella-Rose's hand in marriage.'

'You – are not serious, Lieutenant?'

He coughed into his hand. 'Yes, ma'am. Very serious indeed.'

Demelza perceived that he had had his hair cut and his moustache trimmed. His uniform too was new.

'You are asking . . . my permission to – to – to . . .' She could not say it.

'Indeed, Lady Poldark. I am sorry if it comes as such a – a surprise to you.'

Demelza also observed that he was nervous. Nervous! Lieutenant Christopher Havergal, nervous!

'I still don't quite understand. Do you know how old my daughter is?'

'Yes, ma'am. It is quite incredible. Everyone takes her for seventeen. But I do know how old she is. May I sit down and be allowed to explain myself?'

Demelza waved her hand weakly towards a chair.

He sat on the edge of it, coughed again. His moustache was still long enough to quiver when he coughed.

'I am not suggesting, Lady Poldark, I could not and would not dare to suggest an early marriage. But perhaps in two years, when she is fifteen . . . Until then a betrothal . . . That is what I would like more than anything in the world. What *we* would like . . .'

'So Isabella-Rose knows of this – this proposal of yours?'

'Oh yes, ma'am. We talked of it before she left for Cornwall.'

'And she would like to marry you?'

'Yes, ma'am. It seems to be . . . to be her dearest wish.'

No wonder the little monkey had seemed so bouncy when she climbed into the coach with Caroline.

'I am leaving for Flanders tomorrow,' said Havergal. 'Since Bella left I have been trying to summon up the courage to call. You will see I have left it to the last minute. It means so much to me that I have shirked putting my suit to the test.'

'But Lieutenant Havergal –'

'Pray call me Christopher if you will, ma'am.'

'But Christopher, what you ask is impossible! Although in some ways she seem so mature, she is scarce out of childhood! At that age one is – fanciful, light-hearted, just beginning life. To suggest she would know her own mind so *soon*, on such an important matter as this – oh, I am sure she thinks she does, but in three months she will see some other young man and transfer all her romantic ideals to him! It is – natural! Oh, I am sorry to say this, but may I ask you how often you have been in and out of love with some pretty girl since you were thirteen?'

He had very nice eyes when he looked at you directly; no wonder the naughty Bella had a fancy for him.

'Often, Lady Poldark. I have met many pretty girls – and – if it does not offend you to say so – have had three of them as my mistresses – one of them Portuguese. Many of them have delighted me, but none before has ever touched my heart.'

Demelza glanced round the enormous room with its high windows and its heavy furnishings. Her visit to Lansdowne House was not a great success. Lady Isabel could not have been sweeter, indeed seemed delighted with her company; but it came strange at the best of times for Demelza to do nothing but sit and read or take a constitutional round Berkeley Square or make polite conversation at a tea-table. And this was not the best of times. Her whole life was disrupted, and the proper way, the only way, to counter such disruption was in *work*, sheer physical work such as digging, weeding, beating a carpet; or even milking a cow and carrying the pail back and forth from the dairy. Inaction bred the strangest fancies. She was not happy here but was staying until her allotted time was up.

'Forgive me, Lady Poldark,' this handsome elegant droopy young man said, reclaiming her attention; 'you will think it beyond the world presumptuous in me to say this, but I believe you do not yet quite realize what an extraordinary young woman your daughter is. Have you heard her *voice*? But of course you have! But perhaps you do not realize what an extraordinary fascination and range it has! She must do *something* with it! Perhaps she should go on the stage – or into opera. She would be invaluable, unique, in some branch of the world of entertainment, the musical world. She has a great future in front of her!'

'Married to you?' Demelza was ashamed of the question but it bubbled up in her.

'I think so, ma'am. I think so. Of course we have this little trouble with Boney to settle first. Who knows, I may not survive? And then our betrothal would be irrevocably broken. But if I survive, and when it is over, I have no intention of making the army my permanent career. I shall live in London and pursue some other career.'

'You have money?' Dear life, she thought, what's come over me? Tesn't right, tesn't proper. Shades of Jud!

'Enough money to live on,' said Havergal. 'Some expectations. I read for the bar but did not progress far enough. It could be taken up again. You will see, Lady Poldark, that I do not pretend a special eligibility. But I sincerely believe that if Bella were married to me I could bring her talents to the notice of influential men who would know how to make the best of them.'

Demelza picked up her book. It would soon be four o'clock and Lady Isabel, having taken her rest, would be ready for tea; bright-eyed and chatty and deaf and rather sweet and rather boring.

'Christopher,' she said. 'In the first place I could not possibly let you become betrothed to Isabella-Rose without her father's consent, and that at present is impossible to obtain. You see. In the second place, although I find you likeable and personable I do not think you have quite played fair with us by engaging the affections of a little girl who is still too impressionable to know her own mind –'

'Lady Poldark! –'

'Oh, I know what you are going to say. It was mutual between the both of you. I well can guess how Bella would need no leading on. But you are – twenty-one, is it?, almost twenty-two – you are good-looking, a dashing officer, a – a young man of experience; how could she fail to be swept off her feet? You have not played quite fair with us and you must – must understand the – the consequences. I cannot and will not give permission for any such betrothal like you suggest! It is not possible and pray forget it!'

He sat with his long fair hair falling over his face. Then he looked up and grinned at her – a really wicked grin.

'So be it, ma'am. Perhaps the permission I sought *was* too much to expect. Were I in your position I believe I might feel the same. So let us leave it a while. I will go now. But I trust that if, in a year or two years, your daughter and I should meet again and be of the same mind, you would not find me so personally distasteful or dislikeable as to forbid us your approval?'

She looked at him, part hostile, part won over.

'I cannot say, Lieutenant Havergal. Nor can I speak for my husband. I do not suppose he will at all approve. But what may or may not happen in the future I have no idea. I can only ask you pray to forget about anything you have said to me for a long time to come.'

II

The Royal Standard was the principal hotel in Falmouth. It had a billiards room with fine views of the harbour and a large coffee room, also on the first floor, which was the meeting place for the seafaring folk of the town, though generally speaking it was the captains and masters and agents and factors who met there, not the ordinary seamen. Stephen went regularly and had made it his business to be popular; he had an easy friendly manner, didn't push where he saw he was not wanted, and stood his round. Occasionally he now took Jason with him.

On the Thursday on which Christopher Havergal was putting his proposition to Demelza the room was crowded to its limits, for the weather had turned unfriendly: hazy cloud with a strong south-easterly half gale which was keeping around sixty sail embayed in the Carrick Roads. Chiefly it was a West Indian convoy, and not only were the crews ashore but the passengers, putting up at various lodging houses of doubtful excellence and crowding the narrow streets during the daylight hours as they sought some distraction from the delay.

With only two days to go before the axe Stephen was not the best company, but in Jason's presence he always put on a show; pride in his son's admiration for him impelled him to make the effort. He had not told Jason of the impending crash, but during the evening the young man got a fair idea that trouble of some sort was impending.

'What's amiss, Fa-Uncle?' he said in an undertone after Captain Buller had left. 'Why ask him?'

'Because the *Queen Charlotte*'s being refitted for taking on the New York run – now the war's over. He'll be signing up crew early next month, and there'll be plenty applying. He's got a good reputation and the money's good.'

'I don't want to join the Packet Service,' said Jason. 'I don't want to work for anyone but you. I know I wasn't needed on the *Chasse* – or Blamey did not want for me to be mate – but I'm willing enough to sail as an ordinary seaman on the *Adolphus*.'

'Aye, lad,' said Stephen. 'I've no doubt ye are.'

'There's something serious wrong, isn't there. *Adolphus* has been ready a week an' she's not yet victualled.'

'Nothing to be gained by taking on stores while we're all wind bound. Look at the masters in this room. Everyone's held up.'

'Yes, but if the wind came off at dawn tomorrow they'd all be away by the first tide. We could not be.'

'Mind your own business,' said Stephen, and gulped at his ale. But his voice was not sharp.

They listened together to two captains talking at the next table.

'. . . the breeze died away and we was befogged and becalmed for nigh on ten days. Man, ye wouldna' believe it but ye could hear sailors talking in other vessels and never see sight o' them. Then when the fog lifted we might ha' been part of an armada. Fourteen of 'em we counted gathered there like a flock of sheep by the calm . . .'

Jason said: 'I heard you were thinking o' selling *Chasse Marée*.'

'Who told ye that?'

'It was a word just dropped. Are we doing badly, Father?'

'It is not our fault. I need time, Jason, and I can't buy time.'

'Time for what?'

'No matter. You will find out soon enough.'

'A hundred and fifty-eight barrels of tar,' a voice said near to them. 'Fifty-nine hogsheads of tobacco. Five hundred and fifty mats. Eighty wainscot logs. Clapboards. Laden to the gunnels, we were, and who should come up but this French privateer?'

The Carringtons listened in silence to the story.

Jason said: 'So we're at war with France again.'

'Not yet. I don't know. We may be. But Harrison's talking about the winter before last. I've heard this story before.'

Jason said: 'But it said in the paper last week. It said Parliament said there was a state of war. And it said in another part of the paper that no ships are to go to Ostend except in convoy because o' the French privateers.'

'The lad's right,' said a beery old man, leaning over from the next table. 'They'll be issuing Letters of Marque from this side of the Channel before you know. Wish I was younger. I'd go after some pickings.'

Jason looked at his father who, never down for too long, laughed and slapped the boy on the back.

'Wish we could too. Maybe after the next few weeks, after the dust has settled, we'll go adventuring on our own.'

'What is wrong with *Adolphus*?' persisted Jason.

'Ah . . . There's the rub, boy, there's the rub. Drink up, we must be going.'

Another conversation drifted to them from a large hairy, good-tempered man who might have German or Scandinavian blood.

'I picked up with the *Neptune* in December just before we got the Trade Winds, and for twenty-two days we never lost sight of each other, so even balanced was our rate of sailing. I was just ahead all the time; we were carrying topmast studding sails, but alas on the twenty-first day King Wind said we could carry them no longer and carried them off. Ha! ha! ha! No captain likes to be outdone, me least of all. So the next night we had supper together, McGennis and me. A Liverpool man but no worse for that. Ha! ha! ha! He told me he was homeward bound after a successful trip . . . Thank you, Tonkin. Here's to your health . . . A successful trip. Best part of it, he said, was when he was looking for wood and produce in the Gaboon River. Traders came aboard and offered him thirteen slaves. He took 'em. Carried them across and sold 'em to the Portuguese slave traders. Made more, he said, by this than all his commissions and adventures besides . . .'

There was what passed for a brief silence in the noisy coffee room.

'Tis a felony now, carr'ing slaves,' said a strongly Cornish voice. 'The law were brought in a few year ago, my dear. Tis profitable, I agree, but not if you get ten years' transportation for et.'

'If you get caught, true enough,' said the big man. 'But McGennis was not caught.'

'In Bristol,' said Stephen, 'I'm told they have a device of selling their ships to the Portuguese. Not really selling but a device, ye understand. Then they change their names and sail under the Portuguese flag. Tis dangerous, but the profits are huge.'

'I'd have no hand in it,' said a man called Fox. 'It would be moral blood money. A man who still trades in slaves is no better than a pirate.'

Jason said in an undertone: '*I* wouldn't care. If we don't do it, someone else will. Tell you what, Father. One day we'll sail off in the *Adolphus* together, you as captain, me as mate, see what we can find. That would be real good. Come home wi' gold. If you're in trouble, Father, money trouble, that's the way out of it.'

Stephen looked at the stocky young man beside him. A chip off the old block.

In spite of the vagrant life he had led and the ill luck that had come his way in his earlier years, Stephen had always had a pride in himself, an arrogant belief in his own ability not merely to survive but to become a success. He was confident in his own maleness, in his physical strength, in his good looks, in his ready tongue. There was a unique person called Stephen Carrington and there was no one quite like him. His mind was quick and adaptable, his body was something to be proud of, he walked with the hint of a swagger. And this boy was very like him. This boy, his blood, looked up to him with pride and admiration. And in a few days' time he would learn that his father had lost everything, was to be bankrupted at the whim of George Warleggan.

Well, there was no way out. Of course he was still alive, could somehow begin over again. Scrape together a few hundred pounds from among his friends, lease a small cutter or a schooner, start smuggling crude tin stuff to France, make a bit, add a bit, build up again a step at a time. (Though with the enmity of a Warleggan to face it would be an uphill struggle in this county.) Perhaps go back to Bristol, take Clowance and the boy. (Though he had quite a few enemies there.)

So all his abilities and adaptabilities really counted for nothing. The trap had been set and he had fallen into it. He had been riding high, and the higher the rise the bigger the fall.

Some folk would derive a sour satisfaction from it. Not excluding his father-in-law, he suspected, having no doubt from the beginning disapproved an association with the Warleggans. In spite of Clowance's trenchant rejection of the idea, the old feud seemed the most likely cause of his new ruin. (There was nothing else he had ever done to offend the Warleggans, except to steal money from their bank, a matter on which they could not have the inkling of suspicion.)

The two men left the hotel together. The south-easter met them, whistling round the corner. It was one of those relentless winds that do not take off even at night.

Stephen put his hand on Jason's shoulder, a feeling of warmth and comradeship coming over him. 'I've a difficult time coming, lad. That's why I was wanting you to sign up with Captain Buller. But no matter; I expect we'll get along somehow. Carringtons usually do.'

Seven

I

Jeremy had been away five days on manoeuvres and returned on the Friday afternoon to kiss Cuby repeatedly and to tell her he had planned a picnic for the Saturday.

'Have I spoken of Captain Mercer? I forget. He has invited us to a picnic in Strytem, where he is stationed. It's about twelve miles from Brussels. I have hired a carriage and if we leave at nine we shall be able to spend most of the day with them. Do you mind?'

'I'd greatly like it. Is he in your regiment?'

'No, the Horse Artillery under Sir Augustus Fraser. I met him at the Forties Club.'

'Ah yes. I see.'

There was a brief silence. Jeremy's membership of the Forties Club was virtually the only bone of contention between them. It was a gaming club open only to officers under the age of forty. They played faro, whist and lansquenet, for low stakes or high according to the whim of the players. The principle of the club was that money never changed hands: it was all done by IOU. Once a month there was a dinner and a reckoning. On one occasion Jeremy had shocked her by saying he was two hundred and fifty guineas in debt. Two weeks later, just before the dinner, he had reduced it to forty guineas, but that was not to say he could have been sure of any such outcome.

Cuby's father had died when she was three months old and thereafter her life had been ruled by her brother – who was nine years the elder and who – well set up to begin – had nearly bankrupted himself building a magnificent Nash-designed crenel-lated mansion overlooking Porthluney Beach, and then compounded his error by trying to recoup his losses on the race course. His plan to marry Cuby into the rich Warleggan family had come to nothing, and it was very doubtful now whether he would be able to survive as a Cornish landowner. When, rarely, a sleepless night came to Cuby she would lie quiet beside Jeremy, hands behind her head, staring up at the ceiling and wondering what would happen to her family now.

So, reacting to the sort of life in which she had lived all her youth, when outgoings were always greater than incomings, where essential building or repairs were stopped because no one could pay the bricklayers' wages, where the footmen in the house looked down at heel for lack of a shoe repair or wore a coat splitting at the seams because it had been made for someone else, where the marvellous horse that was going to win the Derby came in fourth or the run of amazing good luck at faro unfortunately changed to an amazing run of ill luck before the winnings could be pocketed, Cuby had, for the first and only time in their married life, exploded at Jeremy.

Afterwards there had been a wildly rewarding reconciliation, when they had kissed and made up, when he had brushed her damp lids with his own and stroked her breasts and kissed her eyelids, and had promised fervently that his gambling and his extravagances should be strictly curtailed.

'*Do* you mind, my sweetheart?' he asked, mistaking, or choosing to mistake, her hesitation. 'It will not be too much for you?'

'Of *course* it will not be too much for me, boy,' she said, using as she sometimes did out of deep affection the name she had first given him. 'Except for this nasty sickness, which your mother assures me will go away soon, I am *very* well. I must not be treated as if made of porcelain! For months and months and months yet it will make *no* difference to my activities. It is *natural* for a woman to have a baby. There is nothing *peculiar* about it. It is not an illness, a complaint, a disease. It is just a natural outcome of – of loving.'

'I am delighted', said Jeremy, 'that it will make no difference to your activities,' kissing her in the small of the neck and then on her hair and then blowing gently into her ear. His fingers stroked her face. 'The natural outcome of loving. What a good expression. Do you not think we should break our five-day fast?'

'Gladly, but it is still daylight.'

'I have no objection to the daylight.'

'And you have not eaten.'

'There are other hungers I would rather satisfy.'

The doorbell rang.

'Oh, *curse*!' said Jeremy, rising from beside her. 'Do not stir. Do not flicker an eyelid, my sweetheart, until I come back. I will send this savage intruder away.'

But when he opened the door a young man in civilian clothes stood there, in the company of a tall young woman. The young man was sturdily built, full lipped, dark haired and browed.

'Goldsworthy!'

'My dear Jeremy! What a pleasure! I trust that we don't call on you at an inappropriate moment? We have but an hour since arrived in Brussels. You have never met my wife, Bess? Bess, this is Jeremy Poldark; how happy I am that we have run you to earth!'

II

The Gurneys were in Brussels just for a week and had taken rooms in the rue du Musée. They had brought their young baby and a nurse and two servants. Brussels at the moment was the social capital of Europe, with Wellington giving repeated balls and much of the British aristocracy there to frequent them and to give soirées and luncheon parties and suppers themselves. Jeremy, used to regarding Goldsworthy as a juvenile and eccentric innovator and surgeon before his time – he was only twenty-two – was surprised that he had come to savour this hectic scene. Probably his new wife, Elizabeth, who was ten years his senior, was the instigator of the trip; though Gurney was no blushing violet. He was, he announced, thinking of moving to London, where all the important men of science congregated.

'Cornwall is a backwater,' he said, 'for what I want to do. Trevithick is there still, but there's talk of him going to South America. Woolf is active and there are a few other good men about, but I believe if you want to make the impact you have to go to London. I can practise as a surgeon there just as well as in Padstow. Not', he added, 'that I shall lose touch with Cornwall. Once you have lived there, nowhere else is quite the same . . . And you,

Jeremy, how long will you stay in the army? How long before we can go into partnership, constructing the next horseless carriage?'

They stayed to supper, with Cuby and Jeremy occasionally exchanging sweetly lustful glances when the others were not looking. Jeremy invited them for the picnic the following day, and they accepted.

At nine the following morning they set off in an open landau and rumbled over the cobbles and out of the city onto the country lane leading to Ninove. Swallows flew high as they passed through rich farmland, patched with woods in which the leaves were brilliantly bursting, a luxurious countryside, unscarred by war.

But a countryside preparing for war. Villages were full of cavalry or horse artillery or men marching behind gun carriages. 'Ninove is Lord Uxbridge's headquarters,' said Jeremy. 'He's the commander of Wellington's cavalry. It's only three or four miles from here.'

All the same, undeterred by thoughts of battle, undistracted by – or uninterested in – the sights of a rich and fertile land, Goldsworthy Gurney spent the trip talking to Jeremy of his plans for a horseless carriage. He was still concerned about adhesion wheel grip on the roads. From his earlier ideas of levers or propellers which acted on the ground like horses' feet to get the carriage moving, he had turned to the introduction of revolving chains fitted with projections which by moving round, as in launching a dinghy, would help the carriage on its way. He had also been experimenting with a new piano which would, he hoped, harmonize with the organ he had built, and which many people said had a specially fine tone. Eventually they could be played together by a single performer.

The two ladies got on as best they might, which on the whole was pretty well. Mrs Gurney had been a Miss Symons of Launcells, and was suitably impressed that Mrs Poldark had been a Miss Trevanion. Cuby was relieved that her new friend knew of John Trevanion only as an ex-Sheriff of Cornwall and not as someone hopelessly in debt.

The carriage turned off the more acceptable road and jolted and lurched among the muddy ruts of a Flemish country lane. Three perilous streams were crossed by bridges on which the plankings were loose. The horses did not like it at all and had to be led.

When they reached Strytem, which was no more than a hamlet buried in tall elms, the moustached Captain Mercer was there to greet them. Two extra made no difference, and he led the way into a large ruined château where his troop was billeted. Inside it was handsome but dark, and soon the party set off followed by a cart containing the food and wine, and tablecloths were laid on the green sward by the banks of a slow-flowing river. There were fourteen of them, including four ladies, and they sat in the sun and laughed and talked and ate and drank in the greatest accord.

Ghent, said Captain Mercer, was crowded with Bourbons, from servants and hangers-on to princes of the blood. It was also a mustering point for British regiments arriving from England and then passing on to new camps and billets. No one, he said, had any idea what was happening so far as a strategy of war was concerned, but all the Belgians, and most of the French royalist officers attending on the King, were convinced that these splendid troops passing through to fight Bonaparte would, if it came to a battle, be thrown back into the sea.

Jeremy, in fact, knew a little more than Mercer, having been out all week on manoeuvres and having seen the Duke at close quarters. This had been just east of the village of Waterloo, and at Halle where the roads from Ath and Mons united.

'I do not suppose for a moment', he said, 'that the Duke will fight unless he has to. At present we are such a miscellaneous crew! There's maybe twenty-five thousand British troops in Belgium but less than a quarter are veterans. Most of 'em are less qualified than I! We're desperately short of cannon and cannot match the French cavalry. Of course we've got the Hanoverians, and the Brunswickers, who are good; but who can rely on the Belgians, most of whom are Bonapartists at heart?'

They left at seven after a day spent in the green heart of spring, making their way back across the bridges until they reached the main road. Here they had twice to draw in to the side while a troop of cavalry clattered past. Then they went through a village in which the Life Guards were taking their ease. Their tall lanky figures in brilliant scarlet tight-fitting jackets contrasted with the brown smock-frocks of the peasants moving among them in the evening light.

In Brussels they dropped the Gurneys off at their rooms, and Cuby made an appointment to meet Bess in the morning to go shopping. Then they drove home.

'Do you find him tiresome?' asked Jeremy. On the way home Goldsworthy had talked of the properties of lime as a manure and had told the sad story of a farmer friend who had burned lime in kilns built with stones containing manganese. Then he had spoken of the dangers of brewing cider in lead vats, this in his view being a common cause of colic.

Cuby smiled. 'I would not say so.'

'Well, I do sometimes. But I also cannot get away from the originality of his mind.'

'Would you go into a partnership with him on the horseless carriage?'

'I think there might be a better future for the steam ship – rivalling the packet ships by carrying mails . . . But yes, I'd go in with Goldsworthy if he put up a reasonable proposition.' Jeremy was thoughtful. 'But the opportunity for me may not be yet. This could well be a long war.'

They reached their apartment and Jeremy paid off the driver. They climbed the stairs, his arm round her waist.

Cuby said: 'It has been a lovely day.'

They went in. In their absence an official letter had been delivered. Jeremy broke the seal and went pink.

'Dear Heaven!' he said. 'A tragedy! I have been promoted to captain.'

Eight

I

Clowance was in her back garden pricking out lettuce seedlings. She was part sheltered here from the relentless wind, but still it blew uncomfortably about her; the two weeks of it had dried the light soil almost to powder and she had given the plants a good watering last night so that those she pulled up to discard would not disturb the others.

Stephen had been out since nine; he had said he would be home to dinner but had not turned up. If he was going to change his plans he usually sent a boy with a message; but not this time.

It was the last day – though, being a Friday, probably the bank would not make a move until Monday. Stephen was as taut as a wire under strain. He had done everything he could: there was no other lever within his reach; but being the man he was it was not natural to sit down to await the blow. He had said he was going down to the *Adolphus*, which, fully laden but still unvictualled, lay in the Penryn River waiting orders. Clowance could not imagine he was still there. Probably he had gone to the Royal Standard, was drowning his sorrows in a conventional way. But she was anxious. Being a man of action, and she well knew sometimes of violence, he might be venting his anger and frustration in some dangerous way.

So when a footstep sounded she turned eagerly, apprehensively, but relieved to see him.

'Stephen! I waited – a long time.'

There was an expression on his face she could not read, grim but with a different light in his eyes.

'What're ye doing, dear heart?'

It was the first time he had used that expression for two weeks.

'You can see,' she said. 'This wind is drying everything, but I think they'll come on now.'

'I didn't get back to dinner,' he said. 'I was called away.'

'Oh? Where?'

He came over and stood beside her, looking down at the ground she had been working on. 'Are they far enough apart?'

'No, but the next time I thin them we can eat the thinnings . . . What is it, Stephen?'

He put his hand on her shoulder. 'What do you call it when a man is due to be hanged by the neck and then at the last moment he is told it is not so?'

'Not so? Do you mean reprieved?'

'Reprieved. That's it. At least, that's what I reckon it is.'

She turned to him. 'How? Tell me what has happened? Is it good news?'

He said: 'This morning. When I was working on the *Adolphus* this morning and reckoning how she could be cheapest unloaded, a man came, a message from Truro. I was requested to make my appearance at Warleggan's Bank at three this afternoon.' His hand tightened on her shoulder. 'It was on my tongue to curse him and tell him and his employer to go to hell; but no, I thought to meself, if this is the last act I'll go see just how they wish to proceed about it; I'll go discover if there is any other mischief planned for me. So I took horse – hired from Greenbank Stables – and rode into Truro, to the bank, was there by soon after two.'

'Is it good news?' she said again.

'Only Lander was there – no sign of George, but he said – and I took care to make double sure what he said – that on due consideration it had been decided to continue to fund me – to a limited extent, on a reduced scale. There's a strict upper limit, a new system of accounting, no this, no that –'

'But Stephen!' she interrupted him, grasping his arms, 'does it mean – does that mean we are saved?'

'In a fashion, yes –'

She hugged him. 'But that – that is the most wonderful thing! You can keep your *ships*, go on with your trading? Even perhaps build our house?'

'I reckon so, wi' safeguards, and a sort of going slow. I have yet to work it all out. He put it all in writing – Lander did – and I have read it through thrice. The upper limit of the loan is rigid and must be reduced by twenty per cent after twelve months. No more accommodation bills but a renewal of those out. I reckon I shall be acting all the time under George's thumb. I don't altogether care for it –'

'But that does not *matter*! Who cares if we have to proceed more carefully? We are *safe! Safe! Safe!* Stephen I have nothing in the house to drink but ale –'

He permitted himself his first smile. 'I reckon I've got a lot of your lettuce soil on my sleeves . . . I can tell you this is the biggest relief off my mind. Even now it is a rare puzzle to me. I had wild and drastic thoughts. We'll go out tonight to celebrate. We'll go to the King's Arms. Mary Commins is a friend of mine and she'll put on a good meal and drink for us . . .'

She rubbed her hands and brushed his sleeves. 'There, it is nearly all gone! . . . You say you did not see Sir George?'

'Not a sign of him. I could not credit it when Lander began to speak. What made him change his mind?'

'Perhaps he meant to all along and –'

'*Never*. Not from George's looks that day . . . I've been wondering – will we go to their house again and be received as friends? Ye see –'

'Does it *matter*? We are safe – and in a little while can reduce our indebtedness! Even what we are getting from Wheal Grace will help! And soon enough you'll be altogether your own master again!'

He kissed her. 'You're wise, Clowance. Always was. Always will be. Twas you who warned me not to get tangled with George Warleggan in the first place. I wonder, d'ye think Lady Harriet would have some finger in this?'

'Does it matter?' Clowance said again.

'Have you seen her lately? Since this happened?'

'I had to go over one day last week. To return those books on architecture. I wanted to give them to a servant but she was on the steps.'

'Did you tell her?'

'She asked why I had not been to the last day of the hunt, so I just mentioned our changed situation.'

Stephen was thoughtful, combing his hair with his strong fingers.

'I reckon it maybe was something Harriet said to George. She has always been specially friendly to me.'

II

Katie Carter, made more clumsy even than usual, if not by her condition at least by her agitation at being in such a condition, upset a pan of boiling water and in trying to save it got a substantial burn on her arm. Cook sliced up a cold potato, slapped it on her arm and tied it in position with a handy strip of duster. Thereafter work as usual.

After a couple of days they took it off and found the arm reddened and bleeding, so she was sent to see Dr Enys. She would have much preferred Mr Irby in St Ann's but Mrs Warleggan caught sight of it and said she must see Dr Enys and she would pay. This was such an exceptional sign of favour in her current disgrace that Katie did not dare to disobey.

Not that she minded Dr Enys: ever since he attended her as a child she had thought him wonderful; but it was precisely because of this that she did not want to see him and exhibit her coming shame. He was likely to know of it – most people had passed the whisper on by now – but it was the face to face encounter she dreaded.

When it came it was not too bad. He had such a handsome way of being impersonal: he was surgeon and she was the patient; there was nothing more between them than that. But then, after he had bathed the burn and dusted it with healing powder and given it a proper light bandage, he spoiled it all by feeling her pulse and saying:

'Is your pregnancy quite normal, Katie?'

She flushed and broke into a sweat. 'Please?'

'You are carrying a child, I understand. Do you feel well?'

'Oh, yes . . . Bit sick in the mornings, like.'

'Are you about four months?'

'Ais.'

'That should be clearing up now then. Let me know if I can be of any help to you.'

Katie fumbled a shilling out of her purse. 'Mrs says I was to pay you this.'

'Thank you. Don't touch the bandage for five days, unless it becomes painful. Try to keep it dry. I'll give you some of this powder to use if you need it.'

Katie put on her cloak, anxious to be gone. Dwight considered her for a moment, uncertain whether to say more. These people were part of the family of Sawle-with-Grambler whom it had made it his business to care for over the last twenty-odd years.

He said: 'They have not found Saul Grieves?'

Katie's flush went darker as she stared out of the window.

Dwight said: 'Your mother thinks he should be sought out.'

'I wouldn't marry 'im,' said Katie, 'no, not if 'e was the last man on earth.'

Dwight walked to the door with her. 'Perhaps there is some other man you will marry.'

'Fine chance o' that, I reckon. Not many'd want me wi' a bastard child. And there's not many I'd 'ave!'

She opened the door, and the sun fell in on her shabby clothes, her heavy Spanish hair, her fine skin.

'I hope this wind will stop soon,' Dwight said. 'It is drying everything up.'

'Ais. Fishing boats put out, they're 'ard set to get 'ome.'

'There's one man would gladly marry you,' said Dwight. 'If you would have him. And make a good father . . . Music Thomas.'

She half stopped, then snorted like a horse. '*Music?* That gurt lump. *He* was put in wi' the bread and took out wi' the cakes, if ever there was! . . . That's a fine jest, Surgeon. Why, 'e's only 'alf a man!'

'You'd be surprised,' said Dwight. 'As you know, I have been helping him, and he has made great progress. He can tell the time now and the days of the week. But you see him yourself quite often. Do you not notice any difference?'

'Can't say's I do.'

They stood then in awkward silence.

'Get along with you, then.'

Katie said: 'Oh, e's always grizzling at me like 'e likes me; but – but I'd be 'ard put before I wed *that* loon!'

Dwight smiled. 'Well, Katie, you are a free woman and I am no matchmaker. It occurred to me that it would be better if your child had a foster father. Sometimes –'

'Oh yes, Surgeon, I'm sure you be right. But, begging your pardon, not a father all the village would snigger at.'

III

The weather at last abating, Stephen decided to take the *Adolphus* across himself on the Sunday. He did not invite Clowance to go with him.

'Ye don't mind, dear heart? It takes a time to get over the shock, to feel things are mebbe going to come right after all. It's like when your leg goes to sleep, the pain begins when the circulation comes back.'

'How long will you be away?'

'I'll be back so quick as I can. But the weather's wayward. While I'm away I want to think things out.'

'What things?'

'How I shall live my life with George Warleggan breathing over my shoulder. Oh, I know he always has been after a fashion, ever since I went to his bank; but I conjected it was a *friendly* breathing, if you follow me. Now I don't know what it is. I feel I'm living – we're both living – on the end of a lifeline, and who knows when he's going to take out his scissors and cut it?'

'He may have done what he did just to shock you, Stephen. So long as you keep to the agreement you've signed there'll be no more trouble.'

'Mebbe yes. And mebbe no. I haven't *seen* him since he changed his mind. I don't know what he's going to *look* like. I only know he looked very nasty when I was told they were going to bankrupt me. Harriet may have persuaded him to change his mind, but what's to stop him changing it back? The sooner I'm out of his reach, the happier I shall be.'

'But how can you be?'

'Not yet. Not this year. But if I can't get out of his hands it will not be for want of trying.'

Stephen was filling his pipe. He looked a big formidable young man, capable in his own mind of taking on the world.

He said suddenly: 'The *Chasse Marée* is due any day. You know I got an offer for her? Well, I shall still sell her; concentrate on the other two. With the money I get from that . . .' He hesitated.

She said: 'What?'

'I have not decided. But tis not going into Warleggan's Bank, that's for sure. Nor is the money from Wheal Leisure. Don't worry, I'll keep to the contract, see Warleggan's are just satisfied. But if I sell *Chasse Marée* I shall have money in hand. Out in the Channel I'll have time to think what to do.'

'You have some ideas?'

'Yes, I have. But I'd better prefer not to say what they are.'

'Until they're decided?' she asked stonily.

'Until they're firmer. I can't be sure yet. Don't worry, I'll talk with you then.' He put his arm round her. 'After all, ye're my partner, are ye not?'

She said: 'If you sell *Chasse Marée* Andrew will lose his ship.'

'That has to be thought of too. I'll try not to let him down. He can always sail wi' me. Or mebbe take the *Adolphus* when I want to be home.'

'You know he wants to get married?'

'What, Andrew? No. Who to?'

'Thomasine Trevethan. George Trevethan's sister.'

'My oh my. So that's the way the wind's setting. Well, good luck to him. Though I doubt he'll be able to set up house with her on what I pay him.'

'He knows that. Before this happened – before Sir George threatened to withdraw his credit – I was going to ask you if you could promote Andrew – somehow – so that he was in a better position to marry.'

'Ah yes, well, we must think around it somehow, mustn't we. If there's some way I can work him into any scheme I launch, then be sure I'll do it. We want to keep him happy, don't we.'

IV

The *Adolphus* left at dawn on the Sunday, following, by a single tide, the West Indian fleet and all the other casual vessels which had been embayed by the relentless wind. Although little above a half gale in Falmouth it had been more severe in other parts, and there had been wrecks up and down the coast. The sloop *Dolphin* foundered near Padstow, the *Concord* off Trevose Head, the *Active*, Captain Dodridge, on passage from Cork to London, was driven ashore at Hendrawna; he was drowned along with two of his crew, the other three were saved. The wrecking was done politely and the survivors well looked after. There was a great shoal of pilchards around the Cornish coast, brought in perhaps by the contrary weather. It was a bumper catch.

Clowance was worried about Andrew in the *Chasse Marée*.

On Tuesday Geoffrey Charles called.

Clowance was startled half out of her life to see him, for she had thought him still in Spain. He laughed at her.

'I could not stay there with the wolf of Europe again at large! Why, if he were to win Flanders he might soon again establish a hegemony in Europe and be knocking at the gates of Madrid before we knew where we were! I have come to offer my solitary musket if the thinking in England is that we should try to stop him.'

They kissed, Clowance feeling the steel in the thin arms, observing at close quarters the tight mouth and the injured jaw.

'And Amadora?'

'Is at Trenwith.'

'Trenwith! Why did I not know?'

'We sailed from Ferrol, and should have put in at Falmouth, but the weather was so foul we had to make for Padstow. We have been home ten days. I have heard about your mother and father from the Enyses. Is there any later news?'

'I'm afraid not.'

'. . . And are you well, my dear? And where is your husband?'

'At sea. What a pity that you have never met him. He will be very sorry. When do you sail?'

'Alas, the 43rd are still in Canada – or somewhere at sea. If allowed I shall join the 95th Rifles, even if it means dropping a rank. They have just arrived in Southampton from America – or so they should be arriving by now, as they spoke a revenue cutter from St Ives. With them are regiments of the 27th and 58th, with three troops of light dragoons. I am being favoured with a lift in a fast sloop which should catch them there, or if not I'll follow 'em to Ostend.'

Clowance had been told by her parents that Geoffrey Charles had been a spoilt child. It was difficult to believe that this hardened but gentle soldier had ever been pampered. How much she preferred him to his half-brother, the elegant but cynical Valentine.

'What will Amadora do while you are away?'

'Drake and Morwenna and Loveday have come and will stay until I return. Pray go over and see her.'

'Of course! As soon as ever possible! For I long to meet Juana.'

'You will greatly admire her. She is so much like her mother.'

She made him a cup of chocolate, and, as the sloop was leaving tomorrow in the forenoon, she pressed him to lie here tonight. He said he had first to call on Aunt Verity, but if he could persuade her to let him go, he would return. They talked of the Blameys and how the younger Andrew was faring, then of Jeremy and Cuby, and she gave him Jeremy's latest letter to read, and also her mother's.

'I will try to look him up as soon as I get to Flanders. I am not sure how difficult or how easy that may be. From what reports I have received there is great activity but also great confusion.'

'Do you think there will be war – a battle of some sort?'

'Oh yes.' He spoke without hesitation.

After a moment Clowance said: 'I shall be anxious. But many people think there may yet be a compromise peace. Even Jeremy in his letter, you see.'

Geoffrey Charles shook his head. 'Bonaparte says he wants only to live in peace with his neighbours; Wellington says there will be an agreed formula without conflict; but in fact they are both preparing furiously for war. Wellington, from what I hear, has such a makeshift army, and Bonaparte is likely to be so concerned to consolidate his rear, that they may hesitate and crawl around each other for a month or two yet; but a trial of strength is inevitable. And when it comes it will be the irresistible force against the immovable object.'

Clowance shivered. 'Do you like fighting, Geoffrey Charles?'

He flexed his injured hand. 'As a boy I hated it, was terrified of *any* sort of violence. But in Spain and Portugal, after a time, one hardened up. And there was such camaraderie, such tests of courage and personal endurance, such a fusion of men into a single splendid fighting force . . . the stimulus of conflict was enormous. I seemed for years to have forgotten how to be afraid. Now I am afraid again.'

'Because . . .'

'Because of Amadora and Juana, of course. I have too much to lose.'

'Yet – you need not have come now.'

He sighed. 'I would not have stirred a foot to go to America or India, or wherever the next conflict showed. But this – this is unfinished business.'

V

After Brigadier Rougiet's visit, Ross found the closeness of his confinement relaxed. He was allowed an hour's extra liberty a day, walking in the garden, with an armed guard a pace behind. The food improved, and he suspected he was enjoying the same vittles as General Wirion. The wine also improved. Twice he even received outdated copies of *The Times*, from the second of which he was very angry to see that the Corn Bill had passed through the House of Lords.

He had one meeting with Wirion, who was pleasant enough, discussed life in France in general terms and asked if there were any specially irksome features to his imprisonment which might be put right. Ross replied, only the imprisonment itself.

He saw no more of Tallien and was not questioned further. Occasionally he caught glimpses of fellow prisoners, but only one, as far as he could tell, was English, an unkempt man of considerable age called Sloper, who the guard said had been arrested as a spy three years ago. Ross never got a chance of speaking to him.

The early summer was advancing and Ross was glad of the fresh air and the extra exercise. To his surprise, the long periods of enforced idleness had done his ankle good, and he was able to walk almost without a limp.

What interested him most about his extra liberty was that he got a much better idea of the layout of the prison, its guards, its wires and its walls. Towards the end of May he discovered where the stables were.

Nine

I

George had never forgiven *The Times* for announcing the baronetcy of Ross Poldark, especially in the Court column, so of late he had been taking the *Morning Post* instead. It didn't much matter – the London papers were all a week late when they reached him and sometimes the local papers cried the news first. There was the particular case when the *Royal Cornwall Gazette* had issued the communiqué announcing the victory at Trafalgar and Nelson's death two days before its London rivals.

But one piece of information which amused him in the paper he was at present reading was an account of an event which had rocked the financial world of London the day before. On the Wednesday a post-chaise decorated with laurels and flags had dashed up the Dover road announcing that Napoleon had been assassinated and that Carnot was forming an interim government for the purpose of inviting Louis the Eighteenth to return to the throne. On the Exchange government stocks which had been very low – three per cent Consols at 57 – had shot up six points, only to fall again when the news had proved to be false. In the meantime the instigators of the ruse, having bought heavily on the Tuesday and sold at the peak on the Wednesday, had made a fortune.

People were such fools, George thought, even bankers and financiers: they rushed like sheep to greet good news, panicked so easily at bad. It was a wonder no one had ever thought of such a simple trick before. Communication was the bugbear. No one *knew*. The owner of a system of fast communication, especially if it was a private system, could make a mint of money any time. The semaphore, which had been installed by the Admiralty in a few towns, should be greatly extended. While it was not, everyone lived at the mercy of rumour.

In London last year George had met a Mr Nathan Rothschild, a Jewish banker who had gained a high reputation in the city and with the Government, and Rothschild always, George thought, seemed to have better information about events in Europe than anyone else – and usually quicker. Perhaps it was because he had brothers in similar influential positions in a number of the capitals of Europe. Presumably he depended on couriers like everyone else. They must just be better couriers.

George had not been to London at all this year, having settled down to enjoy the comforts and stimuli of pursuing his many interests in Cornwall. The journey to London was either bone-jolting and exhausting or – if you suffered from sea-sickness, as he did – only to be undertaken in the height of summer. But he thought he would go soon. There were pickings to be had, he was sure. In 1810 he had lost half his fortune while trying to double it in order to improve his chances of persuading Lady Harriet Carter to marry him. It had taken several years to recoup his losses. But he had learned a lot since then. Look at the way these rogues had hood-winked the market. There were safer and more legitimate ways of making money in the present volatile state of the world, and he was convinced Nathan Rothschild knew of them.

In the last three weeks George had been in a very perplexed state of mind. Or more properly of the emotions. The news that he was to be a father again had taken him utterly by surprise, and perhaps because of the surprise it had shaken him all the more. The total break with Valentine had left him virtually without a son. His beloved little Ursula was the apple of his eye, but she was only a girl. This quite astonishing news that Harriet had conceived meant that he had at least a fifty-fifty chance – he liked to think it more – of having another son. Someone else, someone worthy of him to carry on the name of Warleggan. And a Warleggan with noble blood! Although the Osborne family had never really taken to him, his son would be a part of it. His son would be not only Sir George Warleggan's son but the nephew of the Duke of Leeds. It added a new stimulus in life.

If he went to London and played his cards properly he was sure he would increase his fortune. If he went to London and made more use of his membership of the House and his ownership of the pocket borough of St Michael he could well earn himself the extra reward that Ross Poldark had so undeservingly been given. He might even, with judicious expenditure of money and the political pressure he could exert, become a real baron. Lord Warleggan. While Valentine was alive that could not be passed on to a new son, but he was himself only just fifty-six and might have twenty years of active life ahead of him in which to enjoy such a title!

He had given way over Carrington in order to humour Harriet. Humour, yes, that was the damned word. But suddenly this strange exotic, aristocratic, eccentric woman he had married had become much more precious to him. She carried his child! And if she made as a stern condition to her good behaviour that Stephen's wife, the Poldark girl, should not suffer inconvenience, well, he would accept it – for the time being. That mattered nothing compared to the central fact. From now on Harriet must be 'humoured'. He had lost his last wife in childbirth, and not long before Ursula was born he had engaged in very angry scenes with Elizabeth. It shouldn't happen so this time. Whatever the outcome, he would have nothing *ever* to reproach himself with. Let Harriet have her way. Nothing mattered but that.

Over the longer term, of course, George had no intention whatever of giving up his pursuit and prosecution of Stephen Carrington. It would have been foreign to his nature even to consider such a thing. After all, there was no great hurry. Once the child was safely delivered. Once Harriet no longer needed to be humoured. In the meantime, if it pleased her to have Clowance at the house, or even Stephen, he would raise no objection. His manner towards Clowance would not alter at all. The less he saw of Stephen the better, but when they met he would be impassively polite.

In the meantime he could console himself by considering other plans. Without ever resorting again to the dramatic act of closing Stephen's account with the bank – for that, he could see, by its blatancy would offend Harriet afresh – he could make Carrington's life a burden – an unsuccessful burden – in more devious ways. There were a number of men who had offended George at one time or another, and with only one notable exception they had not prospered after. They had had to leave Cornwall to obtain work or had sunk out of sight doing some menial job. George could make his influence felt almost anywhere. And none had offended him half – one tenth – so deeply as Stephen Carrington.

II

George would not, of course, have considered for a moment using any illegal means for bringing Carrington down. Only once in his life had he sanctioned violence against a man – that was Jud Paynter who had betrayed him after taking money from him at the trial of Ross Poldark – and he had afterwards regretted it. He might have a fearsome reputation in some quarters – and he was proud of it – but it was not the reputation of a man who broke – or even bent – the law.

To 'assist' the law was quite a different matter. He had often assisted the law, and there was no reason on this occasion to give up the attempt because there was no real evidence for what he knew to be the truth. Besides, a man who risked his neck to steal money from a stage-coach might well have committed other criminal acts in the past for which he could more easily be brought to book. If the fox escaped from one lair you might trap him in another. Carrington's past life was shrouded in mystery. Mr Trembath had been instructed to write to a fellow lawyer in Bristol who was to be invited to make inquiries.

Also there was still the question of Stephen's accomplices in the raid: two at least, one a woman. Who were his closest associates, or had been at that time? Clowance could not have been the woman, for she had been thin and dark. Andrew Blamey (another Poldark!) had been very thick with Carrington for some while and was notorious for being in debt. Inquiries had shown that it was impossible for him to have taken part in the robbery, but he might know something about it and George had noticed that he talked very freely when the wine was in him. He must be encouraged to come to Cardew more frequently, however distasteful it might be to entertain yet another Poldark.

III

On the 30th May Andrew Blamey returned to Penryn in the *Chasse Marée*, to be told that it had been sold in his absence and that he was out of a job. There was the offer of his acting as mate on the *Lady Clowance* under Sid Bunt, or second in command on a voyage Stephen Carrington was planning for the *Adolphus*; but with conditions which he found unacceptable.

He said to Clowance: 'He wants young Jason to be second mate, with special concern for hostile navigation. Where does that leave me? We should be running athwart each other at every turn! I have reached the conclusion that Stephen does not want me aboard and never had any intention except to have his nephew in a position of complete authority under him.'

'I'm sorry, Andrew,' Clowance said.

'You know what Stephen is about, of course. It can't be unknown to you.'

'He is going to use the brig as a privateer.' Clowance got up. 'He told me this when he returned from France. Now we are again at war with France he sees a chance of – of making money. He is going to Plymouth tomorrow to get his Letter of Marque . . . I don't like it at all, and I have told him so. I don't want to become a widow . . .' She turned. 'But, Andrew, we have just gone through a very bad two weeks when it seemed as if we were to be bankrupted; I cannot give you more details than that, perhaps I am already saying too much; but it has pushed him into a corner where he prefers to take this chance. I *hate* it and I have told him so! He took the decision while he was at sea and as I am his wife I must stand by it.'

Such a long speech was quite out of character for Clowance and reflected a three-hour argument she had had with Stephen when he returned with the news of his decision. She had attacked both the decision and the manner of it, saying he had broken his promise of discussing it with her first, and that to go on a dangerous hunt of this sort was no longer necessary as the threat of bankruptcy had been withdrawn. He had tried to draw her to him, but she had refused to be touched by him, knowing that he hoped his physical appeal would qualify her judgement. He had admitted that he had taken the decision without consulting her but said that he had to move quickly if he was going to strike while the iron was hot. War between England and France might last for years, or it might all be over in a few months. Two or three such voyages as he proposed, lasting perhaps only a month or so each, might be enough to make their fortune. With a good-sized vessel like *Adolphus*, properly equipped and manned, there should be pickings a-plenty. Fully armed with four six-pounders, a lively crew, and special high bulwarks of elm planking fitted up for protection, they could hardly come to much harm and should bring back a couple of prizes each voyage. The rewards were enormous . . .

'Why do we need rewards? Those kind of rewards?' she had asked. 'If Warleggan's Bank had truly foreclosed –'

'If they had truly foreclosed we should not have been able to mount this! Let's be thankful for small mercies. But we can't *count* on 'em. You didn't see his face, Clowance, that day he told me his bank wasn't going to trade wi' me any more. From now on, I wouldn't trust him farther than I could throw him. He's got it in for us, even if Harriet put in a good word.'

'And what if he knows you have been privateering? Won't this just confirm him in all his prejudices and give him the opportunity to close you down again?'

'Not if he doesn't know in time to stop me. When I've been and brought back a prize or two I can snap me fingers at him and tell him I'm banking elsewhere!'

Clowance had been silent then, knowing that Stephen's mind was made up and that not even she could change it. She also knew his dangerous ability to think that because he wanted a thing to happen it would happen. What was to say that he would not cruise in the chops of the Channel for a month and find nothing – or that he might not encounter a French cruiser and himself be captured? Absolutely nothing except his belief in himself.

Yet often enough, she knew, he had pulled things off; his confidence had not been misplaced. And his eyes were alight with purpose; she shivered a little to think that equipping one of his ships to go on a privateering cruise came more pleasurably to him than organizing legitimate trade. In the end he had silenced her by saying: 'Well and good, I'm going to take some pickings from the French. What's the difference? Your brother and your cousin are going to fight them. Your father's held prisoner of war without just cause. You can't surely be thinking too well of 'em yourself.'

She could not explain all this to Andrew who had dropped in to exchange news. But she did tell him that Stephen had said he had ideas for Andrew if he would but contain his soul in patience.

'It is not my soul that is growing impatient, little cousin, it is my body with its material wants! Incidentally, let me say I haven't got any moral scruples about privateering; it is only a little different from the prize money that all our naval captains seek. Nor do I mind risking the odd flying bullet. After all, twas only the mercy of the Lord, and a little skilful seamanship last month, that saved the *Chasse Marée* from capsizing while she was tender, sailing from Oslo to Drammen to pick up the timber. No, let's say it is just that I cannot get along with young Jason Carrington and his uncle's determination to push him into an authority he isn't yet entitled to! . . . By the way, will you be at Cardew tomorrow evening?'

'No.'

'I have been invited, somewhat to my surprise. But as Thomasine will be there I shall be happy to go along. I have a guinea or two to risk at the tables but at Tamsin's behest will not go into deeper water than I can swim out of. She does not know yet that I am without work. I rather fear her father offering me some position in his gunpowder factory. Though if he did I suppose it would be a sign that he was beginning to accept me.'

'Andrew.'

'Yes?'

'If you go, when you go, I pray you not to discover to Sir George any of Stephen's plans. There have been words between them on financial matters – you know Stephen banks with him – I do not know if he knows of Stephen's plans to use the *Adolphus* as a privateer, but I would especially not want him to know it from you.'

'Have no fear, little cousin. I shall be the soul of discretion.'

IV

Stephen had been busy since dawn. It was not merely refitting the brig for purposes of war, it was arranging for the finance and recruiting the crew. On most of the ventures he had known setting out from Bristol, the financing of the voyage had come from a number of small but regular adventurers, and there were plenty such to be had in Falmouth and Penryn. Men were willing, he found, to put their money into a raiding ship with the prospect of big gains where they had been reluctant to invest it in peaceful trading. But he wanted the least outside investment possible, so that his own gain would be greater. He had chosen four of his friends and acquaintances from the Royal Standard to take ten per cent each, and he, from the sale of the *Chasse Marée* and the income from Wheal Grace, could provide the other sixty per cent.

Nor should he have too much of a problem finding a crew – again, once the news got around, there should be plenty of volunteers – but it must be the right crew. They must be sailors, or have some experience of the sea, for he had no time to knock landlubbers into shape, and a few at least must know how to fire a musket and discharge a cannon. They must be tough, handy with a rope or a cutlass and ready to take orders. Some vessels, he knew, sailed from Bristol with double the normal complement of officers in order to take care of any risk of mutiny, but he decided to take that risk. Even so his complement would have to be over fifty. In privateering it was necessary to have enough force to make a boarding party *look* irresistible, and in the event of capture you had to have enough men to crew the captured ship.

So it would be living in unbearably cramped quarters, eating and sleeping where you could, jostled together in bad weather and in good, searching the horizon for a sail, and no room for grumblers or shirkers. Stephen would have been quite glad to have had Andrew Blamey with him because of the authority of his experience, but Blamey and Jason simply didn't hit it off, so that was that. He'd pushed the boy forward and had put two reliable older men,

272

Springfield and Penberthy, directly under him to give him advice when it was needed.

The more he saw of his son the fonder he grew of him. It's hard anyway to take a sour view of someone who hero-worships you; but Jason was very companionable, and they had the same impulses and feelings about so many things. Indeed in the first few months of their time together Stephen felt he had not quite come up to the image expected of him: the owner of three small trading vessels, commercially sound, content with small profits, hard working and staid, with a home and wife to care for and a respectable place to build in Falmouth's business world. Now it was all changed. They were off on a predatory trip that exactly suited Jason's romantic conception of his father.

He ate at the Royal Standard, alone this time. Jason was still working on board the *Adolphus*, and Clowance was visiting her Aunt Verity. Relations had been strained between him and his wife since his decision. Almost for the first time she had refused his caresses, as if trying to register her protest, make it clear, unconfused by physical contact. It would pass; he was sure it would pass when his adventure turned out to be the success he knew it was going to be. He knew she was not taking any stiff moral attitude, rather that she thought the risks too high and altogether unnecessary.

He had wondered whether to bother to make the tiresome journey to Plymouth – where, he had heard, the press gang was out again – merely to obtain a Letter of Marque. But without it he was a pirate, with it he was legally entitled to board and capture; he must go.

Eating at the next table from him was Captain Robert Buller, the tough, sturdy, middle-aged packet captain of the *Queen Charlotte*, refitted now and ready to sail on the New York run on Friday.

Not an approachable man but a tough, fair-minded seasoned sailor who had made enough money to build himself a substantial house on the newly burgeoning sea-front of the town. He knew Stephen and nodded when they passed; Stephen's recent approach to him on behalf of Jason had not apparently been resented.

'Hope this fair weather keeps up over the weekend,' Stephen volunteered. 'You're sailing Friday, Cap'n?'

'Aye,' said Buller, picking his teeth.

'Full complement, I suppose?'

'Aye.'

'Me nephew I decided to keep with me for the time being. He's young yet. Bit more sea experience before he aspires to the Packet Service.'

'Maybe,' said Buller and took a swig of ale.

'There's a man I know,' said Stephen, 'used to be in the Packet Service, first officer, I believe, or second officer, cannot remember. Opted out. Much regrets it now. Very capable man. Still pretty young. I believe he would like to return to the service, if he had the chance.'

'Name?' said Buller, still busy with a tooth.

'Blamey.'

Someone was shouting at the other end of the room, something about Death to the Frenchies.

'Blamey? Andrew Blamey's son?'

'Just so.'

'Went missing, didn't he? *Countess of Leicester*. Couple of years ago, wasn't it?'

Stephen was surprised at the memory. 'He was in dire straits at the time. Trouble with the moneylenders. You know. If he'd stayed he would have gone to gaol. That's all changed now. A changed man. He'd give his ears to be back in the Packet Service again.'

'What's he been doing since?'

'Sailed with me on a couple of voyages. First-class man. Has just brought me other brig home from Oslo with a cargo of timber and saddlery. He's always regretted leaving the Packet Service, I can tell ye.'

Captain Buller pushed his plate away. 'Gaming and drinking, no doubt, that was his trouble. They say his father was too fond of the bottle once. That was before my time.'

'Never touches it now.'

'Who? The father or the son?'

'Both,' said Stephen, lying in a good cause. 'But young Andrew never *did* drink at sea. Couldn't fault him at sea.'

'Don't know what Captain Faulkner said. Never spoke to him about it.'

'*Countess of Leicester*'s in Jamaica, if all's well.'

'I know that,' said Buller irritably.

Stephen hesitated. But he was never one to be easily put off. 'I hear they're pressing men in Plymouth. I'm off there meself tomorrow so I sh'll have to watch out! I'm going to get me a Letter of Marque. I've already written about it.'

'Oh, aye, I heard tell of this. No trouble finding *your* crew, eh? Make sure they're not all tinners!'

Stephen laughed and ordered another glass of ale for Buller. They sat listening to conversation around them.

'Now the war's on again,' said Stephen, 'good crews will be hard to get. Experienced young officers specially. I've invited young Blamey to come with me on *Adolphus* but he hasn't answered finally yet. I don't think he will come.'

'Why not?'

'He has a fancy for the navy.'

Buller grunted, but it was hard to be sure whether it was a grunt of approval.

'Privateering's a fly-by-night job,' he said presently. 'You toss a card: a quick gain or a quick loss.'

'There's more skill than that in it, Captain Buller. Seamanship and guts.'

'Oh I'll give you guts. Guts and blood. Still, if you've the fancy for it, I wish you luck.'

'Thanks . . . Shall I tell Blamey to come and see you?'

The famous eyebrows came together. 'What for?'

'I thought if he had the chance he'd better prefer to return to the Packet Service than go in the navy. They'd jump at him, of course.'

Buller finished his beer. 'Well, I shall not jump at him. But I tell you frankly, Carrington, I could find room for a reliable young officer. If he really means what he says and is prepared to sail Friday eve, I'll see him if he presents himself at my house at eleven tomorrow.'

V

Andrew had called in to see Clowance again when Stephen burst in upon them. Andrew had stayed late at Cardew yesterday playing cards and at length had been persuaded to spend the night. He had passed the early part of the evening with Thomasine, who was warm and sympathetic about his plight. On departure this morning Harriet had charged him with a message for Clowance, which was to say that Sir George was leaving for London tomorrow and would she care to come and visit her one day soon?

'Where the hell have you been?' Stephen demanded. It could have been more tactfully phrased, but his goodwill had turned to frustration as it looked as if his efforts to help Andrew were going down the drain.

Andrew had a thick head and was only just coming to. He flushed and said: 'What's that to you?'

'I've been seeking for you everywhere – as if I'd not enough to do minding me own business! I even sent over to Flushing to see if you were there.'

'Shouldn't you do just that,' said Andrew. 'Mind your own business?'

Clowance put a hand on his arm. 'Stephen, you wanted Andrew? Was it something special?'

'I thought it was something special,' said Stephen roughly. 'I saw Captain Buller last eve and persuaded him that Andrew would like to return to the Packet Service. He said he needs an officer for his first trip to New York, leaving Friday. He said if Andrew went to see him at eleven this morning he'd mebbe engage him.'

Clowance looked at the clock. 'But it is past eleven now! Where did he want to see him? At his house? Andrew . . .'

Her burly cousin rubbed his chin, which had not been shaven this morning. 'Avast, I don't remember ever saying I wanted to go back to the Service. Let me settle my own life in my own way, Stephen!'

Clowance said: 'But, Andrew, it might be a solution! It – it would give you more standing with the Trevethans . . . if that's what you want. You'd go back as an officer, lose nothing for having been away two years. And your father and mother would be delighted!'

Andrew shrugged. 'You don't live your life to please your father and mother.' He looked at Stephen without favour. 'Where did you meet Buller? I expect he was in his cups.'

Stephen turned away. 'Well, it's up to you, boy. Take it or leave it. Mebbe it's leave it anyhow, as he said eleven and ye couldn't be there until a quarter before twelve. So forget it, if ye've the mind to.'

'Your pony's outside,' Clowance said to Andrew. 'It would take you no more than fifteen minutes. You could explain to him you had been away for the night and only just returned. What is there to lose?'

'If he said no, nothing. If he said yes, I have to ask myself, do I want it?'

'Well, I've no more time to waste,' said Stephen in disgust. 'If ye want me, Clowance, I'm aboard the *Adolphus*.'

'Stephen, it was a kind thought,' said Clowance. '*Thank* you. When Andrew is in a better mood perhaps he will thank you too.'

Stephen patted her cheek and went out. They could hear his hard boots clattering up the street.

After a moment Andrew suddenly laughed. 'God damn, I'll go and see. I've only met Buller twice and twice he's growled at me like a mangey old dog, but he's a good seaman, I'll say that. Faulkner always spoke well of him. And he don't change his crew much . . . New York . . . Hm . . . not a bad run, so I'm told. Wonder if all the American privateers have heard about the peace yet.'

'Go on if you're going.' Clowance took his arm. 'Do not let the chance go by default.'

Andrew stared down at his jacket. 'Spilt some wine down it last evening. Hope it don't show. Anyway, they're my best togs. I wonder if Buller was serious? You know how Stephen can think something has happened when he wants it to happen? I suspicion that when I get up there I shall be turned away at the door.'

Clowance had been fearing the same thing. 'Well, you won't ever know if you don't try. And don't underrate Stephen. Sometimes he can work wonders . . . Anyway I am very obliged to him for doing this.'

They went to the door together.

Andrew said: 'You know, it was fortunate you asked me to keep quiet on what Stephen was about. Late last night, when all the girls had gone to bed, a fat little man – oldish man – sat down next to me, began to talk – Blencowe, he said his name was – thought he was a servant at first. Says he has a son in the navy, asked me a lot

277

of questions about what sort of a life it was. Then, after a while Stephen Carrington's name came up, and he said he knew him and admired him and what sort of man was he to work for? And so on. And so on. Might have been trying to pump me. You know.'

'And you said nothing?' Clowance asked.

'Can't remember exactly what I did say – one gets a bit fuddled late at night. But I can promise you I told him nothing about Stephen's plans for the *Adolphus*.'

VI

Corporal Julien Lemerre, being preoccupied with thoughts of the girl he had met in the village last night, was slow to notice his colleague's late return. Corporal Charles Bernard always took the breakfast up at eight and normally was back by twenty minutes past. At fifteen minutes before nine Lemerre swore and stirred himself to walk up the two flights of stairs and along the corridor to the room where Captain Sir Ross Poldark would normally be eating his breakfast – indeed by now should have finished it.

The door of the room was open, which anyway was against regulations. Lemerre went in and saw the breakfast was untouched. Corporal Bernard was sitting in a chair bound and gagged.

There was not much need for conversation. Lemerre took a knife from his pocket and hacked at Bernard's bonds until he was free. Then he ran out of the room, down the stairs, and pulled the alarm bell.

Ten

I

June 4th was a public holiday in Paris. It was a day of celebration and re-dedication to the imperial power of Bonaparte. Thirty-six fountains provided free wine in the Champs-Elysées, huge trestle tables offered food to all, open air displays had been arranged, with military bands, fire-eaters, tight-rope walkers, conjurers and magicians.

With sunset came a great concert in front of the Palace of the Tuileries, and afterwards a firework display, showing the ship on which Napoleon had landed on the French coast on the 1st March. The Emperor himself watched it all benevolently from a balcony. A week later he left Paris to join his army at Avesnes.

His army consisted of 125,000 men, with 350 guns. It was organized into seven army corps; a homogeneous mass of eager and angry and courageous Frenchmen, fanatically devoted to their Emperor and aware that they must conquer or die.

The Prussian army under Marshal Blücher amounted to 115,000 men and 290 guns; it consisted of four army corps and occupied Charleroi and the country east with outposts as far as Namur.

The mixed army under the Duke of Wellington consisted of 105,000 men and 200 guns. About one third were British, of which 12,000 were his veterans of the Peninsular War, the rest untried and under-trained. Scattered among the various divisions of the army were about 20,000 Dutch-Belgian troops, so scattered that the British elements could help to stiffen them. The rest were made up of 5,500 first-class troops of the King's German Legion, a quantity of Brunswickers and Hanoverians, five Nassau battalions and a Netherland Indian brigade. This army guarded Brussels and the country to the west, particularly the road from Mons.

The Prussian and British armies, by the nature of the distances their defences were stretched to cover, were too far apart to be in touch with each other and contact was only maintained by means of messengers carrying scribbled notes across the intervening thirty-four miles.

On the 7th June, before he left Paris, Napoleon issued instructions that dropped a blanket of iron secrecy over the movements of his army. All frontiers along the Sambre, the Moselle, the Rhine were sealed. No stage-coaches were allowed to travel. Every wagon was intercepted, every traveller held and searched. Only his own agents moved, spreading false reports wherever suitable, even as far as Brussels.

It was into this countryside that Ross Poldark, having broken out and stolen a horse, had to make his way in the hope of reaching the British positions.

II

He'd been lucky at the beginning. He had reckoned on a maximum of fifteen minutes; in fact it was nearly forty before the alarm bell sounded. First there was the knife, the pouch with the small change, the keys, which Corporal Lemerre had unwillingly loaned him, then a flight of stairs and a cupboard where spare uniforms were kept; a tunic and a hat were all he had time for; another flight and a door where the other corporal was supping coffee with his feet up; past that and into the courtyard. General and Mme Wirion, he knew, always went to mass on Sunday mornings at eight: it was worth the risk. The third key he tried let him into the General's house which was on the corner of the courtyard. A woman stared at him, hand to mouth, as he came into the living quarters. A cloak, a better pair of boots, two silver candlesticks, a pistol without cartridges, a map, no money to be seen anywhere, some bread and cheese and a bottle of wine; he let himself out of the front door and into the street. Two old women pushing a handcart, a lad kicking a stone; the stables were round the corner. He chose a pony, which was nearest to hand, saddled him, grabbed a nosebag to hold his possessions, was leading the pony into the street as someone shouted from the back of the stables.

Then it was all straightforward – for the time being. He took his direction from the sun until he came to the River Meuse, then began to follow it downstream towards the north. It was good weather, warm, with an occasional thunder shower. The road kept to the left bank of the river, sometimes leaving it for a few miles as the river described a deep narrow winding arc, then rejoining it. There were a few peasants in the fields, an occasional ragged traveller on the road or a child driving a few sheep; he kept a sharp watch behind but there was no obvious sign of pursuit. He felt conspicuous on his pony, his legs too long; but no one seemed to take any notice at all. Only once on that first day did he hurriedly dismount and lead his pony into a copse while a troop of cavalry clattered past. He spent the first night under some willows, his pony contentedly chewing grass and dozing by the light of a sinking moon.

Early on the second morning he came to a village and spent some of his few coins buying bread and cheese and butter and another bottle of wine. The shopkeeper, looking at his hat and tunic, asked if he was going to join his regiment, and Ross said yes, hoping that no one would remark his broken accent. Nobody did. The shopkeeper wished him luck and told him to make haste. 'The Little Father must not be kept waiting. He is ready to strike.'

It puzzled Ross that there was still no sign of pursuit. Perhaps there was no one to send. France was in turmoil. The armed forces worshipped Napoleon and would follow him to death or victory; but a large proportion of the people longed for peace and a quiet existence. Who knew what General Wirion's private thoughts were? And what in any case did it matter that one middle-aged Englishman should be at liberty when the destiny of Europe was shortly to be decided?

On the morning of the second day he came upon a town of a fair size (General Wirion's map had been discarded, as it did not cover so far north), but emboldened by the total lack of interest people were taking in a lonely, ragged, ill-dressed soldier, he rode straight in and by luck found the kind of little shop that he was seeking. There he sold the silver candlesticks and the pistol, and the boots, which were too small for him. The one valuable item of his personal belongings he had been able to retain throughout his captivity was the gold watch that had belonged to his father. When planning his escape he had decided to sell this to provide him with the money to sustain him on his flight, but when it came to the point he chose not to. The items he had filched from General Wirion would see him through the next two or three days. He would like to keep the watch for Jeremy.

He learned from the shopkeeper that he was in Sedan; that if he followed the river he would come to Charleville-Mézières – not too far distant – maybe twenty-five kilometres. And after that? The shopkeeper shrugged. Far, far to the west was Arras. North and nearer, but still distant, was Charleroi. That, no doubt, was where he should be heading. Troops marching, gun carriages rattling, they had all been through here yesterday and the day before, and the day before that. A great army. No doubt he was one of the stragglers. Where did he come from: he was not French? Poland, said Ross.

He led his little pony away and wandered through the narrow streets, stopped for a coffee and an omelette at a white-washed inn which had some tables outside. It was the first hot food since Saturday night, and last night it had been raining.

Charleville-Mézières was in fact two villages planted on either side of the Meuse with a narrow stone bridge connecting them. He spent that night in an orchard and again bought food on the Wednesday morning in a hamlet whose name he never knew. It was in the late evening that he first saw the soldier.

He had seen others before and kept his distance successfully. This man was a figure at the end of a long tree-lined track, riding in the same direction as himself but half a mile back. Ross would not have picked him out so quickly had he not turned in his saddle to see the inclination of the sun. There was a copse by the roadside and he jumped down and led his pony into the thickest part of it to allow the solitary gentleman full right of way.

As he approached he could be seen to be a tall man, sitting very erect, dark cloaked in spite of the heat. He wore tight-fitting white pantaloons and black tasselled Hessian boots. A well-dressed, well-mounted officer. And glinting plainly under the cloak, where it was open to give the rider some air, was a scarlet, tight-buttoned tunic.

Ross stared unbelieving. This must be some strange foreign regiment, certainly not French; one could have sworn . . . Yet he made no move and would have allowed the man to go by. And the man, who was staring straight ahead, would have certainly gone by but for Ross's pony. Seeing the horse, the little animal let out a snuffling neigh and shook his head until the harness rattled.

The man brought his horse up short; there was a pistol strapped to his saddle and this was whipped out of its holster.

'*Qui va là?*'

The foliage of the copse would not have deflected a bullet. There was nothing to do but come forward . . . Ross led his pony out. The two men eyed each other.

The officer said: '*Qui êtes-vous? Que voulez-vous?*'

In his halting French Ross began the story he had told the innkeeper. He was a Pole, he said in an apologetic tone, who had been delayed by a fever and was now hastening to follow his regiment and hoped to rejoin it tonight. Ross was aware that his uniform would hardly pass muster to a critical eye, and at the same time he was measuring whether a quick leap would enable him to knock the pistol down and unseat the horseman.

The officer seemed willing to accept the story, and with the words, '*Allez-vous-en, donc,*' was ready to let the matter rest.

It might have been better to do just that; ships could pass in the night . . . Yet Ross wanted to hear the man speak again.

With a humility that sat strangely on him he asked if the officer could tell him the direction the French army had taken; and he listened very carefully to the man's reply. Ross's French was halting, this man's fully fluent, but with a distinct accent.

Ross said: 'Do you speak English?'

The officer fingered his pistol and glanced around. The only sign of life were two goats grazing nearby, and a cottage at the turn of the road.

'What is it to you? What do you wish?'

Having made the move, there was no further point in conceal-ment.

'In fact I am British. It is true that I am trying to make my way north, but I am hoping to *avoid* the French and to join the Allied army. The tunic under your cloak – it is very much like a British army uniform. May I ask what it really is?'

'What is your name, please?'

'Poldark. I am an Englishman who was attached to the British Embassy in Paris. But when Bonaparte returned I was arrested as a spy, and since then have been interned in Verdun.'

'And were released?'

'No, no. I escaped last Sunday.'

The man was in his middle thirties, with a bony face, sharp dark eyes, a mouth which given the chance could have been humorous.

'Whom did you work under at the British Embassy?'

'Chiefly Lord Fitzroy Somerset.'

'What position did he hold?'

'He was Minister Plenipotentiary after the Duke of Wellington left for Vienna.'

'What was your mission?'

'I was asked by the Earl of Liverpool to come to France to report on the sentiments of the French army.'

The man smiled wryly. 'I think we know those now, don't we. Who else was at the Embassy?'

'Charles Bagot. Ian McKenzie.'

A moment's silence. The larks were singing in a cloudless sky.

'Your pony gave you away.'

'Yes.'

'He looks tired. Have you come far today?'

'From Charleville-Mézières.'

The officer put his pistol back in its holster.

'I am going north. Ride with me a little way.'

III

On Friday, the 9th June the *Queen Charlotte*, Captain Robert Buller, sailed on her first voyage to New York since the end of hostilities. With her went Andrew Blamey, rehabilitated against his will – or so he made a play of it to his friends, though certainly not to Captain Buller, who was going to be no easy task-master – but privately responding to the challenge and privately satisfied to get his old berth back and privately pleased to tell Tamsin about it and to take a fond leave of her.

Because of it Clowance warmed to Stephen again, and their own separation two days later was affectionate and uncritical, she hiding her anxieties.

The *Adolphus* sailed on the Sunday evening, bristling with men and arms. Stephen had been content with his four long six-pounders. The armourers in the port had tried to sell him some nine-pounder carronades, but Stephen had fired such weapons while in the *Unique* and knew their range to be too short – also they jumped violently and sometimes even capsized when they were hot. Four solid six-pounders would bring most of his potential prey to heel.

Stephen had found Captain Buller's warning all too appropriate. More than half his crew were good hardy seamen, anxious to avoid the press and keen to forage in search of a quick profit; but the rest were a mixture in which out-of-work miners predominated. He made do, comforting himself with the knowledge that most miners had some knowledge of the sea, smuggling or fishing in their spare time, and knowing that if it came to a fight there would be none tougher. Not all could load a musket; they all knew what to do with a cutlass.

The weather was still stormy, the winds fitful, but it was good sailing weather. With his son standing eagerly beside him Stephen set a south-westerly course, making in the general direction of Cherbourg.

IV

'What did you say your name was?'

'Poldark.'

'I think I have heard it somewhere before. My name is Colquhoun Grant.'

'I have heard *that* before, unless there are two officers of that name.'

'There are, damn the feller.'

'But are you not the one who was at Bussaco?'

'I was. Were you there?'

Ross told him. Grant laughed. A snorting chuckle.

'That is where I heard the name. His lordship looked upon you as an unfriendly observer.'

'But you . . . were you not Wellington's chief information officer?'

'Reconnaissance officer. Yes.'

'We never met,' Ross said. 'But your name was well known in the army. Isn't that the uniform of the 11th Foot?'

'It is. And no doubt you wonder why I come to be wearing it deep inside the enemy positions.'

'It had crossed my mind.'

'Because I am a reconnaissance officer I prefer to wear my uniform. I always have. There are obviously greater dangers of recognition and capture but if caught one is not hanged or shot as a spy. As you undoubtedly would be, Poldark, if you were captured in your present garb.'

'Thank you,' said Ross. 'But so far it has allowed me to travel unmolested.'

Grant looked up at the fading daylight.

'We need to avoid Rocroi. This morning there was a heavy concentration of French dragoons there. I do not suppose they have yet crossed the frontier.'

'We are near the frontier, then?'

'Oh yes. But I fear it will not guarantee you safety.'

'Safety I seek. But it would not be the first consideration if this were a crisis in which I could be of use.'

Grant looked at him. 'It is certainly a crisis. Bonaparte has joined his army today just south of Beaumont, which is some thirty kilometres north-west of where we are now. When he will move and which way are matters yet to be discovered.'

'You have agents?'

'I have agents. Not always the most reliable. It was different in Spain.' When Ross did not speak he added: 'Many Belgians have been disillusioned by the peace. They were promised independence and instead have been given over to Holland under a Dutch prince . . . I shall be meeting a *reliable* man tonight, late tonight when the moon has set. Damn the moon.'

They rode on for another twenty minutes and then Colquhoun Grant led the way off the track and into a coppice full of brier and young ferns.

'This is as far as we may go as yet. There are French troops all

286

around here. I have not eaten since morning so shall take something now. You are welcome to share it if you wish, Poldark.'

'Thank you. I'll join you. But I have some bread and cheese and a half-litre of wine.'

They dismounted and unsaddled their horses, tethering them in a clearing where there was good grass. Grant took off his cloak and sat down in his full regimentals as if he were in an officers' mess, except that he squatted in the undergrowth.

'You are an army man?'

'Oh, long since. The American War of Independence. It seems centuries ago.'

'But you have kept up your interest – in military affairs – quite clearly? Are you a major?'

'Captain. My cousin is a major – was a captain at Bussaco – but he has since retired from the army.'

'Do I take it you are a Member of Parliament?'

'That is so.'

'Well, Captain Poldark, I can offer you two choices. Later tonight I can put you across the frontier in the direction of Chimay. From there if you make north-west for Mons you may just steer clear of the French army, which by then should be advancing out of your way. From Mons make for Ghent where the Bourbon Court is, those members, that is, who haven't already scuttled away. After that there will be no difficulty in your reaching Bruges and Ostend. But I warn you, the early part of this trek will be dangerous. And I would strongly advise you, as soon as you are over the frontier, to contrive some change of clothing to avoid misunderstanding on either side.'

The cheese was strong but Ross was hungry. He bit into the bread to soften the taste.

'And the other choice, Colonel Grant?'

'It would be to come with me. I shall rejoin Wellington in two or three days, depending how the situation develops. Once Napoleon has declared himself, the need for behind-the-lines reconnaissance will become less important. But I would strongly advise you against this course. Not only will it be a bloody battle but if you were captured before you reached our positions you would quite possibly be hanged by the neck.'

'It's a risk I prefer to take . . . But I do not think my pony can keep up with your horse.'

'Nor would it. Nor would it.' Grant took a map from his pocket and screwed up his eyes to read it by the light of the half moon. 'It is possible I could use you, by God. If that were the case we would have to find you a different mount, eh? I will see what news André brings tonight. We have *some* friends.'

V

On his third day in London Sir George Warleggan called by appointment to see Mr Nathan Rothschild at his offices in New Court, St Swithin's Lane. They had met twice before, the first time in Manchester in 1810 when George was counting on the prospect of an imminent peace with Napoleon and making his unwise speculations. Mr Rothschild had lived in Manchester when he first came from Germany, and he had been liquidating some of his assets while George was moving in.

George did not like the man. He thought him a cold fish. And for a foreign Jew whose father had been an inconspicuous curio dealer in the ghetto in Frankfurt he was too abrasive. Only thirty-eight or so, stout, rapidly going bald and affecting no wig, speaking English with a guttural Germanic accent, he had already become a close friend and valued associate of the British Government because of enormous deals he had done for them financing the Peninsular War. George resented this. How had it come about that a foreign Jew, and such a young foreigner, had attained such a position of power and eminence in a Christian society?

He should have had a fellow feeling, for he had had something of a similar history. It was true he had suffered few of the humiliations of a German Jew, such as being confined within the Jewish district by chains slung across the exits at night, but he remembered his boyhood when he had been looked down on and patronized by sections of Cornish society as the grandson of a country blacksmith and the son of an unimportant smelter. Like Rothschild he had built upon the enterprise and initiative of an ambitious father, and now there was virtually no one in the county of Cornwall of whom he could not claim to be an equal. And certainly no one would ever dare to *patronize* him!

But this was small beer compared to Rothschild – many years his junior – and a man almost deliberately disclaiming the polish that George considered himself now to have acquired. Of course he had brothers, as George did not, settled in positions of financial strength in most of the capital cities of Europe. Perhaps he felt he could afford to remain uncouth.

George had brought with him an ambitious scheme for the development of water power in the West Country and the extension of the toll roads to open up development there. He did not really mind whether Rothschild was interested enough to help finance such a scheme; it was the opening he wanted for a general discussion in which several times he was able to bring the subject round to Bonaparte and the likely outcome of the new war affecting the prospects for such a development.

For a while they fenced a little, the man with the astutest financial brain of the age, and the provincial banker on whose native Celtic cunning had been grafted years of mercantile and financial experience.

Then Nathan, his cold eyes heavily lidded, turned the scheme down with neither dignity nor politeness; the proposition was too regional for him, he grunted. He had early sensed that the meeting was a pretext, and, once he had seen where it was designed to lead, he gave nothing further of his own opinions away. They parted with a show of amity and assurances of respect that barely hid the lack of either.

Although he carefully chalked this rejection against Rothschild, in case on any future occasion he should be able to do him a bad turn, George came away not wholly dissatisfied. He had framed his questions and rehearsed them beforehand in such a way that even disclaimers could be a sort of admission that the knowledge was there. He was now more than ever certain that Rothschild had better lines of communication with events in Brussels than the British Government, that somehow news was got to him more quickly and more reliably.

After leaving, he strolled north, keeping an eye open for the pickpockets and cut purses who abounded in the area. It was a fine sunny day and the crowds milled everywhere, with hackney coaches forcing their way through, drivers cracking whips; ballad singers competing with fish cryers and the sellers of hot rabbit pies, fresh spring water, quack medicines and cheap penknives, all ringing their bells to claim attention. Beggars crawled in the gutters, elegant ladies were being carried in their chairs, less elegant ones were sharp-eyed looking for a likely man. Dust and dirt and refuse and the occasional stink.

George turned into King William Street and called at an office where a man called Samuel Rosehill was waiting to greet him. Mr Rosehill acted as an agent for Warleggan & Willyams Bank and also for George personally. He was himself a Jew.

'Rosehill, this man you know in the Rothschild office, how far can you rely on him?'

'The few confidences he has given me have proved to be sound, sir. I can hardly say more than that.'

George grunted, and then changed it to a cough, not wanting to sound like the man he had just left.

'The market is very volatile but very low. Nervous, I'd call it. Would you know, could you follow any buying or selling pattern from what this friend of yours could tell you or by observing the actions of the people who trade for the Rothschilds?'

Rosehill scratched under his wig. 'You mean to be able to tell when the Rothschilds are buying and when they are selling? I believe one could discern a pattern, yes. But I question how much my friend could help, sir. Nathan Rothschild uses a number of agents, apart from trading direct.'

'Your friend might know who those people are.'

'He might know that.'

'You would be able to follow any trend at very short notice? Within the hour, say?'

'Oh yes. Given the finances to do it.'

'I'll see the finances are to hand.'

There was a pause. Rosehill said: 'I am not sure if I take your meaning, sir. Am I right in supposing you would wish me, as it were, to follow Rothschild's lead? Buy when he buys? Sell when he sells?'

'Yes.'

'I have to warn you, sir, that Mr Rothschild is infinitely devious in such matters. He knows there are other speculators waiting to follow his lead and deliberately adopts tactics to throw them off the track. Might I make a suggestion?'

'Of course.'

'Mr Rothschild himself frequently comes on 'Change. He always occupies the same place, just on the right as you enter from Cornhill. He will stand there for an hour or two, sometimes more. By observing the men he meets and then what they do to obey his instructions might be the best and most reliable method you could adopt.'

George gazed out at the street. Much as he would have hated to find any common cause with Demelza, he would have agreed that London after Cornwall was unbearably noisy.

'I shall stay at Flandong's another week. Send for me immediately if there is any unusual movement on 'Change which you can ascribe to the Rothschilds. If you are not certain, still send for me. I shall wait at the hotel and can be with you within the hour.'

VI

They had talked in the night. Although sleep came now and again to one or the other, they were both too alert to doze for long. They spoke of their families, their adventures in war and peace, their hopes for the future. Colquhoun Grant said he came of a family of eleven, six other brothers; his father had died young; he had himself been a soldier since he was fifteen; by a strange quirk had been taught French by Jean-Paul Marat when the *sans-culotte* had been a refugee in England from his own kind. He could now speak five languages and make himself understood in three more. The farthest west he had been was when he was stationed at Plymouth. Ross told him of the missions he had undertaken, to Vienna with the Earl of Pembroke in 1807, his helping to escort the Portuguese royal family to safety in Brazil, his trip behind the French lines in Portugal which had ended at Bussaco.

'Lucky you were not captured there. This time, when you were interned in Verdun, did you give your parole?'

'No.'

'Ah. I did once. I was captured in Spain, brought into France, broke my parole, lived for a time as an American in Paris before escaping to England. The excuse was that the French broke the terms of the parole by treating me as a prisoner. But I am still unhappy about it. Of course a French officer of equal rank was immediately repatriated. But I am glad you were able to escape with a clear conscience.' Grant stirred. 'The moon is nearly down. It is time we made a move.'

They resaddled their horses and rode off into the night. Grant seemed to know exactly where they were going. Twice they saw camp-fires, and once drew in to a clump of trees as a squadron of horse artillery rumbled past. They went through a more populated zone, and here they dismounted and led their horses in single file. It was a very mild night with no wind, but a few thunderly clouds hid the emergent stars.

After an hour or so Grant led the way through a stream and to a derelict barn. He cupped his hands and hooted like an owl. Two figures grew out of the darkness, and they entered the barn. Inside it smelt of animals and was pitch black. Horses were stirring. One of the figures began talking rapidly to Grant, but Ross could not follow it for the man was speaking Flemish.

As the conversation continued Ross's eyes grew accustomed to the extra darkness and he could see a table, a bench, a couple of chairs. He sat on one of the chairs while the fourth man sharpened a bayonet and watched him.

'Could you understand that?' Grant said.

'No.'

'French troops crossed the frontier an hour ago and are driving towards the Prussians at Charleroi. This is the move we have been waiting for. Wellington has always suspected an attack such as this, but he has also had to be prepared to counter an encircling movement to cut the British off from the sea. Unless this is a feint, and we shall know more at dawn when we get another report, this means Bonaparte will try to knock out the Prussians before turning on the English.'

'What exactly should we know at dawn?'

'Whether Bonaparte himself has gone. There has also been great activity around Mons, but *that* seems likely now to have been the feint. If once we can be sure that the advance on Charleroi is the main thrust, then Wellington can begin to withdraw his troops from the Lille, Condé and Valenciennes roads.' Grant rubbed his long jaw. 'He depends largely on me for this information.'

'The Duke?'

'The Duke. As Head of his Intelligence I now have the responsibility for giving him this information in time for him to act on it. I shall not go myself as I have a reliable messenger. André will go. But tomorrow I might need a second messenger. These other men are more useful to me here. If you were willing I could send you with a further message. I shall expect to follow about a day later.'

VII

By eleven in the morning the French Imperial Guard had driven the Prussians out of Charleroi. Napoleon sat in a chair outside the Belle Vue Inn and watched his troops marching in to occupy the town. The following afternoon the French massively defeated the Prussians at Ligny, and Marshal Blücher was unhorsed and knocked senseless as the French cuirassiers rode over him, pursuing the Germans retreating towards Wavre. The German losses were sixteen thousand men and twenty-five guns.

Satisfied that he had knocked out one opponent, Napoleon turned all his forces and his attention upon the other.

Eleven

I

The Duchess of Richmond was giving a great ball in Brussels, perhaps the most glittering of a glittering season, to be held on the ground floor of her large rented mansion in the rue de la Blanchisserie. Everyone of importance was to be there, but two days before, Jeremy returned the tickets he had been at some pains to get.

'Do you mind, my love?' he said. 'We have been to so many balls since we came here. I shall be away tomorrow, and fancy a quiet evening with you on Thursday. Just supper and love and sleep.'

Cuby looked at him quizzically. 'I would have liked to go but I prefer to be alone with you, if that is how you fancy it.'

'I fancy it. I may be more away during the next few weeks and would like to make the most of my favourite wife.'

'Do you think there will be a battle soon?'

'Not at all sure. The French have the deal, and we cannot see their cards.'

So on the evening of the 15th they went out alone to the little restaurant they had visited on Cuby's birthday. They walked there from their apartment. In the warm evening the people of Brussels were out in numbers. No doubt there would be a huge crowd outside the Duchess of Richmond's watching the arrivals.

There were also more soldiers about: cavalry clattering here and there, platoons of infantry marching. Most of them were going south.

They ordered a pleasant meal, much on the lines of the one they had had in March; talked in a desultory way, eyes warming to each other, hands occasionally touching.

'Are you more sure than you were on Tuesday?' she asked.

'About what?'

'Bonaparte.'

'Oh yes. He crossed the frontier sometime last night or early this morning. There has already been a skirmish or two.'

'Far from here?'

'Probably about twenty miles.'

'Twenty miles!'

'Oh, don't worry; they were driven back. It was not our fellows: I believe it was the Brunswickers or the Dutch. But the French retreated. I think they are probing our positions at various points before they attempt anything serious.'

'Jeremy, I am a little terrified.'

'Oh, I pray you not to be! There is a lot of noise and smoke sometimes without too many getting serious hurt. D'you know I was training some of my lads yesterday. Me, training them! But the old land pattern musket we have in the army is a very cumbersome weapon. It makes a very loud noise and a great deal of smoke but is monstrous inaccurate. The average soldier always fires it too high because it blasts away in his ear, and he turns away his head and the ball goes winging up in the air. But if you remonstrate with him, and he holds the barrel too low, the bullet will roll out before he fires it!'

Cuby said: 'I am not altogether reassured.'

'Then drink a little more wine and tell me about yourself. Is our baby alive and kicking?'

'Just the first stirrings. You must not be too impatient, boy. It will be December before my time comes.'

'What do you wish for?'

'As to a boy or a girl? I do not altogether mind. Perhaps a boy. And you?'

'Perhaps a girl.'

They laughed.

'Christmas,' said Jeremy. 'I wonder what we shall call her – or him. Noël? I wonder where we shall be living then?'

'Not in Brussels!'

'No. A little while ago I thought this might be a long war, like the last. But now I think it might all be resolved, smack, bang, within a month! I shall not pursue the army as a career, like my cousin. And yet, it is strange . . .'

'What?'

'Geoffrey Charles, they say, was brought up very genteel, pampered as a boy. It was a great surprise when he took so much to the army. As for myself – though the circumstances were very different – I too was brought up soft, I did not really ever fancy to join the army, but now I am in it, I confess I find it rather more enjoyable than I ever expected!'

Tonight Cuby had put on a pale lavender silk frock gathered at the waist with a silver cord. He had asked her to wear it because he said it reminded him of what she was wearing when he had first seen her, and she had sheltered him from the gaugers.

He added: 'Of course my rapid promotion will not continue after the end of the war! It is astonishing that I have come so far without once having to purchase anything and without outside influence! It is solely due to the extreme confusion that has existed since Bonaparte escaped and the dearth of sufficient officers to command the re-formed companies and regiments.'

'I trust you don't deny that it might just be in the smallest degree because you are showing special talent. Come, boy; modesty is becoming until it is so extreme that it mocks itself.'

He looked her over, met her startling hazel eyes under the raven-black brows. Her lips, of which he knew the taste so well, were upturning slightly, a dark pink against the honey-coloured skin.

'Jeremy, I have never asked you. Was it because of me that you joined the army?'

His gaze shifted. 'Very hard to disentangle my feelings at that time.'

After waiting for him to say more she added: 'I think your sister blames me for it.'

'Who, Clowance? When have you seen her?'

'Something Isabella-Rose let drop. But Clowance was unfriendly at Geoffrey Charles's party. Perhaps she just blames me for having made you unhappy.'

'And rightly so.' He patted her arm and then sniffed at her cheek. 'Anyway we'll change that. She has only to meet you and know you. Look at my mother.'

'Your mother is the wisest of women. And one of the kindest.

The minute I set eyes on her at that party I knew we could understand each other. Clowance is more like your father; she will be harder to thaw.'

'I do not think my father will be hard at all! When you know him better you will know that too. But talking of hardness, what of *your* brother and *your* mother? Do you think we shall ever be accepted at Caerhays?'

'Of course! I shall have no hesitation. Do you know, if you can come to ignore their prideful faults, they are really quite nice people! But do you know something else? Even if the opportunity were ever to present itself I do not think I ever again wish to live at Caerhays. It stands to me for a way of life that I have totally lost since I married you. There were many good things in it, many pleasant and agreeable times, but they are so intertwined with restricted and restricting attitudes, limited and limiting views, that I want the return of none of them. It is only since December that I have been free!'

'Tied to me,' said Jeremy.

'Tied to *you*! Where *shall* we live? I think I should like it to be Cornwall.'

'Yes. In spite of Goldsworthy Gurney, I believe sufficient opportunity presents itself to satisfy me in Cornwall.'

'Steam? The horseless carriage?'

'Well, first I shall hope to earn my living at Wheal Leisure – even possibly try something fresh at Wheal Grace. I have been wondering about a small house belonging to my father, called The Gatehouse. When Dwight Enys first came to the district he lived there. Then it was left empty for a number of years, allowed to fall into disrepair. Stephen Carrington and Clowance were to live there and Stephen spent much time and some money putting it in order. Then the engagement broke, and when it was patched up they married and went to live in Penryn, so they never inhabited it. It is possible we could use it for a time.'

'I would be happy to. What is the matter?'

'Matter?' His face cleared. 'Nothing, my love. No more than a passing thought.'

She waited but he did not explain. He hardly could, because the passing thought was of storing the proceeds of the coach robbery in The Gatehouse until they moved it to the cave in Kellow's Ladder.

'And we must have a boat,' said Jeremy, with an effort. 'Do you like fishing?'

'I never have. But I like fish.'

'To eat? Or would you dislike catching them?'

'No, I am not tender-stomached like that.'

He smiled. 'I sometimes wonder if men are not more tender in this way than women. I, now, have never greatly cared for hunting. I do not wish to be sentimental about the fox – and who could be who has found his handiwork in a coop of slaughtered chickens, killed not for food but for pleasure? – but at the end of a run I cannot bring myself to enjoy the sight of him outnumbered twenty to one and torn to pieces. Yet Clowance greatly enjoys hunting, and I am sure Isabella-Rose will as soon as she is permitted.'

'Clemency loves it as much as I do,' said Cuby. 'And no one more tender for animals than Clemency ever existed!'

'Since I joined the army,' Jeremy said, 'I have become very little more inured to the use of horses in battle – I have only seen three killed but that was quite enough. Indeed, a secondary reason for promoting the horseless carriage in my mind would be to relieve them of that burden. Three years even in a stage-coach, and a horse is only fit for the knacker's yard.' He sipped his wine, admiring the colour against the candlelight. 'And yet sometimes I wonder.'

'What?'

'If horseless carriages were ever to become universal we might lose the horse altogether. That would be a worse fate, for them and for us.' He took out his watch. 'Shall we go home?'

'If you wish. Is it not rather early?'

He linked her little finger. 'I think, if you agree, that it is not too early.'

II

They had been lying quietly in bed, the daylight hardly yet fled from the long June sky, when there was a knock on the door. Jeremy lit a candle, pulled on his dressing-gown, went to the door.

He came back after a whispered conversation. 'It is my orderly. I must go. You may see the message.'

Cuby took the paper.

Captain Poldark's company will proceed with the utmost diligence to Braine-le-Comte where he will meet Major Cartaret who will point out to him the ground on which it is to bivouac tonight.
      William de Lancey, Quartermaster General

'My darling,' she said.

'Yes, my darling. I must be off. Just as well we did not go to the ball. They have an uncanny knack, these army people, of keeping ungodly hours and trying to spoil the fun.'

Cuby swallowed back the tears that suddenly, uncontrollably, bubbled up.

'Be back by Sunday,' she said lightly. 'We have that little dinner-party.'

'Of course! I'll tell old Boney. Seriously, *carissima mia*, you have stayed in Brussels like a good wife and I doubt if you will have the least anxiety about the French. But if – *if* things went badly awry, do not hesitate to go with Mr and Mrs Turner and the Creeveys to Antwerp. It is not only yourself you have to think of but little Tweedledum whom you are answerable for. If need be, carry him across the water and I'll join you later.'

'I'll take care of myself so long as you do.'

'When we were very young I used to tease Clowance and she would get angry and throw stones at me. Since then I've always been good at dodging missiles.'

He began to dress. Outside they could hear the shrill fifes and the bugle horns. In the dark of the coming night it was a melancholy sound.

'Is Sanders waiting for you?'

'Yes. And yawning, no doubt. There will be a lot of sleepy soldiers on the march.'

She watched him, eyes darker than usual, the coldest clutch of fear in her heart.

Jeremy said: 'I wonder what my father is doing. *He* is really the soldier by temperament, not I. He'll be very irritable in his camp in Verdun if he knows there is going to be a contest for Brussels.'

Cuby began to dress.

'What are you doing?'

'Oh, it's too early to sleep. I shall see you off and then light a fire and make some coffee.'

Jeremy peered out at the moon. 'Lovely weather for campaigning.'

When at last he was ready and she was sure he had forgotten nothing he came across and took her in his arms, kissed her lightly on the forehead, the tip of her nose, the mouth. After the drowsy abandoned love of an hour ago it was airy, innocent, unemotional.

'Goodbye, Cuby.'

'Goodbye, boy. Come back soon.'

'I know. In time for that dinner-party. I'll tell them to hasten with their skirmish.'

III

André did not come with the dawn, nor until the sun was blazing from a hot sultry sky, a tall ragged man who reminded Ross of the carter who had given him a lift when the diligence broke down on the way back from Auxerre.

He and Colquhoun Grant talked for nearly half an hour; Grant went to the table and wrote out the message the Belgian was to take.

Only then he said to Ross: 'There is no longer likely to be a serious threat to Mons. Bonaparte has thrust his armies into the Charleroi gap and is rolling back the Prussians to begin. There may be time for Wellington to regroup his troops: if this message gets through by late tonight he should have twenty-four hours. Pierre is leaving right away *ventre à terre* for Brussels.'

'And you?' said Ross.

'I shall ride to Namur, where I have two royalist friends. They have a direct contact with one of Napoleon's generals. What information I bring back I will ask you to carry to Wellington's headquarters – wherever they may be by then. It will be a dangerous mission but that is what you tell me you wish to do.'

'You ride as far as Namur in daylight?'

'Three hours each way. The French army will have other matters on its hands. But if I should be captured you will know from my non-return. Then fend for yourself. Marcel or Julius will be somewhere at hand. There'll be food for you to eat and some to carry with you. You will have a fair horse before dark.'

'And when can I be sure you will not turn up?'

'Give me till the moon sets.'

'I do not fancy such a long inactivity,' Ross said. 'Is there nothing I can do here, or in the vicinity?'

'How good is your French? Heavily accented, isn't it? You would be of much greater service by accepting the inactivity. Lie down. Take a sleep, man. There will be plenty of activity for you later on.'

IV

It was a hot sultry day and time passed slowly. Marcel and Julius soon left and Ross was alone with his pony. For the most part he stayed in the barn. The roof anyway was part in ruin, and the sun fell in strips across a floor well grown with weeds relishing the light. His pony cropped in a corner. Twice when he pushed the door ajar he thought he could hear distant cannon-fire.

He wondered if Demelza were still in London. He had received one letter only from her; then she had been staying in his old rooms and intending to remain there a few weeks. By now she would surely be safely home in Cornwall, together with the stout-hearted Mrs Kemp, the precocious Bella and the imperturbable Harry. Jeremy was another matter. He must be involved in this battle which was about to take place. He had been in the army twelve months but had not seen any serious fighting. As a relatively untried ensign he might well be among the reserves. The wonderful veteran army of the Peninsular would bear the brunt.

But Grant had said Wellington desperately lacked seasoned troops; at the most ten thousand were his old comrades in arms who had driven the French out of Spain. Many even of the other English in his makeshift army were untried youths. It was a matter of luck where Jeremy was and how he fared. There was no virtue in comforting oneself with false hopes. The real comfort was to remember all the bloody battles Geoffrey Charles had survived – almost all the bitterest fighting of the Peninsular War – before he married and retired safely on half-pay. God, what a prospect if Bonaparte won this battle! Belgium would be his; the Alliance against him would break up; Austria, to avoid being crushed, would return the Empress and their son; even Spain might again be invaded. Had England the stomach for another long war?

Had it even the stomach to solve its own domestic problems? The two copies of *The Times* he had received had given him a fair sample of the feeling of the House when it was debating the Corn Bill. He should have been there, making his angry protest, instead of allowing himself to become a useless pawn in the international game.

And his other child, Clowance; she was safe enough in Penryn. But, try as he might, Ross could not bring himself actually to become fond of his son-in-law. There was something meretricious about his bounding energy and good spirits; he was so open and outgoing in his behaviour that one never got near enough to him to know him any better. But Clowance did; presumably she saw him more clearly than most, perceived the real sincerity that his slightly sham sincerity served to hide. Of course the sexual lure could distort a woman's view; yet Clowance was a very blunt and honest person and it was unlikely she would marry someone without genuine virtues.

One expected too much. It was natural that fathers-in-law and sons-in-law should have a mild antipathy. Did he feel differently about his daughter-in-law? In the year just gone, when Jeremy had been made so outrageously unhappy by her betrothal to Valentine Warleggan, he had felt the strongest possible dislike for the girl and all her feeble Trevanion clan. When the engagement was broken – by Valentine not by her! – it was he, Ross, who had advised Jeremy to go to Caerhays Castle and more or less help himself to the girl, grab her, take her off, make up her silly indecisive mind for her, and Jeremy had done just this, with the most brilliant of results. Even so, Ross had some ambivalent feelings about the reliability of his daughter-in-law.

At least she had conquered Demelza. Demelza had written how good and charming she had been during her stay in Brussels. And she was with child. Well, he supposed it was time he was a grandfather!

He must have slept for quite a time, for the day was nearly spent when he rolled over in the straw and sat up to see a man in the doorway.

When he came out of the bright light of the slanting sun Ross saw it was André. He was holding his hand to his ragged arm, and there was blood on his hand.

He sagged and came in and sank in a chair and said something Ross did not understand.

'Can you speak French?' Ross asked, getting to his feet.

'Where is Colonel Grant?'

'Gone to Namur. He should be back soon. You are wounded?'

'It is nothing. A musket ball. They are flying very fast out there, and you are lucky if you do not collect one or two even though they are meant for someone else. Have you water?'

Ross took a flask across to him. There was not much in it, and André drained it.

'You delivered the message? You were on the way back?'

André looked at him sidelong. 'It is time Colonel Grant is back?'

'No doubt. But we must wait. Let me see the wound.'

The sleeve was slit anyhow and easily moved up to show the blood oozing from an ugly hole above the elbow.

Ross said: 'Is there water nearby?'

'There is a stream. Turn left out of the barn. But I do not think you need to bother. I have seen many in a very much worse condition today.'

When Ross came back with the flask full he found the thin man sprawled with closed eyes against the side of the chair. He opened them when Ross bathed the wound and wrapped it tightly with a piece of cloth.

'I am not mortally hurt,' said André. 'But I have lost much blood. I think I may faint.'

Ross brought him a cup of wine; he was able to sip it; his eyes were flickering.

'Bring my horse in here – else he may be seen.'

Ross did this, and unsaddled the animal, which was slippery with sweat, foam flecking from his mouth. When he went back to André his eyes were shut and he was breathing heavily. He stood beside him for a few minutes and then went to sit in his chair, ate a few mouthfuls of the bread and sausage, which was all he had left.

Presently the man said: 'Monsieur.'

Ross went instantly back.

'Monsieur, in case the Colonel Grant should be a long time and I have gone unconscious – or perhaps if Colonel Grant should not come back, I must tell you I have not delivered the message.'

'What? Were you wounded and unable to get through?'

'No, no.' André paused for breath. 'I arrived behind the English positions and was arrested by . . . a cavalry patrol. I was identified and told them I had . . . important message for the Commander-in-Chief. Was taken – I was taken at once to the Brigade Commander, General Dornberg, who . . . who took it upon himself to open the message I carried. Thereupon he kept me for some hours . . . and then returned the message saying Colonel Grant was . . . was wrong in his conclusions and said he was certain the main – main attack would still be towards Mons.'

Ross brought back the cup of wine and helped André drink some. As he did so there was a footstep and he quickly turned, aware that he only had a knife within reach. But even in the semi-darkness Grant's stiff figure was recognizable.

He came over and stood in front of André. The man tried to struggle into a sitting position.

'M le Colonel –'

'I heard,' said Grant. And then: 'Where is the message?'

André indicated an inner pocket of his jacket. Ross felt inside and pulled out the letter, on which the seal was broken.

Grant took the letter and held it between finger and thumb. 'Dornberg! God damn the man! May the devil have mercy on him, for I should not!'

'Dornberg?' said Ross. 'A Prussian?'

'A Hanoverian! Like our royal family! Major-General Sir William Dornberg is in command of the 1st and 2nd Light Dragoons of the King's German Legion. Some of our finest troops! He fought for Napoleon until two years ago, when he changed sides! It all smacks of treachery . . .' Grant thumped one hand into the other and tramped about the barn. 'But more likely it just smacks of bungling incompetence. Wellington, in my view mistakenly, gave this fool the responsibility for transmitting to Brussels the reports of the various agents as they came in. He has grossly exceeded his duty

304

by attempting to judge the value of the reports for himself! My God, this might turn the course of the battle! The man should be court-martialled and shot!' Grant turned to the wounded Belgian. 'Are you *sure* General Dornberg did not pass on the report in any letter of his own?'

'That I do not know, *mon colonel*. But the view he expressed in my hearing was that your report only went to prove that the present . . . present attack . . . was a feint.'

Grant swore under his breath again and again. Ross could see his whipcord figure trembling with anger.

'Where are Marcel and Julius? They were bringing a horse for Captain Poldark.'

'They said at sunset, *mon colonel*. They should be here . . . at any time.'

'I will take the report myself,' said Grant. 'It will be late, but not perhaps too late to be of value. André, which way did you go?'

'Through Fontaine l'Evêque and then I struck north. I was trying . . . to avoid the troop concentrations.'

'Would I run into trouble if I went via Gosselies and Frasnes?'

'There is so much movement. At night you might be able to thread a way through.'

'The damned moon is growing.' Grant opened his bag and took out some bread, a cooked chicken, peaches. 'Eat some of this, Poldark. I have no doubt you have been on short commons all day.'

'Why do you not let me take the letter?' Ross suggested.

Grant appeared to consider, then shook his head. 'No. It is a good thought but I must go myself. Unless I personally put this into the hands of the Duke I shall not rest easy. Perhaps I should have gone this morning; but there was more here for me to do, and I did not in all faith believe that one bungling fool could put everything at risk.'

'I shall have the only fresh horse,' said Ross.

Again Grant shook his head. 'I'm sorry, no, Poldark, but I must take it. If you give my mare or André's horse the night to recover you can take one of them. They are excellent beasts. Follow me tomorrow night, or make for the coast.'

'I'm sorry, Grant,' Ross said in his turn. 'Having come this far, I am not to be disposed of like some inconvenient parcel. You are in authority and I cannot stop you taking my horse. The horses outside are spent, but my little pony which has brought me all this way has been resting all day. I can travel on that.'

Grant tore off a drumstick and began to eat it. Then he nodded. 'So be it. Look, if you want it that way, you *shall* take the letter, by God. That is what you suggested, isn't it? I need no letter. I shall report direct to Wellington or not at all. I shall go on the faster mount, but if I am unlucky and am captured or killed, you may bear him the original message, for what good it may do any of us now.'

'Thank you,' said Ross.

'Hush,' said André, stirring. 'That is Marcel. I know his footstep.'

Twelve

I

One of the results of Jeremy's recent promotion was that most of the men in his company were strangers to him. There were about forty seasoned soldiers, most of them campaigners from the Peninsular War, among them the quartermaster sergeant, a rough, tough Welshman called Evans, known as Quack Evans, because he strutted like a duck. Jeremy felt he was much on trial; such men, uncouth and uneducated though they were, knew far more about war than he would ever know. Most of the other men were new recruits, country lads, gaolbirds, poachers, debtors, anyone who would take the King's shilling – or had been tricked into it – whose main awareness of the world was that life was nasty, brutish and short. John Peters, the farmer's son from Wiltshire, who was still an ensign, had been transferred with Jeremy, and Jeremy's batman, John Sanders, had been with him six months. His two lieutenants were called Bates and Underwood. Bates was from Lincolnshire, and he had known him at the Forties Club. Underwood was a stranger.

Braine-le-Comte was a pretty village, but by the time Jeremy and his company arrived there it was crowded with Hanoverian troops and their baggage wagons, whom they had to thread and almost fight a way through. At the other side there was a steep climb to some foothills, and guns were being hauled up there; hussars and dragoons were getting in each other's way, in a picture of such disorganization that Jeremy thought it unlikely he would ever find the Major Cartaret to whom he was supposed to report. Jeremy had ridden all the way on the ungainly but reliable piebald horse Santa, which he had bought in Willemstad last December, it being the practice for officers of infantry regiments to be mounted; but most of his troops were fagged out with the long march in the heat of the day, burdened as they each were with a haversack, a musket and bayonet and a hundred and twenty rounds of ball cartridge. In the way of British soldiers, they brightened noticeably when the sound of gunfire got closer. Presently, almost to everyone's surprise, Major Cartaret appeared, a slim, dapper man, and called Jeremy to him, explaining that they must make for Nivelles. This, it seemed, was where most of the firing was coming from and was about four miles away.

They reached Nivelles, a small town this, and beyond it a battle was taking place in the lush countryside, cannons thundering over the rye and the wheat, musketry crackling, clouds of smoke darkening the sky, soldiers moving here and there, the wounded staggering back towards the town. But this did not dissuade the townsfolk from standing in the doorways or crowding at open windows, watching and staring, some trembling and huddled together, but others cheering excitedly as at a fireworks display. On the outskirts of the town was a tree-lined square, and this was like a clearing station for the wounded. They lay everywhere, the dead and the dying together – two priests trying to comfort and help, some quite elegant ladies; and the wounded helping each other; one with a foot wound squatting and tying up the stump of a man without a hand, most of them ghastly from loss of blood, some crying out, many frightened at the thought that they were going to die for lack of medical help.

Jeremy still did not like the sight of blood, but he led the way forward. Then the road in front of him was suddenly full of soldiers coming the wrong way. A few were wounded but most seemed to be simply following a herd instinct to escape. It was a Belgian regiment and they shouted at Jeremy's company: 'Tout est perdu! Les Anglais sont vaincus! Tout est fini!' It took ten minutes for them to rush past and then the road ahead was suddenly ominously empty. An occasional shell burst overhead and there was the intermittent crack of muskets.

After issuing his orders Major Cartaret had galloped off and had not been seen since. By the time they had gone another mile the sun was low in the sky, peering sidelong among the cumbrous trees. The wheels of a carriage behind rattling on the *pavé*, just room for it to get past, going ahead of them; in it was a single Guards officer, his coat unbuttoned, snuff-box in hand. He took no notice of the company of tramping soldiers nor of the mounted officers in the van. He was presumably on his way to fight the French.

Sight of him seemed to revive the tired men, and enabled Jeremy to have the strength of mind to keep them moving when they came to another hamlet where a large *estaminet* was surrounded by soldiers of all races taking their ease. Through the open windows you could see the rooms crowded with men, talking and arguing and smoking and drinking, and they were sprawled about outside too among their tired horses, drinking, resting, eating.

Once out of sight and sound of this relaxation, Jeremy called a halt. Two food wagons were brought from the back of the column and rations were handed round. It was time the men had a break, past time. They had marched far enough today, but his orders were so vague that he had little idea what to do next. There was still gunfire over the hill. It was no place to linger, this, for they were exposed on two sides, and there was little natural cover. Nor was there a stream, as there had been a mile or so back, where the men could refill their water bottles. He did not want to push on too far and blunder into the French.

The guardsman in the cabriolet had clearly had no such apprehensions.

John Peters came up and squatted beside him.

'Permission to speak, sir,' he said with a grin.

'So long as it's sensible, John. I know you'd rather be back in Brussels with Marita.'

'Well, this grub's not quite up to La Belle Epoque.'

'What are the lads saying?' Jeremy asked. 'That we should have stopped by the *estaminet*?'

'One or two rolled an eye, I can tell you. But by and large, them having marched so far today, they'd like to see a bit of fighting before the day's out. You've got a tough lot, Jeremy, and they don't like to see men running away.'

'The day *is* nearly out,' Jeremy said, squinting at the last glints of the sun. 'Well, I'll give 'em another fifteen minutes and then we'll move on.'

The fifteen minutes was almost up when a horseman came

galloping over the hill from the direction of the fighting. He reined in before Jeremy but did not dismount.

'There's been the very devil of a scrap just in the next valley, place called Quatre Bras. The Duke of Brunswick has been bad wounded and a lot of his men turned tail and ran for their lives. But we've drove the Frenchies back!'

There was no means of telling the rank or regiment of this solitary horseman because he was wearing a suit of embroidered royal-blue velvet and white pantaloons, and his shoes were dancing shoes. Presumably he had had no time to change since the Duchess of Richmond's ball. His horse was dead tired and hanging its head.

'Poldark,' said Jeremy. 'Captain, 52nd Oxfordshires. Major Cartaret is in command but I have not seen him for an hour.'

'Longland,' said the young man. 'Aide-de-camp to the Duke. The fighting's dyin' down now but it's been the very devil of a scrap. I doubt if there'll be much more till dawn. If your major don't turn up I'd advise you to make for Quatre Bras – that's the crossroads; you can't miss it, and bivouac in any convenient field you can find this side of it. There'll be more fun in the mornin', depend on it.' He gently tugged his horse's tired head up and went on his way.

II

So they marched on to the battlefield. A cluster of houses at the crossroads, and there was still some fighting in and out of these. All sorts of noises echoed in the hot evening air, cries of men in pain, the blowing of bugles, the neighing of horses, the crack of muskets, the whistle of bullets overhead, the distant boom of cannons and the explosions of shell. Great clouds of smoke rose from the thick woods beyond, and frightened birds were wheeling and crying. As they skirted the wood to approach the crossroads, they stumbled over corpses hidden in the tall grass. Groups of soldiers moved around the farmhouses, but there seemed no enemy among them now. A troop of cavalry about a hundred strong galloped suddenly across the fields and into the next wood.

Jeremy called a halt and rode on ahead. It was now half dark, with the moon out, and there seemed to be no one in charge, but as he reached the crossroads he could see what carnage there had been. Dead horses, dead men were piled in heaps everywhere. The farmhouses were blasted and pitted with shot. The wounded men for the most part were lying untended where they had fallen or where they had crawled to. A cavalry officer suddenly appeared from the door of one of the houses, unlooped the reins of his horse and began to issue orders. As Jeremy came up to him he realized he was a major-general. Jeremy waited his turn, then saluted and reported.

'Poldark?' said the major-general. 'A Cornishman? This has been something of a scrap, by God. You just come? Yes, water your horses and men – there's a well in the courtyard, though you'll have to wait your turn. Bivouac where you've the fancy; I do not think there will be a night attack, but post sentries.'

In the end they did not, for after watering their horses and feeding themselves from the wagons and what they carried in their pouches, they lay down in the long grass, surrounded at no great distance by great companies of men who were doing likewise; and presently, tired out, fell asleep. Just before he went off, listening to the muttering and murmuring of voices around him, Jeremy thought to himself, was ever a man or men in such a strange situation? Here we are, lying down in the warm cloudy moonlight in the very *middle* of a battlefield in which we have taken no part! Not fired a solitary shot. Quite nearby there are heaps of dead and many wounded, some dying. A few surgeons and medical orderlies are working through the night but their numbers are woefully small. A good man would go and join them, try to succour the casualties. He had heard at the well that the Gordon Highlanders had had a hand to hand confrontation with massed French infantry under Marshal Ney himself, and each side had fought the other to a standstill. There had been no ground given, no quarter asked, until the French had retreated with the fall of night. A good man would get up and try to help those who had fallen. But this good man, though not yet into the conflict, and with only one wounded of those under his command, was yet so exhausted with almost a day and a half of travel and the tension of his new command, that he put his head down on the dewy grass, thought of Cuby for a moment, and then fell asleep.

III

At six o'clock on the following morning with sultry clouds blocking out the rising sun, a group of senior officers were breakfasting in a draughty hut at a crossroads just south of Genappe, and waiting for news of the Prussians. A long table was covered with a white cloth, silver glinting in the morning light, the smell of bacon frying, of coffee; champagne bottles open among the crockery and the maps. The Duke of Wellington was at the centre of the table, other notable and noble figures gathered around him, and indeed there were so many that the numbers overflowed into the yard outside. The Duke's entourage had now increased to about forty men, including his own eight aides-de-camp and numerous staff officers such as Colonel Augustus Fraser, the commander of the Horse Artillery, Colonel Sir William de Lancey, his American-born Chief of Staff and Lord Fitzroy Somerset. Added to them was Baron von Müffling, the Prussian liaison officer, Count Carlo Pozzo, representing the Russians, Baron Vincent for the Austrians, General Miguel de Alava, his old friend from Spain, and a half-dozen assorted English aristocrats, ready to fight if necessary but belonging to no unit, here to see the fray and all of them with too much influence in England to be summarily dismissed from the scene.

On this group came a young staff officer who murmured something to the Commander-in-Chief.

Wellington nodded. 'Send him in.'

A tall gaunt ragged middle-aged man limped in.

'Sir Ross,' said Wellington, 'so you have safely arrived!'

'Poldark!' exclaimed Lord Fitzroy Somerset, getting up and clasping his hand. 'I am relieved to see you. Welcome!'

'Thank you.' Ross smiled. With noticeably less of a smile he added: 'Your Grace.'

'You were not unexpected,' said the Duke, 'so you will have guessed that Colonel Grant has preceded you.'

'I'm glad to know it, sir.'

'But by only a few hours. Six, in fact. He arrived at midnight with information which I would have given a brigade of infantry to have known twenty-four hours earlier. Now it is too late.'

'Too late, sir?'

'Too late to choose more suitable ground before the River Sambre. We must fight where we find ourselves, here among the rye fields.'

'Colonel Grant – he is well?' Ross said.

'Except for a natural chagrin that his message did not get through – which we all share.'

'I shall not need this, then, sir.' Ross took the original message from his belt and put it on the table.

Fitzroy Somerset was at the open end of the improvised shelter. 'Grant said you could muster no more than a pony. If that's your mount outside it looks a very handsome pony!'

Ross's lips tightened. 'My pony was hit by a stray bullet yesterday. I found this horse riderless near Frasnes. It seems that it belonged to a French cavalry officer called Pelet who was under General Kellerman's command.'

Wellington said: 'Have you eaten?'

'Not since yesterday.'

'Then take a seat. Anders will make you some eggs.'

'Thank you, sir.'

Ross brushed some of the dirt off his clothes and took the seat offered him. Until now he had had no time to feel tired. From the conversation as he ate he gathered that Wellington was waiting for the return of an officer called Colonel Gordon who had been sent with a squadron of the 10th Hussars to reconnoitre the situation east towards Sombreffe. The Duke had recalled his advance posts last night on discovering only French and no Prussians on his flank.

'Poldark,' said the Duke suddenly, 'how did you come? Grant took a risk and rode almost directly along the Charleroi road, so he had nothing to report. What was your route?'

'I kept east of that road, but by how far I don't know. I stopped at an inn last evening, being almost too thirsty to care, and they were talking of a bitter battle in Ligny in which the Prussians had been driven back.'

'Defeated?'

'That was the impression I received, sir.'

'Blücher must surely send word soon. We are all ready for the French when he tells us he too is ready.'

Ross finished the eggs and bacon and sipped steaming coffee.

The Duke was looking at him again, penetrating eyes over beak nose. But there seemed to be no hostility in his look; any suspicion of the old days appeared to have gone.

'You have done well to get here, Sir Ross. But you are in effect a non-combatant. You have found your way from Verdun and should now return home.'

'I should like very much to return home,' said Ross, 'once the business here is finished.'

'You do not need to feel honourably detained.'

'Nor shall I for a moment, once this business is finished.'

The Duke sipped at his glass.

'Do you wish to remain as an observer?'

'I would like to take some more active part than that.'

'Colonel Grant is remaining on my staff as an additional aide-de-camp. Perhaps you would care to join him.'

'I'd be honoured, sir.'

'We should fit you out in better clothes,' said Fitzroy Somerset after a moment. 'That's if you do not mind wearing a uniform that the previous owner has no further use for.'

'I am not superstitious,' said Ross.

'There are two Poldarks in the army already,' said a red-haired man at the table with the emblems of a colonel on his coat. 'One's a major in the 95th Rifles, the other a captain in the 52nd Oxfordshires. Major Poldark's a veteran from the 43rd. I knew him in Spain.'

'That must be my cousin, Geoffrey Charles,' Ross said. 'I thought he was still in Spain! By God, so he has come back into it again!' A batman poured him more coffee. 'The other I don't know. My son is an ensign, and I think is in the 52nd but perhaps . . .'

'J. Poldark,' said the red-haired colonel. 'He was promoted last month.'

'To – captain?' said Ross in astonishment.

Wellington looked down the table at him. 'Yes, I observed him myself last month. He has a grasp of things that I find valuable in a junior officer.'

Ross stirred his coffee, the steam drifting before his eyes.

'I have been interned three months. It might be three years.'

An orderly came in and spoke to Fitzroy Somerset.

'Colonel Gordon has arrived, sir. He is just coming up the road.'

A thick-set young man presently entered. Ross could see his horse outside sweating and foam splashed. He spoke in an undertone to the Duke, who however soon communicated his news to the men anxiously waiting.

'Old Blücher has had a damned good licking and retreated to Wavre. That must be all of twenty miles from here. We can expect no help from him today – indeed he is lucky to be alive. So we are on our own, gentlemen, and out on a limb, a promontory, a point, not easily defensible.'

No one spoke. The Duke got up and not for the first time Ross realized he was not a tall man. Only a few inches taller than the great man who opposed him. No one spoke, for they were waiting for the decision which might decide the fate of the battle, the fate of the war.

Wellington said: 'Gentlemen, we must retreat.'

IV

Jeremy had been dreaming of champagne corks popping, and woke to the reality that it was almost full daylight and that the sounds he heard were muskets firing off in the woods to the right of Quatre Bras. In spite of the warm morning he found himself chilly, and he wrapped his cloak around him as he stood up. Men were sitting up all round him, stirring, yawning, stretching, wondering what the new day would bring. Some had already lit fires and were cooking what little food they had left. Jeremy was ravenously hungry, and while Sanders prepared a bite of breakfast for him he munched the remnants of a cake Cuby had given him. Some men were cleaning their arms, others talking and joking; no one seemed to be taking much notice of the smart skirmish on their right.

'Sir.' It was Quack Evans. 'Major Cartaret is here, with orders for the day.'

Jeremy brushed the crumbs off his uniform and walked across the field to greet his superior, who had just dismounted.

'Bad news for us, Poldark,' he said. 'The Prussians have been heavily defeated and we are isolated here. We must retreat.'

'Retreat? We have only just arrived, sir!'

'Colonel Coleborne's orders. But you have some satisfaction. Your company has been chosen to cover the retreat. You will stay here until all are gone, except G Troop Royal Artillery under Captain Mercer. You will then follow the other troops, and we shall expect you to link up with General Lord Edward Somerset when your task of delaying the enemy is done. His brigade of Guards is at present retreating on Genappe; but failing any later information you must find him as best you can.'

When he was gone Jeremy called his two lieutenants, Bates and Underwood, and the ensigns and the sergeants, and told them their orders.

They were not well received, and he could see the ordinary soldiers reacting in a similar way when the news filtered down. After all, you could see the French camping on the slopes in the distance. What in hell was the good of marching all this way and then not having a go at them? Why, there was a bit of hot work going on in the woods nearby – if the company couldn't advance this might occupy their time. Grumbling, they disposed themselves in some sort of order and prepared to wait.

Troops began to march past them, rode past them, artillery rumbling away, one regiment gradually appearing to fill the place of the one which had just left, all retreating towards Brussels.

As the living thinned out you could more clearly see the dead, thickly strewn where they had fallen among the flattened rye or been thrown in heaps to clear the roadways. Some were nearly naked, having been stripped in the night by the peasantry; dead horses too robbed of their valuable harness. It was a depressing sight. About a mile away on the brow of a slight hill were G Troop of the artillery, the only troop apart from Jeremy's company, who were not moving back. Jeremy wondered if it would be suitable to gallop across and have a word with his friend whom he had last seen on a happier day picnicking in Strytem.

Since leaving Nivelles yesterday, there had been little sign of habitation. The few cottages to be seen were empty and were being used only as cover for the opposing forces. People had fled; but the presence of looters showed some still lurked, possibly in the woods or the Forest of Soignes.

Just then it began to rain. The clouds had been thickening since dawn, and now a torrential downpour cloaked off the farther hills. Very soon everyone was soaked through and hungry, the light breakfasts they had had long forgotten. When the rain ceased for a few minutes the only troops still in sight, apart from the battery on the hill, were a score of light dragoons trotting from the woods on the left and what looked like a full brigade of hussars moving through Quatre Bras. It was led by the general Jeremy had spoken to last night. Major Cartaret had said his name was Sir Hussey Vivian.

As he came level with the company of infantry he reined in and said to Jeremy: 'You're covering the retreat in this area?'

'Yes, sir.'

He took out his glass and levelled it at the hills behind. Jeremy could see the ominous black patches beginning to move. White smoke was rising through the trees.

Vivian said: 'That's the French. Lancers, I think. Supported by massed infantry. It's time to leave, lad.'

'Yes, sir.'

At that moment Captain Mercer's artillery opened fire at the advancing masses on the hillside.

Vivian said to his orderly: 'That battery has been left with only sufficient ammunition for a token resistance. I saw their wagons on the road an hour ago. Send over and tell them to begin leaving in ten minutes. Polwhele.'

'Poldark, sir.'

'Ah yes. You're one of the North Coast breed. Is it your father who's MP for Truro?'

'Yes, sir.'

'Thought so. I was born there. Went to the same school as he did – though later. Now look, get your men on the move right away. If the French come within musket shot give 'em a round or two; but no heroics. If you form square you'll be overwhelmed.'

There was a vivid, electric streak of forked lightning, followed by a clap of thunder which drowned the heavy barking of Captain Mercer's five nine-pounders. The storm raged overhead while the 52nd hastily fell into line. They had hardly begun to march when the French artillery opened up from among the trees.

317

V

In Brussels the guns could be clearly heard and seemed to be getting nearer. Crowds of English and Belgians stood on the ramparts of the city watching the passage of vehicles and men to and fro along the Charleroi road, and listening to the approaching battle. Cuby went up for a short time with the Turners. Grace Turner was also expecting a child but like Cuby she was staying with her husband, who was a secretary at the British Embassy.

Gradually the word 'retreat' began to be heard, and, not long afterwards, 'defeat'. The Prussians, it was said, had been swept aside with dreadful losses.

Then Bonaparte had turned upon Wellington. The young Duke of Brunswick, brother of the Princess of Wales, was dead: he had been mortally wounded trying to rally his inexperienced troops, who had broken and fled before the attack of the veteran French; Wellington and his staff had only just escaped capture. The victors were approaching the city.

Soon the Charleroi road was proof enough of the rumours. Few if any troops continued to march out; the road was choked with commissary carts piled with returning wounded, some lying across saddles, many limping or being carried by their comrades. Returning too in broken companies were the defeated Brunswickers, mingling with Dutch-Belgians and elements of the landwehr who had had enough of war and were streaming back into and through the city.

The Mayor of Brussels issued an urgent appeal to the inhabitants for old linen and lint, for mattresses, sheets and blankets, to be sent to the Town Hall. All suitable public buildings would be made available to accommodate the wounded, and rich citizens who showed an unwillingness to help would have wounded men billeted on them by decree.

Many of the English prepared to leave for Antwerp – those who had a means of transport.

'You go,' Cuby said to Grace Turner. 'I shall stay.'

Thirteen

I

The retreat went on throughout the day in pouring rain, with constant skirmishing, a few casualties, but no ferocious pitched battles like yesterday. On the whole the withdrawal if untidy was measured; and the French, as much impeded by the rain and the mud, advanced at about the same pace.

Wellington, having been under constant fire yesterday and in truth having only narrowly escaped capture, dined equably with his staff at an inn called the Roi d'Espagne in Genappe. 'Gentlemen, I advise you to relish this meal for I fancy it will be the last comfortable one we shall have until this business is over.' Ross dined in a second room with Colonel Grant and a few others. He was wearing the jacket of a Coldstreamer, but the trousers had not been long enough, so a deceased Field Brigade officer of the King's German Legion had provided the rest.

Not that the uniform looked much out of the way. All the officers were soaked in rain, plastered with mud and so hardly distinguishable. The first mission Ross had been sent on had been one to General Sir Thomas Picton, who had been in the thick of the battle yesterday and nursed two broken ribs and a grievance because he had been asked to retreat from the position he had just gained. After dinner Ross would have liked to inquire the whereabouts of the 52nd Oxfordshires but could not bring himself to do so. To be invited to join Wellington's staff was a sufficient compliment without his presuming to ask to interrupt the battle to meet his son.

At three the party moved off, following the bulk of the army through what might be called the Genappe gap. In their wake by a matter of two hours came the rearguards, among whom was the troop of Royal Horse Artillery and a company of 52nd Oxfordshires under Captain Poldark. Some fighting took place during the afternoon, and the Oxfordshires lost three men. The Roi d'Espagne, having served dinner to the British, served supper to the French.

Retreat is always difficult and depressing; and the weather did all it could to make either movement or conflict impossible. All except the paved roads became seas of mud. Food was non-existent until the evening when they caught up with a few commissary wagons. Then they squatted round sputtering fires trying to eat and warm themselves. Major Cartaret, who had joined them after Genappe, with a second company under a Captain Allison, said they were lucky to have kept to the centre and made good time; other regiments on the left and right flanks had had to struggle through hilly villages and swamped fields, and some men had lost their boots in the glutinous mud. Rearguards, particularly to the east, had been constantly harassed by French snipers.

This, he said to Jeremy, was as far as they would go today, and it was likely that here they would be expected to make a stand. On their left flank was the main Brussels road, on their right the big farmhouse of Hougoumont. All around them regiments were marching, taking up positions, buglers were blowing, cavalry trotting. Captain Mercer, with his six guns, each pulled by eight horses, his nine ammunition wagons, with six horses each, his baggage wagons, his mounted detachments, his mules and spare horses – over two hundred animals in all – had disappeared into a fold in the land farther back towards Mont-St-Jean.

Jeremy gave the necessary orders to Lieutenants Bates and Underwood and set about consolidating their position so far as they could for the rest of this evening and the approaching night. They had halted in the middle of an enormous rye field, and the soil was so soft and so sodden with the rain that one was standing permanently in inches of mud. Every step had to be taken with an effort, hauling one's foot out and putting it down into another part of the quagmire.

In the distance now they could see the French closing in on them, until detachments of skirmishers in the van were less than a mile away. There they halted and began, it seemed, similar preparations to camp for the night. Some French artillery opened up, and occasionally a ball would pass uncomfortably near; but the main preoccupation was shelter from the weather. It was impossible for men to lie down, or they would almost have drowned; yet they could not stand up for twelve hours. The latest downpour had put out the fires, and there was nothing more to eat. Then Sergeant Evans – the old campaigner – began to gather up armfuls of the five-foot standing corn and rolled it together until it formed a thick mat. This he laid on the mud, then put his knapsack on top and sat on that cross-legged and covered his head with his blanket.

The movement was infectious, and soon at least half the men were following suit, then almost all the rest. Jeremy slogged and stumbled round his company. He had previously given orders for the officers' horses to be tethered to bayonets driven into the ground; all other arms to be piled and no man to leave his position. Satisfied that there was little more to do, he returned in the last of the daylight to a corner where Sanders had magically persuaded a small fire to burn and sat by it with his six officers, smoking and drinking gin and using the sodden rye stalks to cushion him against the worst of the trickling water.

II

It rained all night, and when the sickly daylight dawned the two armies faced each other across an undulating plain of Flanders mud. Ross, so far as he had slept at all, had slept dry; but some of the staff had been moving by 3 a.m. and among them, he suspected, the Duke.

It was still raining but the sky was much lighter, and from his vantage point at Mont-St-Jean Ross could see something of the deplacement for what must be the coming battle: British and Hano-verians and Belgian soldiers already in the positions they were to defend, if not yet ready to fight. The two first defensive positions were the inn at the fork of the roads called La Belle Alliance, and to its right the old farmhouse of Hougoumont, half hidden in its woods and apple trees; immediately behind them, astride the Brussels road, the smaller farmhouse of La Haye Sainte. About six the rain stopped and a hot sun came out.

Colquhoun Grant, coming across to where Ross was standing, said: 'A message from Blücher at last. The old man is alive, thank

God, and has promised two divisions by this afternoon. Pray Heaven the roads dry up, for otherwise they will never cover the distance in the time.'

Ross said: 'Perhaps the issue will be decided by then.'

'They're massing behind Placenoit . . . The Duke wants to see you, my dear feller. I am off to Waterloo with a message, so I hope to be back within the hour.'

When Ross got into the front room of the inn Wellington was just finishing writing a despatch. There were nine senior officers in the room with him and Ross made his way politely forward, bending his head to avoid the beams.

Three men at the table. Sir William de Lancey said: 'I am sure you would wish to know the whereabouts of your two relatives, Poldark. The 95th Rifles are positioned at La Haye Sainte in a gravel pit, supporting the King's German Legion. The 52nd Oxfordshires are positioned in a large cornfield this side of the Château de Hougoumont, with the Foot Guards on their right flank.'

'Thank you, sir.'

'Before that,' said the Duke, spreading the paper and folding it, 'I want you to take this message to Prince Frederick of the Netherlands. I would prefer you to deliver it personally into his hands, but give it to no one less senior than Lieutenant-General Stedman.'

'Thank you, sir,' Ross said as he was handed the paper.

Wellington rubbed his nose. 'The young prince, you will find, is eager for action and will not take kindly to being instructed to stay out of the present battle. If he expostulates with you, tell him that although I am expecting a frontal attack, Bonaparte may still try to turn my flank and capture Brussels. That would be a disaster it will be his duty to prevent.'

The Duke got up and led the way out of the inn, followed at a respectful distance by the rest. He was not in any full uniform but wore a blue coat and cape with white breeches and highly polished boots. His horse was waiting for him and he mounted it and led the way to inspect his troops. At the sight of him men began to cheer, but he smiled coolly and waved them to silence. There would – there might – be time to cheer later.

'Where is Prince Frederick?' Ross asked Fitzroy Somerset.

'At Halle. Take the lane to Braine l'Alleud and from there you can turn up the road from Nivelles. You will travel faster than trying to cut across country in this quagmire.'

'How far is it?'

'About ten miles.'

'My God, it will take me all morning! I shall miss the battle!'

'Don't worry, my friend. If I know the French they will not attack until they have breakfasted. Even then, they may pause a while longer for the ground to dry.'

While Ross waited for his horse to be fetched he gulped a hurried breakfast, staring out through the window at the patchwork of fields and small woods and undulating slopes, all darkened with the movements of men, particularly the French, who were massing in glittering columns less than a mile away. Steel helmets, tiger-skin turbans, blue coats faced with scarlet, green and crimson plumed headgear, pennants fluttering, all the pageant and panoply of the greatest army in the world. It was a menacing sight. From here Ross could see La Haye Sainte, but Hougoumont was out of view in a fold of the hills. It looked as if Geoffrey Charles and Jeremy would both be in the forefront of any conflict which developed. The sooner he was off, the sooner back. Once he had discharged this task he would make straight for Hougoumont. After all, he was under no one's command.

As he left, with the sun blazing down now, fusillades of shots were heard all along Wellington's lines. They were not directed at the enemy, but the troops were drying their muskets and rifles, the easiest way being to discharge a shot out of the barrel before cleaning it.

III

At 11.30, on a halcyon summer morning which seemed already to have forgotten the torrents of yesterday, the battle for Brussels began with a tremendous cannonade from the French guns. The Allied gunners presently replied, and soon the lovely morning was devastated and the sun obscured by black smoke from the guns. Then four battalions of French infantry, preceded by clouds of skirmishers, attacked the farmhouse of Hougoumont and after a bitter fight captured the road south of the house. Without possession of Hougoumont the French could not move up the shallow valley that it dominated and envelop the British right.

They reached virtually the walls of the old house but were driven back with heavy losses by four companies of British Guards under Lord Soltoun. Attack and counter-attack went on for three hours, each side committing more and more troops to taking, or holding, a position which was on the right of the main battle area but which more and more was seen as vital to the outcome of the day.

Then, centrally in the two-mile front, the French advanced under Marshal Ney, preceded again by a great cannonade from eighty of Napoleon's finest guns. At 1.30 sixteen thousand soldiers marched across the blackened burning valley and up towards La Haye Sainte. They came on in stately unhurried masses, two hundred men wide by twenty-four deep, to the dreaded sound of the drummers, *rum-a-dum-dum, rum-a-dum-dum*, a beat which had struck fear into the hearts of all the armies of Europe. The Dutch-Belgians were driven out of La Haye and Papelotte, with almost all their officers killed. La Haye Sainte, though not captured, was isolated, and the 95th Rifles, under Major Geoffrey Charles Poldark, were forced out of their gravel pit and driven to retire towards Mont-St-Jean. A counter-attack by fourteen hundred Scottish infantry against eight thousand French would have been overwhelmed had not Wellington ordered two brigades of heavy cavalry to their rescue. Life Guards and King's Dragoons took part in an irresistible charge which cut through first the massed infantry and then the French cuirassiers and drove everything before them until the French were fleeing on all sides. But impelled by the contagious frenzy of the fight, the two great cavalry regiments ignored the bugle calls to halt and drove deeply into enemy lines where they were themselves surrounded, counter-attacked and cut to pieces. In a single action Wellington lost a quarter of his cavalry.

The bombardment continued, with the weight of gunnery much favouring the French. Three forms of missile were used: first, the solid round shot, an iron ball which bounced and ricochetted and could plough a great trough of death and maiming among a group of soldiers; if it missed them then eventually it came harmlessly to rest; second, the hollow round shot filled with explosive and with a sputtering fuse: these could be picked up and hurled away if the fuse was not too short, but if you guessed wrong you knew no more about it; third, the canister or grape shot, used at close quarters, which burst when fired, spraying the area with pieces of broken metal. Cannon-fire was never accurate but a concentration of it on a concentration of men made certain of heavy casualties. The sound overhead was like the humming of great hornets, blasting the ground and people wherever they landed.

One after another of Wellington's aides went down. General Picton was killed and Sir William Ponsonby. The bitter fight for Hougoumont continued all through the stifling afternoon. Men coughed in the acrid smoke, sometimes lost their way, fired ever more inaccurately through the drifting smoke. Everywhere as far as one could see the fields were strewn with dead and dying men and horses, knapsacks, muskets, broken cannon wheels.

At three o'clock the French cannons, having been dragged forward again, resumed at closer range and with greater intensity. Wellington, expecting Blücher's relieving divisions on his left flank, was not aware that the Prussians, bogged down in mud, were advancing to join him at the rate of only a mile an hour.

In the next ninety minutes four great French cavalry attacks were delivered against the British right centre, nearly five thousand horsemen in the first, over ten thousand in the third. Quarter was scarcely ever given or asked. Again and again they attacked the British squares and again and again were driven off, with bitter losses on both sides. Inside the squares were the bloodstained dead and dying, outside the French dead piled up so much that they became a protection and a barrier.

Napoleon withdrew his brother Jerome from leading the endless attacks on Hougoumont and instead ordered howitzers forward. These set the large house and most of the barns on fire, including the one where the British wounded were lying. These were all burned to death, but the remaining defenders retreated into the chapel and the gardener's house, from which they continued to shoot down the French as they attempted to capture them.

IV

The two companies of the 52nd, defending rising ground to the left of Hougoumont, had suffered badly, Jeremy's the lesser of the two. But both had borne the brunt of the repeated attacks on the British right. In squares the infantry stood, often kept in shape by the long staves of the sergeants, repelling one attack after another. When the cuirassiers failed they came under fire from grape shot. This ploughed lanes through the squares, and the French cavalry charged up to take advantage of the openings. But before they could do so the squares closed again across the dead and dying men, resolutely firing and bringing down the horsemen.

Most of the time Jeremy sat on his horse, where he could see a little more and could direct operations. The bullets droned around him and one cut his sleeve but, surprising himself, he felt no particular fear: it was as if there was some overriding demand upon his mind and heart. But then, in the early afternoon in the middle of a fierce attack, he saw a sharpshooter taking deliberate aim at him from a distance of not more than twenty yards. His mouth went dry and his hands became rigid, but he forced himself not to dismount. The man fired, and missed. Almost at once he was cut down by Ensign Peters.

About 2 p.m. the Duke came up out of the smoke and consulted with Major Cartaret, but while he was so doing another attack developed and he had to ride into the centre of the square for protection. The situation at Hougoumont was desperate. The farmhouse was surrounded by an entire French division, yet still the firing went on. It was all hand to hand now, sword, bayonet, musket-butt, axe, kill and be killed, no orders needed; just fight to the death.

Soon after the Duke had left, the artillery found a better range on the 52nd Oxfordshires. John Peters was cut in half by a cannon-ball, and almost immediately afterwards a huge shell landed just in front of Jeremy. His horse reared and saved his life but at the expense of its own. Seventeen other men were killed or wounded by the blast.

About three there was a brief lull, even in the attacks on Hougoumont. Since early morning the 52nd had had nothing to eat or drink, but now some wagons came up with a cask of water and a tub of gin. All the men rushed for the water, but most took a swig of gin after and then hastened back to the line.

At four the Duke returned, his entourage reduced to one aide but himself miraculously unwounded. Jeremy was with his commanding officer when Wellington rode up.

'Well, Cartaret, how do you get on?'

'As you see, my lord. We are badly cut about and have been in action all day. A relief even for an hour would be a godsend.'

The Duke made a wry face. 'God may send it, Colonel, but alas I cannot. We are stretched to the limits, as you can see. All our reserves are committed.'

Cartaret rubbed a spot of blood off his hand. 'Well then, my lord, we must stand until the last man falls.'

Soon after he had gone, erect and calm on his horse among the hail of shot and shell, the French cavalry launched another attack, but this time the Life Guards swept out from the rear and met them in a head-on clash. It was like a giant blacksmith's shop, Jeremy thought, the clanking of steel against steel, horses snorting and whinnying and falling. Close to the defensive square one guardsman struck his opponent with such force that head and helmet went flying, and the horse leapt away with the headless rider still sitting upright and the blood spurting from the arteries.

As the cavalry retreated the infantry came on again. *Rum-a-dum-dum, rum-a-dum-dum*: it beat in time with the soldiers' steps. Lieutenant Bates, kneeling beside Jeremy, was shot in the jaw. Jeremy detailed Sanders to help him back to a cowman's hut where most of the wounded had been taken. Numbers were now so far depleted that Major Cartaret ordered the few men left to form line four deep. Again the wave approached and again it was thrust back. Then, mercifully, a lull. Such was the smoke that it was impossible to see how the battle as a whole was faring. Cartaret ordered a muster to be taken. Captain Allison had been killed early on, and not one officer of the second company remained in the field. Jeremy, Michael Underwood and the major were the only three officers left. There were three sergeants, including

Evans, and about a hundred men fit to return to the battle.

Then a rider came past to say that La Haye Sainte had at last fallen. Defended to the bitterest end by a regiment of the King's German Legion, it had been evacuated with scarcely more than two score survivors. The centre of the Allied line was crumbling.

Major Cartaret looked up from behind the bank where most of his remaining troops were crouching and saw that in manoeuvring to attack the Guards the French infantry had exposed their flank. He wiped the blood from his face and stood up.

'Come on, you men of the 52nd!' he shouted hoarsely at the top of his voice. 'Now's the time to show 'em what we're made of! Remember Badajoz!' He raised his sword, leaped the bank and stormed towards the enemy. His troops, without food all day and exhausted beyond endurance, rose slowly and then, gathering momentum, stumbled after him.

Under this sudden attack the French wilted and broke, but then the attackers came under a sudden cross-fire from a hitherto unseen company of tirailleurs, appearing from behind the smouldering château. Cartaret was shot twice in the head and died instantly. Evans was wounded in the leg. Jeremy was shot in the back and side and fell flat beside a horse that had both its back legs blown off. The horse was struggling to get to its feet, dragging itself away on its stomach. Jeremy lost consciousness.

V

He half woke to find someone kneeling beside him. He must have been dragged back because he was in some sort of shelter. This man was kneeling beside him. Then he knew he was delirious.

'Father.'

'Jeremy . . .'

The man was ragged and bloodstained and had a week's growth of beard. But he wore no hat and that made him unmistakable.

Somebody wiped the corner of his mouth. The battle was still raging but seemed more distant. In a corner Sergeant Evans was trying to staunch the blood from his leg. It was very dark.

'This – a dream?'

'No. Can you drink this?'

Blessed water. But it didn't seem to go farther than his throat.

'What are you doing?'

'I escaped from Verdun. I would have been with you earlier but my horse was killed. Jeremy, lie still.'

'No choice,' said Jeremy. 'Is the battle . . . ?'

'Still close. But the Imperial Guard have been broken. They came in a great mass and have broken, have given way. And they say the Prussians are in sight.'

'Lost a lot,' said Jeremy with a sigh, 'of my friends.'

'By God, I can't find a surgeon!' said Ross, speaking into the air. 'Jeremy, my son, lie quiet. Can you take some more water?' He wiped the blood again from the corner of Jeremy's mouth.

'These horses,' said Jeremy. 'They should never be in war. If men have to fight – let 'em fight on foot.'

'I will see if I can find someone,' Ross said, his voice unrecognizable even to himself.

'Don't go . . . Is it night yet?'

'No, about eight, I think. I cannot tell you for my watch is broke.'

Jeremy saw now there were a couple of dozen men in the hut. All must be in great pain, but no one was groaning – only the occasional sigh and grunt.

'Father . . .'

'Yes?'

'My love to mother.'

'Yes.'

'Tell her . . .'

'What?'

'No matter. I wanted to tell her – something. Perhaps I left it too late. But I have written.'

Ross felt the tears running down his face. He bent to wipe the blood once again from Jeremy's mouth.

'Perhaps the next war,' said Jeremy, 'will be fought with steam engines.'

Evans was dragging himself towards the door. He knew if he could not get help soon he would bleed to death.

'Father,' said Jeremy.

'Yes?'

'Look after Cuby . . .'

'Of course. I promise.'

'That', said Jeremy, 'is the hardest part of all.'

And then he died.

BOOK THREE

One

I

Letter from Ross Poldark to his wife, dated Brussels, 22nd June 1815.

Demelza,

I have to tell you that Jeremy is dead. I cannot bring myself to write the words, but there is no way I know of breaking this to you gently. He fell nobly and bravely in the great battle just fought in the area south of the village of Waterloo, about twelve miles from this city and won by the British and their Allies in a decisive manner that must finally and forever settle Bonaparte's fate.

I do not know, my dearest, how to begin to tell you what it has been like. In early June I escaped from internment in Verdun and tried to make my way towards Brussels. The difficulty of this journey, though little more than 150 miles, was far greater than the mere distance because between me and whatever troops defended Brussels lay the whole of the French army of the west – some 120,000 men. I was vastly lucky to avoid capture and probably would not have succeeded but for the help of a Colonel Colquhoun Grant, a British officer who was acting as a spy for Wellington, and between us, though we eventually travelled separately, we arrived at Wellington's headquarters as the main battle was about to begin. For the duration of the battle Grant became one of the Duke's aides-de-camp and I was invited to fulfil a similar function. Naturally I tried to make contact with Jeremy's regiment, but was sent first with a message which took half the day, partly because my horse was shot from under me, though I escaped with a bruising.

The carnage on both sides was appalling. I have never seen such ferocity in attack or such utter relentless courage in defence. Just around the farmhouse of Hougoumont, which was where Jeremy

333

was stationed, over two thousand men were killed. In total we are thought to have lost 20,000 men, the Prussians about 7,000, the French about 30,000. Geoffrey Charles survived like me, and did not even suffer a scratch, although he was in the forefront of the fight throughout. All Wellington's main aides were killed or wounded – in total fifteen. Fitzroy Somerset lost his right arm. Sir William de Lancey, the Chief of Staff, was gravely wounded and is not likely to recover. Adjutant General Barnes and his deputy were both wounded. Colonel Gordon and Colonel Canning both died. In the battle the Duke of Brunswick died early, and Lord Picton was killed on Sunday. Two of Jeremy's closest friends were killed, and one wounded. Young Christopher Havergal, who made such a fuss of Bella, has lost a leg. I have also just heard that Brigadier Gaston Rougiet, who visited me in internment and gave me a greater liberty which enabled me to escape, was killed at the very last, fighting the Prussians.

If there was ever a battle fought as savagely as this, I have never known it or want to hear of it.

They say that Fitzroy Somerset suffered the amputation of his arm without a murmur and that the next morning was seen to be practising writing with his left hand.

Dearest, dearest Demelza, I give you all these details not because they can interest you but because they keep me a little longer from the sort of detail that I find it so hard to face. Jeremy died a brave soldier's death; he led his much-depleted company against a French infantry brigade which outnumbered him ten to one. Because of the loss of my horse I was tardy in returning the message I carried to the Duke – who in extraordinary fashion survived the whole battle unscathed – but as soon as I had done this I hurried down towards where I knew Jeremy's company had been fighting all day. I arrived just as a Lieutenant Underwood was carrying him back after he had been shot.

He lived for perhaps half an hour, but did not seem to be in pain. He knew me and sent a loving message to you. That is all I can say.

That night, the Sunday night, I stayed by him, while the French army finally broke and then was utterly destroyed by the Prussians. I did a little to help some of the wounded but am afraid I was too distracted and distraught to have done all I should. On the Monday morning I was able to find a conveyance of a sort to carry him back to Brussels. The road was almost impassable still, for the wounded, the baggage trains, the commissary wagons, the medical supplies, wandering groups of soldiers trying to regain their units; we went with the majority, but a few vehicles were fighting their way against the tide. The road had almost broken up with the pressure it had been under and in some places was a sea of mud. In one place we were held up for fifteen minutes while vehicles were at a standstill. Then, sitting there as I did helpless upon my horse, I heard a voice cry 'Captain Poldark!'

It was Cuby. It seems that Lady de Lancey, Sir William's wife, hearing that her husband was lying grievously wounded in a cottage in the village of Waterloo, had hired a coach and coachman, and, learning of this, Cuby had asked if she might travel with her to see if she could gain news of Jeremy. It was my appalling duty to give her that news.

Dearest Demelza, I have never seen a woman more heartbroken than Cuby was when she realized what I was saying – I know of only one who will be more so and she is holding this letter. What can I say to comfort you when there is no comfort? I try to think of the three children we have left and our duty to them not to fall into utter despair. That many a father and mother through the ages have suffered as we suffer now does not make it easier to sustain. Nor the thought of the thousands of other parents who have been bereaved by this battle. Perhaps we have always been too close a family. To feel so deeply about one's children is a great happiness – and a great danger.

Jeremy is buried in the Protestant Cemetery of St Josse ten Noode, just on the south side of the Chausée de Louvain. It was a simple ceremony but a dignified one. A stone will be put up.

I am returning to England tomorrow with Cuby. She rode in front of me to Brussels, and I thought every moment she would faint and fall. I will remain a day or two in London before returning to Cornwall. At present she thinks she will stay a little while with her brother Augustus in London. She thinks that returning to Cornwall only seven months after leaving it in such happiness is more than she can face.

She bears our first grandchild.

My love, it is only three months since we separated but it is like an age. I long to see you. Perhaps we can comfort each other.

Ross

II

When Clowance heard she left a scribbled message on the kitchen table for Stephen – who had still not returned from his foray – and rode across to be with her mother. Verity went with her. Demelza's two brothers were nearby – Drake at Trenwith, Sam at Pally's Shop. Dwight and Caroline too. Ben was at the mine and all the miners who had known and liked Jeremy so well. Paul and Daisy Kellow, with Mr and Mrs Kellow in the background; Valentine and Selina, just returned from Cambridge; the villagers from all the hamlets around. Letters began to arrive from as far afield as the Harveys at Hayle. A strange, stilted, troubled one from Cuby's mother. So many letters from people in the county: the Devorans, the Falmouths, the Trenegloses, the de Dunstanvilles, the Foxes. Even Harriet Warleggan sent a kind little note. Letters, letters; everyone so kind made the heartache worse.

Demelza took to walking across the beach and back, not to get rid of the deadly sickness and the emptiness and the aching – for there was no way out of that – but simply to tire one's muscles, to exhaust one's body, so that something was registered on the mind besides grief. Dwight gave her tincture of laudanum at night, but it always wore off at dawn when life was at its lowest and coldest. Then she would stand by the window and cry alone for the loss of her son.

Verity did not like walking as far as the Dark Cliffs, but Clowance kept her mother company, most of the way in silence. When it was not Clowance, Drake would go, or sometimes Sam, though he had to be careful not to speak too much of God. Dwight told Demelza to go easy; twice Caroline persuaded her to visit Killewarren and spent part of the day with her.

It was almost only to Caroline that she found she could talk at all – and sometimes in the evening to Verity.

All the beauty had gone from Demelza's face. Perhaps one day it would return, but at present few of her friends in Paris would have taken her for the vivacious, comic, ebullient young woman they had known in February and March.

'Why have I so much cause to be bitter?' she said to Caroline once. 'Folk die all the time – babies, old people, even young people like Jeremy. But I *am* bitter just the same. I don't want to see anyone, talk to anyone, be friendly with anyone. I just want to be left alone to think – to grieve – to think.'

'My dear, that'll do you no good. Though I well comprehend –'

'It does good to remember,' Demelza said. 'It does good to remember a thousand days of caring . . .'

III

But, returning to the county more quickly than his old enemy, came Sir George Warleggan, full of the greatest satisfaction. For on careful calculation he decided that he had added twenty-four and a half per cent to his fortune. His belief that the Rothschilds would know first, and his commission to Rosehill to keep the closest watch on them and to make all the use he could of his friend in the Rothschild office – this had been triumphantly successful. Hardly eating a proper meal for three days, he had haunted the city and the Exchange. The nervousness of the early part of the week had intensified, and the market was like a sick patient with undulant fever, reacting to the lightest rumour.

Looking back on the situation as his personal coach carried him the last few miles through the thickly wooded valley towards his own home, he felt a supreme contempt for the way the government of the country had been run, the singular clumsiness of its communications, its total lack of any attempt to bridge more quickly the distance – at the most two hundred miles – between the House of Commons and the scene of an operation which would decide the fate of the world.

It seemed that the battle had raged for three days, from the 16th to the 18th June. It seemed that on Tuesday the 20th Mr Nathan Rothschild, by means of his swift-riding and swift-sailing couriers, had learned that there had been a victory for the Allied troops under the Duke of Wellington, and being on terms of the closest friendship with the British Government had informed them of this. The Cabinet, sitting in a sudden emergency session so early in the morning, had discounted the information as unfounded. Their own envoys had just brought them news of Quatre Bras, the British defeat and the retreat on Brussels. This had followed the news of the defeat of Blücher. The general opinion was that all was lost.

The same day in the afternoon a Mr Sutton, whose vessels plied between Colchester and Ostend, had brought one of his ships back without waiting for passengers because he carried news of a tremendous battle being fought between Bonaparte and Wellington on the Sunday almost at the gates of Brussels. On the Wednesday *The Times* printed this information and wondered with regret that the Government had not made better arrangements for quicker transmission of the news. Were the Duke of Wellington's own despatches, the newspaper wondered, to depend upon similar vagaries of commercial patriotism? It was not until Thursday that the official bulletin was issued from Downing Street announcing the victory and calling Wellington the Hero of Britain.

But of course it had all happened for George on the Tuesday and Wednesday. Through his friend, Rosehill had been able to obtain the information that the Rothschilds had reported a victory for the Allies and that Downing Street had disregarded it. All that day George expected Nathan Rothschild to make some move. But when he did make a move, it was to sell stocks not to buy them . . . The market, already far down because of the news of Quatre Bras, fell still further. Not only George was watching the influential Jew.

George was puzzled, watchful, upset; for a while bitterly critical of Rosehill who he thought had given him wrong information. It's all over, said the brokers. And so did Rothschild's agents. The battle has been lost at a place called Waterloo. Rothschild, they said, has been hoodwinking the British Government. Then Rosehill sidled up to George with a whispered comment: 'The last hour of trading. Watch that.'

In the last hour that the Exchange was open on the Wednesday Rothschild suddenly bought a huge parcel of shares, among them Consols, which had touched a new low. George, sweating heavily, immediately followed suit. He spent an unhappy morning on the Thursday when shares moved only erratically upwards, stimulated

338

by a few people buying, including Rothschild again. Then the news of the great victory burst on the world – the French army utterly destroyed, Bonaparte making his escape to Paris, the Allies everywhere triumphant.

It was not only the Allies who were triumphant, George thought. Rothschild, by perfectly fair speculation, acting on the information he had already given the Government but which they had chosen to disregard, must have doubled his already immense fortune. And he, George, by astute emulation, had added about twenty-four and a half per cent to his already considerable fortune – or about eighty thousand pounds. It could have been more, he knew; but hedging at the last, still mindful of the disasters of 1810, and fearful of being cheated in some way by the cold young Jew, he had invested only two-thirds of what he might have done. Nevertheless, it was no mean achievement. Every night on the way home he had opened his business case, taken out a fresh piece of paper, and made his calculations afresh.

Just to complete the whole operation he had sent Tankard flying back to Cornwall – more than post haste, killing his horses if necessary – with instructions to Lander to buy all the metals he could, chiefly copper, before anyone else knew of the victory. There was no assurance that the price of metals would go up as a result of Napoleon's defeat – might be the contrary – but if he could virtually corner the market he would be in a position to dictate its movements.

He looked forward to telling old Uncle Cary what he had done. Five years ago, Cary had been scathing in his denunciation of the speculation which hadn't come off. Now, though no doubt grumpy and grudging, as was his nature, he would have to admit the brilliance of the manoeuvre. Nothing spoke so convincingly to Cary as money.

George was also looking forward to seeing Harriet again. In the euphoria of Thursday he had bought her a present, a diamond brooch. It was second-hand and a bargain, but he had paid, if not more than its worth, more than he had intended, and occasionally this little worm of self-criticism came to disturb his sense of well-being. But at least Harriet, who loved jewellery, could not fail to be pleased.

He must be careful not to appear to boast to her about his coup;

indeed he knew it would be better if he did not mention it at all –
if he could *possibly* forbear. Harriet did not pretend to despise
money – indeed, she liked it – but it was not central to her
philosophy; it was only valuable to her for what it could buy; and
he knew if he told her of his successful speculation she would
only congratulate him in an absent-minded way, looking cynically
amused as she did so, and change the subject.

He wondered if Harriet had heard yet about Jeremy. The first
casualty lists had been issued on the 4th July, and his name had been
on it. George supposed the whole county would know about it now.
Personally he was going to shed no tears; he never had liked the
tall, gangling young buck: typical Poldark with his arrogance and his
pride. The women were rather better – at least Clowance was – but
the men were all the same. More fools they for going in the army and
trying to be heroes. It seemed no time at all – though it was actually
getting on for twenty years – since Ross himself had performed some
so-called dare-devil rescue of Dwight Enys and others from a French
prisoner-of-war camp and so had become a nine-days' wonder and the
hero of the county. Well, now his son was gone, and bad luck for him
and for his contriving a baronetcy for his son to inherit – though
George had heard there was another son barely weaned yet; they bred
like rabbits on the North Coast. That miner's brat with the stupid
name; she'd had half a dozen at least.

But talking of breeding; there was his own wife pregnant now,
bearing his son, who, with blue blood in his veins, would live to
inherit all his mercantile wealth and possessions. What should they
call him? George had a fancy for the name of Hector – or Nicholas;
but no doubt Harriet would have ideas of her own. He believed
it would be about Christmas or January; Harriet was typically
vague. It was still a long time to wait. Pray God the child wasn't
premature . . .

The carriage turned in at the gates of Cardew, and George's eye
looked about with critical appreciation, admiring the elegance and
extent of his own property but scanning it for any evidence of
indolence or neglect. When it came to the big pillared entrance of
the mansion, one of the coachmen jumped down and opened the
carriage door. At the same moment the door of the house opened
and two footmen stood there to greet him. It was a warm afternoon

and the coach had been stuffy – it needed to be well cleaned inside with a carriage soap and thoroughly brushed out.

He stretched his legs and his back, glad the journey was over, nodded to his servants and went into the hall. Harriet was crossing, followed by her two boarhounds. She looked up in surprise. Castor growled, and she put her hand on his muzzle to restrain him.

'Why, George,' she said. 'Good-day to you. You're soon back.'

IV

During the momentous days of late June, while the fate of empires was being decided, Stephen was cruising in the Channel hoping to settle some of the problems in his own life.

It seemed the *Adolphus* was out of luck. Fishing vessels and a few tiny trading schooners – the latter just worth seizing but Stephen would not touch them; he was looking for bigger game. The weather was changeable, mainly sunny, almost calm; but then the wind would take off from an unexpected quarter and blow hard, so the crew was kept busy making and shortening sail. Twice they sighted larger vessels but Carter, who had been in the navy, was quick to recognize them as British warships. Then in a flurry of a brief squall they came suddenly in sight of a French frigate and had to run for their lives. The *Adolphus* crowded on all the sail she could and soon was heeling right over, white water along her lee rail, dipping and spouting into the short seas. It was an anxious two hours until nightfall.

Stephen had laid in a generous supply of stores: biscuit, beef, pork, peas, coffee, tea, sugar, flour, pepper, salt, lime juice; and he reckoned they had enough to last a good two weeks. Fresh water might force them in a bit earlier, but he began to hear rumblings of dissension among the crew. It was not, he discovered, discontent with his captaincy, but, with too much time on their hands, they were quarrelling among themselves.

Jason, who was his informant on most things, explained to him that there was a bitter rivalry between men from Falmouth and those from Penryn, and they were dividing into two camps with about a third of the crew uninvolved in either. One day Stephen heard a group of them shouting and jeering.

341

'Old Penrynners up in a tree,' they shouted
'Looking as wisht as wisht can be.
Falmouth men be strong as oak
Can knock 'em down at every poke.'

To which the men from Penryn shouted a more obscene rhyme back.

Looking at them, weather-beaten, long-nosed, hard-faced men, Stephen wondered that they could be such childish fools as to support a rivalry between two towns which were only a couple of miles apart. He'd been careful to lock up all the cutlasses and muskets he had brought and had appointed a man called Hodge as armourer.

Hodge was a little fat squab of a man, swart and jowly, but a bundle of energy and efficiency. Stephen soon saw him as the most valued member of the crew and began to consult him more and more. In his forty years he seemed to have done and been everything, and his experience as a sailor helped Stephen to fill the gaps in his own knowledge. Thank God he happened to come from St Ives.

But there was no knowing how many private knives were carried in secret places or how long it would be before the feud turned into a bitter battle. Jason also told him that they had brought rum aboard: he did not know where it was stored but some of the crew had access to it over and above the daily ration.

So it was a relief on the seventh day to sight what looked like a promising sail.

A beautiful still dawn, with a pearly sun rising out of the early mists, turning them lemon-yellow and then to a grey scarf washed with scarlet. Yet as the sun rose it never came to full health. Anaemia set in, and the mist became light cloud chasing the colour from the sky. The gulls, which were always following *Adolphus*, rose and flapped and cried and settled again into the darkening water.

It was about noon that the look-out reported the sail. Stephen, who was not fond of heights, sent Carter up and then Jason. Soon you could see the sail from the deck.

'She's only got one mast,' said Jason, disappointed, 'but she's carrying a heavy sail.'

Ten minutes later Carter came down. 'Reckon tis a French

chaloupe. She's just put out two headsails; means she's seen us and altered course.'

The manoeuvring of the last few days had robbed Stephen of any idea where he really was, particularly as related to the French coast; but the drift of the *Adolphus* had been continually west, so it seemed likely that there was a great width of the Channel about them.

'Size is she?'

Carter pulled at his bottom lip. 'Bigger'n you'd expect. A hundred ton maybe.'

'Armed?'

'Likely.'

'What with?'

'Could not say. Nothing big.'

'Sure she's French?'

'Well, she's flying the French flag.'

'Jason,' said Stephen. 'Go get the French flags. See if we can reassure her.'

V

They pursued the *chaloupe* all day while the day went off. The sun disappeared about some other business, and cloud gathered and a light rain fell. It would have been impossible to keep the *chaloupe* in sight if the distance between them had not constantly lessened. Her captain clearly saw no reassurance in the flag Stephen flew and bore on a south-easterly course for home. But as the angle narrowed they overhauled him fast. Stephen ordered the armoury to be unlocked, and all men were issued with cutlasses or muskets. The sighting of a suitable prey had come just in time; the fraternal squabbling among the crew had ceased.

She was a strange-looking vessel to English eyes – very heavily sparred with an immense mainsail and a main boom very long and thick. She was steered by a long tiller, had high bulwarks and a wide stern. She should have been clumsy to handle, yet in fact moved well through the water and seemed to answer her helm readily. Her name, it seemed, was the *Revenant*.

Two of Stephen's six-pounders had been fitted as bow chasers, and when the distance warranted he told his gunners to try a shot or two in the hope of bringing down her mainsail, since it was clear that his friendly French flag was not inducing the master to slacken pace. It was then he began to regret not having let the gunners have more practice during the week at sea. (Powder and cannon shot were very expensive.) First the balls dropped far short; then they winged into the air and only a distant plopping indicated where they had fallen. Almost at once a gun replied from the other vessel. Stephen recognized it as a French long four-pounder; it could not reach them yet but could do damage at closer quarters. If only his own damned gunners could aim straight. He ran forward and saw to the next discharge himself. He might not be a first-class navigator but he had had some experience with cannon.

The Frenchman's best hope of escape was the weather. There was a handy, steady south-westerly breeze but the rain was thickening into mist, and visibility was closing in. It would be a disaster to lose touch now. Hodge was the only man who could speak fair French so Stephen sent him up into the bows with a hailer, telling them that the *Adolphus* was friendly and saying that his captain wanted to speak with their captain as he had news of Bonaparte.

The only answer to this was a heavy thump in the bows and splinters of wood flying up through the air. Stephen cursed and lowered the sight of his cannon, ordered them to fire. The cannon reared on the deck, two stabs of flame lit the grey afternoon, but the brig had dipped at the wrong moment and both shots ploughed harmlessly into the sea.

Close to, the *Revenant* was quite a handsome vessel, well cared for and every way in good shape. She was sailing heavy and probably carried a full cargo. Of course she would have to be boarded, and that was what the crew was waiting for – eagerly crouching behind the elmwood bulwarks. They looked a villainous lot, and he hoped sight of them swarming up over the side would persuade the Frenchman to strike and thus save damage and bloodshed. The *Revenant* with her equally high bulwarks could prove a nasty customer if defended stoutly.

Jason was beside him. 'You're firing too low, Father! What range have those guns? If we could smash their rudder . . .'

'Do not forget we want to *capture* this ship,' said Stephen, 'not

344

sink her.' Another shot whistled over their head and tore a clean hole in their gaff mainsail. The *Adolphus* slewed as the sail split, until Carter at the helm brought her up again. 'Now back to your place and no more talking.' Stephen was leading one boarding party, Hodge the other. Jason was in Hodge's party. Carter was remaining in charge of the *Adolphus*.

At much closer range now the two six-pounders fired and this time the shot found their mark. The great mainsail, carrying the full thrust of the wind, was suddenly in flapping tatters. The larger balls and the double shot had done far more damage to the Frenchman's sail; the *Revenant* yawed, and the two vessels closed. Muskets began to fire, and some misfired in the damp and the rain. One ship ran alongside the other with a grinding crump, grappling irons were thrown, men were over and jumping down onto the deck. There was some fighting but it was half-hearted. The man at the helm looked like the Captain, and grouped around him were a half-dozen others, cutlasses out, pistols firing. But one man fell and then another and the Captain raised his hands.

Stephen let out a yell of triumph – it had all come just as he had planned it; a splendid prize! But there was another yell close beside him and a rough hand pulled at his shoulder, tugging him round. On the *Revenant*'s larboard bow something else was looming out of the mist. She was far bigger than either of the contestants: two decks, three masts, a rakish bow. There was ice in Stephen's stomach as he recognized the French frigate which had chased them on Friday.

Two

I

It was luck that they got away at all – the luck being that the *Adolphus* had grappled the *Revenant* on the starboard side, so that the French *chaloupe* was between the *Adolphus* and the frigate and the frigate could not fire at the English ship without hitting the *Revenant*.

A panic retreat for Stephen's men – up and over the side, and back to their brig, hacking at grappling irons that failed to come free, Carter bringing over the helm as the last man dropped aboard; both ships had been travelling at a modest speed when they came alongside; Carter made skilful use of the sail already set, and they had the weather gage. Quite quickly they slipped into the mist as the frigate sent a broadside after them. Some of it landed, and one man, from Truro, was killed, a second lost his leg. Then they were away.

There was still an hour or so's daylight left, and it all depended on whether the mist would clear at the wrong moment. But it stayed, heavy and morose. Stephen wiped the sweat from his brow and looked around. The bitterest disappointment of his life. A prize of real value, virtually surrendered, prospect of a return to England in triumph with a rich reward – and then all to be dashed from his hands. Presumably the frigate had been attracted by the firing. They were damned lucky not to have been captured.

And then Stephen looked around for Jason and found he was not there.

II

'We'll follow them,' said Stephen. 'No choice.'

'I seen 'im with Jago and Edwards. They went forard and got cut off in the strowl. There's the three on 'em missing. They'm prisoners now, I'll lay a crown.'

'Follow 'em?' said Carter. ''Tes easier said than done in this misty wet. Like as not we'll find the frigate instead.'

'It is clearing,' said Stephen between his teeth. 'Look, the sky's light where the sun's setting. We'll follow. All through the night, if need be.'

Rain ran down their faces as they stood by the helm peering into the light fog. A pink haze flushed the mist astern of them; the rain might well lift with the onset of evening. But that was only one of their problems.

'Where are we?' said Stephen.

'Dear knows,' said Carter, 'unless the stars d'come out. And then twill only be at best guesswork so far as the land d'go. But I've a fancy we're nigh in to the French coast.'

'I didn't think so. What makes ye say that?'

'Notice them two French fishing boats coming up as we was going to board the *chaloupe*? They was crabbers. They'd not be far off the coast.'

'Near Dinard, d'ye reckon?'

'Not so far's that. More like Cap Fréhel.'

'The *Revenant* came from St Pierre,' said Hodge. ''Twas on the tiller.'

'Where is St Pierre?'

'Just north of St Malo. I know it well. Upon times when we was running goods to Roscoff we'd come east to St Pierre instead. 'Twas quieter and prices was better.'

Stephen walked up and down, up and down. So far they had been cruising more than a week and now were being sent empty away. And he had lost Jason. To his own surprise this counted for more than anything else.

'Think you could find St Pierre?' he said to Hodge.

'Maybe if the fog d'clear.'

'It would depend upon you and Carter,' Stephen said. 'I've not a great knowledge of this coast, but I know it's rocks. And the tides are lethal. But I've a fancy to follow the *Revenant* in.'

Hodge took out his watch. 'If we're near Cap Fréhel, as Mike says, we could be off St Pierre by midnight. So long as we don't fall foul of the frigate again we could run in and see how the land lies.'

III

At one o'clock in the morning they ran in to see how the land lay.

St Pierre was a fishing village, not unlike its opposite fellows in Cornwall. A horseshoe harbour with stone-built cottages climbing steeply up the granite hillside behind. A harbour wall, a tidal inlet, a church tower showing against the skyline. Even at that time in the morning there were a few lights.

The weather was not unsuitable for a raid. Thick fine rain still borne on a light sou'westerly breeze. The moon had just risen and, though obscured by clouds, prevented the harbour from being altogether dark.

The *Adolphus*, in total darkness, had dropped anchor just inside the harbour wall. They went in in the two jolly boats. Fortunately the sea was light, for each boat was crammed to the gunnels with men. There was hardly room in them to row. Each man carried a cutlass. Stephen had forbidden muskets, even pistols. 'They may squirt us,' said Stephen. 'They won't be able to shoot us tonight.'

But apart from the soaking damp, the essence of the adventure was silence.

There were only three ships in the tiny harbour and they could easily pick out the *Revenant* as the largest and because of its unusual trim. Farther up were a dozen rowing boats stranded in the sand. A light in a cottage. A light in the *Revenant*, somewhere below decks. A swinging lantern as someone moved along the quay.

On Stephen's direction they did not come alongside the *chaloupe* but paddled slowly past it, and each boat attached itself to a weed-grown iron ladder going up the harbour wall. One man was left in each boat. Stephen led the rest up to the cobble-stoned quay.

At the top he looked cautiously around, but the swinging lantern had gone. The village appeared to be asleep.

There was still the chink of light from the *Revenant*, and as Stephen dropped gently upon its forepeak he saw that this came from the main cabin. Followed by six other men, including Hodge, he crept along the deck and down the companion way. A light under the cabin door. Stephen drew his cutlass and went in.

It was the captain, sitting before a desk adding up figures in his log book. Beside him was an elderly man in a dark suit, also with a book open in front of him.

The captain half got to his feet before Stephen was across the room with the knife at his throat. Hodge had come up behind the elderly man, who looked like a merchant. The other men crowded into the cabin; the last one quietly shut the door.

'Ask him,' said Stephen. 'Ask him where he has put his prisoners.'

Hodge spoke sharply to the captain, who was trying to focus his eyes on the knife so close to his throat. A second demand brought a sharp response.

Hodge said: 'They be locked in a fish cellar at the end o' the quay.'

Stephen said: 'Tell him he shall lead us there. If he makes a sound I will cut his throat. You, Vage, and you, Moon, stay with this other man. If he utters a word open him up. *Now* . . .'

The captain was forced to his feet and thrust out of the cabin. Stephen whispered orders to his men still clustered on the deck. They were to stay quiet until he called them, remain where their shapes would not be seen. Then he named the three from the cabin, and Hodge, to go with him.

It was a shambling dark procession which made its way to the end of the long quay. The only sound was when someone caught his foot on an uneven flagstone or splashed into a pool of water. Mindful of his own life, the captain was as quiet as anyone. He stopped before a big stone-built shed on the edge of the village. From here you could see the one light, which was in fact several lights when you got closer, and came from the windows of an inn. Talking and laughter could be heard.

The captain stood before the door of the shed and spread his hands helplessly.

'What does he say?' demanded Stephen.

'That he does not have the key to the padlock.'

The knife came nearer to the Frenchman's throat. 'Where is it?'

'He says the gendarme will have it. He be in Le Lion d'Or.'

Stephen stooped to peer at the padlock. He gestured to Hodge to try to force the lock with his cutlass, but it was clear that the knife would break first.

'Reckon we'd best go,' one of the men muttered. 'They'll come to no 'urt as prisoners . . .'

'Shut your trap!' Stephen snapped. 'Keast, go you back to the *chaloupe* and find a marling spike. Hurry, but stay quiet.'

'Aye, aye,' said Keast and turned and slipped back the way they had come.

Now that there was nothing to do but wait they could take in the noises inside the inn. The sailors had returned safely after a long voyage and were celebrating. Particularly, thought Stephen, they were celebrating the narrow escape they had had this afternoon from capture and a long internment in England.

He bent to the door and listened. He could certainly hear nothing inside, and the monstrous thought came to him that perhaps the French captain was deceiving him. If he was he should pay with his life. Leaving Hodge to guard the captain, he walked round the cellar: there were no windows but there might have been another door. There was, but when he opened it it led into a small room with bags of salt. He came back to the front and stooped by the door again.

'Jason,' he called.

No answer.

'Tell him,' Stephen said to Hodge, 'if the prisoners are not here I will kill him.' Hodge was about to speak when Stephen said: 'Wait.'

There was a burst of laughter from the inn.

'Jason!' he said again.

'Father!' It was a whisper.

Stephen felt a surge of triumph. 'Jason. Quiet, boy. We have come to get ye. Are you well?'

350

'Jago has a bad leg. I am well. And Tom Edwards. Father, can you open the door?'

'Not yet. Have patience. And keep quiet. Can Jago walk?'

There was a murmur inside. 'He says he will try.'

'He *must* try.'

A warning hand touched his arm. The door of the inn opened and two men came out. The lantern light flooded over the cobbled street as they came arm in arm towards the crouching group; then they turned up the quay towards the *Revenant*.

They were both well gone in drink and stumbled several times on the way, supporting each other.

They were half-way up the quay when little Keast slid out of the gloom beside the waiting men, who had been so concerned to watch the French sailors that they had not seen him coming back. He carried two marling spikes. 'Reckoned one might break,' he said.

Stephen attacked the lock with less regard to silence than he had previously shown. There should be plenty of his men waiting to receive the two Frenchmen when they stepped aboard, but whether they could be disposed of without rousing the town remained to be seen.

The first spike bent but the second, forced in on top of it, did the trick. The padlock broke. The door squeaked open. Jason came out first, flung his arms round his father.

'Didn't I say, lads? Didn't I say he'd come for us?'

'Quiet!' said Stephen, giving his son a hug. 'And quick. Now come on, quick. There's much still to do. But *quiet*, everybody!'

Two of the other men were helping Jago out. Edwards too was limping. In all this the thoughtful Hodge was still holding a knife to the captain's throat.

There was still no sound from the *Revenant*, so it looked as if the returning sailors had been taken care of.

The party began to return along the quay. The rain was heavier than ever, misting men only a few yards from each other.

They reached the *Revenant*. Twelve men shinned down the ladder to return to the jolly boats, cast off, pulled round to the stern of the *chaloupe*; four other men ran the length of the ship, dropped lines to the boats, which began to row away. Hodge had gone below with the captain. Jago and Edwards were aboard. Keast and another man had cast off the stern rope securing the *Revenant* to a bollard. Stephen and Jason stooped to throw off the forward rope.

'Halt!' shouted a voice. *'Nom de la République! Qui va là?'*

It was a French soldier who had come suddenly out of the moonlit fog. For a second they stared at each other. Stephen lifted his cutlass. The soldier discharged his musket full in Stephen's face.

The hammer came down to strike the cap and the cap failed to detonate.

Stephen laughed out loud and stabbed the man in the chest. Then, unable to withdraw his cutlass, he left it in the fallen figure and jumped aboard the *Revenant* as Jason cast off.

The two boats began to row the *chaloupe* out of the harbour, and the Cornishmen swarmed up the rigging preparing to make sail.

Three

I

If anyone had spoken of 'the dark night of the soul' to Demelza she would not have known where the words came from but she would perfectly have understood what they meant.

When Julia died all those years ago it had been when she was just recovering from the morbid sore throat herself and she had felt the loss as a mortal blow from which she could hardly recover. Julia had been nineteen months old. But she and Ross were young, and after all the despair, which had included Ross's trial for his life and near bankruptcy, they had somehow climbed together out of a pit, which had never seemed so deep since.

But Jeremy, their second child, was twenty-four. Born in a time of great stress, he had been with them ever since, through all the vicissitudes of life, all their joys, all their sorrows. Because of that, because of his age, he was more a part of the family than any of the three younger ones – even Clowance, who was only three years younger. What she had said to Caroline was only the truth: whenever she thought of Jeremy she thought of a thousand days of caring.

When she last saw him, last December, he had grown better looking. The tall loose-jointed young man with a tendency to stoop had filled out with his army training, had matured, his hair long, his face less clear-skinned, his smile more sophisticated. No wonder Cuby had at last fallen in love with him.

Too late to save him from the army, a captaincy, and a march to his death in the mud of Flanders. Demelza knew that Clowance blamed Cuby for this, saying it was his broken love-affair that had spurred him to go into the army. It could be true; Demelza was not sure; there was another reason which perhaps only she would ever know. Though there were a man and a woman somewhere, one of

353

them probably her son-in-law, who might yet throw light on the subject. (Not that she wanted light. Better for it always to be hidden, as the sacks had been hidden, in the dark cave in Kellow's Ladder.)

Last time he was home he had seemed on the point of saying something to her, attempting an explanation of the unexplainable. 'Perhaps in joining the army I was trying to escape from myself.' And then, when he had seen the loving cup, which she had carefully cleaned and polished and put on the sideboard, he had said: 'Some-day, sometime – not now – perhaps when we are both a few years older – I would like to talk to you.'

And she had smiled at him and said: 'Don't leave it too late.'

It had been prophetic without her knowing it. With the war over it had then been much more likely that she would predecease him. She only wished it had been so.

On Sunday, the 16th July Demelza for once was on her own. Nothing seemed to get better with the passage of the days. This morning she had walked only as far along the beach as Wheal Leisure and then turned back, having neither the energy nor the initiative to go further. A rarely beautiful day, the night wind having dropped as the sun came up, the whole beach in a state of warm confusion as the waves trembled and broke and piled up and trembled and broke again, a magisterial demonstration of power and authority. These were neap-tides, so there was not so much of a run as sometimes, but every now and then a feathery froth of water an inch or two deep slithered up to and around her feet, soaking her shoes and the hem of her skirt.

She might as well go in, she thought, and make a dish of tea; though she was neither thirsty nor hungry. It was something to do.

John Gimlett stood in front of her. She looked up at this unexpected sight.

'The master is back.'

'*What? When?*'

''Alf an hour gone. Didn't know quite where to find ee, ma'am.'

Demelza hastened her step, but not too much. She did not feel quite able to face him.

He was in the garden, her garden, looking at some of her flowers. At first she hardly recognized him, he looked so very old.

She came to the gate, opened it. He heard the click of the latch, looked up.

'Ross!' She flew to him.

Gimlett discreetly went in by the yard door.

II

'Take more tea,' she said. 'You must be thirsty after so long a ride.'

'Your garden,' he said. 'It has lacked your touch.'

'Like other things,' she said. 'But twill alter now.'

'Your hollyhocks . . .'

'Jane said they was damaged by a late frost. And I think your mother's lilac tree needs hard cutting, else it will die.'

'Had you just been to the mine?'

'No, no. I was walking . . . Ben has been very good. Everyone has been very good. You're so *thin*, Ross.'

A cow was roaring somewhere in the valley. It was a distant, rural sound, almost lost in the silence of the house.

'There's so much to tell you,' Ross said, 'I don't know where to begin.'

'Maybe the first day you are home is not the right time.'

'I lay at Tregothnan last night,' he said. 'I put in at St Austell, thought I could reach home, borrowed a nag but the nag went lame . . . If there is one recurring theme in my history it is that every horse I hire or borrow goes lame . . . Or is shot from under me –'

'One was shot from under you?'

'Two, to be exact. But that is for telling some other time. Demelza.'

'Yes?'

'Can you believe it is only in January that we left here? It has been a lifetime.'

'More than a lifetime.'

'Aye, that too.'

She busied herself, pouring more tea for him and then for herself. They both took milk but no sugar. Tea with sugar is not a Cornish custom.

'Little Jane Ellery was bit by a dog yesterday,' she said. 'A stray

355

dog near Sawle. He behaved very strange and snatched and snarled, so I think they have put him down. They called Dwight and to be safe he cut into the tooth marks to make a clean wound and then disinfected it with nitric acid. Poor little Jane squealed her head off, but a sweetmeat seemed soon to set her to rights. But of course they will be anxious for a day or two.'

Ross sipped his tea. They sat quietly in the parlour.

Demelza said: 'On Friday Sephus Billing killed an adder with five young in it. He was drawing potatoes at the time. Side of the Long Field.'

'They were always fond of that wall,' Ross said. 'My father often warned me.'

'Jud used to call them long cripples,' Demelza said.

'I know.'

The brightness of the day outside made the parlour dark.

Demelza said: 'And how is Cuby?'

'She will come later. I told her she must stay with us until after the baby is born. Then she must decide her own life. You would agree with that?'

'Yes. Oh, yes.'

Ross said: 'She was very good most of the time. She only broke down once. I have never heard a woman sob like it. It was – such an ugly noise – like someone sawing wood.'

'Don't.'

Ross said: 'I was so fortunate just to find Jeremy in time. He did not seem to be in any pain. He – he sent his love to you and asked us to look after Cuby.'

Demelza got up, took out a handkerchief and gently dabbed his eyes. Then she wiped her own.

'There is much to do here, Ross. We have been neglecting our home. Some of the seed is not sown yet. And we need to sell some lambs – I waited for you to know how many. And the damp in the library ceiling is getting worse.'

He looked at her.

She said: 'And there's the white store turnips. Cal Trevail was asking me yesterday –'

'Why are you alone like this? I thought you would never be left alone.'

'They did their best . . . Stephen came back from some successful adventure last week. When he heard about Jeremy he came straight over, stayed two nights. He had to go back, then, but wanted Clowance to stay on. I said *no*. I said *no*, you would be here soon, and for a little while I *wanted* to be alone. Twas true. I had no talk left. My tongue has been heavy all the time – ever since I knew.'

'But the others. Verity and –'

'Verity left on Tuesday because Andrew is very slight. It is some heart affection. Caroline's two girls are just home and she has not seen them for a term. Henry is in the cove with Mrs Kemp and they should be back soon. Isabella-Rose is at school.'

'You sent her?'

'To Mrs Hemple's for half a term. I sent her before I – had your letter.'

'How did she take the news?'

'As you would expect,' said Demelza lightly, controlling herself. 'The piano needs tuning badly. The damp air gets at the strings. And this old spinet, do you think we should throw it out, Ross?'

'Never. It is too much a part of our lives . . . The Falmouths sent their love and sympathy.'

'Good of them. I expect they will be concerned about Fitzroy. Many, many people have sent their love and sympathy, Ross. Tis very – warming to have so much – love and sympathy. Even Mr Odgers . . . I think we shall have to do something about Mr Odgers soon, Ross. He took off his wig in church last Sunday, I'm told, and threw it at the choir. He said afterwards he thought he was driving away the greenfly. They have been very bad this year, the greenfly; I think it is the warm summer.'

Ross said: 'And how is Clowance?'

'Well. But you know how she felt for Jeremy.'

'And Stephen?'

Demelza put her tea-cup back on the tray and got up.

'Will you take me for a bathe, Ross?'

'What?' He stared again.

'The sea is heavy, so heavy and the sun is broiling. I have not bathed since last year – I could not without you.'

Ross hesitated. 'It is not seemly on my first day home.'

'Nor is it,' said Demelza, 'but I want you to do it for me – with

357

me. There is time before dinner. It will help – I think it will help – to wash away our tears.'

III

Ross said: 'I am worried about Demelza.'

'Yes,' said Dwight, then nodded his head. 'Yes.'

'She is physically well, so far as you know?'

'She has made no complaints. Of course the shock is still affecting her.'

'Yet not in some ways quite as I would have expected. I am happy if it is sincere but – well, she is so full of interest in all the affairs of Nampara – just as if nothing had happened.'

'Is that how she seems to you? It is not as she has been before you came. She cared for nothing. Often she would not talk even to her family. She spoke to Caroline, but very little. Most times she would just sit there.'

'You think, then, this show of liveliness has been put on for my benefit?'

'She's a very strong personality, Ross. She may feel that she has to be supportive of you.'

'If it is put on, one wonders how long it will endure – and can only guess at what it is hiding.'

'It may not change. Once you have assumed a mantle it may become a part of everyday wear.'

Ross had ridden over and found Dwight in his laboratory, Caroline and the children being out riding. Dwight had walked out with him and they were sitting on a wooden garden seat looking across the lawn towards some trees, beyond which, if you walked a little farther, you could see Sawle Church.

'It is difficult to tell her anything about what happened,' Ross said. 'She heads me off, turns the point, brings up some other subject. Well, perhaps that is natural. One cannot go on probing at a wound – or should not, I imagine. Last night . . .'

He stopped. Dwight said nothing, staring at a squirrel swarming up the branch of a tree.

'Last night,' Ross said, 'she would hardly let me touch her. We lay beside each other in bed, just holding hands. When I woke early this morning just as it was coming light she was gone, standing by the window looking out. When she heard me move she came back, slipped into bed, took my hand again.'

Dwight said: 'When Caroline lost Sarah . . . You remember? She left me, went to London, stayed with her aunt. I did not know when, or if, she was coming back. This is much, much worse – for Demelza *and* for you. Sarah was a baby – like your Julia. Jeremy was just happily married, everything before him. I can only guess at what you both feel.'

The squirrel had disappeared. Rooks were clapping their wings somewhere. They sounded like an unenthusiastic audience.

Ross said: 'Of course there is much I cannot tell her – would not. You saw my letter to her?'

'Yes.'

'I said little enough about that last day . . . When Wellington entrusted me with the message for Prince Frederick of the Netherlands I knew the distance to be about ten miles, but I expected to be back in the very early afternoon. But on the way back – perhaps I was a thought incautious and steered too close to the fighting – I was almost overrun by a French cavalry charge. Then my horse was killed, and as I fell with it a piece of round shot struck me in the chest – just below the chest – and I was knocked out for what must have been half an hour. And for a time after that I could barely stand.'

Ross fumbled in his pocket and took out a piece of crumpled metal which Dwight could see had been a watch.

'My father's,' said Ross. 'It was the one thing the French left me when I was interned. When I escaped I intended to sell it to buy food or shelter or perhaps a weapon of some sort; but in the end I did not have to. Had I done so I should not be here today.'

Dwight took the crushed watch, turned it over. The face had gone altogether, and the gold case was splayed as if it had been hit with a hammer.

'Then that is one piece of extraordinary good fortune.'

'It was intended for Jeremy. If I had given it him perhaps he would be here instead of me. Better if it had been that way.'

'Have you shown this to Demelza?'

359

'No. Nor shall do.'

'Well . . . perhaps not. Not yet anyway.'

The sun came out, warming them as they sat together, two old friends.

'There are many things I cannot tell her,' Ross said, 'even if she would listen. That night after Jeremy's death I could not sleep. I was not hungry but was sickly empty of stomach – and thirsty, so thirsty – and black with powder and stiff from my small injuries. I lay down in the hut for a while, trying to wrap an old blanket round me – just beside him – but after a while I got up again and began to wander about the battlefield. There were many still wounded, crying for attention, but I was too dazed to help – and in any case had no means to help – no salves, no bandages, no water. Have you ever seen a battlefield, Dwight?'

'No.'

'I had. Or thought I had. Not like this. Never anything like this. Of course you have been in a battle at sea, have suffered the horrors of the prisoner-of-war camp . . .'

'Yes . . .'

'Before he died Jeremy spoke of the horses. They were almost the worst part of it. Some were lying with their entrails hanging out, yet still alive. Others dragged themselves around in terrible stages of mutilation. Some were simply wandering loose, having lost their owners. I caught one such and rode as far south as Quatre Bras, where all the fighting had been on the Friday.'

'Was the fighting at Waterloo over by this time?'

'Almost. There were some Prussian troops still about, and not too particular whom they shot at; there were a few camps of them, bivouacking, cooking their meals; but the main body had passed on. Quatre Bras was a ghastly sight. You of all people must be familiar with what happens to a body after it is dead.'

'Yes . . .'

'Those at Quatre Bras had mostly been dead for two days. It was a brilliant moonlit night, with only a rare cloud passing across the moon. In the moonlight they looked like negroes.'

'Yes . . .'

'And swollen into grotesque shapes. Bursting out of their uniforms – those who were left with uniforms. Many had been stripped naked by the peasants; most of those who had not, lay upon their faces with their pockets pulled out and their boots taken, their papers scattered everywhere. Of course it was not just the peasants. The soldiers themselves: the French when they advanced, the British and Germans when the French retreated . . . The stench in the courtyard of the farm at Quatre Bras was intolerable . . . Perhaps you wonder why I tell you all this.'

'No, I think it should be spoken of.'

'There is no one else I would say this to. When I was in America as a young man I saw enough to fill my crop. But not like this. That was skirmishing. This was head-on conflict of a most terrible kind.'

They sat for a while in silence. Ross fingered his scar.

'I found one man still alive. That is why I went into the yard of the farmhouse; there's a well there; I went to get him water. Why he was alive I don't know; his skull was crushed; but some people take a deal of killing. He was a Frenchman, and when he found I understood him he asked me to kill him and finish off his misery.'

Dwight glanced at Ross's lean, restless face. More than ever lean now, and the veins in his neck showing.

'I found I could not, Dwight. There had been so much blood spilt; for three days I had been surrounded by death. And then I thought of the French brigadier, whom I had come greatly to like and respect, even though he was a Bonapartist. And I knew he would say it was only a kindness to kill this suffering man. Perhaps even a duty. But still I could not.'

'I think you were right.'

'I spent more time on him than anyone else on the battlefield. I bathed his face and his crushed head and tried to tie up his other wounds. Then I put a beaker of water beside him and left him – presumably to die.'

'Were there no surgeons anywhere?'

'A few. Working desperately, trying to help the worst wounded. Though from the way I saw them treating men then and afterwards in Brussels, I wonder if they did not help to kill off more wounded men than they cured.'

'Ours is still a primitive science.'

Ross got up. 'By God, I should think so! But you, Dwight, have often said that your profession was over-fond of the leech. You

bleed your patients far less than most of your fellows. These men –
these so-called surgeons – were bleeding men who had lost half their
blood already!'

Dwight got up too, patted his leg with the little riding cane he
carried. 'The medical view is that if a wound is inflamed, bleeding
will help to reduce the inflammation. It's not a theory I totally
subscribe to – as you know – but I was not there and so cannot
speak much against them. I'm afraid most physical treatment is
rough and ready. Not least when it comes to war.'

'The arms and legs that were hacked off! I know it is better than
gangrene – we both know too well that – that anything is better
than gangrene . . . But afterwards, to sterilize with hot tar, and
then, as like as not, a clyster of soap and water and a pill of senna
pods in lard, to clear the humours!'

They began to walk across the paddock towards the distant trees.
After a minute Dwight said: 'Is your ankle . . . ?'

'Well enough.'

They walked on.

'Where is Demelza now?'

'I left her in the garden with Matthew Mark Martin. Jane Gimlett
says she has hardly been in it since she came home.'

'We have never spoken of your baronetcy. I believe it was a good
thing to take.'

'Good? Dear God! It is a cynical twist that Jeremy will now no
longer be here to inherit it.'

'Henry will.'

Ross looked up. 'Maybe. Well, yes. If *he* survives.'

'There should be no wars after this for generations. And if there
were Henry would have no need to take part. You have three
handsome children left.'

'And a grandchild on the way . . . It was strange how I met Cuby.
And horrible. On the Monday morning I was able to purloin a farm
cart and I put my horse – the one I had found on Sunday night –
into the shafts, and I lifted – I lifted my son into the back and
covered him with a blanket. The road back to Brussels was –
impossible, with the sick and wounded, with returning soldiers,
with ambulances and wagons; but we went with the stream. Then
I saw this coach coming *against* the stream with a man riding before

362

it with a drawn sword, forcing people to give way. I paid them little attention, for I was too sunk in my own sorrow. But I remember noticing that the coach horses were screaming with fright. Coming into the battle zone from Brussels, they were not used to the smell of blood and corruption. Then suddenly a voice called: "Captain Poldark!" It was Cuby, my daughter-in-law.'

They stopped at the edge of the paddock. The vegetation here was lush with cow parsley and ragged robin and wild marguerites. Ross wiped his forehead.

'In all those days of battle that was the second worst moment for me. Her round pretty anxious face changed when I told her, she went deathly pale. She jumped down and insisted – *insisted* on seeing Jeremy, on uncovering his face . . . Then – then she looked at me as if I had stabbed her to the heart. Which indeed I had – and would have given my own life willingly not to have done so.'

Bees were humming around a clump of foxgloves, struggling in and out of the bells like fat robbers peering into caves.

Ross said: 'Sir William de Lancey, Wellington's Chief of Staff, had been gravely wounded, and his wife was forcing her way out to Waterloo to see him. Cuby had asked if she might have a lift and had been given one . . . There were other women going out, amid all the confusion, seeking their husbands, hoping to find them alive. Magdalene de Lancey found her husband and nursed him for a week in a cottage in Waterloo, and then he died.'

They began to walk back.

Dwight said: 'It is hot today. Let's go indoors for a while. Will you take a glass of lemonade?'

Ross gave a short harsh laugh. 'In most of the crises of my life, the big disappointments – as when Elizabeth married Francis – the tragedy when we lost Julia – the stresses when Demelza became infatuated with Hugh Armitage – and they all seem to be *dwarfed* – *are* dwarfed – by this; in all of them I have taken to the brandy bottle. Now I am offered lemonade!'

'There is brandy if you want it.'

'I drank very little after Jeremy's death; first because there was *nothing* – except one flask I found half full of *genever*. Then I was preoccupied looking after Cuby. Then there were the burial arrangements. With one thing and another . . . I drank more than usual on the trip home, but the taste was lacking. As my medical man, would you advise a glass of lemonade at this stage?'

'I am going to take one.'

'It guarantees absolute oblivion?'

'As good as brandy in the long run.'

Ross said: 'I'm not sure that I want to regard anything in the long run from now on . . . Tell me, Dwight, one thing extra that has been concerning me . . .'

'Yes?'

'You know Demelza all her life has been a thought fond of drink – some drink – chiefly port. When I returned yesterday there was no sign. Have you seen any sign?'

'I have hardly seen her in the evening, but Caroline would have mentioned it, I am sure.'

'She did over-drink at one time, you know. I came home one night and found her incapable. That was about a year ago.'

'I didn't know. I'm sorry.'

'It never happened again. Perhaps it was a passing phase. Human nature is unfathomable, is it not? Demelza has lost her dearly beloved son and yet appears to stay sober. I am in similar straits and content myself with lemonade. Perhaps grief – real grief – brings sobriety. Or are we just growing old and no longer consider it worth while to make gestures of protest?'

'I suspect you will live to make many more gestures of protest yet,' said Dwight, 'but they are no better for being seen through the bottom of a brandy glass.'

Four

Stephen said: 'It has been a bitter time for you, dear heart; and in truth tis sad for me. All I said to your mother was God's truth. Jeremy was a real true friend. We did – many things together. All through the time when you and I were estranged, him and me, we were still friends. In that year when we was separated he never, of course, took my side against you, but he was never anything but sympathetic to the way I felt. In fact we were both deprived in a similar way. It made for a fellow feeling. He was a brave man and it's bitter, bitter that he should be gone now, just when he was happy married and his wife expecting a baby. An' I'm deeply sorry.'

'Thank you, Stephen.'

He was rowing her back from the *Adolphus*, which she had been visiting for the first time since its famous voyage.

'And thank you for this lovely present,' she added, fingering the heavy coral necklace about her throat. 'It is marvellous pretty, and I want to wear it all the time.'

'So you shall. And others I shall buy you.'

He paused in his rowing, allowed the boat to drift of its own momentum.

'Jeremy's death,' he said, 'Jeremy's death has put a damper on what I did; but I can't but rejoice at the way everything else has turned up aces for me – for the both of us. I can't but rejoice, Clowance, and that's God's truth too.'

'I don't expect you to. In a month – in a few months – I expect I shall be able to rejoice with you.'

'Ye must be able to rejoice now, that we are right out of the wood!'

'Are we *really* safe?'

'Oh yes. Oh yes. By a long haul.'

'Can you bear to tell me again?' Clowance asked, knowing that he would like nothing better. 'At Nampara, in the bedroom, it seemed so unreal beside Jeremy's death, I could hardly take it in. You captured this ship called – called . . .'

'*Revenant*. She was a *chaloupe*. What in England we more or less call a sloop. But bigger than we build 'em in England. She was bigger than we were, bigger than a packet ship, and carried a crew, I reckon, of about twenty-five, and four four-pounders and any amount of small arms. *And* when we rescued Jason and the other two, we bore away with us the captain and a rich merchant who were aboard at the time, and can be ransomed!'

'Why did you take the – the *chaloupe* to Bristol?'

'I knew more people there, see. And to tell the truth I was wary of Sir George. Ye know, the Warleggans have a long reach, and after what has happened I wouldn't trust him as far as I can spit. I thought, maybe somehow he'll try to seize part of the cargo in lieu of a debt – or say it was illegal because of the end of the war and should be returned – or any trumped up charge. I thought I was safer in Bristol. I thought first of Plymouth, but I felt safer going home.'

Clowance shivered slightly; she could not have told why, for the day was warm.

Stephen did not notice. 'Mind, there was a time when I regretted that choosing. Once safe across the Channel, I crept close in to the English coast, not fancying a meeting with a French frigate again; but not far off Penzance the weather turned foul; a strong gale blew up sudden from the south. There was a great peril of being embayed, so I set every stitch of canvas the masts would bear and began to claw off the shore. The *Revenant* was hull down way to the south-east of us and riding it out well. I've never seen *Adolphus* in such a state before. She plunged through the water so fast clouds of spray were frothing to her very topsails. I thought the canvas would any minute carry away. But it did not, and after an hour the worst was over. Both vessels rounded Land's End before nightfall.'

Clowance let her hand trail in the water. 'And the cargo?'

'M'dear, we're rich! Not rich by Warleggan standards, but well found and independent of Warleggans for good an' all. *Revenant*

366

was eighteen days out of New York. Skins, all sorts of skins to make coats; leather and boots; saddlery; 50 tons of pig iron, steel rods, five cases of apothecaries' wares, 36 wheels and axles, 48 kettles – I lost count . . . Aside from the value of the ship itself!'

'And what is happening now?'

'The Cornish Naval Bank has a corresponding partner, as they call it, in Bristol. As the money comes in, twill be transferred into my name in Falmouth. I was tempted to stay on and on, but I felt I must come back and see you, tell you this wonderful news. Alas, that you had such bad news yourself!'

'You have shareholders to pay?'

'Oh, yes. And the crew. But the crew I have now paid off. They're all roaring happy and consider themselves rich, small though their portions are compared to mine.' Stephen shipped one oar and steered past some wreckage floating in the harbour. 'The shareholders will take thirty-five per cent. The rest will set us up very nicely, and *very* independent.'

'Have you seen Warleggan's Bank yet?'

'No. I shall go in tomorrow. All the way home – and twas none too placid a trip for July neither – I have been asking myself how I ought to do it. I thought at first just to tell them straight just what I thought of 'em. I thought over just what I should say. But then I considered further and changed me mind. I've decided to act just as he might act if he was in my shoes.'

'What does that mean, Stephen?'

'I shall act very polite. I shall tell 'em nothing of what I have been doing or what profits I have made – though no doubt they'll hear about it or already have. I shall go in tomorrow and see Lander and simply say: "Good-day to ye, Mr Lander, it so happens that I have been able to obtain finance through another bank, and as they impose no restrictions, well, I think I shall transfer my account to them from the end of this week. Any accommodation bills I have signed, Mr Lander, will be paid the moment they come due, and I will continue, with your permission, Mr Lander, to trade in Penryn and Falmouth as an independent shipper." Something like that, but smoother. "Good-day to ye, Mr Lander," I shall say. "I hope I find you well. Now it so happens, quite by chance, like, that I have been approached by another bank, who offer me all the accommodation I need without imposing any restrictions as to the overdraft I choose to carry –"'

'I am glad you will do it that way because –'

'Well, because of Harriet, in the main, who helped me survive. And also – well, look you, we might still go to Cardew sometime. I reckon if George can go in for being a hypocrite, so can I!'

Coming in towards the quay, they had to row between a couple of rotting hulks long since grounded in the mud. It was half tide and the barnacled ribs stuck up into the warm sunlight, glinting green and black and orange.

'And from now it will be legitimate trading again?'

'Oh yes. No choice anyhow. The war is over. It all just worked in time for us.'

'For us, yes.'

This time he did notice her shiver. 'Sorry, sorry, it will be a sore place for a long while.'

After a minute she said: 'And Jason?'

'Jason?'

'He will – stay on with you?'

'For sure . . .' He allowed the slight current to carry them in. 'D'ye know, it was the greatest moment when I broke into the fish cellar and rescued him. I think then I really came up to his expectations of me as a father! . . . And then to steal away with the *Revenant* right from under their noses! It was Nelson stuff! D'ye know, I've got me quite a reputation, Clowance.'

'Yes?' She smiled at him.

'Yes. When I took me prize into Bristol – that was a brave moment too! We worked into the harbour no more than five minutes ahead of *Revenant*, which, as is the custom, was flying the British flag atop the French flag flown upside down. Lord, when we got to the quay there was a crowd cheering! And the crews cheered too, you stake your life, knowing the pickings that were going to be theirs! . . . And though I took me prize to Bristol all those sailors were Cornishmen, from Penryn and Falmouth mainly, and they haven't been slow to tell folk of the success of the voyage and the way we took out the Frenchman. Why, if I asked for another crew today I should be swamped wi' volunteers!'

The dinghy slid slowly in beside the quay. Stephen hooked the painter over a bollard and jumped out to give Clowance a hand.

'We'll get the house being built again right away. And this time I shall buy meself a good hunter, as good as Nero. We'll have the stables built first so that they'll be well housed . . . Then we'll ride and hunt together on equal terms!'

'Even when the hunt meets at Cardew?'

'Even then. That's what I said. Another good reason not to fall out with Harriet!' He laughed infectiously and they began to walk up to their cottage hand in hand.

Just below them a half-dozen naked urchins were taking it in turns to leap into the harbour, holding their noses as they jumped and squealing with delight when they came to the surface among the floating seaweed and the apple cores and the driftwood.

'And I have a mind too,' he said, 'to buy me another ship when the right one comes along at the right price. Three's the proper number, increases the profit, not too many to look after.'

'Andrew will be back from New York any time now,' said Clowance. 'But if this voyage has been a success I do not suppose he will want to leave the Packet Service again.'

'I was not thinking of Andrew,' Stephen said. 'I was thinking of Jason.'

When she looked surprised he added: 'Oh, I know he is young yet. And he must learn more navigation. I can tell you I'm none too clear on some points meself, but he knows *nothing*. Yet in a year or two he'll be ready for his own ship. Nothing so big as *Adolphus* but maybe the size of the *Lady Clowance*. There was good men on this trip, dear heart, that I'd not employed before. Carter handled the ship real well and Hodge was a godsend. Hodge I must keep in with. Both of 'em I've given special bonuses to. If I buy another vessel one or both of 'em would be ideal to be with Jason on his first voyages, to keep him on course, so to say.'

At the entrance to their house she paused, took off her straw hat and let the sunlight and the breezes play with her blonde hair. He looked at her appreciatively. Pity about Jeremy, of course, but you couldn't grieve for ever, and here he was, with a small fortune in the bank – the reward of a daring and dangerous exploit – and with a very peach of a wife who, by her independence and intelligence and refusal to conform to an accepted pattern, intrigued him the more. He wanted her and knew she wanted him. Life was wonderful and he felt wonderful. No one could blame him for that.

The harbour below them was glimmering, iridescent in the sunshine. Beyond it the bay of the Fal, surrounded by cornfields, looked like a majestic garden. Tall masts swung at anchor; towards Trefusis Point a four-masted full-rigged ship was just shaking out her sails. She fired her signal gun to show she was leaving. Small boats were everywhere. People sat on the wall higher up, gossiping in the summer sun.

'I must go to Flushing first thing tomorrow,' said Clowance. 'Mother tells me Uncle Andrew is serious ill.'

'I'll row you,' said Stephen, happily conscious that for him all the pressure was off.

II

Andrew Blamey senior had had some sort of a heart seizure, with a fast heart-beat and respiratory trouble. He was sixty-seven, and the apothecary took a grave view of the matter. However, a second man, a physician called Mather, recently arrived from Bath, prescribed Dr Withering's new drug digitalis, with mercury pills, and this produced such a remarkable improvement that when Clowance and Stephen went to see the invalid he was downstairs in his favourite chair by the window watching the movements of shipping through his spyglass.

Stephen was a rare visitor in this house, but was now much more welcome, its being known that, although he had aided young Andrew to leave the Packet Service and embark on some far from respectable adventures, he had now contrived to help Andrew return to the Service with no apparent loss of seniority. Stephen too was very much on his best behaviour today, deferring to Captain Blamey in sea-going matters and answering modestly when Verity questioned him about his exploits. Looking at her second cousin – whom she always regarded as an aunt – Clowance remembered something her father had once said: 'Verity was never good-looking but she has the prettiest mouth in Great Britain.' Clowance had also heard garbled accounts of how her own mother, defying Poldark hostility to the match, had contrived to bring Captain Blamey and Miss Verity together.

Anyway, it had been a famous match, and it was only a pity that their one child, thoroughly taking and agreeable though he was, could not quite overcome his weakness for gambling and drink.

Clowance was proud of Stephen today. When he set out to subdue his animal spirits and to attune himself to the people he was visiting it was hard to fault his manners or his behaviour. She was grateful to him. It just showed what success could do.

III

Someone of about Blamey's age on the north coast also happened to be ill at this time, but in spite of having the attention of the best physician in the West Country, he refused wilfully to get better. Old Tholly Tregirls, one-armed reprobate and adventurer, having suffered fiercely from asthma all his life, was now dying of something quite different. Ross had just time to call and see him. Tholly died, as he had lived for the last twenty years, at Sally Chill-Offs. When Ross called he raised himself from his bed and said: 'Well, Young Cap'n, I hear tell as you've had some ill-luck yourself, eh? Sapling cut off in its prime, eh? Master Jeremy gone. Poor jawb. I reckon twas very poor jawb.'

Ross noticed that so far people in the neighbourhood had not changed their form of address to him. He was still 'Cap'n P'ldark', or just 'Cap'n'. That at least was a blessing. But after Tholly had gone there would be no one left to call him 'Young Cap'n' to distinguish him from his father.

'Tis all these 'ere wars,' said Tholly, rubbing his scarred and wasted face with a dirty hand. 'Public wars, I call 'em. Reckon you was lucky ever to come safe 'ome from that one in 'Merica. Public wars is no good. Public wars don't bring no good to no one. Small wars, private wars, they're different, can profit you upon times.'

'Like privateering,' said Ross, 'or ditching a Preventive man.'

Tholly showed his black and broken teeth in a grimace. 'That's correct, Young Cap'n, that correct. You know this surgeon – him we rescued from the prison camp all them years agone; that were a

371

great adventure, that were – you'd think he'd do better for me than 'e 'as – out of *gratitude*. Gratitude, you'd think. But he don't put me on me feet. D'ye know after all these years me asthma have *gone*. Cough too. Couldn't cough now if I wished for it. Gone these last six weeks or more. But I can't *eat*. Can't seem t'eat. Sally bring up good soup. But it don't lie.'

Ross stared round the small untidy room. Tholly followed his glance.

'I took it off, see? Twas irksome.' He waved the stub of his arm towards where the hook and its sheath and leather straps stood upon an old chest of drawers pointing menacingly towards the blackened rafters. 'When I'm gone, Young Cap'n, I want you t'ave it, see? Remind you o' me, see. Maybe missus won't like it so well, but put it in your own room, somewhere where she don't go.'

Ross went to the open window, where the air was sweeter. 'Thank you, Tholly.' He could say nothing else.

Silence fell. Ross thought of Jeremy.

Tholly said: 'Reckon I'll never sell you another 'orse.'

'Oh maybe, maybe. While there's life.'

'I got a long memory for these parts, Young Cap'n. I were born at St Ann's. I mind the time afore ever your 'ouse, afore Nampara was ever builded. Used to be a little pond there, I recollect. There was ducks in it, kept by an old man living in Mellin cottages. Sometimes when twas dry weather, folks in Carnmore – afore Surgeon Choake's time – would send their men with their two cows to drink.'

'Ah,' said Ross. 'How old are you, Tholly?'

'God knows. Or maybe He's forgot too. I mind the two brothers at Trenwith, Charles and Joshua, your papa. Charles were always jealous o' his younger brother. Charles might be comin' in for the big 'ouse and the property, but Joshua were the good-looking one, all the women was attracted to him; then 'e wed the prettiest girl and he came 'ere to live 's own carefree life regardless of the county. I remember Joshua building Nampara. Up it went, block by block.'

'What year was that, Tholly?'

'God knows . . . I were about eleven year old. Ten or eleven. Miners builded it mostly, Young Cap'n, them as worked at Wheal Grace and all around. That's why tis crude built – not like Trenwith. Reckon Charles's great-great-grandfather had proper masons, brought from up-country. Old Cap'n never cared. I mind he said to me once: "The longer I live, Tholly, but more God-cursed certain sure I am that the Wise Men never came from the East!" Made me laff, that. He just wanted a place of his own, see? Built near the cove, convenient for him to fish or smuggle, overlooking the beach where he could line-fish and bathe and walk and gallop on the sands. 'E began a line you've kept up, Young Cap'n. Master Jeremy should've stayed home, kept his house. But he didn't, did 'e. More's the pity . . . Well, mebbe the little tacker will – what's his name? – Henry – twill be a pity if the house don't go on, if it all fall to ruin. Old Cap'n started something you shouldn't neglect. Why, who'd be a king in London if he could be a squire in Cornwall?'

It was late afternoon and Ross could see a few people, mainly ragged village folk making their way towards the inn. Sally was a big-bosomed, generous, now elderly woman who had earned her nickname by being willing to let her customers have a little something on credit. 'Just to take the chill off.' They paid her back when they could, most often after a successful 'run'. Tholly had scraped a living as a horse coper and general picker-up of unconsidered trifles and had lived with Sally Tregothnan – some said sponged on her – ever since he returned from the sea. It seemed, if Dwight were correct, that his tenure was coming to an end.

Tholly coughed, but compared to the old days it was a mere genteel clearing of the throat. 'I mind them old times well,' he said. 'Mebbe I remember your mother better than what you do, Young Cap'n. How old was you when she went around land? Nine? Ten? . . . She didn't take to me, thought I were a bad influence. That's a laff. Whoever thought of influencing the Old Cap'n? He went his way . . . Mind, he took *heed* of she. Good-looking wench. Handsome handsome long black hair. Upon times I seen her brushing it when I weren't supposed to. She 'ad a fine temper. It'd flash out like a sword out of a sheath, silver and sharp and glistening – cut anyone down. O' course it was agin his nature.'

'What was?'

'Being like 'e was when he was wed to she. It never come natural to him to toe the line. It was always 'is way to break the laws, break the rules, break the standards, see. And 'e carried it off in such a style – laughing and joking and devil take it – few folk cared. He was some caution, was Old Cap'n. Yet for twelve year – twelve year, mark ee, I never seen 'im chase another woman. Course he did other things – running goods, sailing 'ere and there on this and that, wrecking if the chance came his way, feuding with landlords and gaugers. But for twelve year she kept 'im faithful.'

'Maybe he wanted to be.'

'Oh, stand on that, 'e wanted to be, else 'e wouldn't 've been! My grandfather's ghost! Not Joshua Poldark. But when she died, 'e went back to 'is old games. Chasing women – it came natural to him. Great man was old Joshua. 'Ard as nails. But a great man, Young Cap'n. He started a line at Nampara that mustn't die out.'

IV

Two days later Tholly died. Although having a pretty good idea of the cause of death, Dwight still wanted to make sure. Tholly's only son, Lobb, the ailing, ruptured, anaemic father of five, had died last year, so Tholly's closest blood relative was his daughter, Emma Hartnell, who kept The Bounders' Arms between Sawle Church and Fernmore. Thither Dwight went to express condolences and to ask hesitantly whether he might be allowed to open the body. Cornish folk, with religious leanings and a belief in The Last Trump, generally had the strongest objection to having any relative of theirs interfered with after death by the surgeons. It came too close to the idea of the Body Snatchers. But Dwight need not have been hesitant this time. 'You can have his *head* off for all I care,' was the reply. Emma, though a nice woman and a kind one, had never forgiven her father for having deserted them when they were young and left them to the Poor House.

So Dwight opened up the corpse and took out the cancerous tumour and carried it home in a jar, where he could dissect it and examine its structure under a slide in his microscope. It was that part of the profession of medicine which Caroline most detested, but she had been unable to cure him of it.

He was reaching some interesting conclusions on the nature of malignancy when to his annoyance Bone tapped on the door and said Music Thomas was here with the request that he should

374

go urgently to Place House where his mistress, Mrs Valentine Warleggan, had met with a serious accident.

While Mr Pope was alive Dwight had been called not infrequently to emergencies in which the old man played the leading role, but since the young Warleggans came to live here there had been no such alarms. He went out to find Music standing on one foot and then on the other and looking anxious. Being an outdoor servant, he had no knowledge of the emergency except that he'd been told Mrs Warleggan had fallen and cut herself.

Since this *might* be a matter of life and death, Dwight grabbed up his case and swung into the saddle of the horse that had brought Music and galloped off, leaving Music to return as best he could.

He was met by Katie, who, more incoherent than usual, led him upstairs to that bedroom he knew so well, where Valentine was sitting beside Selina, who lay palely in bed, improvised bandages wrapped round both wrists.

'Ecod, it was in the bathroom,' said Valentine stiffly. 'I found her there. She has lost a lot of blood.'

Selina was fainting, but when Dwight touched her arm she opened her Siamese-blue eyes and looked her recognition – then she closed them again.

Her wrists had been thinly cut, just where the veins were most prominent, and blood still welled from the wounds.

Dwight sent for warm water, bathed the cuts, put a healing salve on – at which she winced – and gently bandaged both wrists, then gave her a light draught of Theban opium.

'I don't think it is very serious,' he said reassuringly to Valentine, and to Selina who had sufficiently come round to swallow the draught. 'Have you hurt yourself in any other way?'

She moved her lips sufficiently to say, 'No.'

'Did she fall?' Dwight asked Valentine, though he had a fairly good idea of the truth.

'No idea,' said Valentine. 'Damn me, she must have. The maid found her – Katie found her.'

Dwight stayed for another ten minutes talking to Valentine and watching his client; then he rose to leave.

'I'll come down with you,' said Valentine. 'Martha will sit with her.'

They went in to the summer parlour – which also had hardly changed since the tenure of the old man – and drank a glass of canary together. Dwight was anxious to get back to his microscope but he could not leave yet. As Valentine continued a casual conversation about Cambridge he was forced to broach the subject himself.

'I suppose you know, Mr Warleggan, that the cuts on your wife's wrists were almost certainly self-inflicted.'

Valentine crossed and uncrossed his long tapering legs. 'I had that thought,' he said.

Silence fell. Dwight finished his glass.

'More canary?' said Valentine.

'No, thank you. I should be on my way.'

'It really is quite outrageous,' Valentine said. 'My wife slashed her wrists because she was told I had been with another woman.' He yawned. 'What is a man to do?'

'I take it her information is correct?'

'Oh yes.'

After a moment Dwight said: 'Well, I suppose you could refrain in future.'

The young man got up and refilled Dwight's glass uninvited. Then he drank a second himself and poured out a third. 'Refrain altogether? My dear Dr Enys! Isn't that being a trifle naïve?'

'It depends what you want to make of your marriage.'

'This is a form of blackmail,' Valentine said, squinting at his glass. 'My wife threatens to kill herself in order to enforce my marriage vows! From what I could see, the cuts were not deep, were they?'

'Not deep. But a woman has to be distraught to attempt such a thing at all. And she might cut deeper next time.'

'Next time. Exactly! There lies the blackmail. Behave or I will destroy myself!'

'The matter could be put in a more sympathetic light.'

'No doubt. No doubt. Isn't it true, by the way, I think I have read it somewhere, that people who threaten suicide seldom succeed?'

'It's been said so. But have you ever tried to open the veins in your own wrists? It requires a deal of resolution to go even as far as she has this time.'

Valentine hunched his shoulders. 'It is all such a storm in a damned tea-cup. Blood and bones, it is not civilized to behave so!'

Dwight got up. 'Well, I must be off.'

'No, wait. Listen. Finish that canary. You are an old friend, by God. You have known my family for thirty years. If anyone has to hear the truth why should it not be you?'

From the window Dwight saw Music Thomas coming up the track from Trevaunance. It could not have taken him all this time to walk from Killewarren.

'When I married Selina I took her for better or worse and she took me the same. Eh? Eh? I am fully committed to her, as I have frequently told her. She is mine and I want to live with her for the rest of my life! I truly want that, bubble me if I don't. Everyone at marriage makes other vows – take unto me only thyself and forsaking all others – whatever the cursed words actually are. How few even keep that vow? How few?'

'Perhaps not –'

'My only defect is my honesty. A few months after we was wed I spelt all this out to her. I told her that she was far and above the most important woman in my life but that she could not expect to be the only one. I warned her of it and warned her of it, and damn me if she could bring herself to believe it! But ever since I was breeched I have been interested in girls – can't resist 'em. At the beginning every one is different, even if at the end every one is the same! I cannot change my nature, not even for the sake of a damned peaceful married life!'

Valentine was pacing slowly about the room, his long narrow face cynically intent. Dwight sipped his wine.

'After we were married I had a couple of little affairs in Cambridge, nothing more. I imagine she knew about them. But that was over a period of *six months*! Most of the time I was as pure as a parson . . . But then when we came home for the summer vacation I met Polly Codrington. Have you met her?'

'No.'

'No, I don't suppose you would have. Handsome creature, married to some dull clod of a squire in Kent – thirty years older than she is. She came to stay with Miss Darcy at Godolphin Hall. We met her, Selina and I, at the Pendarves. She was only down for a month's holiday, Polly was, and she had a roving eye. I caught it.' Valentine sighed. 'Mind you,' he said, wishing to be reasonable with himself, 'nothing blatant. We both tried to cover our tracks. Me for the reasons stated, Polly because Miss Darcy is a trifle straight in her lacing and Polly did not wish to upset the old dear. Well, we had a couple of meetings and then, not content, agreed to spend a night together at the Red Lion in Truro. I made the excuse that I wished to see my bank, she pretended she was staying with Harriet and my father – she is related to Harriet. And all went well. All went *very* well, I can tell you.' Valentine licked his lips. 'I am not known in Truro. She had never been before. And then in the morning, as we were coming down the staircase together, by the worst cursed contriving of Providence, who should be passing through the hallway but that evil foul scum of a boy, Conan Whitworth. You know who I mean?'

Dwight inclined his head.

'Apparently this odious creature's school was only breaking up that day, and of course he stopped and tried to talk, but I cut him short and hurried Polly off. By then the damage was done. The fat toad must at once have hurried home and told his equally odious grandmother, who must thereupon and with great relish have proceeded to spread it about the county!'

'That does make it more difficult.'

'Very much more, because you see – no doubt you do see – this hit at Selina's self-esteem. However, there it is and the milk is spilt! A mistake like this could happen to *anyone*! But, blood and bones, it is no occasion for amateur dramatics, for slashing one's *wrists* and pretending that our life together is over! Polly Codrington has now gone home to her stuffy husband in Kent and who knows if she will ever return? I am still Selina's devoted husband and intend to remain so. When you come next – you'll come tomorrow?'

'Yes.'

'When you come I wish you will try to bring my wife round to some more reasonable frame of mind – and to understanding my point of view.'

Dwight smiled. 'You are asking more than I can perform.'

'Well try, man, try. I know you cannot leech for a wounded *amour propre* but you can at least advise her how cursed silly it is to resort to such extravagant lengths!'

Five

I

When he came to leave, Katie was holding his horse. She smiled slyly at him, and he avoided looking at her thickening figure.

'Where's Music?' he asked.

'I sent him 'bout his business. He be too long coming 'ome. Wandered off, 'e had, to his own cottage I reckon, to feed all his chets.'

'Don't you like cats?'

'Not so many as 'e's got.'

He led his horse to the mounting stone and climbed into the saddle.

'You are keeping well, Katie?'

'Ais. Proper.'

'Have you thought any more of my suggestion?'

''Gestion?'

'That you should marry Music.'

'Nay,' she said. 'Wouldn't do tha-at.'

He smiled at her. 'You have told me you do not fancy him greatly as a husband, but he might well become an excellent father.'

A breeze was blowing strongly off the land, and she turned towards it so that her heavy black hair was lifted away from her face.

''Ow do I know if he d'want to be a father to someone else's brat or no? 'E haven't said nothing to me.'

Dwight's horse stamped the ground, ready to be off.

'I hear John Thomas has gone to live with Winkey and Peter Mitchell.'

'Ais. He might just so well've gone years ago, mightn't 'e.'

'So Music is alone in the cottage.'

''Cept for the chets. Tha's why he'm always shrimping off to feed 'em; there's no one else now. But tesn right, I d'say. Chets is independent. Chets can forage for themselves. Don't need some poor mazed man stealing time off to feed 'em.'

'It is not a bad little cottage,' Dwight said. 'Of course it has been much neglected.'

'Tis a rare old jakes.'

'But could be done up, put to rights. At present there is no incentive.'

'Please?'

'At present there is no one interested in it; no one to work for. Music put up some shelves for me last month. He's none too bad a man with his hands.'

'Tisn't his hands that are weak,' said Katie with a short laugh. 'Tis his 'ead.'

'Which is improving all the time. He's trying very hard, Katie. Talk to him sometime instead of shouting at him. You'd be surprised.'

II

The following evening Katie unexpectedly had to go to the stables, and Music was there alone and put the question.

At least he mouthed something in a sweaty stutter in which the word 'wed' recurred too frequently for Katie to misunderstand him.

She stared at him in contempt.

''Ave ee been at the bottle, ye great lootal?'

'N-nay! Not so! I'm so sober as a judge. Honest! God's honour, Katie!'

'Then ye did oughter be 'shamed of yourself, thinking such lewd thoughts! *Me* wed *you*? Why I'd 'ave as much use for you as a toad for a side pocket!'

Music cringed, his knees shaking. Then with a sudden burst of bravado he said: 'I dearly love bebbies. Bebbies I d'like. I dearly love the dear sweet sights.'

'You've got plenty of babies,' said Katie. 'All them chets. Look to them.' Then in vexation she added: 'I d'know who's been putting you up to this monkery! Tis Surgeon Enys. Well, he'm a good man, but tis no consarn of 'is what I d'do or don't do. And tis no business of yours neether!'

'Ais, Katie,' said Music humbly, and 'No, Katie.' And 'Yes, Katie,' again. He could not meet her indignant glare.

Katie would have liked at this stage to have flounced out of the stables, but she was not the flouncing sort: her step was too heavy. And, seeing the big young man looking so miserable and sweaty, she said: 'Tis all well meant, I dare suppose, on both 'is side and on yourn. Who'm I to be so hoity seeing as to what I've done and the trouble that have come 'pon me? Still, there you be. Tis no more'n I desarve, and I'll tek my draught wi'out help from no one.'

'I be strong,' said Music, finding his voice again. 'Strong. All ways. All ways, see. God's truth. I'd labour for you and the bebby. *Tha's* no more'n you desarve.'

Katie continued to stare at him from under black, contracted eyebrows.

'Giss along wi' you,' she said at last. 'You can't come mopping wi' me. You're 'alf saved. You know you're 'alf saved. Can't do nothing 'bout that. Even Surgeon can't. Look to your chets, Music. I'll see for myself.'

III

As soon as Clowance heard that her father was home she had to see him. She also felt that Stephen had to go, and Stephen, still in the flush of euphoria, reluctantly agreed. They rode over and stayed two nights.

Clowance was as shocked in the appearance of her father as she had been of her mother, and the visit was a difficult one. Again Stephen was on his best behaviour and did not let his lack of interest in people a generation older than himself show in any discourteous way. He was quite fond of his mother-in-law who had continued until recently to be such a pretty woman and tolerated a father-in-law who was a distinguished man and notable in the county.

Sir Ross, it seemed, had no particular plans for his own future, and intended to live quietly for the next year or two. He had given notice that he would resign his parliamentary seat as soon as Lord Falmouth found it convenient. Lady Poldark spent most of her time in the garden, where the energy she expended was like a counter-irritant to her grief.

Isabella-Rose, fresh-faced from school, was more subdued than anyone had ever known her. Not only was she mourning for her beloved brother with whom she had had a delightful jesting relationship, but she was also deeply upset because her other beloved, Christopher Havergal, had lost a leg. After such cruelty she said she could never sing again.

After dinner on the first day, Stephen and Clowance rode over to Trenwith, but there they found only Drake and Morwenna and Loveday. Mrs Amadora Poldark had just left with her baby daughter for Paris to join her husband, who was to be stationed there as part of the army of occupation. Amadora had been over several times to see the Poldarks and had told them of her summons, but Demelza had mistaken the week she was leaving.

Then they rode on to Place House and drew a second blank. Selina was in bed with a feverish chill and had been told to see no one; Valentine was in Redruth.

In the evening Dwight and Caroline invited them all to supper, which made for a much more cheerful evening than could possibly have taken place at Nampara. Daisy and Paul Kellow had also been invited, and it was a talkative party if not a jolly one.

While carefully avoiding Waterloo, they asked a lot about the months Ross and Demelza had spent in Paris before Napoleon's escape. Ross was incredulously angry that Fouché should have now been elected President of the Provisional Government and had negotiated with the Allies for the capitulation of Paris. There was talk of his even being reappointed Chief of Police in Louis the Eighteenth's new government. 'It cannot be allowed to go on!' Ross said. 'This evil creature must be thrown out!'

'Perhaps Jodie will see to it in due time,' Demelza said. She had had two letters recently from Mlle de la Blache, the second one from Paris, repeating an invitation that they should visit there again, now the bad time was over. Henri, Jodie thankfully reported, was safe and well. She could never thank Demelza enough for her help on that terrible escape, or be more appreciative of Isabella-Rose's innocent but vital intervention.

It was a long time since Stephen and Paul had seen each other, and the old conspirators privately exchanged congratulations, Stephen on his successful adventure at sea, Paul on his potentially successful adventure in the marriage market. They spoke of Jeremy with regret, but, being young, the thought of him being dead and dust and corruption did not so greatly worry them. Death to them was something that happened to somebody else.

Daisy, who had always had great hopes of Jeremy until he became besotted with Cuby, did not appear to repine at all. With the dreaded wasting disease having taken off two of her sisters, she lived too close to the tomb to be overawed by it.

The next day Stephen and Clowance rode home together, Stephen feeling the satisfaction of having performed a tedious duty and the pleasure of returning to the town he had made his own and where his livelihood was always going to be. He had avoided meeting Ben, and need not now go back to the north coast for six months or more. The north coast was a backwater, a dead end, and those who lived there were welcome to it. The future lay in the Channel.

'Look you,' he said, 'being around and about the way I am, I hear all sorts of bits of news that don't become public till they're stale. Yesterday I heard that Coombes's cottage in Flushing was for sale. 'Member him? He worked in the Customs House. Wife died last year; he died Wednesday. Son don't want the cottage, will put it up for sale next month. Reckon if someone went along, offered seventy-five pound, quick sale, money down, he'd take it.'

'Is it the one at the end of the row?'

'Next to the end. The one with the white front door. I have a mind to buy it.'

'For *us*?'

'No, dear heart, not for us. The building of our house re-started last week. I thought to buy it for Andrew.'

Clowance was startled. 'You mean . . .'

'He's overdue now, should be home any day. He wants to get wed – he has no money. I thought to give it to them as a wedding present.'

383

Their horses separated, and it gave her time to take in what he had said.

'Stephen, that *is* generous of you! You are so kind – I'm sure he will be delighted, overwhelmed.'

'Well, he could feel aggrieved that he did not come on our venture, eh?, feel he had missed a big bonus. He can look on it that this is his share.'

Clowance said: 'I can't kiss you, but I will later. Thank you for such a generous thought.'

Stephen laughed heartily. 'And if he don't want it, I can sell it again. But I wouldn't give him the money – he might not keep it for his marriage portion!'

'I conceit Tamsin will sober him up. He'll have responsibilities. I'm told his father gambled and drank too much when he was young.'

'Eh well, ye would not think so to look at him now, would ye.' Stephen flicked at his horse to quicken its step. 'This old nag . . . Next thing is to find me a hunter. I shall wait now till St Erme Cattle Fair in two weeks' time. They say there's some good horseflesh coming up.'

'Let me come with you,' said Clowance. 'I haven't lived on a farm all my life for nothing.'

'Wouldn't go without you,' said Stephen.

They rode on.

IV

Dwight had seen Selina the following day and then called a week later, at her request. No confidences were exchanged, and it would have been against his professional ethics to invite them. Nor, had she told him the facts, would he have been prepared to put Valentine's point of view. On this third visit, when he found her up and about, she spoke rather sheepishly of her clumsiness in breaking the glasses, and attempted to demonstrate to him how she had fallen forward, cutting both wrists at the same time. The amount of blood she had lost was little, and the dark rings under her eyes were no

384

doubt concerned with the cause of the accident, not the accident itself.

He sat chatting for a few minutes, discussing the arrival off Plymouth of the Emperor Napoleon Bonaparte as a prisoner of the British in HMS *Bellerophon*. Selina was of the opinion that he was being treated with too great a respect – it was said that every officer, English and French, uncovered when he came on deck and that the harbour was swarming with small boats trying to get a glimpse of him. Dwight said he was not sure as to the amount of respect he deserved. It was true that, but for him, many thousands of good young men – including one very near and dear to them all – would be alive. But it was the custom of the British to show respect for their fallen enemies and, as well as being a terrible scourge, which everyone admitted, Bonaparte was a great man. For instance the Civil Code which he had introduced into France would probably provide a model for future generations.

On this Valentine arrived, having been out riding. Conversation abruptly lagged, and then Selina, smiling too brightly at Dwight, asked to be excused.

After she had gone Valentine said: 'Not drinking? My wife has caught some of the parsimonious habits of her former husband. I swear you did not like the canary you had before. This is a very good Mountain, shipped direct from Malaga. Try a glass.'

Dwight tried a glass, and for a while talk continued on the subject of the late Emperor.

Then Valentine said: 'Tell me, Dr Enys. What did my mother die of?'

Dwight thought cautiously round the sudden change of subject: 'She died in childbirth. Your sister –'

'Ursula was born on the 10th of December. My mother did not die until the 14th.'

'It is not uncommon, if something goes amiss, for the mother to survive a few days.'

'Do you know what went amiss?'

'She died of blood poisoning,' said Dwight shortly.

'Was that why she smelt so bad?'

Dwight looked up, startled.

Valentine said: 'Well, you see, I was nearly six at the time. They would not let me into her room but the smell escaped into the passage. It is a smell I have never been able to forget.'

There was an uneasy silence. Dwight said: 'I am sorry you were allowed near. The disagreeable smell was due to a putrid condition of the blood.'

Valentine resumed his ramshackle pacing. 'You will excuse these questions, Dr Enys, but you have been a friend of the family, and their physician, long before I was born and you must know more about my family than almost anyone alive.'

'I have known your family for thirty years but I have not been their physician. Your father always had the Truro man, Dr Behenna, and he was engaged to wait on your mother when Ursula was born. I was called in because labour began prematurely while she was still at Trenwith.'

'Prematurely?'

'Yes.'

'I too was a premature baby. Eight months, I understand.'

'I understand so.'

'And so became the cause of great dissension between my father and my mother.'

'I do not know what gave you that impression.'

'A six-year-old boy is not without perception, especially where his parents are concerned.'

'No. Maybe not. But . . .'

'It is good, this wine, isn't it,' said Valentine. 'My wife's money enables me to live off the fat of the land, so no doubt a more moral man than I am would feel obliged to adhere more obviously to his marriage vows.'

'That is for you to decide –'

'I wonder if my mother adhered to her marriage vows?'

Dwight finished his wine and got up. 'I don't think I can help you on this subject, Mr Warleggan.'

'You cannot have lived in these villages for so long without knowing that nothing is ever kept permanently secret. My problem is remembering what I knew in my heart as a child and what I have heard in sidelong whispers since. What I do know . . . Pray sit down again.'

Dwight reluctantly sat on the edge of a chair but waved away an

386

attempt to refill his glass. He appreciated that under the surface gloss Valentine was speaking of something that had been gathering a long time in his heart.

'As a child I soon came to see that I was the bone of contention between my parents. Sometimes all would be apparently well, and then a word would be dropped, a shadow of some sort would be cast – and it always involved me. Sometimes for a month at a time my father would not speak to me, would not even look at me. I might have been some leprous monstrosity which had to be ignored and shunned. Unclean! Unclean! Of course my mother was not like that. Her loving care for me never wavered . . . Naturally all this did not make for a happy childhood.'

'I'm sorry.'

'Did you know that my parents had a violent quarrel only a day or two before Ursula was born?'

'No, I did not.'

'D'ye know, I have a pretty clear memory of the events of December '99. We had been in London and rather happy there. At least, my mother seemed to be, and that reflected on me. She had got much fatter, and I did not understand that, but my father was in a good mood and I was happy with some new toys. I remember specially a rocking horse. I wonder what happened to that? Suddenly it all changed – as it had done sometimes in the past, but never so badly as this – and I felt I was guilty of some terrible sin. We journeyed back to Cornwall, and I remember I was coachsick most of the way. It is not at all agreeable, my dear Dr Enys, being coachsick at the best of times, but when your father looks his utter disgust – indeed hatred – at every fresh retch . . .

'When we reached Truro influenza, scarlet fever and dysenteries were raging, so my mother took me off to Trenwith to see her parents and to keep me out of infection's way. Smelter George stayed behind. It was a dark month. Do you remember it at all?'

'Very well.'

'Trenwith was monstrous dark. It might have been haunted. Do you remember the great storm that blew up during that first week?'

'Yes.'

'It was one of the worst storms that had ever been, but, child-like, I found it vastly exciting. The servants we had, Tom and Bettina –

d'you know, I cannot remember their surnames – they took me out to see the sea at Trevaunance; they got a good wigging afterwards for taking me, for roofs were blowing off and branches falling. But suddenly at supper that night my father turned up with a face like fury. I was so excited out of my usual fear of him that I tried to tell him about the storm. He snapped back at me as if I were an evil thing, and I was sent instantly to bed – in something of a temper myself, I may say.'

Valentine picked a piece of ore off the mantelshelf, weighed it appreciatively in his hand. 'Early assays on Wheal Elizabeth are promising – copper very obvious, but signs also of tin and zinc.'

'Very promising.'

'That night,' said Valentine, 'after I had been put to bed and the candle blown out, I got up again and padded along to my mother's bedroom. But I did not go in. My parents were both there and in the midst of one of their bitterest quarrels. I listened to it all, taking in words but not comprehending them. Only since. Only since, remembering the words, have I gathered their meaning. It seemed that George Warleggan thought he was not my father.'

Dwight frowned. 'Are you sure you remembered the words correctly, that you did not misinterpret the causes of the quarrel? Children can so often mistake these things.'

'Do you mean to tell me that you have never heard whispered doubts in these villages about my parentage?'

'There is always tittle-tattle in villages, Mr Warleggan. Most of it is entirely invented and should be ignored.'

Valentine pushed back his hair. His vivid eccentric manner was at odds with this rather stuffy room, furnished by his elderly predecessor.

'When Ursula was born George Warleggan came into my bedroom to tell me. I was terrified – he had never been into my room for as long as I could remember. But now – for some reason – it was as if the storm – his storm – had passed. He actually patted my hand, told me about my sister, said that my mother was well but must rest in bed for a few days. He talked to me about going to school, about the recent gale, almost as if no enmity had existed between us. I could make nothing of it, remained frozen to his touch. Children cannot change as quickly as all that. I was relieved when he left. I only wanted to see my mother again. This, of course, I did, and also Ursula, but the day after that my mother was taken ill – and the day after that she died.'

Through the open window you could hear the children calling to their cattle in the fields. A horse whinnied in the nearby stables.

Dwight said: 'Your mother was delivered prematurely of a perfectly healthy child. I delivered the child. I did not see your mother again for two days, as Dr Behenna arrived and took charge. Then when I was called in again I was appalled at the sight of her illness. Do not misunderstand me, this could not have been the result of any mistaken treatment Dr Behenna prescribed. Had I seen the complaint earlier I would have diagnosed it more quickly, but could not have halted it.'

'And the complaint was?'

'I have told you. A form of blood poisoning.'

'Gangrene, wasn't it? I have read books.'

'A form of blood poisoning.'

'Caused by what?'

Dwight thought: almost certainly by drinking part of the contents of a little bottle I still have in my cupboard at home. He had no means of analysing it, but he had tasted it and could make a reasonable guess at some of the ingredients. But never could he say anything of this to any human being, least of all to Elizabeth's son.

'Dr Behenna described it as an acute gouty condition of the abdominal viscera which manifested itself in cramp-like spasms and inhibition of the nerve fluids.'

'Do you believe all that medical flummery? You are, after all, well known to be the most advanced and knowledgeable physician in the south-west.'

Dwight stared at the tensed-up young man. 'However knowledgeable any one of us is, we struggle in the dark, Mr Warleggan. We know so little of the human body, even after centuries of practice and experience.'

He might have added: And of the mind, Mr Warleggan, and of the mind.

Six

I

Ellery and Vigus had dropped hints about it at the changing of the cores, though they hadn't dared to face him out. But Peter Hoskin was a more substantial character and when he made a sort of side reference to it he tackled him in the changing shed.

'Well, I dunno narthing 'bout en,' said Peter. ''Tis only what I been telled. Beth Daniel fur one. And others. But it edn naught to do wi' me, Ben.'

'If it edn't naught to do wi' you,' said Ben, 'why don't ee keep yer big trap shut!'

'I don't see as you've any call to take on so,' said Peter testily. 'Why don't ee ask her? She'll soon tell ee nay if tedn truth.'

Katie was normally home on Tuesday afternoon, that being her afternoon off; though she had seen much less of her parents' shop since her disgrace. Jinny, her mother, being a good and respectable Wesleyan, had not taken kindly to a situation in which her daughter should now be preparing to bear a bastard child without making any attempt to bring the scoundrel to justice who was responsible for her condition.

Ben went along and found Katie at home helping her mother to cut up the rhubarb for jam.

Whitehead Scoble, their step-father, was now very deaf and was dominated by Jinny who, though of a naturally amiable disposition, had hardened and toughened with the years.

'Well,' said Katie defiantly, 'what if tis true? Tis my consarn, no one's else.'

'Lord save us!' said Ben between his teeth, 'ye cann't mean it, Katie. Ye cann't. Wed to the village idiot! For land's sake, don't that beat all!'

'I don't see you need to get in such a niff,' said Katie. 'He's not such a noodle as he belonged to be. Ye give a man a name and it d'hang round his neck like a dog collar all 'is life. Besides . . .'

'Besides what?'

'I've the child to think on.'

''*E'll* thank ye, sure 'nough, 'e truly will – or she – to be give a father that don't know the time o' day or whether tis Christmas or Easter! If you wed a pattick like Music ye'll have to keep three 'stead of two –'

'He've got a cottage.'

'Oh, so you're wedden the cottage, are ee –'

'I never said that! I never said nothing o' the sort . . . Anyway, tis my life and I shall lead it as I think fit –'

'But tis *not* fitty. Wi' all the village a-sniggering to bust. They're whispering and sniggering at the mine already. Why, folk'll jeer at *you*, not at him –'

'Oh, leave the maid alone,' said Jinny. 'She've dug her own pit – let her lie in it!'

'What's that?' said Whitehead. 'What's that you say?' He began to light his nose warmer from a spill thrust between the bars of the fire. A cloud of smoke from the shag drifted across the room.

'You mean t'say you don't *mind*?' Ben turned on his mother.

'Course I mind! But I mind the disgrace the more. If I had my way I'd have that Saul Grieves fetched back from wherever he be skulking and *forced* into church. What he did with his self after that would be his consarn. But this way he d'get off fine and free and leave Katie to bear the consequences!'

'I've told ee,' Katie said, near to tears but not giving way. 'I'd never marry Saul Grieves, not if he was to come on bended knee. Music's just a makeshift. But twill make the child legal and give him a name.'

'Well, don't expect *me* to acknowledge Music as me brother-in-law! You must be half saved yerself, Katie, to think on such a thing. What do Grandfather and Grandmother say? They'll spit. I reckon they'll spit.'

Jinny came across to him. 'Don't you go upsetting Granfer and Gran, else I'll give you something to think 'bout, Ben! They're old, and when the time d'come I'll go and tell 'em what I think best they should know. But until then, you keep your spleen to yourself!'

'They'll know about it soon enough,' said Ben. 'You'll find some kind friend'll be along any day, if mebbe they don't already know. Anyway, I'd not like to be there when you d'tell 'em!'

He left the room, and they heard the shop door slam as he went out.

'What was amiss with him?' asked Whitehead. 'He was in a rare taking. I suppose he don't like the idea of Katie wedding Music?'

II

Andrew Blamey returned in the *Queen Charlotte* after a stormy voyage which had taken twice as long as expected and in which they had been attacked by, and driven off, a big American privateer that had not yet apparently become aware of the Peace Treaty of Ghent. He accepted Stephen's gift of the cottage with uproarious pleasure, and they celebrated it at a little supper-party in the Carringtons' cottage, Tamsin being there chaperoned by her brother George. Consent to the marriage by her parents had not yet been given, but everyone at the supper assumed it would only be a matter of time.

Grown expansive on the Rhenish wine, Stephen went into more details of his privateering escapade than Clowance had heard before. In particular when the French soldier had fired point blank at him and the cap had failed to detonate. Stephen now treated it as a great joke, but it had been the luckiest escape from certain death. Clowance could not help but think of another and longer conflict, and wish that the rain had continued at Waterloo.

It seemed that Andrew had enjoyed his trip in the *Queen Charlotte*. In spite of his joviality, Andrew was not the easiest of men to get on with, and so it was notable that he had found an accord with the grumpy Captain Buller. Something in Andrew's character had responded to the stern discipline of his captain, and something in the way he had responded had pleased and satisfied Buller. The success of the voyage radiated through Andrew's spirits, and though he drank plenty he did not become noticeably drunk. They made gay plans for a day next week when they would visit the new cottage together.

On the Friday Stephen and Clowance rode out to St Erme, whose annual cattle and horse fair was the biggest in the county, and Stephen paid what Clowance thought an outrageous price for a handsome dark bay gelding, 'the property of an officer recently fallen at Waterloo'. The two men selling the horse told Stephen that they would get a far better price at Tattersall's but they were selling locally to avoid the cost of the travelling. Moses, as he was called, was a very big animal – seventeen hands – and was clearly accustomed to hunting. A six-year-old, they said, and Stephen could not take his eyes off it. As well as being good at persuading himself that what he wanted was right, he had a similar tendency to believe the persuasiveness of others; and the sale was soon completed.

They rode through Truro and back to Falmouth in triumph, Clowance on Nero leading the hired horse. Even if he has paid too much for it, she thought, it's his money, won by his enterprise, why shouldn't he have the enjoyment? Just as he enjoyed giving me the necklace. Just as he has enjoyed giving the cottage to Andrew. (I hope he has as much money as he says. I hope – I do hope and pray – he will know when to say stop.)

III

The courtship of Music and Katie did not follow a conventional pattern.

For one thing, they did not look at each other as affianced people should. Music gazed constantly at Katie, his pale puzzled eyes gleaming with happiness – he was in his seventh heaven only because there was not an eighth – but he never let his gaze fall below her face. He became alert and experienced in interpreting the nuances of her expressions – which boded ill for him, which tolerance, which – very rarely – liking or approval. He never allowed his gaze to travel anywhere below her chin, for he knew without ever having been told that her corporeal presence lower than the neck was not for him. It was unthinkable territory.

For her part, although she quite frequently spoke to him, she always kept her eyes lowered, as if to reduce within herself the shame of such a match. To meet his adoring eyes would have been to establish a contact, an intimacy which could, of course, never be allowed to establish itself. She went to his cottage, walked around it, made comments, a few suggestions, which he eagerly agreed to. In the end she found he only had four cats. Tom, one of the scabby tabby toms, had been caught in a gin at the beginning of the year, so all that were left were Tabby, Ginger, Blackie and Whitey, which was certainly more than she wanted, but Music was so obviously devoted to them that she decided to tolerate them. In the harsh cat world of Grambler, wastage would no doubt take one or another off in due time, so long as she was absolutely firm about admitting newcomers.

Music went about in a dream world, working every spare moment he could get away from Place House, which was little enough, putting new thatch on part of the roof, clearing out the smelly fishing-tackle, hanging the back door on new hasps so that it would shut properly, mending the broken windows, repairing the fire bars, cleaning out the jakes and laying stones to it across the dusty scrub of the yard. In his excitement he had to be careful not to walk on his toes again or let his voice break into its upper register.

One day when he was trying to repair the table leg his older brother John walked in. He had come over to see what was going on. They were neither of them men of many words, and after a few grunted monosyllables of greeting John spat on the floor and thrust his hands into the upper pockets of his breeches and watched Music trying to get the table to stand steady without rocking.

'When'll ye wed?' he asked presently.

'Dunno.'

'I've 'erd tell tis to be the 1st October.'

'Mebbe.'

'What Katie says goes, eh?'

'Mebbe.' Music stopped to scowl at his table. 'Ais, I reckon. What Katie says goes.'

'Know ye she's only marryin' ye on account that she's forced put?'

'I reckon.'

'It don't fret ye that ee be going to be fathur to Saul Grieves's child?'

'Tes Katie's child. That's for sure.'

'Aye, that's for sure. What do Art say?'

''Aven't asked 'im.'

'Nay, ye wouldn't. Well, I tell ee what ee d'say. He say you'm all mops an' brooms where Katie's consarned. She cares for you no more than for a pail of muggets. Tis just convenience. That's what tis, Music. Just convenience.'

Music stretched up. 'Aye?'

'Aye. He also d'say, and tis the very truth of the matter, that we all three on us own part o' this yur cottage. So if you be gwan set up house wi' this woman and 'ave her child, tis no more'n right 'n proper that you d'pay a rent to we.'

'What?'

John Thomas repeated his words, aware that Music was not taking them in. Eventually Music said: 'You mun ast Katie.'

'Aye, I thought so much. Ast Katie. She'll run ee round like a cocket, I'll tell ee for certain, I sorrow for ee, Music. I sorrow for ee.'

'Ais?' Music smiled. 'Well I bain't sorrowing for meself, see?'

After a few weeks the whispering and the sniggering died down, and people began to accept the match. Music, though a big strong young man, was weak-willed and easily sat on and very sensitive to ridicule. Katie was a big strong young girl, not at all weak-willed, and, when she was among her own kind, a formidable presence. Folk didn't laugh in her face and she cared little for what was said behind her back. Also there was the distant Poldark connection. Her brother was underground captain of Wheal Grace and Wheal Leisure. Her mother had worked for the Poldarks for a long time, a long time ago, and so had her father. Her grandfather, Zacky Martin, who had been a semi-invalid for years, had been Cap'n Poldark's right-hand man through the early troublous years and still lived in Mellin, hard by Nampara. An uncle and an aunt, no older than she was, were employed at Nampara, in the house and on the farm.

It counted for something in the village. It made the enormity of the match greater but it made criticism of it more subdued.

A conversation concerning it took place that evening at Nampara where Demelza, for the first time since her return, had Dwight and

Caroline to supper. For this evening only Isabella-Rose had been asked if she would have supper upstairs.

'It is not that we have anything private to discuss that we don't wish you to hear,' Demelza said to her. 'It is just that we are four old friends, of an age; we have not met like this for so long. We would feel the same if Clowance were here or – or anyone else.'

Bella kissed her. 'One day I shall be grown up and then I shall have nothing more to do with you.'

They ate a piece of fresh salmon, fricasseed rabbits, a blackcurrant pie and syllabubs, with cherries after. At one time Demelza had been a little on edge even when entertaining such old friends; now perhaps her stay in Paris and later at Lansdowne House made things easier; one didn't worry about a servant's gaffe. Or perhaps it was that one no longer cared.

The meal went easily and pleasantly; the room became a little corner of comfort in a black world.

Mention of Zacky Martin brought it up. Ross said Zacky was scandalized and upset by his granddaughter's disgrace, and now by her crazy decision to marry the village idiot.

'He's by no means that,' Dwight said, sharply for him. 'In fact he never was. Slow-witted and amiable, certainly, and at one time he rather enjoyed being the butt of the village. It was a sort of fame. But in the last few years he's been trying to grow out of it.'

'Dwight has been very good to him,' said Caroline. 'Spent hours with him.'

'Half an hour a week at most,' said Dwight. 'But he came and asked what was wrong with him. I was surprised. Village idiots, as they are called, don't usually realize there is anything wrong with themselves; they think it is other people who are at fault. So I thought I would spend an hour or two testing his capacities. I found nothing wrong, physically. He has a good alto voice – but so have other normal people. When he was a child one of his brothers pushed him into the fire and he burnt his feet, chiefly his heels. He got into the habit of walking on his toes, but now he has got out of it. Mentally he's slow. But so are a number of his friends. Recently he has learned to count, and if he concentrates he can tell the time. He knows the months of the year now, and he's good with animals and clever with his hands. It may not be a lot, but I think he is sufficiently normal to have the right to live a normal life.'

'I suspicion that Dwight has been the matchmaker,' said Demelza.

'I'm not guiltless. But in this company . . . It is likely that Caroline and I would never have come together again if it had not been for that man's interference.'

'It's too long ago,' said Ross. 'I deny responsibility. But if it comes to matchmaking, Demelza is in the forefront of us all.'

'Well,' said Demelza, and blew a cherry stone genteelly into her fist, 'that's as maybe. But d'you know, the one I regret was the match I *didn't* make. Betwixt my brother Sam and Emma Tregirls, as she then was. There was such a gap – Sam's religion, you know – so I suggested they should part for a year . . . Emma went to Tehidy. But before the year was up she married the footman there, Hartnell, and so it was too late for Sam's happiness.'

'He's happy married now,' said Ross. 'So is Emma. I do not think it could ever have worked . . . But seriously, Dwight, if you think well of Music Thomas, I wish you might find time to call and see Zacky and Mrs Zacky. They would take greater notice of what you said, and it might set their minds more easy.'

'I will. I would take Music with me, but I know he would be so sweatily nervous that he would show to the worst advantage.'

'If ee please, mum,' said Betsy Maria Martin, of that ilk, coming in. 'Henry d'say you promised to go up and tell him good-night.'

'So I did,' said Demelza. 'I'll come in five minutes.'

Supper was all but over, but they stayed round the table chatting in the desultory way that Demelza so enjoyed. Caroline had sent her two daughters to an expensive school in Newton Abbot but she was not satisfied with it and was considering keeping them at home again and employing a teacher-governess.

'We want someone like your Mrs Kemp,' said Caroline. 'Someone with a rod, if not of iron, at least of birch, to stop Dwight spoiling them.'

'Oh Mrs Kemp was wonderful in Paris,' said Demelza. 'She was a rock. But do not suppose that she is so highly educated that she would suit for Sophie and Meliora. Have you asked Mrs Pelham's advice?'

'Oh my dear darling aunt is at last showing signs of age, and although she loves to have us all there I do not think she would willingly undertake the semi-permanent custody of my two lanky brats.'

'I wasn't thinking that. I was thinking she might know someone. You need someone more like Morwenna, who was so good with Geoffrey Charles.'

They sipped their port. Then Demelza rose.

'Well, I suppose I must not keep Henry waiting.'

'The future Sir Harry,' said Caroline.

'Yes, that's so.'

'Though I trust a long way in the future. And always I suppose subject to whether Cuby's child is a boy or a girl.'

'Oh?' said Demelza. 'Oh, yes.'

'Have you heard from Cuby?' Dwight asked Ross.

'I think she plans to come down next month.'

IV

In bed that night Demelza said: 'Is that true, what Caroline said about Cuby's baby?'

'What was that?'

'That if it should be a boy, he would inherit the title, not Henry.'

'Yes, I suppose so. Does it matter?'

Demelza thought it over.

Ross said: 'It is of little moment to me that I should have a title to pass on. Do you care?'

'I'm not sure, Ross. I think I do. I certainly care that you have a title, as you know. And Cuby's son is your grandson, and it would be well enough if he inherited. But . . . I think that Henry is your *son*, and it would be more proper for him to have it.'

'Maybe. I hadn't thought. It is not important. Anyway nature will make up its own mind.'

The window was open on the warm night, and a moth flew in. It began to make perilous circuitous reconnaissances round the candle.

'Old Maggie Dawe used to call 'em meggyhowlers,' said Demelza.

'What? Oh, did she? That's a name even Jud didn't know.'

'Have you seen him since you came home?'

'No. I must go tomorrow.'

'I went early on, but it was in the first shock and I do not suppose I was as attentive to their complaints as usual.'

After a pause Ross said: 'Did you know that Cuby was in Cornwall?'

'No! Is she coming here?'

'I avoided a direct answer when Caroline asked. Cuby promised to come here for the birth of her child, but that is three months off. She is staying at Caerhays with her family.'

'Oh.'

'She did not mention it when I left her. Perhaps there has been a change of plan.'

'Who told you?'

'I saw John-Evelyn Boscawen in Truro yesterday. He knew Jeremy well, of course. They were of an age. He assumed I knew about Cuby.'

Demelza thought this over too. 'I think she might have written.'

'Perhaps she will.'

'She was some nice to me when I was in Brussels.'

'She may feel a few weeks at home will be good for her first. She was still in a state of shock.'

'We all are.'

'Indeed.'

'Shall you go over and see her, Ross?'

'Oh no. I think the decision to communicate with us must come from her. We must give her time.'

'Time,' said Demelza. 'Yes, I suppose we all have lots of time . . .'

In the warm night you could hear the thunder of the sea on the beach. It was there almost all the time but only on quiet nights did it penetrate to one's consciousness. '*Rum-a-dum-dum*,' said Ross to himself. '*Rum-a-dum-dum*.' Pray God that sound would never be heard again.

'What were you muttering?' Demelza asked.

'I was cursing under my breath.'

'What for?'

'Because I have to get up and push your meggyhowler out of the window. Its suicidal tendencies will prevent me from going to sleep.'

'Put out the candle.'

'Then it will flutter round our faces in the dark.'

'Looking for another flame,' said Demelza.

Seven

Moses was a good mount. He was mettlesome and took some controlling at first but after a week or so he took to his new owner. Stephen was not the easiest of riders: he didn't really know how to gentle a horse along, persuading him instead of ordering him, he didn't talk to him enough. (When Clowance, the unloquacious, rode with Nero alone she talked to him all the time.) But they came to understand each other. It is probable that Moses' former owner, if he was a cavalry officer as well as a huntsman, had treated his horse well, ridden it hard, and lacked finesse. If so Moses, who had a hard mouth, recognized a new and similar-minded master. 'Geldings always make the best jumpers,' Stephen said.

He was delighted. He was noticeable on this horse wherever he went. He temporarily neglected his shipping interests and galloped each morning with Clowance over the moors west of Falmouth. He couldn't wait for the next hunting season to begin. He couldn't wait to show his horse to Harriet.

An opportunity for this occurred earlier than he had expected. Sid Bunt had put in to Penryn, and after reporting and checking his stores he was off with the *Lady Clowance* like the delivery van he was, to complete a half-dozen commissions up the Fal.

Most of these were workaday, but the big house at Trelissick had ordered a harp and two paintings, two late Opies – the painter had been dead several years but his work was becoming still more prized. Stephen was interested enough to see that these all travelled well, and in the ordinary course of events, if he had been free of his other vessels, he would have sailed with the *Lady Clowance* as far as King Harry Ferry for the off-loading. This time, because he was so proud of his horse, he rode overland to meet the *Lady Clowance* there. He superintended the landing of the cargo and met the owner of the house and took a glass of sherry with him before he started for home, full of the satisfaction of having made one more influential acquaintance.

Trelissick is not far from Cardew but it is separated from it by the Carnon Stream. Having dropped down to stream level and crossed by the old bridge, he let Moses amble along at his own pace enjoying the sunshine and the warm air. On impulse he turned into Carnon Wood, remembering the hunt had once taken them through there, and the hair-raising ride – almost literally hair-raising – they had had among the low branches. The wood was not above twenty acres in extent but it had only one decent path through it and a clearing with a workman's hut, part ruined, in the middle. At an earlier season the ground was ablaze with bluebells and wild daffodils. Rabbits abounded and lots of game – hares, badgers, woodcock, snipe.

As he came into the clearing he saw a woman pacing cautiously round the perimeter. She was tall and well dressed, in a purple riding cap and waistcoat with nankeen-coloured skirt, worn short enough to show purple shoes and embroidered stockings. It was Lady Harriet Warleggan. Her rich black hair was in a queue. She carried a riding crop.

'Harriet!' called Stephen in surprise.

She stopped and looked at him, scowling into the sun. At first she did not look well pleased as he rode up and dismounted, taking off his hat.

'Well, well, so it is our conquering hero!'

'What a vastly agreeable surprise!' he said, taking her gloved hand. 'I had not hoped to meet you here – and out walking in your . . .'

He hesitated. Because she was tall and well built, her figure only just showed the child she carried.

'In my present condition, you were going to say?'

'Well, me dear, maybe I should just say I'm gratified to find ye out walking.'

'I shall be out walking for some time yet. Being in whelp is not so disabling as I supposed it was going to be. But do not be concerned: Nankivell is at the edge of the wood, holding Dundee for me. Also Castor and Pollux. I am well mounted and well escorted.'

It was not in Stephen's nature ever to feel awkward – it was one of his charms – and he explained his presence here and what he had been doing this morning and asked her what she was seeking in the wood.

'Foxes,' she said simply. 'We cannot hunt 'em for two months yet, and by then, God dammit, I shall be too far on to participate. But I can still keep an eye on 'em, see what cubs they have. Even if you can't catch 'em at play you can usually tell by the billet they leave. You've spoiled my quest, Master Carrington.'

'I'm not sure I follow.'

'Simple enough. Why else do I leave my escort a quarter of a mile away? It is not the exercise of walking that I so much enjoy. But I had hopes I might see one or two of my little friends and gauge their health and numbers. That is not best done in the company of two clumping horses and a brace of boarhounds.'

Stephen laughed. 'Well, since I've spoiled a part of your quest, can I not help ye with the other part of it?'

'What is that?'

'Counting the droppings.'

She smiled at this. He tethered Moses to a suitable tree.

'A fine horse,' she said.

'Aye,' said Stephen, bridling. 'I wished for ye to see him. Something I bought last week in St Erme. He is quite a special animal.'

'A bit heavy in the hindquarters, do you not think?'

'Nay, tis the breed, Harriet. And he has a fair weight to carry.'

They moved towards the hut, but Harriet turned off sharply to where there was a rift in the ground and a couple of gorse bushes, still in semi-flower.

'You see, there's an earth here. Badgers have made it but foxes are living in it. I'll lay a curse there's a handsome lot of cubs in there. I was hoping to catch 'em at play.'

'I'm in disgrace, eh?'

'No matter.' She allowed the gorse bush to fall back into place and brushed some prickles off her gloves. 'We'll look in this hut and then be done.'

They walked across the clearing.

'How is Clowance?'

'Well and fine, thank ee.'

'She must have been much upset by her brother's death.'

'Oh she was. So was I. Jeremy was a sterling fellow.'

'I gather that while he was fighting Napoleon you were fighting the French in a more profitable way.'

He glanced at her and laughed. 'You speak the truth. I had me narrow escapes, I can vow. But, thanks to you, I got the opportunity to make the venture.'

'Thanks to me?'

'Well, ye must know that Sir George and I fell out – or maybe it is more true to say that he soured of me for some reason and threatened to withdraw all credit. I was as good as a ruined man. Then, for some other reason, he changed his mind and allowed me to continue to function on restricted credit. Twas that that brought me to a situation where I had to go for all or nothing as a privateer.'

'Indeed,' said Harriet at the entrance of the hut, 'so that's how it was.'

'That's how it was. And I have *you* to thank for it.'

'I am at a loss to know why you should think so.'

'I b'lieve Clowance told ye something of our straits and that ye intervened with Sir George on my behalf.'

'What a quaint thought!' She led the way into the hut.

It was a wooden structure, with part of the roof gone and the door fallen in. Inside there was a lot of etiolated grass, a few brambles, some small bones, ashes from a fire.

Harriet stirred the grass with her foot. 'Some tramp has been sharing it with the foxes.'

'Foxes?'

'Oh, they'll come in places like this, especially if their earths have been stopped. We have been led this way more than once and the scent has gone cold. I wonder . . .'

'I mind once last year,' said Stephen, 'last December, we came this way, dashing through the wood. I nearly came off! As usual, you was in the front.'

'Dundee is very sure-footed. And we've been together a long

time; since before I married George. We don't often make mistakes in the field.'

'Was your first husband a great hunter?'

'Oh yes, he lived for it. He was Master for a time, not of this pack, of course, but in North Devon. Nearly ruined himself – and in the end broke his neck at a gate. Well, God rest his soul, it was as good a way as any to go.'

Stephen had not been alone with this cool, articulate, downright woman in quite this way before. She was physically very attractive; pregnancy had given her an extra bloom. She had never spoken so openly and personally. It excited him.

She was stooping, stirring over the bones with her crop. He bent beside her, aware of her perfume, of her queue of black hair, of the flush in her normally sallow cheek.

'Do you see anything?'

'These rabbit bones are new. And these are chicken bones and something bigger. Mme Vixen has been sharing her vittles with someone else.' She straightened up, and he straightened up beside her.

'Harriet.'

'Yes?'

''Twas your doing, was it not, keeping George from bankrupting me? Don't deny it. I have to thank ye.'

'Is it not better to forget it all? Or why do you not give George the credit?'

'Because it is *yours* and I have to thank ye.'

She had her back near the wall, and he put a hand on the wall each side of her, imprisoning her. The wooden shack creaked under the weight of his hands.

She looked at him coldly, great eyes very calm.

He kissed her, first on the cheek and then on the lips. It was a long kiss. Then she put hands on both his shoulders and pushed him away. It was slow but firm; she had strong arms.

She took out a handkerchief and dabbed her lips. Then she picked up her crop, which she had dropped and stooped to turn over the bones again.

'I heard a parson once in the pulpit,' she said, 'state that man was the only creature that killed for pleasure. Damned nonsense.

405

A fox will kill anything that moves, that flutters, that shows signs of life. So will a cat. So will a leopard. Foxes are nasty little brutes, but I love 'em.'

'I can kill things that flutter,' said Stephen.

He followed her out of the hut.

'I think we will rejoin Nankivell.'

Stephen unhitched Moses and followed the tall smart woman through the trees. They came out into the field beyond, where the little groom was waiting with two horses and two dogs. Nankivell got to his feet, taking off his hat; the two big boarhounds rose and stretched and made whining noises. Harriet did not have to bend in order to rub their ears.

'Nankivell, take the dogs back by the road. It will do them good to trot with you. Mr Carrington and I will canter back across country.'

''S, m'lady.'

Harriet put out a hand and Nankivell helped her mount. The two horses, Dundee and Moses, eyed each other. Harriet gathered her reins, adjusted her cap. She had not looked at Stephen since they came out of the hut.

'Well, be off with you.'

''S, m'lady. Beg pardon, m'lady, but Sir George did tell me to see as ee did not go cross-country galloping. He says to me, Sir George he says, mind you see her leddyship don't do any jumping or galloping –'

'Never mind what Sir George said. It is what I say. Mr Carrington will see me home.'

'Willingly,' said Stephen.

'That's if he can keep up with me.'

In silence they watched Nankivell mount and trot reluctantly off, with Castor and Pollux on long leads behind. It was obviously a routine the dogs were used to. Stephen was still standing beside his horse, but now he essayed to mount. Harriet watched with a critical eye as he struggled into the saddle.

It was not so warm out here. The wind was picking up from the east, and they were not sheltered by the trees. But Stephen was warm.

Harriet said: 'If you wish to know, I did influence Sir George in his decision not to withdraw banking credit from you. But I did it

406

for Clowance, not for you. To suppose that I am in any way interested in you as a man is an unwarranted assumption. I have a debt of friendship and gratitude towards Clowance, which I discharged. That is all.'

Stephen patted his horse's neck. 'Maybe I've a debt of friendship and gratitude towards you just the same. Maybe once in a while you'll let me show it.'

Harriet said: 'Your horse is heavy in the haunches. If you're not careful he'll grow fat. I know the type.'

'I reckon he's a wonderful horse,' said Stephen stiffly. 'Every bit so good as yours.'

Harriet tightened her reins and looked across the smiling summer countryside.

She said after a long pause: 'When you married Clowance, it was a big thing for you, Stephen. Be content with it. I do not think it time for you to consider moving farther up-stream. Good-day to you.'

She turned and went off at a fair pace, which soon turned into a gallop.

'C'mon, me lad,' said Stephen angrily. 'We'll catch her.'

He set Moses to the task, and for a short period gained on her. It was uphill and the bigger horse made ground. Then Harriet took a low hedge very gracefully and Stephen followed. Now it was level ground and the two horses galloped at about the same rate, Moses some three lengths behind.

Another hedge, a Cornish wall this, not higher but much broader. Over went Dundee. Moses dislodged a stone as he followed. Harriet looked behind and laughed. Stephen dug in his heels and whacked the hindquarters of his horse with his crop. It was lovely open country, between wooded slopes and tall individual trees. They were galloping now at a thunderous pace.

He knew she should not be galloping like this, and knew that if he halted she would probably slow down. But he could not bring himself to check his horse. Harriet's words had bitten into him like a serpent, the poison seeping and spreading. She had even sneered at his horse.

He knew he must overtake her soon and then, having caught her, he could slow her down and be magnanimous. His horse was bigger than hers and must have more staying power; besides, a woman, unless she is a dare-devil, cannot ride side-saddle at the speed of a man. Harriet was a dare-devil. She bobbed up and down, her queue of hair streaming behind her. Now for the first time she used her whip.

They were coming to the next obstacle. Woods on either side narrowed to a gap protected by a high fence. Beyond it was a deep ditch. Harriet half checked, then slapped Dundee's neck; the horse took a sort of double stammer of hooves and took the obstacle in huge style. He just landed in the rubble and stones on the far side, stumbled and came to his feet as Stephen prepared to take off.

Stephen had been nearer Harriet than he thought; their hesitation, which had really been only a gathering of muscle and determination for the leap, became in him a real hesitation; then he forced Moses forward with a stinging crack of his whip and the great horse took off half a stride early. He made a tremendous effort, cleared the fence by the narrowest margin. But both front feet landed just in the ditch and he fell. It was a great weight of animal to fall, and Stephen was flung off him, clear off him, and landed with a heavy crunch among the rubble and stones.

Thereafter the world went black.

Eight

I

It was on the Wednesday that Ross called on Dwight. It was the first showery day after a long fine spell, and the wind was getting up. Dwight was writing a letter to a Doctor Sutleffe, who had recently been called in to see if he could help the aged King. Dwight and Sutleffe had met in London and had kept up a sporadic correspondence. Sutleffe was prescribing a herbaceous tranquillizer, which he had found successful with many patients far gone in mania, but Dwight, though he did not say so in the letter, was not optimistic of its success when given to a blind man suffering from advanced dementia and now becoming deaf too. The only treatment Dwight would have prescribed was a far greater freedom for the harmless old King to move or be moved around his castle. He could do no damage to the realm.

When Ross was shown in Dwight got up, pen still in hand but smiling his welcome.

'I find you alone?' Ross said.

'Yes, they are all out – I believe on your beach. I think Caroline has gone rather against her will, as she is not fond of sandy feet. You're better?'

'Oh yes. Thank you. We both are. It's – something we shall learn to live with. Or live without.'

'Demelza may be with Caroline. Have you come from the house? They are sure to have called.'

'No, Demelza is away. She has gone to see Clowance. Troubles do not come singly. Stephen Carrington has met with a riding accident.'

'I am very sorry. When did this happen?'

'Yesterday morning. He has recently bought a new horse and, it

409

seems, was putting it through its paces when it fell at a fence and he with it. He was flung clear, but he has hurt his back, possibly broken it. At present he cannot move from the waist down.'

Dwight made a face. 'Where is he now?'

'At his house – his cottage. That is where Demelza has gone. Matthew Mark Martin has gone with her. They –'

'Was Clowance with him at the time?'

'No. Harriet was. I mean Harriet Warleggan. She fetched help from Cardew and he was carried home on a stretcher.'

Dwight stroked his chin with the quill of his pen. 'Who is attending him?'

'A man called Mather. Recently arrived from Bath. He did wonders for Andrew Blamey – old Andrew – when he was ill.'

'Stephen may be better in a few days. Sometimes the shock paralyses as much as a real breakage . . .'

'But if it is a real breakage?'

'Can heal well enough in a few weeks or months. There is always the risk, of course.'

'I'm sure.'

'It depends very much where the injury is . . . Ill luck for him after such a triumphant voyage.'

A shower of rain beat on the windows. Soon over, but it couldn't be the best day for a romp on the beach.

Ross said: 'It does not seem so very long since Stephen was ill before, and you went across to advise and prescribe, and Clowance nursed him back to health.'

'It *is* not so long.'

Ross said: 'Of course Clowance thinks there is only one doctor in Cornwall.'

'I was afraid you might be intending to say that.'

'I have the unenviable task of passing on her message to you. She said: "Do please implore Uncle Dwight to come."'

Dwight stroked his chin again.

'Of course I'll go. It is too late today, but perhaps tomorrow.'

'Thank you. I know how grateful she would be.'

'But I do not know how grateful this Dr Mather is likely to be! To preserve medical etiquette, it should be *he* who invites me to see his patient. Last time it was just an apothecary.'

'If you were intending to go tomorrow, I would send someone over to tell them. I am sure that Clowance, helped by Demelza, would be able to convince any surgeon of the rightness of this course.'

Dwight laughed. 'I'll try to be there by eleven. Mind you, Ross, in the case of an injury of the sort you describe – if it is such an injury, there's precious little anyone can do – surgeon or otherwise – except tell the patient to keep quiet and wait. Is he in much pain?'

'I don't know.'

'Shall you be going to Penryn also?'

'I think not, at least until I have heard what you say. It is a small place and I don't want to overcrowd them. Also, Demelza must not be away too long.'

'Oh?'

'Cuby is coming to stay.'

II

When Dwight saw Ross out he saw Katie moving rapidly away among the trees of the drive, as if not wanting to be noticed. The shower had gone and Dwight was reluctant to return immediately to his letter, so he strolled towards the gates, enjoying the sun and the wind in his hair.

It occurred to him to think that perhaps Katie had brought another summons from Place House, but if that had been the case Bone would have come hurrying. In any event when he had last seen Selina she had seemed to have recovered her health and at least a degree of her spirits. Dwight guessed there had been a part reconciliation between husband and wife. However complex a character Valentine might be, and however mixed up in his own life, he had a great way with women, and there was no reason to suppose that Selina had become immune.

Suddenly Katie was in front of him. She must have dodged round the corner of the drive, and it was as if she came upon him unexpectedly.

'Dr Enys . . . I was nearby and then I seen Cap'n Poldark.'

'He's just gone,' Dwight said. 'Did you wish to see him?'

'Nay, twas you, sur, as I 'ad thoughts to see. But then I thought I'd no right nor reason to come'n bother ee.'

'What is it? Are you unwell?'

'Nay, sur, I'm not unwell. Leastwise, not as no one could say so.'

'I'm glad of that. What is it then?'

Katie's face was down, but he could see enough of it to observe the hot flush colouring all her visible skin.

'I don't hardly know 'ow to tell ee.'

Dwight waited. 'Would you like to come inside?'

'Oh, nay, sur, tedn that. But mebbe yes, maybe yes, I did oughter come in, not bawl'n out in the middle of the garden for everyone to 'ear.'

'Good. Well, come in, then.'

He led the way and she followed for a few paces and then stopped again. He waited.

She looked up and looped a tangle of hair away from one eye.

'I don't reckon tis proper, but maybe tis proper and right. I thinks only Surgeon d'know, so only he can tell me.'

'Tell you what, Katie?'

She put a hand to her mouth as if willing herself not to speak.

'Reckon I've begun me courses again.'

III

'Well, Katie,' said Dwight, ten minutes later, 'without a thorough examination, which I do not think you would wish to subject yourself to, I cannot tell what has been wrong with you. All I can say with certainty is that you are not going to have a baby.'

'My dear life,' she said, breathing out a sob. 'I don't know how 't 'as 'appened!'

'Nor do I. But if what you now tell me is an exact description of what passed between yourself and Saul Grieves, I do not think you could possibly *be* pregnant. You see, merely the male seed . . . Well, there must be a much more definite penetration of the . . . Well, no matter. There are such things, you know, Katie, as false pregnancies. They can be brought on by hypnosis, hysteria, a

412

wishful desire to have conceived, or a tremendous feeling of guilt. And the last is, I think, in your case the one to blame.'

The intense flush was dying from Katie's sallow skin.

After a few moments she said: 'What about this 'ere?' pointing to her swollen stomach.

'I shall expect it to go down naturally, now that you are convinced you have no child to bear. If it is a dropsical condition it can be treated. If tumorous it may be removable. But I am strongly of the opinion that in a healthy young woman such as yourself it is simply a symptom of hysteria and that it will very soon disappear.'

Katie rubbed a hand across her eyes. 'Jerusalem, it d'make me feel some queer, just to think on. All these months – months of sorrow and shame! They was all for naught.'

'It should make your relief the greater.'

'Oh, it do, it do. But I d'feel such a great lerrup. Gor 'elp me, what a great lerrup. Why . . . why I never needed tell nobody nothing! Nobody never needed to know I allowed Saul Grieves any liberties 'tall! Folk'll laugh me out of house an' home. Gor 'elp me. Tis enough to make you fetch up!'

'These things have happened before, Katie. There was a queen of England long ago called Mary who was just newly married and desperately wanted an heir to the throne. She convinced herself, and all the important Court doctors, that she was with child. Alas for her, she was not.'

'She *wanted* a child,' said Katie. 'I *didn*!'

'It is probably derived from the mind in a similar way. I am sure your feelings of intense guilt – and your fear – produced the same symptoms.'

There was the sound of horses outside. Caroline and the children had given up their trek on the beach. At the clatter Katie got up.

'Did she never have no children?'

'Who? The queen? No. Her sister inherited the throne.'

'Well . . . that'll be your family come back from riding, Surgeon. I'll not keep ee no further. Tis for me to live my life – begin it all over afresh.'

Dwight got up too. 'Don't worry. Try not to be upset. It will be a nine-day wonder in the village and in no time at all everyone will forget it.'

'My dear life!' Katie stopped as if she had been bitten.

'What is it?'

'Music!' said Katie, and slapped her thigh. 'I shan't have to wed Music!'

There was a moment's pause before Dwight spoke. 'No. You don't have to wed Music.'

'My dear soul! Well, now, there's a relief for ee! Jer-*us*-alem! I don't have to wed no one 'tall!'

They went to the door.

'Music will be much upset.'

'Ais, I s'pose. Do you think he 'ave ordinary feelings like a real man?'

'Emphatically so. Did you not realize that?'

'Ais, I s'pose. Ais, I d'know he be very fond of me. I like him too. There's no '*arm* in him. Never a bad thought. 'E's gentle and kind. But I don't wish to wed 'im.'

'Well,' said Dwight dryly, 'it is your own choice. It always has been.'

There were more heavy clouds blowing up like angry fists clenched in the sky, but as she was let out of the side door, Katie squinted into a shaft of the expiring sun.

'I can't wed 'im *now*. Twas a convenience. Tis too bad for him maybe. I'm sorry for him, I really am. But there tis. He knew how twas. He'll 'ave to put up with un.'

IV

After leaving Dwight Ross took out the letter Cuby had written.

Dear Lady Poldark,

I am writing this from Caerhays where I have now been three weeks with my family. Perhaps I should first have written to you, but in truth it is hard to know what to say to the mother of the man I loved so dearly and who I know held him at least as dear. When we met last you were much concerned for the safety of Jeremy's father – and thank God he has come safe home – yet I remember it personally as a happy time when we first came to know each other

*and Jeremy was there to make our friendship complete. Now all is
lost, and I propose to come to you carrying his child and carrying
the grief of a bereavement we both equally share. Sir Ross told me
I would be welcome at Nampara, to stay until after the birth of my
child, and I feel sure that you would echo that welcome. But my
constant presence in your household may come to be a too constant
and irksome reminder of Jeremy's death, a lodestone dragging you
ever back to your feeling of sorrow and loss.*

*So with your permission, dear Lady Poldark, I would like to
come for perhaps two weeks, to begin, then perhaps to return to
Caerhays for a little while. Let it be how it seems best and most
seemly to you.*

*If it were convenient I would come next Monday, the 17th. I
would like to bring my sister Clemency for company, who would
stay the night and return with the groom on the following day. But
pray make some other suggestion should this not be convenient. I
am, as you well understand, entirely a free agent.*

*Believe me, dear Lady Poldark, I am so much looking forward
to seeing you again.*

> *Your loving daughter-in-law,*
> *Cuby*

Demelza had sent a note back saying she would be most welcome.

This was just before the young sailor had arrived to tell them of
Stephen's accident.

V

In the afternoon Ross walked up to Wheal Grace, changed into
mining things and went over it with Ben Carter. There was not
much fresh to see, and what there was was depressing. For years
the mine had yielded riches from several floors of tin and now was
played out. The south floor had been closed for two years. The
north, after appearing to be bottomed out more than once, had
raised hopes by revealing smaller pockets and platforms from time
to time, but none had more than postponed the evil day when the
mine had to close.

While in captivity Ross had had plenty of time on his hands to make calculations, and he had come to the decision that if or when he got home the mine should be immediately shut down. By now there were only forty men working in it; all the others who had left had been absorbed into Wheal Leisure as that mine expanded. They could probably now take on another ten.

But Jeremy's death had knocked his calculations – like many other things – out of joint. He told Ben that for the time being the old mine should continue to operate but that the sixty-fathom level – the lowest there was – should be abandoned and such work as there was could be concentrated on the forty-fathom and above. The bottom pumps – installed by Jeremy – were to be disconnected and brought up – and anything else of value before the old floors were submerged. Beth, the engine built by Bull & Trevithick twenty-five years ago, and modernized by Jeremy in 1811, could continue to function on a reduced scale and under reduced stress. Labour force could be pared down to about thirty. It was more than maintenance, but not a lot. It would cut his profits on Wheal Leisure by about twenty per cent.

Ben asked if he would go over Leisure with him tomorrow, but Ross said it would have to be one day next week. There was no reason for this – he was not busy – except that Leisure in the last five years had become so much Jeremy's mine (the whole decision to reopen it, the design of the engine, the leats to bring the fresh water, the development of the rediscovered Trevorgie workings) that he just did not wish to face it again. He had made a perfunctory tour when he first came home, but then the wound had still been so raw that it couldn't be made worse.

It was only about four and a half years ago, just after he had returned from Spain – and they had been down Wheal Grace and were walking back to the house together – that Jeremy had made the suggestion that they might consider reopening Wheal Leisure. He had interlaced his remarks with seemingly innocent queries about the Trevanions – apparently he had just then met the girl for the first time and was besotted with her. Ross knew nothing of this then – Cuby and Jeremy had first met when Jeremy was returning from some adventure he had undertaken with Stephen Carrington and they had come ashore near Caerhays. An ill-fated affair if ever there was one; yet it seemed to have contained within it a short vivid few months of brilliant happiness. Perhaps that was better than nothing at all. And Cuby, although in some ways wilful and perverse, had been a girl worthy of his love.

The other thing Ross had not known that chilly morning in February 1811 was Jeremy's intense preoccupation with the development of steam – and the gift that he had for harnessing the latest ideas. Ross never failed to blame himself for this lack of knowledge, this lack of perception in regard to his son. Yet, as Demelza had said, Jeremy had preserved such secrecy about it that there was no *way* of knowing. It had, as so often happened between father and son, been a breakdown in communication rather than a breakdown in sympathy.

And then, before he died, so very young, he had even begun to distinguish himself in a military career, picked out by Wellington himself for promotion. Another Captain Poldark. Somehow the art of war was the last thing one would have ever expected him to excel at, the tall, thin, gangling, artistic young man with the slight stoop, the joking, flippant manner, the distaste for bloodshed.

God, Ross thought, what a *waste*! what a *loss*! – for Demelza, for Cuby, for Isabella-Rose, above all for Jeremy himself . . .

He was about to leave the shelter of the mine when his temporarily blurred sight picked out the figure of another young man approaching. As tall as Jeremy, younger by three years, long-nosed and narrow-eyed and thin-shanked, dark of hair and skin, a lock showing over his brow from under his hat. His cloak and features were glistening from the latest shower.

'Well, Cousin Ross or I'll be damned! What nasty weather! Were you in the mine? Good fortune for you. I wasn't, as you observe. These clouds just dip the water out of the sea and empty it like a child with a bucket!'

His glinting, easy, charming smile. But just the wrong moment for Ross, remembering Jeremy.

'I thought you were back in Oxford.'

'Cambridge. No, we leave at the weekend. Ghastly journey, but Selina will not go by sea. A pertinent disadvantage to making one's home in Cornwall is the monstrous distance it is from everywhere else!' He got off his horse, glancing at Ross's gaunt, grim face. 'We wrote, of course, as soon as we heard.'

417

'Of course,' said Ross. 'Thank you. I'm sure Demelza replied.'

'I believe Clowance did. It is a sad loss for us all.'

'Thank you.'

Valentine had dismounted. Ross noticed the slightly bent leg.

'Are you walking back?'

'Yes. But I have to warn you, Demelza is from home. She is staying with Clowance for a few days.'

'It was about Clowance that I was come to ask. Or if not Clowance, then Stephen. I have heard he has had an accident.'

'Bad news travels fast.' As they began to walk downhill Ross told the young man what he knew.

Valentine said: 'That is cursed luck. I have come to know Stephen over the last couple of years and find him an energetic, versatile feller. He will not take kindly to a long spell of invalidism.'

'Dr Enys is going tomorrow, so perhaps we shall have more information then.'

The small angry clouds marching in from the north-west had separated, like a military procession before an obstacle, and between them the sky above Nampara had become sea-green and shot through with sunshine. Valentine took off his hat and flapped it against his cloak, knocking away the moisture. He asked about the progress of Wheal Leisure and Wheal Grace, and spoke of his own new venture, Wheal Elizabeth, which by the beginning of next year was likely to need an engine.

'I had been going to seek Jeremy's advice on this. Alas . . .'

'When shall you get your degree?'

'Next spring. We hope to be permanently in residence at Place House from then on. May I ask you one or two questions?'

A change of tone.

'Questions? Of course. If I can answer them. Will you come in?'

'Let us walk down to the beach. Maybe the open air will be better for any confidences which may pass.'

They skirted Demelza's garden and came out on the rough ground leading to Nampara Beach, where the mallows and the thistles and the rough grass grew. The tide was out, and the expanse of sand stretched to the Dark Cliffs, smooth, pale brown, uninterrupted by rock or shelf or gully. The sand nearby was well pitted with footprints, but beyond a few hundred yards even they disappeared.

In the distance a solitary figure moved along the high-water mark.

'Paul Daniel,' said Ross.

'What?'

'Paul Daniel. He shares this part of the beach with three others who go up and down the high-water mark seeing what's come in. When he finds something on the way out he does not pick it up but makes a double cross beside it in the sand. Woe betide anyone who makes off with it.'

Valentine laughed. 'We are both Cornish to the bone, you and I, Cousin Ross; yet I suspect you understand the villagers far better than I ever shall.'

'My early life was more earthy. Certainly until I left to go overseas in my early twenties I had never been further than Plymouth.'

'. . . I have been away so much.'

They leaned on the gate.

'What did you wish to ask me?'

The breeze was not interrupted for some time.

'You mentioned Dwight Enys just now. He attended my mother when my sister was born.'

'I believe so.'

'Did he attend her when I was born?'

'No, he was at sea – in the navy.'

'You know I was an eight-month child?'

'I have heard so.'

'Premature in all things. But you say you have *heard* so. Did you not know so, as you lived so near by?'

'My relationship with the Warleggan family has never been friendly. At that time it was at its worst.'

'Why?'

'Why what?'

'Why was it so bad just then?'

'Is this an examination I have to face?'

'If you please.'

Valentine was tapping on the gate with his long fingers. This young man had been a figure in Ross's thoughts, frequently forgotten and then painfully, poignantly central again, for more than twenty years. Yet in all that time they had never had a personal, intimate discussion. Their contact had been superficial. It seemed peculiarly maladroit that Elizabeth's son should tackle him in this way so soon after Jeremy's death. He had always tended to dislike the young man, his sardonic humour, his mischievous jokes, his great charm, his automatic assumption that all women would succumb to it. He had been particularly disagreeable at Geoffrey Charles's party, had brought Conan Whitworth uninvited and greatly upset Morwenna, had half-drunkenly smiled and sneered through the tense encounter following, when Ross and George had almost come to blows again. Rumour had it that he had married Selina Pope for her money and was already being openly unfaithful to her.

'What are you looking at?' Valentine asked.

'At you, Valentine, since you ask. At the time you were born, the natural antagonism between me and your father was at its height because I had not wished your mother to marry him. He must have known this.'

'You were in love with my mother, were you not?'

'At one time.'

'At that time?'

'I held her in high esteem.'

Ross watched a parade of crows which were waddling in judicial procession towards the cliffs of Wheal Leisure as if about to open the assizes.

Valentine said: 'Did you know – I suspect you did – that I was a constant bone of contention between my mother and father?'

'Later, yes.'

'So you must have known why.' When Ross did not answer Valentine said: 'Because he suspected I was not his son.'

'Indeed?'

'Yes, indeed. All my childhood I lived under this cloud, though of course I did not know what it then was. After my mother died it lifted a lot. It was as if Ursula's birth – at seven months – had allayed his suspicions. After that he made an effort in his own dry dusty way to become an agreeable father. But by then the damage – so far as I was concerned – was done. I feared him and hated him. There was little he could do by then to change himself in my eyes. I . . . I have always felt he was in some way responsible for my mother's death.'

420

'I do not think that could be. Your – George – was very attached to your mother; no doubt, as you say, in his own dry dusty way; but I believe it to have been genuine. Do not forget that it was twelve years before he remarried.'

Paul Daniel had moved out of sight. Ross felt a surge of fruitless anger at the tangle of love and hate and jealousy which had surrounded this young man's birth and distorted his childhood. Whose fault was it? His as much as anyone's. Elizabeth's too. And George's. The one blameless person was surely Valentine. Through the years, and always at a distance, Ross had watched the boy's progress to manhood. Yes, what he had seen and heard had been unfavourable. But too seldom had he faced the facts of his own responsibility, psychological or actual, for the situation as it had come about.

This unsought meeting stung him emotionally, made him feel as if the central fact of his whole existence, the hub from which all the spokes of his later experience led away, lay in the few minutes of anger and lust and overpowering frustration from which Valentine could have been born.

He put his hand on Valentine's arm, briefly. It was an uncharacteristic gesture.

'Why have you come to see me today?'

'I felt that before I left again I had to meet you, try to straighten out certain events in my own mind.'

'I do not think I can help.'

'That was what Dwight Enys said when I spoke to him a few days ago.'

'On this subject?'

'Related to this subject . . . Do you think my mother was unfaithful to George Warleggan after they were married?'

'Good God, no! You demean her memory.'

'I cannot help but speculate. It would explain his extraordinary changes of mood.'

'I'm sure that is not the explanation.'

'Do you then feel equally certain that my mother went with no man between the time her first husband died and the day of her remarriage?'

Ross had seen this question coming. 'Your mother was an upright and honourable woman. I saw little of her, but I should think it highly unlikely.'

Valentine coughed dryly. 'Well, may I ask a final question, then. It is the one I came to ask, difficult as it may be to ask it. Is it possible that you could be my father?'

Ross found he was gripping the top of the gate too tightly. He slackened the grip and then flexed his fingers, looking at them. He knew how much might depend on his reply. And how necessary it was *instantly* to lie, without the *least* hesitation. Instantly. And yet how *impossible* it was to lie whatever the consequences.

'I have no intention of answering your question, Valentine.'

'You mean you can't or won't?'

'Both.'

Wheal Leisure was coaling. Black smoke rose and merged with the cloud drifting above it and began its journey of dispersal inland.

Valentine said: 'Then it is a possibility?'

'God damn you, boy!' Ross stopped and swallowed, trying to contain his anger, aware that it was as much directed at himself as at his questioner. There was silence for a few moments. 'Damn you! . . . Yes, it is a possibility.' As Valentine was about to speak Ross went savagely on: 'But *only* a possibility. No one will ever know for certain. I do not think your mother ever knew for certain. It is a question that I cannot answer for I do not know the answer. Does that satisfy you?'

Valentine said thoughtfully: 'Yes, thank you. I think it does.'

It seemed as if, because of what had happened that moment, the world was moving in a different way, as if a few words uttered into the wind, spoken by a single voice, heard by one person alone, would prevent its ever being the same place again.

Ross said: 'But let me warn you. Let me warn you of this, Valentine. If at any time you speak of this – in public or in private, claiming something or denying something on the strength of what I have said, there will be two men wanting to kill you. That is George Warleggan and myself. And I swear to you one of us will.'

Valentine leaned back against the gate in his usual cynical attitude, as if nothing was more important than that he should seem to care about nothing in the world. But his face was deeply flushed. Returning the gesture, he put a hand on Ross's arm.

'Understood,' he said, 'Cousin Ross.'

Nine

I

When Dwight reached Penryn the following morning Clowance opened the door and showed him into the tiny parlour, where a thick-set blond boy was standing hands in pockets.

'This is Jason Carrington, Stephen's nephew. He has just called to see Stephen.'

They shook hands. Clowance was rather untidy, her eyes blood-shot from lack of sleep.

After an awkward moment Jason said: 'Well, ma'am. I reckon I'd best be getting back. I'll be here tomorrow for sure.'

When he had gone Dwight said: 'I can see the relationship.'

'Yes . . . He is very fond of Stephen.'

'Tell me how it all happened.'

'He was thrown from his horse in the woods below Cardew. Lady Harriet was with him. According to the groom they had not met above fifteen minutes before and were galloping towards Cardew. They came to an awkward fence and Stephen's horse fell. Harriet went for help and he was put in a farm cart so that he could lie flat and be brought home. Even though the distance was much greater than Cardew, they considered it better to bring him straight here.' Dwight thought there was a touch of bitterness in her tone.

'And now? He is conscious?'

'Oh yes. Has been since Thursday. But sometimes confused still.'

'Can he move his legs?'

'He can move his left but not his right. Dr Mather has put him in what he calls a spinal jacket and has bled him constantly. Mama is with him at the moment.'

'And Dr Mather knows I am coming?'

'We told him this morning. Of course he knows your name. He

said he would try to be back by eleven, so that you can see Stephen together.'

Dwight took out his watch. It was only 10.15. 'Does Dr Mather live near? Perhaps I could call on him.'

'At Flushing. I suppose it's three or four miles.'

There was a step outside and Demelza came in. She was wearing a white muslin frock with a black sash, and Dwight thought her looks were already a little returning, almost in spite of herself.

They kissed. Demelza said: 'He is thirsty, and I came down for more lemonade. Tis that good of you to come, Dwight. Caroline did not ride with you?'

'No. She thought it would make a crowd.'

After talking for a few minutes it was Demelza who said: 'Dr Mather is an understanding physician. I do not believe he can be too put about if you go up without him.'

Stephen looked a big man lying in the small trestle bed, much bigger than when Dwight had attended him for the peripneumonia. His face was heavy and flushed. Demelza put the lemonade on a side-table and said: 'I will wait downstairs.'

Stephen's body was bound up in splints, and he grunted as they turned him over on his side. Dwight's fingers travelled lightly over his back, pressing to see where there was pain. The right leg was swollen and useless, the skin dark and bruised-looking. The left leg he could bring up to bend his knee.

They turned him again on his back, and Clowance propped him up a few inches with a couple of pillows.

Dwight took out a glass tube with a small bulb at one end, attached to a thin cane rod for strength. He put this under Stephen's arm. The clinical thermometer had been invented nearly two decades ago but was not in general use. When he withdrew it he saw the mercury well up the scale.

'I'm steering a fair course,' Stephen said. 'Full canvas soon. Rest for a day or two more. That's all. Gi' me the lemonade, Clowance.'

He could hold the glass but his hands were shaky. Dwight lifted his eyelids.

'You should mend,' he said, 'but it will be a slow process. You will need to possess patience. Dr Mather is following the right treatment.' He said to Clowance: 'I think the bruising on the right leg would be reduced with a liniment of camphor dissolved in oil of cloves. But do not cover with a flannel cloth, allow the air to reach it. And I will write a prescription for Peruvian bark. Then I must see Dr Mather.'

'They sent up from the Royal Standard last night,' Stephen said, 'wishing me well. Eh? And Christopher Saverland, the Packet agent, sent his wishes. And others've called. It just shows.'

There were adverse signs here and Dwight wondered whether Mather had been alert to them – and if he had whether he had kept them to himself.

'There's some spinal damage,' he said as they went down the stairs, 'but the recovery of movement in the left leg is a good sign. The oedematous condition of the right leg will have to be watched. I believe bleeding will serve a useful purpose, though at the base of the spine, not on the leg itself.'

'How long will he be bedridden?' Clowance asked.

'It is impossible to know, my dear. Three months, if he is fortunate.'

'Three months!'

'It may be less. He is a very determined man. But first . . .'

'First?' said Demelza, studying the face of her old friend.

'Can he eat? He should be kept on an antiphlogistic regime. Lemonade is the ideal drink.'

'First?' said Demelza.

'There has been some internal bleeding. It may have already stopped.'

'And if it has not?'

'Let us hope it has. When are you returning home?'

'Me?' said Demelza. 'I don't know for certain sure. But I have to go Monday.'

'I think Mama should return home soon in any case,' said Clowance. 'She has enough troubles of her own without bearing mine. And Jeremy's widow is coming to Nampara to stay.'

'Can you manage him on his own?'

'Jason will be here Monday to stay as long as I need him. He can help me with any of the heavy work of nursing.'

'After I have seen Dr Mather,' Dwight said, 'perhaps I might come back and take a bite to eat with you before setting off home?'

II

Aristide Mather said: 'There is a definite fracture of the vertebrae. Palsy was total when I saw him first. I made an incision yesterday in the right thigh and drew a quantity of blood.'

'Yes, I saw that.'

'The swelling was reduced and he seemed eased by it. I also raised the sacrum by means of a levator. That too you will have observed.'

'Did it cause him great pain?'

'He grunted a deal. He is not one, I think, over-sensitive to pain.'

'The right thigh is the greatest concern,' Dwight said.

'Internal haemorrhaging?'

'Yes.'

'I thought of the femoral artery.'

'So did I. But if it had been ruptured he would have been dead by now . . .'

'Well, there's little we can do for that. There is no way of applying a tourniquet.'

Mather was about forty, short, brisk, red haired, with that capable confident air Dwight had always lacked.

'I should like to see him again, perhaps in a couple of days, if that would be agreeable to you.'

'Perfectly. Pray come when you wish.'

'Lady Poldark will, I think, be riding home on Monday. If you would send word by her – in a letter, I mean – that would keep me informed.'

'Certainly. If he is still alive by then.'

Dwight raised his eyebrows.

'Well every day is a day gained,' he said drily.

As they reached the door Mather said: 'I read your article on malign and benign growths and the tubercles of phthisis in the *Edinburgh Medical & Surgical Journal*. I am honoured to meet the author.'

'Ah,' said Dwight, almost apologetically. 'That was last year. I have recently come upon one or two new points, which might slightly amend the argument. But thank you.'

'In the meantime rest assured I shall do all I can to bring this young friend of yours to a recovery. I have always found it as well to fear the worst – in my own mind – so that I am fully prepared to fight it.'

'It is a principle I follow myself,' said Dwight. 'So I am not likely to quarrel with it. I shall await your letter, Dr Mather.'

III

When he got home it was after six and Music had been waiting for him three hours.

Dwight had eaten well at Clowance's, so, having satisfied Caroline's inquiries about Stephen, he was able to delay her thoughts on food until he had seen the young man.

Music said: 'Tedn right fur me to bother ee, Surgeon, but her said yes, Surgeon, her promised me. Her promised.'

He had been crying, but that was a time ago. His light eyes, in which intelligence had only its intermittent leasehold, were dry enough now, prominent, but for him quite hard. He kept swallowing his Adam's apple as if he were trying to get rid of it.

'I'm sorry for you, Music. There is little I can do to help.'

'I d'know that. Thur be nothink nobody can do. But what can *I* do, Surgeon? It d'leave me out of the cold. Worked every hour on that thur cottage. She've been over him wi' me time an' time. Tedn as if I'd *changed*. Bain't no change in me. I 'aven't gone moonstruck nor mops an' brooms, nor nothink. She've just broke 'er promise, that be the whole truth of it!'

Dwight said: 'You realize, I'm sure, that she believed herself to be pregnant and was going to marry you partly for the sake of the child. When it turned out all to be a mistake, the main reason for the marriage had been removed.'

'Please?'

'She is a virgin, Music, if you know what that means. She has never had proper intercourse with a man. She finds herself a girl again. Life for her is beginning afresh. She has total freedom of choice and at present prefers to choose no one – to be what she was before all this began, Katie Carter, a parlourmaid at Place House.'

428

'Please?'

Dwight's mouth turned in a grim smile. 'Come, my friend, do not step back so quickly. But do not think I don't sympathize with you. She agreed to marry you and –'

''Twas a promise!'

'Yes, it was, and she has broken it, and she should not have done. But she thinks everything has changed and that that releases her from her undertaking. I suppose she explained this to you?'

'She said this an' that. This an' that.'

'And did she not say she was sorry?'

'Oh aye. She said she was some sorry and tried to pertend we'd be friends. But that bain't the same thing 'tall.'

'I know. I know how disappointed you must be. And since I encouraged the match I must bear some responsibility. I am very sorry and disappointed this has happened. It is a lesson to me not to interfere in other people's lives.'

'Please?'

'But, Music, you must not allow this to be an excuse for back-sliding. You came to me for advice and help long before your involvement with Katie – or at least long before it became serious. And I *have* helped and advised you, haven't I?'

Music scratched his head. '. . . Ais.'

'So there is no excuse to allow all that to slip away again. You must *not* let your disappointment get the better of you and so return to become the young man you were three years ago. You are so much better. You are normal in nearly every way. You must remain so – even if it means leaving Place House and never seeing Katie again. You must be your own man. Understand?'

'Ais.'

'Now go home and tell yourself you are going to make the best of it. Will you promise me?'

With a large slack hand Music pushed the lank hair out of his eyes.

'Cann't promise to leave Place House.'

'I don't ask that. I only suggest it as a last resort. Promise you will keep up your present efforts to be a whole man.'

Music blinked. 'I *be* a whole man, Surgeon. That d'bring me no comfort.'

IV

When she rode home on Monday there was a conflict in Demelza's mind. The black gaping hole of Jeremy's death was still there in the very depths of her body, like a canker that ate away any sign of a return of her natural high-spirited interest in life as soon as it stirred in her. She was much concerned about Stephen who, if no worse, was certainly no better, and she carried Dr Mather's letter for Dr Enys and was tempted to open it and see what his real opinion was.

But aside from these troubles was an altogether less worthy worry, which she knew Ross would despise her for. Her daughter-in-law was coming to stay.

And bringing her sister, whom she had scarcely met.

The two weeks in Brussels, where Cuby and Jeremy had made her and the other three so very welcome, had passed off beautifully, and if it had not been for her worry about Ross – when in the last six months had she ever been free from worry? – she would have enjoyed herself. The very first time she had met Cuby – only last year – she had felt a certain affinity with and liking for the girl. This had been much enhanced in Brussels, and she had looked forward to seeing more of her whenever she could. After the loss of Jeremy she had fully endorsed Ross's suggestion that Cuby should come to live at Nampara at least until the baby was born.

But now that it came to the point, old feelings related to her humble birth stirred in her.

Cuby had never been to Nampara, which, to face the truth, was only a large farmhouse with a fair range of outbuildings common to a farm, and only one room really, the library, to give it the claim to be called something better. Nampara Manor? It wouldn't do. It wouldn't be true. You don't elevate a thing by giving it a better name.

She had never been to Caerhays, not even to see it from the outside; but Jeremy had spoken of it quite often – a great castle (even if an imitation one which they had not yet been able to afford to finish), set in a superb park, with footmen and grooms and all the panoply of aristocratic living. Demelza knew such houses. She knew them well. Tehidy, Tregothnan, Trelissick. She loved them and enjoyed the company of the people living in them. Bowood, where she had taken Clowance, was the greatest of them all. And she had stayed in Lansdowne House only a few weeks ago. She had mixed with the best. And she was now Lady Poldark.

So why this worry? Well, Cuby had never seen Nampara. It was an earthy place, with a down-to-earth master and an up-from-the-mines mistress. Cuby had been over last year to the party at Trenwith. Now *that* was a suitable house, belonging to Geoffrey Charles. Perhaps Cuby expected Nampara to be another Trenwith. If so, it would be a horrid come-down for her. It seemed that she had become reconciled with her family. Probably after a couple of weeks she would gratefully return to Caerhays and stay there. Even though her mother-in-law was Lady Poldark.

And there was a sister coming. Demelza had seen her at the Trenwith party, along with a rather bumptious brother (with whom Cuby had recently been staying in London). Demelza seemed to remember that Jeremy had spoken well of the sister, though whether this was the same one remained to be seen.

With Jeremy none of this would have mattered. He would have jollied everything along, filled up the awkward pauses, adorned the house, in Cuby's eyes, with his presence. Now there was only Ross, who in his existing mood was more than ever inclined to disregard the niceties.

So she left Penryn very early on Monday, accompanied by the same young sailor who had brought the last message, and was home by eleven. In her reply to Cuby she had invited them to dinner at three, and now wished she had not. There was little enough time to prepare, first, two bedrooms, and then a meal which, while not pretentious, must be pleasantly elegant and well chosen.

All this, as she had instructed before she left, was in train, but much needed still to be done. The parlour was untidy, the dining-room cheerless, the *washing* had to be taken in; and the whole house lacked flowers. To make matters worse a strong south-easterly wind was blowing – always the most difficult to cope with – making windows rattle and doors bang. The tallest sandhills beyond Wheal Leisure were smoking as if they had volcanic properties.

She flew about the house, even making a heart-hurting tidy up of Jeremy's bedroom, so that if Cuby wanted to see it it should look its best. She had given Clemency Clowance's room and Cuby the better of the two new rooms built above the library when that part of the house was altered in '96. This, if she eventually chose to stay, would be where she would bear her baby. It was the least used room in the house and quite the most genteel. Only five years ago they had bought new rosewood furniture, the bed had pink quilted satin hangings and furnishings, with window curtains to match, and there was a maroon turkey carpet.

Into the garden to gather flowers; but they were sparse and looked tired. Cornish gardens were at their best in the spring: the light warm soil favoured all kinds of bulbs, roses, broom, lupins, wall-flowers and flowering shrubs like lilac and veronica. But there was not enough humus to sustain the summer and autumn flowers at their best. (This year, of course, the hollyhocks had quite failed.) Dahlias were becoming all the rage and might have done well in this sandy soil, but Demelza could never grow them because of memories of Monk Adderley.

She had gathered what to her looked a tattered bunch, had thrust them into a jug in the parlour, and hastened out to see if she could find something more, when Ross came into the garden by the gate leading to the sea.

'Back so soon?' he said as he kissed her. 'I had not expected you till twelve.'

She told him between stoopings and snippings the latest news on Stephen.

'I brought a note for Dwight from Dr Mather. I had no time to deliver it on the way home, and I did not like to trust it with the sailor. Perhaps Matthew Mark would take it.'

'I can take it myself.'

'No, Ross, if you please, I would rather you were here when Cuby comes.'

He took her arm. 'It is not the old bogeys rising again?'

'A small matter maybe. But I have never had a daughter-in-law before, and because of what has happened it is bound to be difficult.' She gazed round disparagingly at her garden. 'If I had time I could do better with the wild flowers on the cliffs! There's heather in

432

plenty, and knapweed – and there's lovely fresh gorse at the top of the Long Field.'

'Well, it will take you no more than half an hour. I'll hold the fort while you are gone.'

Demelza shook her head. Sick fancies these days: she had a sudden vivid picture of coming into this house, before she married Ross, a servant girl carrying a sheaf of bluebells, and finding Elizabeth had called.

'Why are you shivering?' Ross asked.

'Was I? It is of no moment . . . I think Stephen is gravely ill, Ross. I wish I knew what Dr Mather had written to Dwight.'

'I will go myself tonight and ask him. He'll tell me. But in injuries like this the surgeons can do little. It all depends on the patient and how bad he is hurt.'

'My dear life!' said Demelza.

'What is it?'

'I think they are here.'

V

'He don't seem to get rid of the fever,' said Jason.

'No. I hope Dr Enys will come again soon.'

'Reckon he did no more than Surgeon Mather.'

'It is just that I have known him so long and trust his judgements. I had hoped . . .'

They were eating some fried soles that Jason had bought, with potatoes and a pease pudding. Clowance had listlessly prepared the meal and ate without appetite. It was the evening of the Tuesday, still light because the sun, though setting over the land, reflected an incandescence from the water of the bay. Dr Mather had been in this afternoon and given the patient a draught which had put him to sleep, and had left another for the night. They were taking it in turns to be with him and had put up another trestle bed in the room so that each in turn could spend the night there. Stephen was in some pain now, but he was too weak to be irritable. All the same his weakness had not prevented him spending a part of the morning planning with Jason the boat that he intended to buy or have built, a smallish brig or a twenty-five-foot lugger, for Jason to command until he was experienced enough to merit something bigger.

Nor had it prevented him seeing three visitors: Andrew Blamey, Sid Bunt and Timothy Hodge. The first had been just a friendly call, a hail and farewell, for Andrew was sailing for New York on the morning tide and came to wish him well. The last two had been on business, for trade had to continue even with the owner laid up.

Clowance had hardly spoken with Tim Hodge before: he was so swart, so dark of eye and skin and tooth, so squat, that it took a time to overlook his appearance; then you couldn't fail to appreciate his practical talents. If Stephen was to be laid up for a long time he was the obvious man to help to run things. If she had not been so preoccupied with Stephen she might have had time to wonder how a man of such parts, now in his mid-forties, should still have had to enrol as an ordinary deckhand in a makeshift privateering venture.

Jason said: 'Father's a real popular man. Folk stop me in the street, say, how is he, seem real concerned.'

'He has a way with him,' said Clowance. 'He gets on well with everyone.'

She looked across the table at Jason, whose appetite was good and who ate with a relish worthy of a starving sailor. Since Stephen's accident she had seen a lot more of his son. He seemed the natural person to help her at a time like this. She saw in him some of Stephen's traits, both unagreeable and endearing, particularly among the former his tendency to fantasize on his own prospects, his ability in his own mind to rearrange the world to his own wishes. He would never be as good-looking as Stephen, nor, she thought, as physically, so vitally, attractive; but he had an engaging manner, an optimism, a resilience that reminded her very much of the man upstairs.

Thinking these things, Clowance said to him: 'Tell me about your mother.'

Jason blinked, then smiled. 'What do ye wish to know, ma'am?'

'Well, do you think you are like her?'

'Nay, she were dark and thin – real thin in later years – and small-boned – like a quail. I've taken from my father.'

'You are not quite as big as he is. Did she have any special abilities?'

'Abilities?'

'Well, I mean, was she, for instance, a good cook? I'm not a very good cook.'

'Good 'nough, ma'am. I'm sure my father love the food you give him. Mother? Yes, she did for us well. How my father liked it I don't know, because, of course, he left.'

'Yes, he left.'

Jason took a draught of ale. 'She was a good sewer.'

'Knitting and weaving?'

'Knitting special. She helped bring me up wi' selling things she made wi' her own hands. This jerkin, f'instance.'

Clowance looked at it and smiled. 'It was the one good thing you were wearing when you came. The stitch is very even.'

'Well, she made it for me. She made many things for me – stockings, gloves. This jerkin was one of the last things she made for me, more'n two years ago.'

Clowance put a piece of bread in her mouth. It was home-made and light, but it lacked something. Perhaps it was salt. She cut another slice from the loaf.

'Two years ago?'

There was a silence.

Jason said: 'Hark, was that him tapping? I thought I heard –'

'No, I don't think so . . . Did you say your mother knitted this for you two years ago?'

'Oh, nay, twas a slip of the tongue. Twas much longer than two year.' Jason had gone very red.

'How much longer?' Clowance asked.

'I think I'll go see if he is awake,' Jason said, pushing back his chair. 'I wouldn't wish for him to think he was alone.'

He went out, and Clowance cut the piece of bread into small cubes. But they still tasted ashen and saltless.

After a while Jason came back. 'No, he's fast asleep still, but I have lit a candle. The light is failing, and when he wakes it will be good to see a light.'

'Jason,' Clowance said. 'When did your mother die?'

'What?' He blinked. His eyes were smaller than Stephen's, sandy lashed.

'She isn't still alive, is she?'

435

'Who? My mother? God's sake, no, she died – oh, some long time ago.'

'When?'

He scratched his head and then took an uncomfortable swig of beer. 'I don't rightly remember.'

'You don't *remember* when your *mother* died? Oh, Jason, I don't believe that! Did your father tell you to lie to me?'

'Oh, nay! But he just said – well, not to talk about her – said it would be like to upset ye.'

Without getting up, Clowance began to tidy the table, putting plates together and gathering spoons. She was doing it instinctively, with no awareness of her actions.

'Well, it does,' she said. 'It does upset me a little to hear your mother died so recent. But now I am upset, I think I would like to know the whole of it.'

'Twas a fool thing!' said Jason. 'A damn fool thing to let it out wi' a slip of the tongue! Twould distress Father greatly to think I had been gossiping behind his back, like.'

'You are not gossiping. And I will not tell your father. Was it last December she died?'

'God's sake, no! Long afore that.'

'I thought perhaps as soon as your mother died you came to tell your father, and so turned up here last January?'

'Nay, nay, she died in the winter.'

'Last winter?'

'Nay.'

'The winter before? You may as well tell me, as I can easy find out.' (She did not know how, but it was a point to make.)

'The winter before,' said Jason. 'I remember snow was on the ground. Twould be in the January.'

'January 1814?'

'Yes . . .'

'Two years ago your father went back to Bristol for a time. Five years ago he *came* from Bristol here for the first time. Was your father living with your mother, or visiting her there?'

'Lord no, we never seen him! I'd never seen him, not for twelve or more year before I came here this January, and that's God's truth! We didn't live in Bristol but ten mile outside. We never heard

436

tell of him until I heard of him at Christmas time, last Christmas time. Then a man, a Cornish sailor called Tregellas, he said he knew my father was newly wed and living in Penryn and was well found with a fleet of ships. So I thought to come, and come I did, as you well know.'

Clowance got up now, carried the plates across to the scullery.

When she came back she said: 'Did your father know of your mother's death?'

Jason looked startled. 'Oh, yes! Oh yes! Well he must've, mustn't he. Before he could wed you.'

Ten

I

The arrival had gone off quite well, and five of them sat down to dinner: Cuby and Clemency, Ross and Demelza and Isabella-Rose. Henry, who usually ate the main afternoon meal with them, was taking it with Mrs Kemp in the kitchen.

In spite of her pallor Cuby looked well. She showed the coming child more obviously than a taller lady on the south coast, who was about as much forward; but like Harriet pregnancy was doing no hurt to her looks. Nor did her bereavement show. Possibly it was the effect of coming to see her late husband's family in their home for the first time that made her vivacious and talkative – much more so than her quieter, plainer, gentler sister. From her green riding costume she had changed into a plain dress of blue dimity, with blue and white ribbons, velvet shoes. No mourning except for a small posy of black artificial flowers pinned to her breast. She had changed her hairstyle, Demelza noticed, grown it, wore it in bracelets of braided hair. Her rather sulky face lit up when she smiled: good brilliant teeth, warm lips.

They were eating hare soup, a green goose, pickled salmon, cheese cake, almond cream, with cider and beer. It was not elegant enough, Demelza thought, but Ross had said it was right.

Cuby said on the way over she had noticed the barley and wheat had been cut but most of the oats were still standing. The ground had been very wet, Ross said; this wind would soon dry it. He supposed crops were a week or two ahead on the more sheltered south coast? Cuby spoke about the excellent carriageway that had been laid between Truro and Shortlanesend, she swore it was the best in Cornwall. Ross said, yes, yes, it was the work of that man from Ayrshire, MacArthur, or MacAdam, was it? Clemency asked

438

about a mine they had passed near Truro, and Ross said, oh that would be Guarnek, re-started last year; it was said to be doing well. Cuby said, was this your mine, the engine that was working as they came down the valley? Yes, said Ross, industry passes too close here to achieve elegance . . . Cuby said she was sure everyone would welcome some industry close to Caerhays if it would contribute to their income.

'In fact,' said Ross, 'the mine you passed, though it has made us a small fortune over the years, is now costing us money to maintain. At one time we employed more than a hundred and forty people, now it is down to thirty. Wheal Leisure, over on the cliff, is the profitable one.'

'But you keep this other, this . . .'

'Wheal Grace. Just in operation. It is partly sentiment, partly that I don't want to throw men out of work. While I was interned I thought it over and decided it must close. But coming home, with later events in mind, I have kept it open. I think Jeremy would have wanted it kept open.'

The name was out. No one spoke for a few moments. Knives and forks chattered instead.

Cuby said: 'Lady Poldark, did you hear that Lady Fitzroy Somerset had her baby in Brussels? In May. It was a girl, but I do not know how she has been named.'

'No,' said Demelza. 'After I left Brussels I did not see her again.'

Ross said: 'I'm told Fitzroy will continue in the army and a brilliant future is foretold for him. He seems completely to have overcome the loss of an arm. The Falmouths say he is in fine fettle.'

'It is not so bad as losing a leg,' said Isabella-Rose brightly. 'Though it may be worse, I dare suppose, than losing only a foot.'

They all looked at this inconsequence in slight surprise, but she was not abashed. 'Do you know what happened yesterday, Cuby? A kite was hovering over the chicken run, quite close, when Ena – one of our maids – rushed out to save the chick. The kite came down and stuck its claws in her cap and carried it off! It was so comical! We was convulsed with laughter.'

You used always, Demelza thought, to be able to rely on Bella to keep the conversation going on a jolly note; but since learning of Jeremy's death and Christopher Havergal's maiming she had been

439

very mopish; often over a meal she hardly uttered a word; so it was a startling and welcome surprise to find her with recovered spirits at such an opportune time.

Now she was asking if Cuby sang, saying that Jeremy had told her she did – using the name without embarrassment – and that Clemency played; so tomorrow they must try duets together before Clemency left; they had a lovely piano – not that old spinet – but a lovely new one in the library that Papa had bought a couple of years ago; and no doubt they would be given permission to play on it for such a special guest.

Demelza went on with her dinner, picking at this and that, and noticing that Cuby was not eating heartily either, but watching her lips part in a smile, those crescent dimples appear and disappear at the sides of her mouth – something which had so enchanted Jeremy, and not surprising; heard her laugh at something Bella said; and she thought: this girl is here in place of Jeremy, my tall handsome dearly loved son, and she was married to him for only six months and is already laughing, and perhaps in a year, two years will have almost forgotten him – as I shall never forget him – and will likely marry again and bear more children by some other man, and the episode of her brief marriage to Jeremy will fade into a sad little corner in her early life.

And looking at Cuby in this way, Demelza felt a spasm of resentment within her that in a flash turned almost to hatred.

Judas God! she thought, aghast and sweating, bringing herself up short, what is this I am *thinking*, what is it I am *feeling*? This girl was the love of Jeremy's heart, and in an ordinary life not cut across by bloody war, would have remained so. She is a *nice* girl, and bearing his child. How can one look beyond that? She has been warm and affectionate to me. Is this feeling I have because, like Clowance, I suspect that if it had not been for her reluctance to marry him, he would not have gone into the army? Or is it something more earthy, more primitive, something every woman feels about another woman who steals her son? In any case it is wrong, wrong, wicked, evil and wrong, and if it is natural to feel it, then I must be unnatural and not *allow* myself to feel it!

I am Ross's wife and Jeremy's mother, not some village woman with mean and narrow and carping thoughts. I am my own person too, separate from Ross, able to choose and decide for myself. Evil thoughts, jealous, mean and petty emotions should be treated like blow-flies, not allowed to settle, driven away. Demelza did not really believe in Sam's circumstantial heaven, with God the Father waiting to greet her; nor really either in Mr Odgers' pallid faith; but if Jeremy's spirit was in any way alive, how humiliated he would be to know that she had harboured such thoughts, even for a moment, about Cuby!

'My dear,' she said, 'if Clemency would wish to stay for a few days we should be some pleased to have her. Of course you must use the piano whenever you want. It will, I suspicion, be badly out of tune, for I have not used it since – we came home. And even Bella has not been quite in the mood. But it would be lovely to have the sound in the house again.'

'That is kind of you,' said Clemency. 'But Mama will be expecting me home. But if I could come again – and soon . . .'

'Then let us make the most of today,' said Bella boisterously.

They made the most of the day, playing and singing for an hour after dinner, and then, under Bella's leadership, took a walk on the beach. Though it was one of the least favourable of days to venture on it, Cuby professed herself delighted with the expanse of sand and sea and rocks, and her cheeks were glowing in an uncommon way for her when she took tea with saffron buns and almond cake in the parlour. Ross talked about the problem of blown sand, especially with north-west winds; down towards Gwithian the sand-banks in some places were nearly two hundred feet high and a mile wide. He went on to speak of the plan to extend the pier at St Ives and build a breakwater and the nuisance that town suffered from blown sand. He did not know if his listeners were interested – or indeed if he was very interested himself – but it was something to say and it kept the ball rolling while someone thought up another subject unconnected if possible with the late war.

So the day passed, pleasantly enough as far as it could, nobody upsetting anyone else, but still inevitably much of a social occasion. Nothing could change that except day to day contact on a basis of ordinary living.

In the evening after supper the three girls had gone to sing duets at the piano, but presently Cuby slipped away, walked through the drawing-room, across the hall and into the parlour, where she found Demelza sitting alone reading a letter.

'Oh, pray excuse me . . .'

'No, no, please to come in. You do not disturb me.'

Cuby moved over to a chair, not sure all the same of her welcome.

Demelza said: 'It is a letter from Geoffrey Charles. I am only re-reading it. It came on Saturday.'

'Oh.'

'You met him of course at his party . . . But not since?'

'Not since.'

'He is now in the Army of Occupation in Paris. His wife and daughter should be with him by now. He fought all through the Peninsular War and was wounded two or three times, but survived Waterloo without a scratch. Could you do something for me?'

'Of course.'

'Those other candles. They will make it more cheerful. Bella and Clemency are playing on alone?'

'Bella is practising that song she sang at the party. "Ripe Sparrer-grass". She has a fine voice.'

'Well, an unusual one. And strong. Her father does not much care for it.'

'We all loved it at the party.'

'Yes, it is at times like that it shows at its best.'

'Do you sing, Lady Poldark?'

'Not now . . . Oh, well, I sang last Christmas – that was the last time. But Bella has quite taken the wind out of my sails!'

'I hope you will sing sometime this Christmas.' When Demelza did not reply. 'I'm sorry. I should not have said that.'

'Perhaps we should all sing because the war is over.'

'Yes. I lost my brother at Walcheren.'

'I did not know.'

Cuby finished lighting the rest of the candles. The old room came into clearer focus, still shabby in spite of new furnishings over the years. It was the room in which all the Poldarks had lived for over three decades. It was the room in which Demelza as a child of fourteen had hidden from her father when he came to take her home to Illuggan.

Demelza was frowning at the letter. 'It is strange about Geoffrey

Charles that he has made such a fine soldier. He seemed at one time a rather spoilt boy. It was not until he went away to school that he grew up of a sudden, began to change . . . But then . . .'

Cuby sat down and waited. Demelza had been going to say: 'Jeremy was the same.' But it was dangerous ground to walk on. It could not safely be explored yet, if ever.

'He has written to us before – since Waterloo, I mean. In this he just says, "I nearly and dearly sympathize with you all in your grief." It is a long, long letter – I think he has specially tried to make it long and interesting – and begins with his account of his march from Waterloo to Paris. He says they marched thirty miles a day! He describes the French peasant women. "They wore lofty white caps with long flaps hanging down to their shoulders, their exposed stays often not closely laced, bosoms covered with coloured kerchiefs, coarse woollen petticoats striped with pink and reaching only to their calves, with white woollen stockings and sabots. Gold and silver rings in the ears and gold crosses on black ribbons round their necks." It is a good picture. He says the English troops were welcomed everywhere as a protection against the pillaging of the French soldiers in retreat and the devastation of the brutal Prussians, who tore down doors and windows and burned the furniture in the streets.'

'Lady Poldark,' Cuby said.

'Yes?'

'May I come and sit next to you?'

'Of course. Of course.' Demelza turned over a page. 'When they reached Paris they were first encamped in the Bois de Boulogne. Mostly the Prussians, Geoffrey Charles says, were allowed into Paris. He says he is now at a village called St Remy, about twenty-five miles from Paris.' She stopped and looked at Cuby, who had come to sit on a stool next to her chair. 'But he says he mounted guard in Paris, Geoffrey Charles says, when the Group of Horses which had been stolen from the Venetians were removed from the Arch of Triumph to be returned to their proper owners. Cuby . . .'

'Yes, Lady Poldark?'

'You cannot go on calling me Lady Poldark. I am Jeremy's mother.'

'It does not matter. I just want you to know . . .'

'What is it?'

'How much I grieve. Underneath. I put on a pretty show. But underneath.'

Demelza said: 'Perhaps without him we are both a little hollow.'

Cuby put her wet eyes against Demelza's hand.

'I wish I could die.'

II

Harriet had sent over twice to ask after Stephen's health. Now she wrote:

> Dear Clowance,
> I understand Stephen is confined to his bed and therefore not suitably to be visited. When he is, pray leave me know, and I will defy the Wrath of God and come to see him. There was a pretty to-do when it was discovered I had been jumping a ditch or so in my present gravid condition; George could not have been more consumed with anger that Stephen had met with an accident riding in my company had Stephen been his dearest friend – which needless to say we all know he is not. A Council of War was held – hardly less than a Star Chamber – with Drs Behenna and Charteris in attendance, in which it was virtually laid down as a Statute that I should not ride again until after I have foaled – though Lord save us, it is probably two months yet to that dreary event.
> So I send sincerest wishes for your husband's recovery, and pray let me know at once if there is anything you lack that I may provide.
> Cordially yours,
> Harriet Warleggan

When Clowance showed it to Stephen he grunted.

'She may keep her charity. We are well enough without it.'

'I do not think she meant charity in any ordinary sense – rather, perhaps, books to read or peaches from their hothouses.'

Stephen grunted again. His face was flushed and his leg painful. 'I want nothing more of her – or any of 'em. I hope she bears him a horse: that'd suit her, I'll warrant.'

444

Clowance said: 'Always before you have been kindly disposed towards each other. We know that she helped to deflect George's intention to bankrupt you. What did she say to you that so upset you?'

'Forget it.'

She waited. 'Well, I must reply, thanking her for her note. When you are better, if you do not wish to see her then, we can always make an excuse.'

'Can you get me more lemonade? I'm that thirsty.' When she had been for it he said: 'Where's young Jason?'

'He went down with Hodge to see the agents. You remember? He should be back soon.'

'Oh, aye, I *remember*. I'm not going to slip my wind yet. Clowance, I been thinking.'

'Yes?'

'This Truro Shipping Company that opened up last year. The shares were twenty-five pounds when it began. They're up to thirty-three now. I thought to buy some. Maybe some folk would see them as competitors, but I know the main shareholders and they're friendly along with me. By buying into their business I help my own!'

'So long as you don't overstretch.'

He shifted into a more upright position and winced with the pain. 'When Swann came up from the Falmouth Naval Bank yesterday he told me what some of the other cargo of the *Revenant* had fetched. Even with the share-out I shall be a richer man than ever I thought. *We* shall be richer. Have you been to the house this week?'

'You know I went yesterday.'

Stephen frowned, then half laughed. 'Ah, yes. And it is coming along well?'

'Well. Most of the outer structure will be finished by Christmas. We could move in, say, March or April.'

'Sooner'n that. Sooner'n that. When am I going to get the use of this leg back? What did Mather say this morning?'

'Yesterday. He said it was only a matter of time . . .'

'Ah, but how much time? That's what I want to know. To come through that privateering venture, wi' folk exploding their muskets in my face, and a French frigate near capturing us, to be floored by

445

a damned horse is the ultimate. Really it is the ultimate . . .'

To calm him Clowance went into details of their house. She had told him them when she came home yesterday, but it lost nothing for him with repetition. Indeed she did not know how much of it he recalled. But when it was over, when she had told him all she could, he was silent for a while. Then he said:

'What'll we call our house, Clowance? Our big beautiful house where we're going to live for the rest of our lives. When we've got those stables up and planted our garden and, maybe, raised our children.'

'I don't know,' said Clowance. 'It's hard to think on a good name.'

'Well,' Stephen said, 'I've a notion. Maybe twill surprise you. But I've a notion to call it Tranquillity.'

Clowance looked at him and half smiled.

'Do you think that's what we shall find there?'

Stephen put a hand up to his brow. She came quickly and wiped it for him with a linen towel.

'I don't know,' he said. 'But that's the name I've the fancy to call it.'

III

The sudden improvement in Isabella-Rose's spirits was not without cause. The letter from Geoffrey Charles, which had arrived while Demelza was away, had been accompanied by a second letter addressed to 'Miss Isabella-Rose Poldark', and as her father was out of the house at the time she had been able to spirit it upstairs without anyone seeing it. It was from Christopher Havergal. She did not recognize the writing, and after she had opened it and peeped at the signature she held it to her breast in youthful anxiety before she could bring herself to read.

My dearest, dearest Bella, (it began)

Since I had the inexpressible pleasure of seeing you last, much has happened – most of it disagreeable. I was devastated to hear of the loss of your dear brother. Do you know, I never met him, much as I should have wished to do so. In a large army I suppose it is not surprising that your brother and I did not meet. He was in the 52nd Oxfordshires and I was drafted late into the 73rd Highlanders. On that fateful Sunday his regiment was holding the ground east of Hougoumont whilst we were defending the Ohain road – a distance perhaps of a mile and a half, but a mile and a half more than a little congested with fighting soldiers! (I was nearer Geoffrey Charles, but never saw him either until the Tuesday after.)

I have also lost a part of myself – though not so large a part as rumour, I understand, first had it. We of the 73rd had had a real set-to at Quatre Bras on the Friday (to think I once complained that I had missed most of the war!) but it was not until Sunday afternoon that a cannon-ball arrived and carried off my foot at such a rate that I was never able afterwards to find it, diligently though I searched. My life was saved by a Mrs Bridget O'Hare, wife of Rifleman O'Hare who, like others of her sturdy kind, always follow their husbands into battle. Mercifully no surgeon was about, so I did not lose half my leg; she applied a tourniquet and bound the wound up in dirty rags, and by the time I was picked up by a hospital cart I did not merit surgical attention.

The outcome is that I am minus my left foot, but otherwise intact. I was very soon on crutches, and now, as the breach has healed over, I am beginning to walk with a leather strap and an iron support which I am told will soon be exchanged for an artificial foot. In time maybe even a stick will be superfluous!

I am writing this, as you see, from lodgings in London, where I have had a wonderous convalescent time being fêted and dined in the best houses as one of the young heroes of Glorious Waterloo. In the last five days I have presented myself at my lodgings punctually for breakfast at 9 a.m. – before I went to bed.

Dearest Bella, before you cut me out of your life for such incontinency, I beg to assure you that very, very soon I shall become sober-minded again. But for a little while I have just rejoiced at being alive and so much in the swim!

I have to confess to you also, dearest Bella, that I am at present living with a lady! . . .

But she is my landlady – forty years old if she is a day, with bad teeth and a stooping posture – a truly curvilinear old maid, who feeds me well when I am there to be fed and who in all other ways *is mercifully unobtrusive. I have seen many charming and pretty and taking young persons since I returned to England, but none has engaged my fancy because in front of them all as I look at them is imposed the utterly enchanting face of my beloved Bella, whose like in the world there is not.*

Isabella-Rose Poldark. It reads and speaks most excellently. Isabella-Rose Havergal. That in due course of time, if you will have me, it shall be changed to. But Bella Poldark will always be your stage name. It runs on the tongue. It runs in the mind. As the owner of it will run on the tongue and in the mind of those who eventually see her.

Three months more I shall spend perfecting my New Foot. Riding shall, I swear, be no obstacle. Dancing may prove a trifle more perverse for a while. Aside from that, and a somewhat loping walk, I swear to you I am a whole man – and wholly yours. In three or four months – perhaps in the spring when your flowers are out – I shall come and sample the salutiferous air of Cornwall. Then, my lovely poppet, I shall hope to see you again!

Your devoted friend – who wishes in due time to be more,
> *Christopher Havergal*

Eleven

I

It was Music Thomas's wedding day.

Or rather it was the day on which it had been proposed he should be joined in holy matrimony to his dearly loved and admired Katie Carter, when they would cleave together and be of one flesh – or at least live together and be of one cottage – until death did them part. Now, alas, not a death but the failure of an expected birth had prevented the union being proceeded with. Katie had let him down, as no doubt she'd the right to do, or so Surgeon Enys said, and he did ought to know. But the rights or wrongs of the situation helped Music not at all. The desire of his life – although it had seemed far out of his reach – had suddenly been promised him. Now it was as suddenly withdrawn. And he had become the laughing stock of the village.

At twelve noon on his wedding day Music stood in his cottage staring round it, all so clean and so tidy and lovingly repaired. Night after night, and whenever he could get away, he had worked to make the place suitable for his queen. Now it was empty except for his four cats.

It was worse being so clean, so tidy; and his brothers would be sneering. The sun was falling through the new windows he had put in. Good glass had been hard to come by, so he had puttied in a piece of bottle-green glass for the lower panes; with the sun shining through it it looked the colour of sea water with bubbles. (Upstairs in the bedroom he had had to make do with oiled paper.)

And the privy was clean and the steps to it new laid, and the back plot was as tidy as could be expected with three hens roaming it, and beyond that Will Nanfan's field and then the moors leading to the cliffs with the Queen Rock looming out at sea.

He knew he should be at Place House, for it was not his official time off, but he did not stir. If he was sacked he didn't any longer care. He'd get a job, some sort of a job, to keep himself fed – if there was any purpose now in staying fed. Many folk, of course, had been against the idea of his wedding Katie; her mother had and her brother had and her grandfolk had; they'd all thought he wasn't good enough. There was a time when he had greatly admired Ben Carter – still did in some ways: that there organ he'd built all by his self in his own bedroom. They was clever folk, the Carters, not like him, the village fool, singing alto and walking spring-heeled and anyone could make a butt of him.

Yet she'd promised. She'd scat her promise. She said she'd wed him and now would not. The Carters were no betterer than the Thomases. In fact worse, for he'd never gone back on no promise to no one.

He'd helped Ben Carter when he'd been in trouble that time, when he'd met him coming out of The Bounders' Arms, with Emma Hartnell propping him up and him as drunk as a newt; he'd helped him back to his mother's shop and helped him upstairs, and Katie had come upon them and had given Music a rare old talking to for helping himself to the asparagus in the walled garden of Place House to take as a present to Dr Enys. But it had all ended beautiful. It had all ended with Katie giving him a kiss – the only one ever, and he had galloped back to Place House like a man who'd found a gold mine.

That was the best day of all. It had never been so good after, with Katie only having eyes for Saul Grieves and Grieves only having eyes for any slip or mistake or shortcoming Music might have or make. It had been sneer, sneer all the way.

Music had never seen Ben Carter tipsy drunk before, nor never since, and his brother John had said it was because Clowance Poldark had gone off to wed that up-country sailor feller, Stephen Carrington. Crossed in love Ben had been, not just so different from Music's own plight now. But ne'er as *bad*. Ne'er as *bad*. Music would have taken his oath Miss Clowance Poldark could *never* have promised to wed Ben, let alone scat it up at the last minute. Ben had got tipsy drunk all the same. Why not? Why shouldn't *he* get tipsy drunk today? He'd pennies enough. He'd been saving for the marriage day, and Surgeon Enys had been generous about those shelves. And that wonderful lady whose dog him and Miss Clowance had helped to bring home in the snow last February, that wonderful lady, Lady Something, had given him more money than he had ever had before in his life.

Rum. That was what Emma Hartnell had said Ben had been drinking all day. Music had only touched spirits three times in his life but he'd never tasted rum. Maybe twas the best thing to fill up a hollow heart.

But where to get it? There was Sally Chill-Off's, just at the head of the Combe. Emma's the other way, past the church. A half-dozen more to choose from. But which might turn him away afore he had had his fill? They cared naught, none of 'em cared naught so long as he had the pennies and they didn't have to chalk up his debt on the side of the bellows. Ned Hartnell was the most likely to see him away too soon. The Bounders' Arms was a bit superior against the rest. But that was where Ben had gone. That was where Music thought he was least likely to meet the village lads. If Ned and Emma would let him he would drink himself quickly into a state where everything would be forgot.

II

Three hours later Ned edged him out of the side door of the inn. Music was a mite frustrated, because he had wanted to be just so far gone as Ben had been, and then Emma could've helped him all the way home. It would have been nice to have leaned on Emma all the way home, because she was soft and kindly and he might have got his arm around her waist even if only in the most chaste way. In fact, though he did not know it, Ned had substantially watered his rum, not wishing to have the young man snoring under his table for the next twelve hours.

Still, he was distinctly merry and the emptiness and grief had disappeared. And he was unsteady enough for Ned to lend him a stick. *And* they'd been all strangers in the inn – that is from places more than a mile away, like Marasanvose and Bargus – so they'd not tormented him with jokes about the wedding.

In the left pocket of his rough smock he carried a small flask. When he got home he reckoned if he finished that off he would sleep his way into oblivion for the rest of the day.

Fine morning, wet evening, that's what it was going to be. The sun had sneered its way behind some mackerel clouds, and there were heavier ones creeping up.

Creeping up, that was the word. Something hit him on the shoulder. It was a clod of earth. He turned slowly, trying to keep his balance, and there was a titter. It was a girlish titter and after a moment or two another piece, half stone, half grass, hit him on the leg. He recognized the black tousled head of Lily Triggs. Then he saw Mary Billing and Susie Bice. Others began to appear out of the rough gorse and outcroppings of rock.

'Goin' church, Music, are ee? Can we come 'long and see the fun? Like to wed one of us, would ee, now? How 'bout Mary 'ere? She'm a fine maid, she be. Just ripe for ee! Heh! Heh! Heh!'

He waved his stick, half in menace, half in fun and then went on. But in front of him he found five big lads barring his way. Another Bice, another Billing, and Joe Stevens, who was one of his long-term tormentors.

'Let's all go church, shall us,' said Stevens. 'Be ee bride or groom, Music?' He tried to hang a lump of turf with trailing ends on Music's head. 'Crown 'im, crown 'im!'

Music knocked the turf away and lost his hat. He pushed his way through the lads and went on his way. He was near the church, and was almost up to the churchyard when his arms were seized.

It was the girls who had got hold of him – hard and noisy as the lads – but because they were women he could not very well knock them away. He struggled to be free, but his fumed head let him down and he fell. Hands grabbed him again and he was yanked to his feet. Laughing, jeering faces.

'Come us on, me dears. Getten wed are ee? Set 'im down in church porch, and ye can wait for yer bride!'

Struggling they lugged him into the churchyard and half-way to the church. Stevens tore up another hummock of grass and clumped it on his head; it stayed there while they howled with laughter. There were now a dozen or more, dancing round him jeering at him and thumping him. He aimed a couple of swinging blows: one landed on Stevens, the other floored Mary Billing, who got in the way at the last moment.

They didn't dare frog march him into the church, but Mary Billing, scrambling to her feet, screamed: 'Put'n in the stocks! That'll learn un. Let'n spend 'is wedden day setten in the church-yard!'

Not far from the porch of the church was a pair of stocks and beside it a whipping post. The post was not often used but the stocks were accepted as a valuable corrective for the minor miscreant.

Struggling and wriggling and dizzy with drink, Music was hauled towards the stocks; he would have been a handful to force into them, but at the wrong moment Mary Billing charged him head down like a bull and knocked all the wind out of him. By the time he began to get it back his ankles were secured, and then it was only a bit more struggling before his arms were fixed into the appropriate holes.

The lads and the girls – six of one and nine of the other – now stood back and looked at their victim. They screamed with laughter, disturbing the rooks overhead. It was the best joke they'd had for years, and into it came a half-realized resentment against the village fool who had striven to shake off his image. While he had been ready to play the idiot, singing alto at the head of any procession they got up, capering like a loon on the balls of his feet, ready to be laughed at because it was the only claim he would ever have to notoriety, he was a popular figure. But these last two years the fun had gone out of him; except for church he wouldn't sing at all; he had begun walking more or less ordinary; he'd put on a few airs, trying to distance himself from his old reputation; and all this had come to a head by him having the cheek to think he could wed a capable girl like Ben Carter's sister. Now she'd jilted him and good luck to her; that'd learn him. And this'd learn him too.

Of all people it was Susie Bice who threw the first handful of gravel at him. The Bices were not a nice family – shiftless and ailing and far from honest – but Susie had always been thought to be the best of a poor lot. It is doubtful now if she thought to start anything serious, but that was how it began. One after another the group began to pick up anything they could find in the churchyard and pelt Music with it.

Then Joe Stevens said: 'Nay, let's play fair. Let's draw a line, see. No one afore that line. No cheaten. We tak it from this yur line, see who scores a hit. See –'

'Stick a pipe in 'is mouth!' screamed Mary Billing excitedly. 'Make 'im into an Aunt Sally!'

'Nay, he'd never 'old un. Leave'n be.'

'Nay, let's dress im all golden like wi' gorse prickles, ready for 'is wedden.'

But Stevens and Bert Bice had no time for frills. They had drawn their line and were beginning to aim. And the one thing available was just beneath a headstone to old Dr Choake. The grave was covered with grey pebbles.

III

The Warleggans – Valentine and Selina, that is – had engaged a housekeeper called Mrs Alice Treffrey to take charge of Place House while they were in Cambridge. Mrs Treffrey came as senior parlourmaid from Tehidy, with the highest references, and there was not likely to be a repeat of Saul Grieves's misbehaviour. Because she was new to the job she did not notice the absence of the stableman; but others did. Katie – whose waistline had by now almost resumed its normal dimensions – could not get away until well on into the afternoon; then she went in search of him. She thought it might be his 'purty chets' that were keeping him. Or, the day being what it was, he might just be sulking. Anyway there was no call for him to lose his job: she would soon root him out, knock some sense into him.

The cottage was empty. Even the cats were not to be seen, though when she went out of the back door she thought she spotted a vanishing tail. She went through and out to the front. In the next cottage were the formidable Paynters, and Prudie was leaning over the wall.

'Looking for lover?' she asked with a leer.

Katie caught a glimpse through the open door of the lamentable Jud filling his pipe.

'I be seeking Music, if that's what ye d'mean.'

'He be gone that way,' said Prudie with a sweep of a fat wobbly arm.

The sweep covered an area of about a quarter of the compass, but there were virtually only two tracks leading in that general direction: one towards the ruined engine house of Grambler and thence to Nampara, the other to the church. Katie chose the church, and very soon heard excited cries and whoops from inside the lych gate. A few strides inside and she came on a group of lads and girls, in their late teens and early twenties, excitedly, hysterically egging each other on to stone her *ci-devant* fiancé imprisoned in the stocks. There had been a number of good hits and blood was running down his face. He was struggling to get out.

Not far from this scene was an open grave, ready dug but not yet occupied. Beside the mound of clay and stones (some of the stone bearing unmistakable gleams of mineral) was the shovel Jan Triggs, the present sexton, had been using. It was a type known as a 'lazy back', having a long handle and a heart-shaped blade. Katie picked it up, twisted it round in her hands to get a firm grip, walked back and knocked Joe Stevens unconscious with a tremendous swing to the head. Then she swung back the other way and caught Bert Bice in the chest, breaking two of his ribs. Mary Billing just dodged a blow that would almost have decapitated her, and the rest simply dropped the stones and fled.

Katie flung the shovel aside and went up to the stocks. Music blinked up through the blood at his new tormentor.

'Get out o' thur, ye great drunken fool!' she shouted in a fine temper. 'Cor, I can catch your breath a mile away –'

'Katie, I done me bestest –'

'Bestest, is it, an? My dear soul, I'd dearly not wish to know your worst! Come us on, come us on! . . .'

She lifted the wooden frame and helped him out of the stocks. A stray stone hit the woodwork as she did so, but she looked up with a glare so fierce no more followed. Two youths were kneeling beside Joe Stevens, who was stretched out on the grass just beginning to groan. Bert Bice was being helped away, holding his chest.

Free of the stocks, Music fell back on the grass and then made an effort to struggle to his feet.

'Lay still, ye gurt fool! Blinded your eyes, 'ave they? I'll see the magistrates 'bout that; have 'em up –'

'Nay, Katie, I can see well 'nough. Tis only the blood from these yur cuts on me 'ead. See.' He smeared his face with the back of his hand and blinked up apologetically at her. He might still smell strongly of rum, but his ordeal had gone a way to sobering him up.

Katie took off her yellow kerchief and began to wipe his face. It emerged through the blood and the dirt.

'Stinking great labbats,' she said, stopping to glare behind her. Two lads were half helping, half carrying Joe Stevens out of the danger zone. Presently they were all gone. She stood hands on hips staring belligerently around her, then turned her attention to the wounded man.

'Get on up, can ee?' She helped him to his feet. He lurched against her, then straightened himself. 'Come us on; I'll put ee home.'

It was not a long way – nothing to the distance Music had aided Ben to walk on a previous occasion. They reached the cottage. Luckily Prudie had gone in, and all the people in the cottage on the other side were at work. It was beginning to rain.

'Ye gurt *fool*,' said Katie again. 'What d' ye want to go get drunk for? Sit *down*!' she commanded. 'I'll get ee a dish of water to bathe off your face. And I'll boil a pan – make ee some tay. Not as I'd not be above one myself!' Her own hands were trembling with the spent anger.

She brought him a bowl and then while he dabbed at himself she lit the fire with some shavings and pieces of driftwood.

She sat back on her heels, looking at the fire. 'My, don't it draw!'

When she had come back from the pump for a second time with water to make the tea, she glanced at Music who had finished dabbing and was drying his face on a duster.

'That won't do! That's a halfy job. Ere take yer shirt off. And yer breeches. You're all caked and cabby.'

He reluctantly removed his shirt and she looked at the muscles rippling in his arms.

'My, what a gurt man ye are! Look, I reckon Surgeon Enys

456

should tend this wound in yer 'ead. Tis gaping like a little mouth.'

'Tis narthing, Katie. Reelly. I'll go Irby's and he'll put some salve on it.'

'We'll see 'bout that. Now yer breeches.'

Music looked at her sidelong. 'Cain't do tha-at. I got no slights on.'

'Well, land sakes, fraid o' me seeing something, are ee? Giss along. Ere – this cloth'll do. Draw off yer breeches and wrap'n round like a skirt. Ere, I'll tak yer boots off. If ye bend too far twill open up the bleeding.'

So presently he was sitting with a piece of old tablecloth round his middle and a potato sack over his shoulders while she made the tea. There were two clean cups he'd bought for the wedding and a half jug of milk the cats had not been able to get at.

They sat there in silence for a few minutes, drinking the hot tea. It was raining heavily now and a rising wind beat the rain against the coloured window panes.

'Them Bices, them Billings,' said Katie, 'they should be learned a lesson.'

'Reckon they 'ave been,' said Music with a half-giggle. 'An' Joe Stevens. He's always one in the lead.'

'Ah. Well, I've give 'im a sore 'ead.'

'I'll mind it fur a long time,' said Music, sipping at his tea. 'I'll mind it fur a long time. You thur striking of 'em, this way, that way, they went down like ninepins.' He relished the phrase. 'Just like ninepins.'

Katie poured out more tea, stirred each cup with the one wooden spoon. 'I'd best be getting back. Else they'll think I've fell down a shaft. I'll tell 'em ye met wi' an accident. Mind you come first thing tomorrow.'

'Ais. Oh ais, I will that. I will that, Katie.'

'Not that Mrs Treffrey will scold. She'm easy-going for time so long as the work d'get done.'

'I'll be there, Katie, sure 'nough.'

Katie looked at him. 'You're a fine figure, ain't you? Gotten more clothes upstairs, 'ave ee?'

'No. Well . . . I've a jacket and breeches 'anging on the wall, but that's for Sunday.'

457

Katie went up and fetched them. She held them up for inspection and dropped them on the table. 'Let's look at yer 'ead.'

She examined him again. 'You should see Surgeon for that. It d'keep welling up. Aside from that . . .'

'Ais, Katie.' He smiled at her.

She stared at him again. 'Reckon if I'd wed you you'd 've drove me mad.'

'Stay a space longer,' urged Music. 'Look at'n. Tis enting down.'

'Put yer clothes on, then,' said Katie. 'You'll catch yer death.'

He dragged off into the scullery and presently emerged in his Sunday best. His face was a mess, three bruises and two cuts, but his eyes clear again, at their most dazed blue.

'Reckon ye need someone to look for you,' said Katie contemptuously. 'You're as fazy as yer cats.'

'No,' said Music.

The firmness of his voice surprised her. It was the first time he had contradicted her.

'*I* want to look for *you*,' said Music. 'All the time – from daystrike to nightgleam. Tha's what I allus wanted for to do. All the time. Tis still what I want for to do.'

An extra flurry of rain lashed on the glass.

'You reckon that, do you?' said Katie.

'Yes, I do.'

Katie thought for a long time.

'You'd drive me mad,' she eventually said.

A smile cracked his battered face. 'Nay, Katie, I wouldn't. Honest I wouldn't.'

Twelve

On Friday, the 13th October Stephen was brighter than he had been for several days, and he seemed no longer in pain. He talked a lot to Clowance, though it was not always coherent.

'I've come a long way with you already,' he said, 'and there's big plans for next year and the year after. I been thinking them over all this time I've been laid up. For you and Jason and the Carrington line. I shall build another vessel, that's what I shall do, one to me own specifications, give the *Lady Clowance* over to Jason. Now the war's really over it looks as if we shall have peace in our lifetime, so we must bend our ways to make the *best* of peace. Peaceful trade's profitable if you get in when the tide's making, before your rivals. Great thing is not to work for other folk but to work for yourself. Then ye don't get paid per week – per month – ye get what ye've earned and it goes into no one else's pocket. I'm thinking to start a Joint Stock Company.'

'What is that?'

''Tis a more modern way of adventuring as in a mine. Or taking shares in a privateer. You establish a Joint Stock Company of say five thousand pounds and you keep three thousand of the stock in your own hands. Others invest in the shares and take a share of the profit, but you always keep control. That way you have the use of two thousand pounds of their money at no cost to yourself. It was the same sort of idea I thought on when I was in hock to Warleggan's. Then no one wanted a share. It will be different now.'

He licked his lips, and she wiped his face and gave him a sip of lemonade.

He chuckled. 'I've been clever in me life, y'know. Clever this last year or so. I reckon you've brought me luck, dear heart. All along, you've brought me luck.'

When did your first wife die? she wanted to ask, and was she dead in 1813, when you were first going to marry me, or were you just resolved to take a chance on not being found out? She wanted harshly, desperately to ask, but instead she wiped his brow again and moistened his dry lips.

He said: 'I've been in one or two scrapes, as ye well know. And some ye know not of. That first time when we were at the races and Andrew recognized me as the man in the bar at Plymouth Dock . . . It was a nasty moment. I've never been too sure of Andrew, y'know. He means well, most of the time, but he talks too much and is leaky in his liquor. Let him drop the wrong word when George Warleggan or one of his creatures is around . . . But now I no longer fear his indiscretions. He's sobering up with Tamsin, and it is all disappearing into the distant past. Like – like something else that happened that he was not concerned in. Others were. Ye'd be surprised if I told you who the others were. Someone quite close to you. But I never will, never can now . . .'

Jason put his head round the door. 'I'll spell you while you take your dinner, ma'am.'

Clowance went to the door. 'I cannot come yet. And – I think you should go for Dr Mather.'

'Why? Is he . . . ?'

'Tell him I would like him to come.'

When she returned to the bed Stephen was smiling again.

'Ye're real good to me, dear heart. I don't know what I did to deserve a wife like you. What was I saying?'

'It does not matter, Stephen. Try to rest.'

'Oh, I know. About me old luck. Look you, there was Plymouth Dock, and I was well out of that. Then there was the stage – the other thing, and I was well out of that. Then George Warleggan and his toadies tried to bankrupt me and drew back at the very last, and I was well out of that. Then there was the privateering adventure, which has made our fortune. And a Frenchie discharged his musket full in me face, and the charge was wet . . . Now I have fallen off a damned, cursed horse and hurt me back, but that is over now and I will soon be well out of that. We're turning up the aces, dear heart, aren't we now?'

'Yes,' said Clowance, sitting quietly down again.

'A leaky ship and the anchor's down. Hurrah me lads, hurrah.' Stephen was trying to sing.

'Hush, my dear, do not tire yourself.'

He was quiet for a minute or so, then he said: 'I reckon twelve pounds for a spring be too much. Why I can take it Plymouth and get it done for less. I reckon tis always the way; your local port'll try to charge too much. In dry dock, ye say? I'm poxed if she needs dry dock.' Then a little later: 'Swedish pitch at eleven shillings a hundredweight and Russian tar at twenty shillings a barrel. Can ye match that?'

Friday the 13th. Clowance was not superstitious but the day had the lowering look of the end of summer, the end of hope. From this window she could see a corner of the cottage roof next door, a piece of sky with clouds as dark as coal smoke shredding across it, and a lip of the harbour curling with spiteful little waves. She was filled with dread for the future; all the warm hopes of last year were gone and she lived in a spider's web of sadness and suspicion. Everywhere where there had been certainty there were shifting sands. She had never felt so much alone in an alien world.

'What I want,' said Stephen, addressing someone outside the room, 'is a smart little cabin for the master, bulkheads half panelled in maple and teak. And then in the corner a fine settee upholstered in crimson plush, see? A neat fireplace and maybe a tiled surround wi' a brass mantelshelf.' Now he turned his head suddenly: 'That suit ye, Clowance? Care to come wi' me across to Brittany? What shall we name her, eh? Now we've got a *Lady Clowance*, maybe we could call her the *Lady Carrington*? The flagship of the Carrington line!'

'I'd love to come,' said Clowance, 'when she's built. Get well first.'

'Oh, I'm coming along fine. Where's Jason?'

'Just gone out to fetch me something.'

'Reckon she'll carry a crew of eight, the *Lady Carrington*. That is about the style . . . Frame shall be of English oak planks; deck, I reckon, of Quebec yellow pine. Very even and hard wearing. The

461

oak can be got from the Tamar River and shipped from Plymouth. Masts of Canadian red pine; yards, topmasts, jib-boom the same. Diameter? I can't tell ye that till we've got the full plan! Where's Jason?'

'He'll be back soon.'

Stephen looked at her with a strange expression in his eyes. 'Tell him to hurry.'

'I will, I will.'

'She shall be laid down in Falmouth,' he said. 'Bennett's is a better yard than Carne's in Looe, bigger. Sorry, for your father has a money share in Carne's.'

'No matter.'

'Will ye hold my hand,' he said.

She drew her chair nearer to the bed and took his hand, which was moist and had no strength in the grip.

'That Frenchie,' he said, with a chuckle that rustled in his throat. 'Ye should've seen his face when the musket did not fire. I stabbed him through the chest. Blade went in so far I could not withdraw the knife. Biggest killing I've ever done, yet folk *praise* me for that. Don't make sense. Clowance, ye're a rare good wife. Where's . . . young . . . Jason?'

His head sank back on the pillows and his breathing became heavy and irregular. When Jason came back with Dr Mather, Stephen was unconscious. It was a long fight then; a man, still young, whose powerful body struggled against the forces of disintegration that attacked it. The hours passed and the night passed in this tremendous contest while the passionate need to live was slowly eroded by a relentless escape of blood. Dawn broke before it was over.

BOOK FOUR

One

Letter from Jeremy Poldark to his mother, handed to her by Cuby Poldark the day Cuby returned to Caerhays.

> *Brussels, 1st June 1815*
>
> *Dearest Mother,*
>
> *I do not suppose you will ever receive this letter – certainly I trust you shall not! – but just in case I thought to leave it in safer hands than mine.*
>
> *In January 1812 I indulged in an adventurous caper that I feel by some alchemy of your own you have already partly apprehended. I will not go into details, for whatever I said your apprehension would never become comprehension. For I do not altogether understand it myself. A serious law was broke by three persons, of whom I was one. I will say no more except to make it clear – and this is one of the purposes of this letter – that I was not unduly influenced by the other two. If anything I was rather the motivating force, and I worked out the plan that was carried out. If you suspect who the others might be, do not consider them more to blame than I and indeed rather the less.*
>
> *Nor should adverse circumstances be held to carry any more than a small load of responsibility. Of course I was disturbed and restless and unhappy. But that was only a scattering of gunpowder on the floor: there was no need to scrape it together and light a fuse! I wish I were able to explain it better than that – I cannot. Did I have an ancestor who ended up as a highwayman dangling at the end of a rope?*
>
> *One thing is certain. You are in no way at all to blame, nor is my father. I had a splendid childhood and a carefree youth-time. Any worm in the bud existed before the fruit was set.*
>
> *That is all – let us not be pompous about it. If, as I trust, I*

465

return with Cuby to set up house together near you, you will never see this – though perhaps it assuages something in me merely to write it down, believing that it will never be read by the Person to whom it is addressed. But then, on my return to Nampara, and at an early stage, I shall reclaim from you a little Loving Cup that you say you found one day on the beach; and I shall look on it as a cup of good fortune and keep it somewhere safe in my own home. If you should read this letter, then perhaps it has rather been a cup of Ill-Fortune, and, since you say you picked it from the sea, to the sea it should be returned.

By the way, last Christmas Valentine was asking me about installing an engine for his new mine, Wheal Elizabeth. If I am not about, tell him to approach Arthur Wolff, who is really the first man nowadays. Tell Valentine on no account to put in a plunger poll engine; they work excellent to begin but the exposure of the whole piston to the atmosphere at every stroke is unsound practice and will lead to excessive wear.

Well, this is about all I have to say! It is my usual custom to end my letters on a jolly note, but clearly this cannot be so in a letter which, if jollity prevail, you will never see! So may I just end with a charge to you and Father to care for Cuby and for our child? I know you will do this without any request from me, so pray take any more as said. Cuby is a wonderful girl and a wonderful wife – there could be no better – who is only just coming into her own. I would not want her to regress under any Influence her elder brother might exert. You, Mama, I think, would be the greatest influence – after me! – in inducing her not to do so.

Love, love, love to you all.

Jeremy

II

Letter to Sir Ross Poldark from George Canning.

Caldas, Portugal, 25th September 1815

My dear Friend,

Thank you for your letter in reply to mine of the 8th July. In expressing our sympathy to you and your wife and family over your grievous loss we were only joining in the chorus of loving friends who must have written in the same vein to try to support and comfort

466

you all. Though I have met none of your family – except briefly your beautiful daughter at the Duchess of Gordon's Ball – I feel that you have always been a close and loving entity, and the loss of your eldest son will be a sword thrust that will wound you to the heart.

But my dear friend, this second letter of yours grieves me in another way because it speaks of your intended withdrawal from public life and your decision to live henceforward in your Cornish home seeing to your own affairs. In large – at least in part – I can only commend such a decision – for what else have I done? – and I know of your long formulated intention to leave Parliament at the successful conclusion of the French wars. That is as it should be. You are not the political animal I am.

But you have so much to bring to public life in some form – a strength of character, a rare integrity, a thinking brain which does not allow itself to be diverted from its true concerns, a passionate belief in freedom and justice, a resolution in all good things: these are in such rare supply today that they cannot, shall not, I hope, be altogether lost to those of us who inhabit the world of affairs.

Peace, I have no more to say, except to ask you in due time, in God's good time, to think carefully on what I write. As for myself, what you may imagine am I doing with my own life to preach to a better man? The answer is little enough. At the end of June I wrote to the Government offering my resignation as Ambassador here, and a month later they accepted it. Now that the menace of Napoleon has finally been removed there is no need to keep such a large embassy in being in Lisbon, so they are going to scale it down and leave it to a chargé d'affaires. And I have become a private citizen!

One of my main reasons for accepting the post in Portugal in the first place was on account of George's delicate health, and in the hope that the warmth should suit him. It does. So I have brought him to Caldas to the warm baths. You will understand – and forgive me for – such a preoccupation with our eldest son. Here it is even hotter than Lisbon, and Joan and the little ones have fled to Cintra where the sea breezes blow. But George prospers in the heat, so I shall stay as long as he is happy here.

For the future? Of course I must return to England, temporarily or permanently, in the new year, if only to assuage my Liverpool constituents, who have seen nothing of me all this time! I do not yet feel ready to resume my political career (nor is there any inducement to do so), so probably I shall return to Portugal and then we shall travel into other parts of Europe – Madrid, Rome, Naples, Florence. Do you know you are luckier in one respect than I am, for I have never been to Paris.

But one day early next year I may of a sudden arrive in Falmouth – on my own, the family will stay here – and I do not know how far your home is from that port but in so narrow a county it can hardly be farther than a day's ride.

By then, my dear friend, I trust you and your wife will have come through the worst of your tragic bereavement. At least let us talk, and if you are adamant in your decision I shall henceforward hold my peace.

Believe me, with all sympathy and much admiration,
your Sincere Friend,
George Canning

PS I am sure you will take great satisfaction from the news that Fouché has now fallen – disgraced, I hear – and Tallien with him. So the stables are being cleaned at last!

III

Stephen Carrington was buried at St Gluvias Parish Church on the 19th October, the Reverend John Francis Howell officiating. A great many people turned out. In his short time in Penryn Stephen had become widely known, and on the whole well liked. Falmouth and Penryn, being ports, were more used to the abrupt arrival and departure of strangers and therefore were less clannish, at least on a superficial level. Stephen had had a 'way' with him, had been free with his money, talked with high and low alike, had put business in the way of the towns, and most recently had achieved a remarkable privateering success which had enriched both those who had put money into his adventure and the men who sailed with him.

There were also mourners from Truro, and Andrew and Verity Blamey, and a large north-coast contingent which included Ross and Demelza and Isabella-Rose, Dwight and Caroline Enys, Will and Char Nanfan. There were a few of his gambling and hunting friends – Anthony Trefusis and Percy Hill and George and

Thomasine Trevethan. His nephew, Jason Carrington, stood beside Clowance all the time, tears running unchecked down his cheeks. On the edge of things, sidling into a corner of the church and keeping her distance at the graveside, was Lottie Kempthorne. Neither George nor Harriet was there, but a slim nervous lawyer called Hector Trembath had come to represent them.

Clowance went through it all with a white, drawn face but tearless eyes. When it was over the Trevethans, whose large house was near the church, invited relatives and friends to a light meal, then everyone dispersed. Clowance had been staying with Verity: she said she would ride back with her father and mother that night and stay two or three days at Nampara, then she would return to Penryn where there was much to see to. Demelza said: 'Let your father do it; he will willingly do it; there is no reason for you to return at all, except to pack a few belongings.'

'I want to see to things myself, Mama. There is so much to think about; I haven't decided what to do about anything yet. *Anything*.'

She stayed three nights and then rode home. She had an open invitation from Verity but she decided for the time being to live at the cottage at Penryn. Demelza persuaded her to take Betsy Maria Martin with her, a solution Clowance said she willingly accepted of. She liked Betsy Maria, and another woman for company was welcome. She told her mother that she would stay at Penryn at least until after Christmas.

Demelza said to Ross: 'I think she may be stopping away because of Cuby.' Cuby was returning to Nampara in November.

'It is not so simple as that,' Ross said. 'I know there is this little bitterness on Clowance's part. But Clowance has suffered two of the hardest blows a woman can receive – the loss of a brother and the loss of a husband – within a bare four months. She's a very brave, honest person, and I think she just wishes to face it alone.'

'Cuby too has lost a brother and a husband,' said Demelza. 'She is more hurt than she shows, Ross.'

'The child may help *her* – it must help her.'

Demelza sighed. 'We are a sorry lot. Thank God for *our* children – what is left of 'em . . . Bella continues to bubble – she has quite recovered her spirits. And little Henry is a joy. One day, maybe, we shall learn to be happy with the blessings that are left.'

IV

In November the weather turned foul; there were storms up and down the coast, accompanied by the usual shipwrecks. A barque was wrecked off the Lizard with a loss of eight lives; she carried woollens and worsteds and refined sugar. Another vessel foundered near Padstow, with Indian spices, ivory, tea and sandalwood. A third with timber ran on the rocks at Basset's Cove. Hendrawna, wide open though it was to accept suitable offerings, only received some of the flotsam from ships lost elsewhere.

Katie and Music were to be married on Saturday the 11th November, which was Martinmas. When the news leaked out that Katie had relented and was taking Music from choice and not from necessity, the neighbourhood heard it first with derision and then with resignation. Sentiment is as changeable as the wind, and apart from a few of the girls and youths who had taunted Music, the general feeling swung in his support. The lad must have *something* about him for Katie to show him this favour. Maybe he'd proved a thing or two to Katie that we don't know nothing about. Maybe she'd best make sure of her man this time before something *really* turns up!

The only actual resentment came from Bradley Stevens, Joe Stevens's father, and some of the girls. Joe Stevens still had dizzy spells and Bert Bice's ribs were mending slowly. The week before the wedding, when the banns had been called for the third time, they got together in a group after church and thought out how best they might disrupt the wedding. They could create a disturbance in church, but Parson Odgers was so much in his dotage he would hardly notice, and anyway Music would only grin feebly and Katie glower; the ceremony would be carried on even in a pandemonium. Also it was rumoured that Dr Enys was going to be present, and although he was not a magistrate he knew all the magistrates. You didn't if possible tangle with the gentry. After the ceremony as they came out of church you could pelt them with mud, of which there was plenty after last week's storms, but again Dr Enys might be there and receive an ill-directed volley. Before the ceremony offered

470

the better chances. Katie had to walk up from Sawle with her mother and her step-father (supposing they agreed to accompany her – Ben would certainly not be there); Music had a much shorter distance to come and might come alone (it was rumoured he'd had hard words with his brothers). They could get some liquid manure ready in pails and swamp him as he came up the hill. Then when he'd gone into church all sodden and stinking they'd barrow in a dozen loads of pig shit and dump it all over his cottage. This plan, the brain-child of Mary Billing, was acclaimed by all.

The day before, Ross had ridden over to the Blowing House near Truro, in which he had a substantial share. He had dinner with two of the other partners and then met Dwight Enys at the Red Lion and they rode home together.

Dwight said: 'From the beginning there was nothing any surgeon could do for Stephen except wait. If a man is injured in the head, one may attempt a trepan, if one of the limbs, at worst one can amputate; for the spine there is virtually nothing. In his case – though neither Mather nor I thought it suitable to ask that we might open the body – we were both certain it was internal bleeding which led to his death.'

'Clowance was devoted to him,' Ross said, 'and they were happy together. He was a brave man and was becoming a successful one. After all his adventures and risky enterprises it is a cynical tragedy he should die in this useless and silly way.'

'I understand from Caroline that Harriet was much upset by the accident and has been more or less confined to the house since, not by infirmity but by George's edict. He is putting much store on the birth of this new baby.'

'They tell me he made a fortune out of Waterloo,' Ross said drily.

'"Dost thou laugh to see how fools are vex'd to add to golden numbers golden numbers?"'

'What is that?'

'Something I was reading last night.'

'Isn't there a verse in the Bible about the ungodly flourishing like a green bay tree?'

Dwight smiled. 'We all must learn to flourish as best we can, I suppose. And it's good to be able to survive, even in a more modest

471

fashion, as we both do, with somewhat clearer consciences than George must have.'

'I do not suppose that George's conscience ever caused him the loss of a moment's sleep. What would cause him loss of sleep would be if he felt he had paid half a guinea too much for a horse he was buying from a starving farmer.'

The track separated them. The mid-afternoon was frowning towards evening, and it would be dark before they reached home.

When they came together again Dwight said: 'You will have heard that Music Thomas is to marry Katie Carter tomorrow.'

'Yes.'

'I hope it may turn out well. I think it might. For Katie to marry Music willingly makes an altogether better prospect of it.'

'Ben does not feel so.'

'It was about that that I wanted to speak to you, Ross. I know you've long had an interest in the Carter family, as indeed I have. We both remember our visit to Launceston gaol.'

'I often think', said Ross, 'it is due to your ministrations that Zacky is still alive.'

'Zacky is alive because he has a constitution which will not give way; my medicaments are no more than a useful prop. But I think Katie will be grieved if no one of her family – except her mother, and she reluctantly – comes to the church . . . I suppose Ben is unrelenting . . . and I doubt if Zacky could walk that distance. But Mrs Zacky is a devout Wesleyan and goes regularly to church. Do you have any leverage you could exercise?'

'Only persuasion. Which I will exercise since it is you that asks. Betsy Maria is in Penryn with Clowance, but there are a half-dozen uncles and aunts – some of them younger than Katie – who might be willing to go. And of course there are the Nanfans. I'll see what I can do.'

'Thank you.'

'I don't recall having seen Music for a couple of years, and then he was still very much the village fool.'

'I've no doubt that if you were to call to see him now, he would be so overcome with embarrassment that you'd think him no better. And I rather fear that the excitement of the wedding may tip his balance tomorrow. But not only has he improved, he is still

472

improving. Rather than being mentally retarded, as we all thought, I am convinced he is just a very slow developer, whose development has been much held back by the part he learned to play and what the village expected of him. I think with Katie's understanding and companionship he may become at least as normal and intelligent as most of those who taunt him.'

By the time they separated the night's cloak had been drawn over the sky with just a scarf of daylight reaching into the sea. Ross made a short detour to Mellin and knocked at the Martin cottage. So he had come one morning thirty years ago in search of cheap labour to work his neglected fields, and so had met Jinny for the first time and become involved in the fortunes of the whole Martin family.

All those years ago Zacky Martin had been a small, tough, wrinkled man – wrinkled far before his time; now with real age and the long struggle against miners' tissick he had become tiny: a cashew nut instead of a brazil. Somehow Dwight kept him alive, mixing hot vapours for him to inhale at bad times, or potions of nux vomica and strychnine as a tonic for good ones.

This was a good one, and Ross, stooping into the small living room greeted them both and sat down. Mrs Zacky, who had delivered Demelza of Julia and helped at the births of Jeremy and Clowance, and who had had eight children of her own, had not shrivelled with the years: she was a stout, white-haired, bespectacled, flat-faced, rubicund, vigorous seventy-one. In the room, as it happened, were Gabby and Thomas, now both married and living at Marasanvose. They had been collecting driftwood (which Ross had stumbled over in the dark outside). The wrecks around the coast were breaking up and distributing their flotsam. Fortunately – from their point of view – old Vercoe, the Customs Officer at St Ann's, was known to be laid up with an ulcer on his leg.

Mrs Zacky said: 'Well, I 'ad thought to go, an' then I thought not. Katie be very wilful; always 'ave been, will not be told. She've never even brought 'im round to see us. I mind 'im in church, o' course but he never come to no prayer meetings.'

'She'm shamed of 'im,' said Thomas. 'That be the truth and no two ways o' looking 'pon it.'

'I aren't so sartin he's so dead'n alive,' said Gabby. 'He's a treat wi' horses. An' I seen him quick 'nough 'pon times.'

Zacky said: 'Katie be wilful but she have her head screwed on. Maybe twill turn for the best.'

There had been many improvements in the cottage since those early days: a good smooth planchen laid over the earth floor, and rugs on that; three comfortable upholstered chairs, a dark oak table, a mirror, a new fireplace; the ovens moved into the scullery. Zacky had prospered with his master. Ross had pressed him to move into a place less cramped for size, but as their family had grown and gone and his own active life became restricted Zacky had been less and less inclined to move.

Gabby relit his pipe. 'I 'ear tell there's like to be trouble.'

'Trouble?'

'Twas only a whisper I picked up but they d'say them lads that was always baiting Music, they d'plan to upset the wedden.'

'Upset it? How?'

'Dunno. There's three or four lads, half a dozen girls, mischief bent, ye might say.'

'What time is the wedding?'

'Nine o'clock,' said Zacky. 'After it they go back to work at Place House.'

Mrs Zacky clicked her knitting needles. 'Reckon I'll maybe go up to the church, if tis your wish, Cap'n Ross.'

'Maybe I'll come along wi' ee, mam,' said Gabby. 'Tis slack time an' I can steal a hour.'

'We'd best not be late leaving this eve,' said Thomas. 'There's a couple loads wood outside. If we can have the lend of your handcart, Father?'

'Anything of value come in?' Ross asked.

'Two spars o' good timber, sur, looks like black spruce or some such. Nought else you'd say of *value*.'

'Think you they've come from the *Kinseale*?'

'They're small pieces, ten foot long, but there may be better on the morning tide.'

'What time is high water? Ten or a little after? Well, it's worth keeping an eye open.'

His mission accomplished, Ross led his horse home. He found Demelza seated before the fire reading to Henry; Bella and Cuby heads together over a piece of needlework; their latest cat, Hebe, licking a delicate back leg at Demelza's feet and Farquhar, nose in paws, drowsing in the steady candlelight.

When he came in all was commotion, movement, talk. Demelza went off immediately to see that supper should soon be served. She still hadn't learned the ability to delegate.

Against the probabilities, her relationship with Cuby had ripened into an easy friendship. There had been some moment of crisis, Ross sensed, soon after Cuby arrived, but that had passed. This peculiarly fraught, uneasy situation could so easily have failed because of the special tensions that operated within both women; and it was a testimony to Cuby, he thought, as well as to Demelza, that they spoke understandingly and affectionately to each other, considerate but not over-polite; they even sometimes differed on things, even shared a joke.

Next Monday Demelza was to go to Penryn to spend a few days with Clowance, and he knew she would try to persuade her to spend Christmas with them. Ross's instinct was against it, but he did not utter a word. The second loss, coming so hard on the heels of the first, had left a raw edge that couldn't yet begin to heal. It was twisting the sword in the wound to attempt to keep up Christmas in any way whatever. If Clowance came she might find it hard to reconcile herself to the prospect of a new baby in the house and a sister-in-law about whom she still had resentful reservations. Dwight said he thought Cuby's child would be likely to be born in mid-January. As soon as possible then Cuby would want to show the baby to her mother. That would be the time to press Clowance to come to Nampara. The longer the girls were kept apart while the first wounds healed, the better chance there was of their finding harmony and understanding.

V

Day came up about seven, with angry clouds which seemed to be a residue of some quarrel of the night. Ross took his spyglass to the window of his bedroom but the sea and beach were calm and unencumbered.

They breakfasted at 7.30, when Bella was full of some rhyme or jingle she had learned, supposing it to be the sounds a nightingale made when in full song. At eight Ross strolled out of the house as if going to Wheal Leisure, but instead walked up the Long Field and its promontory of rocks at Damsel Point which divided Hendrawna Beach from Nampara Cove. The unbroken sand of Hendrawna Beach was a creamy white as the sun broke through, the placid sea, so wild a few days ago,.turning gently over at its edge, playful wavelets bearing no visible cargo. The two Martin men had got the best last night.

He wondered how Katie's wedding would go. He hoped the village lads, who could be spiteful enough, would not interrupt the ceremony, or turn the evening into some sort of a noisy riot. He turned to go back to the house and then stopped to stare into Nampara Cove. By the freak of the tides practically all wreckage was washed up along the great beach, the cove scarcely ever gathered anything of note. Today the position was reversed. The cove was choked with wood.

He clambered down the side of the gorse-grown cliff and came out on the small beach, part sand, part pebbles, bisected by the Mellingey Stream. It took no time to recognize the wood as being good quality timber, more black spruce, red and yellow pine, oak and probably beech. There were also tar barrels and bales of rope and oakum floating around.

He touched nothing but began to limp quickly up the narrow green valley to the house. There were a half-dozen able-bodied men about the farm. They would be mainly in the fields by now. And Sephus Billing. Sephus Billing was this morning repairing the fowl house. He was a fair carpenter but his intellectual attainments would not have put Music to shame. And he was a member of the Billing clan who pullulated in one of the larger cottages of Grambler village.

'Sephus!' Ross called as he came into the yard.

'Ais, sur?'

'There's a lot of good timber washing in in Nampara Cove. Go and tell the other men, I want them to stop work and go down to see what they can salvage.'

A gleam lit up Sephus's dull eyes. He wiped his nose with the back of his hand. 'Ais, sur, that I'll do.' He put down his hammer.

You never had to tell a Cornishman twice to down tools if there was booty to be had.

'And Sephus!' as he made for the gate.

'Sur?'

'When you have told the men you may go on to Grambler and tell your family of it. There should be a little bounty for all.'

Ross walked to the gate and shut it after the fleeing man. With an ironical gaze he saw Sephus running in the direction of Cal Trevail, who was pulling carrots in the field beyond Demelza's garden. Soon there would be plenty of willing helpers. All Sephus had to do then was alert the village of Grambler.

VI

Music and Katie went to church through a deserted village. No young men or girls waited by the wayside to douse them in liquid manure. They were married in an almost empty church, the only people present being Parson Odgers – and Mrs Odgers to remind him not to read the burial service in error – Jinny and Whitehead Scoble, Dr Enys, Mrs Zacky Martin, Char Nanfan, and a half-dozen old women who were too infirm to rush down for the pickings in Nampara Cove.

In the cove itself a fair element of chaos reigned, for the haul was bigger than it first seemed. A freak of tide had carried the cargo of the wrecked *Kinseale* out of Basset's Cove and deposited it several miles north. The way was narrow and people were trooping down and back, some with mules, some with wheelbarrows, some with boxes and sacks – anything that would carry or contain more than a pair of hands. Often they plunged into the water to grab some item of flotsam, often there were arguments, sometimes fights. Everybody came peaceable, but not everybody could contain their greed.

After appropriating for himself two or three nice lengths of wood, Ross left the villagers and his farm labourers to it. Let them have their fun while the going was good. It was doubtful if Vercoe would have hastened to put in an appearance if he had been well; as he was not, there was no risk at all. Cuby went with Demelza and

Isabella-Rose to the edge of Damsel Point to watch. Just for half an hour there was the risk of the crowd getting out of control, but Ross said: 'Let them be. There's no liquor. They'll have cleared everything as clean as a whistle by nightfall.' And they had. Demelza wrinkled her nose at what she expected she would find trampled down in the muddy track of her special cove when she went to look in the morning.

Meantime Music and Katie had returned to their cottage, changed out of their Sunday clothes and walked to Place House to resume their duties. Katie was normally a living-in maid, but as master and mistress were away had been given permission to sleep out for a few nights. So in due course, which was late in the afternoon, they returned to the cottage together, tramping unspeaking through the windy dark. An hour before they returned, unknown to them, the lads and girls, tired out with a day of collecting timber and pieces of panelling and rope ends and paint brushes and a roll of calico and a man's jacket and other odds and ends, had bethought themselves of their old malice and decided – coming giggling out of a kiddley – that, well, they might just so well dump the pig shit as waste it, and they would be passing the cottage anyway on their way home. But they were thwarted by the startling and unexpected presence of Constable Vage, who happened to be taking a stroll in Grambler village at that time. It was the first time he had been in Grambler for a month. Ross, not being a magistrate, had no authority to call him out, but a discreet guinea sent over by Matthew Mark Martin had been enough, and he had whiled away the time talking and drinking with the Paynters until the drunken laughter of the lads alerted him afresh to Ross's request.

So the happy couple slept undisturbed, Katie in the upstairs room once occupied by the three brothers, Music stretched out below in front of the dying fire.

He was perfectly, perfectly happy. She was his wife. She was upstairs in his house, along of him.

If it never came to no more than that, he would be content. If it someday came to the as-yet-unthinkable he would be enraptured. But for the time being he was perfectly, blissfully satisfied with the simple fact that they were wed. Beyond that his patience stretched away into the illimitable distance.

Two

Lady Harriet Warleggan was brought to bed on the evening of Wednesday, the 12th December, and her labour continued into the morning of the 13th.

Things had not been easy between Harriet and George. Harriet was tetchy all the time, plagued by thoughts of the accident and made more angry by George's reactions to it. He seemed to take it as a breach of convention, even an insult to himself, that his wife and this upstart he disliked so much and whom Harriet well knew he disliked so much, who had been guilty of highway robbery against him – that they should have been defiantly and openly riding together; and that she had put their son at risk for the sake of some stupid and high-spirited gallop across hunting country . . . It never quite emerged whether Harriet had challenged Stephen or Stephen Harriet, but there had been some sort of competitiveness involved, of that George was sure. And he was not at all certain that there had not been some sexual undertones.

Indeed he had nurtured a number of suspicions ever since Harriet had virtually blackmailed him into withdrawing his bankruptcy notice. Her overt reason, because Clowance had rescued her dog, had never convinced George. Being a man who disliked dogs and only tolerated hounds because they contributed to a national sport, he was unable to fathom the feelings of a woman who felt as Harriet did. Stephen was a personable man – if you liked the braggart type – and he had made a fuss of Harriet. She clearly had a soft spot for him, and had blown up her obligation to Clowance to hide her real feelings. The fact that they had gone riding – galloping! – together was proof enough that something had been afoot.

Well, serve them both right if he'd broken his damned back. It was a miracle that she hadn't fallen too and taken with her his hopes of an heir.

George had mixed feelings about Stephen's death. It was good riddance, of course, and it wiped the slate clean. All the same it would have been better if he could have somehow been arrested for the crime he had committed and ended his life dangling from a noose. Now he had escaped. And with him had gone any hope there might have been of tracking down his two accomplices. The chapter was over and done with. Only Clowance was left on whom he might vent his spleen.

But that George had no intention of doing. Ross Poldark was winged by the loss of his eldest son. His eldest daughter – yes, there was another one; that one with the raucous voice – seemed bent on continuing to live in Penryn for the time being; and George thought he might well make some gesture to befriend her. Although she was a Poldark with her share of Poldark arrogance, he had always been attracted by her, ever since they had first met at Trenwith when she had wandered barefoot into the great hall blatantly trespassing. Indeed it might be said that it was his encounter with the fresh young Clowance, carrying her bouquet of stolen foxgloves, which had first aroused him to recover his appreciation of women in general, a process which had led to his courtship of Lady Harriet Carter and their eventual marriage.

Of course, apart from a salacious look or two, George had not the least serious sexual intent towards the young widow; but if he did find a way of befriending her it would, he thought, make his old rival irritable and suspicious and might even raise a tremor of annoyance and jealousy in his own wife.

During the period of waiting that dark December night George paced the wide drawing-room of Cardew and nursed his hopes and his grievances and listened for noises from upstairs. His latest grievance was but an hour old. When Dr Charteris had arrived to join Dr Behenna, who was already in attendance, George had gone into the bedroom with them for a moment or two. There had been sweat on his wife's brow, and the midwife was holding her hand. Looking up and seeing him, Harriet had said between her teeth: 'Get out of my sight!'

He had at once retreated, fuming at her rudeness. Very well, it was a painful business and women suffered a great deal and sometimes they were driven to unwarranted comment; and of course as a woman of blue blood Harriet was accustomed to expressing herself coarsely; but it was inexcusable for her to address him thus in front of both surgeons and the midwife! Over the years he had become a man of whom all those with whom he mixed were wary and respectful; even a man like Behenna, who was used to riding roughshod over his patients, deferred to Sir George. Only his wife, his lady wife, could ever have dared to speak to him in this way, and he felt insulted and demeaned by her.

He passed little Ursula's bedroom. Little Ursula was not there, being at school, and was no longer little, being a hefty, heavy-legged, tight-busted girl of sixteen. It had been her birthday last Sunday, and they had given her a party despite the imminence of her step-mother's 'time'. A select group, carefully chosen from among the best in the county; some had stayed overnight because of the distances involved. A pity Ursula was not a more becoming girl, with the blonde hair, frailty and long slender legs of her mother. Instead she was like her paternal grandmother in looks, and sadly looks counted for so much in a girl. She was a chip off the old Warleggan block. But fortunately not at all like her maternal grandmother in a practical or sagacious sense. George's mother, born a miller's daughter with simple beliefs and a country understanding, had never quite moved into the world of opulence her husband had made for her, had always preferred making jam and baking bread to riding in a carriage with two postillions or entertaining on a grand scale.

Such matters would not be likely to worry Ursula. If not intellectual – and who wanted her to be? – she was sharply intelligent and fascinated by commerce and money. An ideal child from George's point of view, if only she had been a son. And, being a girl, it were better had she been more prepossessing.

All the same, he thought, it would really only be a matter of arrangement when the time came. An heiress would have plenty of suitors. It would be a question of his picking the right one; they'd all fall over themselves.

It did not occur to him to recall that the one chink in his own personal chain-armour of self-help had been his weakness for a pretty face. Yet he expected that Ursula would find the ideal husband chiefly on the strength of an enormous dowry, just as he had expected his son to match with a Trevanion in order to secure the land and the castle. *And* there had certainly been no lack of looks on the Trevanion side! Instead Valentine had maliciously and wantonly married a pretty widow ten years older than himself without his father's knowledge or consent. George had made sure that not a penny of his money or property should ever go to Valentine. He had written him out of his will and out of his life.

Now, upstairs at this moment, another life was beginning and if, pray God, it was a son he could begin to reshape his plans all over again. Indeed he had already begun to reshape them. The boy should be called Nicholas after his father. Then he could be called anything Harriet fancied, some favourite family name of her own. Perhaps Thomas, after the first Duke. Nicholas Thomas Osborne Warleggan, that would do well enough.

The house was dark and cold at 2.15 on a December morning. Fires roared upstairs, especially in The Room, and fires roared downstairs, but the house was still draughty; if you crouched within the periphery of one of the fires it was warm enough, even scorching. But if you were too tensed up to remain in one position for any length of time you quickly became aware of the draughts and the dark. Even the candles guttered.

It was a time of night when spirits were low and human nature at its lowest ebb. As he paced about, George recollected that when he had last been in this situation, in December '99, both his own parents had been alive and both Elizabeth's. Now all were gone. Sixteen years spanned so much of his own life, which was fast slipping away. He would soon be fifty-seven. Many men died at such an age. He was filled with a sense of the impermanence of life, with a premonition of disaster. Trenwith was no longer his, had gone back to the Poldarks. This great house which he had bought and repaired and refurnished and extended a quarter of a century ago was now the centre of his life. How long would it remain in Warleggan hands after he was gone? The renegade Valentine was established on the north coast with his own rich widow and his two step-daughters. Ursula might marry and live here. Perhaps, who knew, if he found the right sort of husband for her, he could persuade the young man for a consideration to take not only the Warleggan daughter but the Warleggan name.

But all that would be unnecessary if Harriet tonight produced a healthy son. A Warleggan who could come into everything he did not set expressly aside for Ursula, and who would, in addition to being the son of Sir George Warleggan, be also a grandson of the Duke of Leeds! It was a dazzling prospect. True, by the time he was eighteen he, George, would be seventy-five. But – rejecting the dark thoughts of a moment ago – he recalled that the Warleggans were a long-lived family; both his parents had been around eighty, and old Uncle Cary at seventy-six showed no signs at all of closing his last ledger.

Tock-tock went the clock in the hall. It wanted twenty minutes to three. This damned waiting seemed worse even than last time. Elizabeth had never been in labour long. That had never been the trouble. Harriet of course was thirty-four. It was late for a first child. How old had Elizabeth been when she bore Ursula? He could not remember. Thirty-five, was it? But Ursula had been her third.

The candles bobbed and ducked like courtiers. It was a fine night but windy, a big cold empty night with a scattering of stars among the clouds. Half his staff was abed, but the other half was alert for the slightest pull of a bell. At the moment Nankivell was making up the fires.

'Sur, can I get you something?'

'No.' He had drunk enough brandy, and there was a half-glass unfinished on the end of the mantelshelf.

He sat down at his desk, took some papers out of a drawer and irritably pulled a candelabrum nearer so that he could see. It was on a matter to do with his pocket borough of St Michael. Years ago he had reduced the number of voters in the borough from forty to thirty by the simple but drastic expedient of moving ten of them out of their derelict cottages and rehousing them two miles away in much better property which he had had restored especially to receive them. They could not plead hardship, since their new housing was much better than the old; but they were deprived of their sinecure living by no longer having to be bribed to vote. Their vote was gone, and so was their means of sustenance. As George had dryly observed at the time, some of them might even have to *work*. Since then gradually over the years the remaining number had been reduced to twenty-five, of whom six were members of one family. Mr Tankard, George's legal steward, had called in at the beginning of the month to say that this family was now applying for a loan of three hundred pounds. It was supposed to be to erect a bakery, but everyone knew it was intended to tide them over until the next election, when they would expect the loan to be conveniently forgotten. George had no intention of submitting to this blackmail, in spite of the advice of his friend Sir Christopher Hawkins that he should do so. Hawkins had said: 'It is the price you pay, my friend. Think nothing of it. Think rather of the benefits of having two members in the House to do your bidding.' But George would have none of it. He was not to be held to ransom by a festering family of down-at-heel good-for-nothings, and he was determined to make them pay for their insolence. He felt very strongly about it, and this was why he had dragged out the correspondence, with Tankard's notes, tonight. If anything would take his mind off events upstairs . . .

He pored over it for a minute or so, fumbling for his glasses and feeling the stirrings of old anger; but then he flung the papers down and got to his feet. Even this –

And then he heard a sound, it was a terrible sound, like a wail, like a howl, almost more animal than human. Sweat broke out on him. Supposing Harriet were to die. That would not matter quite so much if the boy lived. But they might *both* die. George found himself confronting a great loneliness which opened up before him like a mining adit. In spite of Harriet's infuriating habits she was a remarkable personality, whose very abrasiveness he would bitterly miss. And if the child were to go . . .

He strode out into the hall and stopped to listen. All was silent now. A log of wood crashed in the hearth and the resultant flames lit up the sombre room where many times there had been so much gaiety and light. Where Harriet and Valentine had organized that great party to celebrate Napoleon's retreat from Moscow; where only a few days ago Ursula's friends –

The same sound again but more muffled. He took out a handkerchief and mopped his brow, started up the stairs toward the sound, then stopped, puzzled, angry, horrified, his heart thumping. A groom crossed the hall, seemed to be coming this way.

'Smallwood!'

'Sur?'

'Where are you going?'

'Up the stairs, sur, beggin' your permission. Lady Harriet said as I was –'

'Never mind what she said, you've no damned business above stairs.'

'No, sur. It was just that she did say I was to look to –'

That terrible sound again, loud now. George's hair prickled.

'Get out!' he snarled.

'Yes, sur. I just had the thought that the dogs making that noise might be disturbing to her ladyship –'

'Dogs? What dogs?'

'Castor and Pollux, sur. Her ladyship give me orders that they was to be lodged in the blue bedroom while she was – while she was in labour, as you might say. Her ladyship didn't wish for them to be roaming the 'ouse while she was poorly and she thought they'd be best out of your – out of the way. I was to lock them in the blue bedroom and see they was kept fed and watered. That is why I was venturing –'

'That noise, that howling,' George said. 'It was the dogs howling?'

'Yes, sur. I thought I'd just go see –'

'Go and see to them!' George shouted. 'Stop their damned mouths, stop their throats even if you have to cut them! Give them poison so long as you keep them *quiet*!'

'Yes, sur.' In fright Smallwood slid past his master and rushed stumbling up the rest of the stairs, then with anxious backward glances retreated down the passage towards the blue bedroom.

George went back slowly down, breathing out rage and relief, and more indignation with every breath. An outrageous thing to happen! Putting the dogs in a bedroom! He'd wondered where they had gone to – how typical of Harriet's arrogance and thoughtlessness for him! He would tell her exactly how he viewed such a ridiculous act. Almighty God, for a moment – for some minutes – he had thought, he had feared . . .

A step behind him.

He swung round. Dr Behenna. Sleeves rolled up. Black waistcoat with gold chain. Grey hair *en brosse*. A silly look on his face.

'Well?'

'I am happy to tell you that her ladyship has been safely delivered of twins.

'*What* d'you say?'

'I had thought this likely since before ten o'clock last evening, but did not wish to raise your hopes. Mother and babies are all doing well. There have been no complications. My sincere congratulations, Sir George.'

George stared at the doctor with astonishment and such a concentration of anxiety and anger as to disconcert him.

'The second child is slightly smaller but in excellent condition,' Behenna hastened on. 'She was born half an hour after her sister.'

'*Sister?*' said George. 'You mean . . . ?'

'You have two fine daughters, Sir George. I am sure you will be vastly proud of them. Lady Harriet has been very brave, and I will give her a further opiate as soon as you have seen them.'

Three

I

Demelza rode back on the 14th from visiting Clowance again. Cuby was out walking on the beach with Isabella-Rose, Henry was with Mrs Kemp. Demelza found Ross in the garden.

'Well,' she said, 'I did not know you knew one plant from another. I hope you have not been digging up my new bulbs.'

'Cuby saw to that,' Ross said, kissing her. 'I believe since she brought them she has been watching every day for them to come up.'

Demelza knelt and stirred the soil with her finger. 'These are late tulips, she says. They do not flower until May.'

Ross crouched beside her. 'Clowance?'

'Better. Eating at last. She has lost a lot of weight. I do not think she will come home for Christmas, Ross.'

'Ah.'

'She said to me: "Mama I will come – of course I will come with pleasure if you wish me to, if you wish this Christmas specially to have all your family round you," she said. "But if it were my own choice I would, I believe, better prefer to remain here with Verity. I do not know quite how to explain it," she said, "but it is certain that this Christmas cannot be a Christmas like last year or any other year we have ever known. So I think it would affect me less if I could look on it as just the 25th of December, another day of the month," she said, "like any other day of any month and *try* to forget it is happening."'

Ross straightened up, aware that his ankle did not like a crouching position. He had had reservations about Clowance coming back too soon for another and altogether particular reason – that is, that in her first bereavement she might see too much of Ben Carter. It was a strange perception for him, and more worthy of Demelza. But under no circumstances would he mention such a feeling to her.

'Shall you mind so much?'

'Not if she is with Verity.'

'How is she dealing with the business?'

'Both ships were out. The boy, this nephew of his, was away in the *Adolphus*, which was being captained by a man called Carter. The *Lady Clowance* was sailing for the Thames with a cargo of china clay. At home, in the port, a strange little man called Hodge is helping her. He is almost horrid to look at, but she seems to trust him. He can read and write and do accounts. And the Naval Bank is also helping: Stephen has left quite a lot of money, it seems, all from this privateering adventure.'

'I'll go over myself next week; spend a night or two.'

The wind was tugging at Demelza's hat. She put a hand up to it.

'She has changed, Ross. I – I think she has been deeply injured – of course by her bereavement, of course, but I suspicion something more than that. It is as if she no longer has confidence in her own judgement – as if she is confused as well as desperately heart-sad. I cannot make it out . . . She is harder than she used to be. I feel she will need careful handling – specially careful handling.'

'By us?'

'I hope so. And by life . . .'

Ross frowned out at the sea.

'Even with the war over,' he said, 'the ships should fetch a good price. If, then, she doesn't want to make her home permanently with us she could travel. She has no family and is still so young . . . It's a grim travesty that we should find ourselves with two young widows on our hands.'

'I do not know that she wishes to sell the ships – at least for the time being. She seems to feel Stephen would have wanted her to keep them. I think they would give her a sense of independence greater than she would have just with the money they would fetch. Also she wants to look after Stephen's nephew, for a few months at least. She says he is utterly lost.'

'She must have time to adjust herself. It will take months, perhaps years. Of course there will be other men in the world. But not too soon.'

'Do you know what she said to me? It was the strangest thing!'

'What?'

'We were just talking, just talking, and I said like you said, that she was so young, she had all her life ahead of her. I'd never've dreamed of saying anything about her marrying again. Twould have been premature and improper and impertinent. But she must've read my thoughts, or twas in the air in some strange way.' Demelza took off her hat and let the wind ruffle her hair. 'She said: "I married once for love, Mama. If I ever come to marry again," she said, "it will not be for love, it will be for wealth or position."'

Ross was silent.

Demelza said: 'Does that not surprise you?'

'It astounds me. You are right to say she has changed. But it means . . .'

'It surely means that her marriage was not altogether successful.'

'A lot of marriages are not altogether successful. Look around. But it is sad if she discovered it so early. And it is the bitterest thing for *her* to say.'

'Yet she clearly loved Stephen. I cannot fathom it.'

Ross took her hat from her and they walked towards the house.

Demelza said: 'Lady Harriet has had twins, I hear. All are well. They are both girls.'

'George will be beside himself with annoyance,' said Ross, not without satisfaction.

'I s'pose he laid great store by having another son. There has been no reconciliation between him and Valentine, has there?'

'Nor ever like to be,' said Ross.

Demelza glanced up at him sharply as they went in. 'Valentine called here once while I was away?'

'Who told you?'

'Mrs Kemp just mentioned it.'

'It was in October. He did not come in. We walked down from Grace together and talked for a few minutes.'

'Did he say they could never be reconciled?'

'He gave me that impression.'

'Never is a long time. I think I rather hope they will . . . Did he want anything when he came?'

'It was just to say goodbye before they left for Cambridge.'

Demelza thought this one through. 'Why did you say they would never be reconciled?'

'A feeling I have.'

'Something he said.'

'Just a feeling I have.'

She was very perceptive of nuances in Ross's voice, but after a moment she decided she should not pursue it.

'I hear Valentine and Selina will not be home for Christmas.'

'Oh?'

'Ben told me. They are going to spend the Christmas vacation in London with her two daughters. Katie has heard and she told her mother.'

'No hint of Ben and Katie coming together again?'

'Not yet. But have you met Music recent? He is quite an improved man.'

'Some people marry and it changes their personalities, it seems. Others marry and it makes not the slightest difference.'

'How do you think it affected us?' Demelza asked.

'We re-made each other after the other's image.'

'That's a little complicated for my small mind, but I hope I know what you mean.'

They went in. He said: 'So we shall be a reduced company in this area for Christmas. Geoffrey Charles and Amadora and Joanna are in Paris. Drake and Morwenna and Loveday will, I am sure, return to Looe, for he has problems at the yard. So there will be just Dwight and Caroline and the girls and a smattering of Trenegloses and Kellows.'

'Perhaps Clowance is right and, just for this year, we should pretend it isn't happening.' At the parlour door Demelza exclaimed on seeing a vase of flowers: carnations, picotees and lace pinks. 'Judas! Where did they come from?'

'The de Dunstanvilles sent them over. They only came this morning.'

'That is so kind of them, Ross! That is kind.' Once in a while Demelza's eyes would fill with tears unnecessarily.

'They have been put in water just as they came. Cuby said, should she arrange them, but I said I thought you would want to do it. And hot-house grapes!'

'I will write. Or *you* will write. Yes, a bigger vase, don't you think? And I can gather some ferns and ivy to go with them. There's time before dark.'

'Just time.'

At the door she stopped, wiped her eyes with an inelegant hand. 'We cannot ignore Christmas altogether. There is little Henry. And Bella. And Sophie and Meliora, who will come over. And Cuby – who may be deeply sad but has a child within her. We shall somehow have to make – a sort of, what do you call it?'

'Compromise?'

'Yes. How you read my thoughts –'

'Long association –'

'Compromise, that is what it must be. No big celebration. But quiet celebration. After all it is to commemorate the birth of Christ.'

Ross smiled at her, for her eyes had briefly lit up in a way he had not seen for some time.

'Just so,' he said. 'Just so.'

II

He went to Penryn the following Tuesday, leaving before dawn and arriving at midday. He had a meal with Clowance and then they rowed down the creek to Falmouth and walked up to Pendennis Castle, where many years ago he had stayed with Governor Melville discussing defence matters. Just before the miners' riots. There had been a number of smaller outbreaks of violence since, but none with that tragic ending.

He did not call this time, but they turned and walked back down the gorse-grown hill towards the town. Clowance remarked that her father's ankle seemed much better; he replied that if it got bad again he would try three months' internment to improve it. All through his visit they had talked long and amiably on many subjects, including details of Jeremy's death and the consequences of Stephen's. They took supper together and he slept there and left to return home the following morning; he would dine at the Fox & Grapes, near St Day, on the way home.

That night Clowance spent with Verity. Andrew junior was ashore until Christmas Eve when he sailed again for New York, but this evening with Tamsin and her brother was attending a small soirée and dance given by one of the other packet captains. Clowance had been invited but had declined. Andrew senior, having had a minor recurrence of his heart affection, had gone to bed.

Clowance said: 'D'you know, it is quite unusual, but since I – since I lost Stephen I have had more single conversations with my mother and father than I can ever remember in my life before. Before, of course, I met them *constantly* in and out of the house. But never in such a concentrated way, if you take my meaning. Most often if it was anything important the three of us would meet together. You must know the – the triviality of daily life. Now we have talked so much, in a different way.'

'Your father looked better,' Verity said.

'Yes, he was, he was. They both looked so dreadful when I saw them first – after Jeremy. But life has to go on.' Clowance smiled wryly. 'Even for me.'

'More than ever for you,' Verity said.

'Yes, I suppose. But at present I'm in limbo. I don't really want to make any decisions at all if I haven't got to.'

'Give yourself a year, my dear. Stephen has left you money enough.'

'Do you know I grieve so much that he was not able to *enjoy* the good fortune. All his life he had been poor – grindingly poor.' Clowance hesitated. 'At least, I think so.'

'What do you mean?'

'I mean that just before he died I discovered an important inaccuracy in something he had told me. And that – and that calls into question some of the other things he told me.' Clowance got up, picked up a magazine, riffled through the pages. 'No, I think I am being unfair. What he told me that was untrue was something important to – to our marriage. I do not believe he would have told me circumstantial stories of his poverty if they had not happened.'

Verity looked up at her tall young cousin. Demelza had been right: the ordeal Clowance had been through, her loss of weight, had aged her but improved her looks.

Clowance said: 'Although I can talk to Papa freely about most things – and I do! – I cannot really talk to him about Stephen, for

492

I do not think he ever altogether cared for Stephen. They were such *opposite* characters, yet in some ways rather alike.'

'Alike? I would not – I don't think I would . . .'

'Well, they were both very strong, weren't they – physically strong, masculine, courageous, stop-at-nothing sort of men . . . After that, no . . . they were not really alike. I wonder why I said that? Perhaps I am trying to make reasonable what to some people was unreasonable, which was my love for Stephen.'

Verity got up to put some coal on the fire.

'Let me do that.' Clowance moved quickly to the fire. Verity saw a tear drop on the coal.

'I am sure your father understands what you felt.'

'Oh, he understands that I loved Stephen. But not why. You see one does not *choose*. I have said this to Mama – oh a year ago, but it comes home even more truly now. One loves a person – feels deeply drawn to love him, and no one else will do. And because you love him you suppose he has all the virtues which he does not have. So one expects more than one gets, and that is wrong . . . I do not believe I am making sense, Verity. It is just helpful to talk to you.'

'Is it Jason who is bothering you?'

'Jason? Oh no. No, not really. You know he is Stephen's son by an earlier marriage?'

'I did not know. Your mother wondered.'

'Did she? Mama has a dangerous intuition. But even her intuition, I believe, will not perceive all that I have in my heart to tell her if I would. But I will not. Nor will I tell you, dear cousin, for I believe it is best buried with Stephen.'

Clowance busied herself with the fire; Verity picked up her embroidery but did not take out the needle.

In a calmer voice Clowance said: 'There was one thing I did not *dare* tell Papa. It happened on Monday. I had a visitor. You will never guess. It was Sir George Warleggan.'

Verity stared at her. 'George?'

'He came with two grooms. I heard the clattering of horses and looked up the street and saw him just dismounted. As he walked down, with one of the other men – I think his name is Nankivell – I was quite terrified. I thought he was going to arrest me!'

'What did he want?'

'Well, when I opened the door he just took off his hat and gave me good-day; I could hardly find the words to speak so I stood aside and he came in. He is not nearly so tall as Papa, but he takes up a deal of room in a small parlour! I said would he sit down and he said no doubt I might be a trifle surprised at his visit, but he just was passing through Penryn and it occurred to him to call to see if he could help me in any way. There had been some ill-feeling, he said, between him and my husband, but now that Stephen was so unfortunately gone he would like to remind me of the goodwill that existed between himself and Lady Harriet and me, and if he could be of assistance to me in my widowhood, either in a social or a financial sense, he would ask me to name it!'

Verity did not speak. She had thirty years of memories of George, most of them bad; but she felt she need not add them to Clowance's own.

'Dear cousin, I was – flabbergasted! I have not seen Harriet since the accident; for Stephen had quarrelled with her for some reason and would speak not a single good word of her. I suppose I too felt that day she had behaved not well, but . . . She wrote to us when Stephen was ill and then again to me after he died, but I had not replied. Now George coming like this . . .' Clowance wrinkled her forehead. 'I thanked him and said I thought I was engaging myself well enough. He said he understood Stephen had left a little money, but if I should be in need of legal advice he would be happy to have it provided for me. And when a due time of mourning had been observed I should be welcome again at the hunt or some other occasion if I should feel the want of company. It was all very gracious, I assure you.'

'George can be gracious enough – and generous enough – when he chooses. But usually with a reason.'

'Soon after that he left, having refused a glass of canary, which was all I had in the place. I have wondered since why he came. Ever since I met him that first time five years ago I believe he has had a very small taking for me. But still . . .'

'George has a weak spot for a few women. I remember particularly –' Verity stopped. 'For fair women especially . . . Though that is contradicted by his second marriage, is it not.'

494

'That is another strange thing!' Clowance said. 'I offered my congratulations, saying I knew how happy he must be at the birth of his baby daughters, and he glanced at me as if he thought I was sarcastic, or deriding him in some way.'

'A daughter for George,' Verity said, 'is near to a catastrophe.'

There was silence for a while.

Clowance said: 'I think I should like a cup of chocolate. Shall I make you some?'

'It would be nice. But pull the bell. Anna is up till ten.'

Clowance pulled the bell. Thoughtfully she rearranged her hair with both hands.

'Papa thinks Cuby's child will be a boy.'

'Why?'

'He says something about the law of averages. Geoffrey Charles had a girl. Your step-son has just had a girl. Now George and Harriet's two! I do not know if averages work in such things.'

'I do not suppose it matters very much, does it? Either will be welcome.'

'It matters about Papa's title, that is all.'

Anna came in and Verity ordered the chocolate.

III

Demelza said: 'Tell me, Caroline, I have intended to have asked you before; what would you say, how would you feel if either of your daughters wished, wanted to become an actress or a professional singer, like?'

Caroline raised her eyebrows. 'I do not believe either of 'em has sufficient talent to shine even in amateur theatricals. Why?'

'I have a special reason for asking, which I suppose you will guess refers to Bella.'

'She certainly has a remarkable voice – even though her father affects not to appreciate it. But has she shown some sudden ambition?'

'She was quite overcome with the theatre we took her to in London. I have never seen her so enchanted. But there is another reason. While we were in Paris we met a young English lieutenant

495

who must have put ideas in her head . . . Oh, it is all over and done with now, but it was some startling how it happened – and to a girl as young as she is!'

So it came out: the jolly camaraderie, the avuncular courtship, and then the sudden visit and the serious proposal.

Caroline listened in silence, playing with the ears of Horace the Third.

'What does Ross think of this?'

'I haven't told him. To begin I was too – too desolate to think of anything but Jeremy. And then came the news that Christopher Havergal had been cruelly maimed. Then it was all struck out of my mind when I knew nothing would come of it. But I often thought to ask you . . .'

'Did Bella know of his proposal?'

'Oh yes. And of course when news came of his wounding she was even more totally despondent: first for Jeremy and then for Christopher. But now more recently she has recovered much of her bounce and good spirits, so perhaps she will forget all about it. But I only wonder if it has not left an impression on her mind which will show in a year or two. And I wondered . . .'

'You wondered?'

'What you would say if you were in my place if next year or the year after Bella said she wished to – to become a singer or an actress for – for money. How would you feel if it were Sophie, for instance?'

Caroline let Horace to the floor with a plop. He grunted a protest.

'You will have to tell Ross sometime, and it will greatly depend on what he feels, will it not. For my part I would look on the prospect with a degree of doubt. Actors and singers are not of any social standing. Some lead a disorganized life and are thoroughly disreputable. Others are respectable but are not generally respected. A few singers, and great actresses like Siddons, they are different; but it will be very few . . . Of course another way to become highly regarded is to become the mistress of one of the Royal Princes. But even then, from reports, it does not seem to lead to a settled or comfortable life.'

Demelza shifted in her chair. 'Christopher was a very taking young man; but in truth it was perhaps all too trivial, too light-hearted to be taken serious. It was unthinkable anyway. But I am greatly relieved that Bella appears to have recovered from it altogether.'

Caroline said: 'It shows how easily the young forget.'

Four

I

'Sweet, sweet, jug, jug, water bubble, pipe rattle,' sang Isabella-Rose. 'Bell pipe, scroty, skeg, skeg, swat, swaty, whitlow, whitlow, whitlow . . . Mama, do you hear me? That is what the nightingale sings. If we could but put it to music!'

Demelza had come into the library. Cuby was at the piano, Bella half dancing beside it.

Cuby said: 'It is almost nice enough as you say it.'

'But Mama is good at finding little tunes; she does not play so well but she has a knack of finding funny little tunes!'

It was Christmas Eve; outside a mild grey day, inside more fires than were strictly necessary, lit to enliven the house. The church choir were coming tonight; tomorrow they were all summoned to Killewarren, where the Enyses had ordered a boar's head for dinner. Aside from the Poldarks, the servants in Nampara had worked their way into a festive mood. Mr Jeremy had been lost, and everyone grieved for him and for Miss Clowance, also widowed. But it did not prevent jollity sneaking in, a condition that Christmas traditionally induced. There were sniggers and flutters and cat-calls. While the Poldarks were out tomorrow there would be a feast in the old kitchen – where Jud and Prudie had once reigned – and gracious knew what noise there would be. Ross wondered how many of his helpers he would find sober when they returned. And little cared.

Demelza was induced to sit at the piano in Cuby's place and Bella intoned over and over the jingle she had garnered from some old woman. 'Sweet, sweet, jug, jug, water bubble, pipe rattle.' So it went on while Demelza tried to find chords to fit it. 'Bell pipe, scroty, skeg, skeg, swat, swaty, whitlow, whitlow, whitlow.' Slowly a little tune came out. Bella crowed with delight, and Cuby and Demelza laughed together.

On this scene came Henry, and Bella gathered him up while Demelza played some of the old carols she knew so well.

The library was decorated with holly and ivy and ferns and a few early primroses, as was the parlour. Yesterday they had all been over to Sawle Church helping to decorate that too. Although flowers were scarce, some had come from Place House and from Kille-warren. Neither Nampara nor Trenwith had a conservatory, and the Tregneloses were committed to St Ermyn's, Marasanvose. Before going to Killewarren tomorrow they would all go to Sawle Church, where Mr Clarence Odgers would read prayers and preach. For this great occasion of Christmas all the servants from Nampara would attend as well.

Dwight and Caroline had promised to be there, even though Dwight pointed out that the 25th December had been a day of festival in England long before its conversion to Christianity.

Christmas Eve passed peacefully enough, the dark coming early because of the gloom of cloud. At seven Cuby said she did not feel well and retired to bed early. But she heard the choir come, and got up and sat by the window listening. The choir, fourteen strong, sang the Dilly Song.

> Come and I will sing you.
> What will you sing O?
> I will sing One O.
> What is your One O?
>
> Twelve are the Twelve Apostles
> 'Leven are the 'leven will go to Heaven
> Ten are the Ten Commandments
> Nine is the moonshine bright and clear
> Eight are the Eight Archangels
> Seven are the Seven Stars in the sky
> Six the Cheerful Waiter
> Five is the Ferryman in the boat
> Four are the Gospel Praychers
> Three of them are strangers
> Two of them are Lilly-white babes

Clothed all in green-o
One of them is all alone and ever shall remain so.

They also sang 'Noël' and 'Joseph Was An Old Man'.

Afterwards they trooped into the parlour and took mince tarts and ginger wine. Music and Katie were of the party, though Music would now only sing tenor and Katie could hardly sing at all. They stood together through it all with an air of indestructibility.

On Christmas Day Cuby was well again, so the planned programme went ahead. Dawn broke misty wet, but towards midday the lips of the sky opened and a drier breath came. All the same there had just been enough rain in the night to make the cobbles greasy, the yard steamy with animals, the tracks slippery with mud. Both mining engines still worked; it was too expensive to shut them down for a single day. In the quiet air their thump and beat became more noticeable.

At church Mr Odgers wore his best cassock which he kept for special occasions, it being plum purple with brass buttons, very tight now, for he had worn it first at his marriage fifty-one years ago. It indicated no doctrinal or ecclesiastical order, for he belonged to none. That morning he was at his best and got through the service with only two mistakes.

The psalm was part of 22, beginning at verse 11. 'Be not far from me; for trouble is near; for there is none to help.' When it came to verse 20, 'Deliver my soul from the sword; my darling from the power of the dog,' Demelza put her hand quietly into Ross's. His hand closed on hers.

After it was over they rode on to Killewarren, a few faint sun-born shadows preceding them on the way.

They had bought Caroline a piece of fine French lace, Dwight a neckerchief, and silk pinafores for the girls; the Enyses had a pair of wine goblets for Demelza, riding gloves for Ross, a finely crocheted child's bonnet for Cuby, a book of songs for Bella, a toy horse for Harry that however much you pushed it over would always swing upright again.

Because of the children they dined early, and laughed a good deal and ate consumedly and drank good wine and generally made merry, though there was ice underneath, ice that clung round the heart.

Shut out thoughts of other Christmases, other shadows on the wall. This was an evil year; there would be others that must be better. Life was to be lived – it had to go on. Chiefly for the sake of the young, but even for themselves, it must go on. And the day was fine and mild and the fire crackled, and food and drink and love and companionship were around them. Do not think of Jeremy lying in the cold Flanders clay.

Darkness fell and candles were brought and the fires remade, and the two Enys girls sang a duet with Cuby at the piano, and Bella gave a little recital of her new nightingale song.

> Sweet, sweet, jug, jug
> Water bubble, pipe rattle
> Bell pipe, scroty, skeg, skeg,
> Swat, swaty, whitlow, whitlow, whitlow.

Her mother did her best to remember the chords she had made up that morning, and somehow it came out as a pleasant little ditty.

By 6.30 Henry was fretful, so Demelza, arousing huge protests from the girls, said they must go. They were away by seven, a small clip-clopping cavalcade, led by Ross, whose old Colley was as surefooted as they came and knew the way blindfold. Bone accompanied them carrying a lantern, though everyone assured Dwight it was not necessary.

A very dark night, unlit by moon or stars, and with a faint freckle of rain again borne on the tired breeze. Demelza carried Henry ahead of her, but as his head drooped in sleep he was transferred to Ross who, riding astride, could keep a firmer grip of him. A quiet ride now, everyone silent after the chatter of the day. In the distance the lights of Nampara already showed up, misting, haloed through the dark. As they clopped down the lane, overgrown with wind-crouching trees, Ross thought how little had changed here from the time he had ridden this way in the autumn of 1783 – thirty-two years ago – returning from the American War to find his father dead and Nampara a stinking shambles with Jud and Prudie in a drunken stupor in his father's old box bed.

They crossed the bridge and dismounted outside the front door. He took Demelza in his arms, then Cuby.

As she slipped close to him Cuby whispered: 'I'm sorry. I think I am beginning my pains.'

II

It was ten days earlier than anyone had supposed, but Ross said, as the lantern carrier was about to turn away:

'Bone.'

'Sur?'

'I am very sorry, but I think my daughter-in-law is unwell. If you would trouble your master to come.'

Cuby went upstairs and undressed at once. It was immediately clear to Demelza that she was not mistaken. Ross went into the kitchen and found less confusion than he had expected. Sephus Billing was under the table and Ern Lobb snoring in his chair, but the rest came to their feet as he walked in.

He smiled: 'You have all dined well? I can see you have.'

There was a relieved laugh. 'Ais, sur.'

'Sure 'nough.'

''Andsome, 'andsome, sur.'

He looked at Matthew Mark Martin. 'I must ask a service of you. Mrs Jeremy is taken with her pains. It is a little premature, but I have sent for Dr Enys. Will you ride to The Bounders' Arms and fetch Mrs Hartnell?'

'Right away, sur.'

Since Emma had moved into The Bounders' Arms with her husband and two children, she had been encouraged by Dr Enys to take over from the elderly Mrs Higgins as midwife to the more respectable houses. It was not unremarked that this 'light' girl (daughter of the rascally Tholly Tregirls), who had at one time been considered to have too blemished a reputation to wed the Wesleyan, Sam Carne, should now in early middle life be looked on as reputable and reliable.

Demelza sat with Cuby to begin, regretting that, not expecting the baby until January, they had let Mrs Kemp take a holiday now, and that Clemency was not expected for another week. She felt nervous and ill-at-ease with this pretty small elegant young woman who was about to bring forth Jeremy's child.

Dwight arrived first, but not long behind him came Emma, riding pillion behind Matthew Mark. Demelza kissed Cuby and left the room. She wanted no part in it. She did not want to see her daughter-in-law in pain. Over the months the rapport between the two women had grown; Cuby told her sister she had never met a woman who understood her one half so well as Lady Poldark did; this understanding was almost though not entirely friendly and full of guarded but sincere affection. Perhaps in Demelza's reluctance to be near her daughter-in-law in childbirth lay the seeds of a fear that the hated sensations she had felt once were even yet not altogether vanquished.

Dwight was upstairs half an hour and then came into the parlour where Ross and Bella were playing a card game. Demelza was putting Henry to bed.

'All is very well,' he said. 'I see no complications.'

'Perhaps we brought you out unduly,' Ross said. 'After leaving you so recent.'

'No, no, it was the right thing to do. The contractions are mild and regular. I would think sometime tomorrow morning. Perhaps early.'

'Your lead, Papa,' said Bella.

'In the meantime?'

'In the meantime get a good night's sleep, as I propose to. I have given her a mild sedative, which should help, and Emma is now making her a cup of tea. Give my love to Demelza again.'

'Of course.' Ross led the ace of hearts.

'Emma will stay with her all night,' Dwight said. 'And have one of your boys close at hand and ready to come for me if there is any need.'

'Your trick, Daddy,' said Bella.

III

At five o'clock in the morning of St Stephen's Day Cuby Poldark was delivered of a healthy six-pound child. There were no complications, and, aware that she was in a strange house in spite of all the warmth and affection shown her, she gritted her teeth and bore the pain almost without a sound. Contrary to Ross's predictions, it was a girl. Dwight patted Cuby's hand and said she was very brave. The man who should have sat beside her bed and held her hand at this time was not there, and never would be. Through a mist of tears, part of happiness but more of sorrow, she was kissed and petted by each one of the family in turn. Henry laughed when he saw the baby. 'Smaller'n me,' he said. Despite Mrs Kemp's efforts, he affected a strong Cornish accent.

So there was another child in the house, another Poldark, even if a girl; their first grandchild, Jeremy's daughter; another generation. A Christmas baby, a Christ child, all that was left of their soldier son.

About twelve Demelza said to Ross she would like to walk to the end of the beach, would he come with her?

'It's a long way for me,' said Ross. 'All that sand. Before I get home I shall be limping like Jago's donkey.'

'Why don't we take our horses, then? Not for a gallop, just an amble.'

'If you've the fancy I'll come.'

'I've the fancy.'

Colley and Marigold were both elderly and would not be restive at the thought of walking at a sedentary pace.

Demelza went upstairs for something, so Ross, while waiting for the horses to be brought round, went to his front door and stared over his land. This was where he belonged. The trees edged his view on the right, with the thin stream, copper stained and running under the bridge on its way towards Nampara Cove. The engine house and sheds of Wheal Grace half-way up the rising ground ahead of him; the piled attle spilling down towards the house, with rough weeds already growing over part of it (the two stamps had been gone some years, at Demelza's request – there were plenty in Sawle); his fields, mostly fallow, waited ploughing in February, speckled with crows seeking any scrap they could find; Demelza's walled garden with the gate leading to the beach, and the rough ground between the garden and the sand. Half a mile distant, on the first cliffs, the engine house and other buildings of Wheal Leisure.

And at his back the house, of nondescript architectural design, with its grey Delabole slate roof, except for a patch of thatch at the rear, its disparate chimneys, its thick granite walls, a house that had been put up by rough hands to meet the needs of the family it had sheltered for sixty years.

'I am ready,' said Demelza as the horses came round.

They set off at a slow pace, the horses as companionable as the riders. Demelza carried a small canvas bag.

'What's in that?' Ross asked.

'Oh, something I just brought along with me.'

It was half-tide, going out, and although there was no wind the sea was showing teeth at its edges. For a while they splashed through the surf, the horses relishing the water. Although the distant cliffs were black, those around Wheal Leisure had head cloths of green and feet of black and brown and purple seaweed. Over all was sky and cloud, ever changing. The scene-shifters were seldom idle in Cornwall.

'So we have a granddaughter,' he said.

'Yes.'

'Does that please you?'

'Yes, Ross. It pleases me.'

'And Cuby?'

'And Cuby. I'm sure it pleases her too.'

They rode on for a while.

Demelza said: 'When she first came to Nampara – that first time – she seemed so composed, so assured, that I almost found it in me to mislike her. But very soon, within a day, I saw twas only a sort of shell. Under it she was soft, vulnerable, damaged, like a hurt animal with bloody and twisted paws . . . Can you imagine what it must be like to have your first child without a husband and among strangers?'

'Loving strangers.'

'Oh yes. But if Jeremy had been here the sun would have lit the sky. She said to me the other day, she said, "No one ever said my name like Jeremy. He has a special way of saying Cuby that was all his own . . ."'

Tears were near, and there had been enough for Christmas. Ross said roughly: 'And so this trumpery title I was so misguided as to accept will descend upon poor Henry.'

'That pleases me too, Ross, except for your way of describing it. I believe it is more fitty that the honour should come to your own son.'

They reached the drier sand.

'Has she given you any idea as to a name she may have in mind?'

'She thinks to call her Noelle. It seems that Jeremy suggested that. And Frances after her mother.'

'Noelle Frances Poldark. It runs well enough. I'm glad she does not think of following the example of the Hornblower family.'

'Hornblower?'

'Jonathan Hornblower, the man who invented the compound engine; he died in March. His father had thirteen children and gave them all names beginning with J. Jeckolia, Jedediah, Jerusha, Josiah, Jabey, Jonathan. I have forgotten them. I used to know them all.'

'You must tell Cuby. She may change her mind before christening day.'

'On consideration,' Ross said, 'it is a pity that George did not have twin boys. Then he could have called them Castor and Pollux.'

Demelza laughed. It was good to hear that sound again.

'Clowance would agree.'

Ross looked over towards the land. 'You see that sandhill? You remember how you and I and Jeremy and Clowance used to roll down it? It was a special treat when they were small.'

'Too well,' said Demelza. 'It was a lovely time.'

'I cannot imagine myself rolling down it with Harry.'

'Don't worry. Noelle will.'

Ross looped over his rein. 'It is a strange feeling, but I do not think I shall ever *know* Harry the way I knew Jeremy. I am not likely to see so much of his life. The gap of the years between us . . . Sometimes I feel like his grandfather!'

'That is nonsense.'

There wasn't another person to be seen; only the occasional congregation of gulls or sanderlings or plovers were disturbed by their approach, waddling out of their way, or flapping a lazy wing to increase the safe distance.

Demelza said: 'I must send word to Clowance and Verity. I am sure they will be anxious to know.'

'I'm sure they will.'

'Ross, I have been wondering about Valentine and Selina in London.'

'What could you be wondering about them?'

'Whether they may see Tom Guildford.'

'You mean? . . . Oh my dear, it is too early to think of anything like that . . .'

'I do not think of anything like *that*! But Tom is a good kind friend of Clowance's. If he came down I am sure he would be good for Clowance, good for her spirits, good for her – her health generally. And do not forget, he is a lawyer. He could be a great business help to her too.'

Ross said: 'In that case perhaps we should send a note to Edward Fitzmaurice so the two gentlemen may start from scratch.'

'Ross, you are *so* vexatious! Why do I bear with you?'

'Well, you said she told you that if she ever married again it would not be for love, it would be for money or position. That would bring Edward strongly into the reckoning.'

'I do not know how you can be so cynical about your own daughter.'

'Is it cynical to face the facts? If Cuby is damaged, so in a similar but different way is Clowance. So we should do nothing, should we, and allow events to take their course?'

They were half-way along the beach by now, past the old Wheal Vlow adit. The Dark Cliffs at the end were coming into perspective; you could see the deep crevices in them, the isolated rocks.

Demelza said: 'And for yourself, Ross. Are you content?'

He was some seconds answering, his face devoid of readable expression.

'What is content? Something more than resignation? I eat and sleep well. I take interest in my affairs. I am content, more than content, with my wife.'

'Thank you, Ross. I did not ask for a compliment.'

'You did not get one. But – I have been home five months – you more. These have been months of grieving. But there is some slow adjustment. Do you not find it so?'

'Yes. And when Mr Canning calls to see us – if he calls to see us – what shall be your answer?'

'My answer to what? He has put no question.'

'But he may do so. He is sure to try to persuade you back into public life.'

'Then I shall not go.'

'Really?'

'Really. I shall continue to look after my own property and my own still considerable family. And my wife, who is not quite considerable enough to please me.'

'Oh, I am putting on weight, little by little. I am having to let out again some of the skirts that I took in.'

'So you too are content?'

'Resigned? – that was the word you used. That is nearer. But you are right: in time it will move by little stages farther away from grief.'

'Perhaps even to happiness?'

'Ah *that* . . .'

'It is not in your nature, my dear, to be unhappy. You are in fine counterbalance with my natural mopishness.'

''Tis harder now,' Demelza said.

They splashed through a pool of shallow water lying among corrugated ridges of sand.

'Old Tholly Tregirls,' Ross said. 'You know I went to see him just before he died? He said two things I have remembered. He quoted something my father said to him. My father said to him: "Tholly, the longer I live, the more certain sure I am that the Wise Men never came from the East."'

'I think he may be right.'

'But something Old Tholly said himself made the deepest impression. It was only in passing. He did not mean it as a pronouncement. He said: "A man is better off to be a squire in Cornwall than to be a king in England."'

She looked across and he smiled back at her. He said: 'Perhaps I have not always appreciated my good fortune.'

IV

Towards the end of the beach they dismounted and climbed up to the wishing well. It was really just a small natural circular pool at the entrance to a cave, with water dripping in plops from the moss-grown roof. It was a place where long ago Drake and Morwenna had come with Geoffrey Charles and silently plighted their troth.

Ross had no idea why Demelza wanted to go there today, picking her way up with greater agility than he could muster among the pools and the sea-weedy rocks. But he went along, content to humour her. When they got to the well they stood for a moment in silence. The cave was in semi-darkness, though the day was bright around the well.

Demelza opened the canvas bag she carried, and took a small silver object out of it. It was the loving cup, bearing the Latin inscription, '*Amor gignit amorem*', 'Love creates love'.

Ross said: 'Why have you brought that?'

'Cuby carried me a little note from Jeremy. It said –'

'You never told me –'

'Twas only a few words.'

'You never told me. He did mention – in Belgium he did mention something that he had written to you.'

'Twas only a note, Ross. It seems he had a sort of superstition about this cup. I cannot explain it any other way. I found it on the beach, you'll remember; it had been washed up by the sea. Jeremy thought it was an omen for him. If he came back from France he would take it as his own. If he did not I was to throw it back, give it back to the sea.'

Ross frowned. 'I don't understand. It was never his, was it? It doesn't make sense to me.'

'It is not easy to understand how he felt, Ross. But we talked about it once, when he was home last December. He didn't say as much then, but when Cuby came she brought this little note.'

'I'd like to see the note.'

'I have burned it, Ross.'

Ross thought this so outrageous a lie that he could not dispute it. Demelza destroying any letter of Jeremy's . . .

'And now what are you going to do with this cup?'

'Drop it down the well.'

'That is not the sea.'

'To me it is better than the sea. And the well is quite deep. No one will ever find it.'

'Is that important?'

'No. Oh no, not at all. But – this is a wishing well. I thought – I really thought it would be most fitty, most suitable.'

'Well, it perplexes me, but have it as you will. Perhaps you have some Celtic perceptions that I lack.'

'You are no less Cornish than I am, Ross.'

'Maybe not. But sophistication has bred it out of me. Or your old Meggy Dawes taught you things only witches should know.'

She smiled brilliantly at him, but there was no laughter in her eyes. She knelt on the stone beside the wall, rolled up her sleeve and put the cup slowly into the water. The cup filled, sent bubbles hurrying to the surface. She closed her eyes as if praying, opened her fingers. The cup sank out of sight. A few last bubbles rose and then it was gone.

It was as if with this symbolic action the ironic tragedy of Jeremy's life and death, which even she could only partly perceive, had come full circle, had played itself out.

She remained kneeling for about a minute staring into the well. Then she got up, careful not to wipe her arm but to let the fresh water dry. When it had done so she pulled down her sleeve, buttoned it, and drew on her glove. Only then she looked up at her husband with eyes as dark as he had ever seen them.

'Dearest Ross, let us go home now. There is a baby to see to.'